avbach@gmail.com
315-729-4910
3040 W. Wellington Ave. FL3
Chicago, IL 60618

EISENSTEIN'S MONSTER

by

A.V. BACH

TETRACULES
PRESS

Cover and interior design & formatting by Phillip Gessert.

Published by Tetracules Press.

For more information or contact info please visit: www.avbach.com or www.tetraculespress.com.

This novel contains portions of Charles Dickens' *A Tale of Two Cities*, James Joyce's *Ulysses*, Lewis Carroll's *Jabberwocky*, as well as Sergei Eisenstein's *Film Form*, *Film Sense,* and his film *The Battleship Potemkin*.

- ISBN-10: 0-9976812-0-9 (print)
- ISBN-13: 978-0-9976812-0-8 (print)
- ISBN-10: 0-9976812-1-7 (electronic)
- ISBN-13: 978-0-9976812-1-5 (electronic)

Portions of this novel were first published in the following places as short stories or excerpts, in various incarnations and titles, under several tryouts of the author's name:

- "Ye Ol'fashioned Olfactory," *Gargoyle* #57
- "Eden" and "But For the Company of Me-rrors: An Infinitum," *Gone Lawn*, No.11
- "I," *Kerouac's Dog Magazine*, Issue 3: Truth
- "The Body of My Work," *Big Muddy*, vol. 10.2 (as "Eisenstein's Monster: an autobiography by Sergei Eisenstein")
- "Making Mickey," *Gargoyle* #60
- "No Names," *Fogged Clarity*, October 2010

The author (me) would like to thank the following: my high school English teachers for teaching me to love the craft; the Creative Writing faculty at Syracuse University for encouraging me to pursue the craft; and the MA Writing department at Johns Hopkins University for teaching me to hone the craft.

Extra Special thanks to Arthur Flowers Jr., Richard Peabody, and George Saunders.

Extra *Extra* Special thanks to my friends and my family, without whom full and absolute lunacy would have surely taken hold.

Dedicated to my Grandfather,
the first great storyteller I ever knew.
"It was a dark, dark night Patagonia…"

"Montage is an idea that arises from the collision of independent shots—shots even opposite to one another: the 'dramatic' principle."

—*Sergei Eisenstein,* FILM FORM

"The construction of this film as a whole, as in this particular sequence, adheres to a basic construction process. Namely: a conflict between story and its traditional form."

—*Sergei Eisenstein,* FILM FORM

EISENSTEIN'S MONSTER
(A NOVEL IN MONTAGE)

by

A.V. BACH

CONTENTS

REEL ONE:
RED TIGERS

"The Japanese regards each theatrical element, not as an incommensurable unit among the various categories of affect...but as a single unit of theater."

—*Sergei Eisenstein*, FILM FORM

I. SHIKAARIYON | THE ONCOLOGICAL ARGUMENT

"Our hulking confrere scraping the wall,
piling the dust over the motionless face:
in the abyss of time how he is close,
his art an act of faith, his grave
an act of art: for all,
for all, a celebration and a burial."

—*Josephine Jacobsen,* IN THE CREVICE OF TIME

Shiva was good—fair, he should say—filling his body with this ambitious decrepitude while this young thing brimming with life sat not ten feet away.

Or maybe she just had a good sense of irony.

From the entrance of the coffee house on the corner with the mismatched salvaged furniture, multicolored walls adorned with rotating installations of local modern art (some of it even good), he watched her, panning his eyes for an open seat near her table, an empty rocking chair or artist's stool, never for an instant losing her in his periphery. There were other women, sure, other girls, but none with that same permeating embodiment of fresh life, as if her cheeks were still flushed from outrunning apoptosis.

No, there was only her; he knew that now.

— § —

In a white room with a solitary window there is a cylinder you enter that pulses and pounds and takes still-lifes of the inside of your body. There are color prints that look like continents in green, yellow, red and orange. There are monochromatic photos that show waxing moons poking through cortextual gray clouds. Regions and continents with their own names and their own moons: there are moons for Wernicke and Broca, a moon for the Inferior Frontal Gyrus, two smaller moons for the Superior Temporal Gyrus and Middle Frontal Gyrus. An explorer named Brodmann mapped these regions.

Dr. David sucked his teeth, "Well, the growths in BA 22 and 45 haven't responded to the chemo; neither have those in 34, 28, 25 or 36—though they're still relatively small. And your entorhinal cortex is grounds for serious concern, Krish. P-p-p-p-p...let's see, areas 20, 40, 44 and 39 are in remission—can't guarantee they won't return—considering the resiliency we've seen—Jesus, did you do something to offend cancer's grandfather in a previous life?! What I'm worried about are the tumors in your Superior Temporal Gyrus—which, depending on how they continue to grow, may push against the insula of your Sylvian fissure...here...resulting in lesions to your temporoparietal junction and your anterior insular cortex—this little guy right here. Could lead to loss of hearing, movement, stroke, TLE...death. Wernicke's aphasia is almost a guarantee with 22 still strong and virile, so to say—or maybe I shouldn't, sorry. The other possibility is metastases extending towards the parietal region, in which case your mobility will be severely impaired and you'll be popping wheelies in a wheelchair. The good news, Krish, if you're at all open to calling it that, is that with the remission in 44, Broca's aphasia might be avoided. Still a possibility, however—which sucks."

The good and bad news about doctors seeing their own is that the bedside manner goes out the window, dissolving into an arguably more natural banter; which is all fine and well, unless, of course, you'd prefer a more formal decorum for certain sensitive topics. Now being one of those times.

"Is that it then?"

"Not...exactly. We found something further in, towards the septum." Did the momentary flicker in the fluorescent panels above mean the room had just gulped?

"Something new?"

"It's small, still; but yes, there is something new."

He took a deep breath, inhaling the disinfectant smell of elementary school bathrooms and another disinfectant smell of something almost pleasurable. "Where is it?"

"Keep in mind it's still very small, about the size of a grain of Kosher salt…but it's adjacent to your nucleus accumbens." And now a moon for the binary system of the nucleus accumbens and the olfactory tubercle.

"Christ! Still nothing in the right hemisphere?"

"Well your right anterior insula looks a little thicker than average, but nothing growing there yet. Look, Krishawn, I know you're a stubborn bastard but I really think you should get back in touch with the ol' Chemo-sabi; *sooner* would be better than later." Dr. David's inflection on "sooner" wasn't the only unnecessary rhetorical device used in that statement—or in their entire discourse for that matter—but Krishawn moved past them all.

"What's the point?"

"Ummm…*excuse* me?"

"Look, it shrank one batch, did nothing for another, and I still have two pea-sized tumors that have only *grown* since the last session—oh, in addition to a newer one on my goddamned pleasure center! So, thank you for the concern—I really mean that—but I hardly see the point of putting myself through that noxious fucking poisoning again—and with even less certainty of success this time. More than likely, David, in two months time, when the nausea wears off and I'm scraped off the bathroom floor by a humorless, Trinidadian nurse from Bed-Stuy, I'll be aphasiac, wheelchair-bound and virtually senseless. Christ, epileptic too!—let's no forgot that."

"There's no way of knowing anything for certain, Krish. But you can always fight; and you can't win a fight you don't wage."

Krishawn looked around the boxy office to see if David was quoting from the litany of reference material that adorned the walls of what would have been the most empirically un-cool of bedroom decorations were David twenty to thirty years younger. The evidence wasn't immediately up for discovery, but that didn't mean it wasn't there. Like an expectant mother, part of him—the part that still lived—wanted to tell David to make him a copy of the scans so he could take them home and post them on the fridge, or bring to work saying "Here's little Timmy and little Billy, growing so big and strong. Don't they just have their father's eyes?"

Dr. David continued, "Look, I understand why you're reluctant. All I ask is that you give it some thought. You of all people should know what I'd like to say to someone so goddamned recalcitrant in his refusal of treatment. Which reminds me, did I tell you about that patient—"

"Can you just give me a timeline?"

"Until when? Until the aphasia kicks in—Broca's or Wernicke's? Global?—heaven-for-fucking-bid. Until the tumor reaches your parietal lobe? Until it pinches off your veins and you aneurysm or stroke out? Krishawn, I don't know. I don't know what direction they may move to, or if they will move at all. I *do* know that some of the tumors responded to the treatment, and who knows, maybe the next time around the others will, too. The only way to know anything is to monitor the growth and take steps towards elimination—which in this day and age is called che-mo-ther-a-py." Dr. David positioned himself in the foreground of framed prints of sailboats and English countrysides and other soft-toned, watercolor visages meant to inspire tranquility, peace, acceptance (not part of the same plastic adornments but nonetheless embodying a certain corporate banality).

"I've already told you my worst case scenario—and the runners up aren't exactly peaches, either. If I only have a couple months left I'm not going to waste them by inducing a different sickness into my body." Krishawn bent his elbows behind him to grip the oaken armrests in a traditional signal of imminent departure.

"And the best case scenario?" Krishawn didn't respond. "At the very least come back here for more scans—or drinks."

Krishawn nodded in appeasement, grabbed a pamphlet on "Coping" and stuffed it under his jacket before opening the door and walking through the waiting room gauntlet of the other terminally condemned. A bald boy in a Goofy t-shirt waved at him; Krishawn didn't wave back; he wasn't one for goodbyes.

— § —

She wore a pair of charcoal Solos and one of those elaborately-decorated hoodies—black and lined with faux-gold thread, a silver-and-white *fleur-de-lis* pattern embossed on the sleeves that made it resemble an early unisex tunic from the Elizabethan era—sitting at a small table in the rear of the cozy shop, her back upright, her left leg tucked under the knee of the extended right, ignoring posture in favor of comfort. It was Sunday, after all. In front of her was an opened black leather folder with her company's initials and symbol, a lower case "a" that became an arrow, showing direction and the perpetual motion of profits; there were loose pages with multi-colored graphs and charts dispersed in a paper Pangaea, subject to the tectonic instability of the table's wobbling legs. She was at one of two small tables in the back, a cove beset with three chairs—a rocking chair in the middle of the two tables that could side with either; her coat and bag rested on this upholstered Alsace-Loraine.

He walked to the table across from her, placed his soft leather bag that looked like a mid-Orlando transformation from briefcase to purse on the fuchsia veneered trapezoid acting as a table and turned to her with his finger pointed at the chair. "Excuse me, are you using this?"

"Oh. No. You can take it." She obliged, removing her bag and her coat and placing them on the floor underneath her table. Instead of seating himself in the chair, or presumably holding it for another party, he merely deposited the hermaphroditic briefcase in the lap and wrapped his coat around the spindled knobs. He sat in the back chair, directly across from her.

She watched this, and as the word "prick" anchored itself around her molar and was about to quietly repel from her tongue, past the stalagmite incisors on her mandible…he began laughing.

"I'm just messing with you. Wouldn't that be the worst, though? The consummate dick move, right?" He rose and turned the chair towards her table.

"Really, it's fine; you can have the chair," annoyance usurping anger, "I was just using it for my coat."

"Here, how about this: I'll hang your coat on this part of the chair, my coat on the other, and put both our bags on the seat?" He repositioned the items as he spoke.

"Perfect." She lifted her head after a moment, narrowing her eyes at him like a McCarthyian inquisitor. "So this was, like, your plan—your play?"

He took to balancing his coat on a lone spindle. "Look at it this way: these tables are too small to work at with coats and bags and such, and, as you can see, the chair is perfectly up to filling both our needs. Come on, I mean, what would you have said if a random man just came over and asked if he could 'split' your chair? Sounds kind of psychotic, doesn't it?"

"Only if you don't explain it; which took you, what, all of three seconds?"

"I guess this way is just more fun."

"Is that to imply you've done some prior field tests?" There was work to be done; she didn't have the liberty, temperance or patience to tolerate, much less nurture, this kind of frivolity. Still then, why did she go with a question?

"Just what are you trying to say?" He looked at her innocently.

"Seems a little contrived, is all." Her pen made a circle in the air, to somehow demonstrate "contrived."

He shrugged, "My desired ends were met."

She felt something cryptic in what he'd just said; wanting to say "And just what ends are those?" she shifted to a less flirtatious quid-pro-quo. "So do you go up to a lot of girls working on their recs and pull this...chair thing?"

"What are 'recs'?" He made a sour-milk face, then focused his attention on the zippered compartments of his bag, plunging his hands inside, pulling out a pen, which he placed in his mouth, followed by a pad of paper, which he placed on the table, before plunging his hands inside once more, keeping his eyes on his tasks.

"Recs. Reconciliations. We go through all our work over the week and work out the financial discrepancies before starting the process all over again Monday."

"And you don't have an office to do that in?" His bag gave birth to a rectangular laptop, a placental power-cord followed after. A different compartment held a circular band of headphones, which he placed on top of the computer.

She realized that he'd dodged her question, that she hadn't been doing any work since they'd begun this conversation, and that even though she didn't want much of a conversation, she'd certainly been the larger participant so far. Sure, perhaps an unconscious procrastination on her part, a submission to a few easy minutes away from the tedium—which is why she was here, at this coffee shop, instead of, say, her living room, with close proximity to her DVR, and her wine. And her weed. The thought struck her that if he was in fact flirting, he probably would have tried pulling up his chair to her table and started staring into her eyes like some necromancer in a 1930s horror film. But he had hardly even looked in her direction; and having equipped himself with the necessities from his bag, he was now preoccupied with the machinery before him, only glancing at her casually and in passing. Frankly, she thought, it was a little rude. She continued though, hoping to approach some entropic realm of niceties and casual amicability—after all, they were leasing a chair together.

"You spend eighty hours a week in an office you don't want to spend your Sundays there. Besides, I know Bertha and she always gives me a free refill or two." She pointed to the elderly Hispanic woman behind the counter who gave no notice of recognition. "And what do *you* do, if you don't mind me asking?"

She said it so cutely, so playfully proper, that he almost told her the truth. "I'm a musician. Composer slash producer, really."

From the expensive-looking hem on his coat, to the similarly priced appearance of the rest of his fashion catalogue—acid-washed, almost-tailored jeans; long-sleeved, red-and-orange California beach-plaid button-down poking out from under a black, half-zip cashmere pullover—she wouldn't have guessed musician in a thousand years. "Cool. Would I know anything you've done?"

"Probably not, it's kind of obscure." He finally looked up at her and gave a self-deprecating chuckle.

"Oh, like Indie?"

"Well, sort of. More…electronic."

"Really? Wow."

"What?" Krishawn lowered the computer screen that had been partially occluding his face.

"I just wouldn't have thought that. I mean look at you."

He pantomimed a mask of offense. "What, too old?"

"No, I didn't mean that. Just, I would have guessed, musically, you'd have been more into Springsteen or Tom Petty, something like that—only more yuppie." She stretched herself over the table to minimize the volume of their voices, which were increasingly attracting annoyed glances from the other patrons at their laptops, those who hadn't brought headphones.

"And yuppie, too! Something *old* like that, you mean? Wow." He frowned and made a mimetic gesture of an arrow piercing his heart.

She smiled, blushing, now blissfully ignoring the black-and-white spreadsheet like a paper jail-cell on her table, a prison sentence of reconciliation and boredom. "Give me a little credit. How many forty-year-old men listen to electronica? I thought your generation was pretty much issued rock at birth and never strayed from the tried and true path."

"Forty? Do I look forty?" His face dropped. She laughed.

"I was being hyperbolic. Don't keep twisting it on me like that. So how old *are* you?"

He took a breath, his hand rubbing against the two-day stubble, the dark pepper speckled on his olive face, as if to think. She couldn't tell if he was Greek, Italian or if she was way off, possibly somewhere far from the Mediterranean; maybe somewhere from the European-infused South America, or possibly Asian of some flavor; something that bordered on Caucasian or was at least infused with it on one side of his genealogy, and something exotic on the other.

"Only thirty-six. Wow, if I look forty I've really got to be scared. Not much after that."

She smiled and he shook off the gravity. "I'm just glad you didn't say Mick Jagger. I think that could have possibly killed me right here on the spot."

She lifted and lowered the tea bag in her mug. "Come on, I'm not *that* mean."

"I hope not; I don't like befriending mean people."

"Oh, are we friends now?"

"I'd hope so. I mean what kind of person would just tell a stranger he looked like a yuppie Tom Petty? Thems fighting words round these parts."

"Well maybe we should fight!" She put up two small fists and waved them cartoonishly. "Take back my chair."

"What, have you been taking kickboxing at your gym? In-between spinning classes and yoga?"

"No, but I used to play volleyball. I've got a wicked spike."

"Oh my God, how old are *you*? Who says 'wicked' at your age? And we're hours from Southey, so don't give me that regional bullshit." He sipped his coffee recently delivered to him in a gigantic, blue, ceramic mug whose handcrafted lopsidedness he couldn't tell was supposed to be intentional or not.

"That's where I'm from, summers anyway. Well, not Southey, the Cape, but you get people saying *wicked* there, too."

"So where'd you live the other three seasons?" Swirling the coffee as if it were good wine.

"Connecticut, outside Hartford."

"Okay. I know Hartford. Played a show there two or three years ago maybe. Listen, I should let you get back to your 'reps.'" He pushed himself closer to the table and raised the computer screen back to a perpendicular position.

" 'Recs.' "

" 'Recs,' right. 'Recs.' Hey, if I'm still here when you finish and you want to continue our talk, I think we can try and work through 'wicked' and any other sophomoric, East-coast, yacht-club, gang-speak you still use."

She feigned a contusion to her psyche before turning back to her work. "Watch it, Mick." She looked up to see if he had heard her quip but found him already ensconced in his headphones and was a little hurt her chide went unnoticed. And then a little confused about the hurt.

— § —

Krishawn was dying, and the act was the only thing he felt beholden to anymore. Sure, he had time enough to try forgetting and denying, for fantasizing, for reinventing himself in the image he would have chosen, with the body he would have chosen: new chest, eyes and nose; bereft of his endemic misfortunes (dental, follicle, carotid and now cellular). But no matter the impossibility of reinvention, the body was built a lemon, designed to fail. So he made time for carelessness, and for carnal indulgences. He had always been a lover of senses, even when they turned on you. It wasn't a matter of feeling alive; it was a matter was of knowing what could exist in life, of knowing what potentials, what worlds, lay just outside the jurisdiction of skin.

But still that thing remained, inextricable, ingrown into the roots of his trees, attached to the cerebral canopies and swinging from the synaptic vines of his consciousness, suffused to his dreams both somnolent and waking. A foreign beast stalking through this jungle with full ease of prey and no fear of predation—save for when the sun's radiated waves found a hole in the canopy.

There was a game his mother used to play with him when he was a kid, and he adopted it for this new beast: "Picture a red tiger," she'd say, "think of the red and black stripes, the red and black face; think of the added terror of a red tiger, out of place amongst the endless shades of green-filtered jungle. Now, imagine yourself in the bush; feel yourself searching through the bramble for a flash of red; feel the fear, the delight, of smelling the beast's breath on your neck, of reaching out and stroking the red and black snout, the red tail swaying like a coral snake. Now, remove the tiger; poach it from your thoughts." The reaction was obvious, premeditated: he continued to hunt, the beast an indelible part of his mind—these days literally, terminally.

Dusk blazed an "A" through the tapered curtains against the western windows as she stretched her neck, unfurled her legs and cracked the middle of her back like a swan going through its pre-flight motions. Most of the customers had gone and the staff looked impatient to close. She looked across from her table and found the man still there, deeply entranced with something on his computer.

She packed her work into her bag, pushed her chair in and drifted to his side as if he were on the way out. He didn't look up. Multicolored waves refracted off the glassine whites of his eyes, his shiny canvas of forehead, his face limp. This was not the gaunt yet cheerful face she had seen before; no, this face looked lost, heartbroken even.

"So what's it like?" but he didn't hear her; she repeated, bending closer to his ear just as the non-conformist lock of blond hair with the interwoven blue feather slipped from the cozy, parental basement of her ear lobe and fell onto the neck below, resulting in a knee-jerk tickle that would prove momentarily awkward for both parties. The moment passed.

"Jesus, don't you know you can give us old people heart attacks pulling stunts like that?" He pulled the right side of the headphones off his ear and looked at her, not the least bit surprised to see her, though still recovering from the, admittedly, emasculated reaction.

"And aren't the elderly all luddites? They'll revoke your AARP card if anyone catches you working on…that." Having only dated a musician once, though his attachment would prove embarrassingly long-term—for both of them—she couldn't remember what to call the Digital Audio Workstation before him.

"Touché."

"So what's it like?" She pointed to the stacks of waves.

He turned back to the screen and thought for a second, "It's like looking at your birth. It's like finding your soul and then watching it crumble and fall apart in your hands. The kind of music that makes you want to commit elaborate suicide." He frowned. They both frowned.

"That's yours? That's, that's how you'd describe your music?" She shifted her feet.

"Mine? God, no. This is a friend's, he's showing me his scratch tracks and improv ideas. Everything he writes more or less sounds like he's scoring the apocalypse. Not exactly the most uplifting of songs."

She exhaled as if she were seven again and she and her older sister had just punched a lungful of spent air into the family car after passing a graveyard. "Oh. Well I think they're trying to close up so maybe you should shut the studio down tonight."

"Are they? What time is it?" He looked around and saw the chairs turned over, resting on the tables so the floors could be swept. He turned to her, "It's still relatively early."

"Sunday, Beethoven; they just want to get home and relax. I'm in dire need of a glass of wine and a nap, myself."

He didn't say anything, just nodded, folded his computer and placed it and the rest of his accoutrements into his bag. In a practiced motion he pulled his p-coat on and swung the bag across his shoulder. "I'd ask if you'd want to grab a glass of wine somewhere but I don't think most places will let you nap—fire hazard you know."

She laughed softly, at least now she didn't have to wonder if he was making an advance. While she was accustomed to being asked out…those nights in college when she would go out and find herself bludgeoned with pick-up lines on some weathered bridge between flattery and disgust, creeping hands and wayward glances of skin across her obliques and belly, the whisper of fingers across her ass when men passed, when she passed men, making her way up to the bar where she knew some fawning lacrosse player or frat boy would let her slide in, smile when she got next to him, offer her a free shot of some sweet-sour, sugar-loaded concoction that he had gotten on gratis from the bartender with the appreciation of prolonged and excessive patronage; and it didn't matter that she had had a boyfriend—when they knew she had a boyfriend—that somehow their words were grand enough, that she could be theirs with just the right amounts of tender adulation and coy mystery interwoven in arched eyebrows, baiting smiles and a peculiar swagger adopted by men in their twenties as a sort of mating call. This man didn't have any of those characteristically desperate, urgent or sordid habits in his conversation with her, at least, none that she could tell. He was confident, sure, outgoing enough and funny in a cocky, aged sort of way that elicited comfort—like an avuncular neighbor; more than anything, he was something new, something different than the professional and social comorbidity of her peers. It was a pleasant meeting, overall. Still, she chose not to respond; she did have a boyfriend, after all.

He stood in front of her, his eyes a few inches above her forehead. "Well, I guess this is it, Southey—"

"Cape," She corrected.

"Right. Well, maybe we'll see each other again, the next time you've got recs and I'm in town."

"Oh, you don't live here?"

"No, I do. Actually only about two blocks from here…I'll be going on the road soon, is all." He looked disappointed at this.

"On tour? Cool. Where are you going?"

He hesitated then gave a singular chortle. "Not quite sure yet."

"When do you leave?" One of the baristas began sweeping towards them with an utter lack of subtlety. The two took the hint and stepped towards the door though not yet through it.

"Two months, maybe three. I have to get some things in order first."

"Well, when can I hear some of your music?"

He thought for a second. "You could try to find some at an underground record store, one that specializes in electronica; they *might* have it. And then you'd have to have a record player. I'm not online yet because of some contractual obligations, unfortunately."

She was slightly hurt by this, and he noticed. He had been hoping for disappointment. "If you wanted to stop by my place I could show you some, but that's probably a little forward."

She looked outside as she thought; there was still enough light left in the day, those in-between hours that exist in the northern cities at the start of spring: the sun's prolonged presence making the cold bearable with the affirmations of hope and the spiritualized sense of conquering winter. It was the time when people opted for a walk in lieu of the subway. "It's close?"

"Stone's throw."

— § —

There was a boyfriend named Raymond who told her that when he finished up at Columbia he wanted to practice Green law, clean rivers polluted with selenium, fight to ban terminator seeds and rBST use in farming, expand funding for cleaner, more sustainable power sources. He would write bills that would reallocate more financial aid to fight malaria or hunger. These were things she liked about him, among many others.

His family was an old one: claiming an American president during the inchoate stages of independence on his father's side; settlers from the *Mayflower* on his mother's. They had three places they could call home: a summer house in Nantucket; an autumn, winter and spring house in Long Island; and a three-bedroom apartment on the Upper East Side that had been in the family since the building's last brick was put in place in 1923. There were other places they owned that they didn't call home: a penthouse in Dupont Circle they used infrequently for lobbying and federal litigation, and as an investment on all other days; a log-cabin in Jackson Hole for winter recreation; a villa in Italy for international recreation; and a flat in Hong Kong for exotic recreation.

Sometimes, like when she was on the couch doing a Sudoku and he was at the table by the window going over a case, she would ask: "Say you're out in Africa or the Amazon, saving the world, and John calls and says 'Raymond, it's time; I'm retiring and me and your mother are just going to sail from port to port retracing Magellan's circumnavigation. Son,' he says, 'it's time for you to step up and take control of the firm.' What are you going to say to him?"

"I'm going to say 'Yes.' Of course I'm going to say 'Yes.' That firm is family and tradition. That law firm goes back to John Adams' grandson. The firm's apple pie, babe. That's why I want to spend my time until then helping people and doing some honest good. You think I'm getting my J.D.M.B.A. because I like the extra work?"

His answer wasn't what bothered her—by all her reasoning she thought it was the right thing to do, the thing she would do had her family a long-running American staple to keep up instead of a line of Midwestern dairy farmers turned East Coast salesmen turned dentists. And it wasn't as if the family's firm was some insidious, commercially carnivorous law firm that reaped the souls of the working men; the firm focused on international and maritime law and worked closely with the UK, Ireland and occasionally some tariff regulations in Asia.

What she didn't like, when it all came down to brass tacks, was the expectation; she didn't like that everything was premeditated, designed to fit into a specific mold. She didn't like that he expected her to fit, to want to fit, so acceptably and gratefully into this agenda. She didn't like that he got pissy when this came up and she wasn't as thrilled as he expected her to be. She didn't abhorrently reject the life Houseman, a lucrative, comfortable institution with a sense of place and purpose. She could find nothing inherently wrong; the family was sweet and welcoming and made her feel nothing but comfortable and wanted. But still…

At his grandparents' 50th anniversary, held at the summer house that doubled as the family archives, Ray's uncle, Francis (the man who married John's sister and traded her Anglican-American name for the Irish O'Brien), had prepared a video scrapbook that showed the lives of the two grandparents: a marriage, a family, with children and grandchildren, condensed to a thirty-minute life of brevity. She watched the video and started thinking about the one that would be played in twenty years for Ray's parents, John and Marie, about the one that would be played for her and Ray, for their children, should they live long enough.

She started seeing herself as every Mrs. Houseman before her and after her, assimilating to the Houseman standard. When she would welcome guests to their home it would be, "Welcome to the Houseman residence." When they had children, uncles and aunts, long-time neighbors and old family friends of the Housemans would hover over the crib and exclaim, "He's the spitting image of his great-grandfather Ernest," or "She's got that Houseman colic." She would wear the Houseman apron and the Houseman summer hat, waving to the long line of butlers and gardeners, and gradually blending into the collage of sepia-toned family portraits, becoming the faded, gold-leafed, paisley wallpaper of the dining room, settling into the ancestral indelibility of the wooden beams fashioned out of the masts of raised ships capsized by British vessels in the War of Independence that had carried tobacco, molasses and slaves. She had excused herself, claiming inebriation, and threw up in the bathroom.

What it came down to, she thought, this upset, was that she still wanted some peradventure out of life; she wanted some excitement precipitated from chance, from taking a risk and diving headfirst into the unexpected, the unknown. At least while she was young. And who knows, some humanitarian work in Asia or Africa could be a source of excitement and dynamism for their twenties and early thirties, but the expedition would all be done with the umbrella of Houseman tradition continually held over their heads to protect them from the dark, cumulous clouds of real risk, of truly living.

Ray had stood outside the door and asked if she was all right; and she had lied and said "Yes."

— § —

He hadn't exaggerated on the proximity; they had barely found a pause in their conversation when he interrupted her with "This is it." *It* was a brownstone like any other, a posh building in an opulent neighborhood she had always thought reserved for CEOs, doctors and the occasional celebrity; the kind of homes that suggested the owner had several—a Housman home. Definitely not what she expected from a musician, especially a musician with the level of obscurity he had suggested. She hesitated a little at the door, thinking the electronica scene couldn't possibly pay this much, then again, he was older wasn't he: old enough to have made a name in the scene; old enough to have sponsors; maybe an honorary Ph.D in the music world, a world she could best describe as generally foreign.

"Coming?"

Her foot stepped off the curbside stair and into the house.

Here, too, she expected something different, as if she needed only to lift a curtain, nudge open a door, and find some seething, incendiary sexuality. Though his dress and bag and speech didn't suggest that mythologized lifestyle, she nonetheless expected broken bottles, used condoms in the sinks and on the counters, dirty needles in the sofa cushions, the aroma of marijuana, stagnant beer and smoldering joints laced with sweet and flowery opium, naked women to suddenly emerge from the doorway interrupted from some initiate orgy. But that's not what she found.

The house was posh yet simple, cozy and classic, furnished the way she'd expected these houses to be furnished: Viking appliances; stainless steel fixtures; Brazilian rosewood floors, cabinets and fridge (adorned with a crayon cherry tree likely drawn by a niece); custom sofa; chic paintings on the walls—the kind you see in gallery windows but never expect to find in someone's home. Houseman through and through, with a slight Eastern tinge. She walked slowly, listlessly following his path as he made his way through the kitchen, depositing his coat and bag on the conservative walnut table in a way that made her realize he wasn't married (something she should have asked before—no homewrecker, she). She looked around again, searching the walls and furniture and accoutrements for corroboration: masculine, yet lacking the tackiness she'd seen from bachelors her own age. There were no empty alcohol trophies lining the cabinets; there were no sports paraphernalia, empty video game boxes, "retro" posters of Babe Ruth, Mickey Mantle or Muhammad Ali, neon beer signs, crinkled bags of stale chips...No, most definitely single; and most definitely adult.

"Sad to say I don't have any wine. Don't drink much these days. I know, right? A musician that doesn't drink? That's like the Kentucky

Derby without mint juleps…or jockeys." He went to the kitchen and opened up the camouflaged door of the fridge. "Can I get you a water or tea or something?"

She was still lost in the contradictions of her expectations, shocking in the most positive of ways, elucidating a feeling of genuine pleasure and surreal enjoyment. She felt like an actor in a play that wasn't quite real but off-kilter enough from the everyday occurrence to incite a feeling of peripheral magic.

"No, I'm fine. You-, you live here all by yourself?"

"I know: a little overkill for a bachelor. But I use the upstairs bedroom as a studio, and the rest…well you can't begrudge a man for indulging in the pleasures of his home. When you're hardly here it seems like the only thing worth your money. Something to come back to."

She nodded and made murmuring sounds until he became visibly aware and stood near the island in the kitchen, smiling and laughing. "You okay over there?"

"No, I'm fine. I just…didn't expect…this."

"We're not getting into that again are we?" He moved outside of the kitchen towards the open stairway at the back of the living room. "The studio's upstairs if you want to listen to my stuff."

She followed him deftly, taking the steps slowly and grasping the wooden rail as she advanced up the stairs behind him in the wake of his cologne.

They proceeded down the hallway to a door at the end. It was hard to imagine the room could have held bunk beds, star wallpaper or found any other kind of usage the way the studio took up the space so comfortably: a large metallic desk took up one whole wall; on the desk was a large mixing board with dials next to a keyboard resting below a 32" computer monitor bookended by two large speakers on the sides; a subwoofer failing to hide underneath; several keyboards lay angled on stands against another wall; guitars, cables and a couple amps took up yet another; there was a shoe rack full of plastic and metal boxes of all colors; several microphones stood on guard in their stands or relaxed on the counters; rivers of cable connected everything, with potential rivers coiled up on pegs, waiting to join the deluge. This was more what she expected, though admittedly cleaner than she thought, and more organized: clasps and plastic zip-ties wrapped around the cables and kept them in neat streams. Surgical, almost.

He couldn't help but smile, loving the astonishment she kept exhibiting (which only heightened her allure), as if he was resurrecting the fire of excitability that had cooled and atrophied since childhood, needing only the proper kindling to incite a blaze; and here he was playing Prometheus. In the few seconds it took her eyes to acclimate to the soft, natural light of the fading afternoon while exploring the room, Krishawn took the opportunity to take her in, cataloging her features: the tint and hue of her blue-green eyes, every dark cut in her iris like the negative of a sun growing from her pupil and spreading its corona (Ponce de León would have given two-hundred more lives to bathe his reflection in the pool of those eyes); a softly dimpled nose and angular jaw rising up to the feathered, almost phosphorescent blond hair falling over her ears; on her temple, a patch of freckles in the shape of Orion's Belt. Her lips spread slightly, covering her teeth but open enough for him to catch a slice of white when she turned her head this way and that, looking at the Les Paul, now the Fender Rhodes. He wanted to hear her music.

"Let me get in there for a second." He moved the mouse and the screen flickered open to a platform similar to what he'd had up before, with wave after wave of tracks stacked on top of each other, him laughing and professing that when a program really had unlimited tracks, it really meant unlimited. He turned the monitors on and, before hitting play, positioned her directly between the speakers and a few feet back from the computer. Then he pressed play and moved backwards, towards the edge of the room, allowing her to become immersed in the music, lost and alone.

The music was soft at first, a delayed beat with the downbeat coming in stuttering bursts, like listening to a drum through a fan. The beat rose steadily and methodically, dropping occasionally and rising again, this time louder, this time with more accompaniment—soft, ambient noises that she couldn't place. A definite melody, but from what instrument she couldn't be sure, as if he had isolated a pure sound, free of timbre and the attack but without the washy, mechanized feel of synth. This felt organic, like a song he had grown in a garden out back, planted among the tomatoes and the rosemary, nurtured with sun and air, watered and then plucked when it was ripe, when the song was full.

The volume swelled and the rhythm pounded through her chest, dictating her heartbeats, her breathing, each exhalation marked with a stabbing staccato of percussion. She got goose bumps and felt the cold precision of each hair on her neck, felt herself collapsing from her exterior shell and pulling into a new one like a matryoshka doll. When the beat split, panning between the two speakers—the subwoofer still undulating subsonic feelings too low in hertz to recognize in stereo—she grew acceptably dizzy. Her heart still pounded but now her emotions rose with the repetition of the beautifully simple melody, so soft, feminine almost, and she could feel herself smiling, elated. When the song pulsed she pulsed. When the bass throbbed she throbbed; she was so engulfed that when the song ended she barely noticed, just sat and waited for it to come back to her like a loyal dog.

"Can you play it again?"

Krishawn smiled and hit play-from-start. Again, she allowed herself to fall under the aural anesthesia. When the song ended for the second time, she stayed seated. The sun was already beneath the horizon and the room was dark but for the glow of the computer screen falling in diaphanous light over the earth-colored walls and instruments, a ghostly light reflecting off the black and silver metal of the digital instruments and off her exposed skin. A cave in orbit with moonlight falling through the crevices.

She took a breath and turned towards Krishawn, quietly watching her from the doorway, arms folded across his chest. "And the title?"

He frowned slightly. "January 27th."

"Any particular reason?"

"None that could be summed up expediently. You know artists: always toying with the obscure." He smiled at her and pushed himself off the wall.

"Can I hear it again sometime? Or some of your other stuff? Maybe you could burn me a copy."

"Fresh out of blank discs. But if you wanted to come back sometime, I could make you a copy and show you some more?"

"Yeah, I'd like that."

She followed him down the hall and back down the stairs, stopping when she got to the door. "So when would be a good time for me to come back?"

"Like I said, I leave in a couple months, so sooner would be better than later." His face was sincere.

"Does sooner have an exact day in mind?"

"Do you?"

"Not especially. Sundays are always good for me."

"Sunday it is. Tell you what, you can use the time to try and think of a better title."

"I'll give it a shot, Mick."

He smiled at her, then closed the door before she had even left the stoop.

— § —

"Fish. Apple. Tree. Cloud. Snake. Lion." Krishawn said the names of the images in front of him, a slide-show of sorts, not of vacations. "Baseball. Mountain. House. Penguin."

Dr. David said "Good" and they moved on to the next test. Like the SAT, Krishawn was given a passage to read. The passage started off with simple sentences and grew to more complex ones. He was asked to interpret each sentence, not symbolically, but logically, testing him on grammar, double-negatives and the like. There were other tests that asked him to place Objects A, B, C and D in order, to stack them alphabetically, then in reverse. They did fMRI testing, where the stills are animated, and David watched the colors of Krishawn's brain move like a kaleidoscope while they did sentence generations out of supplied words: pilgrim, roses, spaceship, library, boat, Florida, tow truck, dog, banana, elephant...

When it was done, David came in and sat down across from Krishawn carrying a clipboard full of papers with markings and printed charts on them; Krishawn couldn't help but feel like he was at the DMV. "Did I pass? Do I get my license? Becky Sue's counting on me to pick her up for the dance."

"Mmm-mostly. We found some inconsistencies with the higher level sentence comprehension. But your image tests were accurate."

"Possible to chalk that up to literary atrophy?"

"Nah. The growth of the tumor has created a lesion on your Pars Opercularis. As it continues to grow, the lesion will most likely spread. You can expect difficulty of reading to increase and trickle down from the harder sentences to relatively simple ones. Have you had any trouble reading lately?"

"Not until you just told me. I haven't been doing much reading, though, mostly newspapers and sheet music. Will that be affected, music?"

"Well, possibly. Music centers in the brain are mixed between the hemispheres and are largely speculative. You know, the mathematical aspect and the art aspect—the language aspect—overlaps several areas. You would actually make for a great case study: give you a piece of sheet music to play and look at your ability to replicate the melody versus your ability to duplicate the melody solely through aural detection. You could even do that at home. Find a piece of music you've never seen or played before, record it, play the selection back and then compare it against the artist's recording." He picked up steam. "It'd be interesting to see how aphasia—or paraphasia, dysprosody, anarthria, conduction aphasia…whatever you might contract—effects music comprehension and performance. Oo, oo, yeah this could be good; 'specially as most believe the right auditory cortex to be responsible for perceiving pitch, melody, harmony, timbre and some rhythm, and your left remains the only affected…"

Sinistire is the Italian word for left, taken from the Latin *sinistra*, named upon the belief that the left was preternaturally evil or sinister. While Dr. David continued rambling, Krishawn wondered whether things would have been different if he had been born left-handed instead of right, if the tumors were on the right hemisphere instead of the left.

David finished with his pitch and returned to his coda, "Krish, man, I really think you should go back on treatment. I know you're adverse to Chemo but it could prolong your life."

Krishawn had his hands in front of him, playing inaudible melodies on a piano that didn't exist. "Ah buddy…at this point, Chemo is just changing the oil on a Chevy too many miles past its prime." His fingers worked an imaginary ostinato and he began wondering whether cars and other machines were subject to mechanical apoptosis, outside of any planned obsolescence; he continued that train of thought as he left the office and boarded the PATH home.

In the week following the Sunday encounter, she found herself stuck upon the song, humming the simple pattern internally from her desk, in meetings, at lunch, on the subway. She felt a twinge of embarrassment when attempting to find him online and realized she hadn't gotten his name. She tried searching broadly through the genre, but, as she had guessed, the search yielded thousands upon thousands of both professional and amateur DJs and electronica musicians, spanning the full gamut from jazzy circuit benders to the "musician" whose playlist accompanied Thursday Night Trivia at his local bar. And even then she realized what she had heard wasn't exactly electronica, either; his music didn't fall easily into any genre or genre-permutation she could think of. There were familiar phrases she had heard before, yet each was executed so differently, manipulated so subtly that it was fresh, lively yet sardonic, if music could be, sensations that were at once invigorating and propulsive yet sad enough to feel an increasing loneliness, a claustrophobic sense of individual beauty and isolating melancholia—a song you wanted to experience on your own, void of any gazes, judgmental or benign.

She listened to other music when she could, found herself engaged in familiar songs and their respective associative feelings, and they satisfied their immediate facilities. But when the quiet began, when she was alone, she felt his song coming back, creeping into her spine when she showered, breathing on her neck while she waited for sleep.

When work ended Friday, she joined her coworkers for happy-hour at the corner bar with the sagging, geriatric ceiling of peeling tin, faded leather booths, an ambience of tea-candles inside smoked-glass sconces. Ray was back in Nantucket for the weekend helping his dad repair the wainscoting in the Master bedroom. She sat in the corner booth stirring a whiskey-sour, feeling the social dissonance of having lifted a new seam in the corrugated lives of this city, peaking into a line of society that was only ever meant to run parallel to hers, never intersecting. She felt removed. Men tried to talk to her and she answered in quick, clipped phrases, not wanting to be cruel or pretentious, just simply unable to muster enthusiasm. The same went for her friends. To be sure, she didn't know explicitly what she was looking for, only that she felt its absence.

When the hour was still late enough into the day and early enough into the night, she excused herself, claiming a fatigue-induced headache, and left the bar. Once outside, she exploited the nascent warmth of spring, walking casually through the streets towards her apartment, warmed in her jeans and top with a thin cotton sweater letting the air breathe onto her arms. The effects of the alcohol heightened her warmth and took the aches and tingles out of her body. This was her first real relief from the work week, the first moment of relaxation and *her* time, so she didn't walk in the most direct path to her apartment but instead took an unnecessary turn here and there, winding her way back home.

She felt his song playing in her head as she walked, adding a cinematic aire to the tempo of her gait and the passing scenery. Rounding the next block, she began to wonder what musicians did on the weekends: that as most of the shows she had gone to were on the weekends, their "work week" would be the inverse of hers, likely not starting until Thursday at the earliest. But that might not be true, either, she thought. Every other expectation she'd had had proven false. He hadn't been what she had expected. She thought, He hadn't been at all what she'd expected. It made her smile, the thought of him. And that made her confused. Her affective history had all been directed at men her own age. She had never gotten the appeal of the older man—and not that he was significantly older—but certainly outside any shared history. She rolled her eyes at the prospect that maybe this was her initiation. Then rolled them at her cognizant questioning and at the silly and pathetic attempt to quantify her amorism, especially into such a binary category: those who were attracted, and those who weren't. He *was* handsome, she'd admit. And interesting.

The light turned and she realized she had only just passed the coffee house and that, if she were so inclined to take a left then a right, would find herself in front of his place. If she passed would she find the house dark? Would she find light and noise pouring from the windows in some debaucherous party? Well there was really only one way to find out; curiosity quickened the tempo of her feet and she crossed the street.

When she got closer to his house, she found herself once more disappointed by her expectations and her flagrant misinterpretation of the music scene. The house wasn't dark—wasn't boisterous either. She lingered in front and watched the kitchen light swim in the sparse strip of lawn out front. His place looked quiet; it was quiet. The neighbors appeared to be more outgoing, filled with light and the polite jocularity of the company; while his house was adorable in its quaint humility, in its reserve and domestic coziness. He appeared in the window then, shuffling about in his kitchen, pouring himself a glass of water and grabbing something out of the fridge. She kept quiet and watched him eat for a few moments.

— § —

There was a bulb growing in a different bed now, germinating between his occipital lobe and his corpus calosum. When it blossoms (two weeks? three weeks?) he will go blind. In two months the bulb will have pushed his occipital lobe into his cerebellum and he won't be able to walk. After blooming it might scatter seeds among the neighboring beds. His body will have shed itself and his speech will already have failed him.

Eating, then, had become more and more an irritating and supercilious event, the minimal pleasures of the tongue outweighed by the uselessness of the task in the long haul—at least the lack of chemo meant he could taste again. But really what was the point? Soon, when his dying body reverts all remaining power to his visual cortex and superior colliculi, when his pineal gland starts firing off like a roman candle...when his consciousness is pared down to a singular column of light, his mind won't be concerned with meals eaten or missed.

Krishawn was the child of divorcees, a second-generation Irishman and a first-generation Indian whose divorce had left her blackballed from her family; they had found each other later in their lives and consummated their new love in the form of a singular child, with a bifurcated name celebrating both of their lineages. They had died years ago, leaving him no half-siblings but enough of an inheritance to put him through medical school without a considerable amount of debt.

Their death—their life, really—was framed in the degrees adorning his office, in the hours he spent working and in the paychecks that accompanied them—which wasn't to say he thought his profession trite or ignoble, he just didn't like to romanticize; at best he thought of himself as an exceptional mechanic. After all, you need only to walk through the cancer ward or the NICU to see the indiscriminating hand of death; and you need only to look at the fecal matter, blood, sweat, vomit and urine left on the mattresses to dispel any beauty or romance therein.

Many nights, when the visitors had left to worry in their homes, Krishawn would amble about the hospital listening to its music: the syncopated beeps of the Plum infusion pumps coupled with the heart monitors; the decrescendo pops of the Vision BiPaps; the electric fuzz of the UV blankets on the preemies; the percussive, double-clutched gulps of air from the forty-two-year-old man with punctured lung and sepsis. The melodic groans of the morphine-induced sleep from the twenty-six-year-old mother of three with third-degree burns and shattered pelvis. The dialysis patients dancing their way through the halls, five-pound weights on the bottom of the stands to keep them from toppling over.

These were the sounds of the place between this life and the next: one's final breath eliciting a flat-lining pedal note; the infant fighting pneumonia waking and inciting a fugue of crying among the other infants; the sustaining hiss of an oxygen hose being unplugged so the woman in the bariatric bed could breathe on her own. He always saw himself the conductor during these walks. In another month or two he'd be just another percussionist in the row, waiting for the cue of a bearded maestro in a white coat for him to crash his cymbals.

— § —

Her first knock was tentative, and he passed it off as a knock at his neighbors' house. The second was more confident. He opened the maple portal and found her standing against the banister, smiling and visibly drunk.

"Hey there?" he said as more of a question, "you come up with a name already?"

"What? No. Look, I've had your song in my head all week and I couldn't wait until Sunday."

He opened the door wider. "Really?"

"Well, sort of, not exactly. I mean it has been in my head all week, but I also kind of wanted to see how a musician spends his Friday nights. I have an overactive imagination."

"It's not too glamorous, as you can probably tell."

"Just you in there?" No sooner had she said those words than she had felt a bend of embarrassment crease her body. "I mean, if you're busy…"

Krishawn smiled, blushing, "Would you just come in already?"

"Umm…yes." She stepped past him into the house and led the way to his kitchen. Krishawn closed the door and followed.

"You know what? I actually have some wine here. My friend left a bottle from dinner this week. You want a glass?" He waited for her to answer "Sure" before he opened the fridge and removed a stoppered bottle of red wine, the cherry tree drawn on Mt. Sinai stationary eight-year old Mary Elizondo gave to him two-weeks before succumbing to non-Hodgkin's lymphoma fluttering as the door closed. He took down one glass and placed it on the granite island next to the wooden butcher's block.

"You're not having any?"

"Like I said, I'm not much of a drinker. *But* I suppose no one really *likes* drinking alone. Too much mythology built around the act." He poured the Beaujolais into two glasses.

"I realized something else, too," she said, taking the glass into her hand and sipping gingerly from the lip. "I don't know your name."

He had planned for that of course, but he made his face into a confused, humorously-shocked expression. "Yeah, I guess you're right. Shawn," he told her, giving her the half of the portmanteau that wouldn't lead to questions.

"Michelle. But my friends call me Chellie. Or Chell. With a 'C.'"

There was that smile on him again. "So what should I call you?"

"I guess we'll find out, depends if your other songs are as good as that last one."

"Well, nice to meet you, Chellie—formally, I mean." He held out his hand.

She used her client posture to accept. They both made overly-professional faces with pursed, serious lips, giving their hands a singular, asexual tug before breaking character; smiles up to canines for both.

Michelle took a sip of her wine, which she probably shouldn't be drinking after the happy hour beers and the whiskey, the combination always made her feel like trampled, Central Park horse-shit the following morning.

"So, you wanted to hear more of my music?"

She nodded. Krishawn took his glass and the bottle and left the kitchen, motioning with the outstretched glass towards the stairs. She rose and he let her pass in front of him, lightly guiding her with a hand on the small of her back, feeling the muscle just beneath the skin just beneath the sweater. He felt himself suppressing a sigh, felt so much of himself disappearing. He watched her climb the stairs and felt the same thing when he heard her steps on the wooden boards, her soft impressions: weightless, ghostly little taps. A chill passed through him smelling the vanilla and coconut of her hair as he followed her up the stairs; her ethereal self entering his nose, his mouth, his lungs.

They entered the converted bedroom and he flicked on a small, dim lamp and pulled a chair from the closet for her to sit in, which she took easily, gratefully after so much walking and standing and lightness of head, holding her glass in her lap, occasionally bringing the wine to her lips while he busied himself with the equipment.

"Do you want to hear something new or would you rather hear the first one," he said after a minute.

"I've had the first one in my head this whole week so you *have* to start with that one. New stuff after, if that's all right with you?" He bowed demurely and pressed play.

As soon as she heard the first pulsing of the beat she felt the same vertigo overcoming her. A mouthful of wine, she let the fermented liquid sit under her tongue, feeling the wave of sublingual absorption fill her head with a rush of lightness. She wanted her senses in unison, in concert. Her head spun and rose and dropped in and out with the song.

He sat next to her in another chair, watching her body sink, her breathing slow and deepen to the bpm of the song. She took another sip and wiped the tannins from her lips with her tongue. Her lips glistened in the computer light pouring over them, as if the crystals in her lip gloss were dehydrated syrup sapped from the Tree of Life itself.

When the song was done she sat quietly entranced before snapping to attention and requesting something new. Krishawn put on a new song and sat back as trilling percussion and syncopated thumps pulsed through the floor into her ankles, traveling up to her chest. The melody entered, a tenor line repeating the same tetrachord, sometimes in time with the song, sometimes not. Another ambiguity to her, the anonymous sounds and sources met with uneasy familiarity, like a song that had been with her through her whole life, as indelible as her shadow and with as much mysterious acquaintance, amorphous incarnations and forgettable simplicity. Chellie wanted to move, to writhe and squirm and undulate against the downbeat: a simple succession of movements so she could breathe the waves. She drank heavily to quell the urge. When her glass was finished, she grabbed the bottle and poured another. He hadn't touched his.

Some halfway through the song, Krishawn stood and walked to the large subwoofer underneath the desk. He pulled the speaker, a cube with an irregular heartbeat, out from under the lip of the keyboard and, sliding his hand behind the woofer, turned a knob that sent deeper waves through the floorboards and into her chest.

"Here," he said, "try this." He took her hand and laid her palm on the cube. She could feel the pulse of the music mirror her own, rumbling through her fingertips and up her quaking arm: a strange numbing feeling not unlike her post-yoga Aums. She laughed exasperatedly and smiled up to her bicuspids, looking into his face. He gave a humble smile.

"How do you make this? It's like nothing I've heard before."

"You want to see?"

With the song still going, he moved over to the microphone stands in the corner and raised them so the mics could look down on him and her. He took a small, silver, condenser microphone and plugged the XLR end into a patch cable, holding the instrument in his hand as he adjusted the levels on the mixer, the motorized buttons snapping to a preset algorithm. The song played lightly. He grabbed a stethoscope from a drawer and placed the ear pieces against the mesh tip of the cylinder, locking them together with a homemade clamp, the diaphragm pressed against the inside of his wrist. Through the monitors she could hear his pulse, a faint thumping with a time signature and tempo just a touch faster than the song's. He used his finger to stop and loop the carotid clip, twisting a knob on the top that made his pulse swell and stutter and shrink; the sound got bright and shimmered as if coupled with thousands of other pulses all crystalline and angelic.

Smiling, he took her hand and pressed the stethoscope to her wrist. The metal ring around the mesh was still warm from him. Her beat increased in the monitors. She closed her fingers around his and he stroked her knuckles with the side of his index finger. With his free hand, he opened a program on the computer and, using a MIDI controller, she could hear her heartbeat shift in pitch; he moved a wheel and the pitch bent and swayed; opening another program she heard the tone reverse, each note a crescendo to the attack of her heartbeat against her veins, rattling through her skin and into the awaiting mouth of the clinical instrument. Every slight shift of her pulse echoed back through the monitors: new, familiar, beautiful; her heartbeat sang to her, melancholic as he dipped the pitch to thirds and seconds, sevenths resolving to tonic. He duplicated the track, made some other adjustments and now there were suspended fourths, added ninths.

"That's amazing!" Molars sparkling.

He laughed and turned on the shotgun mics above. A sharp squelch of feedback kicked through the monitors and he scrambled to lower their levels, apologizing. The feedback pulled out, leaving them in the chamber of an echoing trance. The walls vibrated around them. Every internal act of her echoed through the stethoscope coupled with every external act of them. He clapped and the sound came through in exotic repetitions until slowly dying out.

"Have you ever looked at a reflection of a mirror in mirror? The infinite reflecting the infinite, building on the infinite? That's what I feel like with this, like I'm the conductor of infinity ('finity ('inity ('nity (...))))." His voice returning in overlapping permutations.

He removed the stethoscope and tapped the microphone against her skin, soft patting filled the room—a gallop followed by two half-notes on the up beat: a new loop. He lifted the microphone and let it slide through her hair; a silky shimmering came through in waves.

She laughed. He turned the volume up and kissed her. She kissed him back, lightly cradling his large lower lip in hers, pushing her head forward to take him deeper into her mouth. He cradled her head lightly in his hands, the microphone still positioned between his fingers, brushing against her hair, her face, crackling over her ear.

He rose out of his chair and helped her out of hers. Lying on the carpet, the waves of the subwoofer coursed through their bodies as his hands, microphone fixed between his fingers, stroked her sides. Every crease in her clothing, every ravine and soft hill of her body came through in waves, a tide filling the room with the music of her, seeping into her prostrate spine. The suckling sounds of their mouths coming apart bounced off the windows…her sharp intakes of breath…his baritone sighs invading the ether…

When he kissed her, when he gently squeezed his hand around her breast, when she groaned, she could feel the corresponding sound on her body, upon her body and through her body. The vibrations of his kiss, of her audible pleasure, coursed through her back and nestled her ears.

He removed her clothes in slow sweeps and she took his shirt off in tugs. He kissed her on the neck and undid the front clasp of her bra, cupping his right hand around the beige crest of her breast, allowing her nipples like pink quarters to run through the creases between his fingers. She moaned and arched her back into his chest, wrapping her leg around his hamstring. He took her right nipple in his mouth and let the bumps of his tongue spiral around her areola. The microphone caught the small pop of his mouth releasing her nipple before his lips crept back up her chest and neck. His hand slid to her stomach and read the Braille of her abdomen before sliding under the green mesh of her panties and taking her warmth in his hands. She jumped from his cold fingers, relaxed and let his middle finger slide between her labia, growing wet as his finger rocked between her lips and his warm mouth tickled her neck. She placed her own hand on the clasp of his belt and popped it open, working the button and lowering the zipper. The metallic gate made a sharp ripping through the speakers, and then through their backs. Michelle snaked her hand through the opening of his boxer-briefs and pulled out his penis, feeling another pulse in her palm as she stroked. Krishawn let out a deep groan that spiked the levels of the mic and made the room shudder around them. He pulled her underwear down and let her legs slide out one at a time, hands gliding the fabric along her thighs and knees. He kissed her knee caps and let her legs slide open as he worked his way down her thighs in ghostly kisses, teasing the hood of her clitoris with his tongue before taking her in his mouth. The speakers projected a series of sharp bursts and sighs while his tongue moved inside her. Left hand allowing her fingers to sew lines through the stubble of his hair, her right hand lay across her chest, spinning her fingers in concentric circles around her nipples, creating invisible crop circles on her chest. After a moment, he removed his head and pulled her body forward with a burst of heat as her back rushed against the carpet. He kissed her and she could taste herself on his lips, on his tongue. The alkaloid taste of batteries. She grabbed his dick and brushed the tip against her clit before putting it inside her. He coughed and she could feel his cock give a recursive flex, felt the rigidity of his body against her; Krishawn reached down to her ass and pulled himself further inside. They rolled and she climbed on top of him and mashed herself against him while he brought one hand up to her breast, first the left, then the right, running along her chest and up to her neck, his other hand moving from her ass to make tiny circles of his own with his thumb.

Their voices rose and multiplied through the room, and each pump, each thrust and grinding movement that brought them closer and closer to coming echoed through her ears, inside her body, through her bones and muscles and veins. Here, in this room, she felt him, and she felt herself. And when she came she felt the room coming…and he kept pumping, turning her over now with her back on the carpet, riding the waves of sound.

He made his thrusts slower, his hands moving along her body. He picked the microphone up and cradled it in his palm, running it over her as he continued to grind into her. The speakers sang along with the rustle of skin. Krishawn kissed her, pulling at her lips, tasting her hot breath. He moved the microphone to her pelvis. The cold metal made her jump and twist her body against his cock and she cried out. Gently, the condenser mic crackled against the stubble of her shaved pubis, a static that filled the room with a palpable existence. She could feel herself everywhere: in the walls, on the ceiling, in the window, riding on the light beyond. She wanted to feel this outside, wanted to feel this same sensation, this same sense of ubiquity with the grass and trees, the skies and blankets of clouds. He removed himself and placed the metal against her labia. An initial chirp turned to a coo, relishing the dissonance of his warm fingers against the frigidity of steel. His mouth worked with hers, his left arm cradling her head as they listened to the whispering of the microphone against the folds of her lips. He moved it back and forth against her before slowly sliding it in, first an inch, then pulling slightly back, then a little deeper, and deeper still, until the cold cylinder was completely inside. On the speakers they could hear the amniotic sounds of the mic moving inside of her: the muffled heartbeat, the walls of white noise, the soft suckling, while the cardioids caught her gasps and increasing cries, then the recorded amalgam of each as it recorded the recording of a recording of their sex. He slid the mic in and out fluidly, rocking this way and that. He moved it in small circles, then shallow rapid thrusts. She moved her pelvis into his hand, moved so the mic brushed against her clit in a sawing motion. She smashed her lips against his and held him there with her teeth, allowing a small cry to escape through the corners of her mouth as she came again (and again (and again)) through the speakers.

It was quiet after. They remained on the carpet for some time, the speakers silent, their breathing soft and delicate. His eyes stared at the ceiling; she swirled her finger through the carpet to allow him whatever privacy she felt he needed. After a while, she spoke.

"Have you ever done that before? I mean with anyone else?"

"Yes. No." He kept his eyes on the ceiling. "Not like this. This was different."

"Different how?"

"You were different, this was different…just, everything was different." He turned his head on the carpet and looked at her face still staring purposefully at her fingers. His hand moved towards hers and arrested her figure-eights. Turning his eyes to hers, he reached his right hand over and stroked the soft incline of her jaw, tilting it so their eyes would meet.

"Was this what you had in mind when you met me? Did you, did you plan this?"

"Yes. No. Parts."

"Which parts?"

"The unimportant parts. The parts that didn't involve you."

She allowed him to stroke her fingers; she twisted her thumb into his palm. "When are you leaving?"

His eyes become dopey, his pupils dilated and she felt him disappearing from the room. His mouth flickered and his breathing deepened. "Soon."

She nodded. "When will you be back?"

He didn't answer.

"Will you call me when you're back?"

Krishawn smiled and brought her hand to his mouth and kissed her knuckles, the broad back of her hand, her sticky fingertips. But his eyes stared through her, through the wallpaper, through the sheetrock, the lathe-board, the framing, the brick, all the way through the city, through the stratosphere and possibly way around the curvature of the universe itself before settling back into himself, though now resentful at the restraint of a body. She was no more here than he was, she thought.

"Yes, I'll call you. Of course I'll call you." He said it as if a ghost were operating his tongue. She remained silent and still, and after a while she rose and put on her clothes.

Before she left his house, he held her against the closed door and kissed her deeply, committing every curve of her lips to memory, every bump of her tongue, the alcohol dryness of her mouth. He opened the door and acknowledged her departure with a nod, her hand sliding down the side of his arm, lingering over his hands before allowing herself to be removed from him, neither saying good-bye.

— § —

Outside, the night had gone to winter while spring had skulked home to lick its wounds. The cold bit through the sweater whose porousness had been such a treat earlier in the evening. Michelle picked up her pace, trotting up the sidewalk on her toes, calves knotted up in balls, straight-kneed legs pivoting like the arms of a mechanized compass, unfortunately not pivoting fast enough to make the crosswalk.

She shifted her weight from foot to foot while she waited on the corner for the light to change, too cold to try a detour, mocking the struggles of the straight-jacket bound as she tried to rub warmth into her arms. She hadn't been this ill-prepared for a turn in the weather since that Memorial Day on Ray's parent's boat. Shit, Ray! What was she going to tell Ray?! Nothing, she concluded, and quickly. But how was she going to lie? More importantly, how was she going to live with the lie? If she didn't tell, is that just as bad? Is withholding just a lie in a bad toupée?

A dues-paying member of that elite cabal of meteorological optimists blew through the red light in short-shorts and a tank top, wind whistling through the bike messenger's gauged-out ears, narrowly avoiding the fender of a Sentry and an elderly man exiting a cab. Jesus, if he crashed in this chill…She reached down and rubbed her left knee.

She had been six when she'd learned to ride a bike without training wheels, which, as the only one within two years to master this feat, put her in a sort of limbo: not fully accepted by the older kids to allow her, willfully, to tag along; but she didn't want to neglect her new skill and remain among the training-wheel tethered. She tried to keep up with the bigger kids as they toured the neighborhood and the edges of the forested paths that bordered her subdivision. The older kids rode in packs and Michelle was always forced to ride twenty-feet behind as they made efforts to ditch her, with turns or with pace. And she never conceded; it was part of the fun. Up until one such attempt to lose their tail brought the pack down a particularly steep and eroded path covered in loose pebbles and exposed roots, heavy stones jutting from the dirt. She had followed and fallen, slipping from the bike and landing stomach first on her seat, knocking the wind out of her before somersaulting down the hill, resulting in scrapes and scratches and the birth of what would be an isotope-shaped scar on her left knee. Even now she still felt a phantom sting in her patella when she thought of injuries to that area, bike or otherwise; and even as an adult, when biking, she made attempts to cover her knees, even if just with a corner of summer dress that was sure to slip off.

Christ, she wondered if sex would be like that from now on, too; if she was now conditioned to expecting, not necessarily a substitute penis, a phantom phallus, but something new, un-thought-of, something self-extrapolating and inexorable. She worried whether the kind of sex she had with Ray would ever be enough. And even then, it wasn't the sex so much as it was something…else. She had held something in herself so utterly, pleasantly indescribable, something complex just taxiing in a haze of tangibility around something simple that she had always known or perceived but could never put a finger on.

Across the street, a red light blinked out and a green one blinked in. A blue-tinged halogen man made a vague walking gesture and she resumed her pace, crossing briskly in that mechanical gait, trying to beat the cold, trying to beat the orange countdown that had replaced the man before the red once more took over.

— § —

Even before his condition—likely due to a lack of connection to either as anything but words—Krishawn had always thought it funny how ontology and oncology were separated only by a "c." That somehow the whole of life rested on a single, trivial letter: a simple, curving line, a circle that doesn't connect, a nothingness separating life and death. It was all gloriously absurd. He'd even given the absurdity a cute little name, in passing, in his head as he made his rounds. And that hadn't changed, even after his diagnosis, becoming sharper if anything, as if he could outwit death with a clever turn of the tongue. And now, in her absence, he felt a burgeoning hole inside of him, a nothingness growing and throbbing, and he was grateful, not for the irony, as he'd imagined, but for the hurt.

Upstairs, in the studio, he let the computer be the only light, and he pressed his face against the screen, feeling the tingle of static on his forehead, cheeks and nose. She played on the speakers: her breath coming through in gentle, harmonized heaves; the ambient syncopation of his fingers on her abdomen, letting them fall to her belly in a soft patter while the hallucinatory beat droned through his fingers and chest. He closed his eyes and felt the white light burning through his eyelids, every now and then a flash of red.

Here, in the plasticine immortality of data, was the shape of life where the physical parameters of the corporeal dissolved into an open chasm of infinity; and it was here where, in her increased palpitations, in her sighs and dorsal heaving when his hands moved over her skin, he could stand at the precipice of this life and the next, embrace the emptiness, the nationality of death, and find the face he was saving for God. He turned the monitors up and shut the screen off, standing motionless and alone against the square window whose blinds he'd drawn to keep in the dark.

II. EDEN

nd against the hushed bark of a palm tree, where the orbs of coconuts dangled like stellar satellites overhead, where a creek ran shallow through a labyrinth of pebbles and grapefruit-sized stones, cutting through an occasional boulder, winding through the soft heather where banana trees arched their scoliosis trunks and the Birds Of Paradise fluttered blue then red, black and dotted with nacre spots like so many peacock eyes, where the jagged mountains like moss-covered broken vertebrae dipped in vanilla impaled the terrarium of sky, where pink sand beaches and shallow bays nestled against the breathing of the tide and two naked bodies, sun-bleached hair and a gentle trickle of sweat gravitating from their navel-less bellies to the wooly crevices of untrimmed pubis, mouths crunching on fruits and figs while the beasts meandering through the brush and jungle and plains kept an amenable distance and the sounds of howler and spider monkeys clanging through the python-laden canopies had a rhythm and syncopated melody that the man mimicked in a whistle through his teeth is where her hand rose and made shadows on his chest. When she stopped and the sun slipped its edge into the pocket of the mountains, he mounted her and slid himself inside her and they cooed while

rocking, dangling their bodies together like so many vines twisting and turning and stumbling through the jungle in search of light, ebbing their bodies into the insulating sand, coming quickly and insignificantly. Finished, they laid back and peeled rinds from oranges and suckled on the seeds of pomegranate; and un-sated, they rose—he to hunt animals of the four-legged genus and she to pick ripe blackberries on the beach next to the delta where the sea opened behind the womb of the bay and where they had a fire and spit and roasted boar while floating and drifting against the salinity of the sea, heads bobbing, diving and picking starfish from the coral, puffer fish inflating without terminal recourse, where the wayward nurse sharks trolled only for mackerel and should they tire of boar and deer they needed only to extend the end of a spear for the gracious sacrifice of a squid; and when the sun fell into the periphery of the jungle they've only to pull away from the beach and return to the matted heather where the nights were forever warm and they could count the stars and comets amid the residual death of ephemeral bodies and join in the ensemble of the moon.

Around the fire that night they opened their mouths and tried different sounds, mocking sounds, inflections of their larynx and lips forming the call of panther and macaw and baboon, moderating their inflections to imitate the late crackling of the burning timber, dying down and growing neglected as they explored the mystery of their mouths cooing and making a mess of their tongues. When the fire, finally depleted of oxygen, was left to nothing more than a reduced invalid seeping a littered breath from the asphyxiating pile of ash, the night still burning a vacuum around their concept of home, they kept exercising the flow of air from their mouths until the amber light turned a rough shade of purple and their lips no longer flashed a crimson line with which to measure the movements of the other's mouth, to imitate, to equate cause and action and participate in their emulation; when their mouths waned dreadfully into the night and were swallowed into the mouth of God, they reduced to silence, terrified to continue dabbling in the sonorous mystery of animal and man sans light; and rather than face an incommunicable void they fell back into the physical realm of their bodies, the supple familiarity in which they have all knowable information, when there are no logical barriers between what can be felt by the hand and seen by the eye in day.

— § —

He rose early the following morning, when the blue filter of the pre-dawn light allowed only enough visibility to make out shapes and high-contrast colors, moving into the forest to relieve himself while she lay sleeping. The morning dampness trickling from rubbery leaves fell onto his shoulders and torso as he pushed through the thicket and pulled vines from his face, Old Man's Beard scratching at his forearms as he climbed around a mangrove tree, jumping back to the wet earth just as he caught a flash of something red in the near distance, a heavy push of leaves trailing after. He waited, watching, until the leaves return to rest, and then relieved himself in a dirt hole he would remember to bury and not trample.

She wasn't awake when he returned and he slid next to her in the pressed grass still warm from his body as he got reacquainted with the warmth of hers. They slept dreamlessly until the morning sun coerced their eyes from the dark ocular caves behind the lids. Somnolence left her first this time, and she stared at his closed eyelids, no thought of reading the delta waves that twittered the convex lenses of his eyes, moving the soft skin left, right…finding her fingers and playing with the malleable cartilage of his ears, her fingernails sliding under and tracing the folds before pulling back and twisting a vagrant lock of hair. She pulled sharply and ignorantly. His eyes popped open and he gave a scream and a reciprocal tug, then her hand slapped his stomach and she scrambled upright as he reached out to inflict some adolescent injury to her thigh, missed, and gave chase, her footfalls softly patting along the trodden path to the beach, her mouth barking the uvular ex-plosions she'd taken favor to the night before.

The sea washed the sweat away and provided them with an im-mediate comfort against the sun that never blistered or burned but merely warmed their flesh, demanding only the water from their bod-ies as a tariff, discomfort returning only when they surfaced and the sharp overhead sun bounced off the skin of the water and into their un-occluded eyes, forcing them to squint and dive and cool them-selves in the underlying current where they met and watched the tur-tles swim past, holding hands while stroking the hard shell, feeling the geodesic compartments of the tortoise until the burning filled their lungs and necessitated a return to the surface. An iridescent cavalcade of fish passed below, an ambulating chromatography of reds, blues, greens, yellows and the various permutations of each. They tried grabbing them, inserting hands into the schools as if the thousands of fish were a solitary, corporeal entity, laughing bubbles as their hands returned empty and the school dispersed and reformed outside of their purchase, the barracuda slipping silently and amiably underneath their feet.

In the afternoon they cooled under an eastward facing cove with sharp bluffs overhead to block the light and sloping shores on the sides that met in the crest of inlet and created a soft beach and waist high water where they could sit with their heads poking just above the surface. He moved himself towards her, their buoyant arms finding each other and pulling themselves together in a knot, bobbing aquatically to the movement of the tide, their pubic hair breathing like the coral. The salinity kept them afloat while her head, dangling on his shoulder, turned upward toward the outlying bluffs, vines falling from the trees into the pool, dying roots trying to cling to the rock walls, a few snapped off here and there; she followed the roots upwards, into their trunks and out into the splotchy canopy where her eyes, glazed with the revel of noon sun, closed against the heat, seeing only the nickelodeon playing on the backs of her eyelids.

On a patch of tall grass on a bluff overlooking the sea she sat and ran her fingers through the green blades, feeling the tiny hooks catching on her fingers, a not unpleasant friction, rough but playful, moving her spaded hand in a sweeping motion and watching the grass lightly fall under, springing upright in swathes of white as the sun reflected off the bristles. She used both hands and drew herself in the middle of a figure-eight, positioning herself at the crux of infinity. Plucking a strand of grass and placing it against her nose, she inhaled a perfume of chlorophyll at the severed edge, the taste of Green on her lips and tongue, a tickle at her nose. Another strand plucked, held against the first, and brought to her lips. She blew and sent a squeaking rippling through the air; she laughed and repeated the action again, blowing harder and feeling the sound amplify and a funny buzzing numb her lips, cheeks puffed out and vibrating from the strain. She played with the varying levels of amplification and duration, two soft, short bursts, a drawn-out squeak held to echo off the sun. She grabbed several handfuls of grass, balling them into her hands, and brought them back to the shore where he was napping.

At dusk they sat against a boulder at the meridian of sand and jungle, taking turns at the grass noise and together assembling a fugue of cacophony, reverberating off the rock and outwards to the sea.

While he played with the grass, she put her instrument in her lap and tested the sounds she'd created yesterday with her mouth, a clucking against the buzzing grass followed by a soft "ooh" and "ahhhh," a hiccupping moan, a toccata of the larynx. And when the fire died they slept as soundlessly as the acacia trees breathing lightly in the subtle wind.

— § —

There is another branch, twenty-three feet, reticulated, softly coiling upwards toward the brittle, sun-bleached tips of an apple tree. The rough corrugated bark scraped against the tessellation of scales, the induced friction warming a supple white belly full-up on deer, and then a face breaking through the canopy, forked tongue tasting atmosphere, eyes shut until a distant snap of a twig far below, a synaptic message underneath the glial sheath of bark, tapped a Morse message into its belly. Its face left the openness of the sun and returned to the shade of leaves, retracing its path until the fleshy face and sun-soaked hair were close enough to taste.

It spoke mimetically. Telling her to pluck, bite, eat.

She folded the stem, twisted it apart and severed the ball from its tether, bringing the fruit to her nose, smelling the dry skin, then up to her ear, trying to hear the language of taste underneath. Circumnavigating the red globe with the enamel galleons of her teeth, feeling for inconsistencies, blisters, bruises...she let her mouth dig into the crust, prying a chunk free and holding it in her mouth, feeling the sour cool, the taste of new air, chewing, relishing the muffled crunch against her tongue; and she took another bite, and another, as if with enough effort she could fit the whole of the world in her mouth. She plucked another one after finishing the first and ran chirping and laughing to the beach where he was skinning an antelope and thrust the fruit to his lips—the apple, bitten—and devoured the apple to its core.

— § —

They saw pictures embroidered in the black sari of night. Tiny beads of light, sometimes orange, sometimes yellow, sometimes staying in the sky, sometimes dancing outside the frame of the mountains and trees. She pointed at him and spoke "*eaaauuu*;" he mimicked. They repeated this over and over. She pointed at herself and pushed from her lungs a "*mmmnnneeaa*." He tried to follow, "*mmmmnnnaaayyy*," "*mneeaay*," "*mmnee*" and "*mnai*."

"*Me*," she said.

"*Me*," he repeated.

"*Me*," she said again, touching her hand to her chest. "*Y-you*," touching his knee across the dirt.

"*Hāght...Hāad...Hāadtāmn...Hādām...ha-Ādam...Ādām*." He worked his tongue around and said once more, with hand patting his chest. "*Adam*."

"*Ichch...Isch...Ish...Ishaugh...Ishah...*" She shook her head and proceeded on a new name for herself. "*Haaamma... Haamwā... Haawwā... Ḥawwā... Eewwah... Eewah... Eauwa... Eauvha... Eauva... Ea-va...*" She clapped and patted her sternum. "*Eve*."

They took turns repeating their sobriquets, saying the name and pointing to themselves, to the other; him pointing at her solar plexus, "*Eve*;" she to him, "*Adam*." After a while they settled into a queasy silence, unsure where this moment put them: how they got there, what this meant, and where it would go.

— § —

Names like *rocks* and *sand* and *beach* came easily, with a gentle stroking of the tongue against the palate. There were names like *snake* and *serpent* that recoiled inside of their mouths. *Water* and *coral* cascaded easily from their larynx, cool and relaxed. Their *feet* carried them through *trees* and over *rocks*, cooled at the edges of rivers, scorched on the *sand* hot in the mid day. They caught a *fish* and named it after the bite sized sustenance it offered. They pushed through *leaves* and *bushes* with topographical, semantic fervor and kept their findings mapped out on their tongues and archived in their heads, giving no thought to the nouns that would fall eventually by the wayside for verbs or the tragedy of adjectives.

— § —

There was a non-vocalized nomenclature for the world around them each had come to accept before the burden of naming overtook and brought about the contention of image and label. When he could simply look upon a *plum* and know it from taste and color, when she could pick up a firm piece of earth and not feel the stress of deciding it a *rock*, a *stone*, a *pebble*.

There was a dispute over *legs* and *arms*, and they screamed at each other in preterit tones from their former lives until the matter was settled. There was the problem of *hips, pelvis* and *waist*. There was the reluctant courting of *knees* and *elbows, fingers* and *toes*, the discrepancy of *shins* and *ankles*.

Screaming "*Ears, ears*" she beat him about the face with closed *palms* while he retaliated obdurately with "*Eyes…eyes!*"

They slept apart that night on opposite sides of the hearth, breathing deliberately and stubbornly, unwilling to concede even in sleep.

— § —

When *Eve* awoke, *Adam* was already gone, swimming in the dawn *water*, still dark but brimming with the faint promise of the *day*; the flashes of *pink* and *orange* unbearably differentiated against the dark *blue* of the waves still trying to hang on to the *night*. He floated stilly; large, slow strokes of his *wing*-span keeping his *head* in the air; *eyes* trained to the shore to offer a chastising stare should she chance to enter the *beach*. And when he saw the rustle of the *bushes* in the eastern side of the bay he set his glare and waited for what he thought would be her open *pink* face, dilating and pushing through the layers of *green*.

What came through wasn't *pink* with *brown*ish-*yellow*ish *hair, blue* irises and *red lips*.

Whatever came through was an object of indefinite color, a black effigy eclipsing the inchoate *day* above, a half-risen halo of *fire* surrounding the inset coal slaloming between *conches* and *shells* in the *sand*, coming closer to the shore and always veering away from a position of clarity. *Adam* treaded water and watched the *animal*, transforming from an amorphous blob of motion to a quadrapedal shadow, at times quintrapedal until *Adam* realized the fifth limb was a *tail*. A jungle *cat* of some nature, he could at least make that out, though of different size and stride from the *jaguars* and *pumas*, the *lions* and *cheetahs* or the various branding of *tiger*. Corpulent with slow death, pushing along adjacent to the bramble, walking to the *water's* edge, hind *legs* collapsing to the sand as the animal pointed its *face* towards the bobbing torso in the *sea*. *Adam* turned and paddled backward in case the creature grew an amphibious disposition; but when he turned back around the *beast* was gone, the beaches empty, and the *blue* sand a body of taupe.

Eve made her way to the beach in the late morning, and both apologized in a manner of proffered *food*, physical affection, and a retreat to earlier noises devoid of semantic meaning. They swam and in the afternoon lazed under the sun as a cumulous rode slowly into the sky.

"*Sheep*," she said.

"*Mountain*," he grunted.

— § —

The *sand* was variably monochromatic: *purple* in the morning, khaki in the afternoon, *gray* in the evening. *Adam* made drawings of the *beast* in a *gray* smear before *him* as a full *belly* kept *him* too lethargic to make *his* way into the jungle and bury the uneaten carrion of their meal. Judging the image to be insufficient, *Adam* picked up a burnt piece of coal and submitted the carbon to a flat figure on the surrounding *limestone*, the verisimilitude remained lost and *he* went about ventilating his breaths bitterly, peeling translucent, dermatological wafers from the dorsal region of his deltoids, his first punishment from the sun.

— § —

There was a *river* to the south, *one* of *four* in the region, which curved and jackknifed and opened up to the *sea*; but in the jungle *it* wove smooth, and soundless. *Eve* came here because there was still aquatic cool, the canopy acted as sentinel for the light so *she* could *sit* at the edge, *dip her toes* in the *water* and feel the suckling of the *minnows*. There was *grass* on the floor of the river and *she* twirled the weightless threads with *her* big *toe*, winding a slimy, slippery, and rubbery spool around *her* digit.

While *he* was sulking from the dispute they'd had over *hair* and *hare*, *she'd* bide *her* time here, twisting the stems of *flowers* together into a *one*-stem bouquet, fanning the perfume to *her nose* before throwing the potpourri into the *river to watch* the *colors* float away. *Morning Glory, Lilac* and *Daisy* navigated the slow current, spinning and submerging until disappearing around the bend. *She* lifted *her head to find* a new medium of entertainment and saw a pair of *eyes* across the bank. Squinting and cupping *her hands* to focus *her* pupils, *she* saw the flat, reflective corneas eschewing a fixed glow through the breaks in the thorn *bush*, the apertures opening as the *face* pushed further into the light. There was a *nose she* could see, *ears,* and a *chin* of coarse *red hair*. Lines spread from the snout and split the gap between the *eyes. She* waited for the owner *to come* further when a bit of *pollen* tickled *her* sinuses; when *she* looked up after the *sneeze, it* was gone.

Inquisitive, *she* placed both *her feet* into the *water* and stood *ankle*-deep until *she found her* balance, testing *her* hold with another step forward, then another, letting the *water come* up to *her knees*, feeling a rush of *cold* when *her waist* dropped in. The *water* pushed numbly against *her* and *she* raised *her elbows to keep her* righted as *she* trudged through the *mud* and *rocks*, feeling the gradual incline, the wayward string of *weed* sliding intimately up *her calf.*

On the bank *she* used *her hands to fling water* and sediment from *her body*, muscles sharpened on the *cold*, left *foot* stinging from the vertex of an upturned *rock*. There was some *moss* that *she* used *to remove* what *her hands* couldn't. When *she* was dry *she stepped* towards the *thorn-bush*, tentatively searching the bracken for *eyes*. *She found* the hole where the creature had watched *her* and *found* a wispy *red cloud* stuck to a *thorn*. As *she* pulled the bit of dander into the light, rubbing the strands of *fur* in *her fingers*, working the follicles into a *red ball*, a *thorn* scraped a line into the back of *her hand. She* took the *ball* in *her left hand* and used the swab *to dab* away the blood percolating through *her skin.* The *red* intermingling: *similar, different. She* left the clump of *fur* on the *dirt* and crossed the *river* the way *she* came.

— § —

Eve returned and *sat* beside a hungry *Adam who* had fallen *asleep* under the *heat* and the forgotten *boar* roasting over the spit, waking to a smoking blackness and fumes of a carbon reduction. *He kicked* and screamed and threw *things. She* shook *her* head and showed *him* a bounty of *pears* and *mangos* and *raspberries* and *plums* which *she* divided with equanimity; they set *to eating. Three* cores *lay* before *Adam* to *Eve's one,* preferring *to eat* slowly and *to savor. Adam* finished the last of *his* share, *dropped* the *mango pit,* with bits of viable sustenance still available, into *his* cemetery of *fruit* and *reached* into *Eve's* pile. *She slapped his hand* away.

"*Mine,*" *she* said; *pointing* to *his* discarded supper, "*yours.*"

He shook *his head,* "*Hungry. More. You Share.*"

Eve slid *her fruit* away from *him. Adam reached* again and *she slapped her hand* on a reddened patch of *skin* on *his* back. *He* gasped, then whimpered and made *his* defense. "*Adam bigger, stronger. Need more.*"

"*Food there.*" *She* pointed out the *mango he* hadn't finished.

Adam guffawed, "*Not enough. Sandy. More.*"

"*Waste.*" *Eve* continued *eating* in front of the sullen *Adam.*

"*Not share?*" he demanded.

"*Did share.*"

"*Not more?*"

She put *her hands* in front of *her* as if balancing *two* separate objects and *stopped* them at an equivocal point. *He* still didn't accept *her* notion of fair and asked *her why she* wanted *to fight.*

"*No fight,*" *she* said.

"*Yes fight.*"

"*No fight. Squabble.*"

"*No squabble,*" *he* objected again.

She shrugged, "*Tiff.*"

Looking at *Adam's* lithograph with the few remaining *raspberries she* had, *Eve* took *two* of them and *mashed* them into the *black* and *tan* figure *Adam* had created earlier. Unsure of *what* they were *looking* at, feeling the disparity of nomenclature coupled with the aggravation of familiarity, of an intimate nameless conception, no *word* was proffered by either in the quiet, the dissonance between image and *word*, memory and *name,* remanding them rhetorically and lexically isolated. Then *he huffed* at the *waste* of *food* and marched off *to bury* the remains of the *boar;* he *slept* with *his back* to *her* upon *his* return.

— § —

On the *beach,* after *a morning swim had* driven them to an unbearable *thirst* and they *had to retreat* from the salt *water* inland towards the *river* and a make-shift *gourd,* they *found* a *dove* with both *wings broken* and *blood* coming from *its breast,* the result of some predator *who* for whatever reasons hadn't deigned *to finish* the kill or *eat its* reward. They *stopped* in front of the *bird; Eve* bent *to pick it* up but *Adam* arrested *her shoulder.*

"*Hurt it.*"

She gave him a pleading look. "*Help it,*" *she* insisted.

"*Can't,*" *he* frowned, not knowing how to tell *her it was* too *far* gone.

"*What to do?*"

He scanned the *beach* and *found* a *large black stone, plucked it* from the sand and *carried it* over *his head* toward the *bird. Eve* yelled as *he* was halfway through *swinging* the *rock* upon the helpless aviary.

"*No,*" she said. "*Help. Heellpp.*"

He tried *to demonstrate,* with *words* and actions, how death *was* a form of help, of mercy against the drawn-out and the inevitable. But *she* couldn't understand *his* performance dance and repeatedly *shook her head,* as if the *more* violent *her* oscillations became the clearer *her* point for life would become. Dissatisfied with *her* explanation and obdurate in *his* motives, *he crushed* the *dove quickly* and thoroughly, and *she* refused *to speak* with *him*—in any form—for the rest of the *day.*

— § —

There *were words he tried* for reconciliation, and for grief. *He* didn't *have the* patience *for* commas and *spoke in* abridged sentences, fragmented expositions punctuated with hyperbolic *hand* gestures *to coordinate* purpose and *name.*

When their *words* failed *he hit her* and *she hit him back.*

"Leave," she said.
"Leave?" he said.
She nodded. "Go."
Adam hung *his head* and *left; he lit a fire on the beach. She found pa-paya* and *berries* and *ate* them *on the flattened grass* for dessert.

They had *dreams of things circling* them, of low *growls* and *the* admonishing *rumble of an* empty *belly.* They *dreamt of teeth* and *fangs* and *claws that* could retract. They *dreamt of words* and *phrases that tumbled* over *each* other, *gaining speed* and altitude. There *were words* with *fangs,* sentences with *tails.* They *dreamt of an open mouth like a cave* they could *put* their *head into, reaching past the stalagmites* and *stalactites of teeth, looking down the throat where a vapor of* corroded *flesh sat like a fog* as they *waited for the right words to come that* they couldn't *find on* their *own; when the throat* refused *to answer* they *screamed the words* they *had on hand until* their *throats were cracked* and *brittle. When* they *still didn't come, those words,* they surrendered their *neck to the lower teeth* and *waited for the cave to close.* And *then* they *woke up, alone* and *sweating.*

— § —

She went to the beach because Why shouldn't she. There was water for both. There were fish for her to eat. There were places to lie down when it got hot, coconut oil to stave off the burns. She walked into the water, dunked her head. A jellyfish swam by. She kicked her legs, moving into deeper water.

He dug a hole in the sand with his feet, carved the bottom out with a stick when he hit the wet sand underneath. He saw her swimming offshore, close enough to see her face. She brushed her hair from her forehead to look back at him. He put his feet in the sand to cool. His eyes stayed with hers. A seagull flew overhead, dipped to the water, catching a fish in its beak.

The sun moved slowly up then down. The wind went north then west. When the tide came in it covered his feet in his pit. He moved back to the rocks.

She stepped into the waist-high water. Her belly looked full. Engorged, bursting with life, with new words that would fill the earth. There were still words unsolved, though. Didn't she know this?

Adam left the beach to move to the hills, shade, fields, fresh vegetables, grass for grazing. A bull snake struck at his heels. Adam yelled, recoiled, putting his foot down to crush the snake's head. In the way he took fig leafs to cover his genitals from the elements, Adam wrapped his feet in the hide of a gazelle, using the rest to adorn his shoulders.

Rain came. Adam took cover under a tree with exposed roots cutting into the side of a hill. Eve left the water to hide in a cove beneath a bluff. Thunder rolled in. Lighting struck a dead tree in the middle of the field. Smoke, then fire, came, engulfing the tree, spreading to the grass below. A flaming line cut a swath through their garden, separating them. Eve on the coast; Adam in the prairie.

On his own, Adam had to make shelter. Eve still had the heather to return to, the canopy of the jungle. Adam found limbs, long dead branches of trees to stack up against the hillside; leaves to thatch, to make a roof.

At night: separate fires, separate loneliness. The fire kept burning, severed all paths, kept Adam to Adam, Eve to Eve. Threatening their communion with a flaming sword that would forever rage, feasting off dry grass, oxygen-rent vegetation, living flora killed by the increase of heat.

Smoke seeped into the night sky. Eve watched from the patches of sugar canes, rubbing her protruding belly. Adam stared on from his island of prairie, able eyes trained to the gray tide snubbing out the light, the moon, the stars in patterns yet to name.

Adam looked to his own fire, enfeebled. The coals were going out, tiny embers disappearing into the plains. He set off to collect more wood.

III. NO NAMES

> *"Is there something so innocent in the recitation
> of names that God is pleased?"*
>
> —*Don DeLillo,* WHITE NOISE

The rules they had talked about for a while included that he be in the same room, that they both make the choice, and that they would have no further contact whatsoever with the man they selected, which helped with the last rule: no names: he didn't want any way for them to know each other, and he didn't want any names said during The Act, as they were calling it. There were also stipulations they went over about The Act itself, more appeasements and compromises than straight rules, things that they had felt should stay preserved in their past, such as her drilling her chin into his shoulder or running her fingers through his chest hair; she wasn't allowed to be picked up or taken from behind (which she contented would be hard to step around as it was difficult for her to climax when she was facing him—something the two had never discussed prior to The Accident); there were other things, both more grand and more minute. When they were done they were left with a sort of shot list. The list wasn't really what was important; what was important was that they were trying. A woman has needs a man in his position can't possibly satisfy. He needed to try, as much for her sake as for theirs. Yes, if they were to going to make it, they would both have to make sacrifices.

Still, it didn't feel anywhere close to right, and he knew it wouldn't;

watching the upside-down heart of her ass like two conjoined tear-drops slide and sway, rise and fall, buck and twist against the central pivot of the man's hips did things to his heart for which no amount of preparation would have ever been enough.

Theirs spawned out of a youthful urgency and the acceptance that marriage would facilitate more money and the possibility of safer travels throughout his service career, an extra sliver of hope against the maladies of their friends and cousins and classmates, those mortal and not: begging the question, Which was harder to deal with?

Which isn't to say there wasn't love; they had been attached to each other, had adored each other; it was just they had never subscribed to the idyllic, romanticized couples their parents had read of in the war stories of the wars of their youth.

The first night he had returned home after leaving the VA hospital in Fort Wayne she had bathed him in their tub, dragging a warm wash-cloth over first his legs, then his feet, the bed sores on his hamstrings and calves…two mauve kidneys glowing on the bottom of the cracking porcelain. The crown molding had splintered and buckled, damaged from water vapor and his absence, the framing nails poking through the three-quarter-inch strip of wood like crooked, silver teeth or a crudely assembled crown of thorns. She had painted while he was away and he didn't like the salmon color she had chosen; however, he felt it wasn't the ideal moment to bring it up.

She had taken her time, lightly kneading the muscles with the washcloth and her hands as the nurse had shown her, enduring the start of a career to which she'd never applied, enduring nonetheless. Occasionally he'd take the washcloth from her and clean the parts he felt more dignified to clean himself. Watching her handle his legs, great fleshy submarines floating just under the surface of the salty foam riding on the cooling water, he had cried, out of self-pity and anger and shame and the general calculus of injustice. She dropped the cloth, put his legs down, and cradled his head in her arms; a six-foot-two man weeping and swaddled in the arms of a woman their ethos had sworn him to protect and to provide for; and then he cried harder.

— § —

His grip tightened on the wheels of his chair to contend with the man's grunting, her surmounting sighs and the clapping of the hotel headboard bouncing off the paisley wallpaper (they both agreed it shouldn't be done in their home); the image reversed and doubled in the vanity that faced the bed had an exponential affect. Then the drapery of her hair fell over his forehead and shrouded their faces from him. He hoped they weren't kissing—that hadn't been explicitly said because he felt it explicitly unsaid—yet he couldn't quite bring himself to voice his concern. The end of the first hour beat upon his will and upon the seated muscles collecting blood and formic acid in their unmoving vigil. Early on he had tried closing his eyes, imagining the noises were from another room, from a porno he used to have, from an *a priori* life, all of which only increased his paranoia and so he kept them open, kept them vigilant.

The bed kept ticking, keeping time like a Swiss watch; after each successive rotation he wanted to ask if they were almost done but he'd refrained; he didn't want to ruin the momentum by speaking up as he'd done earlier, when things were just getting started, trying to direct the actions until she'd pleaded with him, in that apologetic tone she gets when she asks his permission to go dance when they're out at the bar with friends and that he sometimes gets from waitresses, that he was being "distracting, sugar;" so he was forced to stop, forced to just be quiet, forced to just watch.

— § —

Their wedding had been a practical event, that is, just their immediate family and a handful of friends with whom they had grown up. The ceremony was done in her church with her pastor because she was Presbyterian not Catholic. Friends of his parents owned a local bar-and-grill and they were able to have the reception there for just a couple hundred bucks, freeing them from having to pay the gratuitous fees at the Marriot or the VFW. Near the jukebox that alternated between Springsteen and Chesney was a table for guests to place cards and gifts inside the mouth of a poster-board collage filled with pictures of toothless smiles, gymnastic competitions, piano recitals, a boy flexing with war paint and Hulkmania T-shirt, a girl wearing her older sister's clothes, football games, soccer games, baseball games, a boy with shaggy hair kissing a bleach-blonde girl in a halter top, a picture of a boy in army fatigues with buzzed head and a girl with brown hair and yellow tips wearing an oversized Purdue sweatshirt, and an empty 3" x 5" rectangle on which his mother had written "Grandchildren ?" in with marker.

Their song had been "Born to Run" because he thought he did a good Springsteen impression when he was drinking and he would often close down the bar with the song and a lip-synced performance, pulling her into the open space allocated for dancing and parading her around the square in exaggerated movements, picking her up, letting her wrap her legs around his waist as she placed her hands on his "*engines*;" they had recited the same dance in a brand new wedding dress and a rented tux, dancing in peanut shells because it was that kind of bar, her hands once again on his "*engines*," his mind elsewhere, imaging memories of the future.

— § —

The pumping increased and he watched the man's knuckles go white from the firmness of his grip on her ass, still buoyant with youth and the absence of childbirth. The man pulled her closer and picked up his pace. He grimaced when her aqua fingernails slid over the man's hands and wrapped around his forearms, assisting his hold on her and allowing more of himself inside her. Blankets glacially spilling from the bed knocked the plastic cocktail cups onto the floor, spilling limes, stirrer straws, empty nips of Bombay. He hated that she still drank gin 'n tonics, it being the last drink he'd ordered before a knife was stuck into his back, something Spanish whispered into his ear and he'd felt so much weight falling under him.

She muttered "Oh God, oh my fucking God" and they switched positions, him on top of her, bending her knees up to her chest, her tongue sliding across her incisors before disappearing back into her mouth, her eyes back behind their eyelids. On the man's shoulder, now the closest body part to him, was a tattoo of some jungle cat or other, a black negative in the red light of the EXIT sign bathing them in a pedantic, admonishing hue from above the door. That the man was only a few years younger and a lifetime removed had bothered him, but she was getting antsy and it was either this guy or a man that just looked way too much like his old XO. Fucking college boys—both of them.

Since their arrival, the room next to theirs had been playing the same lamentable German symphony over and over again in a loop, the same morose piano accompanying the same horrifyingly-sad tenor, crying out through the wall and wallpaper. After numerous repetitions, the German phrases began planting themselves in his head until the song ended, began and came back around again: "*Still ist die Nact, es ru-hen die Gas-sen, in die-sem Hau-se wohn-te mein Schatz… Du Dop-pel-gän-ger, du blei-cher Ge-sel-le, was äffst du nach mein Lie-bes-leid.*" The music was, needless to say, an eerie score for The Event. After so many times, he wondered if perhaps the person next door hadn't killed himself, or herself; it was just that kind of place.

They had tried to work things out on their own. To lasso the feral gorilla that had taken up residence in their bedroom. He had called the initial phase of their psuedo-sexual experimentation "Sexy For Eunuchs." Their first foray required that she lay naked on the bed while he wheeled himself to her side, her head propped up on a pillow against the bare wall so their mouths could meet, close but not touching, breathing the other's breath back and forth in a slow, deep rhythm until they were both drunk on carbon-dioxide; she took his hands and used them to massage her breasts before emigrating them south. The whole time they had never taken their eyes of each other, staring at each other with such determined and ruthless hope that this would be enough for both of them; each knowing, fearing, that it wouldn't.

It was the tantalization that made it erotic, he'd said, which was the goal here, wasn't it?, to find satisfying "non-physical" forms of fucking, like the book said ("lovemaking" was the term the book actually used).

No, it was the high and the anticipation, she'd responded, that's what made it erotic; and whether I come from your fingers or your cock what's the difference as long as it's from you, baby?

Truthfully, he was scared to use even a finger; because sex, like war, thrives off the same basis of escalation; and neither beast responded to a master once born. But he obliged, because he wasn't a deserter, because he had to. Because if your own country won't allow you to fight the good fight you'll find one that will. So they changed their routine.

The sex next shifted to her lying prostrate on his naked body while their stacked hands moved over hers, squeezing and caressing his favorite parts of her, his hands guiding her masturbation, *their* masturbation, like an Ouija board. They tried toys and he would use them on her: his idea, and admittedly one in which her pleasure rode back-seat to the need for him to feel he could still offer her some gratification. But after a while she couldn't come any more and the sex became perfunctory. She needed more than machination, needed more than his elbow and shoulder working in-tune like a piston, needed the raw and idiosyncratic motion of two fumbling bodies throwing each other out of symmetry, hitting each other's pleasure points with accidentals and unexpected rhythms; she needed the passing notes of sexual symphony, needed a force more than gravity pulling her down, pulling him into her—two hands wrapped around her collar bone pulling her into his lap…And how could he possibly give that to her?

She had mentioned a strap-on once, and he had told her to "Fuck. Off!" He had a dick, he wasn't going to shame it even further by using a surrogate cock. Then she asked what he thought the toys were, which made him pout. But she had mentioned it again and he gradually became less reticent.

On a Saturday night after his Tuesday consent she had propped his head and torso up on a couple throw pillows, bending his body to a one-hundred-and-thirty-five degree angle before removing his clothes, one layer at a time: first removing a button, then another; pulling the shirt from his shoulders; sidling his pants down and yanking them—erotically, she had thought—from his ankles as if it were a tablecloth from the movies. If it had been heights he'd have known how to handle the situation. But he'd looked down; he'd seen his flaccid member bowing under a veil of cotton briefs, had seen the tubes coming out the side, one catheter leading to a bag of urine, another to a bag of shit, both dangling from curly hooks extending from the back of the wheelchair sitting beside him. (His chair, what was she? A vigilant nurse? A sympathetic comrade? A beneficent voyeur? His con-joined twin?) She then straddled his knees, one hand balancing herself, the other waving that polyurethane priapus in the air like a gelatinous baton, the peevish smile on her face diminishing his confidence and heightening his apprehension. He stopped her just as she bent down to his waist.

"Wait."

"What's wrong?"

"I-, I don't want that...that thing—look, can we just put a towel or a blanket underneath? And another for the..." he looked to the bags.

"Big baby wants her first time to be special?" she toyed, aiming the phallus at his face with just a little too much enjoyment. She climbed off and disappeared into the bathroom. When she returned, she placed a towel over the bags and another over his hips and spread it out to cover the bulge of his failed masculinity, making sure he could see on-ly his abdomen disappearing into terry cloth shuddering quickly and shallow to match his breath. Then she reached underneath him and fastened the strap.

"Giddy-up," she laughed, unaccompanied.

She didn't object or press the issue when he refused to try it again—which he was truly grateful for—but that had led to other talks that had eventually led them to tonight.

— § —

The volume of their voices went up and his head dropped to his chest (hands gripping the now-warm rails of the wheels) while hers was thrown back, eyes closed, a mouth spread wide with mirth. Her fingers made a lattice with his. The carpet was silent under his wheels as he pulled the chair backward the equivalent of a step. Her head dropped to the man's shoulder and he realized their shot list more of a loose outline, subject to the improvisations of the talent. He glided towards the partition separating the bedroom from the living area of the suite, towards a collapsible bed masquerading as a thin couch as her head pulled back from the shoulder, dragging from her lips a sparkling trail of saliva glittering faintly in the luminance of the night. Silently, his wheels moved along their invisible track and carried him out the bed-room against the primal noises making no acknowledgment to his departure from the station. Gradually his strides became longer, moving him closer to the door on which the edges of the fire escape routes were hastily painted over, opening the door at first only a crack, testing for noise and light from the bedroom. Hearing no disruption in their engine, not even a faint knocking or the rumble of a downshift, he breached the threshold of the room and crossed into the sour-yellow light of the hallway, sconces glowing like scattered coffee-stained teeth whose enamel has been peeling away for decades. Fueled on the coal of his own escape to a blessed absentmindedness, he accelerated down the fake oriental carpet, arms pumping the crests of his wheels and cycling back to apply more pressure, his speed advancing despite the folly of friction attempting to slow him down.

Numbered doors flew past him down the long corridor, doors possibly occluding similar anonymous atrocities. His vision narrowed to only the view of what was immediate: a path and a flight. Which is how he failed to notice the wire-conduit hiccupped in the carpet, catching on his wheels and vaulting him into the stale air. His face rubbed hot against the short bristles of the carpet, scraping away a fine layer of skin; his elbows bruised under his cotton shirt and a sharp sting throbbed in his wrist. He lay on the floor, groaning but trying not to be heard. After a minute, he lifted his hands to his face and felt little dabs of blood on his cheeks and forehead. Down his body, his legs were contorted and folded under each other, the trail of him spreading out in a thin line like a bicycle-severed earthworm: his arms trying to right his body, his legs gnarled and useless, the twisted tubes attaching him to the bags of waste on the back of the chair standing sentinel over his writhing torso. Turning himself until he was on his back, he lay for a while on the coarse fabric, stirring and contemplating how he could manage to free himself from the weight and his entanglement on his own; he rested the back of his head on the carpet and tried to catch his breath before attempting a return to dignity. He closed his eyes and re-opened them, staring at a small brown spot fluttering on the bottom of the sconce above him where a moth had fallen after burning its wings on the light bulb.

— § —

She drove home with the night still waxing darker. There would be no sound sleep in that room. The couch would remain a couch; the bars of soap would remain packed in paper boxes next to vials of shampoo and conditioner, seals intact; the bed would remain as it was, with unfurled sheets and a permeating dampness.

She drove smoothly—slowly and contentedly—looking at him now and then with reassuring smiles as if the night had merely been a trip to the dentist, a tooth pulled, a cavity filled. As she drove, he thought, Would there be others? Yes, probably. Not for a while, he knew; she had seen the look on his face as he had to allow the man's hands, covered in each other's sweat and discharge, to lift him, to carry him and place him delicately back in his chair while she cooed sympathetically, motherly, in his ear, wrapped with ample suggestion in a hotel towel, directing the man's movement and stroking the back of the man's head gratefully when he was back in his chair.

But he knew there'd be other times down the road: other men, other names agreeably supressed and discarded, new men taking up the role of Mr. Anonymous, the Mystery Man, Mr. E, together assembling a solitary, shadowy man known only by function...because, after all, it had worked, hadn't it? Because, simply, she would have to. And he knew he would object, knew they would fight, and in the resolve—a week? a month? a year?—they would talk about it in quiet terms in an attempt to smother the pity and shame and reproach in the other's voice. Then there would be a point when he would give in.

They would find a new man, they would seek him out at another bar or hotel, in classified ads, chat rooms; they would reserve a room somewhere cheap but not hourly. He would sit and watch, maybe he would leave the room again; maybe he would be still and defeated and patiently wait for her to come and shower and get dressed. Maybe, down the road, he would refuse to go with her. Maybe she would put up a fit, saying how she needed him there, how his presence was in *their* agreement, in *their* rules, but she would resign that maybe the best thing really would be for her to go alone, for him to stay, seeing how hard it was on him. And she would leave, kissing him on the forehead, and telling him there were Hungry Mans in the freezer and return several hours later drunk and giddy after he was already in bed. And she would climb in from her side and sidle up to him and stroke the skin behind his ear as if he were a Labrador.

He could see this as clearly as he could see the perforated lines on the road and the bugs splattering clandestinely against the windshield. He could read the future on her face in the light of the dash, in the scrapes on his hands and face, in her lane changing and acceleration, in the diaphanous reflection of themselves in the tempered glass against the dirty, humid night. Yes, months/years from now, she'll leave the house longer and longer, and he'll stay because it's consistent, because it's necessary, because this was how it worked. He'll stay home, picking at his dinner, guffawing at the droll dialogue from the rotation of sitcoms on the tube, listening for the six-cylinder hum of their modified mini-van to crunch up the driveway, pause, idle before cutting out, while he remained inside, dreading, hoping, fearing, praying she's come back with a name.

REEL TWO:
THE HOLE FAMDAMNILY

"Emotional effect begins only with the reconstruction of the event in montage fragments, each of which will summon a certain association—the sum of which will be an all-embracing complex of emotional feeling."

—*Sergei Eisenstein*, FILM FORM

I. WHAT'S IN A NAME?

> *"The Naming of Cats is a difficult matter,*
> ...THE CAT HIMSELF KNOWS,
> *and will never confess."*
>
> —*T.S. Eliot,* THE NAMING OF CATS

It had begun to snow again. Jack was driving as he usually did, that is, more aggressively than I would have liked: under normal conditions, under these conditions, under my conditions. "Slow down, Jack, Jesus; a car crash isn't a vetted alternative treatment to this little ailment of ours."

" 'Little. Ailment?' " Jack sounded mortified.

"That's not what I meant and you know it. Just a little hyperbole. A joke: you remember those, right?"

"Jesus, Gillian, hell of a joke. Sometimes, sometimes I wish you'd prune your diction just a little more…tastefully." He paused for a moment and checked to see if my seatbelt was fastened before switching into the right lane. "And don't use the word 'condition,' okay; sounds as if this issue of nomenclature was the product of an ultimatum."

"Can we not talk about the names we're putting on things and talk about the issue?"

"But that exactly *is* the issue, dear: the names we're putting on things."

" 'Things?' " I said with not a little amount of ironic vitriol, staring at the side of his face that wasn't to the side of the road and the driver's side window: half of a nose, half of a mouth, one eye.

"Him. Her." Each pronoun filled a measure against the *largo* tempo of the road.

I continued, "It's just that I think we'd both feel better if we give it a name. That way we wouldn't have to refer to this incident as 'The Incident' or that 'Slip-up' or 'That Nameless, Abominable It Subletting The Back of the Two-Ton Elephant in the Room.' Wouldn't it be easier if we could just say Tom and we'd both know what the other was talking about?"

"You're assuming this is something we *want* to talk about ever again." There was a moment of quiet as we merged onto the ramp for the southbound highway; whether it was a necessary quiet for the respect of the drive or a signal of the conversation's termination I couldn't be certain.

Jack settled back into the comfort of the middle lane. "Tom, huh?"

"That was just an example. It doesn't have to be Tom."

"Tom just feels like it's a big joke. Or too frequent for us to use. I know Toms. I can't get all worked up in the middle of a meeting because a client has the name Tom. Same goes for Jeff, or Bob, or Steve. Allen."

"You're looking for something a little more niche, then?"

He started doing that thing he does when he thinks: pushing and pulling his flat, upturned hand as if sanding the underside of a table, forward then backward along an invisible grain. Under the bridge below us, locomotives rumbled magnetically north and south, puffing clouds of invisible ions that intermingled with the static white snow.

"Not so much niche as unique," Jack said.

"So if you bring up Tallulah in conversation wouldn't you expect people to ask about such a weird—no, not weird—unusual or-, or antiquated name?"

He raised a finger for each letter. "A: this is not something we should be talking about at dinner parties. B: tell them to kiss my ass, fuck off, inside joke; we're a married couple, we have our own rhetoric. And C: fuck I forgot what C was."

A black Volvo sped up behind us and passed a little too close and too fast, spraying the side of the car with brown slush and dirt. I guess you can afford recklessness with that kind of safety rating.

"Michael?" I said.

"Too biblical. Murphy? Malone? Margaret?"

"What's with this M kick? Does it have to start with an M?"

"Not necessarily, I'm just in an M mood for some reason. Magnusson!?"

"Are you kidding me? Can we make an addendum? Nothing Irish or Scottish, please; it just doesn't feel right and I'll never be able to eat haggis again."

"Getting your fill of it these days?"

"What about Lolita?" It's not that I had been thinking of that name in particular, but when I said the name, somehow, it felt right on my tongue, and I realized that maybe I had been thinking about her for a while—something to do with parallels and role reversals and the unfairness in the tangibility of life and art.

"You want to name it after a sexually abused girl?"

"She never really had an adulthood, or a childhood; fitting don't you think?"

"In a morbid sort of way."

"What part of this isn't morbid, Jack? I've already come to grips with that. I want it to mean something, and I think-, I think it'd be a tribute to name it Lolita."

"Jesus, you're not going to start communicating with the dead and playing with Tarot cards now are you? A bit late to go goth, no? I've never heard you say anything even so remotely dark before."

"Well fucking Christ, Jack; take a guess why."

"We don't even know the sex, Gillie; wouldn't it be better if the name was androgynous?"

"Chris? Pat? Kelly? What? Something bland and utterly forgettable. We're not naming a manila envelope, dear. This isn't about playing it safe. It's about, it's about…" If I kept speaking I was going to cry. We stayed quiet for a while. I kept thinking of bodies and of actually consecrating the necessary, procedural steps from the car to the clinic, into the waiting room, to the office, then back out again, after. A series of entering smaller and smaller rooms inside the same building. It felt a compound fete, which I guess is fitting. I am a compound person, soon made simple. This is just a division of independent clauses. After another minute I made an addendum: a division of complexity: neither of us independent, really.

— § —

"Horus?" I said after a while.

"Going mythological now?"

"It could work. I mean Horus was the product of Isis finally putting Osiris' rent body back together and giving him just enough juice to give her a child, Horus, who would later defeat Seth, banish him to the underworld and become king." He was quiet so I continued. "If you think about it, our marriage was ripped apart and only when I became pregnant did we work to put it right. Today is about conquering the opposition, reuniting ourselves. Maybe surviving as a couple is our kingdom. A kingdom named Horus…

"Or maybe Osiris, go with the more literal interpretation," I added after a moment.

Jack gave me a look of disgust, as if somehow it was inappropriate to acknowledge the reality of what was soon to happen. I shouldn't have been surprised; after all, this is the same man who still wrote the grown children "From Santa" on their Christmas gifts. Changing gears and lanes, he began singing the intro to an old TV show about a talking horse, substituting the words. *"A Horus is a Horus, of course of course…"*

The snow was building across the windshield and clouding the wipers, caking the blades in ice and leaving wet, prismic rainbows across the tempered glass in small, concentric arcs.

"Do you want to go over our reasoning again?"

"I'd rather not." The fan on my feet was too hot and I leaned over to turn the air down.

"It might help to talk about it again, give us a little confidence as to why it can't happen."

"No, you want to talk about what I did again, about what you did again." I wasn't angry, necessarily, just exhausted from having run the marathon of this conversation before.

"So we settle on the rationality of the complexity?" He was trying to sound rational and complex and calm, as if the conversation were about the physics of boiling water in varying atmospheric pressures—which is, incidentally, a conversation we have really had before.

"No, we settle on the rationality of the irrationality. We are too old;

we have some serious personal shit to account for, problems long before the infidelity of the infidelity; it's all symptomatic of each other
and of the same thing, Jack, and it's no basis to have a child based on
the hopes of finding penance and bandaging un-healed contusions. It's
simply not fair."

"Okay," he said, making a shield of his hands.

"Not to mention the complications and birth defects that can arise
having a child at my age. Could be the last egg in my basket and I
don't think nature intended that one to be golden."

We passed a billboard in the stages of being changed. The snow and
sleet must have forced the workers to abandon halfway through: from
the top-left I could make out the iconic bottle-top of Coca Cola, spinning through some arctic landscape, reminding you how refreshing a
Coca Cola sounded at the moment—which did in fact sound pretty
tasty; on the other half, a movie poster for a romantic comedy featur-
ing that British actor all her female students were obsessed with but
whom she's never really seen.

"Our sex life was better, though, you'd have to admit at least that
element of our relationship was healthy, during the turmoil." Jack was
digging deep.

"Healthy? It was only healthy out of insincerity; we only increased
our sex to hide our other sex!" I was laughing a little bit, and Jack
laughed too after a while. "A fake sex life to cover the tracks of our real
sex lives." Amazing, the levels we go to to dupe the ones we love; you'll
never find better actors than your own family, because this is the audience that matters.

Our youngest called from Trinity yesterday and said he needed
more money. I knew he was spending it on cocaine—I found a little
plastic baggie with white residue in the pocket of his jeans when I did
his laundry over winter break—I didn't have the courage to hear him
lie to me so I didn't ask what the money was for, or what he'd spent
the last of his allowance on, and it broke my heart that he was hurt I
didn't ask.

"Plus, it's already a cloaked name. If we were to mention it in public
no one would have any idea we weren't talking about anything but the
book. And if it made us somber, all the more to do with the book."
This seemed the most logical choice for me and I couldn't understand

his obduracy against it.

"Who?"

"*Lolita*. Lo…Li—"

"You're still on about her?"

We had named all our children after our patronage and matronage: James, Chloe, Reilly and Mark. Could it not hurt to have some imagination with this one? I let it marinade.

Apparently he was focused on other things. "They say the soul enters the body on the 45th day, the same day the pineal gland appears."

"Jesus fucking Christ, Jack? Really? Now? You're getting into this *now?*"

"Lighten up, I'm saying it's ironic seeing as we're getting off at exit 45A is all."

"Well poor fucking time to mark the irony, dear."

Outside, the snow kept falling in steadier, heavier sheets. I tried to single out one flake at a time among the hundreds of thousands falling in unison onto the New England highways, valleys and hills. I selected one, but, with the speed of the car, the speed of the wind and the unpredictability of nature, I could only follow its path for a second, then the flake would fall on the car or amongst and in-between the other flakes and onto the frosting covering the ground. When one was gone I found another.

Tiring of the game, of never being able to follow a flake longer than a second, of watching them all fall into a confederacy of anonymity, I closed my eyes and put my palm to the small convexity of my stomach, waiting for the flesh to warm my hand through the cotton shirt. Jack placed his hand on top of mine and held it there long enough to enter into a battle of entropy: his cold hand leeching the warmth I had leeched into mine. Jack took his hand back and rejoined the other at the ten and two. There was still a half-hour or so before we would arrive; I watched him drive for a while.

II. MAKING MICKEY

"As a pupil emulates his master; God
Has as it were a grandchild in your art."

—*Dante Alighieri,* INFERNO, *Canto XI, 100-101*

B ut then there was the time that we came back from the mall
'cause Jimmy needed new shin pads for soccer and found Dad
making papier-mâché out of cum, and Mom was like "Richard, what
the fuck are you doing?!" and he goes "Does this look like Mickey
Mantle if it was sculpted by Goya?" and I told him "Dad, Goya didn't
sculpt, he painted," and he looked at me like I was on to something big
and said "Yes! Exactly, but what if he did? Can you imagine what it
might look like?," and Jimmy went into the living room to watch TV
'cause he said he needed to catch up on *Lost* and Mom just kept yelling
"Where the hell did you get all that semen from, and why is it in my
kitchen, and why, for God's sakes, haven't you at least put a towel or
some newspaper down so it doesn't get on the table?," but Dad just
dipped a brush into a Mason jar full of the stuff and took out a big
heaping load and slopped it onto Mickey's head and said "Dorothy,
I'm afraid your attitude and language are just not conducive to a creative atmosphere, and I'm going to have to ask you to leave if you continue in this vein; anyways, I've been saving up for a while—its protein
strands really make for quite the adhesive—and I especially don't want
it to go bad and have to throw three months worth of jism down the
drain," and Mom laughed and said "That's exactly where it belongs,

Dick" and Dad just scoffed like he does when he watches network television and told her "If you're going to try and be clever I would think you could find less sophomoric avenues" and just went on dabbing at the black and white ball that I didn't want to go anywhere near 'cause, well, shit, who'd want to get their Dad's cum on them, so I crept back towards the fridge where I could still see and hear and protect myself with the fridge door should things go bad and that Mason jar gets tossed around, or if Dad gets angry at his sculpture and starts destroying it and breaking the bottle and shit just starts flying everywhere and then I've got to go to school and explain to Akshay and Damen why I can't wear my Zambrano jersey anymore but can't tell them why, and they'll be like "That's sacrilege," and then Clayton would say something like "Good, you shouldn't have had that piece of shit in the first place, should find a pitcher who doesn't buckle under pressure and has a team to back him up" and I'd say "You can't talk about Big Z like that, motherfucker's big as a horse" and he'd say "Yeah, that makes sense, you didn't like him, just his horse cock," and then I'd punch him and get suspended and Dad would have to pick me up and tell me how I'd just destroyed an entire day's work for him, and I'd ask "How much did you write" and he'd say "Nothing, but that isn't the point; I was deeply entranced in a liminal place and needed only another couple hours of meditation before my breakthrough would undoubtedly appear" and I'd say "Well how do you know it was going to happen?" and he'd sigh and go "You just know these things, you can see them coming from far off; you're too young to understand; maybe your mother and I should put you on a meditation schedule," and he'd say it real depressed-like and I'd feel bad because not only did I get suspended but I also suck at life and can't even get a meditation right, and then I'd remember how when I was a kid Dad used to do his work near my high-chair and call me his colleague and in the afternoons it would be just me and him, he'd stand near a whiteboard that he claimed he borrowed from the university with drawings on it and stacks of books on the desk and say things like "Can we make a determinate progression of Foucault's panopticon for our current decade, and if so, in what ways has the observer been modified and in what ways has the observed changed? Is there any way that perhaps both parties are at once the observed and the observer, that in our modern world it is necessary for the panopticon to undergo a permutation of its intrinsic function in order to protect and preserve the whole; that, as no one can be quantifiably attributed to either party, our behavior is thus modified on a grander scale of the principle? Jeremy, have we discovered the omniopticon?," then he'd look at me in my chair and I'd say "Pizza!" and he'd go "Okay, okay, I see what you're saying; you want me to return to the concept of the circular post and observation, that if there really is going to be an omnioptican it must come out of a center and grow from there? What could that be, though? Because it couldn't be a progeny from the prison itself, sure we took the concept and carried it further, but in our contemporary society where could it have come from? But if it truly is an omniopticon then it reasonably can't have a central point or source, it must exist in the ubiquitous; so you see, I'm afraid your pizza projection missed the mark" and I'd clap and yell "Pizza!" and he'd say "Really, you ought to move past that point, Jeremy, you've exhausted that path," and then when Mom would come home she'd get angry because Dad sometimes forgot to feed me lunch or he would give me spicy tuna rolls that I wouldn't eat and then accuse me of having a "pedestrian palate" and they would fight but I was too young to really know what they were talking about, and I only really found out about it from my Aunt Becky who says her sister is a freakin' saint for putting up with my father all these years, Aunt Becky, who's a paralegal, says she's seen hundreds of cases like ours and that, in her opinion, especially in this state, my mother would be a "shoe-in" for full custody, and then my Mom says that what Aunt Becky doesn't understand is that she loves my father and even though he's quirky—"psychotic" Becky says; "different" my mother corrects—he's a good father and she loves him and the last guy Becky brought home got caught exposing himself to a minor in Bloomington and the guy before that—well, we still don't talk about that Christmas—and who was she to judge our family, and I think "Fuck yeah, Mom" (only of course I don't say it) because I'm remembering when Becky forgot my birthday and to make up for it she mailed me a Christian rock CD because she felt bad that her sister had failed to provide "adequate spiritual guidance"—and she actually wrote that on the card, before the part that says "Love, Aunt B"—and then went on to say that if I ever felt I needed to leave—and Jimmy, too—we could live with her, and here

I am, fourteen and thinking what a fucked up thing to put in a kid's birthday card, and then I get pissed off again because as far as I know Dad's never said anything along those lines about Becky, and I know he can be difficult (my father) and Mom really is a trooper because Dad's got his...proclivities...but he means well and we know he truly cares about us and what Mom doesn't say to Becky is that he never shouts, he never hits us, how when she was sick he forced the university to extend his sabbatical, or how he cut off ties with his brother who would ask (more than once) whether my Dad was pissed because me and Jimmy were closer to Mom's color and if our skin would lighten over time, or if we had inherited certain culinary preferences or physiological "attributes," so Mom just shakes her head and lets Dad continue assembling Mickey and even puts on the radio for him and then she heads upstairs to her bedroom where I know she'll come down for dinner smelling like cigarettes and where I hope she won't notice that I bummed one from her pack and Dad will be done with his project and we can have dinner as a family and afterward we'll all watch *Caddyshack* and laugh, except dad because he'll have lobbied for *The Cremaster Cycle*, but he'll smile and make popcorn because he loves us, because sometimes the answer to a question is "pizza," and because sometimes Goya was a sculptor.

III. YE OL' FASHIONED OLFACTORY

> *"The Lions may roar and growl yet the teeth of
> the great lions are broken/The lion perishes for
> lack of prey, and the cubs of the lioness are scattered"*
>
> —*Job 4:10,11*

I have teeth, and yes they are sharp. And yes there are prosthetics, too; they help me to smile and light my way through the dark. I show these prosthetics to women on the street who blush. They think of my teeth on their insides. They think of my teeth inside them, chomping, gnawing upwards to their bellies.

I have jackets with peaked lapels, ones with double breasts and double vents. I have black ones and camel-skin ones. I keep my wallet in the breast pocket, over my heart. I have nice clothes and they rest between my heart and my money.

I have shoes that cost money. They are pointed like my teeth. These teeth walk down sidewalks and gnaw on concrete, they swallow cement.

I have biceps like incisors. I do curls to keep them sharp. When I am done I flex these teeth in the mirror. The teeth smile back.

— § —

Breather asks, "Do you have children?"

I tell him "Yes, we are all fathers and we all have sons."

"Will they be like you?" he asks.

"Will I be like *them*?" is the question he should be asking.

Breather asks, "What of your daughters?"

"They will be as daughters. Sugar and sweet." Breather nods. He has a hole in his chest; I put it there.

There are seven-hundred-and-thirty-eight steps in my building, none of them creak. They are made of stone. There are panes of glass, two-hundred-and-fifty-six. They are green in the day and black at night. We have a man who cleans them and another man who opens doors. There is a flag outside with our city's colors. Two red stripes and three red stars.

I have a wife who smells like my children.

I have a son who asks, Do I look like you? Sort of, I say. Do I look like Mom? Sort of. Well then who do I look like? I'd say you look more like Benny. Benny is our dog. He laughs. I tickle his stomach. I kiss him goodnight.

My daughter is dyslexic. She sketched the silhouette of her hand puppet, put it on the fridge and labeled it "goD." I pay for tutors and therapists. The lessons are hard for her, she throws tantrums. This makes my wife cry a lot. I cry, too. When our daughter sees us crying we tell her we were just watching a sad movie, the one where the dog died. When we say this our daughter's eyes well up and she cries too and joins us on the bed.

I have another daughter who is smaller. I could always tell she was bright: she never bought the existential jokes of peek-a-boo and got-your-nose. We go to the zoo and she holds my hand. She says she wants to see the Ions, and we watch their manes and tails. In the reptile house she points at the Nake before hiding behind my leg. I show her, Look, there's glass there, the Nake can't hurt you. The Enguins are her favorite, that's where we end our day.

Breather asks, "When will you do it?"

"When the time comes for it to be done."

"So you haven't decided then?"

Breather asks too many questions.

— § —

She asks if I like her pussy shaved or waxed? Does it make her look too young? Do her tits look too saggy? Do her nipples have the right color, the right shape? Are they big enough? Do you think they're too pointy? Can you see the veins? Do they look like little blue rivers under my skin? Did you ever go rafting? Fishing? I had brothers that cleaned their own fish, can you do that? Do you know how? Do you want me on top? Do you want to see my face? Do you want my pussy first or my mouth? You can come in my mouth but do you have a glass of water, a drink or something for the taste? Why won't you kiss me after I give you head? Is it because you think I still have your spunk in my mouth? Is it the taste? I get it; I used to really hate olives when I was young, but now I have at least, like, three a day; isn't that funny how that happens, did you ever have anything that you didn't like that you like now? Olives, oh and salmon, I think it was the smell, you know?

— § —

Breather's shirt is purple, it used to be light blue. His voice is raspy and rheumatic.
  "If I were your appendages, I'd be folded at your brow."
  "Just what in bloody hell is that supposed to mean?"
  I show him. He nods. He prays.

— § —

I used a revolver on Hyte. A Tuarus Judge loaded with three-inch Winchester .410 shells packed with double-aught. I shot him twice in the chest, once in each lung. The buckshot ripped him exit wounds the size of my fist. I know because I put my fist inside of one. On the wall behind him was a spray in the shape of a butterfly. I took a piece of paper and pressed it onto the wall. When I peeled it off it was a beautiful red monarch that I folded and put in my pocket. I gave it to my daughter saying, Look what Uncle Hyte made for you.

— § —

Breather asks, "Will you visit her?"

"That depends."

"On what?"

"Would you like me to visit her?"

Breather's speech is slower; he takes a minute to answer.

"Yes, I rather think she'd like that."

"Then I will."

Breather tries to speak, I tell him to be quiet now.

— § —

My nose hears things, it acts as ears. It hears what's coming. My lungs are a nose: they crinkle, they flare, they sneeze, they drip. My lungs have their preferred smells: gasoline, nitrous oxide, Novocain, ammonium nitrate, bile, burning-radiator fluid, electrical fire ozone, hotel bible pages, snow-blower exhaust, butane torches. My mouth is a nose, it smells benzoylmethyl ecgonine, 2C-I; 2C-B; 3,4-methylenedioxy-N-methylamphetamine; 3,4,5-trimethoxyphenethylamine; Sildenafil citrate.

— § —

Do you want me to face you so you can suck on my tits? You can bite me if you want? Not hard, but a little, if you're into that? Are you into that kind of thing? I dated a guy once who used to bite the meaty part between his thumb and finger when he would come, is that just, like, totally weird? What were your girlfriends like? Did they have any weird habits? Was one of them your wife? How did you meet her? It's okay, you can come in me all you want: I can't have kids.

— § —

Breather asks about my eating habits. I tell him my habits are thus: If it bleeds I'll swallow. If it beats I'll chew.

He said he figured I'd say as much.

— § —

When I killed Creigge, I cut out his neck and the top of his throat, from chin to larynx, so I could stick my hand in and he could talk like God. I squeezed his tongue and flapped his mouth. We had conversations about the weather and about the benefits of the pocket square. I told Breather this; we laughed.

— § —

When I'm done she asks, Do I want to talk? Do I want to rest? Sleep? Would I mind if she touches me, not much, just a little? Maybe just her hand on my chest? Will I call her? Can she call me? Do I know when Breather is coming home; I miss him, will he be gone long?

— § —

"When you killed Hyte, did he talk this much?"

"No."

"Creigge?"

"Sort of. He gurgled a lot." Breather is starting to gurgle too, which is good because I am getting cold. It bites through my gloves.

When Breather is dead I slip my screwdriver in the underside of his jaw. It is a flathead; it is good for prying. It sticks out through his mouth. His eyes look puffy and waxy like a fish's. I grab the end. I pull the screwdriver and his jaw dislocates. His teeth break, they are not like my teeth. The skin rips; it bleeds but it comes off. I keep the jaw.

— § —

I have an artificial heart that beats for me. It flexes and contracts. It sings when it beats too fast. When my oldest complains or throws a tantrum I put her ear to my chest and tell her, I must really love you because you make Daddy's heart sing. Then she forgets what she was complaining about and we eat ice cream.

I have a son who hears the beeping in my chest and tells me Daddy these are the aliens in there. They're super small and fly their invisible space ships down my nose and into my chest. He tells me the noises in my chest are the aliens sending messages to their families, telling them

It's safe, come on in. My wife and I are in agreement, our son watches too much TV. But at least his imagination hasn't rotted, she says, and I agree.

— § —

Do you mind if I take a shower? Will you be here when I'm done? Yes, I'd like you to stay, if you can? I don't have much to eat but we could go out if you like? If you don't want to go out I understand? Maybe we could just watch TV? I promise I won't talk too much, or touch you, unless, would you like to be touched? Breather used to cuddle, but you don't look like much of a cuddler, are you? It's okay, I won't look at you if you don't want me to? Do you want to see the engagement ring Breather gave me? Look, it's got three gold bands that curve around and meet at the top where a silver dolphin holds the diamond, well it's only a C.Z. right now but still looks nice, right? It was sweet of him to get my favorite animal don't you think? Are you leaving? Where are you going?

— § —

I have a family that says I don't spend enough time at home. I'm looking out for your interests, I tell them. You are our interest, they tell me.

I have a wife who wants vacations. I tell her travel is hard on my teeth. She says she wants to rent a van and drive across America. She says she wants the kids to see Mt. Rushmore before it erodes. I tell her I can't go too far from my dentist. She says she wants to drive across the Golden Gate Bridge, she wants the kids to see how big the redwoods are. She says What's the point of having a family if you never spend time with them? She says she's pretty sure our youngest couldn't pick me out of a line-up.

— § —

Outside Breather's house I pull his jaw from my bag. It is dry now, the broken teeth rattle against the bone. My teeth are still strong. In the glove box I keep a pair of pliers. I open the pliers and place the clamp around my number six tooth, next to the prosthetic ones. I squeeze, it makes a cracking-kind-of-popping sound and I bleed. From my mouth I pull another tooth, number eleven, with another crack-ing-kind-of-popping. I clean them off, they are still very white. I place them in the empty slots on Breather's jaw. I put them where numbers twenty-four and twenty-five used to be. My teeth are much whiter. I slide the jaw in the mailbox.

Before Breather died I wish I had said: Even sometimes a bear will leave a fish. Even sometimes the snake belongs behind the glass.

I leave her a note and place it next to Breather's jaw in the mailbox and close the lid. There are bars on her windows. There are gutters that need cleaning, siding that needs to be replaced. I leave her with his jaw and the note. It says: *To the Enguins, From the Ions.*

— § —

I have a Littlest who, on cue, comes out of her bedroom with her Win-nie the Pooh pajamas and stuffed Emperor Enguin and runs up and says, Daddy I missed you. She says, What happened to your mouth? Oh, Daddy's learning to be a Wawwas, I say, and then I flap my arms at my sides and bark through the tampons sticking out of my canine sockets. Then she claps and laughs, and I pick her up and tuck her back into bed.

— § —

Before Breather died I told him this: "The point is, if I were in the for-est I'd be as an eagle, in the rivers I'd find fish. If I were in the plains I'd walk with mane and tail. I would stalk the antelope. I would sniff them out, and tearing and gnashing I would feast on their hinds. If I were in a desert I'd slither and lie in wait. But I am not; I am here. And one must rely on instincts. My hands will act as lions. My eyes will live like vultures. My hands will *be* as lions; their teeth are very sharp."

REEL THREE: EISENSTEIN'S MONSTER

"Here is another organic secret: a leaping imagist movement from quality to quality is not a mere formula of growth, but is more, a formula of development—a development that involves us in its canon, not only as a single "vegetative" unit, subordinate to the evolutionary laws of nature, but makes us instead, a collective and social unit, consciously participating in its development."

—*Sergei Eisenstein,* FILM FORM

I. THE BODY OF MY WORK:
AN AUTOBIOGRAPHY BY SERGEI
EISENSTEIN

> *"Life and death appeared to me ideal bounds,*
> *which I should first break through, and pour*
> *a torrent of light in our dark world."*
>
> —*Mary Shelley,* FRANKENSTEIN

A handsome man, with broad chest and incalculable ambitions, Sergei Eisenstein had spent the week prior to shooting *The Battleship Potemkin* holed up in his Odessa hotel room on account of inclement summer rain, going through pages of notes and essays that, rewritten, would later make up some of the material in his books *The Film Sense, Film Form* and portions of an article called "The Montage of Attraction" in the anthology *Cinema Today* [edited by Alexander Belenson]:

> *It had come to me first while I was involved in theatrical*
> *productions, that emotional stimuli, or viewer response, could be*
> *complicated through a more complex integration of action, action*
> *not just on viewing one particular plane of discourse but of two.*
> *Assisted by my production team, I endeavored to "shock" the reader*
> *into an emotional response that otherwise wouldn't have occurred*
> *without the dualistic presentation: a tightrope walker performing his*
> *feats of agility, and inducing suspense, while an otherwise banal*
> *conversation takes place adjacent; actors moving between two*

"separate" planes of theater; the reproduction of dialogue from one isolated scene on one stage to be repeated in a later scene. What I had found, and to illustrate with just one example (the tightrope walker), was a transference and amalgamation of visceral intensity: where I had wanted the dialogue to induce a certain sense of dread and precipitate consequence, it was not immediately or directly present in the scene because essentially nothing was happening. There was no movement. And yet, with the parallel action of that of the tightrope walker, the intended feeling was complete: a polyphonic experience that consolidates to—well not one because humans rarely ever feel just one emotion, and because the best of human interactions consist of multitudes—an emotional profundity. And this is essentially the basis of the film experience. The eye focuses on these two very different, very individual, pieces of information and the spectator assembles them in his mind to create a composite image, an amalgam meaning; a summative process of information and effect…actor to actor, image to image, scene to scene, image to sound: a discourse. A conflict, comprised of, if not compounded by, personal history and metonymy.

—S.E.

Sergei shoved the note to the portion of his desk reserved for such ramblings, mingling among the letters, shooting scripts, notes and drawings: one, a premature sketch of bodies stacked on top of one another to form the Tower of Timur, a design he would flesh out more in 1939; the other, a rough imagining of the storyboard for the opening of *Potemkin*. Wagner's *Die Walkure* wafted through the vents from the player-piano in the parlor below—a requested pleasure.

Sergei had spent many similarly unaccommodating afternoons in Moscow with Lev Kuleshov—friend, confidant and fellow contributor to *Cinema Today* for his axial system of filmmaking—sipping warm vodka and arguing their respective notions and employments of montage: of manipulating, as it were, disparate parts, images, and weaving them together in a particular order so as to establish context and to maximize the affecting response in the audience. As Lev was in St. Petersberg and Sergei in Odessa, their ongoing discourse was limited to letters; the latest an attempt to convert Sergei's "shock" montage to that more consistent, and as Lev proclaimed, more "successful" style of brick-by-brick, axial montage. Lev was for the more deliberate, overt approach for producing context; instead of filming from multiple angles he would merely change the distance of the shot to highlight emotional or scenic importance indicated through the enlargement of a character's expressions or of a particular object. And though Sergei used the method infrequently, nevertheless, he felt that it was not the end-all-be-all of film experience; that, as in the way the Japanese art students put together a whole image of a cherry branch from various circular, square or rectangular pieces (framed shots) of the branch, so too can space be engineered (in film) through various discordant images and angles; and thus create in the audience's mind a room, a place, a character—and through extension different "shocks" of emotion. But, as Sergei pulled a fresh piece of parchment to the front of the desk, this was not to be the topic of today's letter to Lev.

Glumov's Diary and *Strike* had met with intermittent success, enough to garner higher budgets and expectations for his next endeavor, *The Battleship Potemkin*. Not just a state- commissioned socialist film, *The Battleship Potemkin* was for Sergei a means of establishing himself—as inventor, as director, as auteur—and he wanted *Potemkin* to be a tour de force for his particular montage technique; he needed the audience to identify with the characters in newer, more powerful ways; for the audience to feel a visceral effect in their stomachs and hearts and heads when the soldiers cried out against the tyranny of Russia in 1905 (this year marking twenty years past).

Propaganda was the word of the time, and the word would surely be used to describe *Potemkin*. Sergei didn't particularly like the word; it felt diminutive. Declaration and manifesto were words he liked better, but neither described his aims, aims directed more towards intellectualism and artistry. In a prior letter to Lev he had written:

> *Am I a fool to want for my film an existence beyond the*
> *trivializations of contemporary propaganda? I am a man with*
> *talent, and the ego is naturally to follow, but does it make me a*
> *monster to have ambition? Fathers and mothers imbue their*
> *children with hope and projections of success far beyond the reach of*
> *possibility. Am I any less a father? Am I any less a mother, for as you*
> *well know I bear the burden of my films inside me for months; the*

*reels floating in the amniotic fluid of my heart and my head until I
deliver them with my own hands? Do I not suffer through each of
their births? How can I not hope for them to achieve renown? My
dear Lev, I am sorry if this letter seems petulant, but as well you
know the Proletcult series Towards Dictatorship of the Proletariat,
which Strike was to be one-seventh of, was never completed and thus
my imagining and purpose went unfulfilled. It has aggravated me to
no end. I hope it will be different with Potemkin, and I can
actualize the breadth of my dream.*

—SERGEI

Lev's response had been:

My Dear Sergei,

*We practice the art of illusion, art nonetheless, but inculcated
socially as illusion. I feel most illusionists misunderstood. Merlin,
should he have existed, was merely a man with an astonishing sense
of chemistry and physics. Christ, too, could be seen as an illusionist
in the secular lens. And our beloved countrymen, comrades and kin
have disallowed most forms of illusion. How could our country
prosper under a common goal if all are still under the illusory
enchantment of God and Christ, sitting around, pining for the
rapture? And thus we are to perform our tricks for an audience who,
even if our strings and trap doors remain unseen, never the less keep
their apertures myopically shut to the fantastic. Ours is a difficult
illusion (made more so by the Jubilee Committee's hands on the
strings of our marionettes). The only advantage we have is that our
tricks are still so fresh a medium. I would like to write more on this
but feel I must limit myself for obvious reasons. Be well my mad
wizard,*

—LEV

The letter composed on this particular day consisted primarily of questions of truth and fiction that needed to be considered. Sergei required a considerable amount of realism to sway the people, to illustrate the degree of oppression and hostility embodied in the Tsar's regime, but there was creative license to consider, extrapolations and hyperbole to employ—for dramatic effect.

> *Of course one could consider that to construe vagrant shootings of*
> *soldiers on citizens to that of a massacre is an irresponsible act, the*
> *poetics demand that for me to inspire the intended result (both*
> *emotionally and ideologically) I must extend the carnage and*
> *bloodshed and to capture the injustice and tragedy at a pedestrian*
> *level. I must get close to the audience. I must show one of their own*
> *(and thereby themselves) feeling the full brunt of the violence. And*
> *this demands some fictionalization. So I shall write in a massacre,*
> *ground it emotionally in the form of a baby in a carriage—the*
> *future of Russia, the past of us all, helpless and fragile—rolling*
> *down the steps as his dead mother collapses against the carriage*
> *under a hail of gunfire...*

And Sergei would have a revolution, too, a sailors' mutiny against the
oppressive officers in which their leader, Vakulinchuk, would perish.
The injustice would trigger a call to arms, in both soldiers and citizens. "This happened and we mustn't let it happen again; and hooray
for the Soviet State and their guarantees of this and of a better life for
the proletariat" was an idea he wanted imprinted on his audience, an
idea that would surely induce socialist verve and satisfy his benefactor's
requirement, thereby allowing Sergei to fulfill his own requirements.

Sergei and long-time collaborator Nina Agadzhanova had shared
this vision in their writing of the script, and Sergei wondered if he
shouldn't have more brutalization, perhaps as bloody a death for the
officers as that of *Strike*. But that scene was still far off, and shooting
was to begin in just three days.

— § —

He had arrived in Odessa a month before filming to get reacquainted
with the town and to look for cast and locations he might not have
thought to include, which continued into these final days prior to
shooting. Sergei preferred to use the locals for the majority of extras
and auxiliary rôles: untrained peoples that had the image of the populace, of the oppressed. He hoped it would allow his audience a stronger
connection. Mostly he just summoned the locals the week before

shooting (earlier if he had costumes to employ), but certain rôles required casting.

He needed someone to play Grigory Vakulinchuk, the sailor whose noble Bolshevik spirit leads the other soldiers to revolt, and whose death triggers a nation's upheaval. So Sergei had placed a call to the dashing embodiment of masculinity, Aleksander Antonov, whom he had worked with before. Similarly, he needed equally powerful men to play Commander Golikov and Chief Officer Giliarovsky; he wanted faces that inspired plausibility, fear and animosity, and he went with the tried and true actors Vladimir Barsky and Grigori Alexandrov, respectfully. And while indeed many of the extras and masses were already compiled, there was always the chance Sergei would find someone perfect for a particular rôle or scene, or someone who would inspire Sergei to create one specifically for that individual. This is what propelled him to take walks and explore Odessa, which isn't to say that they were done solely without frivolity and leisure; on the contrary, Sergei found that he became most lucky with new talent when he was at tea, playing tennis or engaged in some otherwise innocuous pastime.

A cobbled path made its way north through the heart of the city, moving away from the waterfront and into the residential neighborhoods full of quaint shops, cafés, bars, butchers, grocers, cobblers, tailors, bookshops and the like. Sergei went into a small family operated café he'd dined in the last time he was in Odessa. The elderly Jewish couple who owned the restaurant were reserved and moderately quiet—'less they bring undue attention to themselves; they greeted the customers, seated them and smiled but otherwise kept to themselves. The only time Sergei had heard the man engaged in talk that wasn't solicitous was when he had come in for an early tea and found the man immersed in a chess game with another elderly man with bushy eyebrows, long grey hair and Greek Orthodox cross strung around his neck. The men talked about God's plan and equated Russian history to the chess pieces, the infallible Tsar-king—they had made a joke about Queen Catherine and her proximity to the knight, horse-head ever defending the queen, or was it the other way around?!—and Sergei had half-listened while scribbling notes for *Strike*. A family restaurant, the couple had a daughter who always tried to catch Sergei's eye, maybe because he was a filmmaker, maybe just because he was a man. Sergei

had humored her, complimenting her on the silkiness on her black
hair and full smile that was surely attracting her male peers, but they
were casual flirtations that never amassed more than the niceties demanded.

The hinges creaked when he entered and he took a seat near the
window so he could keep a vigilant eye out for faces, ordering pick-
les and herring before moving on to a kosher borscht that he sipped
anonymously, watching the faces of the shipyard men coming home,
looking for the face of Russia. He would have to find out what bar
they frequented and send Shirey to ask for volunteers. When he was
done he left a few coins on the table and approached the owner, asking
him if he still played chess with the Christian. The restaurateur said
he played chess with many Christians, and Jews, and should he like a
game he could grab the board from the back? Sergei thanked him but
declined.

"The Christian with the bushy eyebrows and long grey hair," Sergei
said, "I would like to offer him a job on my next film. If you should
see him again, please tell him to contact my production manager, Mr.
Brian Shirey, at the waterfront inn."

"I haven't seen Mikhail in a couple of weeks, but I could call on
him if you should like?"

Sergei nodded and thanked him in Hebrew handed down from his
mother, a mother who had a fondness for disclaiming her son and
would watch with neither pain nor interest as spouse beat spawn.

— § —

The filming went as flawlessly as anything on a major scale can go.
There were days when the light, cues and apertures were perfect. There
were days when he got the most inspired and enlivened performances
out of the extras he had picked straight from the streets of Odessa,
and Sergei would grab their faces and kiss each one of them on the
lips. Conversely, there were days when an extra stumbled, forgot his
cue and ruined shot after shot until Sergei had him replaced, sometimes forcing Sergei to occupy the rôle himself. And there were the
days when the actors spent the evening drinking at the pubs and staying out late into the night, impressing the locals with their intoxicated

performances of Shakespeare and Sophocles, failing to provide satisfactory performances the next day.

After a particularly long day of shooting the soldier's revolution, Sergei, roused with the spirit of his actors roused by the great Aleksander Antonov, agreed to go with his cast of sailors to celebrate the day's wrap with strong vodka and song. Knowing the importance of keeping an authoritative distance from his players lest they think they have directorial rights, Sergei bought the men a bottle, gave toast and drank patiently from a booth in the back next to the restroom. The bar smelled of old leather and many spilled spirits. The men drank too much, and when given to pissing invariably passed Sergei, often grabbing him by the shoulders and embracing him in a hug while slurring the lines of an old Russian drinking song into his ear. Sergei patted each on the back and sent them on their way, returning to the rabble having forgotten the plight of their kidneys. The old Christian, Mikhail, who had accepted Sergei's invitation via the Jewish restaurateur, still donning his black robes from wardrobe, was going from man to man blessing them. Sergei couldn't tell if he was sincerely blessing these pagans or had dismissed his life's beliefs and fallen into atheistic mockery. Sergei hoped either hadn't been his fault.

As the clocks outside began tolling midnight, Antonov climbed onto the bar, flapped his arms to lull the rabble and dropped his voice to a baritone as he recited the brave words of young Hal on the threshold of battle; at which point the hand of every soldier-actor went up in spurious zeal and shouted applause for Antonov and for their Band of Brothers.

Sergei clapped too and stood, "My friend Aleksander, if you are the valiant Hal, who does that make me? Sir William?"

Antonov laughed and pointed to the director puffing out his chest in the Elizabethan style, "Why, Sergei, my wise imparter of truths, so knowledgeable of the world, who has taken us under his belt into the realms of artistry…of course who else could you be…but our own dear Flastaff?!"

The men, most of whom were about the same age as Sergei [27 then] if not older, cheered and Sergei put his hands to his belly and gave a tremendous shake, as if the men were waiting to drink mead from his barrel of flesh. Antonov hopped off the table and the men returned to drown their mouths. Sergei sat down again and took a healthy sip himself.

When more songs had been sung and bottles drank and replaced anew, Antonov stumbled to Sergei's booth and fell into the opposite seat, spilling booze and body onto the wooden bench. "Dear Falstaff, forgive me, I was trying to explain to our young petty officer over there what you told me about the gazes, but I fear the drink has locked my eruditions away. Would you begrudge me terribly if I asked you to tell us again? I promise to keep my ears fully open this time."

Sergei laughed. "Or at least 'til the next dungeon-master locks them away again," lifting his glass to Antonov's. "Bring the boy."

Antonov raised his arm like an elephant's trunk and yelled to one of the younger actors in a jacket much too big for him, "Kosha. *Kosha.* Come."

The boy approached furtively and looked only to Antonov. Kosha was a local whom Sergei had to chide too often for looking like a deer instead of a riotous, undernourished sailor. Antonov raised his left hand towards the boy and the glass in his right hand to Sergei as if to offer introduction and formulate a triangle of discourse.

Sergei began, "So you want to know about the gaze—the gaze*s*? Well, there are three gazes you must consider in the medium of film: you have the gaze of the camera, first and foremost; there is the gaze of the audience, what we see and what we look at on the screen; then there is the gaze of the actor, what he or she sees. Each gaze is individual but complicit in resolving the readership of the film; and we mostly do not realize it, at least on a conscious level. Now, try to follow me if you can.

"As we don't have the luxury of diagetics and cannot hope to hear the brilliantly spoken words of our Aleksander here," who bowed accordingly from his seat, "we have to assemble the meaning of the film in a different manner. You have to consider what the camera shows you and *how* it shows you. Do we film our Aleksander from above, looking down at him like we would a rat or a child? How do we know to feel terror and hatred for the tyrannical Commander," pointing towards the red-faced and impotent Vladimir Barsky nodding off on a stool, "if we film him the same way as the brave Vakulinchuk? Think..." Sergei made a circle with his hand, looking for the boy's name.

"Kosha," Antonov provided.

"Think, Kosha, the audience does not know our story, they have their textual inserts but that is not enough. I am a filmmaker: I cannot rely on the crutch of words to tell my story. So how can the audience understand my film, or any film for that matter? Here, let's try an exercise." Sergei told Kosha to pretend he was the audience. Antonov, who had now remembered the exercise, made his hand into an open cylinder and placed it to the boy's right eye. Sergei said for Kosha to think of Sergei as the actor.

"Close your left eye, Kosha, Antonov's hand will be the camera." Antonov pointed his camera at Sergei's face. "Now, what do you see?"

"Your face."

"And does it appear to look, angry? Happy? Sad? Does it look like there is anything else in the room with me? What are my eyes doing?"

"They're just looking at me."

"Right, and what happens now?" Sergei shifted his eyes to a point above the boy's head. "Does it now look as though I am in a place that has walls and objects that might be outside your awareness?" Sergei didn't let the boy answer, "it is because when my eyes are pointed at you I am removed from the world on screen, I am acknowledging your presence and we become engaged in a direct discourse. But when I look at something else you suddenly become aware of what I am looking at. If I raise my eyebrows, drop my jaw and curl my lips as I look out the window would you not understand that there must be something terrifying outside?"

This was a drill Sergei had run many times for the sole reason of the look on Kosha's face that invariably comes to those unfamiliar with the camera. It was a look that at once made Sergei Socrates and Isaac Newton, a supplicating look of endearment, epiphany and just the right amount of obsequiousness. Of course, Lev had never shown Sergei any of these looks; they had never found it necessary to engage the other in these sorts of pedantic exercises.

Sergei had them switch rôles, telling Kosha to be Antonov's camera, to dictate what Antonov saw and how he saw it. Kosha pointed his hand towards the vodka on the table and Antonov said how it made him feel, "Thirsty." Kosha pointed out the window, "Cold." Kosha pointed to the barmaid, "Warm...very warm." They laughed and

Kosha blushed. Antonov slapped the table and they switched, Kosha playing the actor to Sergei's audience.

Through the hole in Antonov's hand, Sergei told the boy to make him laugh. Kosha crossed his eyes and made a face that wasn't funny but Sergei laughed for the sake of his argument.

"Now, make me think that your mother just walked in from the door and will beat you mercilessly if she finds you drunk instead of helping your father, but don't look at her." The boy shrunk in his seat but kept trying to look over his shoulder. Sergei watched the boy mindlessly following his tasks and wanted to keep the boy like this forever: head bent like a dog waiting to please his master. Now why couldn't the boy have followed his direction so well in front of a real camera, when it mattered, he thought. Sergei moved Antonov's hand away and ended the exercise.

"Now, do you see what I was trying to get at?" The boy nodded. "Each of these gazes is a different self. Were you not three people just now? Film is simply a language spoken by all three of them. An ideogram composed of the three."

"Depends on how big the film is," Antonov said through his moustache.

Sergei nodded, "That can be true. Each actor is a self. In a film as large as *Potemkin* you could have a hundred selves to read in a single shot. But they all amass to that collective self of the Actor. If you want to be a good actor, Kosha, you've got to be aware of these gazes; you've got to play to them. That's how I get a good shot, that's how I get a good scene; a good color if you will. You see, Kosha—and Antonov knows this from *Glumov's Diary*—I am a painter, and the scenes are my paints. Now, how can I make a portrait if I don't have the right colors? I can mix them, sure, and I do, but I can't if I don't have the proper base because unfortunately with the medium of film, I don't have the luxury of simply going to a store and buying it." Sergei nodded until the boy nodded with him in induced guilt. He wanted to tell him about Kuleshov's Experiment: of the repetition of Ivan Mozzhukhin's stoic face juxtaposed to the bowl of soup, the dead little girl in her coffin and the voluptuous woman, all of which produced an effect in the audience which, through transference, they would read in Ivan's face as hunger, despair, longing, etc. He wanted to offer the boy several titles on acting and the employment of bodily motion for the boy to read: *Physiology of Motion* by Duchenne, Nothnagel's *Topische Diagnostik der Gehirnkrankheiten* and Vsevolodsky's *History of Theatrical Education in Russia*. But no sooner was the experiment finished than Sergei, Kosha, Antonov and the rest of the acting party were called once again to the community of song and fraternal inebriation.

Yet, when Sergei went to work the following day he found his words to have made an impression on the boy. Kosha snapped to attention at every bark of the line producer. Sergei shot the soldiers in their perfect lines and Kosha kept his eyes diligently forward, never acknowledging the camera, focusing his eyes on a point in the horizon that Kosha thought showed discipline. He fell right in with the other actors who had once been soldiers in former selves. They were a uniform shape and color that Sergei could work with. And when it came time to shoot the scene in which Commander Golikov shouts "I'll string the rest of you up on the yard," Sergei chose Kosha to be among the few actors who were to look upon the ghostly apparition of Golikov's threat.

Of course, the shots Sergei found himself most concerned with were those involved in the Odessa Stairs sequence. A whole week of tedious coordination and preparation (the two-story wooden platform from which the camera was to film had to be built) tolled heavily on Sergei, who spent most of the nights in his hotel room smoking cigarettes and drinking vodka, terrified of an accidental trampling that would shut down the entire film and potentially get him thrown in the Gulag.

When filming commenced, he threw up between takes. The demonstration, though massive, was easy enough to film, but the citizens stampeding down the stairs required much coordination between the camera, the extras and the subjects. And though they'd rehearsed each scene the night before, if a vagrant extra, one of the citizens or one of the soldiers, got too close to another and tripped or fell, the whole shot would be ruined and the actors undoubtedly injured and thus replaced. Then, of course, there was the boy to contend with.

He found a woman named Katerina Glauberman who was willing to allow her son, Abram, to play the wounded boy on the stairs, just as long as she didn't have to watch them film it. He thanked her and

found another woman, Prokopenko, to play the wounded boy's mother, cradling the boy in her arms and carrying him up the steps to plead
with the soldiers before being shot down.

Filming the scene, Sergei, wearing grey trousers with a fresh, white,
button-down shirt, dark glasses and a megaphone, stood ten feet from
Abram and shouted directions as feet trampled the boy's arms and legs;
at the camera, his assistant, Aleksandr Levshin, swallowed the boy's
torment into the abyss of the lens. "Now you are shot; you collapse.
Now you reach out for help, but no one comes. The people are stepping on you, kicking you. You are afraid you are dying. You want your
mother but she is too far away; she will not come. You might die before she gets to you." The boy acquiesced beautifully at each direction,
and Sergei smiled when the take was done and clapped the boy on the
shoulders, pleased with the verisimilitude. He thanked the boy and his
mother, hugging them and kissing both on the lips.

The boy didn't speak but nodded to Sergei and left his real mother's
side to sit on the stairs. Ms. Glauberman approached Sergei and asked
him "Why do you want to make a film about dead sons? Why can't
you make something happy with dancing and a nice love story?"

Sergei cradled her shoulders in his hands. "Because I never want to
see dead sons again. Because I never want to see tyranny's feet again
trampling upon our youth. Because I don't want people to forget about
the horror that occurred here, nor do I want them to forget how far
we've come. This is bigger than you, bigger than me. This is for Russia, for all of us."

He let her go and nodded. "You should be proud, your son performed magnificently."

Sergei looked to the boy who was obviously shaken and disturbed,
sitting on the steps detachedly rubbing his legs on the marble and trying to avoid eye-contact with the rest of the crew. Sergei was ashamed;
he had exploited the boy and couldn't shake the feeling of vulgarity
and irresponsibility. *But there is a pay off,* he wrote in his notebook that
night.

— § —

When the filming was complete, Sergei set up a dark room, projector
and Moviola editing machine in the attic of an Odessa house that

looked out over the water. Marta K. Imelienev was a widow whose husband, a naval man, had lost his life during the Great War and who blamed the Tsar directly for his death, muttering scathing apostrophes at the wallpaper, the dining table and anywhere she thought could strike hurt. Sergei had found her during principal photography and had used her during the Odessa Stairs sequence, a mother amongst mothers pleading for a halt to the violence. After filming she had approached the director and commended him for his bravery and said that he was a proud son of Russia and should he need a place to sleep she had an attic where her son, Alyosha, used to live before he married and it would be his free of charge.

Sergei had the reels, labeled according to sequence and chronology, delivered to the attic. He'd established when writing the script with Nina that Potemkin would be a dramatic chronicle, a newsreel aesthetic compounded emotionally by a classic five-act tragedy: five separate acts, each different from the last, each with their own movements and emotional shifts. More conflict to drive the viewer into a state of ecstasy. In order to accomplish that he would work on reel, one act at a time, starting with the first and moving towards the fifth; it only made sense to him to work in chronological order, how else was he to know whether he had captured the appropriate feeling of the film if he worked out of order?

He was too anxious to wait for the work-print and slid the first reel of "Men and Maggots" into the Moviola. From the beginning, from his first location scout in Odessa months before, he knew he wanted to start with shots of the Odessa Harbor, of the raging sea: open symbolically, get the audience imbued with the notion of the torrents, of the violence as the water crashed upon the breakwater. He had fifteen minutes of footage to sift through and he played the reel no less than five times looking for the appropriate—nay, the correct—shots. Sergei had selected two locations, one of the rocky coast and the other in front of a jetty where the water exploded along the surface—*for natural volatility*, he told Lev. He wanted an accelerating feeling, a visual crescendo of the water gradually getting higher and more volatile. Sergei removed the reel and brought it to the Moviola but tripped over the head of a nail sticking out above the floorboards and the reel dropped to the floorboards. Several meters uncoiled, scratching on the splintered planks; a quarter of his coast shots damaged from wood and exposure.

From downstairs Marta heard Sergei's fists pound against the walls and a string of profanity seeping into every chamber of the house. She gave a proud smile to the living room furniture and followed suit, slinging her own fetid curses at Ivan in the form of the lamp, the easy chair, the fireplace mantle...

Upstairs, Sergei picked up the reel, cut the damaged film and placed it back in the Moviola to see what he could salvage: a couple bursts of tide against the rocks: all powerful, one more so than the others. His plan of gradual acceleration was clearly bruised; he would have to duplicate the lesser of the crashes and close with the greater shot. Five medium shots in total.

Sergei moved to the introduction of the Potemkin in a long shot and then to Vakulinchuk and the crew. He had scenes of the soldiers attending to their duties, smokestacks billowing pure power. There were shots below deck, the dark offset by the white of the hammocks and the bodies of the soldiers, the petty officer, dark-suited like the night, beating a recruit upon his back.

"There is a limit to what a man can take," speaking the scripted lines as he replayed the reel, repeating the process until he found the right moment, the exact frame when he felt the men pushed to their limits. He cut it, spliced in the intertitles Nikolai Aseyev and Sergei Tretyakov had dropped off and proceeded to the next shot.

— § —

While he enjoyed filming, without a doubt, the reward, and the bulk of Sergei's interests, lay in the editing of his films, and he spent the majority of his post-production days locked in the attic: viewing, splicing, replaying, re-splicing, reviewing... The editing, the montage—this was his artistic order, this was the canvas for his inimitable compositions, where simple images combined to create something truly spectacular: a portmanteau (like that great portmanteau from his nearly blind admirer from Ireland—and whose work Eisenstein himself held in the highest esteem), simple words smashed together to create something complex whose qualities were so much greater than merely the sum of their disparate parts. For, like the ideogram, like the great abstractions that have accreted throughout our linguistic and rhetorical histories, the montage creation embodies so much more than the combined disparity of shape and line; created out of his expert placement, sure, but created more so by the spectator himself—bringing his own personal histories to the viewing, his own connections and history with the image with which to confront and resolve the conflict: in effect, to process, to read, to feel.

Lev was still unconvinced; and his critics bemoaned his excess of formalism and research. But perhaps, yes, perhaps *Potemkin* would change all that—and if not, he wasn't likely to change his tune.

In a recurring quotidian exercise, Marta would bring him supper and tea, rap her anemic fingers on the door, only to be told to leave it on the top step where Sergei would sometimes, sometimes not, open the door long after she'd left and take the viable—though now certainly cold—sustenance. Sergei ate intermittently, absentmindedly, that is, only when necessary; treating his body like a great diesel machine, he worked until he was down to fumes and his body began knocking. But how else could he possibly find the necessary immersion into his work if he was to break from the world of his narrative every time his stomach grumbled? He spent eight unbroken hours replaying the same small sequence to make sure he got it right: the maggot-filled meat, Doctor Smirnov and his spectacles that collapsed into a magnifying monocle, the tension between Vakulinchuk's discontent and the officer's inspection. (Which might well be another reason he wasn't quick to take his meals.) Again and again Smirnov raised a limb of the rotten meat, framing Vakulinchuk's head in a circle of rot—for which the Chinese have yet to fashion a character for. It was good, but after all that time it still wasn't right. He resolved to take a break from the scene for the moment and move forward to the punishment of the soldiers and the start of the revolt in "Drama on the Quarterdeck." He replayed it until his eyes burned; and then he slept, waking when the moon was fresh and he felt he should get some air and a drink.

By the time he had settled into a chair and a vodka most of the heavy crowd had dissipated to take their dinner with their families. The thin crowd allowed him the freedom to remain detached and contemplative. A young man of international recognition, the townspeople treated Sergei with reverence, excitement and timidity. Some of the Odessians whose faces would soon be played in screens across the world charged Sergei in the streets and demanded, in amiable terms, when the film was to be finished or when he would screen it in Odessa (which they were under the impression was to be the first city to view *The Battleship Potemkin*). Politely, Sergei thanked them for their help and informed them that he was still a long ways from finishing his film. Some just stared and kept their distance but it was largely understood after a while that when Sergei was drinking he was to be left alone.

However, he was feeling charged with the day's accomplishments and engaged the other men in conversation, singing along to Russian pub songs, arms around the shoulders of his comrades, drunkenly professing that "all a man needs is the love of his fellow Russian and the endurance to promote equality; and should the rights of the workers come under attack we need to consolidate our strength, form an iron fist and smash it into the faces of the oppressors." Then he stumbled home drunk and replayed the footage he'd edited for the day, impossibly trying to look at it with the eyes of a stranger.

Sergei watched the scene in which the men who refused their soup were awaiting their punishment. He watched the sinister Chief Officer Gailiarovsky twisting his moustache before crying out "Cover them with tarpaulin," the soldiers carrying out the tarp and unfolding it, placing it over the insubordinate soldiers while the firing squad waited for the cue. The bayonets wavered, showing the soldier's trepidation to fire upon their brothers; and Vakulinchuk's triumphant call for revolution. Sergei felt inspiration and the necessity to work.

What he needed was to edit in the ghosts of the men hanging from the mast of the ship as Commander Golikov shouted "I'll string the rest of you up on the yard." He faded the dark images that he shot in another reel: six stuffed effigies hanging from the masts, two up top, four below. Sergei copied the compilation onto the work-print and watched the new scene, satisfied with the duration, the believability and the horror. The black shapes of men materialized in the air above the deck, hanging by their necks above the gaping soldiers.

Then a peculiar thing happened.

Sergei played it again, but when the soldiers turned their heads to look up at the hanged bodies, he thought the image of the ghosts lingered longer that it had before, spread across the face of the old sailor looking on with horror.

He rewound the scene and played it once more. The Commander shouted his threat, Kosha and several other men tilted their heads, six bodies materialized. But when the shot ended and the next shot followed, the bodies still hung in the background. Sergei removed the reel from the projector and brought it back to the Moviola. The reel opened in front of him, Sergei examined each frame with his glass and, as he expected, the bodies were only in the frames he had originally intended. Sergei slid it back into the projector and played it again, but the bodies continued to linger. Chalking it up to a lack of sleep and strong inebriation, he put the work-print down, made himself prostrate on the corner cot and tried to will himself to sleep; after a while, it worked.

— § —

Sergei didn't always leave the house for a drink. Sometimes he would just take a walk to view the city at night. The summer was over and the nights were regaining their October nip from the Black Sea. Wrapped in a light coat, Sergei walked down the side streets and out onto the harbor, lit only by the moon. Odessa always looked loveliest at night, when the sparse light cast the city in blocks of black and pale-orange:

> *…an impressionist's seaside castle; you feel at once real and imagined. Like a living work of Van Gogh or Monet: as if a multitude of discordant pieces can be both something real and still and something fantastic and frantic, but always whole. I wish I had the equipment to capture this scene on film, but I fear that even with the best lighting team I could never reach a level of verisimilitude with only black and white; it has to be experienced, the colors have to be lived.*

Yet lately he had come to regard his nightly walks as being not solely his own. There were shadows out of place for that time of night. There was the constant feeling of unidentified observance, and when he turned to confront whoever may be stalking him, he saw a faint shuffle of light, like a body slipping into the dark cove of a doorway. In shadows cast by the street lights he saw, on the cobblestone streets spread out in front of him or in the windows he passed, a black non-descript figure always disappearing out of focus whenever he turned.

Maybe Stalin had thought his film pornographic and wanted it destroyed. He'd obtained permission through the higher offices of the state to make his film, and indeed they supplied invaluable commission, and although Sergei regarded his film as a tribute to socialism it was certainly possible Stalin didn't want his people to be reminded of the past, or to feel a modicum of rebellion and turn on his word. Sergei had friends like Vladislovksy who'd had to watch his reels burned and his teeth knocked loose from his head upon finding the State's dissatisfaction with his work. An act Sergei knew well enough was a light admonition. Perhaps they had spies waiting to see a first cut of the film; perhaps they worked in teams, waiting for him to leave the house where one man would tail him while the other inspected his film. Then again, perhaps it was simply paranoia.

He asked Marta one night whether anyone had been in the house other than himself.

"What do you mean?"

"I mean has anyone been here inquiring about me? Have you let anyone upstairs?" He grabbed her by the wrists and shouted, "Tell me, have you sold me out!?"

"Stop, you're hurting me."

He became aware of her loose skin, her waxing cataracts, her varicose veins, and he dropped her wrists. A chill collected on his forehead and he had to sit. Of course she hadn't sold him out; of course it was his paranoia. Maybe he was becoming too attached, too obsessed.

"I'm sorry, Marta. Please, please forgive me. I, I…"

Marta, stroked the sides of his arms and told him he was just overworked, he should take some time off, "Sleep, you need to sleep. All the time I hear you pacing and the *click-click-click* of your machine."

Sergei sat on the steps and combed his hand through his wild hair, pulling it upwards from his scalp as if run through with electricity.

"Go up, I'll bring you some tea to help you sleep."

Sergei went upstairs and Marta came several minutes later with a tray of chamomile tea and a glass of vodka that she said "Puts me right down." Sergei accepted the tray and apologized again, hiding that he had no intention of sleeping. He drank the vodka, threw the tea out the window and flicked on the Moviola.

The men were protesting against the rotten meat; again he watched Dr. Smirnov inspect the pig slab and declare it edible despite the men's objections. He rewound it and played it again, trying to feel the disgust of the meat; he wanted to feel his stomach churning, pre-vomit saliva coating the inside of his mouth. He wanted to feel what he wanted his audience to feel, physical revulsion; yet it was impossible for Sergei to feel as they would feel, close as he was to the material. Sergei made a cut, removed it, brought it to the projector and stood next to the screen, watching the squirming and writhing of the larvae.

His camera work was excellent: he could see in great detail the bulbous worms crawling in and out of the muscle, not just in the extreme close-shots but in the close-shots where you looked past the men and the maggots were just little white spots. He put his hand on the screen and tried to stroke the slab. Fingers touched coldness and wetness unlike that of the screen, then shallow movement on the tips of his fingers. The projection of the film was on the back of his hand, but he felt worms moving inside his palm. Maggots climbed through the gaps between his fingers, black heads and white bodies crawling around the back of his hand, enveloping it in a glove of undulating white. He pulled his hand out of the range of the projector, and still the maggots remained. He heard the sound of their bodies sticking and suckling at each other, a wet squishy noise like boots pulling free from the vacuum of mud. Sergei whipped his hand toward the ground and the maggots fell to the floor. He crushed them into the soles of his shoes.

It was November and Sergei feared what most artists feared: cataclysmic obsession. He wondered if his film had become a singularity, pulling into it his blood, his sanity, his life—eventually collapsing into itself. Nothing was good enough, and he couldn't find a way to make it better. He was looking at a cipher, working it backwards and forwards, testing different algorithms of the alphabet, waiting for a key to come along and unlock the correct sequencing.

He felt it too critical, too disparaging, so he put the film away, stored the reels out of sight and walked out to the harbor where the sounds of seagulls and waves crashing against the hulls of powerful ships sounded nothing like the click of a projector.

He composed a letter to Lev, a long letter of unabridged openness
with spots of blurred ink where his selfish and exhausted tears hit the
page. Lev was the only other man who could empathize with Sergei
when he found himself in these fits, as their artistic paths were so
largely comorbid. Despite their bifurcated methods, Sergei had often
thought of them as piloting the same ship; the two halves of Nemo
braving the leviathan-filled waters of the artistic unknown.

> [...]Also, something strange has been happening. This pressure is
> surely seeping into me. Paranoia, perhaps; insanity, I don't know
> which, but I can't discuss it further at the moment. I must say
> good-bye now, Lev; the light is leaving and I fear I've spent too
> much time in this cathartic letter when I know there is no real
> absolution. Not as long as this film remains unfinished. I want to
> make a masterpiece, Lev. But then I'm sure you've known that about
> me; me and my dispositions toward grandeur. Is it vain? I suppose
> so, but then again we all have our vanities, and as my hair has
> begun its exodus from my skull I suppose my vanities are better
> reserved for my craft. I long to leave Odessa; it is a nice place but I
> fear it is draining me of my health and wits. When I return I shall
> tell you all and set up a private screening for you as I value your
> opinions over most. So long my friend.

—LOVE, SERGEI.

Sergei placed the note in the breast pocket of his sable-lined coat and
left the pier, pensively making his way back to the attic like Atlas ever
beholden to the globe. He took a longer route through town to delay
the burden and began to notice a shadow paired with his own, moving in tandem with him, yet no turning of Sergei's ever discovered a
body for the shadow. In a gold-lined mirror displayed in the window
of a furniture shop, in the window reflection of a bakery amidst decorated cookies and pastries, he found the dark shadow of a body, just
above his shoulder, a dark and ambiguous figure watching him from
the other side of the road. He held his breath and his position, waiting
to see if the figure moved; and when the man proved too obdurate in
his vigilance, Sergei conceited to try luring the fellow into following

him, then to give him the slip and wait for him to pass.

Sergei moved past two more doors, residences, before he came upon a book shop and slipped in through the glass doors, walking through the aisles, sharply glancing over his shoulder only to find the startled faces of customers who then kept their distance and continued to stare cautiously at Sergei, attributing his bizarre behavior to that of an artist: imbalanced. He picked up Gogol's *The Nose* and read the first page five times, using it as a means to stay in the store, but the man never passed. When the shop closed for dinner Sergei was forced back into the streets with no more knowledge of his stalker.

He pushed the door open at Marta's, embittered by disappointment and stress, stepped into the entryway to wipe his feet and found Marta sitting on the sofa in the living room. "Marta, I've had a day, would you mind fixing me—" Sergei stopped, having entered the living room and finding Marta with company: a fat man with clean, shaven jowls in a dark suit, sporting a blue tie in an awful pattern of stripes and diamonds, depositing Marta's tea into the basin of his lower lip.

"Mr. Eisenstein, this gentleman has come to see you," Marta pointed to the suited man, who set his tea down on cue and rose to greet Sergei, lips spread across his face in a hideous smile. Sergei did not return the sentiment.

"Mr. Eisenstein, it is a pleasure; I've been admiring your work for some time. Before your films, I had the privilege of attending several of your dramatic works in Moscow. *Le Comte de Monte Crisco, The Veil of Columbine, The Double*—which, if *I* remember correctly, you starred in yourself—also *The Lawsuit* and *The Gamblers* by...Gogol is it?" He kept his smile aimed at Sergei.

The coyness: the keen arrogance of this man: an esoteric threat cloaked in the blubbery lipped smile stretched to its limits on this pale, unassuming face. The bastard! Surely this was the man who had been following him, the "coincidence" of Gogol...and the pause before the name! "Yes, Gogol, that is correct. But I believe those first two plays you mentioned weren't performed in Moscow. If I remember correctly I put those on while in the PUZAP [Political Direction for the Western Front]."

"Ah, well I suppose I do travel so much things just...blend together as it were. But I have yet to introduce myself. My name is Dmitri

Kolov." He extended a firm hand to Sergei, who took it and gave a
cautious pump.

"An admirer, you said?" Sergei took his hand back and stepped towards the stairs.

"Well, maybe a little more than that. I am a representative from the
Jubilee Committee, come to check up on our investment, if you will."
Dmitri gave a sufficient party smile.

The man didn't look like most of the other members of the USSR's
Film Society he'd encountered, who often met his projects and propos-
als (from his early works and more so in his later projects such as *Ivan
the Terrible* and *Qué Viva México!*—which met cremation instead of
projection) with a militaristic and philistine ideology; men with hard,
serious, moustached faces whose filmic aims extended only to the glo-
rification of the nation and who, when authorized, preferred lining
variants up against the firing wall in opposition to re-editing.

"Colonol Kolov—"

"Just Kolov, Comrade Kolov. I am a representative, not the Com-
missar himself." He laughed. "Just a citizen whose public works have
garnered a position of, well of consult, you see."

"Not quite, sir."

"I was a professor in Stalingrad, Classics and German Literature.
Well I still am, really, a professor. I've been enlisted to provide help
with the state-commissioned work and international press, from time
to time."

Sergei held his breath and nodded.

"I've been asked to pay you a visit, make sure you're using our money for work and not spending it on booze and brothels—well, not too
much." Dmitri chuckled; his fat face shook, laugher rippling through
his skin like a bowl of congealed pudding riding on a carriage.

Sergei smiled in appeasement and took another step backwards to
the stairs. "I assure you, Mr. Kolov, everything is on schedule."

"Fantastic, so you expect we'll have the final reels in three-week's
time?"

Sergei lied and smiled for the man. "The film is near completion. It
will certainly be ready for our projected December release," Sergei put
his hand on Dmitri's back and walked him towards the door. Dmitri
stopped, looking over Sergei's shoulder towards the attic stairs.

"I was rather hoping to fetch a look, Mr. Eisenstein, give my superiors a first-hand account, you know. My personal guarantee." Dmitri's face was serious.

"I am sorry, Mr. Kolov, but I never allow people to view my work until it is finished. So you'll just have to go back with my guarantee. It is my responsibility after all." Dmitri raised his chin, to acknowledge that he, Sergei, accepted all responsibility for the work in passing up Kolov's offer. Sergei read the man and nodded, then he leaned in and whispered, "And you can tell your man everything is on schedule." He nodded; wagging his chin to make sure Dmitri caught his drift.

The fat pig bristled. "What man, Mr. Eisenstein?"

Sergei couldn't tell if Kolov was playing coy again or if indeed he had no knowledge of Sergei's stalker. Either way, the man could surely cast some indictment of unease onto Sergei, reporting back that he had found Sergei uncooperative and paranoid. Sergei laughed and squeezed the man's shoulder warmly and affectionately to compensate. "Have a safe return, friend. Give Moscow my love."

Dmitri stepped onto the stoop and turned, "I should like to see the process some day. It's still so very fascinating to me: the machinery, the film, the tedious methodology…next time perhaps."

Sergei nodded and watched the man leave, hoping to find another man emerging from a bush or alley to meet Dmitri. When Dmitri passed out of sight, alone, Sergei frowned and tucked back inside the attic.

— § —

Kolov's visit left Sergei in a maelstrom of stress: he could see the individual torrents spiraling towards the whirlpool center, each with a face and name, and Sergei remained a fixture of the current, steadily losing buoyancy. There was the oppression the deadline created, and the fact that he was still so far from completion. Should the film be no more completed in two weeks, he would remove his name from the film and quietly wait for his punishment. And Sergei hadn't resolved whether Dmitri, like some ingenious thespian savant, had feigned ignorance to Sergei's remark or really had no knowledge of the man following him. If his stalker wasn't from Kolov or the Commissariats what else would he want with Sergei? Was he looking to blackmail Sergei: trying to find something he could use to extol money, political clout or possibly his film? Maybe it was an American, one of D.W. Griffith's men trying to steal Russian techniques. He wished he could write to Lev, but that was out of the question as his mail was surely being read.

He knew he should get some sleep, but he spent his day worrying the dread of supervision to the point of ignoring his film, and the night spent guilting himself to do work that he knew would be trash. He drank to level himself out, and ate only as a means of ballast, when he needed to right his inebriation to the point of functionality. When the need for companionship arose, he put on his coat and stormed drunkenly to a bar.

In the post-midnight quiet of the late hours that vesseled Sergei's return home from one such establishment, the almost inaudible whispering of the Black Sea was upset by the distinct clapping of feet on the cobblestone. Sergei pivoted sloppily, jovially, expecting to see one of his drinking compatriots, and found himself staring into an empty street. He retraced his steps a couple paces, looking to see if anyone moved from a shadow or dark doorway, and when nothing gave a hiccup of motion he turned back around.

When the footsteps returned, Sergei quickened his pace, taking a quick look over his shoulder as he ducked into a narrow side street he knew limited the places anyone could hide; something thick and nondescript passed in front of a streetlight. Fear overcame his sense of direction and he sprinted down alley after alley until, slipping one dark passage after another, he ran out of urban labyrinth and into a well-lit, utterly vacant, industrial park that smelled of rotting cabbage.

He ran towards the first warehouse and got to a small, square, loading bay between two buildings, lit only by a small kerosene lamp, and he called to his stalker. "All right, I've had enough of these games. I know you've been following me. Let's have it then."

He waited for someone to come. A figure moved through the park, occluded by the Black Sea's fog. The figure moved closer and Sergei could see the shape of a head and shoulders. The body walked from the lot and stepped into the loading bay, yet the light of the kerosene didn't unearth any of the man's features. Like looking at a silhouette, there were no eyes, no nose or mouth. And the figure kept walking towards Sergei, mutely.

"Who-, who are you?" Sergei whispered, acid rising in his throat, sweat collecting on his neck and forehead and the backs of hands.

The darkness became shadows, the shadows became manifest shapes—spherical, conical, indistinct polygonal forms. When still the figure moved into the domicile of light and no more features answered the incandescent call of definition, Sergei threw up his hands and yelped a defeated plea for the creature to stop.

And the body obliged.

Horror retreated slightly to make way for the courage of astonishment; Sergei stepped towards the shape, circling the ambiguous body in a weary orbit. The figure was as dark and non-descript as those of the hanged men from his film. After a third tour, Sergei stopped in front of the body and felt his stomach buckle with recognition: the body was his film; undifferentiated, sure, yet Sergei could recognize it fully as *The Battleship Potemkin*. He knew the creature like a father recognizing his bastard son without introduction.

Sergei laughed out of exasperation and paternity. He took another step forward and put his hand out to touch the body, half expecting his flesh to pass through. His hands moved along the arms and chest and towards the face. And the body remained still. Sergei gripped the body harder, warm muscles underneath dark skin that wasn't quite flesh but was indeed organic. Finally, he stopped and said, "We shall have to take you home."

— § —

Undercutting the main roads with more alleyways and side streets, pausing here and there to move the body behind a chimney or stair to thwart the threat of an inquisitive pedestrian, Sergei returned with the body at a time when he was certain Marta would be asleep. He bid the body to follow him upstairs, Sergei stretching across the steps that creaked until the body fell upon such a stair and burned a terrific wooden bellow into the hall.

Sergei winced and, grabbing the body by the arm, continued towards the attic stairs when a soft and surprised "Sergei?" wafted up from the kitchen. Marta, in her white nightgown, unable to confidently haunt the candle she carried, made her slow trek from the kitchen to the stairs. Sergei panicked and scrounged the area for an immediate solution to cloaking his companion, and when no hidden doors presented themselves he blew out the landing's light and shoved the body into the darkest corner he could find.

"Yes, it's me. Late night, I'm afraid."

"I couldn't sleep so I came down to have a little nip of bra—well, what has happened to the light?" Marta stopped at the base of the stairs.

"Gone out I'm afraid. Must've been the wind coming through when I opened the door," Sergei called from the newel-post.

"Well, no matter, I always keep a box of matches in my pocket for this kind of thing. Very dangerous for a lady my age to be caught in the dark." Marta set the candle on the receiving table next to the banister and pulled the matches from her breast pocket. Sergei rushed down the stairs as Marta worked the friction, with a bit of luck and a summons to the best of his theatrical skills, he feigned a slight fall from the stairs, the rush of air banishing the lighted match back to the world of darkness; Marta's candle stifled when Sergei's hyperbolic over-corrections pushed the flame into the wax with a slight sting. "Well, now, look what you did? Clumsy boy. And I've only two more left."

"I apologize, Marta. I'd only meant to offer you a hand. Please allow me. I should think it more dangerous than the dark for a lady of your years to try climbing darkened stairs to light a sconce with only a match." He grabbed the matches from her hand and bounded upwards to the landing.

He struck the first match firmly, snapping it in half. "Oh, no. I'm afraid I've broken it."

"The youth are always so clumsy, even in their twenties they're still trying to figure out how to operate their body. Well, do try and be more graceful, dear, I feel the brandy taking hold and I should like to fall asleep in my bed and not on the foyer floor."

"I could always carry you, Marta," Sergei proffered.

"Out of the question. The only man allowed to touch me is Mr. Imelienov, and that rat-bastard Ivan saw to it that would never happen again."

Sergei had hoped for the conspicuity of darkness but as that would not happen he would have to think of a new plan. He struck the next match, the last match, and made his way to the sconce, lifted it to the light and gave a violent, and utterly false, sneeze.

"Oh, Sergei, my dear, sweet fool."

"Not a moment, Marta. I've a box upstairs brimming with plentiful matches. I'll only be a second, a few frames, my dear. A foot of silver nitrate."

Sergei grabbed the body from the second-floor recess and sprinted up the final flight into the attic, deposited the body into some indiscriminate corner, scrambling through the darkness to his desk where he had last left the box of matches. All kinds of papers and pens and tools fell to the floor but finally he found the worn box and once more propelled his body to the height of expedience. He lit the sconce on the first try.

"Well there you go."

Sergei offered Marta his arm and helped her up the stairs and towards her room. He opened the door for her, and as she turned to thank him and wish him goodnight, a hard thump from above was too loud for either to ignore.

"What was that?"

"Oh, I must have bumped into something while I was looking for the matches. My projector, or perhaps one of the reels, displaced and finally given over to gravity." He gave an awful, peevish smile that Marta, even through haze of midnight, could see through.

"What have you got up there, Sergei? A cat? A dog? I'll have you know I will not tolerate you bringing home any stray pets. The Tsar took my little Ilea and I promised myself I'll have no other pets."

"I assure you I haven't brought any animals with me, Marta."

"Rats then." Marta reached behind the door for a broom whose presence in her bedroom neither would explore. "Diseased little buggers, they come off the ships and scurry into my house—"

"It's not rats, ma'am. It's, it's…ah…"

Marta's eyes widened, glowing orange from the candle. "Ah, a girl then? Well, you're a young man and given to certain needs, but…" and she raised her voice so whoever was upstairs, and surely listening, wouldn't miss, jabbing the ceiling with the broom just to truly make sure, "I would hope some people would exhibit some respect for their body and not just give it over before the blessed union of matrimony." Feeling this a sufficient admonishment, Marta smiled, patted Sergei on the hand and replaced the broom next to the door. "Goodnight, dear."

When Sergei returned to his attic, nerves slightly abated yet still ringing through his body from the adrenaline like a well-struck cymbal in a marching band, he found the body slouched in a corner with his belly protruding and arms slack at his sides; Sergei absentmindedly reached down and felt his own convex corpulence while he sat in a chair opposite.

They sat in quiet for some time, Sergei unsure just what he was looking at, how the film had materialized so and whether he would have to feed the body, though through what he couldn't tell, as there didn't appear to be a mouth—or eyes or nostrils for that matter. Sergei waited for movement, he sat still and watched to see if the body would rise and explore the room on his own accord, but the figure never moved more than gravity demanded. The body sat still; Sergei tried to listen for breathing and eventually fell asleep.

He awoke in time to hear Marta's steps on the top stairs just before the door and he moved just in time to throw himself against the thin wooden barrier as Marta turned the knob to take his empty dishes from the meal he never ate and to ask him what he'd like for his breakfast.

"Nothing, I—I mean to say, I've fallen ill. I suppose I shall remain inside my chamber for the day."

"My goodness, is it bad? Shall I fetch you a doctor," Marta still tried the door, automatically assuming the rôle she'd take when her son was ill and forgetting all about the noise from the night before and the supposed 'hussy' she'd imagined with him. "Come on, open up. Let me have a look."

Sergei pressed himself against the door, "Not necessary. My illness is more a result of the drink than of a bug. An Irish affliction, as they say."

"Who says?" The knob twisting again.

"I think sleep should suffice. Sleep and perhaps some tea, and maybe some toast."

"You young men are all stupid: you spend your nights drinking and your days recovering. What you should be doing is looking for a wife. I know a girl, homely, not much to look at, but she can cook and clean and take care of a man. I'll call on her parents and try and arrange a meeting for the two of you—"

"The tea! Just the tea and some toast, Mrs. Imelienov. That will be all." He didn't like being curt with Marta but, as he'd learned, it was sometimes necessary to end the conversation. He put his ear to the door and waited until he heard her tiny feet descending before his heartbeat could start again.

— § —

After Marta had brought the toast—with tea and a side of vodka for his head or stomach, or both—after Sergei had ordered her to set it on the stairs, after he had waited for her to leave before slipping the tray inside his chamber did he try and approach the day with pragmatism and purpose. He still had no idea what to do about the body, which, no matter the intensity of light, always remained dark and featureless, as if casted in a perpetual eclipse. Sergei told the body to stand, and it stood, then he moved the chair and the body into a corner of the attic, away from the door should Marta come in unexpectedly. He had the final scenes of "Meeting the Squadron" to assemble in his film, which were to be some of the most potent scenes: the soldiers taking control of the Potemkin, mobilizing, preparing their guns and selves for battle. To get the sequence not just right, but perfect, required precision on his part—required all of him.

He turned on the projector and watched the work-print of the footage he'd taken of the smokestacks billowing ominous black clouds. He took the work-print down and placed the strip back in the Moviola. There were eight minutes worth of film and he watched and cut, and watched and cut until he was left with three minutes of what he thought was the most malevolent bursts of smog. Sergei did the same with the shots he had of the gunmen readying themselves, turning the wheel that rotated the barrel, cutting, discarding the excess and moving onto shots of the pistons in the engine room, shots of more smoke. He cut each strip of scene into smaller segments and taped them together in a separate work-print, a preliminary montage. Emotionally, the scene was a scene in which everything had to come together, the maggots, the rebellion of the soldiers, the unjust killings in Odessa…all leading to this moment of Bolshevik strength, of a fight for freedom, of victory. He placed this latest draft in the projector and

watched the film. When the scene was done he rewound the reel and
played it again, and again, looking for continuity, looking for an appropriate level of disjunction, the right conflict. But nothing looked
right, nothing felt right. And the body stood resolute in the corner:
watching him, mocking him.

— § —

Sergei's assistant, Levshin, had stayed in Odessa after the rest of the
crew had left to return to their families, friends, occupations or new
gigs; his aunt was suffering from pneumonia, and death was likely to
be her last gentleman caller—and unfortunately her most intimate. As
she had been ill as often as the change of seasons, marriage had passed
her by, and with that children of her own, leaving Levshin the only
able-bodied man in the family capable of caring for her. Well aware of
the time Sergei dedicated to his editing, the encroaching deadline and
the little time left in his Aunt's biological hourglass, Levshin had never
deigned to call upon Sergei for a friendly lunch or chat; so it was only
by mere chance that Levshin stumbled into the director: the pharma-
cist Levshin normally used in the Northwest part of Odessa having run
out of morphine and antibiotics and sending Levshin inward to another apothecary, one that happened to be adjacent to the little Jewish
Deli Sergei had chosen for his afternoon meal (hoping for the comforts
of familiar and familial cuisine to help the uneasiness that had taken
hold of his stomach and head). Their paths had crossed while Levshin
stepped in for a bite while waiting for his parcel to be prepared.

"Sergei?" Of course he was able to immediately recognize his friend
and employer even though Sergei's complexion had paled dramatically:
a sickly layer of dew collecting on his now nearly translucent skin; the
fully pronounced shape of the bones and veins underneath stretching
along his forehead to newly un-follicled patches of skin.

"My God, Sergei, are you ill?"

Sergei took in the young cameraman through the purple-shrouded,
matte box of his eyes—owing to an acute absence of sleep that had be-
fallen him in the five days since the arrival of the body; cautious and
uncertain of what the body was capable of in his unconscious absences.
He greeted Levshin cautiously, assured him it was just a bug going
round and, though he didn't feel up to talking, allowed the young man

to seat himself at Sergei's table.

"And what brings you to Odessa again?"

Levshin looked at Sergei strangely, as though someone else were donning Sergei's skin. "But, Sergei, I never left Odessa. I'm sure I told you several times that I'm here to take care of my aunt—she's on her deathbed, you know. But I'm sure you have more important things on your mind. How's it going by the way? The film, I mean."

Sergei, for the life of him, couldn't remember any such conversations with Levshin, and eyed him suspiciously; between the ghosts and the maggots, and then Kolov and the body and now this unexplained coincidence…nothing short of an interconnected conspiracy, no doubt. Some collating collaboration of a syndicate out to sabotage him. And now, they've reached out to a trusted friend. Sergei wouldn't abide the pitfall; he wouldn't give in so easily.

"How is it a concern of yours how the film is progressing?"

Levshin was understandably taken aback. "But I…Forgive me, Sergei, I only wanted to see how our work was—"

"*Our* work? *Potemkin* is not *our* work, but *my* work. Do you understand?" Sergei was gripping his fork so tightly that the neck of the utensil bent the prongs from their threat of impaling the ceiling to that of the chest across the table.

Levshin was hurt. Never in the time that he'd spent working with Sergei had he been privy to such animosity directed at a live being removed from the passion of theatrics. Though Levshin had never witnessed Sergei in his editing, and perhaps, he reasoned, this was just how the auteur worked. As he was about to rise and carry out the remainder of his wait in the pharmacy, Sergei caught him off-guard with another scurrilous indictment.

"Kolov sent you, naturally. I could read that man's soul through his jowls, and I saw that he would never be satisfied with my word; that he and his like-minded cohorts wouldn't let me work in peace, they would follow me and tag me until I handed in the final reels or until they wheeled me off and shot me in the field. And now they've sent you to try and filch out some meager little update of my work. Well you won't succeed, my friend. So, my weak minded, sniveling, little Brutus, you can fuck-off and give them your report with my complete assurance that the film is fine: *Potemkin* remains in my capable hands and they

will have it for their deadline." Sergei's raised voice had attracted the
uncomfortable eyes of not only Levshin but of the three other patrons
in the diner, the proprietary couple, and the young daughter whose
shaking hands clutching a pitcher of water sloshed out puddles onto
the floor, the table and Sergei's lap.

"Oh, you stupid, stupid girl! It's no wonder you aren't married, you
haven't the looks to compensate for the egregious incompetence in that
walnut-sized brain nestled in that primitive cortex of yours. You've got
the ego of a troglodyte and the looks to match."

The girl began to cry; Levshin wanted both to put his arms around
her and console her as much as he wanted to scream at Sergei that this
was no acceptable behavior for a gentleman—or even for a 'troglodyte,'
for that matter. This was Sergei, though: his mentor, his friend and
his employer, without whom Levshin might never be able to find a
payable vocation in his field should he challenge him now. And while
he had never known Sergei to be anything other than physically benevolent, he saw a glimmer of suppressed rage, something endemic no
doubt, taking hold the reigns of his somatic system. Levshin kept quiet, as did everyone else; and in the quiet horror Sergei came back
to himself and realized what he'd done. He tried to fumble his way
through an apology, each syllable working itself in queue towards the
precipice of his tongue. The embarrassment surmounted and he fled
quickly from the restaurant to the only recluse he knew: the attic, and
thus the body.

Sergei had been so immersed in ridding himself of the burden of the
film—completion being the only resolve—that he had failed to notice
the development of the body in the corner. Perhaps he wouldn't have
noticed the body at all—set in the dark corner with no sunlight and
only a single candle burning in the room—if he hadn't cut his finger
while splicing a frame and stamped around the room holding the cut
and cursing God, the Devil, Stalin and everything in-between. When
the nature of his pained ambulation forced his eyes to look upon the
corner, there wasn't blackness as he expected, but a shape of gray and
taupe flesh. Sergei, supplanting the pain for the intrigue, picked up his
candle and moved towards the body as silently as the floorboards al-

lowed. The orange light hit the roof of the attic and sharpened its focus in the acute corner. He could see the body fully, that is, he could distinctly make out arms, legs, fingers and toes in the sparsely lit room. The body's skin was a fleshy white like his own, patches of thick brown hair on his forearms and chest. And he could certainly label the body a him, the bulge of a penis squished between the legs. There was still no definition to the face: a mask of flesh where eyes should be, lips, a nose that appeared stock and ventless, faint sprouts of hair on the sides of his head. There was no mouth to feed or hear.

What Sergei felt wasn't fully terror, nor excitement, nor any other polar emotion. When he looked on the body he felt a sense of urgency that he couldn't account for. There was a feeling he got of burgeoning resentment, of angst. Or was it regret? He needed to put his hands on the body; he needed to dig his fingernails into the body's shoulders and shake; he needed to wring the man's throat. He wanted to beat him, to kick his face, his chest, his stomach and groin. He felt overcome by the want of a service revolver. His rage terrified him more than the amorphous body and he refrained from acting on any of these feelings. Instead, he extended a derelict finger towards the body and ran the proffered digit down the chest, pausing over the heart until he was certain he could feel a faint beat, unsure if the pulse was the body's or his own.

Channeling the urgency, channeling his aggression, Sergei worked through the night, cutting and re-taping the end of his film, looking over his shoulder at the body, sneering with contempt and working faster. He placed the smoke stacks, pistons and guns in one series of montage, viewed the sequence, then cut and tried a different ordering. Marta knocked on the door several times to tell him he needed to eat, that he hadn't touched the tray she'd sent up hours ago, that she was worried, begging him to let her fetch a doctor. All the while, Sergei resisted the urge to shout at her, until he found that the only way to quell the woman's concern was to appear in the flesh, eat and show vitality—though he felt up to none of the above. He sat through dinner, and when he felt Marta had been satisfied by his company returned upstairs and sat again at his cutting booth.

The body remained vertical in the corner (Sergei having no better place to put him). Occasionally, Sergei looked back at the corner and found more hair on the body, on his forearms and legs and chest; he saw wrinkles appear in the man's skin; freckles and moles on his body. Sergei viewed his latest cut and looked back to watch a mouth forming, a chasm creeping into the skin and the subsequent formation of lips that separated to show overcrowded teeth. Sergei was more than aware of his fists clenching and his jaw tightening together. He felt himself tearing up, wanting to beat him so badly though he couldn't say why. He pulled himself away from the ever-materializing figure and returned to the screen.

Music would have helped, he thought; maybe the feeling he was looking for could only be achieved when he coupled his film with a score. Perhaps he should get Edmund Meisel involved now. No, unfortunately that's not how things worked: the film comes first. And if he was going to do anything of valor, the film needed to stand alone as Eisenstein's creation. The film couldn't be dependent on a crutch.

Every time Sergei made a cut, frantically, as if the Tsar were back in power and he himself was marching up the stairs, soldiers at the ready to stand him against the attic wall and shoot him then and there, each cut felt no closer to the last cut, the last segment never inspiring the visceral reaction he needed for the film to be complete. In disgust, Sergei turned his eyes away from the screen, turning them over his shoulders so not even his periphery could witness what he considered to be his inevitable failure as an auteur. He shut his eyes that stung from the hours of light and the tedium of reading and cutting the right frames. When he opened them again, Sergei found himself staring into the eyes of the body. Neither moved. Sergei continued to stare from the perch of his shoulder, the body's eyes never blinking, and he was overcome by a sickening feeling of déjà-vu. Though many of the features still existed as an out-of-focused blur, Sergei realized he intimately knew those eyes. Taking a deep breath, he composed himself and crept toward the body.

"Step forward, move into the light," he directed. "Here." And the body did, frame heavy with skin and the jiggling of fat around the midrange and into his chest.

The body moved to where Sergei could circumnavigate it in full benefit of the light, and he made his inspections: he poked the muscles and ran his fingers along familiar scars and moles; he felt the expected, familiar girth of the man's arms and shoulders; fingers splayed into a comb, he worked them through the wild, upright hair; he pressed the body's hands to his and found a stereo match; their eyes met on level, foreheads pressed together in a kiss of two cortexes, occluded by skull and skin.

Yet, the body never moved as it was prodded and squeezed under Sergei's inspection. Sergei circled the body seven times, each sidereal revolution bringing more verve to Sergei's touch, pushing harder against the stomach or arms, groping the man's face, scratching his fingernails along the stubble of the cheeks and chin. Still, he recognized the body as his film, but also as something else.

Sergei pushed the body, which swayed and returned to buoyancy. He pushed it again, harder, finally deregulating his emotions toward the body and allowing himself to exercise the full range of his aggression and anger, his preterit revenge. Sergei punched the body in the stomach. He heard the wind fall from the body as the figure buckled. Sergei hit him again in the chest, grabbing onto the body's shoulder for leverage as he drove his fist again and again into the stomach. He pulled back and hit the body in the face, which didn't bruise or break, and he struck him until his wrists stung and he was forced to use his elbows and knees. Sergei rained blows upon the man, expunging himself. Yet the body remained unmarked, sending Sergei into a heavier rage. He grabbed the body and threw him to the ground, kicking the man's face and waiting to hear the release of teeth onto the floor. When nothing came, Sergei tried to drop his whole weight into the man's face and instead stubbed his toe against the floor. Sergei screamed and cursed the body, giving no heed to Marta downstairs.

He pushed the man's face into the wood, stepping on his arm to keep him there. Sergei beat his fists against the man's back, the unbroken pale skin. He punched the man's ass, kneed him in the genitals, then reached inside his trousers and removed his own member. Sergei shoved his cock into the body's upturned ass, crying and continuing to lash out at the tyranny of the man's un-abating skin, sobbing against the oppression of the body that refused to break and the obduracy of injustice. He came spitefully and collapsed onto the body, sobbing and wailing into shoulder-blades until a few split-seconds like eons elapsed and he rose from the body in a fit of terrified calm.

Sergei buttoned his trousers, straightened his shirt and ran from the

attic. He took the stairs two at a time and pushed against the locked
front door, he fumbled with the latch and was only thankful later, after
he'd found a seat at the bar, that the locked door meant Marta hadn't
been home.

— § —

Sergei drank vodka and smoked cigarettes as if it was his Bolshevik
duty. He refused food and sweated profusely. He feared everything:
from the Stalinist punishment against murder and rape; to the vacil-
lating answer to the question of his homosexuality; to the failure of his
film and theories; to the capacity for violence and hatred he had never known himself to possess in such physical form—the initiation into his endemic burden. He looked at his hands, swollen knuckles and
fingernails filled with dirt. His wrist throbbed and he was certain he
had broken his ulna, along with several carpals. He watched the door,
anticipating the wooden portal to splinter open and guards to pour in
with Marta at the head, pointing Sergei out and yelling "That's him.
That's the murdering sodomite. And to think I tried to set him up
with a nice wife who'll cook and clean for him and who has the hips to
bear as many children as he could sire." If he ran would they chase him
with pitchforks and torches: the trusted auteur demonized and ready
for the pyre, a little seasoning thrown on for good measure; a man who
had created his monster with their bodies and reanimated them on the
silver-screen?

He tried desperately to slip into the anonymity of the brotherhood
of the inebriated, but then the door opened and the face of the Jewish
restaurateur whose daughter he had assaulted only the previous afternoon came from the ensconcing cloak of winter and into the sparsely veiling light of the domestic hearth. Sergei's breath was muted, as
he hoped beyond all reserves of hope that the man wouldn't find him,
wouldn't call him out right here, order his arrest for the assault and the
stolen meal; then, in their procedural follow-through, find the raped,
murdered(?) body in the attic. The man turned his head and rested
his eyes upon the face of the petrified director before taking the initial
steps in his direction.

Sergei threw himself from the table and sprinted through the bar,
knocking larger, stronger men than he who shouted curses and made

to grab him, but Sergei nimbly slipped his arms from their grasp and threw himself into the storeroom, bolted the door and left through the back exit that opened to the alley. He ran to the only immediate solace he knew of, to where chase or a hotel registration wouldn't surrender him to the homicidal masses he was sure were pounding down the pavement hot on his trail, to the place where his fears would have to be met head on, forcing him to end his procrastination and face up to his consequences: Marta's.

Sergei moved as expediently as his necessity for stealth allowed (in case they could hear the sharp clap of his footsteps on the sidewalks), fearful of more bodies following him: either bodies with names, clothes, faces and an address or bodies of perpetual midnight that mocked his sanity, his understanding of himself, his beliefs and the realm of physical possibility (after all, he was an engineer in his earlier years). Possibility brought all manners of fear: What if when he turned the corner he found another of these filmic bodies? Would he bring this one home as he'd done the last? Would he attack him—or her—with the same Bolshevik hatred and sexual effrontery? Throw the body to the floor and tell the tyrant to swallow his socialist cock?

As he slipped through overpasses and the undersides of bridges, tempting to throw off the trail, he was forced to confront the existential causes and consequences that had happened to result in the rending of his superego and the beliefs that he always held as the basis of his character. He was removed from his self: the ideogram dissolved into its individual, conflicting pieces. He felt himself divorced from himself; somehow bifurcated from himself and conjoined with something darker, something insidious, and yet, at the same time, wholly him (the dormant and the active in symbiotic, temporal unity). He saw himself as violated and inviolable; he was the moon: at one time a celestial beacon that reflected the holy light of the sun; and at another, a heavy, lightless bulb.

Sergei was at Marta's door: the painted oak spat in his face. The knob bit his hand when he twisted and pushed it open.

Sergei could tell from the sour smell of boiling water and the bite of chopped onions that Marta had returned and was still up and about. Standing at the threshold of the door, he felt as if he were a seafaring navigator from the future: Odysseus granted with the tragedy of perfect foresight, conducting his journey from Troy to Ithaca with the hellish knowledge of every set-back, every Scylla, every Cyclops and wandering rock that would befall him. He saw everything in four dimensions and it made him nauseous. When he walked into the living room he knew Marta would come from the stairs on her way to the kitchen. He knew that when he saw her she would stop at the doorway and place her hand against the frame for support. And that he would drop onto the couch in supplication and wait for her judgment. What he didn't know was how long he would have to wait or the exact phrasing of the words that would leave her mouth.

"Well, what have you to say?" Sergei noticed the wet towel in her hand.

He watched Marta stumble for words. "I, I'm very sorry Mr. Eisenstein. I should have knocked. I tried to clean up the mess as best as I could."

Sergei nodded, fearing the confirmation of homicide, but was perplexed as to why Marta would make an attempt at covering up the crime. He rubbed his hands against his thighs then brought them up to pull at his hair.

"But, Marta, why? Do you realize what they'll do to you, even at your age?"

"Oh, really it wasn't a bad mess." Marta looked down at her towel and the stain the oxidized color of wet brick. "That's most of it right here. Well, what I could get up before I left."

"How much more is there?"

Marta looked confused. "maybe just a drop or two. The floor will probably have taken it up by now. Nothing to cause alarm, I've never known a little tea to hurt a piece of wood." Marta moved towards him and stroked his shoulder like a child come in from the cold. Sergei cried.

"Everything's fine, Sergei, it's nothing to be ashamed about, it was just a little tea and…" then Marta laughed, "I *was* married; it's nothing I haven't seen before."

"Marta," Sergei stood, confused and angry, "what-, what did you see?"

Sergei grabbed her shoulders.

Marta tried to uncoil her body from Sergei's grip. "What do you mean?"

Sergei shook her, "What did you see, Marta Khrypnouvitch? WHAT DID YOU SEE!?"

"I saw you, Sergei. I saw *you*."

— § —

Sergei took the knob in his hand lightly; he didn't have the dignity to clasp it with strength. He pushed the door in and entered. The projector had been left on but pushed to the side during his violence and left only a dim slice of yellow on the slanted ceiling. Chamomile soaked pine wafted from the doorway. Sergei stepped fully into the attic and slammed and locked the door behind him, lest Marta decided to come up or, even worse, lest the body escape. The body, however, lay flat on the floor: naked, legs spread out exposing the man's hairy genitals. Sergei yielded his breath to see if he could hear another set of lungs working, which the projector thoroughly prevented.

Vacant unfixed eyes, like those encumbered in the deepest of opiate throngs, stared unblinkingly at the floor; the body's unblemished face, resting on an un-swept plank, pointing towards the pale, gray screen. Sergei grabbed the body's shoulders and turned him on his back. Not a mark could be found on the figure. The eyes remained forward but never settled on anything, pupils dilated and mouth puckered like a bloated, dead fish. Crouching, Sergei took the body into his arms and lifted him to the corner that had been his shadowy nook.

— § —

There isn't time. There isn't time. There isn't time. I've this deadline approaching like the indelible hand of death and no penance to offer. It lies in spools in my room and fails to define itself. Were I to return, say from the lavatory, and find it finished and perfect, I would throw my bawling face to the feet of the man that succeeded in the face of my flagrant failure and kiss his boots to mirror-like perfection. Maybe this is it; maybe I've met my end. And maybe for good reason: I've exploited death, children, god and the history of Russia. And here I sit in hand with the shovel that dug me in, spinning and flashing on the screen. Kolov will come to collect. He

*and his men will open the door and find me collapsed on the floor,
soiled, presenting him my service revolver and begging for a decisive
and discriminating end.*

Sergei never sent this letter. Instead he balled it up and gave it an incendiary funeral in his bedpan. In as much as writing his concession
he had willed himself—through anger, determination or integrity he
couldn't be certain—into a frenzy. He yelled to Marta to bring up coffee and vodka—these were to be the last of his provisions for the remaining four days until the deadline—and, picking it up from the step
as he still hadn't allowed her entry into his room, began slamming reels
into the projector, removing them, cutting them and snapping them
back in, watching for minutia. Removing two frames at a time, then
one. After his fourth cup of coffee, with the vodka half-full, he began
yelling at the body while he worked. "Do you like that cut you vile
bastard?" "I bet you wanted me to cut to a shot of the ship didn't you?
Didn't you?" "When this is over I will have your head." The body just
stood and watched the screen, his skin moving like the shifts of tectonic plates, forming a more resolute form with new idiosyncrasies of
freckles and moles and blemishes.

Owing to a lack of food and too much caffeine and drink, Sergei
vomited and tried to kick the bile-laden stew under a table. He wiped
the vagrant strands of saliva and stomach acid from his mouth, found
a pitcher of water and took a healthy sip before sprinting again from
the projector to the cutting board.

He had amassed more micro edits and collected the separate reels
in order and watched the film from the beginning, genuflecting under
the projector's beam of light. The credits started and Sergei's face became speckled with mist from the exploding water on the opening jetty. A wind blew across his forehead and dried his skin with the salinity
of the breeze. "There is a limit to what a man can take," he spoke along
with Vakulinchuk. Sergei screamed and laughed and screamed again.
Maggots poured from the screen to the floor. There was rage such as
he hadn't expended since that night when he attacked the body; yet
when the film finished and the projector flashed only a haze of stale,
infertile light, Sergei screamed at the absence. He was close, he could
feel that at least; however, the proximity to completion only elicited

stronger anger and heightened his fevered state. Should he fail, after coming so far, after enduring so much strain, simply to fall short…he didn't want to think of the consequences, imposed by Kolov and his men or by himself. He picked up the "Odessa Stairs" reel and placed it back on the cutting board, trying to will his shaking hands into making a precise cut. Gluing a new cut, Sergei's hands slipped and spread the sticky polymer over two of the slides, ruining them.

He screamed and beat the floor under him, slamming splinters into the meat of his hands; he wrenched handfuls of hair from his head and shoved them into his mouth while sobbing, crying around a mouthful of hair and curses and fingers.

The body looked on, his eyes never leaving the screen, waiting for something to come though Sergei didn't know what; Sergei took the expression as more mockery. Clothes had adorned the body, gray trousers and a white, button-down shirt applied by Sergei and taken from his own closet, not wanting to stare any longer at the nakedness. There was nothing to shroud the body's smug smile.

— § —

There were only four days left before Kolov's deadline; four days to finish; four days to perfect and birth the behemoth he'd spent the past months incubating and nursing with his sweat, his blood, his nerves and his wit. There was still so much work to be done, so many cuts, so many frames to go through. When midnight struck, signaling the three day countdown, Sergei collected every bit of spare furniture and vagrant piece of lumber he could find and set to barricading himself inside the attic. He would allow himself no reprieve, for water, sustenance or communication, until *Potemkin* lay coiled and completed inside the cans.

Marta repeatedly tapped on the door and tried slipping her pleas in the sliver of space between the door and the floor of the attic. Sergei never budged or responded, barking only once, "I shall only leave this room in two ways: when the film is completed, or when the coroner carries me out on a stretcher."

Sergei's obduracy prevailed over Marta's and by the second-to-last day there wasn't a peep in his direction, and he worked relentlessly, paying no attention to the cuts on his hands from his inattentive han-

dling of the razor, or the smashing of his fingernails while hastily loading the reels into the Moviola or the sprockets of the projector. The
final day arrived, and with dawn came no less feeling of accomplish-
ment. Sergei quickened his pace, if that was at all possible.

The knocking started again in the afternoon, the interruption igniting in Sergei such a severe anger he almost threw the Moviola at the
door. Marta announced that a man and his daughter had come to seek
financial restitution for a stolen meal, an apology for his daughter and,
not the least important, to inquire about the health of Sergei.

"They are worried about you, Sergei. They're not angry with you.
Please, come and talk to them, it might make you feel better."

The announcement of unwanted guests, especially these unwanted
guests, instead elicited in Sergei the height of shame and embarrassment, knotting Sergei's innards tighter, and he trudged on more resolute than ever to finish the film; that all could be forgiven if he could
only present a material product and say "This is why. *This is why.*"

Sergei slid the second reel once more into the projector with trembling hands guiding the film through the machine. The constancy of
the machinery made the attic unbearably hot and Sergei vented the
sweat from his shirt. On screen, the demonstration struck up. The attic room was full of rioting and shouting and the sounds of trampling
feet on stone bouncing off the wainscoting and rafters. The soldiers
came and the room took on the smell of burnt gunpowder, igniting
the air as the bullets narrowly missed his face. Then there was another
knock, someone with a stronger and more confident hand than Marta.

"Sergei, it's Lev." And for a minute Sergei stopped moving and almost went to the door. He wanted comfort, he wanted companionship, but he had to do this on his own: to let him in would only sabotage this final stretch. Sergei felt it best not to respond.

"Levshin sent word to me. He said you looked ill; said you weren't
acting like yourself. He's here, too. We're worried, Sergei; please just let
us in. We can help."

Sergei began to cry and shoved his fist in his mouth as if the physical act would be sufficient to stop himself from speaking.

"At least let me in; I can help you, Sergei."

Sergei took a moment to collect himself, to control his breathing
and reset his will; he went back to work. He took the second reel off,

made a quick cut in the Moviola and picked up the third reel, the reel of the "Odessa Stairs."

The scene began again with revolution and a march, and again the shouting filled the attic so that Sergei couldn't hear the clacking of the machinery. More gunfire, more stampeding as the steps descended from the screen and into the attic, and with the steps the soldiers and the pleading masses. A soldier brushed too close to Sergei, knocking him down to the unforgiving steps; the sharp tips of boots and blunt heels assaulted his chest and arms as he tried to cover himself. He scrambled across the attic floor, dodging a phalanx of marching legs and weaving through the masses of the fallen to find a break in the lines. A cut opened his forehead and blood ran into his eyes and nose, dripping onto the steps. His shirt was cotton and would at least condense the wound; Sergei ripped a strip from his sleeve and tied it around his head as he braced himself against a column of marble that supplied some cover. Then there was the boy.

From his position on the periphery of the stairs, Sergei only made out young Abram in small flashes of visibility through the channel of legs, snapping the image of the boy with a shutter of scissoring legs. The boy was collapsed on the steps and pleading for his mother as a legion of boots reigned over him.

The dying boy reached his hand towards Sergei, "Mother, help me, Mother. I don't want to die. Mother, please, why won't you help me? It hurts. They're killing me." A trampling sound like horseshoes on marble accompanied the cracked celery sound of broken bones as Sergei made his way to the boy; he pulled the boy to his lap and collapsed and wept with the boy in his arms.

Sergei heard a familiar voice shouting, "Now you are shot; you collapse. Now you reach out for help, but no one comes." The boy in his arms, half on the attic floor, half on the steps, Sergei turned to the voice and found the body shouting directions at the boy: Sergei shouting directions at the boy. "The people are stepping on you, kicking you. You are afraid you are dying. You want your mother but she is too far away; she will not come. You might die before she gets to you."

The boy wailed and pleaded with his absent mother, "Please, Mother, help me! Help me. Mother. Mother?"

Then the boy went slack and Sergei rocked the limp figure in his

lap, stroking the boy's face and repeating, "I'm so sorry. I'm so sorry."
He turned to the body, to the other Sergei. "You did this."

Sergei left the dead boy on the stairs, plucked up into the arms of
his mother and carried up the steps as Sergei lunged at the body, wrapping his hands around the body's neck, strangling his likeness as he
shouted "Why, damn you? WHY?"

On the screen, the woman in pince-nez went bloody, trickling from
her jaw and her eye under the shattered glasses. The baby carriage began its descent down the stairs, passing the heaps of dead bodies whose
smells perforated the attic. The beaten woman screamed. The carriage
rolled on. The stone lion woke from his slumber, rose and looked on
with horror. Sergei's grip on the body's throat tightened.

The body, through a constricting windpipe, croaked, "Because I
never want to see dead sons again. Because I never want to see tyranny's feet again trampling upon our youth. Because I don't want people
to forget about the horror that occurred here, nor do I want them to
forget how far we've come. This is bigger than you, bigger than me.
This is for Russia, for all of us."

Another knock hit the attic door, and another voice followed. "Mr.
Eisenstein, it's Dmitri Kolov. I came by to pick up the final reels in
person and now I find that you've locked yourself in the attic? I do
hope nothing is the matter, sir. Please, be a good chap and open the
door for us." Kolov paused to wait for an answer.

Sergei still had his hands firmly around the neck of the body with
no intention, in his heart or in his head, of answering or of letting go.
He felt his fingernails slip into the warm skin and fill with dermatological blood as he bent his mouth close to the body's ear and cursed
him. "You bastard. You fucking bastard! You killed him."

Kolov called again, "Come now, there's nothing to be afraid of. I'm
sure whatever you have is utterly splendid."

Lev must have moved to the door as well, somehow finding a way
to share the tight space with that fat oaf. "Sergei, please. This is ridicu-
lous."

Levshin's voice, smaller, farther down the hall called, "Please, Sergei,
we're your friends."

Sergei tightened his grip and felt aortic blood rush over his hands.
The body's eyes, Sergei's eyes, made a slow journey to the back of his

head. The sputtering of breath stopped and was replaced by the sound of shoulders laying into the barricaded attic door. Sergei continued to sit on the body's chest, stroking the familiar dead face and breathing heavily and triumphantly. As the door beat upon the lock and the furniture barricade, Sergei vacillated between sobbing and laughing, looking from the body to the progressively splintering door frame.

Lev had Kolov take a step down the stairs as he readied himself for what he hoped was the final kick; he felt the wood give considerably, yet the door remained shut. He prepped his leg for another bash when the door suddenly opened and they found themselves staring at a bloodied, panting Sergei, smiling and holding a stack of reels in his hand.

Lev: "Sergei, my god."

Kolov: "Good heavens, man."

Marta wailed.

Sergei continued to smile and tried to catch his breath. "I...sorry...you'll have to...excuse me...just...trying to get it...ready."

Kolov forced his corpulent figure past Lev. "What have you been doing in there, man?"

"Just making the final edits."

"And-, and are you finished then?" Kolov sputtered.

Lev called to Marta to send for a doctor. The father pulled his daughter into his chest at the bottom of the stairs.

Sergei looked down at the stack of reels in his arms, hefting their weight, taking another exhausted breath and smiling, "Yes; yes, I believe I am."

II. FRANKENSTEIN'S DOPPELGÄNGER I

"They shall be told. Ere Babylon was dust,
The Magus Zoroaster, my dear child,
Met his own image walking in the garden.
That apparition, sole of men, he saw.
For know there are two worlds of life and death:
One that which thou beholdest; but the other
Is underneath the grave, where do inhabit
The shadows of all forms that think and live
Till death unite them and they part no more..."

—*Percy Shelley,* PROMETHEUS UNBOUND *Act I. 191-199*

— § —

TO THE VISAGE,—

As I'm sure you well know, I've seen you. And do I assume too much in saying that you have seen me: crossing, as our veiled and secret noctambulations have taken, the same spots of Ingolstadt, the same crannies and repositories of the dead? And have I not seen you, glimpsed, as it were, always slipping back into the shadows as I chanced to turn, allowing myself only to rent the image of a lock of greasy, black hair, skin pale as my own from the feckless ours of toil and study those two years had bleached from my body (stretched to a waxy onion-skin over the muscles and arteries beneath), or the specter of light from a candle or lamp as it refracted off the sheen of your ~~white~~ teeth? Glimpsed—rented, as I said—never purchased, before passing through an alleyway along the brick sheath of a sepulchral tunnel leading to an indiscriminate—and always private—charnel-house, dissecting room, vault, or wagon of the newly dead before their horse-drawn promenade to the graveyard. (Always vacant, as though unmapped in the minds of Ingolstadians; as if built solely for me?) And have your hands passed—do I dare even write it?—over the same freckled leg, the same noose-wrangled torso, selecting the same enlarged liver I required, the same heart, the same pair of enormous hands, gripping the arachnodactylic fingers with intimacy before slipping the curtain from the formaldehyde-entombed brain? I could have sworn, when I placed my hands about the ears of the Marfan head required, to have dipped my hands into a pocket of warmth left from yours.

Could I have found my creation without you? Could I have born the dæmon without your aid, without your seed of selection? Was the life of the monster anything other than the result of our collusion: a coitus in the sacrament of theft, grave-robbery, secrecy, and—I'll say it—perfection of choice? For as I deigned to build the body of a man larger than any before, eight-feet tall, as you surely know, what are the chances of finding such perfect samples, such anomalies, such idiosyncrasies in this town, yet ones that fit together so precisely, as if they had asked for fusion or had reunited with themselves: the perfection of their circulatory systems matching without a solitary leak in the plumbing; the perfection of the body accepting itself without the slightest bit of infection—the infinitesimal possibility that the neurons would work in such resplendent concert and unbroken communication!

Such questions, when compared with my ultimate motive for lifting this pen and writing you (which I feel, should I perish inside this arctic desert, will find you still), such questions become ancillary, topical even. The question I am plagued with is this: Did you build my monster, or did I build yours? And further: Is this inevitable damnation upon my soul or yours?

Perhaps we'll share the hell that waits. Perhaps, as we built a body for a dead soul to inhabit, our souls have built our own habitations in Hell, excavating a new circle in Dante's architecture; I should say it should be a lonely place, with the possibility of more population in later days as I'm certain my folly won't be a singular offense in the coupled trajectory ~~of reason and resolve~~ of inquiry and means, willed to action in the name of the empirical.

Perhaps the punishment will be that I am forced to chase you round and round the circle—as I have done these past months with the monster, with you—trying to catch you but always finding you slipping behind the arc and out of sight; and perhaps your fate—I should hope—is the same, and you are chasing me, always out of reach; and we continue to chase after each other for eternity as the monster watches over us from the crest of the malebolge (mocking us by shouting a false beatitude of Coleridge's *Ancient Mariner* and his favorite passages from Milton's damning verse), standing arm in arm with Prometheus, laughing at our hubris and lashing us until our wounds—compounded by our restless locomotion—concede and our bodies are rent apart—only to be cruelly stitched back together and returned to our track.

I've had a dream that's kept recurring since that fateful November: Elizabeth had joined me in Ingolstadt; I embraced her and we kissed, but when I looked down I found my lips engaged not with her pert, supple forms but with a necrotic, blackened mouth. As I held her, dismayed as I was, she took on the features of my dead mother and I held both as the worms went at their flesh: the woman who gave me life and the woman with whom I intended on creating it. Was this irony the work of your dream, the product of the monster, or my creation alone?

Which made me wonder, was it really you I was following? The other Victor, the other *me*, as it were? Or are you merely a divination of my future, a path in time just slightly ahead, a map to keep me navigating true along the waters of fate? Or, as I've lately begun to think, are you instead the dæmon himself, piecing yourself together, creating your own existence, using me as the puppet or tool?

And going further: Am I, in fact, the monster? not merely for the irresponsibility of the act, but because I have always been the monster? Because I was always going to create him (*you*, if you be he); because his creation was my diathesis; because the creature was always with me, indelibly; and because, of course, as it was my hands that built him/you, as it was my hands that infused the necessary life into those that later wrapped around the throats of William, Clerval—oh God,

Elizabeth!—that of course, transitively, those murderous hands are my own?

Yet I shall say, Could the inverse not also be true: If he you (for as I write I am growing more confident in the identity of the addressee) were really with me as permanently as I suggest, dualistic, as it were, would it not then mean that my hands were your *own* hands that gave yourself life, that took life, that willed themselves into being only to eliminate all the love therein? That you had created yourself only to kill the ones you loved, and I was thus the weapon used? That I was the monster created: reanimated through a teleological, ontological ouroboros coiled outside the parameters of time—creating and recreating myself to feel this punishment over and over? And further, that upon my death, it will be me alone brandishing the lash against myself in Hell; and *I* will wield the needle and thread and stitch my skin back together as I always, and will always, have done?

—VICTOR FRANKENSTEIN.
NORTH, JULY ?TH, 17—.

III. SETTLING A SCORE

"It is not the voice that commands the story:
it is the ear."
—*Italo Calvino,* INVISIBLE CITIES

"Let's take it from the coda" had become more or less a mantra around Sunset Studios in Torrance, California: recited enough by composer Bryne Dogan from behind the glass window of the control room; reprised with a more sarcastic timbre by the recording sextet when taking five in the break room, and only when well out of earshot. The sextet—a percussionist, two violinists, a cellist, a pianist and a guitarist who played his guitar as if it were a keyboard (respectfully, Maruki Kaijima, Svâto Sckoufias, Erin Mielzarek, Joseph Michura, Bertrand "Birdy" Jones and George Holland)—often accompanied said mantra by riffing on a recurring theme that compared Dogan's distracted conducting to that of a surfer Beethoven with ADHD, using an invisible wand to conduct a waltz above their heads until distracted by something shiny floating into view. This was a comparison of both affection and commendation. Their friend and erstwhile employer, Bryne's scatterbrained antics lent themselves to a well-meaning caricature—of course, said antics could become problematic at times, distracting even. While the sextet attempted to perform Bryne's expansive compositions with professional severity, few could avert their eyes from the one-man show framed in the glass theater of the control room: Bryne's lanky, six-four frame scurrying about the cramped room with the lum-

135

bering grace of a drunk giraffe; the childish puppetry of Bryne's
mopped hair the color of old hay bouncing along the top of the desk
like an early run of a Jim Henson sea urchin while he rummaged
around the floor adding vintage talk-boxes, analog delays or other such
pedals into the FX chain; the thousand-yard stare from his perch at
the outboard mixer, back straightened, eyes dilated to infinity, making
painfully-tedious, quantum manipulations as if he were part of Hous-
ton's mission control crew, preteritely trying to correct the miscalcula-
tions of that tragic first-manned mission to Mars, not wanting to replicate their mistake of giving too much juice to the starboard side of
the ship's ballast and upending the pod—after 210 days and 140 mil-
lion miles—just yards from the surface. And so, on more than daily
occurrence, the normally mechanically-precise musicians would find
themselves a bit off-kilter, stumbling through runs, dropping uninten-
tional ritards, falling off tempo or coming up flat, only to find themselves cut off by the intercom's spark of connection as Bryne mum-
bled the count-off to that well-vetted invocation, "All right, um…so,
ah…—Let's take it from the coda."

Riding the saw-wave of that on-again-off-again relationship that had
begun flittering with the first stirrings of electricity—beginning with
the conception of the phonautograph, incubated by the player piano,
the phonograph and the Theremin, finally rocketed out into the
world with the birth of the Moog, developing from the adolescence
of Kraftwerk, Devo or Herbie Hancock to the pubescence of Aphex
Twin, Nine Inch Nails and The Crystal Method, the emotional
teenage years of M83, LCD Soundsystem and Crystal Castles, the
douchey twenties of EDM (excluding their jazzier cousins in Flying
Lotus, Bonobo, Prefuse 73), skipping right over adulthood and into
the telepathic overman of Joy Circuit and his Grubl Tele-Kastr™ (eschewing any kind of digital manipulation in lieu of a goofy helmet)—live instrumentation was once again playing the field, enjoying
a bull market after a long winter of hibernation. Which would have
been a good thing for Bryne, had he just stuck to the instruments and
not attempted to bridge the two worlds: mashing the digital and the
analog together like pieces from disparate jigsaw puzzles, hammering

at the joints to make them fit, recording the ear-piercing whine of a violin's gut-wound string crying from the slow draw of an equine bow in a room with harsh angles and a large atrium, duplicated, delayed, phase-shifted until the tectonic plates of their cycles rubbed against each other with all the insomniac malice of the trembling San Andreas below. Perhaps this was why his work was predominantly commissioned for horror films.

For his musicians' sake, if it was a piecework payment system the players would have stripped the walls of everything even quasi-valuable the second Bryne called it a wrap, but they were card-carrying members of the union and paid hourly, and, most importantly, they were musicians, an endangered species that always hovered around the brink of financial extinction. The more Bryne had them repeat the same movement—the same bar for that matter—the more their checks increased, a comfort for most as it could be a year before another session gig and many resented having to perform in their respective town orchestras, frequented by people more enamored with the idea of being at the concert than with the concert itself (with the glaring exceptions of Bertrand, who played in a popular acid-jazz band in Minneapolis, and George, who did God-Knows-What around California but somehow made a living). And besides the paycheck there was the project to consider, a rescoring of *Nosferatu* [Murnau, 1922], whose mythology kept their interests piqued and their hearts pumping with vital enthusiasm.

Dogan himself couldn't care less about the musicians' mockery or feigned indignation—which he most certainly heard—the day's accumulation of stress was easily quelled by the sacramental lighting of a freshly-rolled joint and good tunes as he hit the stalemate of Los Angeles rush-hour traffic, a journey he enjoyed as long as he remained high and the iPulse on his watch kept him accompanied by jazz, reggae or Afro-pop, blaring from the antiquated stereo system of his even more antiquated '75 Jeep Wrangler—a collector's classic were it not for the electric engine. The Jeep had been a replica of the one his parents used to drive, bought in tribute with the money from his first ReMA; it was a purchase of both pride and guilt.

With his masters in the can so to speak, he left Sunset Studios for the last time and lit the first of his joints as he started the journey back to Santa Monica, opening the sunroof though some ash was still falling from the burning mountains. He took off his crushable, tan fedora and tossed the hat on the passenger's seat, choosing the air on his head, ash and all.

Which isn't to say that Bryne wasn't still floored by the work; the completion of *Nosferatu* had him practically salivating in anticipation of experiencing his work on the silver screen—after all, that's what it was, wasn't it? the pairing of sound and image? An experience, and one that he'd petitioned hard for. He'd hounded David Ricciardelli and Rasheeda Brown of the AFI for the position and somehow beat out the Nobel-winning Michel Cloussant (likely more for his rate than his talent). His idea, which he kept outside the loop of the petulant musicians, was to make multiple recordings of his decidedly more classical score and to put each recording through different mixing and mastering algorithms and run the stereo outputs from the mixer through various post effects, bathing in the warring phases. He used Theremin stingers played through a Leslie rotating speaker outside, and sometimes underneath, the score. He wanted to give the film the familiarity of classical music, a score similar to the early accompaniments, but dilapidated through post-production to make it more unsettling, eerie and, well, more terrifying. "Like a Vivaldi suite left out in the rain," he'd told Rasheeda. It was a touch experimental to say the least, but accessible, in a horrific sort of way, and he was ultimately very satisfied with the product. He just hoped the AFI would be as well.

A century later, the silent film was once again the *grande triomph* of the film composer: the lack of diegetic competition, no dialogue or sound effects to interfere with his score—let alone the dictation of tone-deaf directors. It was a good time to be a film composer these days, composers and editors being the few positions in the industry that still utilized creative expression; the streets of Ventura and Sunset Blvds were lined with out of work directors and actors (those that stuck around, that is, either unable or unwilling to join the Great Migration of 2004), some guiding walking tours in what *The Atlantic's* Dustin Desmond dubbed "Colonial Williamsburg West," others part of the attraction, intentionally and not: Jace Aberdeen, who'd won an Oscar for playing a despondent junkie, shooting up for real this time, tying off on a bus stop in front of a busload of tourists.

There were still "talkies" to score, too. While there were no new "original" films to score, the AFI had taken a cue from the music industry and was finding great financial success releasing remastered and remixed classics (ReMas and ReMies, respectfully) they'd bought the rights to for pennies on the dollar when ALS was making desperate, last-ditch efforts to keep their (studio head's) head above water. The bulk of their income came from the ReMies; after all, who wouldn't want to see their favorite movies cast with their favorite actors, regardless of above-the-line costs, age, scheduling or even if they'd been alive on this planet at the same time as each other. Owing to significant advances in digital video processing and data storage, an actor's likeness and voice could be inserted into the templates of classic movies with relative ease. They'd had plenty of time after the Migration to go through their newly acquired film collection, using Grubl's technology to map, catalogue and store algorithms for each actor's movements, voices, gestures and facial expressions—they even mapped their atmospheres!—an actor's "essence" boiled down to the genome of their craft, digitally stored on a secret server known only as The Vault.

This meant you could watch *The Graduate* [Nichols, 1967] with a young Brad Pitt and Sofia Loren as the alluring Mrs. Robinson, *The Godfather* [Coppola, 1972] with a carousel rotation of its three main stars or *The Sting* [Hill, 1973] with Michael Aughlin and Tony Driver. You could remake *Titanic* [Cameron, 1997] with Willow Strange and Kiera Knightly for the cost of a down-payment on a renovated Cape Cod! With that kind of savings they could afford to throw six- or even seven-figure contracts for things like a new score. Which meant competition was still fierce as ever. Bryne had a solid reel under his belt, and was able to make a respectable living off the mid five-figure advances rescoring seminal classics (with the added help of Veena's ample salary) but he was hoping, with the final mix for *Nosferatu* bagged and clouded, for the chance to work on something massive.

Leaving the studio for the last time, he took the 1 over the 405 because if he's going to be stuck in traffic at least it could be scenic. Despite the waves, the beaches were empty, a sight he never would have seen fifteen years ago when he used to ditch 9th grade geometry for the cylindrical barrels of the morning surf, riding the proofs of nature's geometry. Instead of surfers and babes and beach blankets the shore was lined with an oily black ring marking the phases of the tide like a stopped up bathtub used to clean birds from an oil spill. The chop was certainly doing no favors for the passengers on the ferry coming in from Plastícea, the floating island of trash colonized by the founder of Grubl after the Cascadian Quake of 2012 that had cleaved a wound in the earth from Vancouver to Palo Alto and sent the tech companies scrambling to find new homes. Lucky for them a bounty of vacant soundstages, warehouses and studios was available several hundred miles south thanks to the emigration into Americaland Studios in New Mexico. But Grubl's Tad Ionzeit had had enough of quakes and their persistent growls and had removed himself from their calculus of catastrophe, terra forming the floating mass no country had the courage to claim and building a new headquarters/dormitory/village. The island's general mooring lay in the middle of the San Nicolas, San Clemente and Catalina Island triangle. They had machines to de-salinate the water, plenty of citizens to supply compost for farming, and an unending supply of cold water to keep their servers from overheating—the effects of which meant they could not rely on local fishing to supplement their local vegetation; even in the densest of fogs, the freighters and ferries bringing out their food stores and relatives could tell when they were getting close by the aromatic ring of dead fish that surrounded the island.

Can't say he was surprised by the beach's emptiness: assuming you could get beyond the litter and the aroma, there were still the sharks to consider: the Great Whites, who'd always roamed the coastal waters from Manzanillo to San Francisco and who were already a little mad from the escalating mercury poisoning, had acquired and sustained a taste for man after the quake with all the bodies that had gone in the water; couple that with the waning seal population and you basically made man the filet mignon of the buffet. No, he wasn't surprised by the emptiness, just saddened, like passing the gravestone of an old friend struck down on the side of the road by a careless driver.

He pulled off the highway just before Santa Monica pier and headed inland, flicking the cardboard filter of the first roach out the window, cranking the dial as the iPulse dropped a retro classic, Sleep's "Holy Mountain," and firing up another victory joint.

— § —

The faces of the AFI directors were impossibly open to interpretation. From the boardroom of the diamond-shaped tower that used to house the headquarters for Center Studios, David and Rasheeda sat perfectly still in their green, leather thrones as Bryne's final mix of *Nosferatu* played on the 72" monitor. Though the medium of viewing could have been better, at least they had the Bose 17.1 "directionless" sound system to assist, the sonic ether allowing Bryne's score to breath down their necks, tickle their earlobes, transporting the horrors from the screen not just into the boardroom but inside the theater of their own heads. They were quiet, and though that could mean many things, given the genre, Bryne was understandably nervous. Sunglasses still fixed to his nose, Bryne didn't watch the screen but instead used the tinted lenses to watch these AFI directors whose 'yea' or 'nay' could determine the rest of his career. He'd swear an affidavit he took maybe twenty breaths during the entire screening. When it was done, David and Rasheeda solemnly faced each other, gave each other telepathic, corporate nods and turned to Bryne.

David folded his hands and took a breath, "We love it!"

Bryne let out an audible sigh of relief and an inaudible fart of pent-up nerves.

"It was out there, certainly, but you've retained the integrity of the original," Rasheeda added.

"I think you've heightened it. I remember watching this in film school—as I'm sure you did, too, Rash—and feeling...I guess ambivalent about the whole thing; probably because of the film's failure to maintain relevance to the age and the outdated techniques of inducing fear. But now—with this score—I realize it wasn't the film that induced an emotional catatonia, but the score that I had heard originally. I was blown away, terrified even." David laughed.

"Thank you," Bryne's breathing was starting to return to normal.

"What I like is the continual feeling of being unsettled. The only thing I can think of in comparison was an earthquake I was in last year. I was at my sister's who was having a party for her husband's promotion—they're outside Malibu—so, we're all having a nice time, it's the first time I'd been to their new house, a gorgeous Dutch Colonial, and the earthquake hit. It wasn't anything monstrous, but it was continuous—you probably remember it, the one from last April? Lasted for two-and-a-half minutes but might as well have been eternity. And here I am, a little tipsy from the sangria and their homegrown herb, and thrown into a state of perpetual anxiety. It was horrifying. You've been able to capture that same feeling—and for ninety-two minutes!"

"Do you think it's too much then?" Concerned he's being set up for a beautifully disguised rejection.

"Not at all. Not at *all*. I think it's perfect. I'm going to be honest, most of our reissues don't sell much—not in the way our remixes sell. I think," motioning to Rasheeda, "*we* think, this could be a big seller."

"Very big." Rasheeda spread her arms in a wide hallelujah.

"Great. Fantastic." Dogan's relief left him at simple words.

David and Rasheeda clasped their hands and smiled. Bryne removed his sunglasses and joined the mirth. Eventually Rasheeda closed the meeting, "Well I think that about does it. Thank you again, Bryne. It was great, really great."

A final round of handshakes and compliments, Rasheeda closed her folder and told them she was late for another meeting and asked David if he would take care of the other thing. He nodded and said he would handle it, which aroused in Bryne a strong swell of dyspepsia, terrified of some conspiracy always at the brink of possibility in the mercurial world of show business.

"Is something wrong?"

"No, no." David, realizing the reasons Bryne might find concern, attempted to dispel the imaginative, unspoken horrors by waving them away. "I could see in this industry how any cloaked dialogue like that can be taken as something insidious. But no, everything's fine. On the contrary it could be very good for you. We want to discuss a new project with you."

"Oh?" The inflection belying the urge to shout "This is it! This is it!"

"We're approaching the one-hundredth Anniversary of *The Battleship Potemkin* [Eisenstein, 1925] and, per the director's insistence on generational relevance, we need a new score. Rasheeda and I wanted to see if you might be up to for task?"

He'd been hoping for a ReMi instead of another ReMa, but this was an anniversary edition—*the* anniversary edition—and of a film he knew front-to-back. If he could nail this, no doubt he would have carte blanch on his next projects. Unfortunately, the pre-screening smoke sesh was strong in his system and he could only muster a simple, affirming "Gahhh, yeah, I'm up for it."

"Excellent!" David clapped him on the shoulder, "I knew you'd be on board."

They moved from the boardroom to the poster-adorned hallways, signed one-sheets eighty-years old interspersed with modern digital ones: the violent psychedelia of *The Pinealien* [Di Mateo, 2006], scored by one of his favorites, Michio Kronopolis, and equally as epileptic as the film itself; an adaptation of Morrow's *Towing Jehovah* [Loveland, 2004], one of the more popular remixes starring Kirk Douglas à la *Spartacus* [Kubrick, 1960] as the young Captain Van Horn towing the body of God (Marlon Brando) with Robert Mitchum as his unpleasant father; then there were the posters that inserted the passer-by into the lead role of the respective film: Bryne as Bugsy Malone, as Butch Cassidy, as Hannibal Lector, as Blanch Dubois...

David kept his hand on Bryne's shoulder as they made their way to the elevator banks, inadvertently tracking the same paths as countless actors and camera operators during the building's former life. "Of course, I understand that you've just come off a major project and need some time to gather new ideas...to collect yourself, but the reissue is only five months from now and we need a score in three. And," putting a hand to stop Bryne from talking, which Bryne had no intention of doing, "you're correct: three months is a short amount of time for a project of this scope; and yes, we did have another composer in mind before you—several in fact—but, well let's just say we never saw eye to eye on the scores they turned in."

Bryne tried to think if he'd heard of anyone who'd been working on *Potemkin* but as nothing came, no shoes he was stepping on or bridges burnt by taking a job obviously left unwillingly, he counted it as a blessing and gladly proceeded.

"No, that sounds great. Thank you. Sorry, I'm just in a state of shock. To be honest I didn't know whether you would even accept my *Nosferatu* score, let alone offer me *Potemkin*! I know it well. Very well, in fact. I used to do live improv scores to it back in college, very bizarre stuff."

The elevator doors opened and David walked Bryne in. "Well we're looking for good, not necessarily bizarre, Bryne. Keep that in mind," David said in what he hoped was a non-patronizing manner. "Don't sweat it though; you're going to do great! We've got the utmost faith in you."

Before Bryne could mumble another "thank you" David stepped out of the elevator as the doors closed with a faux-metallic "ping."

— § —

To celebrate his completed commission and his new one, Bryne and his live-in girlfriend, Naveena Miller, went to a new fusion restaurant recommended by one of Veena's co-workers, a Japanese/American cuisine that tried to blend Japanese flavors and ingredients with traditional American dishes. Bryne had a Volcano Roll Burger, essentially a volcano roll, sandwiched between two rice crackers with sliced ginger and wasabi-ketchup, salmon fries on the side. She had something he couldn't pronounce that looked like a pizza with eel sausage, nori and octopus pepperoni on a seaweed crust. The fact that they didn't need a reservation should have spoke volumes about the place. At least the booze was good, and cheap. They both got drunk and Bryne drove home more impaired than he'd anticipated—no Grubl Auto-Pilot on his Jeep, the engine and stereo the only items he'd allowed modernized on the antique (the electric engine not so much allowed as mandated). When they got home they threw on the original release of *The Battleship Potemkin* with Miesel's score and fell asleep on the couch before the second reel even began.

If they'd lived together since the start of their relationship they'd have been well into a common-law marriage by now—and one of them wouldn't stop dropping not-so-subtle hints about embracing the actual sacrament. They'd met in a coffee shop, of all places; Bryne was sitting with a friend talking classical music and counterpoint, Veena was right behind him, waiting for a date that would never show.

"On their own, each line is fine, good, probably not great; but, when you put them together, when you pair the bass and soprano together—pair them against each other—that's when you get something great. And that greatness only increases the more lines you add, when you add the alto and tenor. That's why people still love to study Bach, Beethoven, Pachelbel, Handel…these geniuses writing musical puzzle boxes."

"Geniuses!? Bull shit," she all but shouted, not bothering to turn and address the man she'd just interrupted. "As someone who was forced to play Pachelbel and Handel for every church service, wedding and funeral in town for the better part of her youth I can tell you it's a far cry from genius." The fact that she'd been stood up was settling in and making her a bit aggressive—well, that and the whiskey she'd added to her espresso. "I swear, if I ever hear 'Canon in D' or 'The Messiah' again in this lifetime I'll puke."

"Wow, well that's an aggressive sentiment on two pieces of music almost universally accepted as beautiful."

She finally turned to face him. "Just because it's old doesn't mean it's great.

Bryne turned his chair to face her. "No. But it's only old because it's great. If it wasn't great, it wouldn't have been allowed to grow old. You think those songs would still exist 400 years later if they sucked?!"

"Hey, I get it. Retro is cool. But isn't it like the Model T or a video game? I get it had to come first before the others could exist but do you really think the 8-bit Nintendo is better than the 32k resolution we have now?

"Well, you could make the argument that the 8-bit system is just like the Western diatonic scale from which all of our musical understanding emanates. The only reason we feel how we do about the 16-bit Oriental scale or the 32-bit cacophony of someone like Henry Flynt is because of its contrast to the 8-bit classics."

"Oh here we go!"

And there they went. Five minutes into the conversation, Bryne didn't even notice that his friend had left. Twenty minutes in, Veena hadn't even remembered the name of the guy that stood her up (which, again, could have been due in part to the whiskey). Two hours in, they'd segued to dinner and drinks. Two years in, they'd had their drones deliver their bathroom sundries to the same address.

Naveena had pivoted from the artistry forced upon her as a youth towards one of her own choosing, literature. She'd gotten her degree in English & Comparative Literature, much to her parents chagrin, and she wrote some, here and there; but after a while she found her interests, passions and—she'll admit it—her talents more along the business line, in the editing and marketing of the work. Thankfully for her, by the time she got her M.F.A., fiction had made a resounding comeback after a near extinction—due in small part to a hipster resurgence of the passé artform and the boutique bookstore (the former occurring only to facilitate the latter)—due in larger part to the fall of ALS and the proliferation of ReMies that left literature as one of the few bastions of original storytelling. After a few grueling internships at the bigger houses, she'd gotten a job working at an independent publishing house that specialized in avant-garde literature (principally a marketing job, now that print versions were done with POD kiosks, allowing the reader to choose their own cover design, paper type, font, etc.). Well, profitable avant-garde literature. This was a business after all.

Bryne read some of the work and agreed that there was still something to be said for major publishing houses, something to be said for filtration, shaping and accreditation. He told Veena as much; and sometimes she agreed, saying that it was just her job "to give it a voice at the table and not to steer the literary conversation;" and sometimes, when she felt that Bryne was simply being an ass who had presumably spent the whole of the day high and plucking around on Shelley, she'd tell him to fuck off because her epitaph won't read "Here lies Bryne Dogan, who dedicated his life to getting high and occasionally wrote a song so he could continue his habit." The last time being about three weeks prior to their Trans Pacific dinner exploration.

The morning after their celebration, Veena left early to track down some new obscure author she was trying to sign, and Bryne, still riding the celebration, felt there was no better way to celebrate than by diving straight into Potemkin. He headed back to the couch, queued up the film and packed a bowl, keeping a notepad of fresh staves in front of him so he could pencil in some melodies and chord charts between bong rips.

As he packed the bowl he grew prematurely hungry, and his thoughts drifted to last night's dinner: of the meeting of East and West. He began to consider the possibilities, challenges and insinuations of a Western score versus an Eastern score, of a possible fusion, and what that would mean. What he had liked—and more importantly, what he had remembered—about Eisenstein's concept of the score was that it would change to mirror contemporary political strife; the problem was that only expanded the options. During his morning "constitution" he was confronted by no less than twelve headlines on ten separate stories concerning seven of the nine conflicts our country alone was currently engaged in. To say nothing of the conflicts of other countries, wars civil and non-.

Was he to write a score focusing on each conflict? On just the religious wars? The geographical wars? The socio-economic wars? The ecological wars over fuel rights and the protection of natural resources? The war on tariffs? The war on copyright? The war on drugs? The war on space? If he did anything remotely Eastern would people think he was making a statement about India and Pakistan? If he didn't get the local nuances right would they think he was taking sides? Could he do anything oriental without people expressing disdain for the 'overtly North Korean sympathies' people would surely invent? If he went into atonal atmospherics would people read conjectures into the I.S.S. hostage situation? Was he merely supposed to give an update on the Russian plight? Moreover, if he did anything remotely classical or similar to the first, what would it say about the resurgence and the subsequent re-fall of the USSR? Would any score he turned in be able to escape the gravity of 'pastiche'? The politics were daunting.

Bryne hit the bong as the opening frames of *Potemkin* came on. After five minutes he declared to no one, "You know who'd really be able to weigh in on this? George." Then he stood and shouted "To George's!"

— § —

George Holland lived in a run-down pink Victorian, with unattached garage and a guest house he had converted to a studio and control booth, respectfully. The house was just outside the SC campus, which kept him in weary proximity to all of his vices. Holland had boarded up the walls and ceilings of the garage with spongy, ridged foam-sheets to dampen the sound. A five-piece drum-kit, Jack DeJohnette dark ride and Zildjian A-Custom crashes purposefully (blasphemously) dented with framing-hammers, sat in the corner perpendicular to various keyboards from various decades; there was a wall lined with amps and cabinets and a wall lined with guitars and basses hanging from padded, forked holsters.

He'd first met George ten years ago, when he was a young 25-year old Composer in Residence at the UC Irvine Conservatory. Svâto Sckoufias, Principle 2nd at the time, had tricked him into dropping acid and joining him at a live scoring of *Begotten* [Merhige, 1990], an experience so haunting it still gives his flashbacks chills. After he'd been able to conquer his initial fears, he was able to block out the visuals and focus solely on the music, all of which seemed to be coming from a sampler-laden pedal-board connecting to the guitar on the lap of a man with long, silver-dyed hair peanut-pinched by a Hatchimaki bandana. After an awkward introduction from Sckoufias, the rest was history, and a long strange one at that.

In keeping with that strangeness, Bryne witnessed the following as he entered the studio from the side door: Holland, donning a pair of Zubas and the top-half of a wet suit, in the garage running his guitar through various pedals, splitting the signal into two separate amps, combining their output into one cabinet which was then mic-ed and run through a speaker abutting a fifty-gallon water tank that—via a bubbling, perforated CO_2 hose run through—manipulated the incoming sound waves recorded through a Piezo pickup at the opposite end, which then ran out of the garage and into the mixing console in the control booth. Bryne determined that George had started smoking without him, or that he was possibly back on his acid regimen.

Holland didn't notice the presence of another living body and continued to strum sloppily on his instrument, cocking his head so as to better hear the in-ear monitors relaying whatever sonic monstrosity he'd created.

"What Cageian madness is this?" Bryne's body moved in front of the door's aperture and cast a caricature Bryne on the shag carpeting of the garage floor—a cheap but effective means of sound dampening, comfort, and masking several decades of oil stains.

Holland didn't hear him but saw the rotoscoped Bryne and looked up, taking the monitor out of his ear and brushing long, naturally-colored, salt-and-peppered strands of hair from his face. "Oh, hey, man!"

Bryne reiterated. "What is all that?"

"Oh, nothing, man. Just something I'm playing with." Bryne had to bend to hear him, Holland always speaking too softly, as if cradling the air in front of his mouth, too afraid to raise his voice and awaken the oxygen. George put his equipment down and switched the amps to stand-by. "Come on, step into my laboratory."

Few details remained that could identify the control booth's former utility: several holes in the back wall where the Murphy bed had docked, replaced by a couch whose two-of-three seats were occupied by milk cartons overflowing with patch cables and adaptors; pastel wallpaper peaking out of the few places not covered by posters; the same seashell molds of soap still rested on the counter of the sink in the closet-sized bathroom, now an impromptu vocal booth. The large bay windows that could have held a breakfast nook facing the garage now housed a desk with a thirty-two channel Mackie mixer, dual Event monitors, a Studer A820 MCH 2" tape recorder (which Bryne had no idea how he managed to afford), computer tower, 32" monitor and a MIDI controller, the last three of which surprised Bryne as Holland's analog preferences were vocalized well to the point of ludditism (but really how far could you go these days without digital assistance?). Several dog-eared, coffee-stained books were scattered about the floor or dangling over the edge of his desk; of the titles Bryne could make out were Anthony Braxton's *Triaxium Writings* and Vol. 3 of *Composition Notes*; Steve Reich's *Writings About Music*; and an authorless tape-bound book entitled *Concertinas From the Rabbit Hole: Psychoacoustic Experiments, Effects, and the Neurology of Aural Processing*—which had been retitled with red marker in Skoufias's trademark serif lettering *Codex Gig-Acs*. Holland pointed Bryne to a desk chair while he went to the closet and produced rolling papers, grinder and a jar of cured weed taken from his home garden. Holland gave the jar to Bryne for inspection and praise while he busied himself with the rituals of joint rolling, beginning with the placement of a gatefold LP on his lap to use as a workbench, just as his father had done. When the last edge of the EZ-wider was folded into place, smoothed, twisted and toasted to dryness, he gave it to Bryne to spark, who did so without delay.

They passed the joint back and forth, holding it by the cardboard filter and not speaking other than to compliment the quality and taste of the weed—which they both conferred was true to its sobriquet of Orange Crush. After they had smoked the joint down to just a glowing red nub, Holland began laughing for some unaccounted reason.

"What?"

"I was just thinking: Like, do you remember all those ads and articles and posters and shit when we were kids about smoking pot? Remember?"

"The really over the top ones? Like where the kid gets run over by the car or blows his head off?"

"No, like the research, medical ones. Like where they say the cannabinoids will leave men sterile and can cause testicular cancer?"

Bryne Pavlovially hugged his testicles with his thighs.

"I remember. Why?"

Holland smashed out the joint in a clover-shaped ash-tray and produced and packed a bong. "As an adult it's so obviously a scare tactic, man. I mean, what better way to scare off dumb kids with a permanent hard-on and a recreational habit than to tell them their balls are going to fall off. They use the same platform for sex, too, man. Anytime men take up an activity that isn't explicitly mandated by God or the right-wing, these-, these evangelical fascists go after our balls."

"You know what I read a little while ago? I have a doctor friend that subscribes to all of these journals that publish stuff from electro-cardiophysiology to new drugs to limb and face transplants, and I was over there the other day and found an article on THC as a preventative to cancer. I'm probably butchering the article: apparently, there's this thing called apoptosis, which is the programmed death of cells. See, ordinarily each cell is pre-programmed to be created and destroyed; once its objective is met, the cell dies—like a self-destruct switch, like nanomachines. And so, so basically cancer is a cell whose mutation has hindered apoptosis so they just continue to, like, grow out of check. The cannabinoids, the article said, actually perpetuate apoptosis in cells, so they die when they're supposed to."

"Or earlier." Holland passed the bong to Bryne and began fidgeting with the controls on his mixer, opening some windows on his computer and turning on his speakers.

"Shit, yeah I guess. But isn't that cool? So, like, every time we smoke, we're actually fighting testicular cancer." Adopting a bad Irish brogue, "*Tis one's fer me bahls.*" Bryne exhaled smoke into his crotch. George took the bong and did the same.

Bryne cocked his head like the eponymous spaniel. "What?"

"Nothing, just thinking, like, with these rampant cases of breast cancer, testicular cancer, cervical cancer, is it, like, just a coincidence that all this 'unchecked growth' is going on in our reproductive areas? Like, could they just not sit still and retire? Can they just not stop creating or what?"

George sat forward on the edge of his seat, modulating into that conspiratorial mood he sometimes gets in, "Reproductive areas, or, *or*, OR…our pleasure areas?! Like, after all, no one is born from the colon."

"Really? I've met a couple."

George buckled over in that laugh of his that sounds like a mischievous, cartoon dog snickering before almost knocking the bong over. Once collected, George put the cashed bong back in its holder—the same kind used in the garage to hang guitars but with considerably more padding.

"So what are you working on in there?" Bryne pointed to the studio beyond the window.

"Lemme show ya." Holland hit play and the room filled with strange aquatic music. Bryne pictured an underwater band-shell filled with tone-deaf dolphins playing full-heartedly for an octopus conductor, a different tempo for each tentacle.

"But again, what is it?"

"So I had, like, an idea of, like, putting the signal out of phase then seeing if the signal would rejoin itself or if it would, like, step out of phase even more based on the unpredictability of the water." Holland gave him a visual narration: hands clasped together; splitting into a v; spreading out; wavering, to show interference and water; hands coming back together and interlocking his fingers with a singular, coital shake. "Like, nature affecting music, and, and vice versa."

"Uh-huh. Yeah I'm not so sure I really hear it, George."

"Yeah…I might have to try a different approach. Maybe I should find a way to run the mic directly through the water. What do you think?"

Bryne paused to at least feign consideration. "It sounds like it would either be cool, or really, really bad. No middle ground there. Either way I want to hear the outcome." Bryne opened an LFO-filter plug-in and twisted the band back and forth to see if it produced anything he liked. It didn't. "Where the hell did you even come up with this idea in the first place? You find it in one of those books somewhere?"

Holland looked at the books as if he'd just noticed their presence, like a guest he'd rudely forgotten to introduce. "Yeah. Oh, man, have you read any of this stuff?! It's absolutely fantastic." He picked up the tape-bound book and flipped through the pages, occasionally stopping and lifting an open page to Bryne, displaying diagrams of sonic projection and reflection, absorption mediums, crudely drawn portraits of the inner ear and temporal lobe, all sorts of graphs focusing on phase shifts in wavelength, cymatic shapes of sound. "This one's a whole thesis on stuff way cooler than my water experiment. I mean there's a lot in there about triggering specific neurons and creating a sonic space inside the brain—sometimes creating the perception of music solely out of electromagnetic waves!—but those are almost completely impractical to duplicate in a home setting. There are more applicable experiments, though.

"Like, look at this one, The Wizard Duel! Basically a long range Theremin between two people: one hand the pitch antenna, the other the volume, with the distance as the capacitor. The frequency gets higher and higher the closer you move the antennas together. Requires building and soldering two sets of plates for each hand but it's totally worth it."

"Is it?" Bryne dropped, trying to think of any way this would be worth the time, money and burns from soldering this together, for all of maybe 3 minutes of "fun."

"Or Pi," Holland continued, flipping the pages to another experiment, "where you shoot the sound through a Hula-Hoop at one end, record it at the other and you get the phase-shift of Pi!"

"Far out." Bryne failed to see why the phase-shift of Pi would be particularly desirable, outside of a mystic standpoint, though he was interested in some of the induced perception of sound theories, and in smoking more of George's herb, which he packed into a small bowl.

"Man, this is the one I've been trying to do: the Hydra-Pantheon experiment. You find a big, empty, ovular room and in the focus put a corrugated column with speakers in each of the grooves, and you put an omnidirectional mic at the other foci; then you play a song, or just any piece of pulsating music with a lot of tonal variety—I want to use a recording of Reich's *Piano Phase*, which is already a phase-shift in itself—and you get a different phase from each of the grooves assembled into one recording. I've been trying to find a room over at SC but I think the security guards have caught on; I get, like, two steps into the campus and some tyrannical meathead turns me right back around. Like, how do they know I'm not a professor there or something?"

"Well, probably has something to do with what happened last October. Your face is guaranteed posted inside all the guard shacks after that."

"Shit, you think?"

"Well you did publicly invite the Chancellor and her daughter into an acid-fueled threesome on the quad, and then started without them. They tend to frown on that sort of thing."

"Fucking f—"

"Fascists, I know," Bryne finished for him. He clapped him on the shoulder, "we'll get 'em next time."

Bryne passed the bowl to Holland, Holland passed the book to Bryne. "Sckoufias turned me on to it. You should read it, man. Might find some cool ideas for *Potemkin*. How's it coming, by the way?"

"Well, it's only day one, and I'm here. Still, there isn't a whole lot of time; David gave me three months before it has to be done. *Done*. But so far it's kind of overwhelming; I start thinking about all the possible options and directions it could go in—or should go in—and I just have no idea which road to take."

Bryne put the book in his lap and noted George's bookmark sticking out of the top, the playbill for Reich's "Music for 18 Musicians" played by Carnegie Hall's Robotic Philharmonic. Bryne had gone through the usual adolescence of his career by first loving Reich, Young, Reilly, Glass, moving on to the later polyrhythmic minimalist groups like Battles, The Carousel Question and the Speed of Might before feeling the Lacanian necessity to castrate them in order to "move-on" or "advance," as he had thought he was doing at the time. (Ironically, though not surprisingly, most of his scores of late fit into the paradigms of the former's retro experimentation.) What he had rejected in most of the experimentation was the cacophony and grating effects it produced. Like the early Twentieth-Century composers Stravinsky and Bartok, the atonal and sequential melodies left the audience detached and frigid—which worked perfectly for something like *Nosferatu* but didn't necessarily fit every film. As cool and theoretically inventive and genius as their scores might have been, there was still a necessity for heart, for a connection to life—at least in the score he wanted to produce for *Potemkin*. In that sense, most of those experiments and the ones in this book were creatures without a pulse, vampires that drained the life from their listener. And he was done with vampires. Now was the time for man, more specifically, the working man.

"Bryne Dogan and The Curse of the Ticking Clock." Holland picked up an old PRS that he always kept in the studio, its flame-top sunburst had either been worn or chipped away to the naked maple underneath, and ran through some arpeggios.

"I don't know. I was all psyched to do it—I *am* psyched to do it. It's an amazing film, and an important one. I guess I'm just a little intimidated by doing the hundredth anniversary. Plus, David just sent me a Facemail on my way over—which I'm guessing he thought would inspire me but actually just upped the pressure—talking about incorporating a summation of the past one hundred years of political history and contention, about what's going on currently, about how the score should strive to mirror it all, about how the music should be just as big of a message as the film itself. Like, like how the hell am I supposed to do that?!"

"Hm, maybe you should just take, like, the predominant music from each of the wars. Schoenberg or Strauss for World War One, Irving Berlin and Duke Ellington for the Sequel, or you go the whole pop route and mirror the popular songs from the era. Like 'We'll Meet Again' and 'Der Fuehrer's Face' for World War Two, Credence songs for 'Nam, and so forth."

"Yeah but that only concerns American Wars. I mean it's not even an American film. And how do I blend global political strife seamlessly into one style?"

"Beats me, I was just trying to help." Then Holland started laughing. "Can you imagine, 'Der Fuehrer's Face' playing on top of Schoenberg's 2nd String Quartet? Or as a *Klangfarbenmelodie*?" Holland

arpeggiated some utterly dissonant chord and exhausted every cacoph-
onous integer, then heightened it by tapping out harmonics up the
fretboard.

"It's just intimidating is all." Bryne began playing on the MIDI
controller. It wasn't turned on and the only sounds produced were the
percussive thwapping of spring-loaded plastic.

"Just do what you want, man."

"I will. I just don't know what I want yet."

Holland took up the bowl and did his best Sherlock Holmes while
taking a hit. Eventually, after exhaling, he said, "You should do something like *Zaireeka*."

"What's *Zaireeka*?"

"Wayne Coyne? The Flaming Lips? Same guy who did the parking
lot experiment with the cars and tape decks—and the satellite experiments a couple years back. They recorded an album, well it was four
albums, but they were supposed to be played simultaneously."

"How does that apply to Potemkin?"

"Well you were saying how you wanted to incorporate the world
right? So you write something for each region or country or style, or
something from a bunch of different countries, then combine them!"

"That sounds like pure cacophony. Like an ice cream truck plowing
into a marching band."

"And it might be. But wouldn't that, like, fit the film? All warring
and combative and shit, like an uprising. I mean you'd have to make
it your own, but that's what you do. You just need the gambit to get
started."

Bryne stopped playing on the controller and seemed to consider
this. They passed the bowl back and forth quietly, each contemplating
their own musical ambitions. After a moment, Holland looked down
at his arms and gave a sudden start, "Jesus, why the fuck am I wearing
half a wet suit?"

— § —

Other than Miesel, Bryne barely remembered the other *Potemkin*
scores, even several of the recent editions (recent meaning in the last
forty years, a lot popping up around the turn of the millennium), and
spent at least two solid days going through some of the more popu-

lar scores: Chris Lowe and Neil Tennant had done a score with the Dresden Symphony Orchestra; Club Foot Orchestra and other experimental-jazz bands were performing scores live—probably where Bryne had gotten the idea for his live performances; Russian death-thrash band Apokalipsis had put out a live performance with the entirety of *Potemkin* played on a screen behind them—which the band ripped to pieces for the encore; several other traditional film scores; a few ambient, drone scores in the tweenage years of the new millennium. And aside from Apokalipsis, he thought each of them good by all accounts, yet he had preferred the original for the antiquity of it, for the charge and melodrama that seemed to fit perfectly with the time. After another day of marinading, he tried making his first foray into the score by putting on the Tele-Kastr™ and letting the machine take a first, largely-subconscious pass at it while watching the film on mute; but all he kept getting were recurring fragments of the original score, with bits and pieces of several others he'd heard along the way and a few random funk tunes and jingles that popped up unsolicited.

Contrary to the path George had recommended, his present goal wasn't to combine myriad styles or scores into one jumbled potpourri of sound. To be sure, he still didn't have any clue what the correct path looked like, or if he'd even recognize the trailhead when he saw it. But he was two weeks in without even a bar to show, and that was a problem.

Bryne had arranged the home studio like the editing booths at the AFI, with the desk and workstation in the middle and the TV on the wall directly across so he could screen and score simultaneously. From the TV, moving down the walls in a clockwise fashion, were his implements of creation: a 1965 Gibson ES-335 in honey burst; blonde '59 Fender Strat with '57 v-neck and custom-wound pickups; blue-burst Rickenbacker 4003S with Piezo mod; several Orange rack-mounted preamps for that warm analog tone; other rack-mounted power conditioners, preamps, equalizers and effects; Vox AC30; a tweed Fender Twin 2" x 12" and an Orange half-stack; Fender Rhodes piano resting on top of the cab; a Hammond Organ leaning against the wall; Mini- and Micro-Moogs; a couple Maschine MPC pads; the (32-bit) Tele-Kastr™ 2.2 hanging from a hook on the wall like the souvenir of a fallen Centurion that had perilously tried to conquer *Tron* [Lisberger,

1982]; an ESP custom shop—for when he still wanted to play some metal; a large 15" Leslie rotating speaker cab on the other side of the door, operating as both desk and bookshelf; lastly, his primary writing instruments, the small, 49-key Roland midi-controller he uses when in the lab, and, in the floor stand next to the desk, Shelley, the Martin HD-28 he uses when outside, on the couch or, as more often the case, too high to bother hooking anything up. Despite the value of the goods, the studio was just enough to get ideas across and make demos of his compositions, but offered nowhere near the quality the final recordings required. And now, standing in front of all these amps and keyboards and monitors blinking at him in shared monotony and expectation, awaiting the maestro's cue, he could think of no command to give them, not even the prompt of a tempo, to keep them standing by.

To help him think, he would need a sandwich.

The one thing he had liked most about his house, other than the fact that it was on a hill so he could see the ocean in the distance, was the reverb in the kitchen and entryways, a result of the high ceilings, the Nuevo-art-deco walls and hard-wood floors—which in reality were a synthetic compound made to look like Brazilian rosewood but, nevertheless, resonated phenomenally close to the real thing. Though he'd never recorded anything official within the spaces, he loved whistling the melodies that overtook his head and forced themselves into the open. Some days he would just get high and sit at the kitchen table, drinking Arnold Palmers and whistling at the ceiling. With the stress he was enduring, he didn't feel much like whistling as he took out pesto and cold cuts and slapped them between a pretzel roll; he *did* think that if he got high it would alleviate his stress, which in turn would help him to explore the situation fully.

His porch was made of similar composite wood as his living room; the lack of maintenance required had been a huge selling point. He had a grill and a small outdoor table and a two-meter landing pad where Bryne and Veena stored and charged their personal drones, Otis and Lorraine, respectfully. Lorraine was out at the moment, Veena likely sending her down to Tijuana for more of that skin cream whose active ingredient was not exactly legal in the States—or most active members of the UN. (Lets just say it has something to do with a certain brand of regenerative cell taken from donors who, should they have ever graced a pre-school classroom, would have found the tiny swirls and loops of their finger-paint signatures identical.) Otis was sitting in his dock, whirring like a sleeping owl after a long night of refueling Bryne with multiple burrito runs.

Like his neighbors, he also had a corner reserved for homegrown tomatoes and marijuana. His strain was a cross between Afghan Kush and Juicy Fruit, not owing to his green thumb, but rather because he had placed the two clones too close together and they had cross-pollinated; which gave it a very potent sour-smell that tasted like a sublimating bowl of passion fruit. If you were out on a deck like this when the Santa Ana picked up you could smell everyone's cannabis gardens, along with hints of thyme, rosemary and dill that people occasionally grew, too. Veena had been trying to convince him to add a "legitimate" herbal component; Bryne was reticent for the fear that the herbs would aromatically contaminate his prized crops. He had a cedar box he used for curing and a jar to hold the marijuana in when ready. If he worked it out right, he would have a couple buds hanging and by the time he had finished what was in the jar, the hanging buds would be dry and he could rotate them in, along with new buds. The Middle Ages system of rotation modified to fit the domestic, agricultural needs of recreation. The jar was half-full of his mutt-weed and he withdrew a gram and dropped the conical bud into the grinder, pulled out a couple hefty pinches and sprinkled the coarse powder into the bowl of his favorite bong, a two-foot glass-on-glass piece with Erlenmeyer base, diffusing down-stem and ash-catcher, aptly(?) named Crunkmaninoff. Veena, who did smoke but nowhere near the extent of Bryne (few did), understood the links between creative enterprises and methods of inspiration—the fruits of which paid her salary—still she would've preferred some semblance of moderation, or at least a clean house to come home to.

Bryne threw his SoundBall™ onto the table and let the ball peel apart, scattering and repositioning its six component pieces into a perfect 5.1 arrangement while he finished the last bite of his sandwich. He then cued up a good smoking soundtrack on his phone before placing it back in its Faraday sheath; not a week went by, usually prompted by a horrific visual reminder, that he didn't thank his lucky stars he hadn't had the money available when the implanted devices had hit the market—although the class-action lawsuit would've paid his mortgage twice-over.

True to his word, Kurzweil had been dead-on with the technological trajectory of his singularity—and the implant had been more than willing to accept the merger—but he'd failed in one crucial part: he'd never asked the body its thoughts on the matter. They had developed technology that was more than amenable to integrating with the body, but the organic tissues weren't yet requiting. Just because you can cut and hammer a jigsaw piece into place doesn't mean it fits. You've got a complex organic machine and you're throwing incompatible and inorganic parts & fuel into the mix. The machine isn't knocking when it's a grand mal seizure. Of course complications arose! The body rejected the implants in grotesque and largely intractable ways; growths, benign and non, surrounded the site of implantation like the rounded, vertiginous peaks of Machu Pichu. Those that were able to successfully extract the device were left with a hideous crater in their temporal lobe and a burgeoning hat collection. Those that weren't so lucky...well, some of the kinder comparisons included Dishwasher Teddy Ruxpin, Chernobyl Ken, Microprocessor Potato Head and, likely the most cruel of the kind, a Tourettic Android with an Elephant Man Complex. Both cases were a stark reminder that Orwellian Totalitarianism wasn't handed down from up top; it was something we lined up around the block for three days in advance.

Significant warning signs should have been observed. For instance, the sharp rise in testicular and cervical cancer from people pocketing their phones all those years finally manifesting into an irrefutable causation. Or the across-the-board drop in sperm counts from men whose boys were more or less taking an eight-hour-a-day soak in a spa of radiation. Or that the Q4 quantum processors required a power source that could service a one-man drone flight from San Diego to Van Nuys.

So Bryne was more than fine with the retrograde tech and the ability to someday sire children, which, lets be honest, he didn't see happening for at least another five years, contrary to Veena's readings of the firmament.

The SoundBall™ kicked off the B-side of Brian Wilson's sonic masterpiece, *Pet Sounds*, just as Crunkmaninoff grew thick and milky with smoke; he withdrew the slide and cleared the chamber, holding it, holding it, *holding* it…until opening the valve and slowly expelling the yellow smoke into the brown-tinged air, punctuating the hit with a cough. Already, the inspiration was striking, though leading him not back inside to the studio, but into a vision of the past, of Wilson in the studio working on the Beach Boys' 11th album, then deeper back, to their early work and the start of the beach music movement, and then, to the beach.

With the POD kiosks taking away the physical production costs, the publishing industry was forced to pivot if it wanted to survive. The services one could expect from signing with a publisher included, in descending order, branding, advertising, design, marketing, editorial services and collating the distribution channels. Much like the independent record labels of old, Veena's firm didn't offer large contracts or advances, what they offered was their name, and their name was drawing more and more favor each quarter, their titles finding their way on more and more awards short lists. Babbling Babylon Books, or B3, was known for their eye towards the experimental; the problem was the more experimental works they published, the more experimental their slush pile became—to the point where the company's most important job was simply parsing out the insanely authentic from the authentically insane. And Veena had some of the best eyes in the company—so her boss had said on many occasions, and with dual entendre.

Per the vetting process, Veena was forced to meet with various authors and pseudo-authors, often on the authors' terms and at locations of their choosing; Veena had been everywhere from afternoon strip-club buffets, where both dancers and "chefs" had work to offer, to the horse stables at the track where one would-be experimental author worked—so he had said—out of the necessity to familiarize himself with excrement so that he may better acclimate himself to various sordid climates of literature (a contract had not been extended), to those whose whole aims were to see how much this girl could stomach in terms of petulance, arrogance, solipsism and all permutations of armor for the ego. Some men just wanted to hit on her. Some women did, too. Occasionally she would bring Bryne along so as to deter—really, to minimize—the advances and keep the meeting steered towards a professional vector.

The latest meeting was to be at a dive surfer-bar off Venice Blvd. named the Wet Whistle, where they were supposed to meet one such author who, through his own claims, was trying to reengineer the novel as they knew it.

"I'm just going to say this, if his book's so good and so brilliant, why is it not being pursued by one of the big houses? Have you read even an excerpt yet?" Bryne was driving despite being stoned; Naveena expected this author to be of the type to conduct business through strong drinking, hence the seedy bar best known to have the worst bathrooms in Venice, and had previously agreed with Bryne that, as the agent, she would drink if necessary and he would be her designated driver.

"No, I haven't read *anything*. That's what this meeting is about: he refuses to even show a sentence of the work to anyone unless he meets them first and deigns them worthy."

"How regal of him. How did you even hear about this guy?"

"I'm not even sure anymore. I think he might be a friend of Russell's, or they met at a bar, or he contacted us…I don't know, I stopped asking those questions a while ago, the answers were mostly incestuous or redundant."

"Have you talked to anyone who's read it?"

"Nope."

"Then how do you know it even exists? Maybe this guy, like, just goes around trying to pick up free drinks from willing publishers. Or maybe he just uses the book as a ploy to meet women, or just to build up an air of mystery around him. A tease that never puts out."

"Oh it's all a possibility, babe. That's why you're here."

"Intimidation?" Bryne sat up straight and puffed out his chest. Though still a string-bean, the last time he'd been in a gym was well over a year ago—and that was just to record the sound of iron hitting iron for a film project.

Veena snorted and rubbed Bryne's shoulder, "Oh, babe…you're here to drive me home when I get too drunk or the meeting turns bust."

"I can be intimidating."

"Sure you can, sweetie."

It was a Wednesday so they were able to find parking on the street, yet, despite the weekday, even from outside the bar music pounded like some pugilistic poltergeist on the boarded-up doors and windows painted like a sandblasted lifeguard station. Near the door was a squat, little, palm tree that looked to be, amongst the palm tree society, a grizzled, hunchbacked hermit, with a beard of dry white fronds wrapped around the whole of the trunk. As they got closer to the dendritic bouncer, they heard "Happiness is A Warm Gun" playing in an odd, repeating loop with tape-effect treatments that denuded any such happiness.

"Jesus, nice place. Shouldn't you be trying to wine and dine him at some fancy hotel restaurant?"

"This was his idea!"

"Thirty minutes and we're gone." Bryne pulled out a one-hitter disguised as a ceramic cigarette and took a quick pull. He then lowered his fedora slightly over his eyes to what he imagined was a position of gumshoe intimidation, his blond hair poking through the perforated vents and under the brim like an overstuffed scarecrow.

"Come on, this is my job."

"Not if this is just some bullshit this guy's feeding you."

"Fine, if he's just fucking with us, thirty minutes then we'll leave." Veena walked in front of Bryne and pushed through the batwing doors, which swung back and clapped Bryne on the backside as he struggled to put his one-hitter back in its case, knocking his perfectly configured fedora onto the ground. "Ahhh."

Inside, the bar writhed with the latent contention of heterogeneous communion: two stoned surfers in sandy board-shorts and Wayfarers downing Sol near the defunct jukebox; three frat-boys playing cut-throat on the stained pool table, each with trepanning indentations in their foreheads; a tattooed, bikini-clad, punk girl with gauged-out ears wide enough to fit two fingers standing at a small rack-mounted amp and mixer (the sole individual responsible and attentive to the music); two men at the bar who either looked like they owned motorcycles or wanted to own motorcycles, indeterminably sipping bottled Pabst Blue Ribbon; the bartender, a tall, slightly overweight black man with a large, neatly trimmed beard, jeans rolled into capris, white tank top with some faded silk-screen print underneath a cut-off fishnet T, both of which Bryne thought were for the sole employ of showing-off his left, double-pierced nipple befitted with skull and crossbones: all candidates viable and all viably candid.

Bryne half contemplated approaching the surfers to see if they wanted to smoke while Naveena met with the supposed author. Veena had preemptively thought this, too, and grabbed hold of Bryne's sleeve, shaking her head that she was not to be abandoned.

"Do you have a description of the guy?"

"Nope. Wait here, I'm going to ask the bartender."

Not being blessed with space, Naveena was forced to get closer than she would like to the two motorcycle enthusiasts, one of which stared unapologetically at her breasts, cautiously covered in a sweater, while the other appeared not to have noticed her existence at all and sat there picking at the label on his beer bottle until he was able to slide it off in-tact and affix it to the table with about ten others roughly in the design of a Union Jack. The bartender had his back turned while he was cleaning the fruit flies off the spigots of the hard liquor and forced Naveena to tip-toe and lean over the bar to get his attention.

"Excuse me. *Excuse me.*"

The bartender turned back and put the browned towel on the bar but didn't speak. Veena continued. "I'm looking for a man named Merv; do you know him?"

The bartender stared at her, and she stared at his nipple ring. "What do you want Merv for?"

"I'm supposed to meet him about publishing his book." Naveena lowered herself so she wasn't straining her calves, and so the man next to her would stop looking at the tuft of carmel skin exposed where the sweater pulled away from her jeans.

"Veena?"

"Oh, so he told you I'd be here?"

"Something like that. I'm Merv. Give me a second I'll meet you at a booth. You want a drink?"

"Whatever you're drinking."

Merv moved away from the bar to conduct some business with the register. Naveena turned to find Bryne staring at the punk girl, trying to make out her tattoos: holographs of optical illusions which appeared to be some ornithological movement on her tricep and bicep, an exact replica of Allyson Grey's "Chaos Order and Secret Writing #4" on her lower back and a pair of wings taking up the entirety of her upper back designed to be viewed with 3-D glasses. Bryne was grinning and maybe even drooling slightly, as he sometimes does in moments of stoned awe.

"Excuthe me, Misth," the man ogling her lisped in a faux-British accent, his four upper front teeth missing, "but is thisth puthy taken?"

"—", Veena's throat double-clutching in aphasia.

"Puthy's not gonna eat itthelf!" The man cackled, flicking his surgically-forked tongue through the gummed-over gap between his upper canines. She left and rejoined Bryne at a booth near the door.

"Fifteen minutes."

Bryne nodded, "Have you seen this girl's tattoos? Complete mindfuckery. Why hasn't anyone else thought of doing that?"

"I'm sure they have, sweetie."

Merv joined them at the booth carrying a fistful of PBR by their necks, setting them on the table before seating himself with strange grace for a man of his size. He pushed a beer in front of Veena and one in front of Bryne, who reluctantly pushed it back into Merv's vicinity.

"Isn't there somewhere quieter we can talk?" Veena hoped he had an office or outdoor patio in the back, somewhere they might actually be able to hear each other.

Merv nodded and turned his head toward the punk girl, "Kimmy." She turned and Merv made a slice with his hand across his neck. Kimmy turned the music down but remained at the booth toying with the envelope filters.

Naveena smiled in appeasement. "Great, thank you. I'm Naveena, as you're aware, and this is my boyfriend, Bryne."

Bryne acknowledged the man sitting across from him for the first time and extended his hand enthusiastically, all attempts at being the strong, brooding, tough guy apparently forgotten with the arrival of Kimmy's tattoos.

"So what do you do?" Merv took a swig of his beer, downing half of it.

Veena answered for him. "He's a composer. He does film scoring."

"Anything I might have seen?"

"Probably not. I just finished a new score for the release of *Nosferatu*," Bryne answered for himself.

"Oh, nice, I just watched that last night. Not a bad score."

"It hasn't been released yet, how'd you see it?"

Merv shrugged, "It's a small city: friend of a friend of a producer."

"That sounds about right."

"You didn't happen to hear what that prick over there said to me, did you?" Veena pointed to the assailant.

"Oh, Sam and Lily? I wouldn't worry about them. You wouldn't know it but they're queerer than a snake in snow." Merv finished the first bottle and took up another from the collection in front of him.

Not wanting to linger any longer than humanly possible, Veena jumped right in. "So, tell me about this novel. What's it about?"

"Everything."

Oh here we go. "Okay, can you try to be a little more specific?"

Merv narrowed his eyes as if practicing for an optometric exam, or perhaps, more accurately, as if getting into character. "Well first you have to consider the direction of novels in general. One novel precipitates another that zigs where the other zags—

"Zig-zags?!" Both dismissed Bryne who, ignored, went back to staring at Kimmy's tessellations, which appeared to be in migration, ambulating in a first clockwise then counterclockwise motion, from her tricep to her bicep and then back.

"So, the next novel does the same, and so on, and so on, until you get the breadth of every possible story and style. Then they got experimental and started inventing different styles until that, too, eventually ran through all possibilities."

"Enter postmodernism."

"Right: postmodernism and the pastiche, then Re-modernism, the Re-Postmodernism. Etcetera, etcetera. I mean you can only go so far, right? Everyone has done everything, all stories told and retold, and our progress has recycled to a matter of pastiche."

"What about science fiction? I guarantee you those stories haven't been told," Bryne proffered.

"But they have. Discard all the planets and warp-drives and shit and you're still left with stories revolving around the human affect. Jealousy, betrayal, love, greed, etcetera. They just have different decorations."

Merv took another sip; Veena waited anxiously for the Reveal; Bryne went back to his people watching. The batwing doors swung open and a couple Trashlanders walked in; though their time on Plastícea had given them ample sea legs, you could always tell a Trashlander on the mainland by their walk, as if the gravity of terra firma was significantly heavier; more than likely their legs were not used to ground that doesn't, in some way, bob and spring back with each step. Rubber legs mirroring the plasticity of their home. The Trashlanders ordered fruity cocktails—their penchant for scurvy-fighting libations the Trashlanders second give-away—with Kimmy serving as the interim bartender, and took a seat at the bar at a wary distance from the two patrons Veena had experienced.

Merv continued his pitch, "Right, so all we're doing is just rewriting the same story for different models and contemporary purposes, adding a new layer on top of an existing cake, building new flavors on their existing allusions and themes and arcs..." Merv twirled his hand to pantomime the ellipse. "I mean, if Book A references Book B, and Book C references Book B, doesn't it transitively reference A, too? Doesn't it absorb both of their allusions, both of their flavors?" He didn't give them an opportunity to answer. "Now, wouldn't the next step then be collating Book F—made up of Books D and E—with Book C to create Book G? And then wouldn't the natural progression be to extrapolate that until you have Book X, a book that encapsulates all Books before it? Pascal's Tetractys collapsing into itself, going back to just the one overall, encompassing piece?"

"That just sounds, well...a little...contrived, don't you think?" Naveena trying not to appear too combative this early; Merv nodded in expectation.

"Well isn't it all? When you consider the parameters of what constitutes a story, the four main conflicts of story and the basic twenty-four tools of the English language, do you really think there are infinite possibilities?" He turned to Bryne, "You're a musician, how many possible combinations can be made with twelve tones to choose from? Eight if you're going straight diatonic?"

Bryne leaned forward, suddenly put-on, "Like, mathematically?"

"What about Joyce?" Veena retorted, "*Finnegan's Wake* wasn't based around the limitations of English. That book blew open the limitations of all language and etymologies and their amalgams; there's virtually an infinite way to interpret that book. Scratch that, an *absolutely* infinite way to interpret that book."

"I'll get to Joyce; let me go back to what I was saying though. Now, if the proposed difference between modernism and postmodernism is that of creation versus destruction—metaphor versus metonymy—in accordance with the increasing limitations of language invention, wouldn't a work that incorporates all works not be the ultimate embodiment of destruction? After all, isn't reduction the most flattering form of destruction? If we do that, what we get is a reduction of all work and all language into one book. And if that book can be reduced, if we repeat that process—reducing chapters and paragraphs and sentences—what do we get? One metonymical semantic for all of literature. One absolute reduction into an elegant, one-inch line that permeates everything, from the microcosmic to the macro. A sacred literary geometry. A fractal linguistic solution. They say the Tetragrammaton hasn't been spoken since the Second Temple of Jerusalem was destroyed; maybe it wasn't saying the name of God they deemed sacrilegious, but simply because they weren't pronouncing it correctly. And maybe that's because, if the reduction is true, it would require all works of past art and all future art consolidated into one *objet d'art*. If people are searching for the word of God, maybe that's it, the Reduction."

"So...you're book is the word of God?" Had she said fifteen minutes? Better make it five, grandiose, deistic arrogance being more often than not the usual precursor to bullshit.

"Baby, baby, baby. No, I'm just talking about the end game of literature and art. I would hope that my book is one of the first steps towards the Reduction, a cornerstone of the Holy Trinity, so to speak. Although, it would likely take more than three books to accomplish that fete."

"So what *is* your book?" Veena had been impatient, now, with Merv still dancing around the point, she was feeling near furiously anxious.

"It's the first collated novel. It's a story solely made of bits and pieces of just about every novel I could find. A remix, of sorts. I haven't added a single word of my own. Outside of chapter headings."

"Then how is it yours?" Bryne rejoined the conversation while surreptitiously sliding a beer into his possession, hoping Naveena wouldn't notice, which, of course, she did; though if chipping away at the pile of bottles got them out of here faster, so be it.

"Man, I could ask you the same thing. You invent all those notes you use, motherfucker? No, they already exist, you just rearrange them. Even if it ain't a Remix, it's a remix. It's just organization, man, architecture. Shit, you of all people should recognize the merits of that."

"Well, yeah, point taken—but it's not the same thing."

Given the current climate, Bryne assumed hitting his one-hitter indoors was more than acceptable and took a generous drag. He assumed correctly, and even offered one to Merv, who shook his head no, then yes, then no; he had a pitch to continue.

"Look at art—no, first, look at technology. Look at what we've built, from computing power to AI, robotics to regeneration—cloning! Shit, each and every one of those innovations is just us playing God. We built technology to better understand ourselves, to better understand where we came from so that we figure out where we're going. And the best way to check your understanding is by replication. So we ape God, and then we ape him again by refashioning ourselves in the image of our creations. Need I mention the whole implantation wave? An ape aping an ape: what I call the Möbius Ape—that's Chapter Two."

"Pretty soon we'll be writing Zoloft prescriptions for our drones," Bryne nodded, suddenly concerned with Otis's state of being.

"You joke but it's not that far off. If we modeled them after us, you can bet your ass they got our flaws, too."

Bryne pictured Veena picturing Bryne on the couch, sharing a bong with a robot.

Merv turned to Veena, "Art is the same thing. If our art—and I do mean all art—is a creation of man, who is a creation of God, would not reverting back to the one, pure art not in a sense be a retreat back to God? To God's own art? The essence of creation itself? A creation singularity!? Maybe there is a preliminary inertia and a kinetic limit to art, a limit to what we can produce; and when we've hit that final inch of creation, art begins to collapse back on itself. Art is just mirroring the elasticity of the universe, baby, but that doesn't mean that art is done."

"So when is that supposed to go down? Did the Mayans mark it on their calendar, too?" Like Veena, Bryne found himself similarly irked with the *auteur* (as apparently "author" couldn't be the appropriate word). If he was forced into coming, he felt himself granted free reign of his opinions.

"Well if we're starting to revert now, maybe it's already begun. Maybe pastiche is the beginning stage of the inversion; or maybe it's the last...the deceleration. I don't know; I'm not a scientist."

"No, you're a bartender." Veena glared at Bryne and dug her fingernails into his thigh.

"Ouch!"

"Watch that attitude of yours, friend. You're in my bar. We got rooms in back for people like you. Ask Kimmy about her last boyfriend."

Bryne gulped and played with his hat, pulling the back of the brim down to expose his eyes, lifting the veil from his helmet. "All I'm saying is that as someone who hopes to have a long and lucrative career as a musician, I hope to God that we don't collapse anytime in the near future."

"Here, here." Veena raised her beer. Bryne clinked his bottle to hers, forgetting he was trying to keep the beer under wraps.

Merv placed his hands flat on the table and leaned in to Bryne, his beard kissing the sticky table, "Broheim, you should be as concerned about this as I am. You're a musician, a writer in a different language. You really think you've got more means of ingenuity? That you're not gonna run the tank dry one day? How many original chord structures you think are out there?"

"So you're talking the inherent limit of all art?" Veena deflected for Bryne, running an abacus in his head.

"Yes, exactly!" Merv finished his beer and grabbed the last one on the table, the empties in the corner standing like an abandoned glass city whose luster had dwindled to a dull brown.

Veena shook her head. "But you need limits, limits are a good thing. A lot of good art is created specifically because of limits. Think about it, the limits of the paper, the canvas, the key signature, the limits of the range of colors and sounds we can see and hear, the limits of our bodies—what are sports or dance but an exploration, a testing, of the physical limits of what our bodies can do!? Without limits you just have a vast abyss of possibility. What would Guernica look like if it was just a small corner of a football-field sized canvas? How do you account for all that negative space? How can any art be completed if you have all this possibility left on the table?"

"The universe all over, baby: just because it's dark, doesn't mean there's nothing there. Negative space is just the dark matter of art. And even at that, there's a finite amount of dark matter, too. Conservation of matter. And even that will get compressed."

The conversation settled into a natural lull. Veena took out her phone and pretended to read an email, accidentally reading one on the way. Merv rehydrated. Bryne tapped a new rhythm on the side of his bottle. Aside from the frat boys who were chalking their cues and pressing blue circles into the divot of their trepanning indentations, the rest of the bar was operating at the same level of entropy as when they'd entered.

Bryne was the first to jump back in. "Here's how I see it: Magellan and Columbus and Galileo and the pre-colonial notion that the world is flat—'That's it folks, we've mapped it all out, be sure not to sail off the edge.' But those dudes proved otherwise. Then it was only a matter of time before the earth was fully mapped and every square of the globe graphed and locatable through satellites. But did we stop there? Did we just up and say, 'Oh, now that we've solved that one, guess we'll just rest here?' No, man, no: we went to space, mapped the solar system and our galaxy; we sent probes and manned ships towards our inter-stellar neighbors. Then we went *inside* our planet. We found water underneath the oceans and made an algorithm for the tectonic shifts underneath our crust. We predicted earthquakes—not the Big One, but still…Look, there's never a stopping point, man, there's just dead ends and wrong turns that spin you around, and even if you back-track a little, you still end up on a new course. Like underground rivers man, they always find a way out into the open." Well, well, well…look whose afternoons spent smoking and watching the Discovery App finally paid off.

Merv appeared to be considering this; Bryne, taking advantage of the space, gathered momentum. "Yeah! Look! Okay, so music is basically split into two groups: performers and composers. Originally, we composers needed orchestras to play our compositions, and orchestras needed compositions to perform. It's…symbiotic," he looked at Veena to make sure he'd used the right word and waited until she nodded to proceed. "We applaud the composers for their creations, and we applaud the musicians for being able to play them. We watch people play Chopin and Paganini not because we like the music—I mean there is that—but because of the acrobatics needed to pull it off. Now, used to be you needed to be able to do a little of both to be considered a good musician, but now, after the advent of multi-tracking, sampling—shit, the Tele-Kastr™!—hell you don't need to know a damn thing about music to make it. And then on the performing side—well, look at the old adage: Classical performers can't improvise, and jazz performers can't replicate. Performing versus composing. With this new technology, the wall between the two is gone; it's rubble. See, music found new ways to exist inside of your limits, and without just remixing the notes."

"Ahh but there you go. The destruction of performing has already begun. Performing and composing are merging." As if on cue, Kimmy started playing some Joy Circuit, choosing one of the tracks off his last album before his on-stage death two years ago from ingesting a lethal amount of MDMA and suffering a stroke; his affliction went largely unnoticed as the helmet occluded any visual signifiers of the apoplexy and whose continual synaptic firings dropped, quote, "one of the sickest grunk beats ever!"

"But people are still performing. People are still going to performances. Look at Carnegie Hall, they've been filling shows for their Robotic Orchestra for years."

"Yeah but you just proved my point!"

"Shit. I did?"

"Those people that are attending those performances aren't going for the music. They're not going for the humanity of the score, for the art. They're going to watch robots pretend to be human. They're watching to see how close they come to the real thing. And they capture the score with, literally, laser-like precision. But it's not about the art. The robots can't capture the nuances of the music, and even if they can, they don't feel it—emotion makes no difference to the robots—a heartfelt performance would only exist to satisfy spectators and their creators. Just elephants at the circus, man. Parents at their kids' recital."

"So you're saying it's not art because the performance is perfected, perfunctory even?" Veena asked.

"No, I'm saying perfection isn't art any more, or at least, it's not the goal any more. Perfection stopped being art as soon as we achieved it, even transitively, through our creation's creations. See, as soon as we hit the limit, art started to collapse on itself.

"Look at the story of...oh what was that Italian motherfucker's name? Grotto, Ciatto—oh yeah, Giotto," Merv continued, "Right, so Pope Something the Nth asked all the local artists for a demonstration of their artistic skills. So what did Giotto do? He drew a perfect circle, freehand. And out of all the other artists' entries, the Pope selected his as the best because he knew the skill required to create something perfect. If they did that today, with both a human and a robot drawing a perfect circle, the robot would win hands down; the best a human could hope for is a tie. Does that mean the robot is the better artist? No, because it's not about the product, it's about the process?"

"Is it?" Veena, whose commissions certainly came more from selling the product than the process, asked with not a lack of sarcasm.

"Yes, because it's about the human pursuit of perfection. That's why it's art."

"But if we've already accomplished perfection, what's left? Why even keep creating art? It can't just be for the paycheck 'cause I'll tell you right now, even if we decide to publish your book you won't exactly be building a palace with the advance."

"Yeah best case is a new scooter." Bryne had peaked at his fair share of contracts Veena had left out on the table, mostly to assure himself that he'd chosen the right artistic path, financially speaking, which, looking at the contract, he most certainly had.

Merv ignored him. "We create because we're still exploring our humanity, and more than our humanity, creation in general."

"And these robots aren't artists?" Veena's voice was taking on that timbre again, the one she'd had when her and Bryne first met, and the one that had once gotten Bryne a black eye while defending her honor. "*Can* a robot be an artist? Is that even possible in your estimation?"

"Sure they can, just not in that instance."

"How? When? In what instance?"

"When it's exploring its 'inner robot,'" Bryne answered, making sure to air-quote accordingly. Merv nodded.

"Same with an elephant, if it's exploring its own 'elephant-ness'" Merv added. "The point is art is now the pursuit of the imperfect. Perfection isn't the focus any more. Creation isn't the focus any more."

"So what is?"

"Organization. That's the new frontier, organization, consolidation and abstraction. After all, ask a robot to draw 'grief' and see what you get."

"I did. It was….horrifying," Bryne stared at the table in grave recollection, remembering that time he'd been strolling through the mall after smoking a full gram of the sativa-heavy Afternoon Delight and got pulled into the Grubl kiosk for an AI demonstration. Never again! "It was like a lawnmower ate an H.R. Giger painting and puked it onto a Dali."

"See?! There you go; even abstract expressionism isn't solely our own any more. We have to pivot."

"But pivot to what?" Veena asked, "Theft?" Which was what they were really talking about, weren't they? Seeing as, by his own claims, he hadn't written a single word of this book.

"Organization. Organization as destruction. Destruction as reduction. A reduction of our humanity. Then, a reduction of all life."

Well at least that elevator pitch could actually be accomplished in the span of an elevator ride, Bryne thought. If he had to run through this whole damn thing every time someone asked him for a synopsis of his book he'd need to be in a hand-cranked car in the Burj Khalifa or Jacob's Spire—should they ever complete that "tower to heaven" (rumors of union holdups). And even then he'd run the risk of the other party clawing his or her eyes and ears out at some point.

Veena, still unsure if this is something she can, or would want, to publish (the licensing alone sounded like a headache—a very expensive headache) decided to ask, if for nothing more than shits and giggles, "How do you account for other countries and cultures? What language is this final artform supposed to be in? I don't think English is the first language of God."

Merv grew pleased and smiled. Bryne thought Merv's nipple ring might have been mood oriented as it seemed to be glowing bright green, though that could just be a reflection from one of the numerous flashing lights Kimmy had turned on, the DJ and sole participant to her own private dance party—though the forked-tongue biker, who Bryne guessed was Lily, was starting to bob his shoulders.

"Well that's it, isn't it? It wouldn't be just writing. In the final stage there would be one book for all books, one painting for all paintings, one sculpture, and so forth."

"So how does that combine to form one *objet d'art*?"

"Maaaan, if I knew I'd have done it by now and I wouldn't be working at this goddamn shit hole. Maybe Joyce was the first prophet. *Finnegan's Wake* the first step to an amalgam language and book, arguably the best step with the possibility of *Y* in 2013. We just need the legal disparity over rights and ownership dissolved and we're finally free to open the floodgates on the coagulation of literature. We're on the precipice of the apocalypse, baby! The artpocalypse!"

Merv downed the rest of his beer and settled down. The biker must have been a Joy Circuit fan as he'd gotten off the stool and was taking up one of the Trashlanders as a dance partner. Judging from the stiff movements—let alone the terrified expression on his face—Bryne guessed the dance card had been reluctantly punched; stranger, still, the Trashlander appeared to be leading. "The question is this: Is language, art, a perpetual motion machine, or did God just supply us with enough potential energy to keep it running for a while?"

"Apoptosis," Bryne said in an aside to himself.

"What was that?" Merv turned to Bryne as of he'd just dropped the password for Merv's bank account.

"Like, an apoptosis, but for language: a pre-programmed, built-in death."

Merv's lips stretched into a wide smile, "Motherfucker, you must've read Chapter Five!"

— § —

They drove away from the Wet Whistle with a copy of Merv's manuscript in Veena's lap, *[Dis/Re]Assembling the Godhead* by Merv Griffyn.

"Griffyn!? Are you shitting me?"

"Keep your eyes on the road, dude; I saw you snake that beer. Don't want to blow your whole advance on bail."

"I'd rather keep them on your lap. Shit!" Bryne hit the brakes as an Auto cut him off in a silver Beamer. A metallic hand emerged from the driver's side window and slowly extended a shiny middle finger; the car's owner joined with an organic finger from the other side of the car. "Fucking Agro Mods."

After deigning Veena worthy, Merv had Kimmy fetch the manuscript from behind the bar and deliver the parcel—wrapped in brown paper, tied with twine and sealed with wax—to their table. As soon as they got in Bryne's Jeep he begged Veena to open it, and after some ten blocks she consented. The manuscript was a hefty one: no less than 500-pages, hard-covered with two pieces of laminated mahogany, home-bound with wire and glue. Both the title and author were branded onto the cover, along with a strange geometric symbol in the center.

"Well let's hope he's got an electronic copy because I'm not running this through the scanner."

"So you think you're going to publish it?"

Veena sighed. "I don't know; I'll give it a read and make a recommendation but it's really Russell's call. I mean he's built up enough mystique among other publishers by now. Even if the book's shit people might read it just based around his persona."

"I love your optimism."

"At least he's got his spiel practiced. If it picks up, he'll certainly entertain people on the tour front."

"Like a sideshow: Step right up folks, come see the amazing, tattooed, pierced, post-modern prophet. Hark, for his nipple shall speak the word of God. So what's it look like? The actual writing?"

Veena turned the first few pages and began to read to herself. "Jesus this is going to give me an aneurysm. It's like someone dropped an entire library into Burroughs' cut-up engine. Faulker one sentence, Joyce the next. Fitzgerald…I see some Dickens, Pynchon…This one's gotta be German, maybe Goethe or Rilke. Poe! Jesus, I don't even know if this one even counts as language."

Veena flipped more pages, shaking her head. "I guess there might be some fun in going through here and seeing how many passages you recognize."

"So it's like a word-find? Er, sentence-find I guess."

She flipped to the last page, "Like a six-hundred-and-forty-two-page sentence-find? I wonder if we'd be able to link all these. People reading the book could just click on the sentence or phrase and be brought to the original text. Actually, that might increase our sales if it promotes readers buying other works. I'll see if Russell can look into some click-through royalties."

"Go synergy. Is there even a story in there?"

"Fuck, I don't know. I suppose there might be an arc somewhere, but based around that convo I'm guessing it's just a lot of name-dropping for the entirety."

Bryne laughed, "All that work for the literary novelization of *Where's Waldo.*"

— § —

A month in and the creative constipation was holding strong, and it appeared no amount of inspirational laxatives would remove the blockage. Just to have something, anything, a start that would hopefully transmute into a legitimate idea, Bryne had been working on a version of Holland's suggestion of a composite score, sitting in his studio, writing a couple lines each of variegated musical styles and then playing them together to see if one worked better with the whole, if he should try and coordinate a melody or chord structure within the different segments: an Amsus4 over three different instruments and voices; a re-imagination of the *klangfarbenmelodie* produced from four distinct melodies. An implied melody? In those few moments when honesty peeked through the gown of optimism, he knew in his gut the music wasn't any good, that David and Rasheeda would not be pleased; yet he would have to keep going on this path until he found the next phase, something more organic, and something that would hopefully come soon.

Just because the laxatives weren't working (yet), wasn't any reason to give up; Bryne packed the little bowl he kept in the studio, ever so cleverly named Smokezart, and began considering the music of language itself—prompted, no doubt, from the preceding night's conversation with Merv. *Planet of the Apes* [Schaffner, 1968] was playing soundlessly on the screen in the corner, and Bryne leaned back in his chair and took a few puffs while watching the bipedal apes haul the manacled

George Taylor through their camp. Without the benefit(?) of an office and the eponymous banter, Bryne often kept the monitor on just to give the illusion of companionship. As the good Dr. Zaius was examining the intrepid astronaut, suddenly bursting into speech thought impossible and astonishing the loquacious apes, Bryne couldn't help contemplating the stubbornly human aspects of music. Primates could learn sign language, sure, we've all seen the videos, but they have no concept of rhythm. He remembered a study Berkeley had done some years back trying to get gorillas and chimps to keep time. They had given the ape a tambourine, and while the hominidean liked the jingling of the instrument, liked banging it against its hand or on the ground, they could never get the animal to play on time, even with human coaches playing along.

Bryne liked that music remained solely a human attribute; and the fact that he made his living as a sonic architect of affect made him feel as if he had the keys to humanity. If he was truly a good composer, as he thought himself, he should possess the master key capable of unlocking any and all human emotions. Perhaps the locks weren't turning lately because the key was dull or gunked up. If only he could polish and sharpen that skeleton key he'd be back in business. This was precisely the kind of thinking he needed to get out of his introspective funk. Water in a cave, he thought, just working through all the dead ends until rejoining the river. He laughed to himself; Merv was out of his fucking mind.

He took another hit to cash the bowl and made a lemon face from the taste of sour ash.

But instead of diving back into the writing, Bryne put on Tom Waits *Mule Variations*, which his grandfather had turned him onto, and took a bathroom break when "What's He Building In There" came on.

— § —

When the first week of the second month passed, and with it no more progress than a couple versions of his quadraphonic score, Bryne decided it was time to try tracking down the other composers who had worked on the score prior to him. He needed to know how they saw the project, what they attempted and why it had failed. Not invasive or a cop-out, or to steal their work, Bryne felt it absolutely necessary to know what had failed lest he repeat their same errors and lose the contract. There wasn't much time left and *Nosferatu* couldn't float him forever.

But David wouldn't give the names out. "Why would you want to talk to them?" Bryne explained his reasons, the ones that didn't display a lack of confidence or progress. "All the same, Bryne, I'd rather not. Wouldn't want you to get any bad ideas," David laughed.

"But that's just what I'm trying to do, David, get rid of the bad ideas, avoid replicating their mistakes."

"Believe me, from what I'd heard, I don't think you'll have to worry about replication."

Bryne was pacing on the deck, using the SoundBall™ as a speaker phone. "But what were they doing? What track were they on? I'm sure you can imagine, there are many, *many* roads to take with Potemkin, I just want to make sure I'm not going down the path through the dark and haunted woods."

The mountains in Topanga State Park just northwest of him were on fire again. The ash fell in soft, quiet flakes, dusting his crops and hair and covering Otis in a fuzzy, gray dander.

"Look," David continued, "we put our faith in you, Bryne; we firmly believe you will produce a tremendous score. But I have to say, your insistence on contacting our former contracts is…well…a little disconcerting— no, I shouldn't say that—a little disheartening. If you don't think you can handle the assignment please let us know now while there's still time to find a replacement."

"No, no, no, no. Nothing like that, David. This score, it's-, it's going to be epic! Brilliant, maybe. I just want to make sure I'm not going into any territories that failed in the past. I don't want to invest my time in a failure, and I'm sure the same could be said on your end."

"Indeed it could."

They'd ended the conversation after another minute of Bryne convincing David everything was on schedule and promising he'd send out demos in the next couple weeks. Instead of solving his problem, he'd just upped his timeline. If David wasn't forthcoming, he could bet Rasheeda wouldn't be either; he'd have to find the names another way.

Luckily, Bryne was able to secure the names quite easily from one of the kids at the front desk with nothing more than a gift basket of his finest home-grown herb, delivered by Otis with a pair of Wayfarers taped over the serial number. (He was pretty high when he executed the mission.) Bryne's stomach dropped as he read the sheet of paper Otis brought back in his nylon papoose. Only two names made up the list, names both impressive and depressing: Wyatt Wade and Michio Kronopolous. If these Olympians of composition couldn't produce a satisfactory score, how in the hell could Bryne hope to not only produce an acceptable composition but a better one at that?

The first name on the list, Wyatt Wade, was surprisingly easy and accommodating to track down, answering his own phone and inviting Bryne and Veena to attend an upcoming house-party that weekend. Dressed to the nines, Bryne and Veena posted up on Wade's patio overlooking the Stone Canyon Reservoir and Los Angeles from its perch in the purple, sage hilltops of Bel Air. Wyatt's mansion was a newer home, built on an area that had suffered immensely from a battery of fires over the last two decades, culminating in The Great Conflagration of 2022 that had burned up most of the residences on the mountainside. In the aftermath, developers installed fire-retention walls of concrete and glass, with faux-wood veneers of decadent walnut running along the vertical facias; the walls still facilitated the breathtaking views their residents had come to expect and pay out the ass for, but created a barrier between the incendiary flora of the mountain and the mortgage-paying fauna. Wyatt's house was built in a similar schema to the walls and resembled a government bunker in a not-so dystopian future. The landscaping, an assortment of rocks, ranging from small beach pebbles and lava stones to giant boulders and red slats of earth taken from Death Valley or Joshua Tree, filled a similar purpose, an inverse moat designed to drown any encroaching flames in its dearth of fuel. Inside the C-shaped structure of the house was an oasis of ferns, palms and plants with purple, orange and yellow buds and flowers—offshoots from the infinity pool that seemed to extend beyond the cliff face and quench the parched city below, shimmering and dancing in the heat.

Veena—in a short, white, tennis skirt where the pleats crossed in Xs, a red-and-orange, flower-print, halter-top with a gold band positioned tastefully, and voluptuously, at the beginning descent of her cleavage—was enjoying herself, having taken to the posh view and the osmotic associations of wealth. Bryne, though usually one to condemn the lavishness of the uber-rich, was finding it hard to deny that he, too, was enjoying his time among the upper echelon, donning the dress fedora he rarely finds an opportunity to break out. Though, for Bryne's case, much of his enjoyment had less to do with the ornate beverages (intricate glassware holding six-inch swords impaling absinthe-soaked exotic fruits, served to them with obsequious care by tuxedoed men and women of their same age (an "Is everything to your liking, sir?" or "Shall I adjust the angle of the umbrella to get the sun out of your eyes, ma'am?"), and which Veena couldn't slurp down fast enough), and more to do with the company of the party. Scattered among the grounds and patio were a colloidal mix of musicians, artists, writers, designers and producers from all points of the spectrum; a single endorsement from any of them could garner Bryne an inexhaustible supply of job offers. And there, strolling along the perimeter of the yard, in a blindingly-white Stetson, with plaid flannel and a taupe vest, sporting a pair of barndoor-red boots of a brand of cow not yet on the market for clothing or consumption, was the man himself: the Cowboy of Chord, the Maestro of the Mesa, the Shane of Sound, the Hero of the A-OK Chorale: Mr. Wyatt Wade.

A two-time Oscar winner and four-time nominee, Wade had been a disciple of Reich and had taken many of Reich's innovations (stacked polyrhythms, incongruous melodies, pools of harmony, disparate rhythmic structuring and the complete dissolution and reinvention of melody as a simultaneously rhythmic, harmonic and ambient machine) to levels both more experimental and more ingrained in the conventions of pop music. Amid a maelstrom of swirling time- and key-signatures, a torrent of impressions struck the ears with both chromatic cacophony and resplendent aural beauty as, say, two out of the five key signatures paired together in a sort of sonic eclipse, while another parallel line of music, one more familiar and with a "classical" hook to it, moved independently from the solar system and exhibited no parallax. No matter how far out into space you were, he always provided something to hold onto, a tether to keep you within safe reach of the ship. Probably why he'd always enjoyed both critical and commercial success.

They'd been there almost an hour and Bryne still couldn't find an opportunity to speak to their host. Wade, whose aberrant mane of black hair poked out from the back of his Stetson like a petrified groundhog under the shade of a sun-bleached pueblo, was making his way through a queue of people far more important than Bryne, greeting each pod of big-wigs, shaking hands, attentively listening to each guest while stroking the sides of his black handlebar moustache specked with red and gray. Veena couldn't care less about meeting Wade (except to thank him for the invitation) and focused on enjoying herself, getting punch-drunk off the cocktails and exclaiming about the view and the absurdity of the tuxedoed caterers forced to keep the image of formalism in the ninety-six degree heat, wiping their brows so often they reminded her of elephants swatting flies in an everlasting dance with the elements. At least the fires had calmed down today and they didn't have to put up with the ash on top of it; no chance the catering company would have covered the dry-cleaning costs.

The company at their small garden table had rotated often, and, like the guests, vacillated between seeming normalcy and flagrant oddity. The sweet, producer-couple with three alliteratively-named children, who specialized in family-friendly ReMies, had, within five minutes of meeting them, propositioned Veena for a threesome—but were kind enough to offer Bryne their Swedish *au pair* if he was interested. "Um, do you have a card or something I can take?" Then there were two-thirds of a three-piece band called Bif Hellerman & the Aporianettes who were so hung up on experimentation and compositional music theories that they became, essentially, theoretical musicians: songs and performances that existed only as intangible ideas and that would never have the privilege to be performed, heard or, at best, overlooked. (And perhaps most infuriating of all, there was no Bif Hellerman!) And lastly, the heroin-skinny rocker in her late thirties who, through what sounded like an inflated tongue, drawled on and on about Mexico City being the last bastion of human primacy against the hedonistic West—whatever the hell that meant—before nodding off and being escorted to the guest house.

As Bryne continued to wait for an opening with Wade, a former actor whom both had seen in various supporting roles (both before and after The Fall), and who would invariably elicit a tongue-tied search for the names of the other places they had seen him whenever he appeared on screen, took up the rocker's vacant seat and conversation. His (stage?) name, he was pained to produce, was Ulliver Treadwell. They talked briefly about their jobs and the weather; they talked in more duration about the hauntingly depressing condition of the Pacific beaches and about how the most dangerous thing a person can do is to read a good book while on a solitary journey through the outback or foreign lands.

"Because you're so removed from yourself in terms of social application, that on your own, you're allowed to fully slip into the narcissistic identification of the character without having to leave and return to yourself. You become lost in their—the character's or the author's—consciousness and absorb it, adopt it, like that alien in *The Thing* [Carpenter, 1982], and pretty soon you can't tell your innate self from the new one. That's why you always have to pack for the person you want to become, not the person you are."

"And you're speaking from personal experience?" Bryne asked. Like the occupants before, the conversation appeared to be dipping once more into the territory of the pretentious or the bizarre, too early to tell which just yet.

"I am indeed, my friend. It happened while I was doing a month-long solo camp in Iceland. Messed me up good," Ulliver shook his head as if the thought of his identity crisis was too disturbing to go into on such a nice afternoon.

"What book were you reading?" Veena asked around an alcohol-infused starfruit dangling from the corner of her mouth.

The actor laughed, flashing his pearly whites. "*That*, I'm afraid, is too embarrassing for me to say."

"But you're an actor? You're not supposed to get embarrassed."

"Well, if I was a better actor, I wouldn't get embarrassed." He combined his self-deprecation with a laugh and playful pat of his hand on Veena's knee. "But I'm not talking about a character here, I'm talking about me—my own personal life. You have to separate the two."

"Oh come on, tell us." Veena fawned.

This was certainly not the first time Veena had been flirted with in his company—hell, he'd almost be offended if she wasn't hit on, a girl as gorgeous as she; Veena's flirting back, however, was a different sto-ry. But the real issue, the one he saw rising as steady and predictable as the black tide, was her drinking. This far into their common-law marriage he knew she became flirtatious whenever she got drunk off sugary drinks, just as he knew that sickness inevitably followed. He didn't have to worry about any flirtations as they would soon, like her lunch, be thrown out the window. In these instances, Bryne only had to worry about getting her safely to the bathroom and then to bed.

"Nope. Can't do it. Lips are sealed."

"So, what'll it take to unseal them?" Bryne was a little taken aback by that one; even Ulliver blushed.

"Yes, dear, what *will* it take to unseal those lips?"

Veena, realizing the charged entendre, altered her course, "At least give us the author's name? Give us that much."

"Nah, still too revealing. I would die of shame. Look, you ever hear the one about The Leading Man?"

"What's that?" The starfruit was gone and she was trying to spear a soggy lychee at the bottom of her drink, alternately keeping an eye out for the nearest waiter to bring her another.

"It's just some anecdote my old theater professor used to tell us." Ulliver leaned back in his chair, resting his left foot on his right knee. "So, The Leading Man arrives on the set of his new film and the di-rector comes up and says 'We've made some adjustments to the scene today. I'm having my assistant bring over the edits. Give them a look and take an extra hour to prepare if you need; though, I doubt a man of your caliber will really need that much time to prepare: five Oscars, two Golden Globes and a Tony!' The director smiles, claps the actor on the back and takes off. The actor, understandably flattered, smiles to himself and thinks 'Hey, that's true, I am one of the top performers in my field. I reinvented the pathos for King Lear. I defined Faust. I made Uncle Vanya a household name. I've juggled twelve selves in one role and made women and men break into uncontrollable sobs. I can do this, how difficult could it be?'

"So, the actor goes to his trailer, all confident and happy because of the faith bestowed upon him, and he finds the revision sitting on his table. He picks it up, still smiling, and as he reads through the new scene his smile fades and his face grows pale." Ulliver drew a hand over his face, trying to pull away his leading man face and replace it with a flushed one.

" 'Well, this clearly has to be a mistake,' he says. 'This just simply will not do; I don't even see how the union will allow it!' So off he runs to find the director, passing the fawning female extras who would have otherwise been lined up outside his trailer for a turn at the Don Juan Thespian.

"He finds the director at the video village and pulls him aside. 'Glen,' he says (or Bob or Jim or whoever—it doesn't really matter). 'Is this a joke?' as he throws the new pages onto the director's chair.

" 'Joke? Of course not. Now, I know it's a little unconventional but you are the greatest living actor, are you not?

" 'Yes,' he says, not calmed but also not immune.

"And you wanted to be the Marquis de Sade, didn't you? You said you wanted to capture the full, sordid essence of him, right? Isn't that what you signed on for?'

" 'Yes, but...this can't be right, Glen. This is pornography!'

" 'Not pornography, Billy Boy (or Jeff or whatever), history. Art! And you are my artist, are you not?'

" 'But, but *Glen*, you have me performing homosexual sex in this scene, with a number of men!'

" 'And women.'

" 'And a few other things, some of them not even alive!'

" 'Well, it's the story, is it not?' "

" 'You have me taking a dick in my ass, Glen. You have me inserting champagne bottles into my anus!' Now the actor gets really pissed, 'You've even written in the notes: NO DOUBLES. NO STAND INS. NO CGI. FULL PENETRATION! With an exclamation point for Christ's sake!'

"But the director retorts, 'It's about the integrity of the story, Irv. Everything in here is straight out of *Justine* and *The One Hundred and Twenty Days of Sodom*. It's for the— '

" 'Glen, I'm not a homosexual.'

" 'No, you're an actor—and a splendid one at that. You're our Leading Man!'

" 'Yes, exactly. I am the Leading Man. How do you expect this will look to the public? Everyone will think I'm gay with a thirsty, insatiable asshole; and by all technical accounts they'll be right as rain.'

" 'But you're not in love with the man, I don't require you to be attracted to him as you, Malcolm Langston. As long as Malcolm Rutherford Langston doesn't find any longing for him this doesn't make you a homosexual. This is basic theater, Mally; this is Acting 101: The Separation of the Self. I mean, didn't your teacher ever tell you the story about The Leading Man?' "

Ulliver ended his soliloquy with a big smile and a slight bow. Veena clapped, then signaled the waiter, pointing to her empty glass and giving a thumbs up. The way Ulliver was smiling, Bryne guessed the author wasn't some ascot-wearing, classical, theater professor but the man in the linen suit sitting in front of them undoing his third-from-top button.

"And this explains you not telling us the name of the author how, exactly," Bryne said.

"Bryne's just being coy." Veena, apologizing for him.

"Am not. We started talking about a book he was too embarrassed to name, and the next thing you know a champagne bottle's getting shoved up someone's ass! And how would that story apply if you were a female actor?"

"The gender isn't important here—

"One could beg to differ." Veena shot Bryne a reproachful raise of her eyebrows.

A waiter with a large knit cap covering his head like a sweater on a partially deflated basketball approached the table. "Excuse me, would you care for some, would you-, would you-, would-." he placed the tray on the table and smacked himself on the side of the head, "Beg your pardon but would you care for some bacon wrapped dates?"

"Sure," Veena said, as if taking a date would in some way alleviate the man's pain or embarrassment. "Thank you very much."

"Poor bastard," Ulliver said, watching the Implanted waiter move on to the next table, a twitch in his step, "in a different era, he might have made it to a national deodorant commercial, or at best a recurring character on some CW soap opera."

Ulliver leaned forward to take Bryne's hand, which Bryne quickly retracted. The actor went on as if the hand were still there, even appearing now and then to stroke the imaginary knuckles. "All I'm saying is that for an actor to be really successful—or even to be considered acting—there has to be a separation of the individual and the character. A sort of duality that happens to occupy the same body; for actors, this is where so much of the trouble comes from, because some got into the game just to be stars and have their face on billboards and the accompanying fame and sex, and others got in it for the art. 'All thespians are actors, but not all actors are thespians,' as the great Jacob Christi once said. Those in it for the art, however, have to be able to divorce themselves from their characters; they have to be able to take a little vacation from themselves. Which is why everyone loves and hates Method Actors—because they're on perpetual vacation and can't turn it on and off. It's on and it stays on, until it's over. They live the part; they don't actually *act* the part.

"Now, the minute the individual steps out of character and says 'No, I will not do this,' for his or her reasons—and not for the sake of the character—he or she has failed as an actor. I regret to say that I haven't developed the ability to fully divorce myself yet. I still make distinctions between my life and my characters. For example, I'm more uncomfortable telling you the details of some embarrassing story when I can, in full comfort, discuss sodomy and other vulgarities as easily as if reading off a menu. Unless of course the menu is in French." Ulliver laughed again in Veena's direction, reaching for her hand as well, which she would have allowed him to take were it not accepting a fresh cocktail from the waitress.

"You shouldn't be so adverse, Bryne. This applies to you and your line of work, too."

"Why does everyone keep saying that? What does this have to do with me in the slightest?" As Treadwell's inflection and tone progressed through the course of their conversation from colloquial surfer to veteran storyteller to the elocution of a nineteenth-century dandy, Bryne became more and more confident this was all a script, and one that Ulliver probably used most often to get women to sleep with him; the only thing Bryne wasn't certain of was whether Ulliver was the script's author. He was also quite sure, based around Ulli's filmography (Cop 1, Cop 2, Surly New Yorker, Jailbird, Sports Dad #3, Abusive Step-Father in that MOTW, etc.) that Ol' Ulliver here probably hadn't attended any formal theatrical training, other than maybe an improv class

Tuesday nights at the YMCA. Bryne guessed that, much like the rest of this town, nepotism had opened the door for Ulliver, and had likely opened the door to this party as well—surely the nephew or godson of one of these titans.

"I'm not trying to tell you to divorce yourself. All I'm saying is that for all great art there is a pivotal point where you have to give up part of yourself to the art, an abyss you have to cross. I have a writer friend—well, had a writer friend—who says in order to be a good writer you have to be like Orpheus and plunge yourself into the underworld, you have to dig into the most terrifying and sordid recesses of your soul and try and transmit them onto the page. I'm sure the same goes for great painters and sculptors and I'm sure it applies to musicians, as well. You've got to give something of yourself over to the work if it's ever going to have a life of its own. And then you have to cut the umbilical cord."

Maybe it was the apocryphal authenticity of the speech, maybe it was the smug vessel it came from, maybe it was the fact that he'd abstained from smoking anything prior to the party, maybe he just simply didn't like the ilk of his silk, no matter how you cut it, Bryne wanted to punch him, and he was not a violent man. The last time he had hit anyone (but not the last time he'd been hit) was almost ten years ago and his one punch resulted in a broken hand and an ass kicking from a guy who barely came up to his shoulders. Even during his high school tenure in the metal scene he'd never been big into moshing or slam dancing, opting to stay outside the ring of death at a vantage point that would allow him to watch the fingers of the guitarist(s)—which, considering his height, was more or less anywhere in the club, hall or basement. In Manchurian he'd never even flirted with playing the menacing frontman, preferring to play his guitar from the back of the stage, less out of playing the haunted, Pageian figure—the brooding source of their creative energy—and more out of stage fright and an almost paralyzing self-consciousness of his lanky appearance and awkward movements. "Imagine if Animal mated with Thurston Moore and the kid got really heavy into the heroin-steampunk scene," his old vocalist, Len Spazz, now fronting the rotating lineup of grind outfit Death Fissure, had described to Veena upon meeting her, always eager to hear stories of Bryne's mythological, dreadlocked past.

But no, to leave would be better.

Wade was over by the pool talking to a small group of people. After watching Wade for the last three hours, Bryne knew he was never going to find Wyatt vacant of company. And if he knew anything about Veena, he had about another hour before she'd start feeling nauseous and demand to leave.

"Veena, let's go talk to Wyatt. He's the only reason we came here and I don't want to leave without speaking to him."

"Wheredju think we're going?" she slurred.

Bryne wanted to say "Home in about an hour, less if you have another one of those drinks," but he held his tongue.

"I just think it's time we talked to him."

"You're the one who wants to talk to him. I've got nothing to say. I'm perfectly fine here, sipping my drink and admiring the view." Veena smiled and pursed her lips to the straw.

"Don't worry, Bryne, Ohl stai hea 'n' entertain the missus," Ulliver said, dropping into a horrid cockney accent by way of a Made For TV English orphanage.

"Oh, we're not married," drunken Veena ever wanting to be factual.

The idea of leaving Veena in lecherous reach of Ulliver incensed Bryne more than anything he could otherwise think of, but there was also the strong probability that if Veena accompanied him as he tried to talk to Wade she would make a drunken mess of herself and destroy why they'd come here in the first place. He would have to leave her, but hopefully not for that long.

— § —

"Excuse me, Mr. Wade," Bryne reached for the man's shoulder over a smaller, Italian man on Wyatt's right flank. An extraordinarily tall Japanese woman stood to Wade's left; an androgynous rotunda of an individual dressed in white, overtly bland clothes with blond bangs that came down to his or her bespectacled eyes stood across from Wyatt, closing the gap. Wyatt had told Bryne to call him Wyatt, but as they hadn't yet met in person, it didn't seem appropriate. "I'm Bryne Dogan. I spoke to you on Thursday…"

Wyatt turned and smiled at Bryne as if he'd known Bryne well enough to pick out his musk. "Bryne! Glad you made it, m'boy. And please, *please* call me Wyatt—I'd rather sound like a famous cowboy 'an a pensive swimmer." Wyatt, who was surprisingly only a couple inches shorter than Bryne (Bryne thought he had a "short" voice over the phone, a Napoleonic cowboy), pulled him into a very cordial hug and, upon releasing him, turned back to the crowd with his left hand draped over Bryne's chest, "Folks, this the man who's score we jus' heard on *Nos-fer-a-tu* las' night."

There were a couple nods and some minimal chatter. Bryne started saying "How did you..." before realizing who he was talking to and shut his mouth.

The tall, Japanese woman nodded gravely to Bryne. "I thought the score made the film splendidly tragic. I felt for the vampire, as if I'd carried him in my own womb and suckled him to my breast." She seemed to hold that last word longer than the others; or maybe it was just Bryne's imagination. More likely it was the fact the dress she wore threatened to reveal the sustained word at the slightest breeze.

The Androgynous broke the spell, speaking in an alto that gave no further evidence of the speaker's gender. "Personally, I didn't enjoy it at all. I found it too grating and self-indulgent. Maybe if you raised it by a half-step it would work for me, but as of now I can't applaud it."

"Posh." Wyatt's voice was so percussive the bristles of his moustache trembled as he spoke. "If it don't just scream o' Nietzsche for you 's rubbish."

The Androgynous shrugged in concession; the Übermensch indeed.

"Now, what where we talkin' 'bout?"

The Italian man was about to speak up when Bryne cut him off, "Actually, Wyatt, I was wondering if I could briefly talk to you about the work you did for the new *Battleship Potemkin* ReMa?"

Bryne could tell by the reprimanding scowls on the faces of Wyatt's friends that this was not a subject they wished to discuss, nor something for Wyatt to discuss. And even in Wyatt he noticed a shadow of discomfort cross the man's face, like being forced to recall a treacherous voyage where not everyone made it back alive, and those that did make it back weren't necessarily the lucky ones.

"Yes, well, I s'ppose we'd better." Wyatt nodded, as if he really were the eponymous cowboy, hell-bent on justice, sent out to meet certain death on the streets of Tombstone, if not for honor then for a sense of duty. The others objected but Wyatt put up his hand. "No, I've got to. Be back 'fore you know it."

Wyatt draped a hand around Bryne's shoulder and ventured outward from the others along the side of the infinity pool whose water was a bizarre desert orange.

"What's going on with the water?"

"Oh, damn thing's broken. And I jus' had her installed two months ago. Damn Grubl piece a shit." He raised his hands above him, "My Kingdom fer a Competitor!"

"The pool?" The pool looked very high quality but judging from the spiderweb cracks in the corners of the concrete it looked as if it had been at the house for some time.

"Not the pool; the lighting system. I got one o' them systems reads the body o' whosoever swimmin' in't, and, through a series o' LEDs, phosphorescent nano-chemicals an' some other such science talk, changes the color to the color o' the water you want t' be swimming in." Bryne looked confused so Wyatt continued. "Say you wanted t' be swimming in the Mediterranean off the coast Ibiza, it'd turn 'at exact same color green. Or if'n you wanted to be 'n the dark blue o' Maine..."

"So how did it end up orange?"

"Somebody must've gone 'n an' wanted t' swim in the apocalypse; which should 'ave been fine, but it ha'n't changed since. Forebodin' don't you think?"

"Bummer," Bryne said. "So about *Potemkin*—"

But Wyatt cut him off, "Unfortunately, Bryne, ain't much I can tell you. I didn't make it very far in't—well, in a way I did—*very* far into't, too far—but I never came up 'th a full score. Tha's why I quit."

"Quit? I thought David said he fired you, well, not fired, but 'didn't accept your score' were the words he used."

"Did he now? Can't say I'm too surprised."

"So what happened?"

"I happened." Wyatt chuckled, plucking a strand of hair from his lash. They were facing out towards the valley, the view broken up by alternating layers of smog and smoke.

Bryne looked at him with a strong sentiment of confusion.

"What I mean is—and I'm sure you're going t' find out you stick with it—you get to a point where'n you really ain't just scoring some ol' black and white film; you ain't scoring some concepts that you want t' get across—I'm guessing David sent you a list o' somethin'r'other to that effect?" Bryne nodded. "What I mean is, what you're looking at, what you're trying t' create, i'n't jus' a piece o' soundtrack or jus' a film."

"What is it? I mean I only vaguely remember the political ramifications of the film. I guess I could do more research…" Bryne nervously adjusted his hat.

"I'm not talking 'bout the goddamned politics o' the film. I'm not even *talking* 'bout the film. You get me?"

"Not really. I'm trying, though."

"I'm talking 'bout something darker, something more profound. You hit th' wall. Jus' think back to 'at ol' quote 'bout the abyss from the philosopher Kai's been so lately obsessed with. Least this new phase o' his is better 'an his Pyrrhonic phase. 'At one was a nightmare I tell ya!"

Wyatt continued, "Now, all m' friends tried to convince me it's cursed or some such hogwash—an' if you've talked t' Kronopolous he's likely t' agree with 'em. But here's the thing, ain't no curse or ghost or supernatural thing going on. Contrary, what happens is very real, as real an' cerebral as you're ever going to get, boy-o. And 'at right chair 's the problem."

This was not the kind of explanation, or help, Bryne was hoping to find. Couldn't anyone just come right out and say what the hell they're talking about? "Look, I guess what I really want to know is what kind of score were you working on? Was it more experimental? Is that what you're saying?"

"Bryne, my friend, you ain't listening t' me. You've got the youth an' persistency inherent t' ride this here project down t'your last drop o' sanity. At's why I know even if'n I asked, even if'n I pleaded with you t' let this go, even if'n I paid what they're offering, you'd still continue."

Bryne disagreed with that last part, and hadn't felt nearly the obsessive stirrings Wyatt described—at least, not in the way Wade was describing. Not yet at least. He wanted to know what Wyatt was talking about, wanted to press on from the vague and abstract towards something concrete—hell, even a "stay away from anything half-diminished" would have been a treat at this point. And he was just about to ask for one concrete example, but a quick glance towards the patio and the now empty table beckoned him to investigate Veena's whereabouts instead of further investigating the vagaries of Wade.

"Ahh shit."

"See, I think you're startin to get it," Wyatt smiled, clapping Bryne on the back.

"No, it's not that, my girlfriend is missing."

"Oh," Wyatt hung his head, embarrassed for Bryne, "happens to the best a us, my friend. Why I never put the ring on—'cept for those two times, a course."

Bryne thanked Wyatt for his help and the invite and excused himself; Wade said something as he left, but it was in Japanese and went right over his head.

Bryne entered the house through the open patio where the servers kept buzzing in and out of. Passing through the doorway, he narrowly missed the Implanted waiter carrying an especially loaded tray of those fruity libations, skirting the server only to hear him suffer another twitch; Bryne turned back just in time to see the entire tray spill onto the head and lap of the Aporianettes' drummer. Hopefully his dry cleaner was more practical than theoretical.

Inside, the house embodied the same architectural coldness of the exterior; where he was expecting Remington sculptures and paintings he found nothing but modern decadence and technological flare, nothing of the Cowboy vibe he'd imagined would inhabit Wyatt's abode. The hide of a spotted cow draped over the brown leather couch in the living room and a pair of Navajo-inspired huaraches with black, yellow, red and turquoise beads hanging from the wall made up the most "Western" accoutrements in the whole house. Bryne pushed on through the house, searching first the bathrooms, then bedrooms and finally opening the door to Wade's secretary's office.

"Vee?"

"Hey, baby!"

"What are you guys doing in here?" Veena was sitting at the desk with Ulliver draped over the chair pointing out something on the monitor in front of them, everything seeming to be on the level: meaning clothes on and hair still in the last place he'd remembered. Judging by the redness in her cheeks and the glossy tint to her eyes, she'd had another cocktail during his talk with Wyatt.

"Guess what? Ulli's got a book he wants to me publish!"

"*Americaland Refugee*," Ulliver offered. "It's a working title."

"By—who's Will Slaughter?"

Treadwell shot her a look as if it was a daft question. Though between Will Slaughter and Ulliver Treadwell, who could say which was the more plausible pseudonym?

"He's showing me the first chapter."

"Just the tip," Ulli winked.

"I'm sure he is, babe. But I think we should get going."

Veena started to protest, then hiccupped and changed her tune, realizing it wasn't long until gas wasn't the only state of matter leading an exodus from her stomach. He'd gotten Veena halfway to the door when Ulliver called to them from the desk, "Virginia Woolf. That's all I'll say."

"Ah ha!" Veena shouted, smiling and pointing an accusatory finger at the actor, before turning back towards the door and irrigating the potted ficus in a fertilizer no botanist would ever recommend.

"Ohhh-kayyy...Let's get you home."

They were halfway down the hall when Treadwell shouted after them, "Call me!"

— § —

Maybe it was the mounting pressure of the ticking clock, or maybe something inside Wade's enigmatic admonitions had provided the kindling, whatever the final impetus was didn't really matter, what mattered was that the spark had taken and Bryne finally felt the flames of a true creative fire take hold.

He'd sent David some demos, as promised, of the few audio tracks he'd recorded thus far, early incarnations of the amalgam score. David, unfortunately, hadn't been too enthused, though he'd phrased it in a very supportive manner.

"You know, when Rash and I first thought about offering you the contract after hearing your early *Nosferatu* demos we said 'God, just think of what a guy like Bryne Dogan could do on *Potemkin*!' We wanted that Bryne Dogan treatment, you know? So far, I gotta say, this just doesn't feel like an authentic Dogan to me."

"Oh, don't worry, Dave; this was just the first idea to gauge where you're at. Believe me, I've got plenty more ideas cooking. None I can send right now—still all in sheet music form—but don't worry, you'll get that Dogan brand on it soon enough. All part of the Process." Then he'd hung up and spent the remainder of that day figuring out just what in the hell the Dogan brand was, and the Process, for that matter.

Now, though, his most pressing task was trying to figure out how to blend the Western components and the Eastern components of his galvanized score, which he felt, somewhere in their melding, would yield the alchemy he's been looking for. He took up a deck chair and spent the morning flipping through the pages of theory books from college left to yellow in a cardboard box in the basement, contrasting them to the books on Indian and Arab music he'd picked up a couple days after talking with Wyatt. Despite Bryne's disappointment, he'd been spurred on by Wade's esotericism, and was hoping to find out what in the hell the composer had been trying to tell him, figuring the only way to do so was to completely submerge himself into his work. Apparently ignoring the important parts of Wade's advice.

He had always felt the thesis of Western music—and something his theory teacher had verbalized for him—was all about the creation and resolution of tension, of an expected anticipation of both. Western music's progressions and cadences were designed around the anticipation of the dissonance: the dominant-7ths; the diminished and half-diminished chords; the subtle differences we notice when hearing an IAC compared to a PAC (Imperfect Authentic Cadence and Perfect Authentic Cadence, respectfully)—to say nothing of suspensions, tritones and chromatics. They had described the different cadences as musical punctuation: the Plagal-cadence as a semicolon; the Half-cadence as a comma, a transition that doesn't close or complete an idea but moves into a tangential thought; the PAC having the finality of a period (the IAC a period at the end of a fragment). The language of expectation had inundated Western culture for the last four hundred years. He thought, maybe Eastern music carries the colons or the parentheses, the ellipses or the m-dash. But there were challenges in the consolidation. The alphabet was different, for starters; the twelve tones of the West versus the twenty-two of the East. Where he had half steps between acceptably differentiated tones, they had quarter steps. Would it be possible to merge the two and form a conclusive, definitive language? Is there a musical Rosetta Stone that has the East, the West and the amalgam? Was there music in Babel, a whole from where the two styles diverged?

After pouring over multiple books looking for an opening to crack the oyster, he found an entry point, a place to bridge the two worlds. He would use several heptatonic *melakarta* of Carnatic music, *ragas* that focus on *madhyama* in *sadharana*, then gradually move the *madhyama*, the fourth, from perfect position (relative to tonic) to the *prati*, an augmented mode. Bryne could use the *katapayadi sankhya* circle and go from the *Rutu* variations of numbers thirty-two through thirty-six (*ragavardini* to *chalanata*) then switch to thirty-seven (*salagam*) in the *Rushi* and explore those numbers, using the differences in the *ārohana* and *avarohana* to make the shifts. Or, he could use the *chalanata raga* and interpose the *prati* to transfer it to the *rasikapriya raga*. Then interpolate the score with the *thāt*, blending the emotion of the *raga* with the emotionless *that*: implying both rules and breaking both rules. He would then blend that with a Western key. D Mixolydian with the *chalanata* and *rasikapriya* starting on D, too, perhaps? Or would A be better? No, D, definitely D.

All this research was starting to give Bryne a headache, the kind that can only be cured by the inhalation of high-THC marijuana; luckily he was pharmacologically flush at the moment. He brought the book Holland had given him, the *Codex Gig-Acs*, out onto the deck and began looking through it as he smoked, resolving that there was far too much talk of mathematics and physics and hardly the relaxation, or inspiration, he was looking for. Yet he continued reading. The abstract opened with a discourse on the sounding board of a piano and on the fundamentals of sympathetic resonance, two principals, the author informed the reader, whose basic conceptual understanding was necessary before undertaking the rest of the book. The abstract then went on into the realm of advanced calculus for which there was apparently, unexplainably, no prerequisite, as if all musicians (of whom the book was assumed to be the primary audience) were as familiar with physics and integrals as with the pentatonic scale and the sixteen-bar blues progression.

After scanning a few more paragraphs, he laid the book on his lap and used the flat surface as a table to roll a joint.

Bryne Dogan was a Flower Grandchild through and through. Like many children of the Free Love Generation, his parents had disavowed the lifestyle of the Flowers that pollinated them, always quick to dispel any endemic "hipness" from their lives, and, aside from their wine collection, generally led a chaste and upright existence. Both were engineers: his mother, a professor of mechanical engineering at Berkeley; his father, head of R & D for a private firm in Oakland that developed construction equipment. In fact, it had been their mutual interest in engineering that had sired and named Bryne, his parents having met each other at a summer internship with the venerable Brynehoffer Industries. They'd waited until they were in their 30s to have kids—only the one, it would turn out—waiting until they'd won the opening gambit of their career aspirations and with it modest financial stability.

And maybe it had been his parents' rejection of their parents' lifestyle that had pushed Bryne into music in the first place, falling into the great ironic cycle of many families with a history of rebellion. The childhood visits to his mother's parents' ranch in Sebastopol were acute indulgences in the artisanal, from the hand-churned ice cream and saltwater taffy to the candle-dipping and free-association painting sessions his grandmother led every afternoon. (These visits would later become his first forays into the realm of the psychotropic; aside from their homemade kombucha, his grandparents also grew, harvested, cured and baked their own marijuana—hell, the first time he'd done mushrooms was with his grandfather at the Solstice Drum Circle they hosted!) But more than any other indulgence on the farm was that of music. Records—and we're talking 140 grams of wax or more—were constantly rotating on and off the turntables. Aside from the gap between flipping and brushing the next side, there was rarely a silent moment in the house; and even then, someone would usually take up the slack by whistling, be it human or bird. It was only a matter of time before those indulges started stowing away with Bryne on his trips home.

III. SETTLING A SCORE

His parents had been initially worried when he'd returned from one visit at the age of twelve with his grandparent's guitar and a freshly tie-dyed haircut, like a virologist forced to take a parking stub from an attendant with blotchy, rice-paper skin seeping fluid out of his sallow face as if a pipe had broken inside, exclaiming, in congested lisp and inflated tongue that "he muth be cubbing down with a colb." And they'd been absolutely petrified when the albums evolved from jam bands to the airborne pathology of punk and metal, when the records changed from The Dead to Green Day, from Metallica to Slayer, Sleep to High on Fire, expanding beyond the Bay down the coast to Tool, Intronaut and Carry On before taking that great road trip cross country, picking up Pantera and God Forbid in Texas, moving into the bayous of Thou, Eyehategod and Down, a deathly dip into Tampa before rerouting north to Georgia's Mastodon (where he started his side family with hip-hop, beginning with Atlanta's Outkast), up the Appalachians into North Carolina's Horseback and Between the Buried and Me—and into a tangent of other prepositional bands—continuing along the shore into Virginia (Clipse) and the entire Richmond, VA scene, up to DC's Darkest Hour (Little Brother), Philly's Turmoil (The Roots), through New Jersey's Dillinger Escape Plan, taking the Staten Island ferry (Wu Tang) into Manhattan's Krallice (Big L), over the Brooklyn Bridge to Candiria, Anodyne and Tombs (Gang Starr, Jay Z and Talib Kweli) (moving deeper into Long Island for an extended stay in Queensbridge with Mobb Deep, Nas, Cormega and Kool G Rap (Queen's A Tribe Called Quest introducing him to the immortal beat poet, J-Dilla, and sending him down a parenthetical trip to Detroit's Slum Village and Black Milk)), sidling back up the mainland to All Out War, working around the Sound to New Haven's Hatebreed, blowing his ears wide open upon reaching Massachusetts with Isis, Cave In, Converge, Unearth and The Hope Conspiracy (Made Men) before stamping the passport of his first European tour with Black Sabbath, Electric Wizard, The Ocean, Cult of Luna, Opeth, Decapitated, Meshuggah, Behemoth…a brief foray into Nordic Black Metal until realizing the recurring threads of anti-Semitism didn't really jive with his maternal lineage…on to Japan's eerily occidental Boris…diving into the dangerous waters of Australia's Portal, New Zealand's Ulcerate and Tasmania's Xul…flying back home by way of the Pacific

Northwest's Botch and Wolves in the Throne Room, crawling down the coast to Yob before finally settling back home in Oakland's OM.

He had taken quickly to the guitar and gradually expanded his range of instruments to include the bass, the drums and the keys, but never vocals. He started a crust-core band, Manchurian Candid Hate, in high school, playing shows in basements and dives of the greater Oakland metal scene. Such is the nature of the empirically ugly: it was a time of staunch virginity for Bryne and the other members of the band. And while he acceded Manchurian would soon hit its half-life (if it hadn't already), he truly thought his future lay in on-stage musical performance; and he thought studying Jazz Guitar Performance at USC would drop him right into the Los Angeles post-metal scene, a scene he hoped would provide the chrysalis for his impending musical monarchy. But plans, it seems, are big proponents of improvisation.

As it turned out, jazz was pretty cool after all; he'd only embarked on Jazz as there had been no Metal option at the time and he thought jazz would at least make him better at soloing and expose him to more "fucked-up sounding chords" than the Classical or Studio options. Within the first semester his teachers had opened his ears to a world he'd always heard of but never truly appreciated, starting him down a general path of sonic, spiritual and artistic exploration—a different haircut for each leg of the trek. They started him on the standards—Dizzy, Bird, Armstrong, Brubeck and Bassie—before moving on to Miles Davis and John Coltrane, which would provide the jumping off point into virtually every other subcategory of jazz. He hung posters of John McLaughlin and John Abercrombie on his walls; they didn't exist, unfortunately, a problem indicative of Jazz's greatest threat, obscurity, so he had to make them. True to form, Miles and Trane segued Bryne into a deep sojourn of the free- and acid- varieties of jazz, turning him onto Alice Coltrane, Pharoah Sanders, Sun Ra, Ornette Coleman and Yusef Lateef, which paved the way for his appreciation of composers like John Cage, Steve Reich, Terry Riley and Philip Glass. His girlfriend at the time had taken that propulsive ball of kinetic open-mindedness and steered it into her world of jam bands; pretty soon Bryne was crunching and grooving barefoot to the sounds of Moe, String Cheese, Umphrey's McGee and Phish, taking disco biscuits at Disco Biscuits, dropping out with the Drop Out Boys.

Then, one fortuitous night-in, he was introduced to Angelo Badala-menti's work via an acid-fueled David Lynch double-feature of *Blue Velvet* [Lynch, 1986] and *Mulholland Drive* [Lynch, 2001], followed up a few weeks later with a Cronenberg residency on his TV that introduced him to Howard Shore. From there he was on a tear of film scores, diving ear-first into Morricone and Mothersbough, Green-wood and Elfman—Wade!—Marianelli and Giacchino; he'd actually taken the time to transpose and perform Trent Reznor's electro-hyp-notic work on *The Human Animal* [Gorman, 2007] into a guitar and cello duet he and a friend performed at a local coffee shop. The fire for music was still there, but the blaze had changed direction; he switched majors from Performance to a BM in Composition, still keeping his minor in Accounting—if he'd learned anything from the underground music community it was that you should always have a real vocation to fall back on. The completion of his BM automatically ushered him into their Scoring for Motion Pictures and Television one-year gradu-ate program and his work was some of the most talked about, if not always the most applauded.

So there he was, freshly graduated with two degrees, making a name for himself as the go-to guy for student filmmakers looking for that off-the-beaten-path score, diving into the electronic music scene on the side and interning at a production company when it hit, the Big One, the Cascadian Quake. It was so immediate and sudden and full no one had been able to even prepare to prepare themselves to han-dle such complete devastation; the last words he'd spoken to any of his family had been "Yeah I'll give that recipe a shot" to his mom two days before. In the aftermath, months after, clearing first the cities and ex-panding outwards, they'd been able to find and bury his grandparents, crushed under the roof of the chicken coop. His parents, like most of the fallen, were never found, interred among the great wealth of rub-ble and chaos and water that marked the mass grave of a city and the paradigm of safety that never quite returned. He'd stayed down here ever since. No way to go back and nothing to go back to.

The life insurance in the form of a bi-weekly dispersed trust (his parents ever the engineers, even in death) made the burden of an un-paid internship manageable, and gave him a buffer when he quit to go freelance, earning a very intermittent living scoring commercials and shorts until landing his first ReMa. He promised himself when he landed his first ReMi he would start transferring the trust into one of his own, for the kids that would someday arrive, when he was ready, "And not a second before," he told Veena whenever the subject broached its bonneted head. But perhaps now, with *Potemkin*, there was the chance to do something more, something beyond the lines of simple career advancement and financial duty. Now was the chance to change the affect that accompanied every automated credit to his checking account, gradually conflating their memory with a fixed-interest disbursement. "Survivor's Guilt," a psych-major ex- of his had said once; "Survivor's Debt was more like it." But, if *Potemkin* worked, if he was successful and created something powerful, something even half as epochal as Eisenstein's film, wouldn't it be possible to usher in a transubstantiation of that money into something deeper? Work into honor? Loss into tribute? Pain into love?

Though self-assured he was on the right track, there was still a nagging need to hear the other side of the coin, to hear Kronopolous's take on the score and see if that could further illuminate the path whose flagstones Bryne could at least now make out. Still, he wanted to see the full path, down to the grout.

Bryne placed several calls to Michio Kronopolous before even making it through to his voice mail. The Greek-Japanese, first-generation American composer was known to be considerably less gregarious (publicly so) than that of Wade. A middle-aged man who didn't give his number out except to producers, agents, managers and a few select individuals should have made acquiring his number the most arduous part of the task—except for the fact Michio never answered. Luckily, another of those select individuals had a girlfriend who had published—and had made a killing—with Babbling Babylon Books and an address was secured by Veena, who Bryne was most-assuredly leaving behind this time.

Noon sounded like the most opportunistic time to try and catch the reclusive composer at his Beverly Hills home, and Bryne arrived a quarter-to on Saturday. The front gate was locked and the electronic intercom appeared to be covered in bubble gum and confetti, the

LEDs dark and non-responsive. Bryne walked around the corner property's gate and found a dip in the fence at the Southwest end a person of his height could easily scale, and Bryne did just that, scratching his shins and forearms on the fig trees bordering the property.

He made his way through the backyard garden filled with iron-and-glass sculptures and furniture, though the former looked more accommodating than the latter. Michio's "pool" was a pair of unconnected rings of water separated by twenty feet of patio space, circular moats each with a fifty-foot diameter surrounding fifteen-foot circular patios inset with uncountable inner rings of lapis lazuli winding around the fire-pits in each center: a pair of eyes, seen from above, and at least one with some virulent form of conjunctivitis. The first pit in one of the pupils was smoldering, spewing a tendril of black smoke and a noxious, toxic effluvium. Bryne pulled his shirt-front over his nose and mouth and jogged towards the sliding-glass door in the back.

After a couple quick, unanswered knocks, Bryne took advantage of the unlocked and slightly ajar door. The frame was well-greased and the door slid soundlessly. The house was quiet and dark though the sun was going strong overhead; the smoked windows were still set to dim.

"Hello? Mr. Kronopolous?" he called in his best Eddie Haskel, poking just his head inside. "Anyone home?"

With no answer, Bryne stepped inside the house, moving pensively from the kitchen entrance into the living room dark as the rest of the house, inching his way towards a side door near what looked like a fireplace when a voice spoke up from somewhere in the abyss: "The funny thing about pet owners is that they always prescribe their dogs, cats, hamsters such human traits with the glaring exception of responsibility; as if the act of owning a pet—which requires maintenance and money and the virtue of patience—allows the owner to slip from the identity of a human to the identity of the animal, free of responsibility but with all the same human attributes bestowed. We should give our pets their own pets, teach them something of responsibility, and just get this whole transference over with."

"Mr. Kronopolous?" He still couldn't see the figure, though he could tell the voice was coming from the couch he just banged his knee on.

"Please, Mr. Kronopolous was my mother. Call me Chi [key]," opting for a Greek pronunciation.

"I'm sorry to intrude—I didn't mean—it's just, I talked to Wyatt and he was so damned cryptic I just needed to—Oh, my name's Bryne."

"Hiiiii Bryyyyyne, " he said with the inflection of an infatuated teenager with a *Tiger Beat* crush.

"Right, well, I came here—"

"For *Potemkin*."

"How'd you—"

"Wade called me; he said you'd probably try calling me, too."

"So you got my messages? Why didn't you answer?"

"For the same reason I'm not calling the police and having you arrested: a promise I made to Wade; a 'duty,' he called it. And believe you me, Bryne, I had every intention of avoiding that duty. But since you clearly didn't take the hint from my voicemail, and seeing as you're willing to risk a trespassing charge pursuing this little quest of yours, I suppose I can't avoid it anymore, this 'duty' as he puts it. God, he really is just so hung up on this whole cowboy thing of his. You know he's from Burbank, right? *Hardly* the frontier."

Bryne moved towards the source of the voice, cautiously, unsure of his footing, the space or even the corporeality of the strangely muffled voice—images of Chi in a subterranean bunker, watching him on closed-circuit TVs and speaking via intercom cropped up in the ol' noggin. "Why a duty?"

"He thinks it's a duty for anyone involved in this project to forewarn the next person working on *Potemkin*. He called me when I took it over. Naturally, I didn't believe him until I saw—well—until later. And now I'm telling you, but of course you won't believe me, and you'll invariably end up telling your replacement this same nonsense."

Well with only a month left he doubted there'd be a replacement, should he fail. "What is it you feel you have to tell me?"

"I don't *have* to tell you anything? I don't *want* to tell you anything? If I did I would have picked up one of your hundred-and-twenty-seven phone calls! But since you're here I suppose I can't avoid it or I'll have to put up with more of Wade's diatribes on 'morals and responsibility.' Honestly, I feel like this will be the lesser headache."

Before he began, Chi directed Bryne to the opposite wall and the touchpad panel next to the bay of windows. "Use the dimmer and only bring it up to about seventy-eight-percent luminosity. Gradually, dear boy, gradually."

Bryne obliged and, tripping and slamming his knee into various obstacles, found the wall and the meter for the smoked-glass windows. As the light grew less and less opaque, Chi's house emerged from a world of off-blue darkness: phallic lamps that spat an upwards arc of glowing, incandescent pearls (each a blinding two-hundred-watts should they be turned to full voltage); a blown-glass coffee table of two, naked, female contortionists (where one could reasonably set a glass was a complete mystery); a tie-dyed leather couch; an installation piece by *avant garde* artist Yosenia Brafton, *Ghost in Translation* (a series of panels showing the input and output of a poor speech-to-text software); piles of clothes for all sizes and genders; a mechanical bull with Hawaiian Leis around its neck, horns poking through a sombrero pitched forwards in the direction of the foyer; on the ceiling, a mural mocking the Sistine Chapel, where God extended his finger not to Adam but to a vintage Beta video player; and finally, the living cornucopia, Chi himself, in full, Swiss, ski apparel—a pastel candy-cane dropped out of a 1960s Blake Edwards film sprawled across the couch.

"My God, aren't you hot?!"

"Conditioning. I'm acclimating by body to the heat. There's a retreat at Joshua Tree I need to attend, three days in the desert tripping on a fantastic assortment of entheogens. I don't want to ruin the trip for everyone by overheating."

"Naturally." Bryne stood awkwardly by the light-switch, unsure whether to move towards the couch, to continue standing or to try making an exit.

"Would you stop fidgeting and take a seat already? You're making me nervous, and getting nervous is just increasing my heart rate. Or are you trying to tack on murder to breaking and entering?"

Breaking and entering?! Wasn't it just trespassing a minute ago? Bryne lumbered over to the couch and sat on an edge of crunchy cushion near Chi's feet. "I didn't really *break* anything, the door was—"

"Do you know Alexander Shulgin?" Chi interrupted, still prostrate on the tie-dyed sofa.

"Like, personally?"

"Or his wife, Anna Shulgin? Though if you knew Anna you'd have to know Alexander."

"Can't say that I do," Bryne said, checking his cuticles for a patch of dirt or skin to pick at, some innocuous task to alleviate the awkwardness.

"Well, he was the pharmacologist who found MDMA, the 2C-family and a variety of other delicious psychoactive treats."

"I'm really more of a weed guy myself."

"To each his own. Doesn't matter. Anyway, I was reading through his books the other day. I can't remember if it was *PiHKAL* or *TiHKAL*—that's *Phenethylamines I Have Known and Loved* and *Tryptamines I Have Known and Loved*—respectfully, of course...books that focus on the couple's lives and their synthesis of psychoactive compounds. A romance of the utmost beauty, Bryne. You see, I'd been trying to cut out the middle man in my—well, my extra-curriculars—and started producing them on my own: such fun substances as alpha,N-DMT; MDMA; MMDA; DOM; LSD_{25}—LSA!; DMT...what else? ...TeMA. Those sorts of things. So I was reading the book—well not in this room—or was it this room? There was a TV, I remember..." He picked his head up and looked around to see if there was a TV in the room, of which there were multiple; he shook his head and laid it back on the pillow, "Could be—either way, it doesn't matter. So, I was reading and fell asleep while *Fantasia* [Ferguson, 1940] played. You ever watched *Fantasia* high, Bryne? And not high but *high*, if you catch my drift? Well, I was out of my gord on Amanita Muscaria watching it and I fell asleep with the book on my chest. And when 'The Sorcerer's Apprentice' scene came on it sort of infiltrated my dreams. Directed them, you know? I dreamt Mr. Shulgin was the sorcerer and I was his assistant. I watched him work in his laboratory, making all sorts of drugs that made your bones disappear, ones that made your muscles rubbery, ones that made your cock three feet long and seeping strawberry juice. And then, of course, Mr. Shulgin left, and it was just me in the laboratory. I became inquisitive and, still in my robe—we were wearing thick, dark robes, mind you—began grabbing all sorts of beakers and Erlenmeyer flasks and graduated cylinders dripping molar amounts of these beautiful drugs into test tubes. I stuck my tongue out and collected several healthy drops of this mysterious substance I'd created. Like collecting snow flakes. I remember it prickled; it didn't sting. No, it was more like Pop-Rocks on my tongue.

"Strange, isn't it," he segued, "the sensations we supposedly 'feel' in our dreams? Oh well, moving on." Bryne could only imagine the sorts of sensations Chi might get into.

Chi continued, "I swallowed and nothing happened, at first. Then, as I was mixing a new compound, I began to feel all strange and tingly. I looked down and saw arms poking from my stomach; then came shoulders; a neck, a head, a whole body pulling out of myself, with my face and wearing an identical robe. The other Me went about making more chemicals and I, happy to have the added help, went about swallowing more and more of the drugs (I believe the dream took on a *Willy Wonka* motif at this point). Sure enough, more Me-s were popping out of my chest and out of the chests of the other Me-s. Carelessness overtook them, the Me-s, and they began knocking things over, breaking all sorts of glass and equipment. 'This won't do,' I shouted to them, 'Professor Shulgin'—as I had begun calling him in the dream—'will have our hides.' Of course, at that moment, I looked down at my hand and found I was holding a mallet, large and oversized, like something out of *Looney Tunes*. I smashed one of the Me-s, then another. But they kept coming back as more Me-s, then more and more as I kept smashing. I resolved that I had to create a compound to rid myself of them, but they were breaking nearly everything around me, filling up the room, suffocating all the air around the lab so that I couldn't breathe, couldn't move, and then..."

"And then...?"

"Well, I woke up of course."

"Of course." Bryne was growing really, really tired of finding his questions met with obscurities and eccentricities. At this point he was wondering if he was at fault for ever getting his hopes up. "Why are you telling me this, Chi?"

On the back of one of the women making up the glass coffee table Bryne noticed a green bruise on one of the kidneys, which turned out to be not an inconsiderate amount of ground marijuana, no doubt spill-over from a hastily rolled joint. Bryne pointed the pile out to Chi.

"Be my guest. I'm telling you because, in a way—in every way, or in some ways—maybe it's just me—but this is what happened, what resulted from scoring *Potemkin*."

"A bunch of You-s?"

"Yes. No. More, a confrontation of Me-s. It was all me—don't you see?—that I had confronted in the score. I was forced to contend with myself, with every iteration of me."

Bryne pressed the tip of his finger into the pile and transferred the shake to the One Hit Wonder. There was enough weed to pack the little bowl tight and full. He took a healthy hit. "Forgive me…for sounding…rude," he exhaled, "but this is a lot of the same cryptic nonsense I got from Wade. And to be honest, neither makes a whole lot of sense to me."

"It shouldn't, I guess; it won't, not until you've really immersed yourself in the score. Felt the full weight of possibility on your shoulders. Wade said it was our responsibility to forewarn the subsequent, and probably infinite, line of composers who naively take on the task. I tried telling him it was impossible to convey but he insisted—through various threats, if you can call them that—that I make an effort to warn you, should you contact me.

"I thought, 'Well if I just make it so you can't contact me, I won't have to tell you a thing.' But…" he spread his mittened hands in front of him, here you are.

"Look, all I really want is to know what kind of techniques you guys were trying? Maybe your scores were too similar and that's somehow what…went wrong, I guess? Can you understand, I just don't want to waste my time repeating the things you each did?"

"Oh Bryne, Bryne, Bryne, Bryne…do you really think our scores would be that familiar? That that's what caused the problem? Wade's a minimalist at heart; I am not. Do your research, dear boy." Chi swatted the air, the sound of his nylon ski suit swishing against the couch.

"If you'd just let me listen to what you had, maybe it would make more sense." For the love of God, Bryne kept from adding.

"No sense can be made, Bryne. The issue is entirely a personal one, can't you at least understand that much?" Chi fit a pair of goggles over his eyes and sat upright, alternately examining the fabric through the filtered lens and through his naked eyes.

"One track. If I could just hear one track. One *bar* even."

"Impossible."

"What? Why? How?" Bryne was getting angry, despite the weed.

"Because I burned all the tapes, all the data, silly boy."

"You burned your work?" Bryne's mind did a smash-cut to the burning toxicity near the pool.

"I had to. You obviously can't understand. Perhaps you should put down your herbal recreations and pick up something more mind-opening, something that will stimulate your pineal gland, perhaps. Perhaps," Bryne waited for him to add something but Chi never did.

"How could you burn your data? I mean if you wanted to get rid of the score, at the very least you could have just deleted it."

"I needed the whole thing gone, Bryne," staring at Bryne through his goggles like some sort of Suessian Praying Mantis.

"I saw smoke outside. Was that it? Did you just burn it last night? Did you think I would come?"

"My, someone thinks highly of themself. This isn't a Bryne-centric universe. Look, we were having a splendid party and one thing led to another and when we ran out of firewood, well, I saw an opportunity to solve two of my needs." Chi swept the left wrist of his suit away and read the blinking blood-pressure monitor. "Right on track."

"Your guests must have loved that." Bryne was bitter. But could you blame him?

"Please resist the impulse to play the pissy child and try to come to the realization that I did it for your own good. Christ, were you this bad with Wade?"

Bryne cashed the little pipe and tapped out the ash on his jeans. Chi stood and looked about the room as if only now waking up, shocked by the light and the circumstances of the hour; he found a remote on the table, pressed a button and the veiling on the windows further dissolved into a burning, alien light. An urgency rose in Chi's voice, as if he suddenly remembered an appointment he had to make. "Well, Bryne, I think you're done here today. Please feel free not to break into my house again."

Bryne nodded, feeling to use words would only be an exhausting act of wastefulness. Rising and pocketing his still warm ceramic piece, he made his way towards the back door.

Chi cleared his throat. "Um, Bryne, the front door this time. And do mind Vincent on the way out. A gift from Otto after I scored his *Son of the Matador* [Hearst, 2002]. He's very sensitive—Vincent, not Otto. Otto has the temperament of a warthog, or a wart."

Bryne made his way around the mechanical bull barring most of the path to the hallway and slipped out the front door. The September afternoon had turned into a scorcher. Veena would probably be at Kersa's pool, sipping margaritas and listening to Kersa rifle through her new rolodex of PR clients she thought would make a better partner than Bryne. He thought about joining them until the impending October dead-line and the colossal amount of work still to be done made its way through the haze of his high as a clear and un-navigable obstacle.

— § —

Crunch time. No more day-time TV or *Planet of the Apes* marathons, *Potemkin* was on a perpetual loop in his studio. Three weeks left and he still had to finalize his sheets, book studio time and pick his musicians. More than that, he still had to finalize just what in the hell he was going to do for the score.

He'd made progress in the days since leaving Michio's, stretching his composite score further and further like bands of spaghetti, equally replete with empty calories. He hated his score, hated the entirety of his work on it thus far. There was no heart here. There was chaos and theory but nothing for the film or for the audience. *Potemkin* required passion and heart, and all he was serving up were passive head games. Staring at the computer screen, the dog-eared *Codex Gig-Acs* and the pages of staff paper scattered around the studio with nothing but contempt and shame, Bryne wavered his finger above the delete button, wanting the courage to depress the plastic tab and send his score to a binary sepulcher where he knew the music belonged.

Jesus, was it this hard for Sergei to make the damn movie?! He doubted it. And really that question didn't matter as much as the others plaguing him: Was it possible to back out gracefully? Was it too late to call David and say "Maybe this film is cursed, or maybe I just lack the talent to get the score done?" Could he somehow fake his own death and keep the advance and respect? Or just the respect? Or just the advance?

Bryne knew the answer to all of those, and when he got down to it, quitting was really not an option. Despite the obvious contusion to his career should he quit—Bryne thoroughly wanted to finish the score, to answer the challenge failed by Wade and Michio and prove his merit as a top musician, to be able to sit at the table and see his name written in gold calligraphy on the place setting. He wasn't void of personal connection either: the project had certainly taken him on as much as he had taken it on; he knew, should he quit, every subsequent score would be underwritten with a grace-note of regret, as indelible as the five lines on which the music would be written. Plus there was that whole transubstantiation thing, too! Let's not forget that.

Bryne's cowardice prevailed, and instead of diving into the delete button his finger performed a half-gainer into a save macro.

"Bryne, you about ready?" Veena shouted from the bedroom down the hall.

Bryne looked at his clothes, which appeared to be socially appropriate, meaning void of stains, "Ahhh yep."

A little dubious, Veena told him to come into the bedroom for inspection before they left for her boss's party; any simple task of Bryne's lately required supervision, he'd been so locked into his work. Bathing, shaving and general hygiene were the first things tossed out the window, dressing and feeding himself, the second—which spoke volumes about his state of mind as she knew his marijuana consumption had only increased over the past week and there was nary a burrito wrapper or spent sushi tray to be found. Otis looked like he hadn't left his cradle in what had to be at least two weeks, judging by the solid film of gray ash covering all four propellers.

Before peeling himself away and reporting to the drill sergeant, Bryne took one last look at the computer screen, one last look at the stacks of discordant lines in the cell block of his pardoned score, wondering, in all that mess, whether there was anything worth rehabilitating.

— § —

Russell was hosting his quarterly barbecue for the company, and though billed solely a social event, the party always ended up business related. It was a common, and unspoken, knowledge within the company that a good performance at the barbeque translated to raises, promotions or simply getting more high-profile authors. A competition whose true competitiveness had to be hidden under a façade of amicability: smiling and laughing while holding a knife behind your back. It was an understandably stressful event. Veena therefore rejected Bryne's attire of tank top and the corduroys he'd been wearing all week, forcing him into a button-down, slacks and a blazer. His dress fedora was similarly rejected and Veena dragged him into the bathroom to comb product into his hair and style his mop into something respectable. Bryne had protested all week, saying he needed to stay home and work, but, as Veena reminded him, she'd attended Wade's party for his career, so he was damn sure attending this party for her career—after all, an absent significant other was deemed a sign of weakness—even if it did give Russell an opportunity to make more passes at Veena.

Per usual, the barbeque started with amiable introductions to spouses, fiancés, etc., banal chit-chat regarding the occupations of the non-B³ guests and of finding a dessert that wouldn't melt or curdle in the heat, followed by invitations to the snack bar and drink requests, then dinner, shots of Sambuca and The Lighting of the Tiki Torches—which gave way to dessert talks of art and movies, which of course set the dialogue vector to a discussion of literature, and, like clockwork, finally to talk of the business. While Veena and the rest of their boutique band of marketers and A&R reps discussed earnings and potential clients and new marketing venues, Bryne found the trampoline and joined Russell's two kids, the three of them each wielding a firecracker popsicle—Bryne's of a THC variety.

By this time it was almost expected for the non-employees to take their leave of the sandalwood dining table in the solarium that had become the de facto conference room, and most gathered around the pool or the fire pit or took turns tending bar. Bryne, personally, was a little talked out and was happy to be away from their company for the moment, bouncing thoughtlessly along with these kids who wouldn't ask him about his current work or make well-meaning suggestions in a field they didn't fully grasp. "Why don't you just use Beethoven?!" "Beethoven? No, no, no, you should use DJ KwikS&—he's super hot right now!" "So it's like a mix of east and west? Like *Big Trouble in Little China* [Carpenter, 1986]? But in Russia?" "My niece plays the cello;

maybe she could write something for you?" He wasn't annoyed that they didn't understand the nature of his work; he was annoyed that they didn't understand that they didn't understand.

The kids, for their part, seemed to enjoy Bryne's company, too, if only for his willingness to double-bounce them. In high-pitched pleas they begged Bryne to use his weight to depress the trampoline just before they landed, resulting in a deeper, elastic snap that propelled them twice as high into the cricket-serenaded night. With popsicle syrup coloring the lips and fingers of all three, they popped up and down on the polypropylene screen like corn kernels in hot oil, each at his and her own frequency—though forcing Bryne's frequency to accommodate a double-bounce for every other jump of the youngest and every third jump for the oldest, giving both a double-bounce on every seventh and thirteenth jump. At the fifth and tonic, Bryne thought, arpeggiating a chord of the twelve-tone system with each of Bryne's bounces counting as a half-step. A chord in the key of Bryne: a Bm°7add$^{\sharp}$2, $^{\flat}$ 4,6,$^{\natural}$7. If only they had another to jump every three jumps and hammer home the minor third and the tritone of the diminished fifth. Or a big, fat guy that only jumps on the tonic, once every twelve jumps. Jesus, he thought, the *Gig-Acs* really could have included a chapter on trampolines: show me a better example of sympathetic resonance you can actually touch and feel.

He wanted a trampoline ten times as big, with enough people to jump at 8va and 8vb the thirds and fourths and fifths, one at 15va above the tonic. He wanted the trampoline to be as taught and laden with sympathetic potential as possible, a purely mechanical form of resonance. They would be the un-dampened strings and aliquot scaling of a Steinway's sounding board.

Bouncing along to the soundtrack of the kids' glee, Bryne went deeper, thinking about the sympathetic resonance in the fibers of the stretched canvas, in the springs attaching the tarp to the metal frame, going deeper still, down to the molecules in steel I-beams, to the frequencies involved in laser surgeries, to the pitch of water molecules amplified in the microwave—the built-in biological diathesis for resonance in all water-based life. He wanted to find ways of effecting resonance in his audience, of inducing a frequency (sans lethality) in their hearts and minds, manipulating their heartbeats like an inverted version of his iPulse DJ, which, on the ride home, went wild from Bryne's excitement and kept putting on metal upwards of 200 bpms, queuing up one of his old Manchurian Candid Hate tracks:

"BARDO BE THE SHIVNER"

They rode on the back of moonbeams,

Sweet Vairocana and Samantabhadra chomping at their heals;

Force fed by the scruff toward the Desert Eagle barrel of her cunt,

Positioned in her womb like a bullet:

Haloed be thy name (hollow be thy point).

Rag-choked and mainlining fumes

Leftover from the beer-battered ballistics that trickled down after,

She removed the safety and oiled the slide

While teams of marauding deities repelled 500 feet from the ceiling

And sequestered her Federal Reserve,

Matching faces with deposit slips,

Demanding routing numbers and

Pillaging the registers, shouting:

> *"The accounts are invalid,*
>
> *The accounts are invalid,*
>
> *The accounts are invalid."*

Veena shut the stereo off—before the breakdown, too!—and stared at Bryne with not a lack of concern, especially considering the circumstances of their exit, which could best described as...suspicious. Not until he'd made it down to the last licks of his popsicle did Bryne notice a curious absence of the indelible marijuana flavor even the best bakers and confectionists could barely mask in their infusions; and when the youngest stopped bouncing and said "I feel weird...like a big, fuzzy balloon," he'd quickly hopped off the trampoline, found

Veena and told her they needed to go—now!

"Stomach things," he apologized to the crowd, going no further into detail when he and Veena were back in the Jeep, leaving her baffled and a little worried as he sped down Sepulveda.

"What has gotten into you?"

"I got it, babe! I figured it out—*Potemkin*! I finally cracked it!"

Cracked something, she thought. "Goddamnit, Bryne, I told you not to smoke. It's my boss's house for Christ's sake! And-, and did you do a line with Ryan, too? I kept seeing the sneaky bastard dipping into the bathroom every fifteen minutes."

"Everything has a pitch, Veena. And the great thing about music is that with a Western lexicon we only have twelve distinct pitches to choose from, anything in the heptatonic system, which also includes some Indian and Asian scales."

"Jesus, slow down, Bryne."

"Oh, right, so, many Indian scales are actually pretty similar to western modes, just with a little tweak here or there—

"No, I meant on the road, you're going to kill us."

Bryne ignored her and continued, mostly for his own benefit, needing to formulate his ideas aloud in order to ensure their existence. "What I want to do, Vee, is create a layer of melodies and chords in every key, simultaneously! Each done on an instrument tuned to a certain key: guitars, basses, harps, pianos, drums, violins, violas, cellos...only *real* instruments. I want to put them all in one room, each playing their melody at the same time. Or no, wait, maybe what I want to do is put them all in one key and have each instrument tuned to a different note of that key, or to part of a certain chord." He paused and looked over at Veena, her mouth agape and eyes searching, "Why aren't you writing this down?"

He continued, despite no motion from Veena to take the dictation, "Record it. Phase them out. Cut off the attack maybe. Then do it for chords of a different key—every key! Blend it all together, right? Every key, every chord, every note. Record it in analog and then play it all back in the recording studio and re-record them together! Think about it, every possible option of sympathetic resonance will be achieved!"

Based around his frightening level of enthusiasm—a truly rare event—Veena let him continue; better out than in, she'd learned from past experiences.

"Or—*or!*—I'll have them all physically perform it, rent out a church or warehouse and segregate the different keys. Everything bouncing off everything. Everything coming together and coming undone. Imagine it, every minor-sixth possible played inside a cathedral with the same 5/8 ratio! Think of the architectural resonance we'd add!" Bryne took a breath as Veena continued staring at him in marked disbelief before rubbing his shoulder as if he needed consoling. He'd definitely not joined Ryan for key bumps in the bathroom; no, this was something else.

"I'll mix it all down to a soft, distorted fuzz played continually throughout the film. Just out of focus. Each person will hear something different, subconsciously picking out their own melody. It will come in waves, like, like, it will seem like some innocuous, static drone, then gradually they'll pick up a sliver of melody and then *boom*, like that it's gone again, off to some new melody, like someone's working a mixing board in their heads! An implied melody. Think about it, Vee, each person who watches the film will experience their own individual soundtrack! Their own idiosyncratic score! And a different one every screening! Think about it babe: it will create a limitless interpretation—no, no—a limitless *generation* of music. Ah ha—take *that*, Merv!"

And it's got the spirit of the original, Bryne thought to himself, after they'd returned home and he'd b-lined it straight for the studio—not even remembering to put the car in Park, which Veena had to do for him as it lurched towards the garage's shared wall with the living room. Veena, for her part, went straight to the cabinet for some aspirin and then to bed, leaving Bryne to deal with himself.

Bryne's discourse continued in the studio, subvocalized, though if you looked closely, you could occasionally see his lips moving. It's mutinous, it's contentious, it's revolutionary and now it's relative not just to one particular plight, but the plight of all! The score is transnational, transcultural—even transtemporal, if he be so bold—it appears as it wants to (as the audience subconsciously, or, hell, maybe even consciously, allows or dictates). His score would include all melodies and no melodies. The pure melody of the human spirit? Of God?—well maybe that's a little bold. Or wait, maybe that big, tattooed bastard from the Wet Whistle *was* on to something; maybe this was what he was talking about: an amalgam score; a collated composition. He should maybe try to bring Merv in on this. Later though, no time now; there was too much work to be done presently. Far too much work.

— § —

"*Hola, mi amigo,*" Holland spoke to Bryne's back, accompanied by a quick galloping knock of his knuckles on the door frame before stepping into Bryne's studio and the sonic maelstrom that assaulted him. From no less than at least eight speakers (the SoundBall™, both desktop monitors and at least one amp were the only ones Holland could confirm) came different parts of Bryne's "score." Overlapping melodies enharmonic and non-, polyrhythmic and non——speaking more to one's bowels than one's ears—emanated from a perimeter of speakers pointed centripetally towards Bryne, sitting on his knees in the middle of the room before a pile of books and crumpled staff paper. "My God, man. What pickled hell is this?"

After a moment of shuffling some more papers, Bryne finally turned and acknowledged Holland. "You ought to know, all that *Zaireeka* talk of yours. And that damn *Codex Gig-Acs*! Basically your idea, right here. Well, not fully, but, you know, they were the…" he moved some papers about in front of him, as if the word he was looking for was somehow written amongst the various clefs and chord structures, "…progenitor of it all."

Holland picked up one of the SoundBall™ speakers and held it to his ear, impossibly trying to hear a singular sound. "I thought you were going to try using music from various periods. This…this is…I don't know what the hell this is."

"Like I said, 'progenitor,' I've sort of expanded on the concept. On the whole concept of music, really." Bryne began to dig through resonance charts then scrambled to his feet and punched something into the computer.

"Anything I can help you out with?"

"No, not really; unless—do you read fan?" Bryne shot him an expectant look void of any sarcasm.

"Read what?" Bryne shoved a printed diagram into his hand with chords written around the edge in marker:

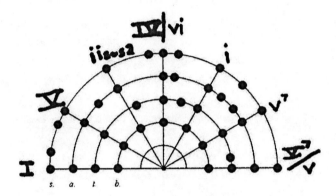

Bryne shoved a printed diagram into his hand with chords
written around the edge in marker.

"But...but what is it?" This was one of the few times in his musical history that Holland had been genuinely baffled.

Bryne shot him a disappointed frown, as if it should have been obvious, "It's a Bottle Organ, George, played with a fan. You fill the bottles up to hit specific frequencies, using different-sized bottles for different notes, suspended in padded, wire hangers and arranged from bass to soprano. The fan sweeps back and forth, playing it one way, then the reverse. Like a musical palindrome—although, it's not really the same forwards as backwards, not this one anyways. See, a PAC one way becomes a Half-cadence the next; suspensions become anticipations; appoggiaturas resolving upwards one way, downwards the next. Look, look, there's even a 3-against-2 polyrhythm in the i-v^7 wedge. You see? You see?!"

"Um, yeah...But, like, what happens if you're fan doesn't open all 180-degrees?"

"Well ideally you'd have something like the Grubl Blade—a fan with a beam—or else you'll have to make an adapter. And if it's not 180 then you adjust, squeeze it in a little tighter."

"I don't remember seeing this in the *Gig-Acs*."

"Oh it's not. This one's my own invention. Radial counterpoint, I'm calling the technique."

"Um, far out," George set the diagram down and continued on to the next exhibit in this museum of madness. Bryne went back to the pile of notes in the middle of the floor.

"Good lord, this sounds like the noon parade march at the gates of hell."

Bryne looked up to see which nightmare-scape Holland was standing in front of. "Ahh haha, you're not far off!" He'd taken a sample of the new Death Fissure album Len had sent over, *The Scales Beneath the Flesh*, a concept album about the Cabala of Reptoid overlords ruling Washington with a slimy, green fist, and slowed it down to 33bpms, phase-shifted to the frequency of the mothership's thrusters.

"Jesus, what bpm is this?" Holland had moved down the wall and had his head bent to the AC30 spewing sounds like that of a coke-addled microprocessor out for a night on the town.

Bryne squinted in his direction, flaring his nostrils as he thought, trying to remember which score he'd sent to the amp. He raised his hand when the answer came to him, "Three-thirty-four."

"Fucking hell!" Holland's voice actually approached normal amplification.

"Yes, but wait 'til you hear *this*." Bryne clicked a button on the computer then looked to Holland, who was waiting for something to happen. "Do you hear it?"

"Hear what?"

"Exactly!" Bryne turned the volume up and the floor began rumbling. "Negative-thirty hertz! I've moved beyond audible sounds; I'm all about feelings now. About *internalizing* the music. Come." Bryne picked up a remote and motioned for a pensive Holland to follow him out of the studio.

They moved into the living room where Bryne had arranged two four-by-twelve Marshall cabs and three Ampeg fridges (with their price tags still dangling from the handles) in a ring, enveloping the microfiber couch and bullying the rest of the furniture. Bryne made a couple quick finger movements on the remote and the sound—the noise and vibrations—popped over from the studio to the set up in the living room. There was an immediate reaction; dolls of porcelain and glass deities handed down to Naveena rumbled suicidally towards the edges of shelves, tabletops and armoires. Everything immersed inside the terrarium of Casa Dogan was drowning in the waves passing through every cell and membrane of entities cognizant and not, the alive and the inanimate alike entombed in this sonic sarcophagus, prepped and bound by Bryne standing in the middle of the room, twirling and laughing as the inaudible ghosts of melodies moved about the room: poltergeists *moving* the room.

"Jesus man, turn it off. Turn it OFF." Only twenty seconds had passed, certainly more than enough for Holland to gauge the terrain of this new path of Bryne's, and certainly more than Holland would have ever liked to hear. "BRYNE!" he had to yell, but still to no response.

The tinkling of broken porcelain and the image of an exploded, hand-painted Shiva were what made Bryne finally hit stop, bending to attend to the broken heirloom and cradle the jagged pieces in his hand, uttering a profoundly quiet and drawn-out "fuuuuuuuck."

In many ways, Holland was relieved by the broken doll.

"This is the second goddamned time this has happened. The first time Veena was sleeping and I tried to pass it off as an earthquake. She didn't buy it then, either." The first piece that had fallen was an eight-inch figure of Christ (arms outstretched in an embrace, Sacred Heart exposed) her grandmother had been given by the missionaries who'd sponsored her arrival into the states in the 1950s; and for a moment, Veena had raised the dagger-like arm of Christ and advanced upon Bryne with the malevolent righteousness of the crusades.

Holland stood behind Bryne, gratefully looking down at the pieces that had saved him from that auditory malebolge, still trying to regain his balance and assure his organs all was right with the world. "Why didn't you just remove them?"

"Huh?"

"Why didn't you just take the pieces down before you started playing with this...this...whatever the fuck you're playing with?" Holland had settled back into his soft voice so as to set his world right.

Bryne rubbed the back of his head. "Hmm, guess I must have been distracted."

— § —

George helped dispose of the remains, finding a nice receptacle (his empty cigarette box) for the shattered deity before guiding the bereaved Dogan towards the deck and possibly, hopefully, towards a fresh round of medication. He thought they could both use a dosing.

While Holland dug through Bryne's cabinet of paraphernalia for the appropriate piece of glassware, selecting a vintage, three-foot, triple-percolator PURE (simply named Ralph), packing the bowl and topping it generously with kif, Bryne sat in his deck chair like a child waiting for Dad to come home and dole out the impending punishment. At first, Bryne refused to smoke, saying that getting high would only aggravate Naveena more, that there was too much work to do, that he felt awful and wanted to feel awful. Holland's persistence, or maybe Bryne's internal discourse, got the better of the increasingly fragile refusals and Bryne eventually gave in. They sat there quietly smoking for a while.

"So what the hell was that in there, man?" Holland said after the bowl had been cashed and he'd drummed the opening bars of Zeppelin's "Heartbreaker" with his fingers on the side of the pipe.

Bryne's pupils were dilated to their max, focused on the horizon like he was trying to read a street sign in Plastícea, "Everything."

"Ugh, doesn't that just feel wrong coming of your mouth?" Holland was inadvertently holding the bong in both of his hands, pointing the top slightly towards Bryne as if the pipe were a microphone.

"Everything in the sense that the music is everything that music can be, and at the same time all that it isn't; or, I guess, all that it could be, elevated beyond the standard means and thoughts of music. I wanted to make music something…something…" Bryne trailed off as a scab on his forearm usurped his attention, "How in the hell did this get here? Huh." He shook his head and continued, "Something physical, you know? Like, I wanted music to switch from being *affective* to being *effective*. Like, instead of the old tricks I'd've used for tension—stingers, mu chords, ninths—I would manifest the tension internally! Give them the raw materials and let them build their own tension, a tension that plays inside their muscles, in their organs, in their actual beating hearts, man!" Bryne tapped his left breast for emphasis, well away from his heart.

As can sometimes happen, the kif high sparked a sudden detour through paranoia and Bryne went on the offensive. "Wait a minute, how are *you* criticizing me, Georgie-boy? Johan Sebastian Aquaman?!! Of all the people who'd appreciate it, or who'd at least *understand* what I was going for, I would have thought you'd be leading the freaking parade."

"But that's just it, man. If *I'm* saying it's too much…" George brushed some ash out of his silver hair, streaking some of the white strands and dulling the luster.

"I mean, all I've done is take what was in that book of yours—along with some stuff from a couple of other books—and with some of my own, you know, like theories and shit—and just combine it, tweak it, in order to come up with this."

Holland began cackling, "Holy moly, I've created a monster."

"Hey, man, I just want to do for music what Eisenstein did for film."

"But Bryne, there's *music* and then there's that. What you got in there, man, it's something different—I'll give you that—but, man, in the spirit of full disclosure, I came about to the absolute brink of shitting myself. No joke." Holland had leaned in, speaking just above a whisper—even for him—so Bryne knew it must have been true.

"But don't you see? That means its working? That score was for the 'Men and Maggots' section—I *want* people to shit themselves. Well, not really, but I do want them to feel that kind of disgust and internal distress, so—well, yeah I guess I do. Sympathetic resonance!"

Holland looked horrified. "Do I even want to know what you've got written for the stairs scene?"

Bryne flashed him a devilish smile Holland had only ever seen on Svâto Sckoufias before—who both were convinced, though they'd never shared it with even each other, had been Mephistopheles in a past life—well, that or Richard Nixon, either/or. He let the look expire, his face settling back into its normal shape. "I'm not finished with it yet, George, not by a long shot. I mean, I'm close, but there are still so many possibilities to explore to get it right, just right. I have to craft the layers to better exploit the audience: their histories with the film and with the music; their knowledge of musical styles; can they hear the Carnatic *ragas*? are they familiar with the 'minimalists'? do they have an understanding of the film's history, or are the scenes personal enough for the audience to swing the mood this way or that? It's the Kuleshov effect, but with music, man! *That's* the future!

"I've been reading this author Vee's working with. His stuff's, well, actually not any of his own, but that's besides the point. He's got some ideas, George. Actually, you might like him."

"What's that supposed to mean?"

"Nothing, he's just very…progressive—er, regressive…technically. Jesus, it was a compliment!" Bryne leaned forward in his chair. "Regardless, that's not the point. The point is we've reached the end of this era of music, man. I'm all about the future now, and you should be, too." Bryne ended with a hard look at Holland, expecting nothing less than the man to rise to his feet in enlistment of the cause.

Holland merely blinked, shrugged and began looking for more marijuana.

— § —

Since Bryne had taken to spending almost every waking hour in his studio or at the kitchen table pouring through books, making diagrams and calculations on everything from legal pads and newspapers to the back of the electric bill and the table itself, Veena had given Bryne some distance. Quite a bit of distance, actually. She worked extra hours, ate dinner with friends and clients, went to sleep at an earlier hour, only making contact with Bryne when she wanted a status report or to check if he'd eaten. Shaving had gone completely out the window, not that he was ever much of a beardsman to begin with, a soft blond heather covering his face like a hairy archipelago. She already knew he wasn't sleeping; Bryne hadn't slept in their bed but once since leaving Russell's party (and certainly no other bedroom activity), and unless he was getting in an occasional nap on the sofa while she was gone, that made it at least two weeks since he'd had a decent night's sleep.

Last week she'd walked into the studio only to find the ground covered in flour, speakers rumbling at tectonic frequencies. She'd taken half a step into the room when he'd shouted "Don't come in here! I'm trying to find the cymatic shapes of the score!" And she'd withdrawn her foot and refrained from asking any further questions about the work.

But what was really nagging on Veena was Bryne's inattention to her absence: never a "where have you been?" or "why didn't you call?" or even a "should we send Otis out for Chinese?" What made it even worse, what she was really scared of, was the lingering possibility that he might actually prefer her gone. To the point where she even found herself suggesting—though she never thought she would—that he smoke some pot and relax, take a break and visit with her.

"Ahh thanks, babe, but I don't have time to smoke," he'd responded cheerily a few days after she'd chewed him a new asshole or seven for breaking her grandmother's Shiva figurine and stuffing it into an American Spirits box. (As a very vocal hater of all things tobacco, Veena thought it odd there was an empty pack in the living room trash bin, opening it only to see if this was one of Bryne's latest additions to his carousel of oddities or if he'd merely used the case for joint transportation, certainly not expecting to find the shattered family heirloom.) This bubbly disposition of Bryne's in all this madness made Veena wonder if maybe he'd switched from pot to lithium. "There's simply too much to get done."

If his refusal wasn't so un-characteristically Bryne, Veena would have been otherwise pleased with his ambition and newfound sobriety. Such as it was, Busy Bryne was unpredictable, obsessed and so disturbingly chipper and wound-up he exuded a pink noise of anxiety and discomfort into every nook and cranny of the house, like a nest of mosquitos hiding in the air ducts.

On Saturday, Veena told Bryne she was going to meet up with Kersa for brunch, hopefully leaving Bryne enough time alone to finally finish this fucking score. The house to himself, Bryne took full advantage of the space, pushing out all the furniture in the living room so that he could better map his final studio plans and play with more acoustic experiments. He made diagrams of how he would set up the space: an outer ring of timpani drums each tuned to a different note, several doubled-up in the diatonic key of D and at the dominant, some even tuned to the quarter pitches of the *ragas*; in the next ring, baby-grand pianos fixed with aliquot scaling not on just the high strings but on every string, rubber stoppers inserted in several to "tune" it to D, another round of stoppers in several other pianos to facilitate reverberation of the fifth and seventh; fifteen guitars tuned to open-D, five with capos on the fifth fret, another five with capos on the 12th; violins, violas, cellos and double-bass, each tuned to open-D and fixed with an EBow to keep them vibrating at a low volume, establishing a drone and prepping the atmosphere. Sarangis, sitars, hardingfeles, gottuvadhyams, bazantars and an h'arpeggione similarly tuned to D; a hurdy-gurdy with a mechanized wheel to keep it constantly in motion. He placed the stringed instruments in the centermost ring, sounding holes centripetally facing the speaker suspended from the ceiling. He would use a damaru to sound the AUM: striking both triangular sides of the hourglass-shaped drum (male and female, delta and nabla); he would then isolate them, striking the *lingam* and the *yoni* individually, then add chorus or a flanger with maximized speed and depth...an oscillation of *sabda* and *asabda*, sound and non-sound, a going-in and going-out of being. Bryne, be-clad in tiger skin, would take the trident into his hands, and with grand, sweeping gestures, supplant the role of Shiva, bringing these frequencies in and out of existence.

Other pages lay spread before him of various theory and chord structures: a diagram of the Circle of Fifths, inset with a triangle showing triad relationships within the circle:

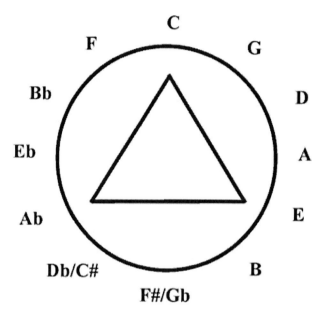

Other pages lay spread before him of various theory and chord structures: a diagram of the Circle of Fifths, inset with a triangle showing triad relationships within the circle.

Other copies of the diagram penciled in with squares showing $^\varnothing7^{\text{ths}}$ and hexagons which produced an assortment of dissonant and otherworldly messes with one fell polygon: $G^\flat$ m7($^+$5)add4add6, $E^{\varnothing}$7add4add4, $A^\flat$ m7($^+$5)add2add4, $C^{\varnothing}$7add2add6, etc., a chord made from the entire hexatonic whole-tone key; Prometheus chords both inclusive and beyond the Elektra and mu variations, with hand-written labels such as 'Leviathan' scribbled inside the shape.

But how to isolate the produced sound of his symphony? Piezo pickups fitted to each instrument, graphic equalizers and pink-noise distributors, preamps, phantom-power boxes, noise-gates (both open and closed), several condenser microphones and cardioid microphones run through filters to cancel out the originating frequency. (Or does he keep the original? Keep the feedback and the amalgam frequencies?) Moreover, he would need a space big enough to accommodate all this. Maybe one of the Pre-Fall studios owned by Sony or MGM or Paramount. It will be expensive, surely. Two-grand-an-hour, maybe more. He'd have to petition David for the money. But would he pay? Of course he'd pay. If not Bryne would have to fund the rental on his own dime—more ammunition for The Great Transubstantiation.

His new plan for the "Men and Maggots" sequence included inverting a sound and hard panning it across from the original, creating the feeling of a bunch of squirming worms crawling through the meat of their brain. But how to work that in with the rest of the score? He'd figure that out later.

Back to the primary score. He would need an instrument to keep a pulse, to denote some kind of rhythm and pace. Then he would need to shift the pace to different tempos depending on the part of the film—

"How's it coming?" Bryne hadn't heard Veena enter. She stood at the edge of the living room, fidgeting with her doggy-bag, looking, *trying*, to be optimistic. "You almost finished?"

"Are you kidding me? Does this look like I'm done!? No, just some more plans, sweetie. Prep work." He winked at her and went back to the notebook in front of him.

Moving into the kitchen, Veena deposited the tin of Eggs Benedict in the fridge—how she'd reheat the dish she'd no idea. She grabbed a beer out of the fridge and went back to the living room, leaning against the door jamb. "So, you'll never guess who we ran into today. Ulli Treadwell! You know, that actor from Wade's party?"

"Uh-huh." Bryne remained bent over a stack of notes.

"Yeah, me and Kersa were eating on the patio and I saw him walking by. He stopped over to say 'Hello,' and then Kersa invited him to have a drink with us. Remember how he was talking about writing a book? Well, he said he'd been approached by a couple publishers, but that he'd give me first dibs if I wanted."

"Uh-huh, that's nice."

"Looking really sharp, you know?"

"Yeah, grab me one next time!"

Veena heard the pencil resume its scratching. "Umm, yeah ...so he said if I wanted, I could go over to his place and pick it up." She gave him a window to respond, or to at least stop writing, to give *some* indication that he was still there, lurking inside this shell. "I was like, 'sure.' So I ditched Kersa and went back with him. He showed me the manuscript...showed me some other things..." Nothing? "Showed me his big, fat, steaming cock."

"Oh that sounds nice, babe."

"Yeah and then of course I just dropped to my knees, put that ol' cock right in my mouth. Sucked it clean, too! Got his whole cock right up in there, balls down to the molars." Her heart jumped as Bryne sat up, then deflated as it was only to compare two sheets of paper he'd stuck together to see how the diagrams overlapped in the light. "Yeah, and then, you know, he sucked *my* dick. Then he sucked on my tits, all four of them. Gave him my pussy..." pencil still scribbling, "then my ass"—which should have at least made the pencil jump, that orifice being one he's been trying to gain access to since they'd started dating. "And then the Martians came down and everyone was fucking and sucking everyone. I think Eleanor Roosevelt was there, too, working the camera—"

"Ahhhh! Jesus Christ, Bryne, if I was talking to a goddamned wall it would have perked its fucking ears by now!" She threw the beer can on the floor, giving absolutely zero fucks for the suds seeping into the rug, infusing the room with an aroma of cereal malts, pineappley mosaic and dank simcoe.

Startled more than anything, Bryne stopped writing and looked up, but only looking at her as if she were a child asking a riddle he didn't have time to answer, "What is it, honey?"

Veena slumped against the door frame into the puddle of beer, either not noticing or not caring, rolling her head to signal the director to cut, this take had gone on long enough. "Fuck, Bryne…" She wiped her face, laughing neurotically. "*We* haven't even had sex in over a month."

"Oh, is that what this is about?" Bryne began unzipping his fly.

"NO, THAT'S NOT WHAT THIS IS ABOUT!" Bryne zipped his fly back up. "Well, it's about that, and everything else. It's about you, and me—and *us*! More than anything it's about all *this*," she pointed to the swath of lunacy surrounding them. "What is all this, Bryne? I mean, I've seen you work before—I've seen you obsess even—but never anything like this. Never on this scale."

Bryne bent to add a new note on the *ragas* before returning his gaze to Veena, apparently waiting for her to pick up a ball that was very clearly in Bryne's court. She shook her head incredulously, aghast at his silence and unwavering cheer. "Are you even there?"

A cauldron of exhaustion, confusion, concern, fear, heartbreak and anger boiled over and tears joined the cheeks still fluttering up and down in hysterical laugher. "Tell me, in the course of your day, how often do you even think about me, Bryne?"

At this, Bryne walked over and wrapped her trembling frame in his arms, kneeling beside her in the beer, stroking the back of her head as she sobbed into his shoulder. "Of course I think about you, Vee. I love you." He pulled her head back, cradling her cheeks in his hands, smiling a deep and earnest smile, rubbing away the tears with his thumbs before leaning in and kissing her forehead. He pivoted to her right side, keeping one arm draped over her shoulder as he picked up a nearby sheet of paper with his other and brought it in front of her. "Now, take a look at this, I have each instrument set up so—"

"AAAGGHHHH!" Veena pushed him off her and stood up "What is WRONG with you?!" When the look he gave her promised no answer, or even receipt, she ducked back into the kitchen, snapped up her purse from the counter and stormed towards the garage. "You're a shit, Bryne, a fucking shit."

She put her Auto into Agro mode and the hybrid left a bacon stripe of rubber on their driveway as she peeled out.

An Organ!

Yes. Could he find a church with a good organ to use? Hook up Piezos to each of the pipes? No, that might interfere...He'd be better off using condensers at the output of each pipe, which would cost more, sure, but well worth the price. If they had a choir maybe he could record them singing, drop the pitch to below 18 Hz, where it can only be felt, see what sorts of psychological effects the human voice could produce when brought down to those depths.

And what if he arranged them into different cymatic patterns?! Would that have an effect on the sound? If the auditory has an effect on the visual, could it go the other way?

And if only the film were in color he could have matched the audible frequencies with their respective visual overtones: an A at 440 Hz to a yellow at 483,785,116,220,000 Hz; an orange for the major fourth of G; and so on. Music is just diluted light, he thought. Or slower light, light you can hold and morph in your hands. As the score is written in D, would it be too much to ask them to put an indigo filter on the film?

— § —

David called three days after Veena returned from her weeklong furlough at Kersa's—Byrne had called her at four a.m. the day before her return, apparently returned to his wits, pleading with her to come home, that he was sorry and didn't know what had come over him, that it's this goddamned score, but it's over, it's *almost* over, the end is within sight, and he'll be angry if she wanted him to be, that he *was* angry, at himself, at the project, that maybe this was what Wade and Chi had warned him about, and such and such, ad infinitum. Veena returned after work the next day and was surprised to discover that her half-serious expectations of finding the house in utter shambles—or burnt to the ground at this point—were unfounded, at least from the outside perspective. She came in through the front door, expecting to find the interior covered in a layer of flour, with Bryne dancing naked in the middle, head shaved and doing his best Brando from *Apocalypse Now* [Coppola, 1979].

But she'd found none of that. In fact, the house had been vigorously cleaned (an outsourced job most likely—still, that showed initiative, for Bryne); and not only was there no scent of weed or extinguished flames but the smells of dinner wafting from the dinner table (most definitely outsourced), set for two with candles and a bottle of wine. Bryne had showered and shaved as well. They ate and drank and talked and eventually went to bed where they screwed like soldiers home from war—taking out the full spectrum of their emotions that had amassed since their last time together, well over a month ago. Then they cuddled and talked some more and eventually fell asleep in each other's arms as the pint of ice cream melted and dripped off the nightstand, gluing her slippers to the floor with a raspberry sorbet bonding.

Things went well the next couple days. And then the call came.

Halfway through her week at Kersa's, Veena had placed a call to David, leaving an irate and desperate message with his secretary, demanding to know what more they needed from Bryne, when the project would be over, when they could be rid of this and go back to a normal life. David had never gotten back to her. And, after returning home to Bryne's fugue of apologies and the promise that he was close, so *goddamned* close—just a couple days away, she'd forgotten all about the call. Making a few concessions herself, she allowed that there would still be a few more days of Bryne holed up in his studio, putting, as he said, the finishing touches on the piece. As she'd tried to put that week behind her—as well as the two bottles of wine she'd had before making the call—Veena didn't recognize the unsaved number when the call came in the Sunday morning of her return.

"Hello?"

"Hi, this is David Ricciardelli. Am I speaking to Naveena?"

Suddenly filled with the embarrassed pangs of intoxication recall—that "oh shit, that really happened" moment—Veena felt her face flush as she sat up straight and spat out a fastball of apologies. "Oh, yes. Sorry. Hi, David. Yes, yes. Sorry about the call the other day, I was…a little worked up, as your secretary probably told you. And please apologize to her for me, too. It's just, Bryne and I had some issues—frankly, and don't take this the wrong way, issues stemming from his work. It's fine, though, he assured me he's almost done. And it really won't be a moment too soon, David. Oh my God; I'm so sorry; I must have sounded so neurotic."

"Hmm, ahhh...see, that's sort of why I'm calling. I didn't get your message until just recently because I was out of the country...Odessa, actually...for a premier screening of the one-hundredth anniversary of *The Battleship Potemkin*." David left a considerable pause there, a hanging static he must have deemed pink and hoped Veena wise enough to read.

"I don't understand; Bryne's not finished with the score, how could you have premiered it?" Veena left the kitchen and went into the living room, looking at the closed door of Bryne's studio, hearing the madness behind the door, willing all of her neurons to focus intently on David's next words.

"That's really why I'm calling. You've hit the nail on the head ha ha. Bryne never finished the score. It was due a month ago; we even gave him a couple of extra days to get the final score to us but he never produced. He never even called us back, as a matter of fact. We had to go with the original Miesel score, remastered of course. So if you could have Bryne return the advance at his earliest convenience that would be great."

Now the pause was on the other end of the line; David broke it this time, "Say, ah, you wouldn't happen to know if Bryne talked to a Wyatt Wade or Michio Kronopolous at all, would you? Hello? ...Veena?"

— § —

Two double-red-eye coffees pressed on Bryne's bladder and forced him to temporarily abandon the studio. Veena was sitting on the armrest of the sofa, phone pressed to her ear, brows bent in that trademark "V" of worry. Probably Russell wanted her to follow up with some difficult client, maybe even Merv. Before turning down the hallway towards the bathroom Bryne shot her a wide smile, like a zealot at the rapture, and held his thumb and fore-finger a centimeter apart to suggest he was on the absolute verge of finishing his work, which may or may not be a lie—Bryne didn't really know. He felt close to finishing, yet every time he got within feet of the finish line he found some new facet—through research or experimentation—that absolutely had to be included. This was to be perfection; this was to be his masterpiece. Of course, he hadn't actually recorded anything for the final composition yet, hadn't sat down in the control room with his instruments at the ready, hadn't even obtained the instruments for that matter. But that would come later. The trick was getting the idea of the piece completed in his head, the concept, and then, and *only* then, flushing it out into a real recording. Cheaper that way, he reasoned.

He pissed quickly then spritely made his way back to the studio, bouncing on the balls of his feet. Veena was off the phone, slunk into the sofa, staring at the carpet; maybe something was wrong with one of her relatives—her aunt had recently been diagnosed with Alzheimer's. He'd comfort her soon enough, when he was finished; there simply wasn't time now. Speaking of which, he still had to watch the film again and note the markers for the tempo cues. Maybe he'd drop in an allusion to John Cage with a tempo change at the four-minute-thirty-three-second mark—or maybe just a few seconds of silence. A little bit of esotericism for the truly observant and dedicated. Are there other allusions he could employ? He'd have to do more research. Perhaps something from Odessa itself, or just Ukraine if he had to broaden the search. Isn't Mykola Lysenko from Ukraine? But then the question is whether to focus on his piano music, which is much more classically oriented (à la Chopin), or his vocal music, which is of a folk derivative? Then figure how to work that into the nature of this score. Maybe if he just found a local instrument from Ukraine and worked that in with the others? Bryne looked for a notebook or a blank sheet of paper to write on, found a partially marked piece of staff paper and began scribbling notes into the margins. Maybe he'll use that instrument to play both a Western and Eastern piece of music, so that the timbres match, a bridge for the two worlds, a road. The Silk Road to the Orient!

Yes, maybe he could try and record silk, or try and record something that might sound or remind the audience of silk, of the gateway to these two worlds. And maybe, yes, maybe, just maybe, he could find…

REEL FOUR:
THE APOCRYPHAL BODY

"It is art's task to make manifest the contradiction of Being."
—*Sergei Eisenstein*, FILM FORM

I. THE PHANTOM PENANCE

"I brought you into this world, and by God I can take you out!"
—Parents the world over

I.

It was supposed to be a routine operation—just a quick in-and-out—but all was ruined with a hyperallergenic sneeze and the removal of the cornerstone piece of anatomy that entitled "Big" John Johnson a man. If only that had been the end of it...

— § —

You see, Dr. Gabriel Aranda had just recently moved in with his girlfriend, who'd been withholding access to the more adventures parts of her body until they'd moved into that DuPont brownstone she'd had her eye on; which meant Aranda acted swiftly, though not necessarily carefully. And unfortunately for the hyper-allergic cardiologist (to say nothing of the ill-fated patient or the litigation-averse landlord), the maid service hired to clean the apartment, having been slipped the high hard one before by both the landlord and tenant decided not to dispose of the bounty of cat hair, but instead balled it up and stuffed the Cheshire cantaloupe as deep into the master bed's central air duct as their slender Eastern European arms could reach (hoping for a bit of that American justice they were always hearing about).

Not a week had gone by before Aranda began sneezing uncontrollably and watering about the eyes, popping Claratin like Tic-Tacs and never leaving the house without a pocket of tissues. The doctor, and (now ex-) girlfriend, of course scoured the apartment for traces of mold or pollen or the ghostly follicles of a four-legged beast with an affinity for yarn and scratching but found no plausible culprit(s). Aranda asked (accused) the landlord whether he'd been as diligent as he'd contractually promised and had the apartment professionally cleaned, or had instead pocketed the money like the low kind of person Aranda thought him to be. Aranda made very specific threats of lawsuits, which the possibly-illegal landlord promised he'd do just about anything to prevent. "I've got surgeries to perform, god damnit. I have *li-i-i-ives* to save, you base baffoon!" And yet despite the healthy recompense for saving said lives, Dr. Aranda chose not to ride out the domestic ordeal in the sterility of The Willard: out of pride, and obduracy.

Now, the consummate sneeze occurred after a solid week's worth of exposure, as Aranda went to make the angiogram's initial incision into Johnson's leg and—perhaps instigated by an acute reaction to the halogens or the dislodging of a stray hair—perhaps simply the expectation of the sneeze was enough—whatever it was—the precipitate was a most vicious nasal eruption that sent Aranda's hand flying x-wards in a horizontal guillotine.

Big John was awarded only one piece of luck that day: he had been fully anaesthetized and was not awake for the procedure. And what was perhaps most astonishing yet, was that—like the decapitated of olde—after the fateful slice, the head continued to blink.

— § —

Waking groggily, and to what he hoped was an answer to his frequent chest pains, Johnson instead found himself greeted not by his wife of eight years but by an obsequious Dr. Aranda sitting on the edge of his bed, holding Johnson's hand in his lap. "Mr. Johnson, good morning, sir. And how are you feeling today?"

Johnson noticed the centripetal rings of suited men and smug nurses standing behind the doctor, "Confused."

"Mr. Johnson, there's no easy way to put it so I'll just come right out and say it: there's been..." he turned towards the ring nearest him, waiting for the paternal nod of his lead counsel's chin before continuing with the approved rhetoric "...an incident."

And maybe it was the sizzle of the word's sibilance but it was at that moment that Johnson noticed a peculiar tingling in nether-regions and made a horrifyingly empty scratch with his free hand at his Johnson's Johnson. "What the..."

Jenny Johnson—who had been apprised again and again of The Situation, and more so of the faultlessness of the physician—pulled her husband's hand away from a second groggy investigation and coiled it within hers. "We'll get through this, honey. We'll-, we'll make it work." Big John turned back to the doctor.

"You see, Mr. Johnson, I am a man of honor, a man who believes in the convictions of man, of their inherent decency: so when I entrust a man to his word that he will, say, clean an apartment I expect it to be done and done thoroughly, now—"

As a matter of security in what will already be a considerable malpractice settlement, Aranda's lead counsel, wearing the Martha's Vineyard whale-pattern bow tie his wife, Mrs. Bernard Flanagan, Esq., had gotten him for this year's father's day, cut Aranda off before he started digging with dynamite. "What my client means to say, Mr. Johnson, is that during the surgery, to which you'd elected to undergo [holding his admission form in a plastic bag], a situation arose which proved effecting to your person and is, at this point in time, irreversible. Having discussed the matter at considerable length, we have resolved to award you a monetary compensation for your loss."

"What loss? Honey, what loss?" The anesthetics were operating locally, and allowed only a short-wave buzz of information to reach his head.

"Your-, your-, your *penis*, dear." As if the word were blasphemous.

"[gulp]"

Understandably, there was a considerable moment of shouting and screaming and cursing in languages that were English and of Mr. Johnson's own invention; even a few of the more seasoned nurses found themselves taken aback by some of the more creative installations. While Johnson was preoccupied with his paroxysm, Aranda leaned in to Jenny, "Again, Mrs. Johnson, my apologies, but all of this all could have been avoided by the diligence of a certain landlord taking some goddamned responsibility," surreptitiously slipping the landlord's business card into her hand. "I hope you find justice with the truly responsible parties."

When Big John had fully expunged his anger and calmed down (?), he took a deep breath and addressed the doctor in a more hospitable manner. "Where is it, Doctor? I want to see it, please. I-, I would like to say goodbye."

It was as if the whole room had pulled the collar from their collective throat.

"What? What is it?"

"Your penis…" Aranda began.

"What about it?"

"There's no other way to say this: I'm afraid your penis is gone, sir."

A beat. " 'Gone'? What do you mean 'gone'? I mean it couldn't very well have just gotten up and walked away!"

"—", all.

— § —

The Penis had no sooner hit the floor of the operating room than he'd stood, stretched his youthful body, and high-tailed it out of the OR and into a life of his own: unshackled from the burden of Big John; finding himself, for the first time since college, limitless; staring unblinkingly at all the potential the world had to offer.

Once clear of the hospital's automatic doors and the threat of pursuit, The Penis caught his breath and took up an easier stride. He strutted down Pennsylvania Ave alongside the mall, taking in the warm summer air and admiring the coeds from George Washington University tanning themselves on the Washington Monument's neatly trimmed landing strip. Feeling the freedom to mingle of his own volition, the Penis didn't hold back, winking at the first girl that he passed, a fourteen year-old with pig-tails and freckles who shrieked and ran for the emergency phone. Afraid of incarceration after only an hour of liberation, the Penis scrambled and fled for the cover of the M St. Bridge, making his way into Georgetown, the waterfront and another batch of young talent.

— § —

"Now, don't worry, Mr. Johnson, we've put your Penis on a No Fly list and instructed the Megabuses not to pick up any suspicious Packages. He's not going anywhere," another be-suited man, whose lesser cut of cloth signaled law enforcement, informed him.

"But how did you lose it?!"

Aranda's nurse chimed in from behind the litigious barricade, "I looked everywhere for it, Mr. Johnson! Scoured the floor under the gurney, checked the corners, the hoses…it was just gone!"

"No, what I mean is how in the fuck did it just walk away?!"

"Well, now, sir, for the moment we're chalking that up to a real pickle."

Another lawyer stepped forward and cleared his throat, "An un-known-unknown, if you will."

Instead of asking what in the hell that meant, Johnson focused on something more prudent, "So, my penis is just wandering around DC? On his own?"

— § —

II.

"He's on the move!" Johnson burst from the crust of a deep sleep ex-actly one week after his discharge from the hospital. It was early PM hours; he'd been sleeping a lot lately.

Jenny came in from the bathroom, cinching her robe shut and drip-ping water from having taken another one of her long baths, a recent addition. "Who is dear?"

"My Penis. He's, he's moving! I can…*feel* him."

Before Johnson had been given his discharge papers, and his check and Aranda's promise that should he—or Jenny—need anything, *any-thing* at all, day or night, please don't hesitate to ask, the nurse had de-livered a stack of pamphlets on the towel resting over Johnson's waist: two on coping with the loss of a loved one and one entitled *What to Expect When You're Expecting Not to Feel a Tickle in Your Missing Limbs.* Jenny read from the inside cover " 'It is not uncommon for people, in the event of a separation, to experience sensations or 'phantom pains' in their missing appendages.' The doctor said you might experience these following the incident." "Execution," he'd corrected. Jenny had read the entirety of the crumpled pamphlet after picking it up from floor and, gently rubbing her husband's back, tried to recall what she'd read and offer some comfort, "Now honey, they said it's totally normal to feel—"

"This isn't like feeling cold on my veneers, Jen, or feeling a scratch on my shaft!—It's not *pain*, Jenny, it's-, it's *movement*. I can feel him...walking around, maybe in a park somewhere," he sniffed," somewhere where there is grass." Johnson threw himself from the bed he'd scarcely left since leaving the hospital, rattling the nightstand full of flowers and cards from well wishers: *Truly one of a kind; the world lost a real beaut!/Uncle Peter";* on a card whose cover read "Heaven Holds the Faithful Departed" his dad had written *"It'll get better, you just/have to take it one day/at a time, Dad/ 'Bigger' John Johnson, Sr.";* and *"Remember,/one may still lead an extraordinary/and even full life without the/element of sex. ¶ I mean, I don't even see what the big deal is anyway/ just a bunch of skin/slapping against skin/...sweaty, sweet, supple skin.../I mean sure sometimes/there are mounds/of tender meaty flesh/you just want to sink your teeth/into, but we're not savages/are we?! ¶ Frankly, I think we'd all/be a lot better off/without the* ~~desire~~ *burden of/that torrid, just really icky affair/Yours,/Father Pat/p.s. One of these days you/won't be able to refuse/seeing my model collection of Victorian bathtubs—/I've recently acquired a neo-gothic claw-foot you just have to see to believe!"*

"And where do you think you're going, mister?" Jenny pushed him back onto the bed and picked up the (formerly) frozen bag of peas that had fallen to the ground.

"After him, God damnit!" head lifting up against his semi-prostrate position; Jenny's hands applying compression to his chest.

"Ohhhh no; you're not to be going anywhere, buster; not in your state."

"But he's out there! If I can just find him..."

She stroked his forehead. "Now, babe, the doctor said even if we find him, too much time has elapsed; the tissue won't bond. You've got to accept it: he's his own Penis now."

"But, but—Oh God, is he? Is he?" Johnson's face flushed, growing splotchy and red, his eyes dilated and drew half closed, taking ecstatic, opiated breaths as his head oak-leafed back down to the pillow. "Oh, God. I think," his eyes went from half moons to new moons and back, "yes…yes!—I think he's having sex!"

— § —

And indeed he was. Recently the Penis had been shacking up with a single mother who'd found him curled on the stoop of a house one rainy day in Georgetown and brought him back to her rent-controlled apartment in Woodley Park. They bonded quickly, staying awake late into the night, sharing their feelings about each other's recent divorces. Beverly, as she was called, was quick to defend the Penis when her Ex had come by to take their daughter for the weekend, asking her if she "was really seeing this half-pint," to which she'd snapped "Yes; and he's twice the man you ever were!" The sex that had come over Johnson occurred that same weekend, when, despite an empty house, they'd decided to have an afternoon picnic in Rockcreek Park.

They brought a basket of aged cheese and a seven-year-old bottle of Kistler she'd taken off her husband in the divorce. With no mind to the neighboring picnickers, they kissed and petted and, not long after, he silently wriggled up her skirt and they began making love. When he was finished, they packed up the basket and started again in the empty apartment—which almost made Johnson spill his cream of mushroom soup at the dinner table.

Unfortunately, the romance was short-lived: the Penis, drunk on liberation and his first taste of a woman other than Jenny in seven [sic] years, pulled a real dick move and quietly slipped out of the bed the next morning: unseen and unstoppable.

— § —

Some three days later, after Big John had exhausted his sick and medical leave and was forced to return to work on the Lobby front, he experienced another ineluctable twang of ecstasy. It happened just as he was sitting down with the head of the Health, Education, Labor, & Pensions Committee, hoping to "influence" the Chairman into pushing through a bill that would allow fast food and pharmaceutical companies exclusive rights to advertise in children's text books. Upon feeling that oh-so-familiar rush of excitement, Johnson began rubbing his chest and moaning, grumbling "yes…yes…*yes*" until standing up and shouting "take it, take it, TAKE IT YOU FILTHY PIG!" just as his partner had begun telling the philandering Chairman to "take the deal and the girl's family is just as soon the owners of the best burro in town and welcome to all the McSleazy's Guatemalan customs can clear."

The next incident regrettably took place in the company break room while Johnson was pouring creamer into his coffee. Shortly thereafter, Johnson was kindly asked to work from home.

III.

It didn't help assuage Jenny's worries about the new quinoa risotto recipe she was trying that John suddenly doubled over in his seat, rushed to the bathroom and began vomiting.

"What is it honey?" biting her thumbnail with hope, "was it the chicken?"

"It's him, he's—yes, I think he's having sex with a man." And at that he roiled again into the porcelain mouth like a sparrow feeding an adopted pelican.

"What?! That's preposterous. How can you even be sure?"

"We were together for thirty-four years, Jenny. This is something new."

"I mean *we've* certainly never done it before, but how do you know he's not just, um, having—that kind of—with a woman?"

"I can tell; something about the diet."

"Oh come now. It can't be affecting you that badly. You two aren't even together anymore. I mean it's not as if *you're* having sex with a man."

Johnson's face soured further. "It's the principle, Jenny. It's like he's using my car to rob a bank. It's like he's cheating on me!"

There was a knock on the front door. Jenny left her husband and found Dr. Aranda standing on the stoop with a rose for Jenny and a bottle of Macallen 18 for the men. He'd been coming around often, trying to get on their good side and directing them—whenever the issue came up, which was a lot—that, again, the real perpetrator of all this suffering was that insipid landlord. He was also there to counsel Big John through his trying time, though he had no proper training and even his bedside manner, which you might have observed, begged overhaul.

"Thank God you're here, doctor; maybe you can talk to him."

Delivering the rose and bending to kiss Jenny on the cheek, his moustache digging into her skin, "What seems to be the problem?"

"It's John—well, his Penis—apparently it's having sex with a man and John isn't handling it well."

Aranda gave a stern, "I see. Let me speak to him. Where is he?" Jenny led the doctor to the bathroom where Johnson sat the toilet like many a college freshman.

Aranda came in and sat on the edge of the tub. "Hey, buddy."

"Oh, it's you. Of course it's you," Johnson was less and less happy of the doctor's pop-ins.

"Jenny tells me you're having some trouble coming to...*accept* some of the behaviors of your Penis." Johnson dry heaved; Aranda continued. "Now, what you have to remember Johnny, may I call you Johnny? I feel like we're there now—what you have to remember, John Boy, is that he's really his own Penis now. These are his decisions to make, not yours anymore. And as such, his actions reflect on him, not on you. Are the faults of the son the faults of the father? Of course not; how can they be? Especially if that son decided to squander every opportunity afforded him by his doting father, wasting years of private tennis lessons and tutors and apparently opting to take a giant piss on all of his father's ample connections for a career in 'meditation studies!' " He cleared his throat, "Er, what I mean to say is: Remember when you left your parent's home for college: no longer under your parent's control, you became a man. Well, buddy, that's what's happening here: you're Penis is becoming a man, his own person. Now, while you might not approve of all of his actions—and what father does!—you do still...*love*...him don't you?" Aranda's question didn't seem to be solely for Johnson.

Big John sniffled, "I guess."

"And don't you want him to be happy?"

"I suppose." Big John used the back of his forearm to wipe away the dribble from his mouth.

"All right then. Now what do you say we get out of this bathroom and help ourselves to that exquisite feast Jenny's spent so much time preparing? Maybe a snifter of scotch as well for us men?" Aranda led him by the shoulder back to the dinner table.

— § —

IV.

It hadn't been easy, but Johnson had gradually come to accept the Penis's behavior; or is perhaps coming to accept the behavior. As Jenny told him: "You've been a real trooper, hon!" But that was until the Saturday when Johnson, watching the US Tennis Open on his couch, was struck with an entirely new, and disturbing, feeling in his phantom self. A rough, grating feeling not unlike sandpaper. When Jenny came home an hour later, she found Johnson slumped on the floor, pale, crushing the macramé catalogues he'd ordered in his fists.

"Jesus, what is it sweetie?"

"I don't know! That's just it. The Penis, he's doing something I can't figure out. Something horrible."

"Him again? I thought we agreed just to let him be?"

"But—I think he's having his way with a tree!?" Panic creeping through the uncertainty.

"Excuse me?"

"A tree, Jenny! A goddamned tree! A-and this isn't the first bizarre episode I've felt, either. I didn't tell you this but, a couple weeks back, I suspected he was having sex with an animal. A, a goat if I'm not mistaken. Does any other animal bleat?"

"Oh, dear."

" 'Oh, dear' is right. What am I going to do? I mean he still has my name, my DNA, for Christ's sake—"

"Language, dear."

"Technically, it's me out there committing all these horrendous, lecherous atrocities. It's still my Penis, Jenny!"

"Well what can you do?" Getting thoroughly tired of the argument.

"I have to go after him. I have to put a stop to all of this. I brought him into this world, I can take him out."

"Well, technically he came with you at the same time but you just go get him, hon!"

— § —

The Penis, for his part, had been going willy-nilly with experimentation of all forms of intercourse, starting with the culinary circuit (jell-o molds, jelly donuts, warm biscuits and croissants), quickly followed up with the hot and steamy (used diapers, sewage holes, hot towels at the Marriott). Then there was the cylindrical obsession: toilet paper rolls, PVC pipes, the holes of a fountain in Columbia Heights, the organ pipes of the National Cathedral; the exposed sides to the rungs of monkey bars on a playground in Southeast. Tires, fences and certain types of ruffled lamp shades were thrown in the mix. Traffic cones, waffle cones, snow-cones. He wormed his way into concrete holes where the rebar had fallen out. He found holes of a more surgical variety: stomas, tracheotomies, abscesses. He hit the road: getting road-head, road-kill, road-signs. Road-ways!

It had become a Penis sans ego and superego: a raging id, serving coitus to all willing, unwilling or incapable of cognizance let alone consent. And at each digression, Johnson was struck hard in the stomach with the pangs of responsibility and the torment of unseen pleasures.

And when he would invariably get caught, the Penis would extricate himself and shuffle on down the road, finding street vendors and hiding out from his pursuers among plastic replicas of the Washington Monument. Which is how the Penis first evaded capture by Johnson, who, having brunch on Connecticut one day, heard a wild shriek from nearby a vase of tulips and gave chase; the Penis only breaking away from the souvenirs some thirty minutes later when an unfortunate tourist reached out for a little something to remember America by.

— § —

To capture the Penis, Johnson needed a plan. He felt he should devise a list, mark out all of Johnson's old haunts and stomping grounds, then all the places he'd already discovered the Penis, followed by all the places he might expect the Penis to go. He made a map of DC and color coated it as such: red, yellow and blue, respectfully. Unfortunately, when he stood back, Johnson realized he was looking at a large, pre-dominantly blue, diamond. His next realization was that in order to thoroughly search for his Penis, he could no longer do so from indoors; if he wanted to truly find the Penis, he would have to get into the field, he would have to get his hands dirty.

v.

"Excuse me, miss, you haven't by any chance seen my Penis, have you?" Johnson asked a gorgeous young woman in Foggy Bottom, a woman that, were his Penis still under his ward, Johnson felt would have surely have given him a rise. The question was his second mistake, and he was rightfully reprimanded with a firm slap to his left cheek. His first mis-take—exacerbated by the second—and why the woman was now run-ning towards the police officer on the opposite corner—was his choice of attire, suited, he thought, to sleuthing: a khaki trench coat with up-turned collars wrapped tight around him despite the soggy August cli-mate; dark sunglasses that spoke of time spent in truck stops; and a fake moustache he had to keep pressing back to his upper lip. Johnson had only made it past the maître d' at a kitschy brunch spot when he felt his legs going out from under him and the heat of concrete scrap-ing his chin, tripped by the cane of an elderly vigilante who'd done so without ever having to rustle the shih tzu in her lap. The click of the handcuffs was an unfamiliar sound for Johnson, outside of the televi-sion.

Awaiting booking, Johnson tried to explain his situation to the jaded Desk Job that'd been in that post ever since finding the wrong Con-gressmen in the wrong kind of congress on the Congressional steps, and making a stink about it. "You don't understand. My Penis is out there terrorizing the city…terrorizing me! My Penis must be stopped!"

"Heard that one before, pal. Brodsky'll be here in a minute, you can tell him allll about it." Then he went back to the crossword puz-zle—which wasn't going to solve itself. He turned the radio up, which just happened to be playing a certain track by King Missile regarding a certain detachable body part. Johnson was forced to sit next to a man deep in the throws of a hallucination, trying to conduct the populace of the floor.

Officer Clayton Brodksy was never short of bad fiction in his line of work: "We were just role playing; she *wanted* me to use the cat"; "I told you, the wind from the metro blew the dress off and the street sweeper sucked it up! It's just a damn turn of bad luck that I don't wear no panties"; "These pants? These are actually my cousin's pants, man; that's *his* pipe and rock, I was just wearing them to keep them warm on my way to pick him up from the pool." And apparently now "My Penis has run off and is committing colossal acts of sexual depravity all over the city."

"Uh-huh. Now, let me get this straight, you say your penis was cut off in surgery and is running amok all over this fair town of mine?"

"Yes! And I have to stop him."

"Mm-hmm. And you wouldn't happen to have another person who can corroborate this here story of yours would you?"

"My wife, yes. A-and Dr. Aranda! Yes, call Dr. Aranda; he can explain this whole thing!"

Reluctant as he was, Brodsky placed a call to the good doctor, keeping a furtive eye on Johnson the whole time. "I see...yes, I see," Brodsky's face, scanning Johnson up and down, shot up quickly with alarm, and soon fell grave. "I see. I *see*. Well I suppose you have a point there. It is tragic, I agree, but that's really not my department. No, I don't think you can prove RICO on a landlord and two cleaning ladies. Well for one, there aren't enough people involved; and secondly...Right, okay, goodbye."

"What'd he say?"

Brodsky blew out a large breath, "It's going to be tough, but he says he can prove fault lies with a certain Mario di Silva.

Johnson's face reddened. "Not that. Did he tell you what happened?"

Brodsky acknowledged the gravity of the situation and squeezed his thighs together. "He did, Mr. Johnson. And on behalf of the whole Metro Police Department, I'd just like to say we're all very sorry for your loss."

"So am I. But for now the important thing is that we find him—find him and stop him."

"Agreed. We'll work out a description and I'll put out an APB on him. We'll need to work up a dossier as well. Tell me, what's this guy into? What kind of pre-versions are we looking at here?'

Johnson gave him a quick run-down of the major points, which he frequently interrupted with defensive interjections: analogues of "Keep in mind this is him not me! I-, I would never do those things!"

"Hm-mmm."

"Honest."

"Watever you say, pal."

"Really, I swear!"

"Hey, it's your Penis. So we got ourselves a real freak, huh?"

Johnson went on the offense, "Enough about him, what are you going to do?"

Brodsky slowly turned his chair to face the window behind him. "I'm going to go out there, root him out. I'll start searching the local bars," Brodsky sucked in his cheeks and turned his head to the side, "see if I can't," pouting, "*lure* him out."

"You're going to what?"

Brodsky spun around "That's official police business! I'm going to track down this Penis of yours, boy-o, and I'm going to do it by the book! Solid detective work is going to bring this one in. And in order to do that, I've got to get in the field."

Johnson stretched forward in his chair, "Well that's what I said!"

— § —

VI.

Disregarding Brodsky's demand that Johnson leave the police-work to the police, Johnson left the trench coat and mustache at home and continued his search in a more pedestrian fashion. Using what he attributed to divination or telepathy, Johnson tried to hone in on the whereabouts of said Penis. Seated on a bench in Meridian Hill Park, Johnson closed his two external eyes and opened his third, entering a liminal state, waiting for any relevant information to roll in: key sounds, smells, textures…

Then something cold began to wash over him, something cold and smooth and rock hard; something grooved, like a pipe, but open. He felt air, a breeze. Then he started to hear voices, the patter of feet. Heavy reverberations. Chatter bouncing off high ceilings and hard floors. The squeak of a sneaker on waxed marble.

"A monument!"

Johnson bolted from the park bench and b-lined it for 16th Street, where his skin color quickly hailed a cab; he stuffed a handful of dollar bills into the driver's gloved hand and shouted, "The mall, and step on it. Oh, and also turn down the radio; I need it quiet. I have to concentrate."

The cabbie accepted the money and the order and proceeded down the hill in the direction of the White House. Johnson closed his eyes and tried to narrow down the possibilities. More echo, water in the distance, a Midwestern mother's recitation of *"Four score and seven..."*

"The Lincoln Memorial!"

— § —

He hoped to all manner of deity that the Penis was still there, that it hadn't gotten spooked, caught or, god-forbid, satisfied, and moved onwards; Johnson thusly approached the base of the steps pensively, cautiously, whistling and slyly undoing the cap on the mason jar in which he planned to contain the feral creature. Lincoln towered in front of him like some alabaster Egyptian god; Johnson sucked in a tear of American Pride just as the spark of a shriek in the adjacent chamber ignited a high-pitched blaze of panic. Johnson pushed against the grain, trying to juke his way into the room while the stampede raged around him.

Johnson sprinted towards the scream's origin and found the exposed Penis shuffling along the far wall towards the ledge. They made eye contact. Johnson's feet moved fast. The Penis, looking back at the escalating footsteps of chase—for only the third time running towards him instead of away (there was a bachelorette party a few days ago, and that one night in DuPont...)—sped up his stride and pushed towards the monument's vertiginous edge, vaulting from the marble and pencil diving towards the lawn, narrowly evading Johnson's outstretched fingers as the man slid in head first, desperately reaching for his member.

The mason jar in his left hand hit the ground first and shattered upon the fall; at least it was empty.

"Fuck. Damnit!"

As Johnson pushed himself to his feet and brushed the beads of broken glass off his trousers, readying himself for the next heat of pursuit, he once again found himself pinned to the ground by the strong hands of DC's finest.

"You don't understand; my Penis, it's right there!"

"Oh we understand all right, pal" came the sardonic reply of the clean shaven officer with the particularly pronounced nose. The following noise was the onomatopoeic click of handcuffs securing Johnson's wrists: an increasingly familiar and diegetic sound.

VII.

"I thought we talked about this." Brodsky slapped his hand on his desk, which sent the bobblehead of *South Park*'s Sgt. Yates nodding in agreement. Johnson sighed. Brodsky, with pink blossoms of rouge haphazardly rubbed from his cheeks, continued, "Did I not tell you to stay out of it? To let the professionals handle this? Now I've got a lobby of angry mother's asking me why their Girl Scout Troop had to see some philandering dick getting off on Lincoln when they're supposed to be learning about American history!"

"But if we only just explained it to them—"

"Explain what? That there's a Penis running amok in Washington causing all sorts of sexual indiscretions? Christ, we'd have a pandemic on our hands."

Johnson rubbed the sore rings around his wrist; though Jenny and he had experimented once or twice, the ones he'd been donning weren't nearly as fun, or furry. "Well what do you want me to do? I can't just sit on my ass knowing what he's doing out there. And let's face it, you need me."

"Need you?"

"Yes. You need me because I'm the only one that has a connection to the Penis. I know how it thinks. I know its habits, its hunting grounds—its *modus operandi*." Johnson paused, hoping the cop lingo would land. When it didn't, "I can feel what he feels, officer. Smell what he smells. Hear what's around him. It's as if he were still a part of me. How do you think I found him today? You think I just happened across my Penis by accident?"

Brodsky appeared to be considering Johnson's claim. "Well I do suppose it is a pretty big coincidence: you just happening to be in the same time and place as your Penis. But what are you proposing?"

"Just cooperation. If I keep getting arrested every time I'm close this thing is never going to get resolved."

It was quiet for a moment as Brodsky, who, without admission, knew he would need Johnson if he was to catch the Penis, considered the proposition. Brodsky kept a bag of baby carrots in his drawer (at his wife's insistence) and he removed a handful of the orange fingers and beheaded the first with a clean chomp. Johnson, with no distraction of his own, could do nothing but wait. He played with his cuticles as the cop ate until he was hit with the sudden scent of hot dogs. He sniffed again, stronger.

"What in holy hell are you doing, Johnson?" addressing the man turned 180-degrees in his seat, scanning the floor through the window.

"I think there's a hot dog vendor outside. Or maybe someone's eating one at their desk; either way it's very strong."

Brodsky gave him the stink eye and went back to his carrots, mulling together a plan until a knock on the door, followed by the protruding face of a younger detective, announced that there'd been a phallic breach at the Capital. "Could be your guy," the knocking detective added.

Then it hit Johnson, "The vending machines! The hot dog vending machines!"

Brodsky spat a slurry of orange into the air, "Let's move."

— § —

VIII.

Johnson rode along un-handcuffed, though forced to ride in the back of the unmarked car. Turning off Constitution Ave, the large white breast of the Capital rising into view, Johnson was visually accosted by the orchestra of red and blue police lights and the percussive blackness of the Secret Service SUVs parked on the western entrance; Brodsky drove past.

"What are you doing? Shouldn't we stop and tell them what's going on?"

"You want to stop so we can tell the Secret Service your Penis is the perpetrator? You barely got me convinced, ace; how you think it's going to go over with them? Humorless bunch a bastards."

"But then what are we supposed to do?" Johnson poked his fingers through the grated partition.

"I'm taking a different entrance."

Johnson shook his head. "You mean *we're* taking a different entrance."

"Like hell I do; you're staying in the car. Just be glad you're not cuffed."

"Have you been inside that place? It's a goddamn labyrinth in there. You're never going to find him. Brodsky, when are you going to realize you *need* me."

— § —

It had taken another five minutes and one grown man's tearful tantrum before Brodsky consented to allowing Johnson to accompany him. They entered through a back door and made their way to the second floor. Brodsky un-holstered his gun as they stalked the carpeted hallways, passing offices where the female interns who'd seen the Penis sat in shock and lightly wept with blankets around their shoulders and cups of hot tea in their hands.

"Is that really necessary?" Johnson asked Brodsky.

"Right?! As if they've never seen a delinquent penis in the Capital before!"

"No, I mean the gun. You don't-, you don't have to shoot him do you?"

Brodsky stopped and placed a fraternal hand on Johnson's shoulder. "Look, I know you still think of him as your Penis, but he's not yours anymore. You've got to understand that. Look at it this way: if he's still your Penis, then you're also on the hook for his crimes. You want that?" Johnson shook his head. "I didn't think so. I don't want to shoot him if it can be helped, but he's a menace. He's a terrorist, Johnson, plain and simple. And we have to take him down any way we can, even if it means lethal force."

Johnson gulped but gave a nod for them to move forward.

They turned down another lengthy corridor and found the Secret Service (two of which were in hazmat suits) taking apart the hot dog vending machines, bagging hot dogs as evidence, spraying the carpet with ultraviolet solution to determine the Penis's path. Without the proper clearance for Johnson, Brodsky avoided the judicious Servicemen and quickly pulled Johnson out of their sight. It was still his case, after all.

Then there came a choir of screams from the vestibule. Brodsky and Johnson sprinted down the stairs and into the large opening. A group of tourists, sequestered for their own protection, were pointing skyward and gaping. Brodsky, who didn't have his glasses with him, grabbed one of the tourist's cameras (with tourist yoked to the strap) and used the zoom to scan the rotunda; Johnson didn't need ocular proof, he could feel the Penis making its ascent towards the zenith: feel him climbing…then, air.

"Fuck, I lost him." Brodsky released the camera and tourist.

"He's outside," John said slowly.

"How can you tell?" But the man merely nodded.

One of the tour guides, a young, unpaid college student, overheard Brodsky. "Excuse me, officer. A bird hit one of the windows earlier this week. They still haven't fixed it; could have gotten out there."

"Thank you, miss."

The student shrugged. "Hey, I just want it to be over so I can go on my lunch break."

"You're not shaken up?" Brodsky asked.

"Eh, it's just a penis. Seen plenty of them and that little guy isn't going to cause me any harm."

"Hey!—"

"I mean would any of you be terrified if it was a vagina running loose?" She laughed, and expected the two of them to join, but found Brodsky slightly paler, crossing himself, and Johnson embarrassed and beet red, steaming from the previous insult.

"Let's go." Brodsky pulled Johnson by the arm and the two moved towards the stairs that would take them to the roof outside the rotunda.

— § —

IX.

The Secret Service had beaten them to the deck and barricaded all lower law enforcement agencies. Johnson and Brodsky were forced to watch from behind the yellow, police-tape barricade as snipers took position and a senior agent produced a megaphone with which he'd try to reason with the Penis, a vain assignment.

"This is your final warning. Come down peacefully or we'll be forced to open fire."

The Penis, however, climbed un-impeded towards the building's aureole. The agent nodded to the gunman at his left, who slid a round into the chamber of his rifle.

"Fire a warning shot." The rifle acquiesced.

Hearing the shot, Johnson felt a sickening blow to his stomach. "Stop, stop shooting! For the love of God don't fire!" Brodsky tried to hold him back but Big John broke through the tape and made his way towards the agent. The guns moved to him.

"Stop. Get back," the agent shouted.

"Sir, you don't understand. That's my Penis."

The agent, dubious, lowered the megaphone. "Sir, if that's the case, I'm going to need some evidence."

Unhappily, but for the greater good, Johnson unzipped his pants and showed the agent his pelvic scars. "Dr. Aranda," He said.

The senior agent, retired Army Staff-Sergeant Victor Slayton, nodded sympathetically. He then unzipped his own pants and showed Johnson a similar, though slightly more aggravated, pattern of scars. " 'Nam."

Brothers in harms, Johnson breathed a heavy sigh of relief as Slayton signaled to the female agent with her 9mm trained on Johnson; the agent lowered her gun and radioed the information in. She put her finger to her earpiece as the dispatching came in. She removed her finger and nodded to Slayton. "Checks out, sir; although it appears the blame may not solely lie with the physician."

"Oh Jesus," Johnson spat, but allowed the anger to slide over, feeling confident that, in the bonds of empathy, Slayton would allow the Penis to be taken quietly. "Listen, I think if you just let me, I can talk him down—"

The sound of the rifle's report cut him off. Johnson pivoted and looked back to the Capital's nipple just in time to see the Penis buckle, stumble and fall, screaming a solitary "NOOOOO!!!" before the world grew dark around his eyes and consciousness slid off his shoulders as his body hit the deck.

— § —

x.

Dr. Aranda's face was the first thing John saw when he regained sight and cognition. The second was his hands straining against the hoses of the infusion pumps as they reached out to strangle the good doctor, completely overlooking the bouquet of flowers from one Mario De Silva.

Arrested by pain and narcotics, Aranda completely misinterpreted the gesture. "Now now, my boy, there is no need to offer your thanks and gratitude. It was my distinct pleasure. Really, happy to do it. I just hope that the past indiscretions can be wiped clean and this mishap will be looked upon as a—well let's say a funny little ordeal Jenny, yourself and I will be laughing about come Christmas."

"What in God's name have you done to me now?!"

"Come, that's hardly the attitude I would expect from the man who just received elective surgery—*pro bono*, I might add—from a dear, dear friend."

"What elective surgery?" Johnson was suddenly too terrified to lift the sheets and explore what mutilations befell his body this time. Perhaps the doctor had turned that grizzled patch of skin he'd had into something more x-chromosomal. He gripped the edges of the bed. "Where's Jenny? Jenny!" he shouted.

"She'll be along shortly; she's at my place for the time being. I knew the surgery would have been too stressful had she been present. I gave her some valium and told her to take a nap in my bed—which, with one-thousand-count sheets, she should have found most comfortable—and when she woke it would all be over."

"Doctor, what did you do to me?"

"Why, Mr. Johnson, what are you playing at? I have reattached your penis."

Johnson remained confused, "But, doctor, I saw them shoot him—I mean…"

"Merely a flesh wound, John Boy. A grazing. Sure there was a lot of blood and some considerable scarring but such are the attritions of a battle such as yours. And I daresay you emerged the victor. And, as they say, to the victor go the spoils." Aranda held his hands in a sort of chalice shape towards Johnson's pelvis, imploring him to explore said spoils.

Johnson finally resigned to lift the sheets and found his Penis, though slightly off-center and heavily stitched together, nonetheless attached. "My, God. My-, my God."

"Now, John John, you shouldn't blaspheme. I enjoy the compliment but I am merely a man, not a God—though, I'll admit, my practices do share some similarities."

Johnson examined it from another angle. "Jesus did you attach Frankenstein's cock by accident?" Surely Jenny would never allow this stitched-together abomination anywhere near her Vicinity.

"If by Frankenstein you refer to the ambition, the beauty and alchemy of such a complicated process as reanimation, I'll take that as a compliment. If you are referring to the stitches, they will heal in time. We might even be able to do some laser treatments for the scars."

"Where's Jenny?"

Aranda pressed a button on his phone and speed-dialed Jenny. Jenny picked up and Johnson reached up for the phone. Aranda pulled it out of reach. "Yes, he's just woken…no…yes…yes…well he's a little more aggravated than I would have thought but that could just be from the medicine…okay, well I shall see you shortly…yes, of course. You, too."

He hung up, "Jenny wishes me to send her love."

Johnson put his head back on the pillow and made his demands to the ceiling. "Please, doctor, can you just leave me alone for a while."

"Certainly, I expect it's a lot for you to take in. I'm sure you'll want to catch up." Aranda rose from the bed and made his way towards the door. "I'll just let the two of your get reacquainted. But I should say, with the stitches fresh, I wouldn't advise any 'play' if you get my meaning." Aranda shut the door behind him when he left.

There was a sort of quiet in the room that Johnson was grateful for; the beeps and grunts from the machinery didn't bother him nearly as much as the prior dialogue. After a moment of rest and some light revel in the morphine, Big John lifted the sheets once again to look at the Penis: *his* Penis once again.

But is it really, he thought. I don't know where you've been, what you've done. It looked extra-corpus and unfamiliar. An alien growth, something parasitic perhaps. "Reacquainted, my ass." The Penis gave a twitch Johnson hadn't intended, flopping from a right delineation to a left.

What now? To make amends? To forgive and learn to cope? How will it ever be mine again? Yet it must be, attached and thriving off my blood. The real question remained, and it cut through the haze of morphine into the deepest bowels of self: *How will we ever be me again?*

Johnson put his head back on the pillow and counted the tiny black pecks in the ceiling tiles as he was sure many, more terminal cases, had done before him. Counting two-hundred-and-seventy-one, two-hundred-and-seventy-two, Johnson's mind drifted towards the legal repercussions of his Penis's actions: Would there be a trial over the battery of sexual impropriety that took place? And who would be the accused, Johnson or the Penis? Would he have to testify against the Penis? Could he even be forced to do that? After all, they can't make spouses testify against each other. At least, that's what the mob movies of old (and new) had taught him. Perhaps he could invoke the Fifth Amendment.

And what would be the punishment if found guilty? A sort of muzzle maybe? But then, by now, it should be under his control, Johnson's Johnson, once again operating under his own volition. He felt his stomach flop over as he thought of the whole cavalcade of victims endlessly parading through the courtroom doors; "And where on the doll did the defendant assault you?" Then there were the victims without a voice: surely traffic cones and trees couldn't take the stand, nonetheless accosting him with memory every time he drove past construction or jogged through the park.

"It's too much. It's simply too much." He looked down at the haggard member sutured to his crotch. Yes, he resented the Penis. Matter of fact, he might even hate it. He certainly hated what it had done: to others; to animals; to objects; to Jenny; to himself, then and now, mocking him by living off his blood, by claiming sanctuary in his skin. Though he would have never thought it a week ago, he wanted his Penis to become, again, an ex-Penis, an ex-Penis in all senses. "It must go."

Yes. Yes, the Penis would have to go.

II. THE BALLAD OF TOKYO ROSE

"Neither culture nor its destruction is erotic;
it is the seam between them, the fault, the flaw,
which becomes so."

—*Roland Barthes*, THE PLEASURE OF THE TEXT

The ballad of Tokyo Rose doesn't begin with Iva Toguri, either with her work on NHK's *The Zero Hour* or with her unjust incarceration following the collapse of World War II, nor does it begin with Major Charles Cousens and his nationally heterogeneous compatriots thwarting the Japanese agenda with their careful utilization of script and pun, nor does it even begin with a catalogue listing of rumors and here-say surmounting to a vague sketch of the supernatural villain ideized by American G.I.'s scattered throughout the Pacific; no, the ballad of Tokyo Rose truly begins with a small beachside apartment in San Diego circa 1939; it begins with an entrepreneurial young woman doing her best to provide for herself and for her familial charge; it begins, as many have suspected, with a birth defect: an especially pronounced case of *vagina dentate*: an anomaly concurrently charged with Rose's preservation and destruction; and, for her broken heart, a typically paradoxical cause and cure. It begins, as all things do, really, with an absence and a need. But let's begin.

Katsumi "Tulip" Tsutsuji, the girl that would come to be known as Tokyo Rose, was first known to the enlisted men as an attraction for thrill-seeking sailors on leave from the 32nd Street Naval Station from August of 1936 until December 7th, 1941. Under a hand-painted "Lady Tulip's Asian Quisine" [sic] sign hanging 5-degrees askew from the second story railing of what had once been a moderately respectable motel in the '20s, the soldiers got in line alongside other edible experimentalists, fringe fetishists, sideshow surveyors, and other curious courtneys (male and female) that extended from the parking lot of the bank across the street, wrapped around "Madame Ruperta's Palm Readings & Farmer's Market" on the first floor, and snaked up the stairs to the small two-bedroom apartment/office—blackout curtains ever the brooding sentinel in the living room/waiting room windows—where a young Japanese male assistant (Katsumi's mute cousin, Yoshi) took payments and led them individually to a dark bedroom that smelled of balsamic vinaigrette and opium-scented incense. There they would watch a small woman with sharp forehead, bushy eyebrows and clicking rotator-cuff spread her legs and insert carrots, radishes, cucumbers, and, for an extra five dollars (owing to overhead expenses, size, and a general aversion to the saltiness) salami, one at time into her vagina, spitting the mulched cuisine onto a bed of iceberg lettuce. The dinner and show cost each patron a total of fifteen dollars for the standard meal and invaluable stories and photographic documentation. Her second, and most famous calling, came several years after the Quisine first opened, following closely on the heels of FDR's famous speech about a day of infamy.

Precisely two weeks after the attack on Pearl Harbor—the Asian Quisine a fortnight closed out of fear of misguided retaliation—Yoshi took his time returning from his errands, taking the scenic path along the boardwalk where he could see the ships and soldiers in their pressed white uniforms and the gorgeous women on many of their arms. He bobbed and weaved through the crowds, daydreaming of the day he could call them soldiers, brothers, friends...when his shoulder was wrenched a violent 60-degrees backward by a passing mechanic, knocking the bag of groceries to the floor. Yohsi used universal mimetics to apologize to the aggrieved man and his cortege of white t-shirted friends, all taking umbrage with the boy's actions though none had been accosted. "What's all this [mocking the boy's movements]? What, you sayin you're sorry. Oh, you solly? You Solly, are ya?"

The swarm of white men in from Tucson circled Yoshi, who kept offering bows and apologies in his gestures. The verbal abuse quickly took a physical form. "Yeah, you so solly ain'tcha," one tormentor shoving him from behind, another from the front.

"Go back to Slantsville," shouted another assailant. The celery and carrots crunched under their feet.

"Yeah, why don't yous just go back home, Slanty," his primary tormentor suggested. "Just fly on home, pal." He looked around at his men, "Here, we'll even help yas with the take off." The men fell on him, grabbing him by the arms, then the legs, hoisting him into the air with his arms outstretched in slender wings; the lead bully flapped his lips like a propeller as they ran him to the edge of the pier, shouting "Bonzai" before sending the human plane nose-diving onto the rocks below.

When Yoshi hadn't returned by evening, Katsumi grew frantic and enlisted the help of the gypsy below to search for the boy. Madame Ruperta—who didn't have paranormal abilities but *did* have a working AM radio—twisted the tuner until finding a scratchy news broadcast relaying the story of an Asian boy murdered on the pier by an unidentified band of assailants who'd fled the scene (not exactly); Katsumi held out hope until forced to identify the cold body lying prostrate on a metal slab. Very shortly after the incident, just as rumors of internment camps began creeping around the corner, Katsumi left California and returned to her grandparent's birthplace of Kyoto: there, she sharpened her vaginal teeth on a file, reprised a certain set of vocal exercises, and turned the dial on her heart to Vengeance.

A fete she felt too grotesque to use in a commercial capacity, the promise of justice offered a more than suitable arena for Katsumi to exercise one of the more spectacular aspects of her "condition," as her family had always referred to it, discovering the anomaly one disastrous Thanksgiving—her uncle forced thereafter to try the Herculean task of using chopsticks without the use of index and middle finger. She had, through the course of her post-adolescence and early twenties (locking herself away in the attic of the house she shared with her mother, grandmother, Yoshi, Yoshi's mother, and Yoshi's father, the aforementioned/abridged uncle) (with careful practice and considerably disciplined muscle exercises) fastened the ability to pull air into her vaginal cavity, store it near her cervix, and expel said air past her vaginal teeth and carefully contracted labia, eventually constructing consonants, vowels, and fricatives…then words, phrases, and independent clauses. Under the impetus of pain, Katsumi once again reenrolled in her (understandably) autodidactic courses. When, after several months of training in a secluded apartment above a restaurant in Kyoto even the stray dogs in the alley knew to avoid, when she was finally able to recite monologues in almost idiosyncratic English (you should have heard her rendition of Beckett's "Not I"), in a haunting accent a crossbreed of West Coast American combined with the cadence, syntax, breathing, and emphasis of her maternal Japan, only then did she make the phone call to the uncle who ruled the intelligence community with an iron (and complete) fist; her uncle, ever the skeptic, required a preliminary demonstration of his niece's talents—which left the hibiscus flowers below the front window covered in emetic goo—before he passed her promptly up the ladder, looking for just the right officer to develop (pimp) her talents, until falling on the obvious choice of Lieutenant General Yamamoto Oshiri: a mon applauded for his ruthlessness, renowned for his obduracy, and feared for his "outside the box" thinking. Oshiri quickly crafted a special niche for Katsumi in his band of secret weapons, the likes of which wouldn't be seen again until the advent of JIEDDO in 2006: crafting the girl not so much a niche as a career, should she want it, in broadcasting.

She shed her birth name and chose the field name Kerria, after the Kerria Japonica, a dually gorgeous and vicious yellow rose she used to see from the window of her Kyoto dojo; the double-toothed yellow blossoms seemed a more than fitting handle. Oshiri forced her to use the American vulgate Rose for her broadcasts, to make it more memorable, adding the geographical forename although Katsumi had never once shadowed its grounds.

Under Oshiri's command, Tokyo Rose and her Japanese forces slipped their frequency (broadcast at a sizeable 250,000-watts) as a ghost frequency just a mere 2khz difference from the NHK's Radio Tokyo, parasitically fooling those who were trying to find "The Zero Hour" and its patsy Iva Toguri (or her Sunday fill-in, Ruth Hayakawa), which aired daily at 6PM, and in so doing, subverting the plans of the captured British-born Major Charles Hughes Cousens (a broadcasting celebrity of sorts in Sydney) and his consortium of fellow POWs (Captain Wallace Ince and Lieutenant Norman Reyes [American and Philippine, respectfully]) who had been charged with producing a radio program designed to decrease the morale of the Allied Forces, and who thought they were cleverly succeeding in their own subversion—a subversion of the subversion—via their puns and sarcasm, not realizing that their subtle revolt (leading only to a popularization of the program for American G.I.s!) was actually leading them—corralling them, as it were—towards the real subversion, the real Japanese agenda: Tokyo Rose, harbinger of dissent.

So, to illustrate, in years down the line—on May 7th, 1942, for instance—while sitting around the radio aboard the USS *Lexington* [CV-2], taking in sun after their afternoon chow, a gunnery sergeant and two petty officers exchanging leave stories on the deck, one petty officer talking about a woman in Hawaii who gives blow-jobs while keeping a hula hoop constantly in motion, the gunny discussing a cousin stationed in Honolulu who'd contracted warts from a prostitute that had, after failing to seek treatment, become so prevalent that when he urinated the stream came out as if from a shower head, just after their C.O., overhearing them, began regaling them with tales of a certain salad he'd eaten in San Diego, the other petty officer squirmed and turned up what he thought to be "The Zero Hour;" at which point a soothing voice came across the airwaves, greeted her listeners—specifically the crew of the *Lexington*—thanked them for listening, and informed the entirety of the crew—with utter accuracy and a cruel listing of names—that they were all going to die. Fear stayed with all who'd heard the broadcast the remaining sixteen hours until the *Lexington* was torpedoed and began its sepulchral descent into the Coral Sea.

As much as Rose treasured the moral debasement of the American troops, especially adored recalling specific names of soldiers who had visited her shop, and absolutely loved when she could remember the names of girlfriends and wives mentioned in passing, Rose's vengeance, and corresponding pleasures, went beyond the microphone and into the field. Dropping into Midway and taking the name of Keiko, she took up ranks with the local prostitutes and similar operatives of Os-hiri's command; offering low rates and good times, Keiko led the sol-diers (often singing Walter Kaner's theme song, "Moshi, Moshi Ano-ne," a counterforce against Rose's theme song sung to the tune of "London Bridge is Falling Down") down an alley where the sounds of screams and watery guillotines were drowned out amongst the com-peting bustle of debauchery and commerce, the two often converging. Rose's two distinct voices allowed exclusivity from one agenda and the other; sometimes a sailor became privy to the duality only when, ly-ing and bleeding to death on the ground, he heard her vagina cack-le "Thanks for listening, my lovelies." The recognition would never speak beyond the grave.

She had experienced the vaguest pangs of regret after a kill only once. One of the first soldiers she'd dispatched had been a Navajo Code Talker who, upon discovering the denticularities of her vagina, hadn't shown the least bit of surprise or fear, chuckling to himself, telling her that long ago Coyote had removed the teeth from women's vaginas, leaving only one little tooth at the top for pleasure, that Coy-ote had "invented" the clitoris and that he must have passed her over, "poor thing;" dropping to his knees and lifting her skirt he whis-pers that the Navajo have known about that last little tooth for eons, and that sometimes "just a little flick of the tongue can glaghalghal-ghahg glahglhg…Ahhhh AHHHHH!!!! Glethuth! Glu glut gly gluck-ing glongue goff!" While the man lay on the ground, one hand clutch-ing his mouth, the other searching for the lost tongue, pity crept in-to her heart like water through a missing shingle and she quickly eu-thanized the soldier by slipping her blade into his basal ganglia; Rose felt bad about terminating the Navajo soldier—a brother in cultural devastation—but training was training, muscle memory and so forth; and besides he *was* aiding the enemy, and this was war after all. The hole was plugged and Rose continued to conduct her missions in a dry clime, for a while that is.

It was on a routine mission in the field some months later when the roof of her heart sprung another leak. She would always remember the salty evening breeze on the night she encountered 2nd Lt. Ryôichi An-derson, a young Japanese-American naval officer whom she couldn't bring to dispatch in her usual methods—couldn't solicit either, for that matter, though she had tried. Ryôichi kept assuring her that what he wanted wasn't one night of payment and sexual compensation, that he could tell she was different from the other girls on the boardwalk, that he could tell she was unique and had more to offer and could she not imagine herself his wife in America, a place she could start anew, a place she could reinvent herself where they could raise their children with all the same beautiful Japanese culture but with all the privileges and opportunities of America. It wasn't that she had fallen in love with him; it was that he had elicited in her a sort of pathetic sympathy, churning up memories not of the Code Talker but of Yoshi and a puppy she'd had briefly in her youth, before her mother's allergies forced them to give it away. And even though she wanted to push him away, told him repeatedly to leave, told him that she couldn't spend her time talking to American "queer-boys," he remained obdurate: which was terrible for both of them, because, as Rose well knew, she hadn't been sent alone, unwatched.

Every operative—from the clairvoyant Madame Midway, to the knife-wielding working-girls, to Rose, to a woman whose mammary glands produced not a nutrient-enriched milk but rather a potent analogue of mustard gas—was accompanied by up to three high-ranking Japanese Intelligence officials whose positions and rank were designed to throw off the Americans should their plan become exposed. The man who pretended to be their pimp was no more than a page of sorts, powerless and void of information; whereas the toothless emaciated "teens" that washed the floors of the small apartments or peddled fruit were actually the XOs, relaying orders back and forth via banana messages (kanji characters scratched onto the peel, manifesting an hour later into a bruise-message). And so the Japanese-American soldier had no clue that the seemingly innocuous banana peddler, whose presence around Rose increased concordantly with Ryôichi's, wasn't trying to sell off his rotting fruit, but was, in effect, gauging the severity of the soldier's threat and formulating the proper punishment: not only for Ryôichi, but for Rose, as well.

"なぜあなたは彼を実行しないか？" The officer asked through banana message early one morning—which, due to the time allocated to writing each message, as well as the transportation delay, carried this conversation through all of the morning and into the late afternoon.

"彼は日本だ、私は"日本を殺すしない she'd written back on a banana. "とは、日系アメリカ人であり、彼は日本を殺す。彼は裏切り者です。あなたは裏切り者を殺す。"

"してください、彼は無害で、私はこの1つだけを残して聞かせている。" "アウトの質問の場合は、今夜彼を殺すか、または私が悪いエンドの両方をあなたの表示されます。" written on all five sides of a particularly long banana.

"あなたは彼を殺すと私はこれ以上放送することはありません。"

"あなたは位置要求を作成するのです。"

"これは私の才能だ、私はどうすればフィット参照してください それを使用することができます。" she wrote back in a last defiant effort.

"我々はそのことについて表示されます。"[1]

But of course her superior was right, and her talents—and by extension, her person(ae)—were no longer hers to met out at her own discretion.

—§—

That final bananagram arrived just minutes before Rose's nightly taping, done so from a boat shed at the northern, peninsular tip of the Island, what she thought would be an act of faith on her part before returning to the front where she truly hoped Ryôichi would finally have taken the hint and abandoned his pursuit, for both their sakes.

"Hello again, my darlings. I'd like to begin by saying goodbye to my dear, dear friends aboard the USS *Chicago* [CA-29], my favorite Heavy Cruiser in the Solomon Islands. I hope you boys are enjoying

---

1 "Why would you not execute him?" "He's Japanese, I don't kill Japanese," "He is Japanese-American and he kills Japanese. He is a traitor. You kill traitors." "Please, he's harmless, let me just leave this one." "Out of the question, you will kill him tonight or I will show both of you a worse end." "You kill him and I won't make any more broadcasts." "You are in no position to be making demands." "It's my talent; I can use it how I see fit." "We'll see about that."

the water off the coast of Rennel, but I wouldn't do too much swimming if I were you, you'll get plenty of swimming come the 29th of January. Chief Warrant Officer Herman Van Horst, I certainly hope you and your lovely wife, Brenda, practiced your backstroke and water treading on that Florida honeymoon of yours. Our show's music will be dedicated to you boys tonight. I hope you've enjoyed the most of your 1943, however brief it's been..." [USS *Chicago* sunk by torpedo on January 29-30th, 1943 off Rennel, Solomon Islands.]

When the taping was done Rose killed the amp and the lights and returned once more to the boardwalk, hoping for nothing but a tide of unfamiliar faces.

Unfortunately, the 2nd Lieutenant had indeed come back that night, this time wielding a wedding ring, a diamond beset with volcanic rock from Mount Fuji—believing that she was rejecting him based on his lack of a firm commitment—approaching her almost as soon as she'd taken her post. She had tried to tell him one last final time to go but that was before he pulled out the ring, upon which point pity swarmed Rose's nerves and she switched tone (reverting to her American dialect) and told him to follow her immediately, that it wasn't safe for him, pulling at his arm and trying to drag him towards the American base through alleyways where she hoped she could lose her tail(s). Ryôichi protested and kept stopping to ask why she was talking like this, how her English had gotten so good, how she could have lied to him, who she really was, etc...Rose just pressed on, telling him there wasn't time and that they needed to keep going for his own safety. Anderson finally halted as they came upon a dark stretch of beach and refused to take another step until she told him the truth, any truth. His answer—indeed the truth—came in the form of a chloroform-soaked rag applied to his mouth and nose by a dainty fish monger in a red Hawaiian shirt, accompanied by other pedestrian operatives who then wrapped the unconscious body in a black blanket, shoved him into a large wicker basket, and carried him off the beach—at last joined, though not in the method he would have preferred, with a similarly detained Rose.

— § —

When Rose awoke a good many hours later, she found herself in a steel cell she'd never been in before, strapped in an obstetrics chair, feet locked into stirrups, arms and chest bound together, mouth firmly covered with tape, naked below the waist but for a Nady PCM-100 placed in front of her crotch. Across from her, seated in an old dentist's chair, sat a still-unconscious Ryôichi, naked and doubly bound.

The chloroforming "fish monger," a.k.a Tetsuo Oshiri, a.k.a Lieutenant General Oshiri, a.k.a the Okinawa Ox, who looked much more formidable without the prosthetic nose and teeth, dressed in brown aviator attire, fitted with the souvenir of an American Bowie knife tucked into his belt, entered the cell not a minute after she'd come to; so she was being watched, as well. "As Captain Wakahisa had to remind you, last you two spoke, and as you can clearly see," Oshiri smiled and pivoted with his arms held out like a bellhop showing the room, "you do not call the shots here." Rose tried to speak through the tape covering her mouth. "Ah, you want to speak? I should think so, after all, isn't your show about to start? Any minute, so I'm told. And what's more, I hear it's to be a live broadcast?! Well, Rose, that's so splendid, we haven't had a live broadcast from you in ages—what with all your time spent in the field! I know you must be thrilled to be able to get back to your calling, now that you've got ample time to just sit, and reflect, and really consider your audience. And I don't just mean the guest in-studio [pointing towards the still unconscious Anderson with his Bowie knife], but all your American listeners out there in the blue Pacific; and of course for your family—cousins, aunts, uncles—in Kyoto and Nagasaki and Tokyo, too; and, say, I've got it on good authority your mother even listens! Never misses a show, as I'm told. Tunes into it on that little garden stereo of hers, the one right next to the rutabagas." Oshiri smiled at Rose, his snaggletoothed canine winking at her.

Rose strained against her gag, pleading towards the Lieutenant General, who put a quick finger to his lips and then grasped her avuncularly by the shoulder. "Ah-ah, quiet now, you're almost on. We wouldn't want you to waste your words prematurely. And no worries if you get a little lost, you've only to look right over there, just in front of you, and the words will come." Oshiri read the look on her face, "And if you're thinking of catching some last minute stage fright, I can see if the soldier here can give you a hand," Oshiri drew the blade of the knife in a circle over Ryôichi's hand, "or two."

Rose gulped as Oshiri pointed to the second hand, "But I can see that won't be necessary; not for a performer of your caliber." Oshiri slipped the knife back into his belt and stood against the steel door, "Now, break a leg, as they say! And remember, Rose, 'Loose lips sink ships,' so let's make sure we're nice and limber out there."

After another reassuring and terminally-serious smile, Oshiri left the room, several pieces of machinery turning as the door closed tight behind him. Rose squirmed, testing her restraints for loose bolts, searching for anything that could be turned into a make-shift tool of egress, before hearing the click of fuse boxes, the sound of a generator powering up somewhere deep inside the hull of what she realized was a ship of some sort, the tungsten filament of a light bulb clicking on, focused and funneled into a beam of light shining directly on the wall above and behind Ryôichi's head, numbers flashing a countdown as the microphone in front of her crotch went hot: four, three, two...The numbers switched to text, big and bold; Rose didn't have to squint to read the prompt, and her muscles and teeth reverted right back to their familiar labial consonants, her dental plosives dashed with a clitoral lisp at the end of each autonomous cervical egressive enunciation. The product of good training and muscle memory.

"Hello-hello, on this beautiful February First. I'd like to start by saying 'Hello' to all my loyal listeners aboard the USS *De Haven* [DD-469], as this might be my last time I get to speak to you. I'm talking about you Petty Officer Third Class Jonathan Remner, you Seaman Luther Steig, and even you Ensign Milton Hughes. I'll miss you all. Oh, don't worry about ol' Rose here, she's not going any-where, boys. I'm just sad to hear that the *De Haven* and her brave crew won't be making it through the night. Don't feel bad boys, especially you CPO Coleman Hayes, I've been informed your pretty girlfriend, Justine, is being attended to by a nice boy down the road..." [USS *De Haven* sunk by Japanese aircrafts on February 1st, 1943 off Savo, Solomon Islands.]

Anderson woke some thirty minutes into the broadcast, still groggy from the extra tranquilizers administered throughout the course of the journey, lolling his head about, murmuring permutations of "that voice, that fucking voice!" into his gag. As his senses slowly came back, he was able to roll his head upright and take in the visage of Rose: first her gag and bounds then finally—regrettably, tragically—the microphone between her thighs and the coalescing clarity of aural and visual information.

"No, no, no, no, no...No! It can't be. No, it isn't true. It can't be!" he spoke into the cotton. Anderson wept for quite some time while Rose stared right at him—specifically, at the prompt right above him—spouting this filth, this immoral propaganda, this lottery of death against his brothers. And even after the mic went cold and the lights went dormant, after an anonymous soldier entered and placed a wooden block in Rose's pelvic mouth (so she couldn't chew threw it), Ryôichi continued to weep into the gag until eventually the muffled sobs were no more differentiated than the ambient backdrop of the ship's pipes and pumps gurgling through the night.

— § —

Their incarceration by no means an ephemeral punishment, Rose's broadcasts continued in their regular time slot:

"It's that time again my lovelies. It's a beautiful March day outside. I hope the crew of the USS *Triton* [SS-201] has gotten a chance to emerge top-side and enjoy the sounds of the White-naped Friarbird, the Pied Cuckoo-dove, the Meek's Pygmy Parrot, hopefully with a glass of fresh coconut milk. Because you won't be able to enjoy St. Patrick's Day, I thought I'd give a shout out to a couple of my favorite Irish fans. Staff Sergeant William Fitzgivens, Private John Patrick Lafferty, Seaman Recruit John "Jackie" Ennis, and Lance Corporal Francis Keagen. At least the waters are green." [Sunk via destroyers off Admiralty Islands on March 15th, 1943.]

"...happy belated 4th of July to my avid listeners; our antennas were out the past week, but as you can see, I'm back now. Just in time for the crew of the *Gwin* [DD-433] to unfortunately succumb to torpedoes in the Kula Gulf. We'll miss you, Admiral Armitage, and the whole crew of the destroyer..." [Sunk by torpedo on July 13th, 1943 in Kula Gulf, Solomon Islands.]

"...Crisco *Cisco* [SS-290], your mothers' baked you all a good-bye batch of chocolate-chip cookies that unfortunately went overboard before they could reach the Sulu Sea. Looks like all those sharks and marlins will have to eat them. I do hope they're not allergic, it'd be a shame to lose such noble and respectable creatures." [*Cisco* sunk on September 28th, 1943 in the Sulu Sea.]

The captives' dialogue of their first seven or eight weeks of internment consisted mostly of Anderson's ejaculations of anger, remonstration, despair, and self-pity (his gag only utilized during Rose's broadcasts: an experimental torture of affect Oshiri had designed, hoping to facilitate a one-sided speech that would in turn hurt both parties); and, of course, of Rose's pro-Japanese broadcast rhetoric (her cephalic mouth only slightly decluded when her meals were brought to her and a small slit was made for her to sip bites of rice, ginger, and stale tuna before masked once again with fresh tape, never allowing her the faculty of her larynxial voice). With the banality of the hours, Anderson eventually found himself talking just to talk, more or less removing the restrictor plate from his id and spilling everything that floated across the bridge from internalized to externalized speech: a mass of words and clipped phrases banded together with clauses of sometimes indeterminate nationality keeping a steady cadence as they crossed the cerebral planks (held together by synaptic vines gone weak with use); trudging and swaying as they crossed, held high above the cragged rocks of consequence, mediation, suppression, and restriction; always crossing safely to the other side and into the smothering air of their cell. As was Oshiri's intention.

Ryoichi wrung out everything in his mind to spill upon the cement and steel floor between them, to soak into the sound-absorbing blankets tacked to the walls and ceiling and stuffed with hair—which smelled of soggy dog as the humidity crept in and took up permanent residence. In all manner of absurd confession he disclosed to Rose the fifteen-degree twist that occurred through the length of his penis ("I measured the twist with a protractor one day"); that his stomach had been accustomed to American cuisine and their current fare was causing him some serious digestive concerns and the imminence of soiling himself. That one day, when he must have been about ten or eleven, he had played a game of hide-and-seek with his neighborhood friends and he had hidden himself in his parent's closet behind the pin-striped and hound's-tooth curtains of his father's sport-coats; and he had remained there for hours after the game surely had ended—possibly because he relished the thrill of hiding, of the sort of drama of hunting, sport, and wit; possibly because he felt cozy nestled amongst fabric laden with the olfactory signatures of his father and mother, the American smells of Old Spice and Brute and his mother's silk robes that smelled of aloe and lotion and boiled rice. He was remanded so, among the clothes and corrugated afternoon light falling through slats in the closet, when the door opened and his parents came in, and he had remained hidden as he watched his father remove his jacket and place it on the chair at his mother's vanity, watched his mother disappear behind the paper screen in the corner; he watched as his father then removed his tie and unbuttoned his shirt, stripping himself down to trousers and cotton A-frame, waiting at the edge of the bed, face towards the window as his mother came from her dressing screen and seated her naked self before his father, taking him into her mouth and then slipping under the covers…He told her that for some reason this was the memory he was focused on, and that all he wanted was to be back there inside that closet interwoven with the smells and textures of his parents as they made love quietly before him, and he confessed how strange this all must sound, and how embarrassing it would have otherwise been to tell this to anyone. And so how most of his musings and affectations of tongue and teeth progressed, each admission taking him further down the spirals of shame.

"Boys, boys, boys…no hard feelings. Remember who loves you, *Grayback*! [SS-208]. Take comfort there are still plenty of good, strong American boys to take care of your ladies after you're gone, and I'm sure they've already treated them to a sweet Valentine's Day—I even heard a certain Joanna Hochstetler of Baton Rouge gave an extra-big, good-night kiss, if you catch my drift, to the piano player who took her out to Sully's for a night of dinner and dancing." [Sunk February 26th, 1944 in the East China Sea by Japanese aircraft.]

— § —

"I was engaged before," Ryôichi began one day, ready to confess his next bout of embarrassment. "Well, to be honest, I only thought I was. This was back in San Francisco, when I was studying to be an architect. Did I ever tell you that? Not the engagement thing, the architect thing? My mother's father was an architect back in Nagasaki, I guess you could say it was the family business—which is accurate in a less linear way because my father was a journalist—well, translator really—working for the *San Francisco Chronicle* translating copy from Japan and also translating articles from the *Chronicle* to a newsletter for the Japanese neighborhoods, helping to construct a community—which, as my mother told me, is what my grandfather said was the sole goal of an architect. I never met him, my grandfather, strange how much of my life I've dedicated to, or how much of my life has been shaped by, a person I've never known; it could have been anyone, really, I mean to base my life on. I mean, what if they had lied to me and he wasn't an architect but a dancer, would I have been a dancer? Would I have wanted to become a dancer? I wonder if there's any way in that scenario that I'd have ever become an architect—and if not, how badly did I really want to become an architect in the first place?"

As their time had progressed into months, the months gestating into years, Rose was able to communicate herself rather aptly through her eyes, through the expressions of her brows and lids and the general revenue of the intensity of her gaze; she had confessed to him the reasons she had gotten into this business of deceit and vengeance, of her work back in San Diego, of Yoshi and his death (to which Anderson had apologized on behalf of all Americans and Men); she had went on to tell him that she was sorry that this had happened to him, that if he had only just backed off like she had told him he would have been fine, probably back on board his ship, alive ("There's still the outside possibility that I would have been killed, Rose. This is war, remember?" "But you would have been free," she'd blinked. "Would I?" he'd responded). And of course there was the ineluctability of the clockwork of her broadcasts, and their conversations were always interrupted—sometimes picking up right where they left off once finished, sometimes growing quiet when the particulars of the rhetoric got to them. They had talked of other things: the innocuous details of their lives and where they would like to visit were they allowed freedom unencumbered by war ("Paris." "Milan." "Kyoto." "Johannesburg." "Helsinki." "Anchorage." "Des Moines." "Des Moines?" "Yes, Des Moines. Why not?"...) So, as Anderson's speech trailed along unchecked, as it often did, Rose used her eyes to prod the 2nd Lieutenant back to his original statement. "The engagement?"

"Oh, right. Thank you, it's hard to stay on track when there's only one *real* voice." He paused to think, conjuring the mental mapwork of the appropriate stones that laid the path for his story. "Her name was Edith—Edie, as she liked to go by. She was a mix, like me, but of the American sort. Her Father, part Anglican Jew from one side, part French and Iroquois on his other; her mother was Dutch and Irish. She was gorgeous: this long slender body with skin like pampered cream—I mean even her skin color!, it was as if she came seamlessly from the Earth, just one day climbed out from the wet-sand of the beach. She had this amazing hazelnut hair specked with blond and black that looked like it was made for the California sun. She taught me to surf and convinced me to change from structural architecture to landscape architecture. She was—well, you have to understand—I mean, I was never the first name on anyone's dance card, Rose; I just didn't have the right aesthetics or personality to capture their attention; besides the fact that I wasn't American enough for the Americans, or Japanese enough for the Japanese, I just wasn't—I'll say it—that good looking, and I was extremely shy, to boot. I suffered all the usual, you know, adolescent hopes and spurns and ridicule so that I'd almost wondered if just maybe I wasn't supposed to be with anyone (and even—I'll admit, Rose, and I can't believe I'm telling you this—for a small while I thought that perhaps I wasn't meant to be with the *female* sex—though when I put away the divinations I realized my heart was always set upon women). But that thought transmuted to another: I felt I was meant for an asexual life dedicated to the pursuits of science; mine was ordained by God to become a Pythagorean life of mathematics and structural design.

"So, my father got me into the University's architecture program—I think from some acquaintanceship from the newspaper—and I met her my freshman year. We were muts, Edie and I, peripheral to the

rest of the student body—or maybe I had just imagined that, romanticized the notion of our individuality, establishing in my head further
grounds for us to be together. She was nice to me in a way that no
one else really was; and, of course, I had taken that nicety for affection.
We would talk about our futures as if they were synonymous, with
the variance that she would be an engineer and poet and I would design the landscapes where she would write her poetry: a little koi pond
down a secreted flagstone path beset with aspens and tall firs, with a
small red pergola and Shinto arch overgrown with ivy, and a hand-
carved wooden bench that proclaimed the title of the space: 'EdAn' (a
mix between Edie and Anderson, get it?). I was in love. I was naïve, yes,
but I was truly in love and I took our time together, our cozy friend-
ship, our talks of conjoined longevity, as a sign that she loved me too,
and that we would someday be married.

   "She met my parents, my father, who was ever anxious to befriend
Americans of mixed ethnicity, plaguing her with questions about her
family's occupations and lineage and story in America, my mother
silent as always. Edie adored them, which I took for further corroboration. I remember we were in Fish Alley, walking along the wharf,
sometime after, maybe a week or so, and I had told her that I was trying to think of a way to ask my father for a loan to buy a wedding
ring. And I remember the look she gave me, at first it was sort of confused, and then she smiled and grabbed onto my arm and said 'Why,
Ryô, I had no idea you were such a romantic. That's so sweet. So who's
the lucky girl?' She was clutching my arm with her head on my shoulder and smiling, I thought she was just giving me a little joke. Playing
along, I pointed to a plump, red-faced, Scottish woman with butter-
bean shoulders like a boxer, stripping the guts from fish, and I said
'Why, that's her right there!' And she laughed and we continued on.

   "When I gave her the ring I had made sure to buy a brand new suit
to go with it, and I hadn't eaten more than two crackers that day as
my stomach felt like sharks were swimming around inside and it was
everything I could do to remain calm and keep them from becoming
agitated and ripping through my chest. I told her to wear something
nice, that I had a surprise planned for her. I brought her to her favorite
place to write poetry, a small clearing in Golden Gate Park near the
Rainbow falls. 'Why did I have to get dressed up to come here, Ryô?'

She was laughing, as if this was some sort of practical joke. 'Seriously, why am I *here* in this dress?' And that's when I got down on one knee, opened the box, and she just looked heartbroken and pitying, going 'Oh, Ryôichi…oh, Ryôichi…you poor, *poor* thing. Oh, I'm so sorry, sweetie, but you've got the wrong idea.' "

"I'm sorry, too, Ryôichi," Rose nurtured with her eyes.

"Turns out she was going with her poetry professor the whole time! And you know, once the broken heart and all that had healed, it was…it was the embarrassment and the naïveté that ended up hurting the worst. I just kept going around asking myself 'How could I have not known? How could I have been so stupid?' And then it was, 'cause I had been so hopeful, so sure, and it was just as it had always been; and I just thought 'I was right before, maybe God just doesn't want romance for me? Maybe I am supposed to be alone and my life is meant only for study and work.' I kept the ring with me to remind myself of that.

"And then the war started and I enlisted. And then I met you and it just seemed—it just seemed we were so similar. You know? When I saw you I just saw—I just *felt*, really, I can't describe it—a damage, a loss, an otherness on parallel to my own. Which isn't to say I think you're damaged or anything! I just felt: a home doesn't have to be a beautiful, shiny new building; no, sometimes the best homes are fashioned out of older, overlooked buildings, as long as the inherent structure is still solid. That it's the history that makes it beautiful, that makes it a home. And even though I promised myself after Edie I wouldn't fall so simply, I stupidly pursued, and, of course, here we are."

Rose was crying, and now it was her turn to apologize for her gender and for the situation, at which point the light in the corner began to blink and the hiss from the microphone picked up and it was time for another broadcast. If she had had time she would have told him she had never been romantically in love with anyone, either, that her condition precluded trust and ambition and the closest she'd ever come to love was with her late cousin—platonic, romantic, whatever love was without sex—and it was precisely this aversion to her condition and the resulting deficit of love, compounded through the death of Yoshi, that had led her to accept her body, and to weaponize her sex; but there wasn't time for that, and Rose had to stop crying so she could read the transcript floating above Ryôichi's head as her vagina barked the familiar tune.

"Our listenership lowers again tomorrow—and six days before Halloween, too! What would you Carrier boys of the *Gambier Bay* [CVE-73] and the *St. Lo* [CVE-63] have gone as? And you, men of the Destroyer *Samuel B. Roberts* [DE-413]? I was going to dress up like Dorothy, I was; put my hair in pigtails, put on my Ruby slippers, and click my heels three times—but wait, that's silly of me, I'm already home. Oh I wish I could have lent out my slippers to you boys, but we haven't the time and I don't think they'd've fit you. Well, maybe you can still try clicking your heels together as you hit the water of the Leyte Gulf…just take off those life-preservers and click until you're home. So allow me to play a little number for you boys: '*We'll meet again…*' " [Sunk off Samar, Philippine Islands, on October 25th, 1944 in the Battle of Leyte Gulf.]

Ryôichi was particularly quiet after this last broadcast, broken morale coupled with adrenaline exhaustion from so much confession; he sat slumped in his chair watching his toes while Rose tried blinking her way into his attention—that she would talk and maybe he would be cheered up, or maybe he would just feel less alone for the moment—but Ryôichi kept his eyes floor-ward, and time passed extraordinarily long; she became impatient waiting for her next heartbeat.

In the following days, Ryôichi begged Rose not to broadcast, confident that her punishment would be in the fashion of his release from this plane of existence and not hers. He was tired of the menu, tired of the scenery, and tired of talking, talking, talking…tired of the preterit embarrassment that surfaced well after the exercises of his tongue. "They might even let you go," Ryôichi opined, "without having me as leverage." To which she had to remind him that Oshiri had made well-informed threats on other members of her family, that his wasn't the only life she was protecting. When she remained adamant that she would not facilitate his execution, Ryôichi refused to look her in the eyes, castrating any other power Rose might have held, and remanding her mute. The silence lasted for five days; broken only by Ryôichi after catching Rose's eye post sneeze and finding the only glimmer of companionship and solace his imprisonment afforded; her eyes said simply one word, "Stay." And he did.

— § —

"I want to wish my friends on the USS *Reid* [DD-369, sunk by Kamikazes on December 11th, 1944 off Limasawa Island, Philippine Islands] an early Merry Christmas. Sorry to say, you boys who've been practicing your swimming will be spending Christmas in the waters of Limasawa—well those who survive, anyways. No, that's not the Christmas star you'll see rising into the sky on the eve of the 11th, it's our own—"

"Don't listen, boys! Be brave! Take heart—" Through the degenerative failures of several key, load-bearing teeth, Ryôichi was able to exert his tongue just enough to push the cloth gag from his mouth and get out a few meager (but hopefully inspiring) phrases to his brethren before Oshiri's main patsy was in the room and smashing his hands around Anderson's mouth. They remained that way, hands pressed against the American's twisting, straining head, until Rose's broadcast had finished and Lt. Gen. Oshiri himself strolled into the room, munching on an Asian pear, and swinging his bowie knife from a lanyard.

"Don't give me that look, Lieutenant; I'm not angry with you. On the contrary, I'm very glad that you've brought the issue of the inadequate bondage to my attention before more serious consequences could arise. I shall have to reward you." Oshiri took a bite of the fruit and rolled it around in his mouth while thinking of a proper consolation for Ryôichi. "Ah, but what better gift could I give you than the freedom from having to worry any further about the integrity of gags and so forth, of the burden you must feel should you find your tongue free in the future? So, we shall simply eliminate the root problem, eh Lieutenant?" Oshiri motioned for the patsy to produce Anderson's tongue (which he did) and stretch the muscle as far as it would go (which it did) while Oshiri rotated the knife to his dominant hand.

"Don't hurt him!" her vagina yelled, the gag not yet replaced as the patsy was busy restraining another mouth.

"Shh, shhhh," Oshiri trying to calm the American's eyes as they attempted to leap from his face and strangle the Lt. Gen. with their optic nerves, "there's no need to thank me, soldier. You've earned your reward!"

The knife cut quickly, though not everyone in the room shared that same perception of time.

— § —

Never much in the company of the deaf, Ryôichi had to devise his own manner of sign language (considerably clipped as his forearms were bound to the chair) with which to communicate with Rose, and by April of 1945 he had assembled enough rudimentary mimetic nouns and predicates, a few phrases and the occasional ejaculatory clause, so that they could continue their weary discourse. Ryôichi's hands once again became a train wreck of id. Rose's feelings towards the lieutenant, again, vacillated between feelings of guilt and grief, pity and resentment, disdain and longing. They squabbled like any couple, and, when the animosity passed, they talked of innocent longings, movies they'd like to see again, food they'd like to eat again—though this of course caused some additional despair in Ryôichi.

But April of 1945 brought another problem to their already crowded table of discourse, undercutting their minor communicative victory; the first serious incarnation of which (outside of a few minor stumbles as could befall any performer) reared its Gorgon head on April 7th as Rose's broadcast was focusing on the Motor Mine sweeper USS *YMS-103*:

"And to my lovelies, my lovelies, to my, my, lovelies. To my. My lovelies my, *love*lies aboard the *YMS-103*. Sorry there, I don't know what came over me. Perhaps I was choked up over what's going to happen to you tomorrow off the Ryukyu Islands, Islands, I lands I, lands I—I want to wish you farewell, my loyal listeners…" [Sunk off Okinawa, Ryuku Islands on April 8th, 1945.]

Rose's next broadcasts continued to roll along the down slope of vaginal aphasia, sometimes repeating the same word over and over, sometimes confusing her diction into an incoherent casserole of words, as on July 28th when Rose was supposed to be informing the crew of the USS *Indianapolis* [CA-35] that they were going to be sent to a salty, shark-laden, Philippine grave the following day:

"A woablly that is that is such a lovelie my twonkt can if he light but lovelies, love lies my, my, *my* lovelies, mymy…can fovever…if mungtd if not come out the football Philip were on MY *lovelies* cigarette—" before the feed was understandably cut and a young male soldier with an effeminate voice eerily identical to that of Myrtle Lipton's (a.k.a. Little Margie from *Radio Manila*) finished the broadcast; and then the lamp went out, leaving only the sliver of occluded porthole light; and then the gain drained from the microphone and the cylinder became just an inert piece of cold metal between her legs.

An unhappy, and uncharacteristically quiet, Oshiri visited their chambers a good twenty minutes or so after the broadcast, approaching her with reserve, lowering his head towards Rose, examining her taped mouth, her eyes, pulling one eyelid up, then the next, bending his bald head down to her pelvis and bare crotch, sniffing for yeast or some other form of biological interference that could have perpetrated the aphasia before returning to an upright position; his initial quizzical looks dipped into the far reaches of disappointment and finally resignation as he drew the knife and drove the butt-end into her mouth, knocking the rotten teeth from their final, pathetic holdings and filling her mouth with a cragged potpourri of enamel and blood. Oshiri removed the duct-tape and Rose, too hopeless to cry, gently pushed the teeth from her lips and looked expectantly towards the Lieutenant General, challengingly, as if to say "What more can you take from me? What more could I possibly give you;" Ryôichi, meanwhile, attempted to assail the brute with linguissected curses, a volley of stumbling vowels without the violence of fricatives necessary to inflict damage. Oshiri just shook his head and left the room like a teacher leaving two pupils who'd spurned his tutelage and concern at every turn.

Two nights later the ecliptic of the moon nestled itself into perfect concert with the small opening in the porthole where the circular cardboard cutout didn't cover, a large crescent moon thrown into the middle of the floor between them, allowing just enough light to make out the whites of Rose's eyes, the flashes of Ryôichi's fingernails and cuticles. Removed of gags (what purpose could they possibly perform any more?) they remained unable to properly express themselves over the past days: a vast tundra of things needing to be said, needing to be unsaid, needing, at best, to disallow any arbitration between the two poles and remain in that tract of silence Wittgenstein scribbled his claim on two decades prior. They remained that way, silent, for most of the time: unsure what words could possibly be said; unsure what words would even want to be conveyed, manifested, born between them. A child, stillborn, of language. The crescent light grew longer and thinner as it slid across the floor, flexing and contracting; before it slid away Rose whispered to Ryôichi "Savannah."

"Boise," he responded with a flash of cuticle.

— § —

No longer of any formal (or convenient) use, Ryôichi and Rose became systematically abandoned: their meals slipped off to one bowl of rice for the two of them, brought only twice over the next five days; the lights were out, the bustle of electricity hushed; Oshiri's visits, in person or by proxy, stopped completely. The sound of feet scurrying over the steel hallways, as though the arrival of August had lit fires under their feet, increased to a sound like hail beating down upon a tin roof, though no one ever entered their little compartment. (Even the meager sustenance supplied to them was done so by means of a trap door and a healthy push, most of the rice finding its way onto the floor; no thought as to how the two bound parties were going to find the logistical means to dine.) Something was going on in the ship, in the sea, in the war, something more crucial than propaganda—or, more precisely, their failed propaganda; and the tools—now useless, dull, and outdated—were left in their shed to rust.

Eventually, Ryôichi, through means of emaciation and determined wiggling, was able to slip his right arm through the twine rope purposed for securing his elbow, and upon liberation began working furiously at the knots that held his left arm (knots unaccountably tighter). Once free of both arms, Ryôichi untied the band around his throat—coughing and gagging as he had to strangle himself to slip the knot—moving to his pelvis, legs…Once free, the unencumbered lieutenant cackled to himself and rubbed the worn skin, the bondage indelibly tattooed upon his muscle fiber, before crossing the room and working to provide Rose similar alleviation—freedom not exactly the proper word.

Though touch was implicitly necessary to remove Rose's restraints, it wasn't until after they were both locomotively freed—first shoveling pinches of stale rice, whatever the cockroaches and rats had left, into their sore and tortured mouths; then scurrying to the inside corner behind the door to get the drop on Anyone should Anyone decide to come for them—that they set to ravenously embracing the other, pulling the other's body into their own, through arms and fingers and mouths, vampirically trying to absorb the other in order to ensure or qualify their own existence in the seeming vacuum of their cell: a love in the manner of fusion on that 5th of August (day?, night? who could say the hour?), emitting a cloud of emotions more profound and complicated than either would have thought possible. They kissed in spite of the pain in their mouths, kissed because of the pain in their mouths, hands at once caressing and gentle, urgent and violent. Bruises created, sores rubbed, hair pulled and smelled; limbs constantly trying to wind around one and the other. A conversation more honest than either had ever experienced. And then of course, as the day passed, the 6th of August crept into the clock and the real fusion began, unbeknownst to them; after that, the two were utterly forgotten, not even a bowl of rice or a quick visual check—not even the rainfall of feet above or below them—yet their door remained electromagnetically secured.

After almost an entire week spent in darkness, they set to the discussion of light, the porthole, and the proper time to remove the cardboard obstruction. Gradation was necessary, both conferred, and dawn would more or less provide the best path to once again court the sunlight. While Rose tried finding a comfortable, prostrate position to rest, Ryôichi went to the window and pulled the cardboard from the small hole, night still enjoying its reign outside, and returned to Rose. Morning on that 9th of August crept up and light began to slink its way inside and burgle the navy and violet sections of the floor and walls, of the two empty chairs, absconding with the *palette de frigidité* and leaving a calling card of redpinkorangeyellow warmth. Rose slept while Ryôichi watched the progression of the light with the dedication of a child's virgin trip to the cinema. Crumpled underneath the porthole so as to get the most indirect exposure to the light, Ryôichi put his hand in front of the beam and felt the sun stirring his melatonin; Ryôichi placed his heated hand on Rose's cheek below him; she purred. When Ryôichi had gathered enough courage, he made a perforated shield of his hand and through the slits took in the world beyond: the sea below and towards the crust of shore was heartbreakingly blue; above them, gulls flew in loose, peacetime formations. The smells of salt and algae sticking to the hull crept upwards as he undid the latch and swung the window open. The sun was coming up in front of them, stifled through clouds and smoke on the horizon...a mess of information that Ryôichi eventually pieced together to mean that they were facing East with a slight delineation towards the North, that the ship wasn't moving, that they were somewhere near land, though which land he had no way of knowing. At about eight o'clock in the morning, he began to open the lattice-work of his fingers and let in just a speck more light. Still too strong, he returned his fingers to a more private aperture and kept them that way, viewing intermittently over the next three hours, watching the waves, picking out a crest and following the white cuticle of sea, speaking in its own right, until crashing into the ship, reforming into a new wave and moving on.

At eleven o'clock, Ryôichi—tired of the safety of his fingers, confident that his eyes could handle the full brunt of light still shrouded by a sheath of clouds and some outlying smog of war-time industry—removed his shield. For the first minute Ryôichi felt fine; then, at 11:02 AM, approximately 1,650 feet above the city at the tip of the horizon, a new sunrise sprang into existence without any sort of visual premeditation, vaporizing the clouds and filling every visible surface before him, every molecule of salt and air and water, the hull of the ship, the sky—each surface reflecting the other and the amalgam—every element of every viable surface becoming its own sun, rising unfiltered, unhampered, and filling the ubiquitous with an unsolicited violence of light. The ubiquitous unfortunately included every rod and cone of Ryôichi's macula and fovea, and effectively flash-fried his retinas. Anderson screamed and screamed again—waking Rose, who'd settled into a comfortable nap—before collapsing to the floor while trying to dig the burn from his eyeballs; Rose summoned all her strength to keep him from exacerbating his injury. After an hour, he slept.

As nightfall settled into their cell, Rose held the broken soldier in her lap and kept up her discourse of huddled consolation (Ryôichi too pained to speak to her with his fingers and unable to hear her with his eyes), doing her best to take on the communicative burden. She traced into Ryôichi's back and shoulder kanji characters of serenity and peace, maternal and romantic aphorisms, beatitudes of hope and perseverance, none of which Ryôichi could understand on a semantic level but nevertheless understood on a level of intention and care. Even the stir of the waves seemed to offer their condolences, carrying the wails and sirens of the decimated city on their back.

After he had finally fallen into a steady, restful sleep, Rose gently disentangled herself from Ryôichi to stretch her muscles screaming for euthanasia and to better assess their situation, hoping to collect her wits and find some mode of escape. She paced around the room, first clockwise, then counter-clockwise, looking for any debris she could use to pick the lock, muscles audibly creaking from atrophy. There wasn't a vagrant strand of metal or wire to be found. She pried at the construction of their thrones but her fingers were too weak to remove a single nut or bolt. Defeated, she collapsed against the cell door, which subsequently fell open and deposited the unassuming Rose into the hallway.

Her head struck a handrail behind her and the first several moments outside the confines of her hell for the past several years were spent rubbing her head and trying to wince away the pain before opening her eyes and fully realizing this fresh liberation: a promising diathesis for actual freedom. What's more, there was no follow up sound of inquiry. The ship was empty.

The hallway was dark, only slightly more illuminated than their cell, though with actual means of incandescence—steel-wire sconces on the walls protecting bulbs anywhere from 50-100 watts, all gone cold and dead, not a sparkle of reanimation when Rose found the switch at the end of the hall and gave several rapid toggles. Without light, she crept along the hall, using the railing for support as she tried to make her way up to the deck. The staircase at the end of the hall was a challenge, and it took Rose a good twenty minutes before she successfully ascended and found herself facing the ice-rink shaped portal to the outside. The moon was barely visible from the deck, but the conflagration on the shores provided a solid enough haze to make out the basic shapes of the ship. The slight breeze was a welcome chill on her shoulders; she remained outside, chilled, for quite some time before returning to Ryôichi and telling him of their fortune.

— § —

They had to wait for daylight before they could begin exploring the ship. Though still quite sizeable at eighty-five feet, the boat was smaller than she'd always imagined: no hope for relativity inside an eight-by-eight, foot windowless chamber. From what she could tell from the tight quarters (three rooms no bigger than hers, each designed to sleep six), the control booth (where only those blessed with exorbitant agility and the endurance of keeping one's self to a five-inch width could fit), the galley (quaint even by quaint's standards), and the steel doors labeled—in English!—"engine room" and "freezer," the vessel had been at one time a large American freezer trawler, gutted and refitted by the Japanese with a reinforced steel hull, painted with faux-wood grain pattern, then stained again. (The idea of camouflaging a Japanese communications ship as an American tuna boat well past American fishing jurisdiction seemed something of an aporia for Rose, but, then again, so was most of what she'd encountered during the war.) The sky was still burning in the daylight as they stood against the gunwale; Rose painting an image of the landscape on his back with her fingers. Rose left him on a bench to at least smell the fresh air while she examined the deck. The winches designed to hold trolling nets were almost-well-hidden retractable antennas—designed to relay their broadcasts to a 250,000-watt station on land that could transmit in their desired radius; the freezers, their large mechanical doors, gaping at her and eschewing a thin effluvium of smoke and ozone, held in the stead of crab and lobster gigantic generators, fried and useless. Every piece of mechanized equipment onboard had, it seemed, been called to its own electromagnetic rapture; and apparently the crew went with them, though through the expedient of the ship's life boats, as Rose sadly discovered. No power, no engine, no sail, raft, or barrel they could ride to shore: they were marooned on this dead and buoyant island of steel and peeling wood.

And though marooned, there was one consolation of hope which finally dawned on Rose and made her break the inquisitive, hardly empathetic, gaze she had on the vibrant colors of the horizon—the slaughterhouse grays and browns bedecked with pupils of cooked paprika and neon-orange hellfire; toxic greens like the next evolution of chlorophyll (vibrant, transcendent, and painfully organic); blues of the Atlantic-drowned, floating into the clouds, becoming the clouds, and disbursing into the air to become something more—and she moved below deck to find the galley in the barest of hopes that the food hadn't vanished as well.

What would have been moderate rations for a crew of approximately eighteen to twenty men was quite a considerable pantry for Rose and Ryôichi. Rose brought the blinded lieutenant, through a considerable ambulatory burden, into the galley where she wet a dishcloth and wrapped it gently around Ryôichi's eyes before setting to fixing a meal of freeze-dried miso soup with pulverized salmon for the two of them. Rose tried using her skin-kanji techniques to tell Anderson of her find, of the ship, the bounty, the destruction—onboard and coastal—but, again, not understanding the endemic characters, Ryôichi could only make inferences based on the dynamic intensity with which she wrote them. It was an acceptable gist. At present, he understood only that there wasn't much to worry about in the ways of further torture from their captors. And for that, he was grateful.

Through the coming days, spent mostly eating and nursing the other, sleeping on the pseudo-mattresses in the bunk rooms, Rose and Ryôichi developed their discourse of drawing pictograms on Ryoichi's skin. She traced a vivid portrait of the horizon she'd seen; she made a picture of the state of the ship they were in, the former utility of fishing and the various metamorphoses undergone; towards the end of the first week sans cell, as a strong breeze cut across the deck and threatened to blow Rose overboard, an idea blossomed in her head like any of her eponymous names. She rushed below deck where Ryôichi was resting his eyes, rolled him over, and began scribbling on his back, trying to ask him if he knew how to sew. Eventually he understood but shook his head "no." In rapid fingerstrokes she had to repeat multiple times, Rose told Ryôichi she had an idea: if he knew the basics of sailing—if he could teach her and help her assemble a sail from constituent parts of sheets, forgotten uniforms, flags of all denominations (the real camouflage she guessed), semaphore signals, and netting—if he could help her unload as much unnecessary weight as they could—they might actually be able to move the ship without the motor. They could escape from the bay, sail off, just the two of them, to wherever they wanted to go. Later that night, after they'd committed to the plan, Rose drew pictures of how she imagined Bali to look, Sri Lanka, Cape Town, Monaco, Nice, Anchorage, and Helsinki—some of their dreamed-of itinerant destinations obviously impossible.

Using his fingers, Ryôichi instructed her on the rudimentary basics of sailing and on how to read a compass and plot a course; they took turns, when their bodies were up to the task, hauling every piece of extraneous equipment (transistors, amplifiers, spools of cable, guns, mortars (yes, there were mortars on board), every item of the crew's personal possessions) and threw them overboard. Ryôichi would fill his arms and Rose would guide him through the ship with a strip of silk wrapped around his waist. The generators were far too heavy and would have to stay, but they removed every antenna and radar on board—even those relegated to nautical duties. Rose taught Ryôichi to sew and he did so while she was out doing the more acrobatic tasks that required sight and coordination. The stitching wasn't pretty, but it would hold. Their sail, once assembled, was a mess of nautical aphasia: Kilos courting Foxtrots (which became interchangeable pet names, drawn into backs and forearms); Deltas, Indias, and Charlies beset with numerical pendants; a web of nationalities and signs with a burning Juliet at its center. And once they set sail on the morning of September 4th, through some majesty of wind and chance, the other vessels on the water seemed to understand a message from their vessel, a semaphore based not on position but in disposition: chaos that appeared to decry their intentional alienation and nautical innocence, a plea for reciprocal benevolence and sympathetic aversion. The Holy Fool of the High Seas.

The bow cut through the morning chop as Rose and Ryôichi embarked on as close to a primitive journey they could, divorcing themselves from their former technology and nationalism that had pandered to their trust and pimped them out. They sailed as far as they could, traded what they could, stole what they couldn't trade for, and spent their nights telling stories in languages all their own…making love when their bodies allowed, when the foreplay of their digital mimesis granted their wounded and still pensive bodies trust and entrance of one another, Rose's vaginal teeth pressing on Ryôichi's penis with the same playfulness as an aged yellow lab mawing its owner's hand: for Ryôichi, a pain both erotic and familial. Their ship consoled the waters of mournful jetties they passed, negotiated the animosity of vertiginous straights, drifted platonically along seaside caves and bluffs and cliffs; the hull conversed with the sleepy icebergs in timid whispers, the lullabies of the rudder modulated this way, then that, while Rose and Ryôichi remained dry and aloft, carried safely in the mouth of their domesticated chimera, pushing them ever towards a whole only they could know.

III. BUT FOR THE COMPANY OF ME-RRORS: AN INFINITUM

> *"The pleasure of the text is that moment when*
> *my body pursues its own ideas—for my body*
> *does not have the same ideas I do."*
>
> —*Roland Barthes*, THE PLEASURE OF THE TEXT

I n a bathroom that smells like steam, I am before a mirror: in my hands: a mirror. A matryoshka mirror of infinity and self. There is a smaller me in my chest, and a smaller me in his, and a smaller me in his; pregnant with self. In the mirror: An arm moving, an arm moving, an arm moving....A hand that waves, a hand that waves, a hand that waves....In the company of Me-s I speak to give voice to the multitudes; I speak: to synecdoche, to pundit.

'It was a dark, dark night in Patagonia, and the captain said to his mate, "Mate, mate, tell us a story so we may pass the time. And the mate began: "'It was a dark, dark night in Patagonia, and the captain said to his mate, ""Mate, mate, tell us a story so we may pass the time."" And the mate began: ""It was a dark, dark night...""'

A chest breathing, a chest breathing, a chest breathing. Eyes blinking, eyes blinking, eyes blinked. —! An arm moving abreast, an arm moving abreast, an arm standing still. I stop, I stopped, I stare.

'It was a dark, dark night in Patagonia...'

"It was a bark, bark night in Perrogonia..."

"'It was a stark, stark night in Purgatonia...'"

A mouth agape, a mouth in shock, a mouth in mirth. A self agape, a son *agapêton*, a pet *agapazomenoi*? Right hand waved, right hand still, right hand fingering the eardrum. In an echo betwixt the mirrors:

'I...'

"Me..."

"'Mine...'"

Three voices heard. (Maybe others, higher pitched, out of reach.) And there are six eyes to be certain, more if we count the rings. I stand, standing, stood. I will stand, once standing, once stood. Mirror tucked in belt to free the hands. Hands touching hands touching hands.

'Malone?'

"Malloy?"

"'Malarkey?'"

My hands on a glassine, smaller my-face. A polyseme? I says to myself (us (we.)) A metonym? Meanwhile, a hand scratching head, a hand scratched head, a soon scratched head. The royal We, standing perplexed amongst the linoleum and pink bath towels.

'To whom do I address?'

"To whom did I redress?"

"'To whom will I undress?'"

Laughter inside laughter inside stoicism. There are answers I demand. Is it masturbatory to reprimand the self, though thy self be smaller and analogous?

A ghost in the machine and other things obscene.

A soon scratching hand did scratch will scratch.

Anger for certain, for starters: for jocularity, for recalcitrance. Raised blood pressure reddened face. A face red, a face white, a face pink.

'I demand—'

"I remand—"

"'I unmanned—'"

More laughter, more games from the me inside the me, et al(lii(li-ae?—oh god!)). There is a hammer in the bathroom drawer. Don't ask why. Now, to hope for the safety of infinitives. Now, to raise hammer: to threaten with kinesis, to threaten with kenosis, to threaten with epiklesis. Must to coordinate the tenses. Must to threaten. I to sing, sang, sung:

'Who are you?'

"Who were you?"

"'Who will you?'"

'What have you to say?'

"What have you said?"

"'What will you have said?'"

To produce another self-serving *Kristallnacht*? To destroy the has been and the will have been? No. To reign in. Control: the word of the moment.

I to raise hammer. I to tap lightly on the glass. To smirk: Shape up or ship out.

In the mirror a man with fear, a man feared, a man had feared. A name to call myself. Right. A name to call they-self. To revoke/re(de)-nomenclate/repute/un-recalcitrate the *voi*; or is it the *noi*?

'Speak. Tell me a story so I know you to be me.'

"It was a metonymical sunrise like any other, a palatable blend of colors that one invariably comes to expect, an overlapping crispness of air that dangles itself in front of your tongue like so many uninspired appositives. A cyclical, teleological event forcing figurative words upon itself. To paint with preset algorithms how the corona refracts through air and water vapor, to reiterate with an olfactory lexicon how the pine and musk and sweet dew adumbrate your chemoreceptors, I took notes. It was a morning replete with ornithological aural accompaniment: a songbird singing songs, a mourning-dove in mourning (crying over spilt eggs), a meadowlark larking across the meadow. Brewed coffee that tasted like burnt toast, baked toast that tasted like stale coffee, poached eggs that tasted like gelatinous nascent chicken: I ate my breakfast by the window. And then, with an implied sense of its proprietary optimism and a sluggish affinity towards the zenith, the sun began to rise as a lothario for the opposing horizon, a horizon complicit with relativity whose sunset would only serve as another's metonymical sunrise."

"'Penelope (short: Penny) sat in wait at the kitchen table with the bowl of lathered cream holding a milk-frothed requiem for his platonic, burnt-kidney brother that had slipped from the table in the late morning. As a cloud passed over the sun, as a yacht left harbor and coasted up the lake-shore, Penny had gotten distracted, had knocked the plate over. And all the tongue burning coffee and all the chocolate covered biscottis couldn't make her remember why. Why she married him, why she allowed his philandering, why even with her infidelity they held any idea of why they should remain together. Tilly, their amalgam daughter, who had been the consecration of their union after the failures of their first marriages, a girl who went about life with the luxury of strong social interactions that limited the amount of time spent at home, had forgotten to change the ""Word of the Day"" calendar on the fridge; Penny pulled off the last date to the new one, June 16th, ""metempsychosis."" A woman who'd left the working place for the working house, a mother who'd lost and found and lost again the pleasure of domesticity, Penny was left to spend the day wondering what was left in the collective ""their"" of life, coaxing cream into her coffee as *Don Giovanni*

played on the kitchen stereo, fearing what was next in
the navigations of her life like a ship charting a course
through wandering rocks. The implied ""We"" of
ourselves. *Sinn fein*.'"

Lies, all: recited and rehearsed in voices not our own. To raise the hammer once more. To truth.

'Have you a person? Have you a self, damnit!? I want the truth. Tell me something about me [us]. Something only I [we] would know.'

To scoff. To re-raise. To wince. Defeat?

"I have an enormous head. Okay? Like, for my body height
and shape, I ought to have a smaller head. It's just
off-putting, you know? And it's really humiliating. I mean,
I would look so much better if, say, my head were about
two-point-four inches less in circumference. Then I would
look fine. My body would look better because, you know,
I'd look more proportional. As it is, it just looks like a
smaller body's propping up this great big head. And when
you realize your head is bigger than you think, you forget
that when you make certain gestures you've got to
compensate for the bigger head. Like, in some situations,
the face I'm making isn't the face I feel, or the face I want
to be making; the face I should be making with this kind of
head. Like, I'll be thinking I'm making this face that's like
I'm Thinking About Something and Trying to Tell
Whether It's Funny or Not, But It's Not Really Too
Important And I Want You To Understand That. Only the
face I'm actually making, because my head is so big, is
something closer to I Just Stepped In A Puddle On My
Way To A Second Round Interview And It's Bad Enough
I'm Not Even Wearing Fresh Socks But To Have Them
Wet As Well…You know? Like, I want to apologize to
whomever I'm making the face to, right? Like, I should say
to them "'Hey, this isn't the face I meant to make. I'm very
sorry. Have a pleasant rest of the day.'" I've become very
self conscious, you know? Like, if I'm trying to pick up a

woman at a bar or bookstore or something, I'll be too
overwhelmed by whether or not I'm making an appropriate
face. You know? Like, am I making a face like I'm A Very
Serious And Smart Individual, With A Little Bit Of
Mystery To Make Up For The Fact That I'm Not Better
Looking, But I Also Have This Very Funny Side To Me
And Don't You Want To Find Out? Aren't You Curious?
But I could really be making a face like Einstein's Theory
Of Relativity Is All Wrong, And No One But Me Knows
It, And Where Is the Nearest Restroom So I Can Pop This
Cyst On My Upper Thigh? I mean, how do I account for
this? Usually I'll just go up to her after I've realized what
I've done and apologize profusely, but I don't think she gets
me. Most times she just looks disturbed, like I'm not
well—mentally—and she doesn't know if she should, like,
call security or wait it out. I either get that one, or the
sympathetic one, like she thinks I'm autistic, which I feel is
worse because she'll make more of a pitying face. Do you
get me? I think you get me? You get me. Yeah, I don't think
you get me."

"'So I have…this thing…I do. Like a safe-word…of
sorts. Let me back up. Okay, right, so when I was like
sixteen I had gotten into the local rave scene—hold
your judgments. I'd been taking a lot of E, eating
some acid, which would come on these little blotted
pieces of note-card paper (Very camouflaged, right?
'Cause if a cop happened to pull us over he'd find the
note-cards and just think us studious amongst the
pacifiers and glow-sticks and neon clothing and
science-fiction haircuts!?), then there was the
Ketamine and some other kinds of pills that we would
just take without any prior research. So one day this
guy just up and gave me this pill, said it was called a
Peanut. ""Why?"" ""Like what they give the elephants
at the circus, man; it's just like taking a trip to the
circus, man."" Something happened, I don't
remember what, but I didn't take the pill that night,

just put it in my pocket and forgot about it until I was doing the laundry some weeks later. It was...what was it?...a Wednesday, I think. I was bored so I took it...two hours *later* I'm lying on the floor in a pool of sweat and vomit, my skin all blotchy and swollen. My parents came home and found me collapsed on the kitchen floor. They took me to the emergency room where the doctors said if I had gotten there just one half-hour later I would have died. ...So I tell this to girls when we're intimate. I tell them the story and say ""Now, every time I hear the word """peanut"""" I get cold chills and a small spasm of nausea."" I tell them, ""But this is a good thing. It only lasts about fifteen seconds, then it passes."" I tell them ""So, if I look like I'm about to come, or you just want me to slow down, just say..."""peanut."""" "" It's weird, she admits, but sure enough she does it and every time """peanut"""" gets said I stop, shiver, take a couple breaths, and jump back into it fresh as a cucumber. When she sees the effect work, she has a little fun with it and starts shouting """*peanut peanut peanut*"""" until I almost throw up. Then she feels bad and uses it sparingly. Except, and here's the thing: I was never into the rave scene; I never did E, or X, or whatever it goes by; I never took Ketamine; and I've never even heard of a drug called Peanut. I know what you're thinking: ""Oh, so it was just a peanut allergy that you tried to cover up with a story about drug use in order to impress the ladies."" And I'd say: ""Yes! That makes sense doesn't it? That's what you would think, right?!"" Except, I'm not allergic to peanuts."

Victory?

  I, to lower the hammer from the mirror—but to keep in reach. Now to settle the One. A brow raised, a brow raised, a brow rising. Hammer to raise in admonition once again. A hammer raised, a hammer raised, a hammer raised.

Once collated, now collate:

'Let us begin.'

  "Began."

    "'Begun.'"

'It was a dark, dark night in Patagonia…

  "It was a dark, dark night in Patagonia…

    "'It was a dark, dark night in Patagonia…

REEL FIVE:
GOD'S BEST MAN OR MAN'S
BEST GOD

"Oh enough with the goddamned epigraphs already!!!"
—*Anonymous Reader*

"...Mmmmm, no."
—*Anonymous Author*

I. TOWING JEHOVAH

C hrist rode cruciform on the back of Lou's tow-truck barreling through Chicago's forest of coniferous glass and steel, deciduous concrete flaking onto awning nets below, the road ahead known to none but Fate—and she was staying coquettishly tight-lipped. [Josef Olcyzk] Bierczynski rode shotgun with the window down, tapping his scabrous fingers against the passenger door's peeling vinyl sticker:

GOLGA~~THA~~ AUTO REPAIRS:
RESURRECTING VEHI~~CLE~~S IN THE
MIDWAY FOR O~~VE~~R 30 YEARS.

And business was booming in the city of disrepair.

"*Inferno Santo!*" yelped the maitre d' of the *Nostra Vita Cucina* as Louis Cifferetti banked a hard right onto LaSalle from Division, narrowly missing the man's heels as he leapt for dear life back onto the curb. More curses followed; Virgil's horn sent back his own. His hands otherwise occupied, Christ couldn't offer his upturned palms in supplication, nor could he wipe the sleep from his eyes to read the deeper nuances of hatred in the man's face; however, he could still make out the broad strokes of the host's curses sent their way. (Sometimes a well-gestured fist is stronger than any verbal vulgate.) Christ tried to apologize, but his words were drowned in the whine of the Chevy as Lou gunned it through their first of many red lights.

On the ticket that would come to be ignored two weeks later, the black and white tri-folded photo will only show a fading glimpse of Virgil and the cruciform man upon his back, the snarl of Virgil's throttle opening up evident only from the covered ears of those on the sidewalk behind. The truck had inherited his handle after the loveable(?) old codger that had been both mentor and tyrant, father and parole officer, to Lou; and a "he" there could be no doubt: a hulking, graceless, piss-yellow carnivore stalking the streets for benevolent reprobates that might have overlooked a sign, lost track of time or simply missed an elevator. Never one to retire, Lou'd had to wait 'til the old bastard croaked before making a sizeable offer to Virgil's Old Lady, Sibyl, that would allow the wrinkled battleaxe to live to be a thousand, spending her twilight surrounded by her jars of homemade preservatives and framed prints of Michelangelo and del Castagno. (Had the old bastard not suffered a surprise(?) coronary, he surely would have had Enid—as he'd called the truck before Lou reworked her—burned, shredded and scattered across the grounds of his Georgian birthplace.)

Seven-tenths of a mile down the road, Lou made another hasty turn onto Erie and Christ had to really hold onto his nails to avoid being thrown off. Christ yelled up to the cab but they couldn't hear him above the brackish swarm of horns and velocity. Berny stuck his head out the rear window to better hear the garbled complaints of the cruciform man requesting that Lou drive like a civilized, conscientious being and not like some goddamned simian with a hard-on. Berny relayed the message.

"Fuck off, yous said yous wanted da lift so stop bitching."

Lou floored the accelerator as they rode the ramp up Lake Shore Drive, slamming his back into the gold-and-nacre plastic beads that covered his seat like a loose-fitting sock. A Chicago Wolves billboard growled after them. The final rays of the sun, obstructed or refracted through the columns of skyscrapers, ignited their foreground into a prismic conflagration as they made their way south, passing mindlessly over Grand Avenue where the fly-laden homeless slept and groaned and echoed their schizophrenic wails off the tile of the underpass, munching on the wriggling offspring of their winged adornments.

The traffic slowed to a determined trudge through an ancient bog. Christ picked the tune back up, his voice able to carry at this snail's pace, "What I was saying, *Louis,* is that I volunteered myself for this position counting on you to behave fucking rationally."

"What?" Bierczynski yelled for him to speak up.

"Rationally."

"What?"

"*Rational!*"

Again, "What?!?"

"I said you're an *asshole!*"

Christ had hoped to live through his bachelor party long enough to get to his betrothed in the Quad Cities tomorrow, where Magda was working as a showgirl on a riverboat casino (having moved up the ladder from working as a lot lizard in the largest Truck stop in the country, several miles down I-80). He'd met her years ago, back when she was going by Beatrice (short: Trixie), rescuing her from an unruly John chasing her across the blacktop of Iowa 80; Christ had pulled her into his Camaro and peeled out, kicking dirt in the John's face and sparking the ignition of a full-scale car chase down the highway that would end in a bullet-ridden showdown 100 miles down the road in Montezuma.

Lou swerved into the left lane, cutting of a 4-Runner and giving the bird as the driver honked behind him, scrunching his face to try and read Lou's bumper sticker: "ABANDON ALL HOPE, YE WHO TAILGATE." Christ's left flank put him next to a Pathfinder whose left back window featured a metal outline of a fish with the word "tacos" written inside.

"Shit man, that's brisk." The late-March wind picked up as they moved slowly over the Chicago River, battering the scantily-clad Christ and the broad side of the truck.

"Don't chu worry, buddy, we'll stop and grab sometin' ta help with da cold," Berny hollered back.

— § —

After the traffic abated and the rubberneckers had gotten their fill of the two-car collision and a slick of what was either transmission fluid or blood, Virgil found a couple miles of unhampered speed on 41 before Lou pulled off in Hyde Park. He pulled the truck over in front of the first liquor store he could find, double-parking alongside a rusted Volvo with doors that didn't match the body or each other.

"Where you goin?" Christ yelled, who couldn't see their location due to his position.

"Outta beer."

Bierczynski yelled out the window, "And get some scotch, too."

"Da fuck you think dis is? Scotch?"

"Not da good kind you shit-heel, just a pint a somethin generic."

Lou shook his head; he looked at Christ, "Any requests, Nails?"

Christ thought for a moment and said he wouldn't mind a taste of gin.

"I'm not running a fuckin tavern here," but he came out with a case of Old Style and a pint for both of them.

They continued down Hyde Park Blvd, towards the looming Museum of Science and Industry; when they got on 57th, wrapping around Burnham's converted Palace, Bierczynski opened the window in the back of the cab and stuck his torso through, holding the opened pint of gin in his hand.

"Berny, you've the gift of divination." Christ said as he tipped his head back so Bierczynski could toss a little of the cure down his throat.

"Tother?"

"Hit me."

Bierczynski tipped the bottle back and gave Christ a bigger pull. Gin spilled down his chin onto his bare, and surprisingly hairless, chest. Berny pulled the bottle back; Christ let out a howl of manic joy and shook his head to try and free the beads of liquor from his face.

They turned onto 59th from Stony Island, riding along the thoroughfare of the University where even in the cold, early-spring weather poetic hipsters collected on the Midway Plaisance to imitate Bukowski or discuss post-Euclidean physics, isolated inside the ageless liminality of college.

"Fuckin' fags," Lou muttered.

"I know, Lou. And to think they could have turned out just like you," Christ yelled.

"Fuck off, I got all da education I'll ever need."

"Oh, did Stroh's finally start printing some Plato on the side of their cans?"

"Smart ass," Lou, laughing.

As 59th neared Cottage Grove, traffic came once more to a standstill. Berny finished his third beer and cracked open another, no real desire for expedience. Lou didn't share the sentiment and edged uncomfortably close to the car in front of him, hoping some kind of intimidation upon the late-model Geo would part the sea of iron and polymers.

"Hey, in't at your cousin? Da one from Crete?" Lou said after another minute of non-movement. Berny leaned over the dash to have a look. Positioned at the crux of the congestion, directing the chaos in an orange vest, was indeed Berny's cousin, Allen Minoski: his gimpy leg, along with the reconstructed cheek bones and orbital socket, to say nothing of the third degree burns—a hero's attrition from his attempts to free a downed pilot and his son whose plane had crashed inside Minoski's neighborhood after take-off—forced him to direct traffic now instead of driving a bobcat. Both father and son had perished; with no return on his heroism, Minoski begrudgingly settled into his disfigurement; a permanently-fuming, perpetually-snarling, gnarled beast none were overjoyed to take in on holidays.

"Hey, Minnie. *Minn-ay*," Berny shouted from four cars back in the queue. Minoski looked up, contorted his twisted skin into a scowl and turned the "Stop/Slow" sign in his hand to move the southbound traffic ahead. "Hey, Minnie, hows about chu let us true, huh?"

Minoski twisted the sign enough for one westbound car to pass but then they were stopped again. "Shit, Berny, your cousin's a real prick."

"Yeah, but if you'd—"

"No no no…he was a miserable cocksucker before the accident, and just because he looks like Freddy Friggin Krueger now don't give him an excuse ta be an even bigger one."

"What are you talking about? Of course it does!"

"All this talk of fire's getting me a little thirsty back here, Bern," Christ chimed in.

— § —

Eschewed onwards via Minoski—after another twenty-minute

wait—they continued west on 59th after a slight detour on 60th until Lou turned onto the southbound entrance of 90/94.

"Da fuck are you getting on da Kennedy at dis time a day?"

"Relax, Berny, I'll ride up da shoulder." Lou flicked on the lights and in a minute they were speeding down the side of the highway where the rush-hour, butt-to-nut traffic stared and cursed as they passed, the flashing yellow lights casting a jaundiced pall over everything.

"Can we get some music back here?" Christ yelled into the still open cab window. Berny flicked on the radio and Dido & Emimen's "Stan" came on mid-verse. Berny hummed along to Dido's refrain.

"Hey, how about something with a pair of testicles on it?"

Lou turned the dial despite Berny's protestations and "Pour Some Sugar on Me" replaced the tune through the window; "Yeahhhh, now that's what I'm talking about!" Christ bobbed his head and sang along, serenading the faces in the windows of the cars they passed, until Virgil slowed to avoid a blown tire on the shoulder and they settled next to a particularly busty woman slumped behind her steering wheel applying nail polish. Christ gave her a wink and a smile; she made a gesture with her hand and her mouth not commonly found in most sign language manuals.

"Ooh, you dirty girl..." Christ smiled. He turned back towards the cab, "This song always reminds me of strip clubs, you know?"

"Shit, dat's what we shoulda done, gone to da Admiral," Berny said.

Lou piped up, "Fuck dat yuppie, pussy, seventy-five-dollar-cock-tease shit. You really wanna do a strip club lets go down ta Harvey and hit up Sky Box. We ain't too far away, needer."

"Place any good? Never been der."

"Shit yeah! You remember Bubba Zeeble? Ran dat waste water plant out by Lisle? We went der a cuppa weeks ago and he got one of 'em ta blow him in da parkin lot."

"No shit?"

"How much?" Christ asked.

"Not sure 'xactly. He'd been tippin her consistently and towards da end of the night she come up and tell him she's goin on her 'cig-a-rette break,' ask him if he want ta join her. Well, he come back with dis shit-eating grin on his face, and we're all like 'What da fuck,' and he just laughs and sticks his fingers in Paolo's face—and Paolo almost puked. Bubba starts laughing, tells us he fingered her asshole while she sucked him off."

"You check on him lately?" Bierczynski asked.

"Why?"

"Cause I wanna know if his dick fell off. Ya put yer cock in some bush-league skank from a South Side strip club ya might as well drop er in formic acid."

"Hey, you don't want em ta touch ya, your own right hand can save ya; howz bout dat?!"

Christ piped up, "Fuck it, I'm game."

"Course, you're game. You just wave your little hand and dem blisters'll all go away." Berny felt spited; his fingers absently scratching at the scabs on his forearms, the aftermath of a boil infestation that had covered him from head to foot: just one of the many cruel jokes the universe had deigned to pull on him lately, starting two years ago with the stillborn birth of his daughter that had driven his wife into deep post-partum depression and the subsequent dissolution of his freight company, the dispatcher and brains of the operation too despotic to do much other than weep into the phone.

Lou hit the accelerator and barked, "Den it's decided, We're Going Ta Da Sky Box!"

— § —

They took 90/94 to 57 and got off on Us-6/159th Street for two miles before turning south onto Halsted where Lou slowed Virgil's pace and turned "Stairway to Heaven" down—in mid solo!

"What in the fuck, Lou?!" Christ objected.

"Shut up, dis is important; li'l heads up for yous: So last time we come up here bouncers kicked da piss outta a couple o' Juan-Carlos got a little too grabby. One a da little fucks pulled out a piece on dis bouncer, big bastard name a Peor or somethin; and dis Peor guy, he presented dem a little artillery of his own: two eagles of an Israeli-made variety, you catch my drift?"

"Where da fuck is this going?"

"Alls I'm trying ta say is watch your shit and don't fuck around, man. Dis ain't da place to play tough guy." The crunch of the parking lot's gravel and broken glass added an ominous punctuation to Lou's admonishment.

Bierczynski's voice got shaky with nerves and anger, "What da fuck you bring us out here for it's dat kind of place? I just want some…" his fingers bent like claws sinking into some fallen, portentous prey, "some goddamned *flesh*, man, not some hassle."

"Cause it's fuckin golden, Berny—each brick dug outta heaven itself."

"Fine, but you're paying for my first dance. I don't wanna come down here and pay ta get shot 'fore at least having some titties in my face."

"You're such a pussy. Fine. And I don't suppose you got a wallet hidin in dem robes, Nailsy? Need me to pick you up a dance?"

"Well, seeing as I'm a little 'hung up,' if you will, can you use that silvery, forked tongue of yours and see if you can't get one of those sweet young thangs to make a house call? It's still early, after all—well, strip club early."

"You got it, chief."

Lou and Bierczynski went inside (not before Berny stuffed half a box of Solomon Sleeve® condoms into his jacket—slipping one into Christ's robe with a "better safe than sorry" shrug). After a couple of minutes Lou came out with a curvy, black girl in matching bright-green thong and fishnet bra, make-up like Cleopatra on a bender, hugging herself against the chill. He brought her to Christ, who smiled and whistled. "Well aren't you a sight for blue balls."

"Ain't you a little cutie," the girl said, slipping into character.

"Girl you got cute enough for the both of us!"

"Thank you, sweetie." She leaned in to hug him and ran her fingers through his beard, the All-American 34DD breasts that had gotten her pregnant at sixteen rubbing against Christ's chest, an ass any hetero man would be happy to use as a floatation device bobbing buoyantly behind her.

"I should be calling you 'sweetie'—you smell delicious."

"Sweeter than syrup, baby: why they call me Jemimah. So, your friend over there got you a little present."

Christ looked at Lou and smiled, "You're the man, Louie."

"The Best," he corrected. Lou went into the cab to turn the stereo on and grab the pint of gin. He straddled the hoist from behind, wrapping his arm around Christ's shoulder, feeding him sips while the girl danced to "Start Me Up" then "Dr. Strangelove." She pulled her bra off and rubbed her oversized breasts along Christ's chest and down to his pelvis, tantalizing the hard-on poking through his robe. Lou danced and hollered; Christ did the same. The girl slid her panties down and pulled them off her ankles, slipping them past her red stilettos with dead goldfish bobbing inside.

"Hey, baby, watch this." Christ winked and the goldfish somersaulted and swam back to life. The girl shrieked and rewarded him by stuffing his face between her breasts and shaking vigorously. When the song ended, she picked up her clothes and carried them back towards the door.

"Wait a minute. You think we could work something else out?" Christ looked at her, then down at his pelivs, then back to her.

"Nuh-uh, baby. You want that you gots to talk to Keren—I mean Candy—she inside."

Christ stuck out his bottom lip at Lou.

"No way, man; Berny's got me leakin enough money as it is."

"Come on, be a pal."

"You can't do it yourself? Like, you know…"

"I'm not telepathic, Lou."

"Whatever da hell it is."

"It doesn't work like that."

"Fine, I'll talk to her but you owe me big time."

"That's the spirit."

Lou stuffed a few bills into Christ's robe before heading back inside to get some treatment for himself; after another couple of minutes a white woman pushing forty-five emerged. The fresh air seemed to confound her as she wobbled outside the entrance like an astronaut in alien gravity. To right herself, she lit a cigarette, ripped it down to the butt in one fell gulp and tossed it to the ground before staggering across the parking lot; the appendectomy scar running perpendicular to her naval danced a two-step. Her eyes were dopey and unamused, like the eyes of someone who's seen it all before and still never found what she was looking for.

She stopped in front of him and scowled. "Your friend inside said you wanted to see me?"

"Yes, Candy, is it? I was wondering if maybe I could get some…special services?"

She sucked on her teeth and eyed him up and down. From somewhere off in the city came the reverberating snap of either gunfire or fireworks: strangely, neither out of place at this time of year. "Thirty bucks, twenty if you showered today. Up front."

He nodded towards his waist.

"What?"

"It's down there."

"I know what's down there. That comes later. Money cums first, baby; always does."

"That's where the money is. Or maybe there's something else I can do for you that isn't, ah, monetarily associated."

"Huh?"

Christ laughed, "I'm referring to that scar you got yourself. Bet if you didn't have that little flesh hiccup you'd pocket a little more cash each night on the take-home."

"You some sorta surgeon or somethin?"

"Or something." Christ sneezed and the flesh of the stripper's belly became taut and uniform. She smiled, said "lookitthat" and bent her head to his pelvis.

— § —

Which is right when the door burst open and out came Lou and Berny, the latter zipping up his fly, hauling ass to the truck at a speed neither had hit since JV Baseball, "Let's go; let's *go*."

"Man, Peor is pissed!" At which point one of the largest bastards Christ had ever seen kicked the door open and followed the two fleeing men at a slower, yet more malicious, pace, a baseball bat in hand.

"You've got to be kidding me…" Christ groaned, "What'd you do?!"

"Squirt McGirt here couldn't keep it in his pants."

"Hey yous said it was 'dat' kinda place, didn't you?"

"What kinda place lets you blow a load into a stipper's hair, ya fuckin nut?!" On cue, another stripper with a shaved head emerged from the club in a pink bikini to join the ruckus, her wig pinched between her fingers like a used diaper, stomping after them as fast as her five-inch heels would allow.

"That him, Kezia?" Peor asked the bald stripper, pointing the bat at Berny's back as he fumbled with the door handle.

"Uh-huh; that's the sick motherfucker right there."

Candy backpedaled from the truck to join the fold of her people. Lou sucked the last bits of coke off his key before sliding it into the ignition, Peor not ten feet away. Virgil, much like his namesake, gave an asthmatic wheeze before rolling over.

"You, get out here," Peor shouted at Berny as Virgil's transmission ground into gear.

"Sir, maybe I can be of some assistance," Christ offered.

"Oh, you want some too?" at which point all efforts to appease the man and de-escalate the situation went out the window as the bat cracked against the side of the truck, once, twice, denting the ribcage and sheering off Lou's sideview on the third.

"Shit. Go!!" Berny and Christ shouted. The bat struck the base of the hoist and sent the vibrations rattling through Christ's body, which did nothing to neutralize the erection. Lou peeled out as Peor swung and missed, the bat striking only the black exhaust. The bouncer chased after them as they fled the mostly empty parking lot. Just before they made it onto the road, just before they were free and clear, Peor sent the bat hurtling after them, striking Christ directly in his still-erect passion stick.

Christ winced; Peor continued to fume; Candy waved after them, "Bye-bye-ee."

— § —

"So what's next?" Lou asked once free of Peor's range of malice, driving slower than usual, more relaxed, like a man who'd just had his face nestled in the wealth of Silicon Valley.

"Don't know bout yous, but I'm starving," Berny said.

They found a Fish House before leaving Harvey; Christ said it was his treat—with the concession that they bring it out to him, and feed him, of course.

"Always, something witch you, ain't it?"

They each ate three baskets, stuffing their maws full of fried cod and some microbrews heavy on the roasted barley.

"Got a feeling dis is gonna come back and bite me," Berny said, rubbing his belly.

Heading north on 294, they each popped a handful of antacids and washed them down with warm Old Style. They'd only gone a couple miles before their progress was halted yet again by traffic congestion, putting them at a stand-still over the Midlothian turnpike.

"Christ, it's almost nine o'clock, da fuck can dis be?" Lou poked his head out the window but couldn't see anything. Berny did the same through his and found the source of the commotion: a Ferrari had rear-ended a Mercedes and the two drivers were standing on the shoulder shouting at each other.

After thirty minutes, and as many feet, they were alongside the drivers.

"Da fuck are dey saying?" Lou asked.

"*Nowa kasa chuju or nowe pieniadze chuju*," the Mercedes owner shouted.

"*Wez sobie wsadz te sanki nazistowskie w dupe!*" the Ferarri owner, with a twinkling necklace of a golden wolf, shouted back.

Berny rolled down his window and stuck his head out. "*Hej moze nareszcie zaczniesz ja pieprzyc! Moze zrobcie nam spektakl jak tak dlugo sie zabieracie do tego.*"

They both turned their heads to Berny and advanced on the boxed-in truck.

"Uh, oh," Berny said.

"The fuck did you say, Berny?" Christ asked, nervous and defenseless.

"I just asked for a little show while we waited. Didn't think they'd take it so hard."

Berny scrambled to find some kind of weapon in the cab; finding only a full beer, he shook it up, pointed the can out the window and popped the tab as the enraged men approached the passenger side. The pressurized foam hit both men in the face, and as they recoiled and wiped their faces, Berny took full advantage of the distraction, yanking the necklace from the Ferrari owner as Lou ripped the truck onto the shoulder, clipping the side of a Mercury Sable and completely removing the entire front fender from the Mercedes as Virgil chugged along the shoulder toward an ignoble freedom.

A triumphant Berny stuck his head out the window and shouted back to the two men, "*Do wygrywajacego ida nagrody.*"

— § —

"Come Sail Away," blared as they rode the shoulder over the Cal Sag Channel; soon after crossing, the song crackled and became mostly static. Lou cycled stations until hearing Judas Priest's "The Number of the Beast."

"Shit yeah!" Berny reached over and twisted the volume up.

Lou said, "Da devil's greatest trick was convincing da world dat da devil's greatest trick was convincing da world dat he didn't exist."

"Fuckin-A," Berny said while shredding an invisible fretboard, then abruptly stopping. "Wait, what?!"

Lou kept driving and turned the volume up.

"Got anything heavier," Christ chimed in.

Lou smiled, "I believe I got da perfect thing for ya, Nails." He slid a CD into the dash and skipped to the sixth track, after a few seconds the cabin was permeating with shear brutality.

"What is this?" Christ said, "I like it."

"Converge. 'Towing Jehovah.' "

Christ laughed. "Fuck yeah, Louie—all ironic and shit. You hit the nail on the head, buddy. Blast this shit."

"Please don't," Berny requested, covering his ears.

"Aw, is it too heavy for da wittew Joey?" Lou mocked.

"No, it's just—what happened to da classics, man?"

"What happened indeed, Berny?" But Lou only chuckled and turned the volume clockwise another 3 hours. Lou sped up and rode the ass of a Jag in front of them. Bierczynski drained the last drops from his can, crumpled it up and threw the empty beer out the window towards the Jaguar ahead, the can falling short of Virgil's fender. Lou roared.

Christ, who couldn't see, had to turn his head and shout up to the cab, "What happened? What'd I miss?"

"Nothin. It was Berny who fuckin missed somethin. Got an arm like Barry Manilow."

"I'll show yous a fuckin miss." Bierczynski picked up a full can from

313

the little cooler on the bench seat and hurled it at the car ahead, gouging green paint and leaving a dent in the trunk. "How's dat for a fuckin miss?"

The Jaguar immediately pulled away from Lou into the middle lane then dropped in back of the truck, presumably to copy the license plate and call the police. Lou tapped the brake and bucked the truck backwards towards the car. Christ was facing the driver: a pale, mousy, terrified, little man sweating nervously and holding a pensive thumb over his phone in case he needed to press that other -1. Christ smiled to him and mouthed an apology while little beads of blood flew from his wrists and forehead and splattered across the windshield. The man flicked his wiper blades, smearing the blood before washing it away, the small cracks and divots in the tempered glass growing smooth and uniform; still, the man left the highway at the first exit. Christ heard Lou mumbling something about yuppie cunts and he rolled his eyes.

The night sky was clear and to their right loomed the glowing antennae of the Sears Tower above the tombs of the Holy Sepulcher Cemetery. Beyond the cemetery and all around them the sky was cut with the minarets of refineries, an iron city of oil production, plastics and gasoline. Spires of commerce shooting up into the black.

"Jesus, dis smell is fucking awful." Berny put a hand over his mouth.

"Well at least you've got a sleeve to use, you selfish bastard. How do you think I feel?" Christ coughed, hoping it could somehow clear away the smell. It didn't. Berny climbed out the back of the cab and put his sleeve around Christ's face.

"Dis better?"

"No it's not fucking better. Now it just smells like Polish sweat-cheese. Shit, do you *ever* shower, Berny?"

Hurt, Berny pulled his hand back and tucked himself back into the cab. "Fine, you wanna be insulting go right ahead and breathe dis shit in. Tryin' ta do a friend a favor, and dis da shit I get."

"Christ's right, Berny; you really wanna do us a favor, take a fucking shower. Unbefuckinglievable—again?!?" Lou threw his hands against the wheel as they were forced to stop against the wall of construction before them. The 95th Street exit was just beyond, not their intended road but an option to forego the traffic.

Not a single car went through the clogged artery in the first twenty minutes of hitting this latest gorgon of congestion, giving Christ plenty of time to appreciate the airbrushed van to his left bearing three buxom and serpent-wreathed beauties wrapped lasciviously around the parapets of some gothic castle. On minute twenty-one, an orange-and-yellow construction worker, presumably the foreman though impossible to tell, came to the head of the traffic, raised his hands and the bulldozers and blinking pickups pulled to both sides of the highway, leaving a single lane open for the traffic to pass.

Unwilling to further subject themselves to the tortures of Chicago interstate traffic, they pulled off onto 95th Street (Rt. 12-20) as soon they'd cleared the foreman's path. Driving through Oak Lawn, passing the Rusty Nail (eliciting a joke Christ couldn't pass up) and Frankie's Beef (a sign outside saying "Jumpin Jehoshaphat, now that's good beef!" which Berny seconded as having "tasty Guido food"), they headed towards Cicero, which they could take north to 55 and then east back into the city.

Halfway through "New Millennium Cyanide Christ," Berny, sick of the metal, punched the radio to AM's KLM 666—the same station that featured the war-advocating, conservative program "Moe Locke in the Mornings," whose flagrant xenophobic malice got him fired from covering the Sacramento Kings and the Oakland Raiders but found him a comfortable home in the pocket of the GOP.

The station was currently broadcasting their late-evening slot of self-help guru Dr. Lucas Mammoneli-Hu: "…you must be true to yourself and seek the good from within your situation, however inopportune it may seem; your present trials and disadvantages might, in the future, become your trophies. Ultimately it comes down to personal responsibility; you have to understand your actions ultimately effect yourself. You can't shift blame to the external entities of the world—whose workings, though mysterious, aren't effected by you…" Berny nodded along.

"Da fuck is dis shit?" Lou popped in another CD and in a minute "Locust Reign" constructed a sonic pandemonium within the cab. Berny frowned and looked out the window, unwilling to concede any merit to Lou's apparent dissertation on dissonance.

— § —

Heading north on Cicero past the airport, Lou looked down at the gas gauge and found the needle dipping into "E." "Ol' Virgil's thirsty, boys; gotta stop," he said.

The curb at the gas station was steep, and Christ took a painful bounce as Lou pulled in. While Lou went in to pay, Berny rifled through Lou's stack of unlabeled, pirated CDs, trying to find something less "Love as Arson" and more "In-a-Gadda-Da-Vida," leaving Christ to bide his time staring out at the Cicero Avenue scenery: cracked streets; crack heads; bullet-proofed fast food joints; no-contract cell phones; the check-cashing/wire-transfer "bank" next door, into which pulled a Lincoln town car, barely coming to a halt before four horse-faced youths in oversized baggy jeans, flannel shirts and backwards flat-brimmed hats poured out, wrapped bandanas across their faces, whipped Tech9s from their waist and ran into the store, the clomp of their Timbs echoing across the asphalt. They entered and ordered the people inside to put their hands up; the people did. The youths went from customer to customer, forcing them to hand over their cash, beating an obdurate middle-aged man in the back of the head when he hesitated, taking a fat envelope of cash from a man presumably on his way to the Bulls game—his face painted like a bull and sporting an imitation home jersey.

Their driver remained in the car, smoking a mango-flavored blunt, which he dropped as his team sprinted back into the car. Forgetting that he was already in drive, the transmission bucked as he threw the shifter into reverse, then into park, and finally into drive again, placing all their attention on the car and not on the Bulls' fan stepping out from the store and pulling a .44 Magnum on them. The fan took a quick, un-aimed shot at the car, which missed and ricocheted off the street.

"Motherfucker, move your ass," One of the men in the backseat shouted, as their driver finally gunned it into the street.

The fan shot again and clipped the engine; red transmission fluid poured out. He shot two more times, shattering the rear glass and igniting a firework of blood and brain matter onto the passenger side window. The car veered right and slammed into a parked car in the right lane and didn't move again. Transmission fluid continued to spill out in a steady stream into the gutter, joined by a similarly colored liquid. The right rear door tried to open several times but couldn't find enough clearance with the parked car six inches away. The bull fired again and the door made no further attempts.

"Fuck me!" Lou all but shouted, getting back into the car. "He killed 'em; he fuckin killed 'em!" Which is when the bull turned his attention—and his weapon—to the three wise-men/witnesses.

Lou slammed the car backwards, driving Christ towards the raging man and ripping the gas hose from the tank—the nozzle protruding from the side like a skin tag on Virgil's neck—unleashing a torrent of gasoline into the parking lot, the bull's face and into the gutter where it mixed with the crimson fluid and quickly found the smoldering blunt and ignition.

"Woa-ho-ho-ho" Berny said, watching the flames spread from a river to a burning lake as they continued up Cicero in reverse at forty miles-per-hour. Lou laughed. Christ screamed, the only one keeping an eye on the road in front of them, as cars and trucks swerved to avoid them.

"Ah, Lou?" Lou didn't answer. Instead, he cut the wheel, spinning them around one-hundred-and-eighty degrees, switched to drive and slammed the truck northward. A devilish grin spread across his face, Lou whooped and hollered. "Shit man, dat was wild! My heart's pumping like a sonofabitch. Feel like I just blew an entire eight-ball, then stuck my dick in a vat o' Tabasco."

"Fuckin-A," Berny seconded.

"God damn, my nerves are *quaking*. I need something to take me down. Shit. We got any more booze?—no, wait, we got any weed? Berny, open da glove box."

Berny pulled out a plastic baggy full of stems and resin. "*Nada.*"

"Well, shit. My guys all da way out in Aurora. Any o' yous know people out here?"

"You know everyone I know," Berny said.

"Nails?"

"Not my scene, man."

"Fuck. Guess we're goin' ta Aurora." Lou switched to the left lane. Bierczynski passed him a beer from the cooler as they got on 55 West.

— § —

Things were calmer on 55. More tranquil despite the caustic scenery. They passed industrial parks and smokestacks and refineries, graffitied freights and underpasses—and in between them, billboards of models in underwear: European super-model Theseus Thammuze standing halfway-naked over the industrial furnaces below; *Hercules* star David Narcís advertising sunglasses while donning a European Speedo in the middle of the Parthenon.

Eventually industry was supplanted with suburbia and the stench and air cleared. They moved along by the lights of shopping centers and neighborhoods, until the land south of the highway abruptly cut off into a pitch of blackness.

"Hey, in't dat dat fuckin' Argonne Lab? Wit dat forest preserve attached?" Berny asked, referring to the Waterfall Glen County Forest Preserve that wrapped around the Argonne National Laboratory.

"Fuck if I know. What about it?"

"Dat's where dat fuckin' engineer, ah, Abu-Raheem offed his fucking kids. Slit both of der throats and den offed hisself."

"Yikes!" Christ said.

"Dat was here? Shit dis is where Zanche's campaign manager blew his brains out. Further down in the forest. Remember? He was just about ta get indicted. Dey found chunks of skull embedded into da fuckin tree; would've had to cut out half da tree ta get it all."

"Dat was here, too?"

"Yup."

"Wasn't there something kind of sketchy about the whole thing?" Christ asked. "Like they thought Zanche might have had something to do with it?"

"Hey, Zanche said he had nothing ta do with it. Straight from da horse's mouth."

"Well of course he's not going to tell *you*. Shit, he's probably got more bugs on him than a cadaver wagon. He's just gonna open up at the Christmas table, Louie?"

"Zanche is a good guy. I don't care what anyone says," Lou defended.

"I met him, gave me da creeps. Plus I think he was tryin ta fuck my wife."

"Dat's a load a shit. Don't nobody wanna fuck your wife, Berny. Not even you."

Berny pouted and chugged a beer.

— § —

They left 55 and hopped on Rt. 53, heading north through Boling-brook. After a couple miles of stoplights, Berny told Lou to pull over somewhere so he could cut a piss. Lou turned left onto Royce and pulled into the deserted stone field where they used to process grav-el and sand, parking the truck under an old sand Rotopactor. Berny dipped around the edge of a warehouse and Lou hopped out of the truck to stretch his legs.

"Hey, Lou, any chance you could top me off? Growing a little parched back here."

Lou dug in the cooler for another beer. "Only three left. Make it count." He cracked the tab and put the can to Christ's lips.

"Jesus!"

"What?" Lou and Christ both said as Berny bounced back from around the warehouse in a run, tripping as he tried to zip up his pants while making a mad dash for the truck.

"What is it?" Christ asked.

"You catch some sand in your foreskin?" Lou chided.

"Fuckin fairies, man. A whole band o' em back der; all fuckin and suckin each other and shit." Berny hopped back into the truck and quickly fastened his seatbelt. Lou and Christ chuckled and stared at the spooked man.

"Shit, I seen people in *Night of da Living Dead* looking calmer than yous."

"Just go, man. Lets get da fuck outta here."

"Well nows I'm kinda curious…"

Virgil inched around the corner and, sure enough, the loading bay was filled with a whole slew of men in a deep congress of fucking: all manner of men: from blue-collar truck drivers and machinists to closeted employees of the Financial District in sunglasses and base-ball caps, unidentifiable other than by the emblems on their designer clothes: initials beset in a horizontally-striped eagle, an inscribed nabla,

Gs and Cs crossed in a Venn diagram, crests of charging bulls and rampant stallions; men in all manner of copulation: standing against the sides of the building, gripping the surrounding machinery for support; or down on the ground, grappling in par terre; some even laying facedown on the ground—

"Holy shit!" Lou yelled. "Berny, look at dat!"

Berny kept his eyes down, "I already seen enough."

"No, Berny look at dat one. Ain't dat Father Grabassi?"

Now eager and inquisitive, Berny craned his neck at the figure Lou pointed out, and indeed there he was, their childhood cleric, Father Bruno de' Mozzi, being defiled by a man in a John Deere hat, pressed into the sandy ground, cursing God in pleasure at the consummation of coccyx and cock.

"No, fucking way!" Berny said.

"I fuckin knew it," Lou yelled. "All dis time I fuckin knew it!"

"Enjoy da pink sock, Fadda," Berny yelled, which drew immediate attention from the man in leopard-print standing before some anonymous stockbroker kneeling on the pavement, taking in a mouthful of the feline fairy and trying not to drip anything on the large blue lion plastered across his sweater.

"You boys looking to sit in?" The feline said in a husky voice.

"Ah, not at da moment. But I think dat one's asking for reinforcements," Lou pointed to de 'Mozzi.

The man, with a nose like a toucan, looked over at the priest and nodded. "Be with him in a moment."

"Much obliged," Lou said.

As they began to pull out from the meeting ground and head back to the road, a bell was struck from somewhere and all the men stopped, pulled apart, made a circle and gave chase, running after one another in a philanderous analogue of musical chairs.

"You can bet da first one ta get tired's gonna get da cock," Lou postulated.

"Yeah, but so is the last," Christ said. "Everyone wins."

— § —

With Bolingbrook long passed, they drove down New York Avenue, heading toward the heart of Aurora, the street signs fading from English to Spanish, fog settling in as they neared the Fox River. They continued on, driving in cosines across the lanes with no regard for the sparse traffic. A neon-yellow eel swimming through the mist. Once they'd passed the river-boat casinos and the patch of restaurants, the fog cleared and the view opened up to the hookers and pimps, sharp-dressed preachers driving around in their Rolls Royces, kids that would one day become one or the other.

Berny pointed his finger at a pregnant Latina girl standing along the curb in a mini-skirt. "Lookitatone! Knocked up by her pimp and still working da streets—now how's dat for da American spirit!" He then spotted a hulking prostitute whose adam's apple was as big as her biceps and he burst out laughing, "Hey, sweetie, how *do* yer dice roll?"

Lou grinned and swerved into a puddle, splashing water up to her/his sequined belt and then gunning the accelerator while the tranny ran after them for half-a-block before being called back by her pimp.

"Tiresa, get your fucking hairy ass back here."

The smell of dead skunk infiltrated the cab and sent Lou and Berny scrambling to roll up the windows. Christ was once more shield-less against the odor.

"Oh, you dirty motherfuckers," he yelled at them.

They pulled off the main streets and into the neighborhood of one-story brick houses. The air cleared and they opened their windows. Two blocks down the side streets whose houses featured gray blossoms of concrete where bullet holes had been patched, Lou pulled the truck to the side and parked. "Dis is it."

"Dis is what?" Berny said.

"My florist, you fucking retard. What d' you think it is?"

Before they could bicker too long, Christ was shouting at them from his post: "...guys...*guys*...GUYS!"

"What—" They turned to see no less than ten armed Satan's Disciples surrounding the truck, tattooed with pitchforks and six-pointed stars, guns raised to each of their heads. One S.D. even extended his assault rifle and gave Christ a swift goosing. The rosacea-ed gangbanger poised his rifle for another poke.

"Ruby, cut that shit." The teen stopped as their enforcer, adorned in a red-and-yellow T, pushed his way through the circle to Lou.

"Hey, Mal—" Lou pandered.

"Don't you 'Hey, Mal' me, motherfucker."

Sweat perforated Lou's brow. "What gives, man? Why da hostility?"

The enforcer wrapped his tattooed knuckles on Lou's window and leaned in. "Little birdie told me you're cousins with a certain Senator Michael Zanche—who's also a close business partner of Don Logodoro of Rosemont. And you come to me trying to snag grams and eighths—on credit!? You a cheap, lyin', snake motherfucker, Lou. Now you better have something for me to eat, a goddamned brick of cheddar for back pay and emotional damages or my boys'll be using their pitchforks to make me some swiss. And I'm hungry for a Reuben, Lou. I'm fuckin *famished,* esé!"

"Excuse me," Christ chimed in, "But are you talking cheese? Or are you talking bread?"

"The fuck is this motherfucker addressing me?" The enforcer moved around the back of the truck and faced Christ, who was twisting his head around toward the cab and demanding a c-note from Lou.

"But—" Lou attempted to plead.

"Just do it!" Berny grunted, nervously farting in his seat—a foul odor that Lou was too frightened to address.

Lou put a hundred dollar bill in Christ's hand and Christ turned back to the humorless S.D. standing before him.

"Now, I don't know much about cheese and the like—I try to keep Kosher—but I do know a little bit about bread." Christ closed his fingers around the bill and when he opened them, two Benjamin Franklins were staring up at Mal. "But that's only a couple slices and you want a loaf, don't you?" Christ closed-and-opened his palm several more times until there were sixteen bills in his hand. "Now, you tell me, how much bread do you need for you and your boys to have a solid meal? And perhaps for us to get a little something to eat as well?"

Mal looked from Christ's palm to his men, first in disbelief, then in nothing short of bliss.

— § —

"Well fuck me sideways: a quap for a bit of fancy fingerwork? Shit, Nails, whyn't you tell us you could do dat? We coulda been knee-deep in snatch 'n' scotch all fucking night!" Lou said a little while later, after they'd been given safe-passage and a quarter-pound of marijuana in exchange for five-grand (Christ's max, he told them) and the promise of a (safe) return.

"What, am I supposed to do everything around here? And just what the hell do either of you have to offer anyways."

"A lift."

"Our winning personalities." Berny was still riding the back of the adrenaline high, giddy as a schoolgirl.

"And wait a fuckin minute, yous still owe me for Sky Box!"

Lacking proper paraphernalia, Berny told Lou to pull over to the little liquor store at the end of a strip mall. Bernie ran in, energetically grabbing a bottle of Mad Dog 20/20 and a package of Dutch Masters in front of four county sheriffs, each weighed down by heavy bullet-proof vests, patrolling the aisles themselves for a tug of something strong to keep the night away.

Freshly stocked, they hit the road again, smoking and passing the Mad Dog back and forth. They blared Slayer's "South of Heaven" in its entirety, noncommittal to any set direction as they toured Aurora's subdivisions. The Mad Dog went quicker than expected and disappointment followed. Christ instructed Berny to dunk the empty bottle into the stagnant water of Lou's cooler and pass it back to him. He then gave the bottle a tap and Lou and Berny cheered raucously as the water transfigured into the blue-green fortified wine whose flavor, though advertised, could never truly be identified.

— § —

It was well past midnight when they finally decided to leave Aurora. In their path of egress, Lou took a wrong turn and they were forced to clamber their way through roads of gouged asphalt, climbing over rocky paths and dirt fields before they were again on civilized ground. They drove down Orchard, passing houses with crocodile lawn ornaments and squirrels crawling on stone lions whose teeth had eroded, until reaching the on-ramp to I-88 west, into the plains still hardened from the harsh winter—where they knew there would be little traffic or cops.

Thin Lizzy's "The Boy's are Back in Town" came scrambling across the FM and the three of them harmonized the chorus and guitar licks. Berny rolled another blunt and they did cannonballs with the Mad

Dog.

Not far into their drive, the night again became infested with a thick curtain of atmosphere. "Fucking fog," Lou grumbled.

"Not fog, my friend," Christ coughed, "smoke. Look."

Christ pointed to a spot south of the highway where, testing the dexterity of their retinas, a small patch of orange cut its way through the bramble of gray carbon. "Controlled burning."

"Dat's an ox-moron if I ever heard one," Lou said.

"It's 'oxymoron,' you shit-bird," Berny corrected.

"Wouldja lookit da little scholar we got on our hands."

Berny ignored him and put on Incubus' "Pistola," humming along with the verse, waiting for the chorus before raising his confidence to actually sing along, when from behind them came a rumbling of thunder gaining Doplar treble by the second.

Motorcycles raced out of the smoke, flanking them on the outside lanes. One biker, with a snake tattoo that wrapped from his wrist, up his arm and around his neck, looked up at Christ, gave him a nod of approval and sped up to rejoin his serpentine phalanx of riders—some riding two- or three-deep, legs smashed together, bodies indecipherable from one another, leather centipedes with Softails and twin-cam engines. Virgil hung back, and after a few more miles the bikers were out of sight.

They continued down 88, passing another prairie fire whose burning was more pronounced. "Speaking of burning, I gotta take a piss," Lou said.

— § —

The rest stop on 88 at two in the morning was a sordid sight. Christ, who had much better bladder control than Lou or Berny, was forced to stay back with the truck, outside in the air among the cretins. From the diesel pumps, dressed in army fatigues, a vet in his fifties or sixties—his mutilation made dating a challenge—limped past Christ. Amid the scars and lacerations on his face and arms were the more pronounced injuries: an ear burnt down to nothing, a severed nose and deep damage to his throat. He was carrying a small, plastic jack-o'-lantern, which he pointed toward Christ, and, lifting a microphone to his throat, croaked an automatic greeting, "Possibly separate you from some unwanted change, sir?" But, seeing as Christ had no pockets (or ability) to inventory, he shuffled on down the lot.

A daughter and her (step-?) father flanked Christ's ride side: a pair of junkies complete with pasty skin and emanating a stench of gangrene and oniony b.o.. Scratching at the scabs on their arms and face, they stopped along the outside wall and the man pulled out a couple bucks from his jeans and handed them to the younger girl.

"This ain't enough for pseudo." The girl pointed the fist of money toward the man and outstretched her hand to his crotch, rubbing his bulge.

"Well then, Mira," the man grabbed a thick handful of the girl's ass, "improvise."

"For the love of God what took so fucking long?" Christ said as Lou and Berny emerged from the store.

"Fucking Mu-Ham-Ed in der's charging eight-bucks a pack. And sonofabitch only had Newports." Lou got back in the truck. "If I wanted menthol I'd smoke a fucking candy-cane."

"Berny?"

"All dem baskets took their revenge, man. Swear I just shat Da Creature a da Black Lagoon."

"Let's just get the fuck out of here."

— § —

They continued west for another thirty minutes until hitting 39 and turning south. Fog returned, which turned to mist, which turned to snow. The snow lit up the dark, but only minimally; they could only make out the faint vigil of the moon and the outline of the towering silos jutting up from the fields.

Christ was given a sudden quick jerk. "What the fuck, Lou?"

"Fuckin' black ice. Can't help it."

"Maybe if you weren't driving so goddamned *fast*."

"Pussy. Hey, Berny, why don't yous twist us up another 'l,' calm our friend's nerves a bit?"

Berny took out the last cheap cigar and began unraveling the outer leaf, wrapping it around the Mad Dog bottle to keep it moist. He cracked open the inner leaf and began dumping the tobacco: one half falling onto the trampled floor-mats, embossed with naked, monochromatic women; the other half flying out the window, getting caught in Christ's hair and crown.

"What the fuck, Berny!"

"Oh shit; sorry man."

"Fuckin-A, man, watch it with that shit. Puh—it's in my mouth, man."

Berny crawled out the back opening and brushed the blunt guts out of Christ's hair. He pricked his finger on one of the thorns; he cursed and started sucking on his index finger.

"What now?" Christ asked impatiently.

"Your fucking crown stabbed me," muffled through the finger nestled in his mouth.

"Give it here."

Berny pulled his finger back. "No. What are you gonna do to it?"

"Would you just trust me?"

"Just tell me what you're gonna do?" Berny began squirming, half in the cab, half out, kicking Lou and causing him to turn and punch Berny on the ass. Berny flailed more.

"Berny. Relax!" After one last punch, Lou returned his eyes to the road, "Fuck. *Fuck.* FUUCCKK."

The truck had swerved into the right lane, bearing down on a slow-moving, late-model Saturn. Lou hit the brakes, which grasped only ice and, skidding, slammed into the right rear wheel of the maroon car, spinning the little sedan around one full rotation before the front collided with the guard rail on the right of the shoulder.

Spinning and counter-spinning, Lou gained control of the truck and stopped some hundred yards in front of the Saturn. Berny, who'd been thrown from the cab and forced to hang on to Christ for dear life, unraveled himself from the man.

"Shit."

"Should we do something?" Berny asked Lou.

"Fuck."

"Should we go back? See if she's all right? Call an ambulance?"

"Are yous crazy? All dis fuckin booze and weed? And judgin from da damage ta dat tiny piece-a-shit..."

Christ, who from his position could only hear the carnage, was now facing the damage full on and ordered Lou to go back to the other car. Lou declined and Christ reiterated more forcefully, "Go back right fucking now, Lou."

Lou reversed down the shoulder, giving Christ a good push view. As they got closer, he could make out one woman in the driver's seat; she was not moving. Lou stopped the car about fifteen feet away; he and Berny inched their way reluctantly out of the car as if the woman's injuries were contagious.

Some fifty yards from the crumpled sedan was a wind turbine, funneling the snowfall straight into them. The snow collected on their eyebrows, mustaches, hair, beard and crown.

Berny went no further than Virgil's rear axle, rubbing his sore-ridden, shaved head and mumbling an *ostinato* of, "Oh fuck, oh fuck, oh fuck…" Christ ordered Lou to the driver's side to check the status of the woman.

"Is she hurt?" Christ asked.

"Dat's pretty fucking obvious, ain't it?"

"Is she fucking *badly* hurt, Lou? Are there bones poking out of her goddamned skin?!"

Lou rubbed his high-and-tight and wiped the snow on his coveralls, "Shit, man, I ain't no doctor but I'd say she's pretty messed up."

"Here, get me down." Lou and Berny moved to the winch. Each took one of Christ's arms and, as gingerly as befits them, removed each nail from Christ's wrists. Christ's feet were still impaled; Lou grabbed his crowbar and, heaving and swearing, twisted the nail free. Christ yelled.

"Try a little less finesse. Fuck," Christ said, rubbing his aching feet. Blood trickled out his holes. "Berny, grab a flashlight."

The three of them moved to the car and looked inside, pressing their faces together for a better view. Despite the front of the car being severely damaged—the engine block dislodged, possibly crushing the woman's legs—the door remained relatively unaffected and opened without mechanical assistance, allowing Christ to get a better assessment of the damage; Louie C. flicked on his Mag-lite and scanned the car. She was middle-eastern and middle-aged with blood on her face from the broken nose incurred by the airbag. Strewn across the back and the passenger seat were books on TOEFL and architecture (a diagram of the Pisa Tower on the cover). Christ figured she must be a student at Northern, coming back late from the lab, and wondered if she hadn't fallen asleep at the wheel, or if she was too tired to see them, or if, as he feared, it was entirely their fault.

Berny sat on the guard rail, nauseous, "Is she dead?"

"Not quite."

"Well do something, man."

"I'll see what I can do, but I'm no doctor."

Christ reached his hand towards her but it was stayed by Lou. "Wait, what if she's Muslim or somethin.' "

"All are my children, Lou."

"But won't dat be, like, against her religion or somethin."

"I think the gift of life is universal in all religions, Louie Boy. Please, for fuck's sake, try to be a little less provincial."

"But I bet she's not Christian. Aren't yous only supposed to save Christians?"

"I think you've dramatically misinterpreted your history." Christ reached in and pressed the bar on the bottom of the seat. He pulled the seat back and tried to pull her out. "Fuck. Little help here?!"

Lou and Berny came up, each grasping her with both hands, and helped Christ pull her from the wreckage. She was breathing, shallowly, but breathing nonetheless. Christ laid her on the highway and put his hands to her broken legs, ribs and nose. The blood receded. She opened her eyes just enough to see the light from Lou's taillights reflect on the bristles of Christ's beard, thorns and hair before losing consciousness.

"So she's alive? Thank Christ." Berny was leaning over her and drooling from pre-vomit salivation.

"You're welcome."

"That's not what I—I mean—yeah…"

Christ turned to Lou, "How bad is the truck?"

"Truck's fine. Dat's strong, 'Merican engineering for yous."

"Can you get her car up on the hoist?" Lou nodded, lowering the crucifix of the hoist to the ground and running the cable and hook to the front axle. Christ, to Berny, "Give me a hand, let's move her to the cab."

Berny looked at her but didn't move.

"Berny! Fucking get over here." Berny shuffled over and grabbed her legs while Christ carried her torso. They rested her in the middle of the bench, Berny climbed in after to keep her conscious. Christ shut the door.

"Is the car ready?"

Lou was at the hydraulic switchboard. "Yeah, just about. But where yous gonna fit?"

"I'll be fine for a while. Keep driving south towards Peru and get her to a hospital; then come back and pick me up."

"So we gotta come back here? Can't you like…"

"I can't fucking fly, Lou. I'm not Superman, you idiot."

Lou huffed and put the lift into action, murmuring, "Well how in the hell am I supposed to know what you can and can't do…" The Saturn bucked and slid towards its place at the head of the hoist. The hoist whined, the car hiccupped, and then there was a loud snap; the car slumped down as if it was shot, resting halfway across the back.

"Fuck." Lou moved to the cable and tried to hook it around part of the chassis.

"Lou?"

"Not now, I'm trying ta fix dis fuckin thing."

"Lou…I'm hit."

Lou came around to the other side of the truck and found Christ, prostrate on the icy ground with a six-inch piece of steel poking through his ribcage where the bit of fractured axle had shot off and called home. "Christ!"

Lou knelt beside him. "Berny get out here, now. Christ, he's hurt."

Berny opened the door; Christ shot him down. "Don't come out. Stay in there with her." Christ coughed blood onto his face. "Lou, give me something to wipe this off."

Lou opened his coveralls, removed his flannel shirt and passed it to Christ, who pressed his face into the cotton and passed off the blood and sweat. Lou put the shirt in his back pocket.

Christ coughed and more blood followed. "Ah shit…I think this is it, Louie."

"Don't say dat. You'll be fine. Don't say dat." Lou's eyes were watering.

"It's true." Blood poured out of Christ's chest like a hot spring. Lou tried to apply pressure but the blood continued to pour onto the ground, collecting about his waist and starting to freeze.

"It's not fair, man!"

"But this is happening, regardless," Christ's eyes moved past Lou in-to the sky. "The stars are out."

The chaos of the snowfall had receded and left an array of lights up above them: Venus was just starting to rise in the horizon, Jupiter tow-ered above them and Mercury was blocking the path of Andromeda's rescue.

"Is he okay?" Berny asked from the car.

Lou turned to Berny, "Does he look fucking okay?"

"How'm I supposed to know from in here?!"

Christ pulled Lou close. "Lou, I want you to tell Magda—"

"Yes?" Lou leaned in.

"Tell her we'll always have Montezuma."

"Da Revenge thingy?"

"Yes." Christ turned his head to cough up another spat of blood.

"Yous want me ta tell her you'll always have Montezuma's revenge?"

"Yes," Christ laughed and a thick stream of blood left his chest. "Yes. I want her to smile when she remembers me. Everything else is too…morbid."

"What's happening?" Bernie shouted, still inside the truck.

"Goddamnit will yous stop interrupting da man?"

Lou turned back to Christ, awaiting more instructions or testa-ments from the dying man, but Christ was dead before Lou's eyes re-turned to him. "Ahh, no…ahh, no…fuck!"

Lou lifted his chest up and held Christ's body against his belly, sucking in his tears. "Well fucking now what!?" But there was no an-swer, no one to give advice.

Lou looked around at the surroundings. It was a dark night in the middle of Illinois and he didn't want the coyotes getting to Christ's body before the red-and-whites could come. Lou looked around for someplace to store him until they arrived and found a dry drainage pipe under the road; Lou wrapped Christ in his flannel and hoisted the dead man over his shoulder while he climbed down the small em-bankment. The body fit nicely.

Lou came back from the pipe and peeled off the Saturn's hood from its remaining bolt, then disappeared back down the side. Lou placed the hood snuggly against the entrance and went back to the truck. Berny was weeping softly with his arm around the woman, her blood-less head sleeping against his shoulder; he jostled her a bit to wake her up, but she made no further move toward consciousness.

Puffing his moustache to counter the quiver in his lip, Lou was silent as he got back into the cab. In the rearview mirror, the first light of dawn was breaking upon the wavy landscape behind them—bathing the crests of the wrinkled fields in orange and pink. Lou put the truck in gear and drove south, hoping to see that little blue sign with the white "H" on the side of the road before too long. Yes, the sun was coming up, but its rays were still a long ways off.

II. ASCENDING THE HOLY MOUNTAIN

"The text of pleasure is a sanctioned Babel."

—*Roland Barthes,* THE PLEASURE OF THE TEXT

— § —

I.

Six went up the mountain looking for God; *a* God, *the* God, *which* God could not be confirmed.[1] The Intel came in from a patrolling AWAC and made its way up the conduit of rank and office, whereupon a threat assessment was ordered, a protocol put in place, and, trickling back down the ranks, a team was assembled to greet/intercept/assess/engage the deity. Because of the high costs of the operation and the lack of federal sponsorship available what with the seven-front war, financing for the expedition was provided—with markedly high interest—by hedge-fund mogul and amateur dentist J.R. Holmes-Manley, whose terms dictated he accompany the team up the purportedly holy mountain in addition to handpicking them, "My money, my choice." The team he selected was not necessarily the best crew money could buy, but the best crew he could buy with the money he was willing to spend—which put them somewhere between the economy option and business class. On loan from the army were theoretical-

---

1 Okay, more than six, but six had faces, names, a purpose.

physicist Lt. Lawrence Hendrix Higgs, heading up the intellectual and existential components of the mission, and Major Michael T. Carbine, who, with an unmatched militaristic perspicacity, attended to the safety of the party. Dr. Bogdan Zdravko ("Goran," he asked all to call him while on this venture) was the onboard physician. Chef de cuisine Télesphore de Périgord-Bouchon not only provided the meals but was in charge of linguistics, a man whose New Orleans background gave him a Creole, French, Italian, and English base, and whose formal culinary training in the Far Far East provided him with a satisfactory Asian lexicon—not to mention varieties of other languages he'd picked up along the way; and he was a solid Catholic to boot. And to cover all bases, Unitarian Priest Dominic Pigro[2] was sent to handle negotiations with the divinity. [3]

The mountain of concern lay several miles east of Mt. McKinley towards the Talkeetna Mountains, due north of Sovereign Mountain. A volcanic range with minimal pitch, this was no K2 they had to ascend; still it would require wits, discipline, and above all a respect for the terrain...

CLACK CLACK CLACK CLACK CLACK!

Forced to wait out a storm at Base Camp 4 before attempting the final summit, all were sharply woken from their beauty rest by a melee of gunfire—and not for the first time since embarking on the mountain.

"Jesus, has no one read of the importance of sleep to the digestive track!?" Bouchon yelled through the canvas walls of his tent, though giving little sign of waking outside the squeak of the air mattress[4] as he rolled over.

In this latest threat, Carbine had found a squirrel approaching his knapsack with what he would have called "hostile curiosity" and un-

---

2 A former Catholic Priest converted to Unitarian Universalism yet keeping most of his Catholic practices, including title, abstinence, and the administering of Eucharist and confession should any member desire.

3 Then of course there were the Sherpas to handle the heavy equipment and the inglorious labor involved.

4 ?

loaded three clips from his standard issue Beretta into the furry creature. Carbine blew the smoke off the muzzle, letting it tickle the Velcro
Band-Aid of his moustache, apologized for the harsh cock's-call, and
requested that he not be disturbed at his tent while cleaning his barrel. And though no one approached, none could escape the sounds of
the ritual: the smooth tap of a lubed barrel joining the slide group, followed by a dry moan and whimper as he slid the barrel bushing over
the recoil spring plug...

"I guess we're up now," Pigro announced without any reciprocal
confirmation. Slowly, the remainder of the party stirred inside their
neon wombs of blue and yellow, and one by one begrudgingly birthed
themselves out into the indifferent morning air.

Dr. Zdravko spent much of his morning revising a poem entitled
"A Zembian Shade of Love," written under the pseudonym Uroš
Radomir, while keeping a casual eye on the young Sherpas brought in
from Nepal, packing and repacking and hauling the sacks of provisions
and equipment, his pen drooling on the paper when one such porter
had to squat to pick up a heavy parcel. Dr. Zdravko looked at his poem[5] and found many incarnations—several of which he would have to
eliminate out of redundancy—of "hulking brown thighs/delivered un-
to a sacrifice/for the waxwing swain."

"Hold on a tic," Uroš brought the pen up to his lip and mawed the
tip for several moments, "Yes, really more 'gold flake' or 'oxidized nick-
el' than 'brown.' "

While the good doctor followed the perfume of a new muse[6], Higgs
emerged from his tent, billowing Apache signals of yellow marijuana smoke into the gray mountain air as he struggled to close the flap
behind him.[7] In the following order, Higgs scratched the back of his

---

5 More or less a cache of largely stolen or slightly manipulated lines from many
   canonized works.

6 The porter was sensible enough not to ask why the doctor was following him
   into the provisions tent.

7 Whose three columns of smoke would have belied an arguably less dire emergency, were any Apaches watching, than those that ailed him; namely "a debit
   of blue kush and a credit of blue balls," as J.R. quipped to the Sherpa undergo-

neck, his left temple, his right testicle, his left armpit, and finally the tendrils of hardened cocaine and snot infused into his moustache. He looked horny, or so Zdravko (or anyone) could have guessed. Somehow or another, Higgs had found the only woman within a-hundred-and-forty-seven miles of the summit and consecrated wild and raucous acts of sordid love with her in his tent at Base Camp 1[8]. Well, it'd been three weeks since ascending, and based around the steady increase of his drug regimen, Zdravko estimated that his libido must be approaching epochal restraint.

"Good morning, Lawrence," Pigro chirped, standing upright from his morning calisthenics—a global workout, to be sure. Higgs eyed the diminutive man and nodded; Pigro couldn't tell if Higgs had actually registered the words or even the face addressing him. Higgs, for his part, was staring directly into the preterit demerits of a fourth-dimensional insurgency: every former lover occupying the same feeble body addressing him, faces changing kaleidoscopically: Lauriethelips-Lesliethelegs-Zoeythezit-Mollythemole-Friedathefreckle-Heatherinbadweather-KarenintheLebaron-Katjewhocaughtya-Sarahwiththescar-Sarawiththescarf-SierrawithKaharaathersister'squinceanera-thewitch-thebitch-thelawyer-thelech…rolled into one wagging finger, all accusing him of not spinning The Great Wheel, of being too afraid to take the ride, that their sexual exhibitions were merely a cover up (projection, transference, repression) for his Lacanian castration—and that he'd left the kitchen lights on in his apartment; he nodded towards the Amalgam Woman, an act he hoped she'd take as, not confirmation or penance, but more so an acknowledgement that her words were met.

"Um…Larry?"

Higgs made no further comments, merely about-facing and heading to the Comms Tent to see if he could find some music and to fur-

---

ing a quick root canal at his right.

8 God being Man's business, after all, a woman obviously had no place on the actual mission; still, Higgs would have tried to get her on board as his amanuensis had she not turned her ankle in the Comms Tent during an especially wild (and broadcasted) session.

ther contemplate the God he would soon be meeting; *Cannubis* came into his mind: an Egyptian god with the head of a jackal and five-pointed leafs for pupils; large, swelling golden breasts; shouting fire and sweet/sour smoke from the empire of the mountain...

A man corpulent by corpulent standards, Bouchon, having finally roused from his tent to put the breakfast on the burner, was at the other end of the camp reading a New York periodical in which Yosemite Sam, NRA spokesman, was under intervention for amphetamine, firearm, and anger issues. *"Gol darn it, now I'm a telling ya dag blasted, varmit-feltchers I ain't got a problem; and if y'all keep on at it you're gonna find yourself facing the meanest, keenest, Yankee-stompinest, pill-poppin' popper o' conies this side of the Mason-Dixon. Now, Daffy, get my gun!"*

So while the rest of the party was prepping themselves for the day's trek, breaking down camp, packing and repacking their rucksacks, coordinating with the Sherpas how best to load themselves down for the day, Bouchon remained seated, selectively oblivious to the goings-on about him, reading and chortling in his seven-tongue language.

"Bouchon, what in fuck's name do you think you're doing? We are rolling out at 0800 on the fucking dot." Major Carbine took a break from re-fitting his knapsack with ammunition and affixing his M-60 with a makeshift holster to chastise his problem child.

Bouchon grumbled some galvanized string of profanity from around the world with a mouth full of some private dish.

Carbine put down his task and stood before the orange-clad Buddha, "Come again, Bouchon."

"I said, I'm researching refrigeration methods for conditions such as these: how to keep meat cold without risking freezer burn; how to avoid excessive heat, and thus rot! Altitudinal pressure-cooking timetables. Or perhaps you think food poisoning and spoiled *bouffe bourguignon* no great threat to our mission?"

"Now we talked before about that attitude of yours. I know you're here for some bullshit linguistic purposes—a goddamned spectacle if you ask me—and you do make a mean soufflé, la-di-fuckin-da. It's in my SOP to get you up there, keep you safe, and get you back. But you keep on like that and I will frag your fat fucking ass right off this mountain; and so you know I'm not kidding, I'm sending the porter carrying your auxiliary—and completely fucking unnecessary—ration-pack back down the goddamned mountain. Now do you read me *now*, Bouchon?"

Bouchon dropped the mag to his lap and grew several shades pinker. "I should have expected someone with your profligate sexual proclivities to resort to base threats, sophomoric weight jokes. Now, if *you* don't want to find yourself on the receiving end of *my* Damascus, I would advise you to reconsider the porter. I am a man with a wealth of needs, and they are to be met if I am to carry out the task bequeathed to me from *our* President, as well as those of neighboring, yet inferior heads of state. Scamper off and play with your guns; a real man prefers his wit as his weapon, or the gentlemanly intimacy of a blade." Bouchon put his face back into the magazine and produced a cold eggroll from his pocket, which he ate with zero fucks to give for the Major—or anyone else, for that matter.

Before Major Carbine had a moment to counter Bouchon's diatribe, or possibly strike the individual that daily brought his blood to a viscous sludge, dredging through his hardening veins, Zdravko approached to complain about Pigro's lack of physical support[9], placing his hand on the small of the Major's back. The Major promptly stiffened and turned the hand away.

"Major, we are in the middle of a tedious, perilous, and entirely paramount event in the course of our species—nay, all species—and I understand his reasons for being here, but for the love of Yeats may the man carry his own weight?" He extended his hand to Carbine's shoulder and began kneading his trapezius, from which Carbine likewise withdrew himself.

"I understand your concern. I'll talk to him about it?"

Holmes-Manley was passing by in his elk morning robe, brushing his teeth, when he overheard Zdravko's plea. "No worries, gents, I'll have a little talk with our chaplain; there are other things I wish to discuss with him as well."[10] He turned on his heels and brushed his way

---

9 Who, even though he had the body of an anthropomorphic mouse from a Saturday Morning cartoon, was still expected to haul the minimum of his weight—which, as you can imagine, wasn't much.

10 The following conversation between Holmes-Manley and Father Pigro: "Open

towards Pigro's tent. And despite the harsh mountain winds, his blond locks, combed to the side of his head like a frozen golden tsunami, never moved a follicle; his hair was so uniform, so precisely mapped and maintained throughout the expedition that Higgs had become certain it was some kind of advanced, plastic hairpiece made available only to the extremely wealthy; Higgs had also been quick to catalogue the financier's chin as well, likening it to an expertly-shaved nutsack, with not even a trace of stubble in this mountain clime. Zdravko concurred.

Zdravko went back to Carbine, "Well if he's unwilling, would it really be that much trouble to send for a few additional young men to provide us their powerful bodies: incited by their nascent maturation to facilities both stronger and of more endurance?" He ended the dialogue with a tap of his nose before Carbine could answer, in the hopes of rendering the question rhetorical, and therefore the correct course

---

your mouth for a second. Uh-huh, uh-huh, nice. Nice. Did you ever notice how perfectly shaped your top incisors are? I mean 8 and 9 are utterly flawless; ditto 23 and 24." "Glach gluugh." "Number 25 is a little crooked, though; I could probably do something for that. Also, it appears your lower canines, numbers 22 and 27, are just a hair-lip too pronounced and could be filed down easily." "Gleeze glon't." "I don't have my diamond sanding paper handy but perhaps we could use the Major's file; I saw him using it on his .357 last night." "Glongk." "What? Oh. [releasing the man's jaw from his pincers]. You were saying?" "I was saying, I appreciate the interest but that won't be necessary. Perfectly satisfied with the set God gave me." "But that doesn't mean it can't be improved upon!" "Let's not get scholastic; just chalk it up to wearing one's faults with pride." "So it's an issue of pride, is it? Well, it isn't pride when it effects your bite and the posture of your jaw. It's a matter of mechanics my friend: yours is an engine that's not firing in all cylinders." "My bite is fine." "Okay, I exaggerated a bit. But at least let me set you up with a new set of headers, maybe bore out the cylinders a little?" "J.R., I am not subjecting my mouth to your recreations—" "Recreations? This isn't some stamp collection!" "Have you a license or a degree? Do you charge people for your work, sir?" "Charge people? Hell, man, I have enough money as it is; I don't need petty sums just to polish an enamel statue! To practice the one true crown molding!" "The answer is still 'no.' " "Cock tease."

of action. Zdravko then headed off to pick up Holmes-Manley's trail and inquire about the origins of the robe and whether by chance the financier had ever rowed crew in his college days.

"Goddamn civilians…" Carbine grumbled, trudging back to break down his tent. A half hour later, at precisely 0807—a time both irritating and relieving for Carbine—the bags were loaded onto the shoulders of those that would bear them, standing at attention and waiting for the Major's signal. They were to climb within spitting distance of their maker, to start up the narrow path that led to the new residence of God[11].[12] Six were to call upon God and answer for the shape of man, to demand God's deposition and deploringly chastise or reconfirm the drafting of sin and the precociousness of human resolve. Then they would lunch and discuss how best to proceed.

To mark this major event, each climber celebrated in their own manor the beginning of the journey's true commencement: Higgs had rolled himself a large joint with most of the rest of his weed—he still had to make the trip back!—stuffing it so full the band of glue only just wrapped around; he plucked the cylinder from the band of his helmet decorated with various mathematical theorems, graphs, equations—Complex Scalar field theory, Lagrangian density, The Klein-Gordon equation, and a crudely drawn graph of The Mexican Hat potential at the top front of the helmet—and roasted the perfectly conical tip. Carbine lowered his M-60 and shot into the cliff-face of the opposing mountain, which produced a not inconsiderable hard-on. Goran recited a lyrical poem of his own creation. Bouchon slurped a mussel he'd kept chilled for just this particular occasion. Pigro, easily the most anxious, heading into a veritable performance review, burped a gaseous ball of indigestion. Holmes-Manley took one last look at the LED watch that displayed his securities. They were to cross the tree line, a very tangible line between life and death, to trespass the border nature had drawn the world over that firmly decried to the living "Like, not up here, man." They would leave the trees and become men

---

11 —a residence, *the* residence, again inconclusive.

12 And who could say if he was just subletting or had perhaps bought property at a variable interest rate?

of snow and rock, crossing the line that separated path from pilgrimage.

— § —

II.

Of course, he wasn't really Higgs, or, not of the Higgs lineage he would have preferred to share phenotypes with; and perhaps it was precisely that proximity (linguistically, if not genealogically) to the famed physicist and founder of the eponymous boson that had gotten Higgs interested in physics in the first place, somehow striving to become the adopted heir of Higgs, to become the son of the God-particle founder. Stopped for a brief rest, Lawrence took the time to urinate a Feynman's diagram into the snow of two decaying gluons producing the Higgs boson, splitting into a top/anti-top pair and combining to form the Higgs boson; the diagram worked well as, after forming the two decaying gluon lines with looping spirals of bright piss, the branching of the gluons into the two top/anti-top pairs at the triangular center of the sideways 'W,' a couple quick pinches to make the letters, he still had enough paint in his can to finish the perforated lines that finalled to the bladder-draining "H" that is the Higgs boson. He had only a moment to zip and admire his work—the vitamin-supplemented canary and neon-green urine blazing triumphantly against the perfectly refracting snow—before Bouchon—in a hurry to drop his pack and binge heavily on the port in his canteen—barreled into Higgs, forcing him to re-center his gravity with both boots submerged in the heart of his diagram.

"*Baise il mio huevos!*" Bouchon spat in his amalgam language, adding that he would not advance any farther without a sufficient snack, which of course meant a full-on meal; nor would he prepare said meal without a proper sous chef. And so they found themselves taking sixty versus five.

Pigro found himself conveniently stricken with another bout of altitude sickness and was laid up, "resting his eyes," and thus could not assist with the meal. Eager to get the show on the road—and get paid—one of the Sherpas, forced to carry Pigro's load on top of Carbine's, hindering his peripheral visibility, had unfortunately placed his foot in a snow-covered cranny, which resulted in a fall, a twisted ankle, and the contents of Carbine's bag spilling out onto the snow. Feeling it his Unitarian duty to ease the man's pain (spiritually), Pigro rose from his pallet of coats and provisions but soon found his mission realigned by the discovery of a certain piece of paper that had fallen from the Major's pack.

Pigro picked up one of the seventy-pages that made up the mandatory Expedition PREDICAMENTS, Pre Deity Confrontation Assessments: a religious and moral test from the keepers of the MMPI, required by all key members of their group to have completed, then properly reviewed to assess prejudice, existential beliefs, morality, and faith. Pigro picked up the singular, dog-eared, snow-soaked, dirt-clodden questionnaire and found that, other than abuse, it remained free of marks.[13]

Pigro stormed off to confront the Major as to why he had failed to complete the test, and, as such, why he'd still been allowed to go along.

After a long and testy reprimand as to why and how it had come about for Pigro to be in sight, let alone possession of Carbine's person-

---

13 Question 22: A man makes a machine. The machine has a purpose: it is laden with saws, two-foot serrated blades and the general machinery of death to be used in a programmed function of entropy: with only thermo-visual abilities, its program is to identify sources of high entropy and with the "general machinery of death" eradicate all aberrant sources of thermal unrest until the entire area has achieved a balanced thermodynamism, which would essentially assure zero entropy. The question is: If the machine kills a squirrel to satisfy the entropy of the forrest, if a child is killed to keep the concrete at a static temperature (Note: the chalk drawings are still intact), if the machine performs as programmed, do we:

   a. applaud the creator
   b. blame the creator
   c. crucify the creator
   d. blame the machine, acting as programmed, and charge it with
       the facilitation of death?

22A: If the engineer charged with making this machine finds his math out of date and cannot create the aforementioned machine to run "successfully," is he or she:

a. a failure
b. a savior
c. just a man
d. none of the above
e. all of the above?

22B: If the machine, by way of miracles, nanomachines, God or other anomalies on the part of the programmer, were to develop a conscious and instead of dispatching a grove of woodland animals it instead stops its machinery, puts down its tools and learns how to love, is the machine:

a. to be blamed for not following its programming
b. to have the blame transferred to the creator, who will thus spend a month in the hole
c. to be chastised for developing a sense of self and morality
d. to be rewarded for developing a sense of self and morality
e. to be condemned, in that the engineer had promised his benefactors to deliver an entropic machine and by this chain of events the engineer's failure has been unanimously considered seditious, of which the resulting consequence is to be placed against the firing wall and shot six times in the genitals with elephant guns?

To answer correctly show your work.

Question 23: If a 1992 Dodge Stratus is built, disseminated and sold to a man, Y, and Y is found parked near a baseball field molesting a child, gets incarcerated, sells the car to Y_2, Y_2 gets drunk and runs over a thirteen-year old boy on the eve of his middle school graduation, then proceeds to drive on drunkenly, dragging the boy 5.1 miles before finally being pulled over and arrested, the car is repossessed and sold through police auction to Y_3, who drives the car at 23mph down 119th St. while the men in the passenger seat and backseat open fire on five gang-related youths, of which they kill two and pierce the lung of a five-year old girl playing with her Barbie Big Wheel inside her Grandmother's living room, before being impounded yet again, which gets bought in 2001 by a day trader, Y_4, for his sixteen-year-old son who blows his head off in the backseat, but the transmission is still good so the carpet is cleaned and sold to a divorcee, Y_5, who works as a board member on a failing insurance company and who, upon losing his job, dresses in a Santa costume, rings the doorbell on his ex-laws Door County cabin, where nine-year-old als, the Major went on to explain that he found no use for an intangible God, that the only spirituality he considered potent had to be held in his hands, had to perform at his discretion.

"It's like this, Padre: God created man, and man created the M-16, which in my opinion stands for Man-16, the sixteenth installment of man (each revision approaching the asymptote of perfection, from the A1 to the A4): sleek, sexy, powerful, and designed to one specific purpose—none of this fartin' around, 'trying to find your-self' horseshit—perfection."

"Oh, hogwash. Do you honestly feel the M-16 superior to the Kalashnikov? No jamming, no shells rupturing in the chamber; capable of withstanding sand, jungle, mud, snow, all manner of conditions; parts easily replaceable; and it's cheap, accessible to everyone and anyone," the good doctor objected while attending to the medical needs of the Sherpa, extending a thorough examination of the man-boy's leg.

"The Kalashnikov's a hussy. Plain and simple. I'll allow that the MP-7 might be a superior firearm, but I prefer the classical beauty of the M-16A1. As for how I got here, I'm Major Michael T. Carbine, and that should motherfucking suffice."

"So what is it you expect to find up there, then? At the top?" Pigro piped in.

"What God has always been: the world's greatest weapon. Now,

---

twin girls answer and yell with a mix of exasperation and disbelief, "*Santa!?*" before he shoots them each in the face, then proceeds through the house spraying bullets and homemade napalm out of a portable gas container and super-soaker before exiting the house, Santa suit melting onto his flesh so that he pulls over next to an orphanage and succumbs to the burns, but the trunk is booby-trapped to explode should anyone attempt to open it, at what point can we hold the car responsible?

Question 24: If Schrodinger's cat has a name, how does the experiment change?

   a. greatly

   b. very little

   c. not at all

   d. both a & c

someone please assist Bouchon so we can eat and get the fuck up this mountain."

And though Higgs agreed to assist Bouchon[14] with their "lunch" of brandied pheasant and Wagyu dumplings in a balsamic-honey vinaigrette, they would advance no farther up the mountain that day; no sooner had they sopped their plates with the last bits of dumpling than their path was besieged by a strong wind hauling a train of portentous storm clouds.

"We can still make it," Carbine implored.

"There's no way this poor boy can make it any farther," Zdravko still cradling the Sherpa's head in his lap, pinning his arms down as the lad tried to escape.

"Fuck him."

"Well I don't see how that would help. But if you think—"

Carbine vocalized his malcontent by emptying yet another clip; although, with no helpless animals in proximity, he was forced to deposit the bullets into the ominous cumulous.

It appeared God would just have to wait one more day.

— § —

Though none would ever commit to a verbalized agreement, in case Bouchon should overhear and ransom the sentiment for less work, all were immensely pleased to have their linguistics officer be, first-and-foremost, a world-renowned chef somewhere near the upper-ninetieth-percentile of his field.[15] As such, Bouchon was allowed to select the provisions for the trip, barring certain items according to logistical possibilities of transport, refrigeration, cost, and "necessity," as Carbine had said, referring to ingredients such as sea squirt, tapioca multodextrin, *gianduja*, agar agar, *hato mugi*, nepitella, lecithin, *akudjura*, ingredients used to make certain molecular-gastronomy dishes like pillows of cinnamon air, hyacinth vapor, *wasabi* foam, *yuzu* fluid gels, candied *idiazábal*...Despite the setbacks on the garnishes and tertiary

---

14 For a tincture of pure nutmeg.

15 Especially those who'd ever had to rely on MREs for their sustenance (Carbine, Higgs, and Zdravko).

sustenance, the team was served roasted-duck risotto, *miso*-grouper/ Chilean-seabass *ceviche*, powdered-sangria-seared veal *tapas*, and deconstructed shepherd's pie with Guinness-braised short-rib and carrot/corn/pea-*purée* on fried potato wafers died with squid ink (the vial carefully hidden from Carbine). The meals provided not only caloric necessity but a morale boost and insulating warmth of the belly to put each member into a cozy slumber before the ensuing sub-zero chill of night—as well as providing sufficient calcium enrichment as Holmes-Manley pronounced when he demanded a second serving.

"One serving per," Bouchon said with menacingly arched eyebrows and flaming, orange-sienna beard, brandishing a small paring knife in the face of the middle-aged financier. "There will be no free market enterprise in my kitchen."

"My good man, I simply ask you to hold your light to my teeth and examine for yourself. Now, you see there, and there—the white spots?—this isn't attributed to a build-up of plaque, rather it represents an increasing deficiency of calcium in my enamel, making them brittle and susceptible to cavities. I simply ask that you give me another serving so that I may treat my condition: after all we're simply beasts if not brothers."

"*Kutabare con caliente* rusty *sizo!*" Bouchon stabbed the knife into his cutting board before turning to the serving pot, which still contained a sizeable amount of truffles, mushrooms, and lamb cutlets in roux-thickened *velouté*, upended the pot and slapping the dish onto the impacted snow floor. He smiled triumphantly through his beard and jowls, the white fat surrounding his blood-ripened face gave him the uncanny resemblance of a strawberry-jam *kolachke*.

"Well then, I see you're just being difficult." Holmes-Manley huffed about for a minute to show his indignation before marching off to his tent.

— § —

At night, while everyone was sated and slumped around the bonfire and the portable ceramic heaters, Pigro took to musical duties, serenading the camp with his acoustic bass—having never acquired the patience and perspicacity for chords. Though a man of several cloths, Pigro's musical auralography was composed of mostly secular music;

he chugged out the bass lines and sang songs like "Judy Touch Me Two Times," "My Love Lies in Newark," and the 5/8 samba, "Tijuana, Don't'cha Wanna, Love Me A-Mor-eh?" After a while, when Pigro's lack of harmonic accompaniment, needless to say, fell short, Carbine joined in with a resplendent (and surprising) alto and Bouchon thwapped a beat on his belly—occasionally lifting his shirt and slapping the bare skin to form a piccolo-snare. The sherpas danced in the manner of their homelands, and the good doctor Goran joined them, eager to appease his anthropological passions and establish a tight fraternity with this group of men; when he had sufficiently mocked their dance, he set to teaching the men the dance of the Western world, starting with a traditional Serbian *kolo* from the Kraljevo region, forcing them to form a circle and hold each other about the waist. The task proved too difficult (Goran trying to get them to recite the specific nuances of the lower-body dance) and he was forced to move on to similar dances of the outlying Balkans, the *hora*, the Vranjski *čačak*, and a variation of a fast 2/4 *hasapiko* called the *hasaposerviko*. When these failed, Goran moved further west and introduced them to the line dances of the Hustle and the Electric Slide, which, fortuitously enough, they not only learned, but relished. Higgs smoked a joint from his reserve stash with a couple drops of laudanum applied to the paper and tapped his foot along.

The evening was of rapture, frivolity, and general optimism, of celebration and verve, and, unfortunately, of individuality, as it was not to be repeated.

— § —

III.

Due to the nature of one of the party's members having a physical disposition...less than ideal for mountain climbing[16], certain tools and procedures were necessary to maneuver the individual along the more vertiginous faces of the mountain; and certain individuals who

---

16 One Télesphore de Périgord-Bouchon.

had such specialized training[17] were charged with the administration of these tedious and crucial tasks. The system required a knowledge of rock climbing, knots, mechanical physics, hoists, anatomy, gravity, practical application of a fulcrum, and strength enough to provide auxiliary manual support should the trusted motors and pulleys fail. To say that it required one's full faculties would be an understatement; to say that full faculties were always on hand would be an even greater understatement.

As it happened, the morning they were to once more ascend the final stretch, the morning after the dancing and singing, Lt. Higgs awoke with a troubling war occurring in his gastrointestinal tract; evidence of the troops' mobilization could have been found in a simple analysis of his dreams, had he remembered them, where his conquests, each more attractive than the other, were killed by the continuing need to excuse himself and run to the bathroom...and the nightmare of the conquest where the bowels struck in situ. He replayed the events of the night to find the cause of the strife: there was the singing, the dancing Sherpas, the opiated cannabis, the subsequent hunger, the search for a means of snack, the locked provisions, the smells of umami and buttery mushrooms wafting through the air, the finding of spilt dinner seeping into dirtied snow, the test of smell, a tentative taste, another, acceptance, indulgence, overindulgence, the relighting of the joint, the prompt sleep. A peristaltic battle of ingress and egress was waging inside of Higgs, the opium induced constipation slave-driving his bowels inwards, the turned supper in his small intestine battling to burst forth into the mountain air.

"Entropic irony!" he said as if addressing an enemy he knew all too well, the kind of enemy who had run off with his wife, impregnated his sister, surpassed him in a fellowship, and then stolen his notes and files on a patent that would have put his children's children through a bachelor's degree and as many post-graduate degrees they could muster. Higgs was still buckled over in his sleeping bag when Carbine came through to make his morning wake-up inspections.

"0600 hours, Lieutenant. Up and at 'em. You're going to puff like

---

17 Messrs. Maj. Michael T. Carbine and Lt. Lawrence Hendricks Higgs.

an Ingine you're goin' to climb like one, too."

Higgs assembled a weak, "Roger," and Carbine bent his ear to the tent flap, all too aware of conferring to mountain etiquette that one does not enter another man's tent without invitation[18]. He pressed his ear to the canopy tent and listened for sounds of stirring, which Higgs provided by squirming from his sleeping bag and trying to worm his way into the appropriate attire. Carbine took the noise as progress, nodded, and moved on.

When he was fully dressed, taking easily three-times as long as normally required, Higgs un-zipped the tent flap and poked his head through the hole and into the biting morning, looking for signs of the doctor as inconspicuously as he could, hoping, somehow, that his orange climbing suit could camouflage him in the battery of snow. Only several moments needed to pass before Higgs no longer felt his nose and his jaw began playing the spoons, his cheeks saved by the mutton chops that harkened back to the psychedelic era he wished he was operating in; it was a full two minutes before he spotted Goran returning from his morning calisthenics.

"Psst. Psst."

Of course, in twenty-miles-per-hour head wind not even Higgs could hear the plosive call—much less reach the doctor some twenty yards beyond. He would have to amplify, but how to do so with a manner of secrecy, a way to catch only the doctor?

— § —

Zdravko[19] had made his way back to his tent just positively enraptured with the elation of his muscles: his anterior and posterior deltoids, pectoralis (major and minor), trapezius, biceps, triceps, teres (major and minor), flexor carpi (radialis and ulnaris), latissimus dorsi, quadriceps

---

18 Goran, a truly intrepid recidivist of the code; his most recent infraction occurring in Holmes-Manley's tent that very morning, when the financier had discovered the doctor trying on his elk robe in the buff. "Well how are you supposed to feel the quality of the fabric if you can't *feel* the quality of the fabric, eh J.R.?"

19 Ahem, sorry, Goran.

(femoris, lateralis, and medialis), gluteus (maximus, medius, and min-
imus), hamstrings (semitendinosus and semimembranosus), psoas major; from all areas of his pectorals, inside sternum to the ridge above
his obliques and wrapping around the outer cliff-face of his nipples, to
the chimney shoot in his calves dropping to his Achilles: all warmed,
taught, well-oiled, as it were. One mustn't neglect one's morning rituals in this kind of expedition, especially rituals designed to keep one
keen and sharpened, whetting ones muscles on the stones of exercise, so as to be ready to slice with ease through whatever physical
brush might befall their path. He was stepping into his tent to retrieve
a whey-protein bar when the call of a female, red-breasted swallow
passed through his tympanic membrane and into his cochlea. Goran
turned to find the source of this ornithological aberration, only to find
the chill-battered face of Higgs surreptitiously sounding the animal,
then rotating his head left and right as if weary of discovery.

"Why you little scamp, for a minute I actually believed a swallow
had made it this far—"

"I've got a pain in my stomach, doc, what can you give me?" Higgs
had no time for Goran's merry-making.

"Oh, dear. You look a mess, Lawrence. Are you feeling well?"

"I just told you, Zdravko—"

"Goran, please."

"Look, man, I just told you, my stomach is in pain, something intestinal, what can you give me?" Despite the cold, sweat fell free from
the physicist's forehead and nose, his skin gone clammy and pale, from
a concentrated toffee to the water of a thin riverbed after a storm.

Goran put his hand, then both hands, to Higgs' face, clucking his
tongue before adding, "You really aren't well, my young man. In my
opinion, clearly not fit to go on. I'll recommend to Carbine that you
stay behind and allow me to tend to you." Goran turned to go, Higgs
grabbed his shoulder.

"I'll be fine; all I need is an antacid."

"My boy, I suggest nothing less than a laxative or enema, and a day
or two of rest."

"Negative. We need to move today, we've come far too close to be
held back. I won't let this mission be jeopardized on my account."

Goran wanted to say, "I should think your recreational habits the more likely candidate to jeopardize this mission," but felt too much sympathy for the pained man; and they were to be a band of men tight as the Spartans, were they not? Goran simply said, "Then, instead of out, let's keep it in..."

— § —

Towards the late morning, they had come upon the first of the two major rock faces in which a hoist was to be deployed for Bouchon, requiring a small contingency of their party to ascend, via crampon and ice-axe, up the escarpment, secure the motor (a fifty-pound machine that was hardly an easy burden) to the ground, then rig up and lower the hoist to Higgs, who would fit Bouchon in a custom saddle and operate the guide rope that would keep the portly bastard from slamming into the wall, or to navigate him away from jutting rocks or slabs of ice. Carbine, Holmes-Manley, and three of the Sherpas—each laden with a knapsack of food, climbing equipment, and two tents, respectfully—had made the first climb and were lowering the rope to Bouchon, who, having learned the drill, was settling into his saddle, coughing as Higgs pulled at the straps and took up the slack around his chest and groin before fixing the lead with a Prusik knot, a safety line with a Carabiner to a double figure-eight knot, and Higgs' steering line fixed with a clove hitch at Bouchon's belt. Pigro stood with his back pressed to the wall, praying, as Bouchon's feet slowly lifted from the ground; Goran yelling praise and positive reinforcement for the whole company while standing at the back of the pass the way they'd come, with four of the porters and yet more bags and cases needed for their intervention with the deity.

The present vertical obstacle was a total of seventy-seven feet, and just as Bouchon was nearing the fifty-five foot mark, the Imodium demanded by Higgs wore off. The returning rumblings struck quickly and viciously, forcing Higgs to drop the steering rope and make a mad dash to the fore-front of the pass, fumbling the eager attempts to disrobe himself like many a prom date, then violently, and vociferously, expelling the blitzkrieg assailing his bowels into the unassuming snow. The time didn't exist for castigation or disgust, for no sooner had Higgs dropped the rope then Bouchon swung like a flesh pendulum towards the blue and gray wall, slamming into a large, nose-shaped piece of ice that fell and scattered the Sherpas below; Pigro prayed harder; Goran dove, somersaulted, and took up the line[20], overcompensating to right the course and causing Bouchon to crash into another precarious formation of frozen water; Bouchon all the while shrieking like a mad hyena against the amphitheater of the mountain; and soon the air wasn't filled with the rumbling contention of man, but with the rumbling chaos of earth and ice. The avalanche bellowed into the ravine and valley below, sheets of white occluding all visibility, pummeling them with the malice of geology, mingling with the sounds of human screams dropping in red-shifts down the mountain.

A lesson in the sheer power of nature's brevity, when the thirty-eight seconds were up, Bouchon, still dangling from the rope, called out to the party in all languages at his disposal. Carbine was the first voice Bouchon heard, coming in a harsh whisper from somewhere close above him, telling him to "Shut the fuck up. I will not have another avalanche, do you read me?"

Bouchon looked up to the voice and found Carbine, as well as Holmes-Manley, dangling ten-feet above him from the precipice of the escarpment, suspended by Carbine's acumen for knot tying and following protocol. Below Bouchon was a slight stirring in the mound of white from where they had ascended, thin dustings of snow falling, then larger wet tufts and the peeking of black gloves. Pigro's head emerged first, sucking in great helpings of air. Goran, clasped tightly to one of the porters, emerged second, and had no sooner surfaced than he turned around and dove into the snow to search for more of their party, surfacing with just one more of the Nepalese mountaineers.

"Good God," Pigro said when he had caught his breath and evaluated the situation. The path they had come was completely destroyed, the thin slice of rock on which they'd sidled across was chipped to a smaller ridge barely the width of a foot and covered with ice and rock. "Good God!"

"God comes later. Right now, we need to assess our situation, take inventory of personnel and materials, and get our asses off this here cliff face."

---

20 His spryness no doubt a result of his morning training.

Pigro, somehow the only one curious as to the whereabouts of their missing physicist, in a rare display of action, made a spade of his hands and plunged them into the snow, pulling out scoops of rock and ice and throwing them over his shoulder into the chasm, "Lawrence? *Lawrence?!?*," his hands a windmill, one hand throwing while the other dug. Finally, his hands came upon something bristly and warm; he seized upon Higgs' mutton chops and pulled the shocked and breathless physicist back into the light of day. Pigro hugged him and kissed him on both cheeks; Goran blushed with envy.

"Mother-fucker," Carbine said, looking down at the exasperated lieutenant expressing several different shades of relief. Then a heap of snow fell on the back of his neck and Carbine turned upwards to a proffered hand taking hold of his rope and the smiling face of a Sherpa haloed[21] in the sun behind them.

The Sherpa pulled Carbine over the edge first, then reached down to help J.R.

"My God," Holmes-Manley beamed as the porter's face pulled up next to his, "your teeth, they're-, they're positively exquisite!"

— § —

IV.

Higgs had been saved by precisely the thing that had caused the whole damn accident in the first place, that is, his pants around his ankles; when the snow hit and pushed him towards the edge, the crotch had snagged around a rock and kept him firmly planted, with the build-up of snow locking him in place; however, while securing him, the snow and ice also stretched the limits of the composite material.[22] Temporarily collected post frozen-deluge, Higgs searched the thin shelf for a new garment, finding little options but to improvise one with the skin of a similarly shredded tent found in one of two remaining bags on the ledge[23]. With Higgs acceptably clothed, they would have to di-

---

21 Coincidentally?

22 Think "ass-less" chaps of a more alpine variety.

23 A gray tarp wrapped around his body somewhere in-between a diaper and a to-

rect their attention to the next obstacle: getting the hell off this ledge.

Carbine, Holmes-Manley, and the toothsome Sherpa had managed to get Bouchon up and over the ledge without sending too many ice shavings onto the heads below. Though eager to share his disappointment and general indictments of all but himself on the actions that led to his ignominious treatment up and over the wall, none listened to Bouchon's squawking as they lowered the harness down and secured the first of the surviving packs, using the motor to haul them up the side of the escarpment before sending the line back down to pick up the first of the human cargo.

Once everyone had ridden express elevator up the wall[24], the party reconvened and conducted an inventory of the remaining equipment: one CB Radio; Higgs' Geiger counter (in case God proved radioactive); all seven of Bouchon's sauce pans, none of the pantry; Pigro's bass; the Comms tent, poles bent to shit; several of Goran's poems and his medical attaché; Holmes-Manley's dental kit and fused copies of *Female Financier Monthly*; Carbine's rucksack of small arms and ammunition; three of their personal tents; four sleeping bags…

They found themselves logistically hosed as well: The satellite phones provided by J.R. were either lost or smashed on the rocks some ten-thousand-feet below, which meant they had no way of reaching base camp and informing them of the dire situation facing them, them and more importantly the mission. There would be no aid, and as Bouchon stated, no replenishment to their food stores. Unable to go any further, either to the site of the deity—for the present lack of time and the lack of equipment, as they'd discovered during their previous inventory—or back the way they had come, they were forced to make a tentative camp in a small ravine toward the western edge of the mountain, uncomfortably close to the southern side of the mountain and the mercurial geology of the southern face. Sandwiched between going up or going down, the nine remaining members of the party pitched what tents had survived and set about discussing the sleeping arrangements, all suffering a spiritual and cerebral deficit in morale.

---

ga.

24 Except for the fleet-footed Sherpas, who'd scaled the ice in ten minutes flat.

So, with one tent used to clothe Higgs, that left nine men to share three tents, tents technically labeled as having a two-man capacity but which, in practical application, and in conferring to appropriate levels of comfort, were really only meant for one man each. One normal-sized man, that is; Bouchon once again found himself the exception and the problem.

After a lengthy, *lengthy* discussion,[25] it was decided that Bouchon's tent would be shared with the smallest of the party, a Sherpa of fleet foot but small stature who looked more than weary of bunking with the large, irascible man[26]. Carbine, Holmes-Manley, and Santosh Nischal Mahesh[27] would make up another tent. Pigro, Higgs, Goran, and the remaining Sherpa would make up the final tent, a hideous affront to recreational outdoor architecture, stitching together the skin and broken bones of the Comms tent to add a separate "wing." Though utterly exhausted, none looked forward to retiring for the night.

After only an hour of feckless boredom since setting the sleeping accommodations and helping themselves to a paltry dinner of protein bars, the evidence lying in a small snow pit of multicolored foil wrappers, Bouchon decided to lend his tongue to vocalize everyone's unspoken thoughts: "I'm just going to say what everyone else is thinking. I think it's high time we devote a serious discussion to cannibalism."

Immediately the ravine was filled with shouts of objection from most of the party,[28] but Bouchon went on.

---

25 If you can call a fugue of screaming, shouting, and threats, veiled and non-, a discussion.

26 Though a different variety of weary than the Sherpa sharing Goran's tent.

27 They all found it fitting that they should learn the name of the Sherpa who had pulled them to safety, as the other Sherpas were quick to resent.

28 Messrs. Carbine and Pigro were particularly quiet, though that doesn't necessarily mean in collusion with the idea. Holmes-Manley objected more than most, yet approached Bouchon later in solitude and confided that he had merely objected for the sake of appearance, and that sometimes it was indeed better to serve the greater purpose of the party via sacrifice, especially as certain mem-

"Oh, please; you're telling me no one among you has ever sampled the succulent delicacies of Siberian Long Rat? Pasta a la Kosta? Dr. Zdravko, surely you've dined on Boris Borscht?! Mandingo Muffuletas, Major?!" Throwing an eye at Carbine, who was considerably taken aback, though not necessarily for the dietary implications.

"Now, I don't want to call out anyone as being particularly ancillary to our objective, but there are certain of us who, if we still aim to accomplish our goal, don't have a particular..." Bouchon gave a subtle nod to two of the Sherpas, "...skill set to offer, if you get me."

"Sherpa too stringy," Santosh said pulling his clothes from his body to suggest a lack of sustenance, "need someone meatier, rounder." Santosh glared at Bouchon.

"And I suppose you have a breadth of languages at your disposal should you meet this God of ours?" His face again taking on that rubicund pastry hue.

"God speak English, fat-boy. Everyone speak English."

Bouchon made to lunge for Santosh but gave up half-way through, telling himself it was the lack of adequate food that arrested his movement before his hands had even passed beyond his knees.

Goran spoke up, "And I speak Hebrew—my homeland required as

---

bers of the party attained—well, I'll just say it, a quantitative superiority—and should they decide to eat one of their own, he was more than confident in Bouchon's abilities to create a dish favorable to the palate; then impressing into Bouchon's palms vials of allspice, kosher salt, and paprika he had managed to secure from one of the packs before all contents were deposited into a communal bin, which was consequently catalogued and locked. Goran, too, had approached Bouchon when an appropriate time presented itself, and reiterated, almost verbatim, J.R.'s confession. Higgs had approached Bouchon, too, though not in the vein of the others' reasons; he had run out of "herbal remedies" and was wondering if Bouchon had any more nutmeg or morning glory seeds he could...borrow...of sorts. Bouchon, who had been far from the favorite, relished the newfound attention and power, but not without his own reservations: fearing his size made him a viable target should the group change their mind; following the discussion, he sequestered himself in his tent for much of the duration of the day.

much—should that old tongue happen to be the language of God." Bouchon stared at him. "I mean it only makes sense that's the language He would choose, right? The language of God?"

"Judas!" Bouchon cried.

— § —

The following morning—on the heels of a night full of restless slumber, suspicious tosses and coldly-calculated turns—while Carbine was trying to formulate Plan A, to either press on in their mission, or Plan B, to work their way back to an area where they could call for a heli evac, the rest of the team, sans Bouchon, who chose to confine himself to his tent "to ration [my] energy," enjoyed the morning on a moderate inclination of the mountain, throwing snowballs at each other and assembling snowmen in their likenesses. Santosh joined them[29], having been overjoyed in his acceptance through the simple rite of naming, and spurned by his compatriots, who sat in camp begrudging their decision to sign on to this party and wondering if they'd ever make it home; he took to his new circle with verve, but still took up his old duties in the mission, rolling large balls of snow, heaping them on his back and carrying them along the mountain to where they were deposited, stacked, and shaped, each a frozen effigy of their maker.[30] The altitude and temperatures ensured the permanence of the ice statues, as long as the sun didn't come around demanding his take. Holmes-Manley, donning a lion parka that had survived, cheered Santosh on, keeping him in high spirits to keep him in smiles, exclaiming on the

---

29 After an impromptu tutelage from Holmes-Manley: going over basic dental care and accounting; teaching the Sherpa A.L.O.R.E.; proper brushing techniques; advanced gum hygiene; the effects of debits and credits, and how to prepare a proper T-chart to aid his savage brethren.

30 Or rather, their contractor, as Santosh in his quest for praise and continued acceptance gladly performed the recreational task. Higgs, Holmes-Manley, and Goran were equally grateful to outsource their labor; Pigro made the objection that should his hands not have been so cold, and his arms so tired, and his eyes so sore from the glare, he would have given some assistance, and therefore didn't want to be grouped, ideologically, in the same category as the others.

perfection of his teeth again and again, raising the man-boy's self-esteem to no end.

In the afternoon, Goran, or at the moment, Uroš Radomir, sat looking on the statues and composing an overly long ballad on the morning's fete, turning it into a sort of aubade, unabashedly stealing and manipulating lines from poets far greater than he. Aside from the base, they had tried making the snowmen proportionally accurate, from their chest size, to their arm length, bicep/tricep circumference, etc.; making the faces as detailed as one could with snow. The first four stanzas—twenty lines each, detailing the peculiarities of the light and air prior to the building—were followed by another two stanzas on the start of the building, moving on to dedicate one stanza each, these ones roughly forty-five lines long, to each of the statues and respective men, before arriving at the description of his own; and it was here his pencil stopped, on line two-fifty-eight, as he was about to delve into a lengthy description of his chin, when he realized there were significant problems with the verisimilitude of his sculpture. He looked at the statues of Higgs and Pigro—and even Santosh's, himself, who'd finished last and in half the time—and found every one of them to be more physiologically accurate than his own. And he was supposed to be the doctor, an expert on the physical human form! It enraged him to no end, and he shut his eyes to the matter, blocking out the mockery and indignation, snapping his pencil in half before trudging back to camp, sullen and defeated. Goran waited until it was dark before slinking out of the camp and making his way to the sculptures, rubbing his palm over Pigro's nose until it was as impacted as a sorry boxer, snapping off Higgs' left hand, gouging a hole in J.R.'s chest and stuffing a wad of snow in Santosh's agape mouth (whose snow-white teeth were even perfectly cast). Only then was he proud of his work; and he had an extra bounce in his step as he slunk back to camp.

— § —

Carbine was angry; he'd lost an entire case of guns and ammunition[31]

---

31 Which did not mean all of them, of course; but honestly, what could he/anyone really accomplish with just two Walthers, a Heckler and Koch HK45, a .38

and still had no plan as to how they were going to finish the mission or make it out of here alive. Luckily, he kept his aluminum tin of cigars at his breast pocket at all times and now paced the perimeter of the campfire, puffing violently and caustically, enveloping himself in a cloud of smoke that no one dared approach. Pigro tried to take his mind off of their situation by engaging the group in a conversation all considered to be the worst way of appeasing Carbine, asking each member of the team what they had expected to find in God had they been able to complete the mission.

At first everyone held their breath, expecting Carbine, who was sure to take the tense of the question not only as an admission of failure but as a personal effrontery, to jump across the snow and strangle Pigro with his necklace that was once a rosary, now befit with Star of David adjacent to the cross, then the golden elephant head of Ganesh, a silver-loving Jupiter symbol, the crescent moon of Islam, even the goat head of Baphomet...a veritable charm bracelet of deities sanctioned and pagan. Carbine continued puffing away, possibly angered to the point of (s)elective deafness.

Holmes-Manley—who'd never once divulged his reasons for funding the trip or ever attended one of Pigros masses—surprised all by speaking first, not bothering to look up from his work on the mouth of the Sherpa he'd given a root canal to the day before, testing the occlusion of the molar's filling, "It's simple really: a commodity. I expected to find a commodity. God is just a commodity, bartered and traded the world over: from the mud huts of Cambodia, to the Vatican, to L. Ron's Palm Springs Prison Camp. And if this one proves real, it will not only replace the gold standard, but establish an entirely new basis of market. After all, there's no money like God money, as I always say.[32] God is just a market like any other, and I aim to corner that market."

Special that held a special place in his heart, and a Derringer .22 that had once literally saved his ass while on special assignment in Bangkok?!

32 In fact he doesn't; he'd stolen the line from the Rev. Robert Preen, a popular televangelist recently incarcerated for bilking his parishioners out of $15.4 million dollars in order to build a private waterpark on his Atlanta estate.

"Pshh. Commodity? Please. God is the omniflavor, a flavor that contains all tastes and all flavors before it; the source from which all flavors derive, and yet a flavor like no other, and one no one has ever tasted. No word exists that can possibly describe the flavor and texture. It will have the calloused tongues of every insipid food critic from Timbuktu to Timbuk3[33] knotted at the back of their throats until they asphyxiate on the inability to air their mediocrity," Bouchon yelled from his voluntary quarantine in the tent.

"Oh. Kay." Pigro followed; there were no wrong answers here.

Goran spoke next, disregarding the chef, "I may be a scientist, but I am still a man of God. If we are indeed made in his image, then I suspect the divinity awaiting us to be nothing short of the embodiment of the perfect specimen of man. Perfectly proportional: the one true Vitruvian man. An utterly flawless physique: biceps as dense as planets...tendons that could hold up the Golden Gate Bridge...skin as taught, golden, and glistening as a Thanksgiving turkey...hair so silky and smooth it'd make a horse spit...*teeth*! [pointing to Holmes-Manley], teeth of such perfect architecture no dentist, or -dontist would dare utter its sacred alignment. I wonder, I wonder if his eyes will be blue, like the water, or maybe brown like the earth, green like the color of life...or maybe something more elusive, like the orange of the sun: maybe his eyes will hold the true color of creation—life—the thing that sets us apart from Him."

"And are you not at all worried that God may, in fact, be a woman?" Higgs proposed somewhat hopefully, raising a spoonful of ethanol lifted from The Good Doctor's bag to his nose and inhaling; the smashed palm into his forehead as his sinuses exploded meant the alcohol was working. Goran's mouth tried to wrestle a bitter taste. Higgs continued, "Perfection, as you said, but-, but feminine."

"Preposterous. Simply preposterous! I know we are not in the best of situations but now you sit here trying to get a rise out of me?! I shudder to think how *He* sees us now."

---

33 A posh NYC eatery Bouchon had briefly haunted until one reviewer said he couldn't poach an egg if he was sneaking up behind it with Ernest Hemmingway and Crocodile Fucking Dundee [sic].

And like that they were at each other's throats, a powder-keg of ideology combusting in an emaciated "poof!," all too tired and hungry for their squabbling to rise to any respectable conflagration. After they'd settled down, both physically and psychically winded, Pigro somehow thought it'd be a good idea to kick the battered shell and shake out any remaining embers, "Am I the only one who just wants to be in the presence of the God for the simple sake of God? Is it wrong to want to just bask in His—or Hers—awesome glory, in whatever shape It might come?"

"And just what God are you talking about, Father?" they shouted in unison.

"Does It really have to be just one God? Can't It be composed of many? The bearded face of Christ, the skin of Mohammad, the hair of Brahma, the arms of Vishnu? Can't It have Yahwey's sense of humor? The musical ability of Apollo? The knowledge of Saraswati?"

The ethanol was doing its job; cheeks hot, eyes hazy, Higgs fell on his side laughing. After he was able to stop himself long enough to catch his breath, he puttered, "Y'all hear the one about the Man went up the Mountain looking for God?," and resumed laughing.

— § —

The following morning was broken by a shrieking Holmes-Manley. It appears the financier had thrown his back out while trying to creep towards the box of provisions, a key stolen from Carbine in his mouth[34], crawling so as not to make foot impressions in the snow. They found him in the middle of the camp, flat on his stomach, moaning and griping for help, though not to be lifted, merely for a shelter to be built *around* him.

Goran looked him over, dragging his fingers down his spine,

---

34 In fact, the key had been "purchased" from Carbine, Holmes-Manley promising the Major his own personal Bradley Tank when they get back from the mission, provided he make it back from the mission, and therefore needed access to deeper replenishments. I say "purchased" as there was no damn way in hell Carbine was going to cop to the bribe in front of any of the living team members, or even to the dead.

stroking just a little too tenderly, until rolling across a bulbous, slipped vertebrae. He licked his finger then circled the bulge again. "Uh-huh. Now, I want you to imagine the futures market on your favorite commodity, I want you to picture what it will sell for in five years. Have you started?"

"Yes, but what is the—"

Goran slammed his palm into the bulge and snapped the disk back in place.

"YAAAAGGHHHHHH!" J.R. screamed again, out of shock, and took several relieved breaths before speaking again. "Jesus, man. You could have told me that was your game."

"What game? Now, I'll try and rustle up the remnants of our first-aid kit and see if I can't find a steroid in there to reduce the swelling; and if our boy Higgs hasn't gotten to them by now, I'll procure for you an anesthetic or three. I don't recommend you move from this position for quite some time. Boys [addressing the Sherpas], let's get some snow in a cloth and ice this poor man's back some, yes yes?"

Goran scampered off, and his voice was replaced by a bitter and frightened Bouchon, "You mean he's been stealing the only, sub-human food we have left? Well I say it's high time we resort to cannibalism and I can make a suggestion as to who we should start with."[35]

Bouchon passed his tongue over his chapped lips, picturing how to best prep the indisposed capitalist: turn him over on his belly and tie his arms and legs behind him; stuff his mouth with those disgusting dehydrated apple slices he'd tried to pass off as a meal; dig a pit in the snow and pressure cook him for the entire afternoon...My God, he could make a hamstring *confit!*, coated in gun-powder and flash-seared, wrapped with bacon from his belly and topped with a tartar of meat from around his spin! A dash of salt and pepper. Oh, and then what of a dollop of Worcestershire aioli?! He could make braised short-ribs cooked unilaterally in his own fat and marrow!—with a reduction from the raisins in their emergency trail-mix and J.R.'s own stash of brandy! Yes! *Yes*, and they could have sweetbreads and blood sausages, liver *torchon* and, oh, if they only had some cherry tomatoes and a cou-

---

35 Some linguistics officer, he! A prime example of the caliber of J.R.'s spending.

ple cloves of garlic...They could eat for weeks! And eat *well* at that!

A trail of saliva glittered from Bouchon's chin as it touched down onto the snow between his feet

"We are not—I repeat—*not* eating members of our party. No matter how deserving." Carbine was stroking his gun, not pointing it at anyone, just calmly stroking the sidearm that never left his side.

"Come on, Major, we both know that gun is useless from the snow. It probably has more snow than gunpowder in the shells."

Carbine slid a round into the chamber. "And just how sure are you, Bouchon?"

As long as Carbine had that gun, or, as long as Carbine was Carbine, Bouchon's feast would remain forever out of reach.

They had a fire that night, for morale. Stockpiling all extra clothes (none of which included a pair of pants for poor Higgs), paper accessories, garbage, and anything that would burn and wasn't deemed "absolutely crucial."[36] The fire broke the tension and reinstalled jocularity into the group, and they set about teasing each other and singings songs of their respective regions. After a few rounds of song, Pigro popped up, sprinted to his tent, and returned with his acoustic bass, his smile and excitement met with curiosity, anger, and hunger.

"Wait. No. Surely you can't mean—? Oh God!"

The blaze burned higher than their heads with the addition of Pigro's bass, coupled with the vest and Bouchon's bowl, the accelerants of silk and gunpowder throwing greens and blues into the flames. Pigro was still upset, and Goran cradled him in the nook of his armpit,

---

36 All had something they were hard to part with: Higgs, an 1,100-page tome on his eponymous, theoretical boson; Goran, er, Radomir, had several chapbooks of poets he'd long memorized and stolen from; Bouchon, a large wooden mixing bowl that would burn for hours; Holmes-Manley, various articles of cotton and silk that would provide ample tinder and kindling; Carbine, reluctantly parted with several boxes of shells to provide the igniting gunpowder; Pigro, a wicker vest made for him in Western Africa by medicine-men; Santosh and the Sherpas, small wooden figures—a lion, a vulture, and a chicken—they'd taken to carving in their downtime, which made them relatively undifferentiated knobs of wood.

rocking him slowly and pointing out how happy the fire was making everyone—especially with his contribution—how J.R. was mobile despite the morning's setback; how Carbine and Bouchon were getting on, well not amiably, but better than they ever have; how Santosh was hard at work leading his fellow Nepalese in his variation on the Electric Slide, entitled the Santosh Shuffle; how even Lawrence…wait, where did Lawrence go?

Goran looked about the campfire circle and found no trace of their hedonistic physicist, looking back towards the tent he saw…something…moving about; and then he was forced to duck and cover as Higgs' naked body vaulted over the good doctor and priest, planted, and then made another mad leap over the fire, screaming and hooting like an animal. Soon the rest of them followed, stripping off their clothes and jumping like a bunch of pagans at the solstice, shouting all manner of obscenities as they threw themselves through the fire.

v.

In the tent later that night, Pigro, pressed uncomfortably close to Higgs, who was rifling through 3" x 5" pictures of women he'd known and loved[37], looked on the montage of women passing into existence, and then out, with a ping of regret. As the conquests cycled, a small bead of jealousy crept along Higgs' spine, thinking of all the men who might be with these women at the moment, while Higgs was remanded to this incarceration of ice and rock, his sex-life approaching absolute zero.

"Maybe I should have, you know, been more promiscuous with my amorism," Pigro said, looking to Lawrence for a sign of affirmation; receiving none, outside of a rolled eyeball at the word "amorism," Pigro continued to lament his choice of celibacy, stating that maybe what God really wanted was for us to spread love, in all forms of love, and that way know Him, and man, and each other in a most carnal and intimate way; knowing both the primacy of man and the evolu-

---

37 In some capacity.

tion of love—listing several examples of love's progression from platonic love in ancient Greece, to the emergence of romantic love during the Bubonic Plague, to free-love in the 1960s—and that perhaps it was through the physical act of love that we become closer to god, to godliness, and maybe, just maybe there could be as much sacrament, as much of a Eucharist in taking the body of Christ as in taking a woman's supple breast in your hand, putting the nipple to your mouth, of moving downwards to her feminine parts and then—

"Pigro!" Higgs shouted. "Come on, man. These are close quarters, Padre!"

"Right, sorry, sorry." Pigro fumbling around in his sleeping bag, trying to find a posture where his erection could hope to be less intrusive, apologizing profusely.

"Maybe you should go outside, cool off or something."

Flushed, feeling like his face had never experienced a temperature such as this, "Yes. That sounds the ticket."

— § —

Becoming a sort of custom where sonic disorder supplanted alarm clocks, the morning following the blaze was introduced by a war-cry from Bouchon,[38] followed immediately by an entrée of pure, concentrated terror coming from the Sherpa Bouchon was bunked with. Carbine was first on the scene, having already woken that morning to watch the sunrise gleam off the chrome of his Walther (forced to settle for the visual beauty of the gun as any auditory expulsion might create another avalanche).

When Carbine came upon the tent he found the Sherpa halfway through the zippered opening, trying to scramble away from Bouchon who was holding the Sherpa's leg—Bouchon's Hiromoto 240mm Gyuto knife[39] plunged hilt-deep into the side of the quadricep—Bouchon biting into the bronze flesh and growling like a dog. Carbine kicked

---

38 "Veni, Vidi, Comi!"

39 Of the Tenmi Jyuraku Damascus series: the handle fashioned out of lapis lazuli and jade, built by Mr. Nagao himself and inscribed with Bouchon's name in kanji.

Bouchon in the side of the head and the chef recoiled and snarled whilst Goran pulled the bleeding porter to the side and began applying pressure to the wound(s).

"I will have my meal, damnit!" he roared, "even if it means cutting you all limb from limb, I will have my meal!"

Though Bouchon had intentionally confined himself to his tent prior to the incident, it was now decided by all that he remain forcefully sequestered from the group, which of course represented some difficulty, mountainside jails not exactly part of the REI winter catalog. Goran had small, numerical locks that he used for his luggage, which they removed and bound to Bouchon's zippers.

"Please, this is an insult to my superior intelligence. I could use any one of my knives—or even my apple-corer—to cut an exit."

Higgs responded, "Then you'll get mighty chilly come lights out."

To which Bouchon made possibly the deadliest of threats, "Then I suppose I shall have to take up space in a recently vacated tent."

Rethinking their logistics, they decided to hog-tie Bouchon using some of the climbing rope and, should he somehow free himself with a knife well-hidden from their search and seizure and escape the tent, lined it with a series of IEDs made of empty toilet paper rolls, gunpowder, dental floss, black and cayenne pepper, and just a tinge of that wasabi foam found squirreled away in his knapsack: an explosive pepper-spray cognate of his own machinations.

While Higgs, Carbine, and Holmes-Manley handled the detainment, Goran and the rest of the team spent much of their attention on the partially masticated Sherpa, huddling around the man and giving him extra rations of water and protein bars. Noticing the newfound attention, Santosh tried to reallocate their gaze back to him by performing a litany of fetes: cartwheels and acrobatics, juggling the camp canteens, reconciling a balance sheet…

"Will you stop that, you fool. We've overdrawn our karmic credit line as it is, I'd hate to think of the interest of shit you'd be adding should one of those pop," JR snapped, affixing one of the pepper charges on a piece of tent pole. Having been scolded by the very man who'd taken such a strong interest in him only two days before, Santosh hung his head and slunk to the edge of the ravine, where he sat and waited for either an apology or a call to action; he waited for quite a long while.

— § —

Without the proper medical care—compounded by the added insult of malnourishment and a generous helping of hopelessness—the Sherpa conceded to his wounds; held aloft in Goran's arms, he passed from this life to the next with no lack of affection. After an hour of preparations, grief, and a snowy burial, Goran sought the remaining nameless Sherpa, finding him sitting near Santosh's ice sculpture, breaking off bits and pieces of the porter and rearranging them,[40] occasionally staring off to the east, towards home.

"I'm truly, very sorry for your loss...er-, son. It isn't easy dealing with the death of such an accountable male companion." He clapped a hand on the man's shoulder, "It isn't much, but I've composed a prose-poem in his honor, an elegy of sorts I hope will offer you some relief in this cold night of loss." Goran, rather Radomir, deposited a page of parchment into the man's lap.

The Sherpa looked down at the pages, mysteriously typed in Times New Roman, and gave the doctor-poet a dubious smirk. "Sir?"

"Well I didn't say I wrote it *now*," his forehead flushing under his cap.

The Sherpa looked back down at the poem and, with the doctor standing behind his shoulder, apparently not moving until the poem was read in his presence, begrudgingly tried to read the foreign words aloud. He hadn't made it an iamb before Radomir plucked the pages from the man's hands and orated the poem for him.[41]

---

40 Namely, moving certain ventral bits and placing them in certain dorsal crannies.

41 *Year of the Dog*

The Reanimate (Playing Dead):

It took eleven-and-a-half minutes before Black Ears was revived. That was 1939. The longest I heard of was nineteen minutes but I don't remember his name. Her name maybe. Black Ears was the daughter of revived parents herself. I wonder if that wasn't the reason she was able to play dead so long.

Myself, it was only seven minutes dead. Tops. I can't say I remember it. Or any of them.

I get stuck with something and then everything gets real slow. One breath comes, then it's a while before the next one. And then I don't remember the one after that. When I wake up there aree tubes in my heart and veins.

We play dead a lot; I'm a very good dog.

I have an address at the Institute of Experimental Physiology and Therapy in the USSR. Mail envelopes, care packages and letters c/o Muffy.

The Head:

I am the head: with ears, whiskers, snout: yellow fur, not yellow hair: would bark were I with larynx: would growl, too: they have cotton swabs with citric acid that goes on mouth and nose: a burning, a foul: tongue that licks foul: a different foul in ears: ears that like low sounds but they put high sounds in them: snap fingers: bang hammer: I shut eyes: I snarl lips: I would bark were I with larynx: I would claw were I with feet: there is light that goes in eyes: were I with tail it would not wag: I would bark were I with larynx.

The Lung:

There is an accordion…that plays…my lung…the tempo…is *largo*…it moves…in…then out…in…and out…I have…no blood…to give…no air…no veins…no heart…to enrich…no movement…no body…to give chase…to jump…to excite…no…instead…the breath…is steady…useless…I wait…for a plug…to be pulled.

The Heart (The Blood):

If (Always moving) I am (enriched, depleted, enriched, depleted) elated (in, out, in, out), will a (body, rubber, glass, rubber, body) tail wag (mechanized ouroboros) somewhere?

Spineless:

—a messenger with no—

—phone lines without—

—no discourse between—

—junked nerves—

—plead for a signal—

—bought out—

—discarded for synthetic SCAB—

When the poem was done, the Sherpa just kept his eyes on the man, hoping for some kind of further clarification as to just what in the fuck he'd endured.

"Well I suppose it's not so much about your friend's death, *specifically*, really, it was inspired by a film I saw back in medical school of Dr. Sergei Bryukhonenko's 'Zombie Dog' experiments with reanimation; I had *hoped*..." looking down at the man with marked disappointment, "it would have given you some comfort on death and the afterlife, and maybe, dare I say, a swell of hope. But I can see you're—"

"What's this?" the Sherpa pointing at the heading.

Goran looked to where he had written, in pencil, his pseudonym and smiled as if posed a question by some daft child. "Ah, well that is my pen name. You see, some authors will use a pseudonym to fend off the status of celebrity. Pride should nev—"

"No. This," tapping his finger below the graphite sobriquet to a redacted line of text, the tip of a "Z" the only pronounced letter.

"Never mind that. The important thing is that you're comforted." Goran smiled, as if to tell the boy thanks and gratitude were not necessary, that they were felt in the invocation his words surely had upon the dumbfounded porter, in the enrapturing words of Radomir.

"Sir, you no write that poem. Do you?"

"Well, certainly the voice is a departure from my normative—"

"Sir, is *ripped*," pointing to the frayed left side of the paper, divorced of its binding.

Goran huffed, "Well, I might have taken some inspiration, made a few corrections and such…If you ask me, I've improved upon it."

"Stealing?"

"Well, if one must steal so as to improve, than I shall steal as much as I can, as often as I can. And you will know the towers of my keep, the span of my empire, by the golden hue of their words." Goran's hands cupped piles of imaginary bounty, his eyes emitting a golden re-

---

Leftovers:

A body with space for a head, heart and lung. A furnace to keep me warm. A limp tail in want of wag. Somewhere a wag in want of tail, of lung, of heart, of head. *Put us together, love. These holes are cold. And this cold ain't holy.*

flection. "And if they're stolen, so what?, what empire wasn't built on thievery?"

The porter suddenly found himself called by a dinner bell only he could hear ringing and promptly excused himself from the good doctor, who didn't even turn his head as the man scampered off, too busy basking in the glow of his perceived treasures.

As an added precaution against Bouchon's escape, and a subsequent murder spree, they would each take a shift guarding the tent, using a sharpened tent pole[42] for defense and offense should the need arise. Holmes-Manley was supposed to take his watch after Pigro, but as it came within fifteen minutes of his scheduled duty, J.R.'s back pain, which had coincidentally been dormant throughout the day, returned with a vengeance; the financier stating that through no amount of medication would it be possible for him to take his post. So Pigro extended his shift while J.R. took to his tent and Vicodin. After only the first hour Pigro found his thoughts once more pulled by some sort of pagan divining rod towards Higgs' photo collection and the thoughts of all the missed opportunities he could have had, all of God's love he could have given…

Around one in the morning, Pigro was snatched from his reverie by a curious noise downhill, towards the fresh grave, something like a crunching and smacking of lips. Pigro inched down the bank, fearful some carnivorous creature, having smelled the blood and gore in the air, had made its way past the tree line and terrain out of nothing shy of sheer bloodlust. Approaching stealthily, Pigro lifted his spear, closed his eyes, and threw it at the sound of the feasting beast. He heard the spear strike home and the beast produced an eerily human scream.

"Yaaaaaghhh. Jesus H. Christ on a cracker!"

Pigro flicked on his small flashlight and saw a naked Carbine writhing in the moonlight, congealed blood smeared around his mouth, clutching the spear impaled in his right knee, then to the free-

---

42 Carbine refused to be cuckolded by having one of his guns in the hands of another.

flowing blood shining off the light and disappearing around the bend as it slid under Carbine's thigh and the Italian-roast coffee of his skin. Panning his eyes right, Pigro saw the unearthed corpse of the Sherpa and a bicep missing several bite-sized chunks of flesh. Carbine continued shouting, which naturally woke up the rest of the camp, who soon dressed and made their way to the source of the commotion.

"What is it? What's going on out there?" Bouchon yelled from his tent.

When the others had surrounded Carbine in a semi-circle, Carbine admitted, of his own free will, his purpose. "Damnit, I needed the sustenance. I needed the energy so I could complete the mission and get us the hell off this mountain. And now you've gone and ruined it, Pigro, you and that goddamned spear. You don't contribute a goddamn thing all trip. Now, all of a sudden, you decide to man up?!"

"Me? I thought you were a bear or a wolf or something. I struck out of our own protection."

"It took us all manner of pulley's and rope to get up here. How in the hell do you think a bear is going to make it?"

Pigro began to retort, "Well—"

"Will someone please tell me what the fuck is going on down there?!"

Higgs finally answered Bouchon. "It appears the Major here was out for a midnight snack."

"What? Wait. No. You can't mean?" Bouchon began screaming with the most harrowing regret, the most grizzly betrayal. His treasured meal ruined and so far from reach. He began screaming in unshakeable lamentation: "No, you fools! I could have prepared him! I could have prepared him!!!"

"And you didn't feel like sharing, Major?" Holmes-Manley demanded, suddenly cured of his backache.

"I couldn't. I needed every spare bit of food I could get."

"You hypocrite. You goddamned hypocrite." Then Bouchon's voice got lower, pleading and desperate. "Maybe it's not too late. Maybe I can salvage it and we can eat. Won't somebody let me out, for the love of Child!"

"I think it only fair, given that the Major here has already had a taste, that we divvy up the body and each receive a share. It's the fair thing to do." Holmes-Manley ever the pragmatist and adjudicator of equality.

"A surprisingly Marxist statement coming from an unfettering allegiant to Adam Smith," Higgs muttered under his breath.

"Say something, Lawrence?" Holmes-Manley snapped, his hands placed firmly on the hips of his elk robe.

"I'm just saying it's not very free market of you."

"How dare you bring up the market here! Now! Damnit, man, this is about survival!" Holmes-Manley's speech was taking on a political cadence.

"Fuck! Will somebody get me back inside? I'm freezing my fucking ass off out here."

"Ha. A little bit of karma perhaps." Goran grasped the tent pole and cut the elastic joint holding the individual shafts together before sliding it, not too gently, out of Carbine's knee, the Major screaming throughout. "Pigro, give me a hand here."

Carrying the naked and bleeding man back to his tent, Goran and Pigro slowed their pace to hear Bouchon sobbing away in his nylon prison.

— § —

VI.

"I've a good mind to draw up a little sign says 'Infirmary' and place it outside," Goran joked to the humorless Major. Taking the lack of laugher as a lack of understanding, Goran went on, "What, with you and J.R.'s back, and of course this was where we kept the unfortunate, late Mr...well you know who I mean."

Carbine became the second member of their team to be confined to his respective tent, though out of necessity instead of force; unable to walk, forced to a prostrate position, leg elevated, a large and continually renewed amount of snow heaped onto his thigh to keep the swelling down, the only thing Carbine could do was watch the heads of the snow statues as they appeared through the little window, occasionally barking commands to the party and snuggling up with his guns to keep his mind off the pain—disassembling and reassembling the weapons with astonishing grace. Higgs came by around noon for a sober chat.

"Of course by now they've realized that we either haven't succeeded in our mission or that we've perished along the way—both, most likely. You and I both know they had plans for a backup team in the event of our failure," Carbine grimaced at the word, "I guess what I'm asking you is, How long after loss of radio contact will it take to mobilize the second team and send them up?"

"Mobilize? They were mobilized the same time we were. Should Bouchon have sharted himself at base camp there was a man there to take his place before he could change his drawers. The question you should be asking is why we haven't seen them yet? You don't know the general[43] like I do. This mission, though privately funded, is of the utmost importance to Us—though they'd never let J.R. know, bastard'd hike up the goddamned vig even higher. Now, under normal conditions, he would have sent the second team out a day after us, shadowing us; in the event that we encountered the slightest hiccup there would be a team ready to overtake us. The fact that we haven't seen anyone, heard anything, is, to me, the most unsettling." Carbine tried to fight through the pain to a terrace of reason, expecting some sort of wisdom to rain down from the snow totems.

"Isn't there a high probability that the path is inaccessible? If our path down is barred, it's only likely that other paths will have been effected—whole passes likely wiped out."

"That's what I thought, at first, but there are always means of circumnavigation, nature has a fetish for equalization: if one path is destroyed, another will have formed."

They sat on that, weighing the options their brothers in arms had likely taken. After a moment, Carbine put the vehicle into a different gear, "Let me ask you, what did you expect to find up there?" Carbine for the first time in a while finding himself concerned with someone's opinion.

---

43 Gen. Barry R. Winter-Weiss, an ardent commander whose equal penchant for sacrifice bordered on the sadistic kept him, publicly, to only three stars—while behind closed Washington doors, he was the first called for matters of sensitive execution or prejudice.

"Expected or hoped?"

"Both."

"I expected to find an answer to the existence of the Higgs Boson." Growing embarrassed, "I hoped the answer to be the affirmation of the particular boson—a mass giving sub-atomic particle. If we could harness it, synthesize it, we could essentially create mass. Fuck alchemy; not only could we print gold, we could manufacture entire worlds, entire goddamned universes."

"Then I guess what you expected to find is the same as me, a cognate of the same concept, and Holmes-Manley as well. A weapon. An economy. Not a whole lot of difference when you get right to it." Carbine was clearly bitter. He wanted to be the man responsible for weaponizing God, and now either someone else would take that honor, or no one would take it at all. He wondered which one was worse. The former, definitely the former.

Higgs shrugged, having really only been concerned with the scientific coefficient of the mission. "I suppose."

"Well then think about it. Every country and faction and fucking back-woods, inbred militia on the planet would love to get their hands on this."

"So you're thinking maybe our team was overtaken? But wouldn't that mean another team is on their way up, foreign or not? In which case, wouldn't we have heard something by now?"

Carbine nestled up to his guns, not unlike a child with a teddy bear,[44] "Its unsettling is what it is. This silence, this lack of, of...anything. Which brings me to conclude two possible options, and you're a...bright soldier, I bet you can guess what those are."

Higgs thought for a moment, his mind cycling through all the various protocols he'd had to memorize, until the similarities mounted and it all really became the same thing in every situation. "They're going to bomb it. Either figuring the entity hostile, or out of a scorched earth defense. Which one do you think it is, Major?"

"Does it really matter?"

---

44 With the glaring exception of the Major's erection.

— § —

Now that they'd popped the cherry on cannibalism, all queuing up for their turn and demanding an equal distribution of goods, Bouchon's sentence was commuted and his talents subpoenaed by the state of their bellies. Carving the slow-roasted body, Bouchon kept casting reproachful stares towards Carbine's tent, inconsolably envious of the man who had eaten the succulent cheeks of the Sherpa and had thoroughly destroyed the bicep and shoulder with his haphazard, and untrained, bites. Still, the cheeks angered him above all; he had had special plans for them, should he have been allowed to fulfill his calling; he had fantasized about those juicy morsels since his first bite into one of those godawful protein bars. Now it was ruined, wasted on the unappreciative palate of that gun-crazed philistine who couldn't tell a *tuber melanosporum* from a *tuber unicinatum*! Sulking, Bouchon wrapped himself in his gray blanket and set upon sloppily filleting the body and over-seasoning the meat out of spite.

With Carbine's leg attended to, and really nothing more to do for the day, Goran lifted a cigar off Carbine and walked the perimeter of the camp, puffing (and coughing, unaccustomed to smoking at this altitude), going over again and again the comments on his poetry, the supposed "theft." What right was bestowed upon that little pissant to question not only his artistic talent but his whole philosophy and manner in which he produced his art? Sure, his words weren't always his own, but really, couldn't that be said for every auteur at some point, when you really got down to, well, the origin of origin and the whole discourse on inspiration and intellectual property and so forth? And wasn't there some Socratic aphorism on originality? If not there damn well ought to be! And yes, maybe more often than not, he lifted text verbatim, but isn't it really in the way one *speaks* with his work that really makes the difference? Say, if he were to rewrite, re-speak, Eliot's *The Waste Land*, with, say a Prussian accent, or maybe a bit of apoplexy, would it not be entirely Goran's—Radomir's—work? And could he not similarly take possession of things he thought he could have made, or works over which he felt almost proprietary, as if it had been written either specifically for him or possibly even by him in a past life, another dimension? Yes, of course he could. And fuck all those that thought otherwise—at which point he swallowed a large nicotine-infused wad of saliva that began spinning inside his stomach and turning him green.

Goran dashed past Santosh—who, having been spurned, was lying face down on the snow, invisible to all labor and all members of the party made invisible, caring for no one but himself and his concussed ego—as the good doctor vomited his breakfast onto a nearby rock.

Night fell, and with it came a feast of man and a dessert of quiet as each contemplated the consecration of human flesh into their G.I. tract, worrying the moral implications: if they ate too quickly; if they savored; if they had compared the meat to others they had known and loved, and how it ranked.[45] Pigro was perhaps the most disturbed[46], spending the majority of his life preaching love for one's fellow man, only to devour him like hungry lions on an obdurate Christian. (And had he licked his fingers? Oh, God!) He could think of only one thing to cheer him up, and as everyone was lethargic with satiety and guilt (or so he imagined/hoped), Pigro slinked off to his tent and searched Higgs' bags for his photos.

Higgs, himself, was far too concerned with the thought of impending death from above—would it be napalm, concussion blasts meant to entomb the God in snow, something of a nuclear flavor?—and for the extermination of truth that would follow: he would never know the answer as to the boson question, never know whether or not his name was truly the name of God; and he had gradually come to accept that prior to the morning's conversation, sated only with the hope that *someone* surely will discover the answer; it didn't matter that it would be another group, the truth would exist. That hope was over now, and the only thing that could comfort him was the small bag of victory marijuana he had set aside, not to be smoked until they had concluded their meeting and assessment of the divinity.

"Pigro! What in the fuck are you doing in my bag?"

---

45 Eighth for Higgs; second, for Carbine; third for Holmes-Manley, who'd sampled more or less every edible (?) fare the world over.

46 Okay, he was easily the most disturbed, most of the party having devoured their profligate meal with gusto and a, presently, clean conscious.

At that moment, flat on his stomach, hands stuffed into the rucksack, Pigro's fingers settled on the rubber-banded stack of photos and wrenched them from the back, clutching them to his chest for security. "Mine, now, you've had them for long enough. It's Pigro's turn, damnit. *Pigro's*!"

Ignoring the slip into the third person, Higgs moved towards Pigro with the hope of reacquiring his property; as a last act of desperation to attain the prized photos, Pigro shoved the stack into his underwear, below the balls, into the humid cavern of the Grundle.

Higgs halted, then retreated. "Jesus, man. I guess they're yours now."

Pigro smiled the smile of victors, his precious spoils secured and warming against his genitals: a Fort Knox Higgs wouldn't dare to breach.

"I hope they give you a fucking paper cut." He pushed Pigro to the side of the tent (refusing to budge from his prostrate position of victory), reached into the second flap, grabbed the two-point-four grams in their decorative baggy, and left Pigro to Pigro, making his way to the doctor's tent, planning to snort and pop everything in reach that could take his mind off the impending death.

Ever since he'd heard of the 1960s clinical experiments with LSD—of their integral role in the formulation of the microprocessor and as the veritable progenitor of Silicon Valley—when he was fresh out of boot camp and pursuing his doctorate in mathematics and physics on Uncle Sam's dime, he had taken drugs only as a means of expanding his understanding and to hopefully facilitate the formulation of new theorems and concepts; and he'd continued in that vein once the degrees had been awarded, the dissertation argued, and made the return to his Uncle's farm—who looked the other way as long as his work outpaced the Ruskies. And, sure, perhaps there were the occasional instances when his medication could be considered…overindulgent, but as it was all coming to an end now, he would take them as a last hurrah and as a veritable 'fuck you' to the powers that be, and he would take them as ravenously and as selfishly as he wanted.

That was the plan, anyway.

Carbine was in the tent, as Higgs should have known, but, after giving an initial pause, more out of conditioning than fear, he made for the doctor's bag without fear of reprimand. "I'm taking anything I can find and there's not a damn thing you can do to stop me."

"On the contrary, it's everything I can do to assist you, as the last of the morphine is swimming through my bloodstream and it'd take a goddamned lot of my blood—probably the whole damned circuit—for you to drain, filter and extricate. I hope you're a whiz at reverse-osmosis and got a real steady hand for dialysis."

"You lie!" Higgs said with a ripe amount of fear.

"Go ahead, take a look through that bag there. You think we came up here with a goddamn pharmacy? Shit, that Sherpa Bouchon went at got more of the juice than I did. Holmes-Manley, too, he's been popping Oxies like breath-mints, though I think he's fresh out.[47]"

"Son of a bitch." A thorough audit of Goran's bag corroborated Carbine's statement. There was nothing left. Higgs threw it at the ground; well, at least he still had some weed, and he began rolling a joint of considerable girth.

"I'm not exactly happy about it, either. My leg is hurting like a sonovabitch." Carbine winced, having felt a sharp increase in pain as his mind went back to searching for it, allowing the pain to return simply by acknowledging its existence; already he was forgetting his training, and the chaste life that had led to his position, but what more did it matter now? Their mission was over. His impending death would write his epitaph as having gone out of the world a flagrant failure in a mission of the utmost importance. Cannabis entered his nostrils and Carbine had an idea. "Mind if I take a toke?"

What neither Higgs nor Carbine knew, was that earlier in the day, just after their discussion on the terminality of their situation, Holmes-Manley had been returning to the tent for another round of OxyContin and, having heard the cloaked cadence of the conversation, paused, listened, and after hearing the prognosis went about the rest of the day succeeding where Higgs had failed, cornering the narcotics supply in the camp and debiting his supply on hand every fifteen minutes. The

---

47 Having exhausted the Vicodin supply.

cumulative effects of the drugs struck—taking him through the varied stages of opiate use, from euphoria to deep introspection to nausea, back to euphoria, to giddiness, to Godliness, and finally to the heightened libido stage—just as most were regaining their energy after dinner. Rejoining the party were Pigro, Higgs, and Carbine, carried out of the tent on a travois of tent poles, apparently feeling well enough to join in some good old fashioned camaraderie—as it might well be their last.

"Come on, let's have a party. Some singing, some dancing, what do you say?" J.R. was all smiles and pupils, dilated to their elastic limits, standing and grabbing the two men closest to him and wrapping his arms around each, sucking his lips into his teeth and then smacking them as would a dog trying to work through peanut butter. No one was in the mood for dance or merriment, so Holmes-Manley tried to convince them. "We're all dying; any day now we'll be wiped clean off the map as the Major's people pummel us with rockets. So let's live it up while there remains a few hours left."

Pigro grew nervous, "What in the hell is he talking about?"

"I say, J.R. is just having a little fun with us—though I say the fun is solely on his side, taking advantage of us as our morale is scraping the bottom. If there was any merit to his words, surely Carbine would have informed us."

Under normal circumstances, Carbine could have kept a secret to his grave and beyond, but under the current conditions, he broke into a laugher so hard tears began pouring out his eyes. Admitting, between giggles, "It's true, it's true." He laughed harder and wiped his eyes, "We're all gonna die! The failsafe is to wipe the whole cocksucker off the map!" Carbine heaved with laugher and pointed the nine-hundred-some-yards up the mountain to where the God was supposed to be. "I guess we'll be meeting you after all, ole buddy."

"Good God, Lawrence, what have you done to the man?" Goran ignoring the pressing issue.

"Did you not hear him? He's got it on good authority—well, on sound logic—that the general in charge of this operation is more than likely going to choose to blow the whole thing up." Higgs demonstrated the mountain blowing apart with his hands, accompanied by a "Poww," "Whooosh," and a crumbling "Pchchchchchshshsh."

In no time at all, they were squabbling and arguing, lashing out, dealing the lowest of blows, a vindictive listing of the mothers ensued,[48] each going after the throat of the other's existence. Necks were throttled and offences laid which would have taken a lifetime to retract, screaming and shouting without any heed towards avalanches. Carbine was crawling back towards his tent to retrieve his gun while the rest of the men were on the absolute brink of homicide—some slightly crossing over as Bouchon's sausage-fingered vice cinched around Pigro's Adam's apple—when someone shouted "Gentlemen, please! May I have your erection?" All turned and found a naked Holmes-Manley, far too opiated to feel the cold, smiling and holding his arms out so as to pull each member into an imaginary embrace.

Hands were released and animosities abated as they stared at the naked and jovial and—well, erect—financier, teeth set in a wide grin as a man about to carve the Christmas roast. "Gentleman, it appears we've all come to the same conclusion as to the merit of Major Carbine's assessment, and have instead taken to expediting our terminal prognosis. Now, I'm not one for speeches,[49] far too much time has been wasted tonight on the words of tongue and brawn, and I shan't add any synergistic obfuscations of the point...like a giant, opulently-decked purple hand covering the amoeba mouths of these etherized hours of larcenous fraternity.[50] No, *nien*, *net* as our Ruskie yang might say. Gentleman, I say, now is the time for life! Now is the time for celebration. Now is the time to look into the red-rimmed iris[51] of death and say, 'I have more life to spend,' and 'When you write my name in your ledger you will write that I went out with my liabilities unpaid,

---

48 Mary Margaret Pigro, Janice Guinevere Woodsman Manley, Martha Robinson, Candice Carbine, Joséphine Renée Bouchon, Andjela Draženka Karadžić.

49 He most certainly was.

50 The opiates were strong in him, starting to veer back towards the more hallucinatory states, which Holmes-Manley demonstrated as he put his hand out to brush the hair of some invisible plasma-beast before him, inserting his hand and pulling it back while saying "whoooooossshhhhhh" before continuing on with his speech.

51 Iris?

that the value of my stock was mark-to-market, and that my last check will surely bounce!' Gentleman, in the coming days, hours maybe, we will all go out in a bang, and I say now is the time we launch one of our own. To life, *mes frères!*" He finished with both his index finger and his erection pointing triumphantly towards the stars.

There was a "hoor-rah" of support, and at some point in the conjugal darkness, Higgs began cackling, "Y'all hear the one about the Mountain went up the Man looking for God?"

VII.

Before they had time to rise and face the awkwardness, the embarrassment, the guilt, the fear each had going to bed of looking one another in the eye—of those who had joined the call and those who'd abstained—before Pigro could flagellate himself, before Goran's calisthenics could work out the kinks, before Higgs smoked the very last of his weed, before Carbine could give his gun a quick once-over with a file and brush so as to dissuade anyone from touching him, ever, before J.R. could wake with a vicious and throbbing intestinal irritability and runny nose, before the Sherpas could castigate themselves for ever agreeing to sign on with this party and attempt to dip out on their own, before Bouchon's belly could growl loud enough to be heard across the camp, a synthesized thunder rent the morning sky, and all raised their eyes in time to see two F-22s bank around the peak of the mountain, clasping their hands to their ears against the deafening lightning that followed.

The sky lit up with all spectral colors of visible light, the locus of the God swirled about in a maelstrom of fire and sublimated ice, expanding and accreting oxygen—the top of the mountain bedecked with a clown's afro of energy, follicles rapidly reaching out towards the camp.

Each looked on, able only to muster a few token last-minute remarks of despair[52] as the God-infused blast barreled down the moun-

---

52 "My God," "My Man," "My Boson," "My Weapon," "My Flavor," "My Commodity!"

tain in its own fiery avalanche.

Ever the jocular member of the party, Higgs got in the last quip before their voices were muted by the roar of fire and ice and God, "Y'all hear the one about the God went up the Mountain looking for Man?"

But there was no one to answer, or to laugh.

III. THE REITLINGER SOLUTION

> *"And the pupil cuts out from this whole,*
> *With a square, and a circle, and a rectangle—*
> *compositional units…he frames a shot!"*
>
> —*Sergei Eisenstein,* FILM FORM

COLLECTED DATA FROM SAMPLE OV.2 E.121
SUBJECT# 0112358132IA-6823
NAME: REITLINGER, JOHN D.

[Slightly abridged for the benefit of the Assessor]

S.R. 720

[V.N.] A prompt comes in from the panels: left-square, middle-circle, right-circle. I follow protocol and send the proper transmission: right-circle, middle-square, right-circle. There are no more transmissions for the day.

S.R. 745

[N.B.] My schedule, Eleanor, is as such:

- I wake—the time of waking varies, Eleanor: I sleep in intervals of 4 hours, then 5 hours, thereby shifting my waking time, my transmitting time, so that I am not always transmitting inside the same time period.

- I rise, as it were, from my Personal Chambers (an oval approximately 1.5m wide and 3.5m long) that adjoins the Common Room through a narrow passage; the room functions as a mess-hall, gym, rec-room (8m diameter and about 5m height); the Library (an identical 1.5m x 3.5m pod) sits directly across the Common Room from my P.C., accessed through an identical narrow passage.

- I take the morning inventory of myself.

- I dispose of my waste(s), strapping myself into the wall-mounted commode, pressing the triangular button when I'm finished, sending the gastric carrion into the vacuum beyond.

- I move to the MRE Dispenser, press the octagonal button, and a cylindrical pouch of food dispenses.

- I remove the foil.

- I eat.

- By way of a ladder nestled between the treadmill and first-aid station I take my position in the Observation Room held inside a dome at the top of the main chamber—accessed through another, slightly wider, tubular passage. (The ladder merely serves as a guiderail in the void of gravity.) The room is simple: it has a large trapezoidal window with a dilatable coating that acts as a Sun Shield and one ergonomic chair that pulls up to a semi-circular panel filled with various geometrical buttons and indicators: rectangular buttons controlling the Sun Shield; an incoming display panel (a 3x2 matrix containing a top row of circles and a lower row of squares); an outgoing transmission panel (the same matrix as above); a subset of smaller geometric shapes for internal diagnostics (O_2 levels, CO_2 levels, etc); finally, a large red hexagon with small white lettering in the center that reads "Panic," which I have thankfully never had the displeasure of pressing.

- I dilate the Sun Shield aperture to 26° to induce a UV morale boost. The window behind the shield is interactive, I can run my fingers across it and zoom in on various parts of the firmament.

- I work 4 hours, awaiting data obtained from the ship's panels measuring gamma-ray levels (so they tell me) to transmit back to Earth. Some days there are many transmissions; others, very few.

- I take a break, descending the way I came.

- I eat again. The food is technically different but functionally the same.

- I sleep 5 hours.

- Rise again.

- Exercise: run for 34-minutes on the treadmill (exactly 3 miles running and a ¼-mile cool down lap); weight training (cable/resistance exercises); stretching; cardio kickboxing.

- Return to Observation Room for a period of 4 hours.

- Close down Sun Shield.

- Descend once more to the Common Room.

- Eat again.

- Leisure time is divided between a mandatory reading period (how leisurely if mandated?) or otherwise lost in thoughts while performing some liminal task: cards; puzzles; recording my thoughts on these notebooks (once an engineer always an engineer); or using the microphone on my wristband to dictate letters to you on voice notes that I will have to wait until I return home to share. The transmission board is my only means of actual contact with Earth, and its shapes the only lexicon with which I can communicate—and really, who's heart can be expressed in circles and squares? The reading selection is mandated by The Library. I've breezed through the initial fare: a Will They/Won't They between Jane and her erstwhile suitor Richard; the trials of an intrepid quadruped named Spot with a diathesis for running; a somnolent moon.

- 4-hour sleep interval.

- Repeat.

S.R. 766

[V.N.] Today's transmissions: left-circle, left-square, right-square; left-circle, middle-circle, right-circle; middle-circle, middle-square, right-square; left-square, middle-circle, right-circle; left-circle, left-square, middle-square; left-circle, middle-circle, right-circle; middle-square, right-circle, right-square.

S.R. 794

[N.B.] A note on the Library, Eleanor: I should inform you, the Library is less a library than a vending machine. It is not a series of shelves laden with aging paper and worn spines. It is a library of plastic, metal, and data. At any given time there are 23 electronic tablets divided between 7 shelves (why they thought to omit a final tablet to make the shelves uniform I'll never know), each containing just one book; as soon as a book is finished, a new one takes its place. (Why The Powers That Be felt they needed to waste 23 eReaders instead of embracing their intrinsic function—to store—is beyond me. But who am I to questions the motives of The Powers.) Very strange, but refreshing, no? You can go back and reread, if desired, but who wants to do that? Currently the Library has me on a natural kick, following Jack London, Gary Paulson, Mark Twain, touching on the pastoral with Ms. Ingalls Wilder; we'd only just returned from the fantastic a la Juster, L. Baum, and Lewis Carroll; before that, the absurd wiles of Seuss and Dahl, Silverstein and his erstwhile Tree of Life. I'm looking forward to moving on to the next books, Eleanor, to seeing what more the Library has to throw at me; I hope I won't regret that sentiment.

S.R. 849

[N.B.] I've begun to wonder, Eleanor, whether this post was a reward or a punishment. I can't even remember the details surrounding how I got to this solitary confinement: something about two panels converging notes and recommendations, exchanging vitals on my physical and mental perspicacity, informing me with a loud rubber stamp that I had been selected from a very large pool of applicants for this assignment.

The life before was a different one: a different past: bifurcated by my arrival here in which my history and temporality have changed. For I say, Eleanor, time passes in a much different manner than it did under the terrestrial persuasions. 220 miles above your quaint garden I orbit the blue marble at 17,500 mph. My sidereal day is 90 minutes, Eleanor; that means I get to watch the sun rise and set over the earth 16 times during the same 24-hour period. Can you imagine the beauty, Eleanor? 16 sunsets a day, every day, for the 9-month duration of the mission; 4,383 sunrises in all.

Relativity at its finest, my dear. Though I dare say your absence will be sorely felt. I have only my memories to tether me to you.

Perhaps those preoccupations are underscored by a larger question: What exactly is my purpose here, Eleanor? They've build this pod/ship/what-have-you for swift and user-friendly ease; one cannot possibly hope to make mistakes, misinterpretations, or be confounded with the complex engineering on board. Should a problem arise, Eleanor, it is not I who would be digging into the panels or infinite streams of code, that task is outsourced, managed from a remote location; and when the need for physical intervention arises, the pod's robotics will handle the job. What is my task then, Eleanor? I transmit, yes, but what else? And is this not a task that can be handled by an entity devoid of heartbeat, head, and soul? Furthermore, I have no knowledge of whether the transmissions are even going through. There is no record of communication and I receive no communication as to their receipt from Earth. Again, the point is welcome to present itself any time now.

I know what you're thinking, Eleanor, "Why not spend the time reading and send the transmissions later?" Because, my dear, the transmissions must be sent immediately, within fifteen seconds of the incoming prompt. While I may not be certain as to whether Earth receives my signals, the pod is equipped for reprimand—as I unfortunately learned from one late transmission last week—taking the form of violent shaking, flashing red lights, and a siren…a full-on attack of sensory hell. The alarm also sounds if I stray from my schedule: a missed meal, an extra moment of rest, improper workout, chapter skimming, etc. Therefore I must remain vigilant, taught of body and mind.

Or maybe that's precisely the point, Eleanor, the human integration, the human observance. In which case I ask again, was this a punishment or a reward?

S.R. 896

[V.N.] Oh, you'll be happy to know I've shaved my moustache, my dear. I know how you always hated the ol' caterpillar; I figured to count myself as the only pallbearer in that funeral. God, you know, Eleanor, it's been years since I'd seen my naked upper lip. We shall have to spend some time getting reacquainted, him and I. Although the laser burn is making it all puffy and glossy and pink. Like a kid fresh off the Kool-Aid. So it'll be yet a little while before I truly see my face again sans stache.

S.R. 951

[V.N.] Eleanor, I know that when I press the octagonal button a parcel of food will dispense. It will say Teriyaki but it will not taste like it. I know that when I press the yellow triangular button my waste will be released into the vacuum. A trapezoid gives me sunlight and takes it away…my life is operated by the mandates of shapes. I used to be disturbed by this, but now I think I am comforted. Yes, quite comforted.

S.R. 1,009

[V.N.] Having long ago exhausted the catalogue of espionage, crime, and mystery (some books containing all three), and a brief jaunt through the novels of the American canon (Hemmingway, Fitzgerald, Faulkner, and the like), the Library has followed with an anachronistic choice. My current literary fare is of the Mediterranean cuisine: Ovid, Homer, Sophocles, Virgil...

I must say, I find the form of the play very refreshing; I find the language anything but.

S.R. 1,024

> AUTOMATED DIAGNOSTIC ASSESSMENT
> #121814: Subject is positioned vertically inclined; tucked; knees extended at an 85-degree angle; elbows resting on top of the knees; subject's head bobs up and down from his shoulders; the head is tucked then untucked, turned to the side, then righted. Subject's feet appear to be tapping. Heart rate spikes occasionally but quickly levels out; blood pressure, stable. All other vital signs stable.

S.R. 1,032

[V.N.] Something strange happened to me earlier, my dear. I was...indisposed, if you will, when the walls of the pod lit up with some sort of red ether, a bright red ring moving from the top of the Pod down to the bottom. I realized it must have been some kind of scan, a protocol check-up from the Powers—still, they could have warned me. I was in my P.C. when it happened, working out the attrition extoled from these horrendous MREs. I would have liked to have been better prepared, groomed a little, or at least caught in a less ignominious position.

S.R. 1,285

[V.N.] Incoming: Right-square, middle-circle, middle-square. I transmit: right-square, right-circle, left-circle. Left-circle, right-circle, right-square: middle-circle, right-square, middle-square.

S.R. 1,584

[N.B.] I'm beginning to see why the Evelyn Wood Speed Reading course was a mandatory part of my training. (Perhaps this is my true mission, the effects of reading comprehension at zero-gs! Though a practical application for all the money spent researching this phenomenon I can't honestly justify.) However, I am anxious to return to these new books the Library has me on, though a little wearisome, like a good evening spoiled by the reminder of the coming morning's rigorous labor. There's the terminally English writers: Austen, Bronte, and Dickens—to say nothing of their Samurai of Syntax, Virginia Woolf. The ruminative Ruskies: Tolstoy, Dostoevsky, and Solzhenitsyn. There is a large part of me that would have preferred never to have left the admonishing tales of Golding, Lee, or Orwell; or to jump back into the hostile American frontier of Salinger, Miller, or Steinbeck.

S.R. 1,664

[V.N.] My transmissions are sent through a sequence of shapes. I know that, should I displace the order, a different message is delivered, a different task performed. But the transmissions are limited, the combinations finite: thirty-eight possible combinations, thirty-eight possible transmissions. They designed the system specifically to eliminate the misinterpretation of conventional rhetoric, supplemented by preconfigured forms to allow for concrete analysis. Never should a situation arise from which there is no appropriate algorithm with which to respond. Never should a transmission be sent that cannot be interpreted back on *terra firma*. I want you to know, Eleanor, that I find this firmly beautiful. But I say, what should happen should my observations fall beyond what they have accounted for?

S.R. 1,684

[V.N.] My P.C. is equipped with several basic tools of rudimentary grooming. I have a brush with which to clean my teeth—no liquid toothpaste, however. There are clippers for my fingers and toes, designed to trap the clippings so they don't float away and jam themselves into the instruments on board; I haven't had much course to use these yet. There is the "razor" for my face; I say "razor" in that the handheld device, which produces a shave clean as any razor I've ever met—though a touch hotter—has no blade but rather a small laser running the length of the head, burning the follicles off instead of allowing even smaller particles to run amok. Then there is what I can only describe must have been a long history of bad ideas and certain egregious trial failures that, somehow, was still allowed to evolve into this barber-in-a-bag we have today. A nodule-laden cap—one that looks more in line with giving Victor's Monster a perm than coifing the modern man-slips over the top of the skull and is secured via chin strap; the nodules, a series of circular electronic blades, then buzz and turn and systematically deforest my head with the uncompromising speed and uniform efficiency of a prophesized deity Amazonian tribes had been warned would one day arrive to herald the end of days. A hose at the basal ganglia sucks out the mulch and, presumably, spits it out into space. (I have another theory as well, one that puts the Barber and the Dispenser in cahoots.)

I have just used the Barber for a second time and, let me tell you, he received no tip and my business will be as scant as possible. (Adrenaline and hair-cuts are odd bedfellows.) One take-away though, with my hair shorn down to lengths no longer than two millimeters, is the patterns you find when the thicket is cut. For instance, I just discovered I have two cowlicks on either side of my head in the shape of spiral galaxies.

S.R. 1,710

[V.N.] Today's transmissions: middle-circle, right-square, middle-square; left-circle, left-square, right-square; left-square, middle-circle, right-circle.

S.R. 1,790

[N.B.] I almost forgot to tell you, Eleanor, the Library has gone rogue! Surely The Powers would never sanction the subject matter—let alone the syntax—of this new batch of books! They're government men, after all. And this, this "modernist" and "post-modernist" "writing"…it's anarchy, Eleanor! Pure mental anarchy, and I won't stand for it.

A good story (any story!) starts with a capital letter and ends with a period, with some others in between. It is a river starting at the top of an "A" and trickling down the mountain to the placid lake of the period. It is not a Mobius strip of language—if you can even call some of that language! That horrible gentleman should "river run" himself to a dictionary, or a shrink. A Wake, indeed! Pynchon, Brautigan, Burroughs, Gaddis, Hawkes—an obfuscator's obfuscator if ever there was one.

S.R.1,798

[V.N.] I received a message today—crawling across my tablet as I was reading the latest punishment from the Library—that I am no longer to use our Thirty-Eight Code Transmission System. The Powers That Be have conferred and resigned to collate the data into a simpler set of eight combinations. From now on the sequence will only read: one-left, one-middle, one-right. It will still vacillate between circles and squares, but there shall be no more columnar overlapping: no left-square, left-circle, middle-square; no middle-circle, middle-square, right-square—which I confess to have been my favorite transmission…I don't know why so much, only that I felt something heartrending in the aesthetics.

I shall have to make do.

S.R. 1,863

_____

[V.N.] Transmissions: circle-square-circle; circle-circle-square; square-square-circle (which I feel is just hideous—primitive, really); square-circle-circle; and once again that abominable square-square-circle.

S.R. 1,899

_____

[V.N.] I admit the simplicity of the new system is wearing on me tremendously. I feel my brain is slower, as if someone has injected cold molasses into my dopamine and serotonin. When I finish with my transmissions, I am little more than a zombified cosmonaut, forcing myself to internally dictate each of my movements before making them: press the octagonal button for food, grasp the foil wrapper, peel, pull, bring to mouth, chew, chew, swallow…press the triangular button that releases my wastes…illuminate the rectangular eReaders whose serif lines of text look like the vulgar squiggles of a lesser Esperanto, intricately tied tube worms approximating glyphs.

I was abruptly extracted from my disgusted revelry by the intrusion of the Alarm, who had caught me dozing, and I was forced to press on.

S.R. 1,945

[V.N.] Settling deeper into the literature of the obscenely obtuse and the hopelessly dense, I've been forced to endure the Library's course in philosophy: from the Greeks to the Scholastics; to Kant and Descartes; then on to Hume and Hegel before tackling the existentialism of Kierkegaard, Sartre, and Nietzsche; only to be subjected to the semiotics of Eco, the linguistics of Husserl, the, sheer *lunacy* of Wittgenstein. It's like my mind is doing pushups but I'm too out of shape. I find myself incapable of carrying on for more than a few sentences before my mind wanders down some path of its own accord, reading and rereading the same clause, phrase, word…slowly going over every syllable, taking the phonic expressions of every seme down to just above absolute zero. And the Library is swift with its reprimands. I have to put it down, Eleanor, I need some reprieve, some respite.

S.R. 2,021

[V.N.] Transmissions: circle, square, circle; square, circle, circle; square, circle, square.

Perfectly simple, perfectly elegant.

S.R. 2,034

[N.B.] Jesus, and here I thought the philosophy was bad enough: the Library has been on a mathematical kick lately. Starting with books on Thales' pedagogy passed down through Anaximander, Pythagoras, Euclid, Archytas, and Aristotle; following a vector towards early calculus with Democritus, Eudoxus, Archimedes…moving down the timeline to works by Barrow, Pascal, Newton, and Leibnitz; onwards to Eisenstein, Gauss, Riemann, Grothendieck; taking a turn towards the logical with Gödel, Aristotle (again), and books on developmental, semantic, and modal logic.

The Library, it appears, has some knowledge as to my preferences. And my tricks. If I happen to "skim" the pages and place the book back on the shelf, in what is surely not enough time to absorb the material, the Library merely replaces the work with a different translation of equal or greater obfuscation. I swear, Eleanor, I heard the Library grunt, a mechanical "ahem," and nudge an eReader back into my hands as I had merely doodled over the last chapter with the stylus. I half-expect the next phase to be the Library extending mechanical arms, opening my head, and force-feeding me this overabundance of information.

Who the hell decided to put a library here in the first place!

S.R. 2,080

AUTOMATED DIAGNOSTIC ASSESSMENT
#021915: Subject inconclusive; position indeterminate. Heartbeat elevated. Breathing heavy.

S.R. 2,084

[V.N.] That goddamn scan came again, just as unannounced and unsolicited as the last time! Now, before They tell you what They think They saw, let me first explain something: it gets lonely out here, Eleanor, very lonely. Sometimes…in order to account for the absence of any reciprocal companionship one must…become that reciprocal companion. Do you follow, dear? Am I making sense? If not, well, best to just leave that one I think.

S.R. 2,322

[N.B.] No transmissions today, my dear. Four hours and not a single one! I ended up spending a majority of the time holding my hand in front of the Sun Shield, opening and closing the aperture, watching the way the sun turned the skin pink, then orange, then red.

There must be something more productive I can do if I'm to have many more of these days.

On another note, these eReaders are getting very gummed up with fingerprints. Would it really have killed them to have a piece of cheesecloth to buff them out with?!

S.R. 2,466

[V.N.] I dreamt the other night, or I believe I dreamt, of a four-legged spider that had either accompanied me onto the ship or had stowed away somehow. The spider weaves large, elaborate grids, each intersecting at a perfect ninety-degrees. Each grid a perfect square. I have chosen either to name the spider Gibson or Tetracules, I cannot decide. The latter feels perfectly descriptive and of a somewhat scientific nature, subscribing to the physical direction of the prefix and having all the will, resolve, perseverance, and what must be unimaginable strength in order to make it here, in order to survive these conditions on his own, to earn the suffix; but the other name is Gibson, which feels more familiar and comforting. Plus, there is the physiognomy of the spider to consider: the spider's bumbling gait, owing to the extra-bulbous abdomen, distributed over half the normal limbs, causes the spider a greater swing of momentum at each penduluming step, resulting in a sort of bow-legged strut; his haughty head raised up in a distinguished pose, donning what appears to be a large, white mustache that curves ever-so-slightly around his mouth...with all these attributes, how could I not think him a Gibson?!

I believe I would enjoy the company of a Gibson over the company of a Tetracules, but I can't be certain. Possibly I would feel too formal around a Gibson, owing to his almost certain aristocratic background; with Tetracules I fear I would be too intimidated by the associations I have conjured for that name. But I also believe Gibson would make me feel as though I am in the company of an acerbic sidekick, loyal to a fault, dedicated to seeing through to my mission—which is, I realize, the role I must also have charged Tetracules with, a reliance on his strength.

And I know what you're thinking, Eleanor, "Why couldn't one be a proper name and the other a surname? Why couldn't the spider be Gibson Tetracules or Tetracules Gibson?" Because, my dear, neither the one sequence nor the other could appropriately describe the spider—he is not a creature of two names, not of our social order of naming. Perhaps the spider himself has a name, though I doubt he'd ever tell.

Perhaps that name is Gibson. Perhaps Tetracules.

If that name is Tom or Gary I shall be thoroughly disappointed.

S.R. 2,548

[N.B.] I have seen the antichrist, Eleanor, and they have shelved his work in my library: Philippe Sollers' *Nombres*. Were I still a terrestrial man I would voluntarily incarcerate myself after slaying that Beelzebub Sollers and his axiomatic Bourbaki apostles. Infinite interpretations, posh! Infinity is just an ouroboros with a twist in the middle. A snake like any other.

The bastards have also perniciously included Derrida's entire bibliography (*Glas* for god's sake!) as well as that of Barthes and Hegel, Wittgenstein and Husserl, not to mention fiction dense as a meteorite. They've left me, centered on the shelf, glowing from the light above, *Correction* by Thomas Bernhard. I feel as if I've done something terribly wrong to these people. They have locked me up on Crete in some syntactic labyrinth, chased by a hulking Minotaur of rhetoric.

Do they want my suicide, Eleanor? Seppuku by way of self-induced aneurysm?

S.R. 2,598

[N.B.] Please, Eleanor, allow me to apologize, not to you, my dear, but to the transmission system for ever doubting her. Whence love was lost, it has returned anew, a-brim, for the language of my transmissions, for the simplicity inherent, for the precise articulation of the meanings. No doubt a reaction to this "leisure" reading: works that solely confound the mind. I cannot imagine how I once loathed a language in which all was clear, in which there was no anxiety of false interpretation, no threat of infinite meanings and understanding.

I swear to you, Eleanor, I've begun to dread my leisure time; my hand trembles, actually trembles, over the cover of these works. I feel as though a watermelon seed were gestating in my stomach as I fall back into the literary malebolge; and if I could option a name for the thirteenth Malebranche, it would be *Glasida*. Yet I read on, what else could I have done? I only wish, my dear, there was some way to subvert this system I write in, think in, that though I now loathe the rhetoric with which I try to communicate to you, my love, there is no other method at hand—the irony has been keeping me awake through most of my resting periods, the sleep I do find consists of dreams regarding some new expedient of communication; well, that, and the frequent returns of the Spider.

Speaking of which, I find that perhaps a slash can accomplish for me what indecision couldn't. For with the slash I can have both names, each isolated from the other, dichotomous. The spider is thus a polyseme meaning either Gibson and/or Tetracules, but never Tectracules Gibson or Gibson Tetracules, or even dashed versions of the sequence. Gibson/Tetracules: separate but equal.

I had considered using a pipe to eliminate giving the appearance of preferential treatment in the ordering, but the "|" has far too much symbolic history associated with it, far too much linguistic overlap across the sciences: from the language of logic (the Sheffer stroke) to the language of computation (the bitwise "or" of C), the language of the physical (the bra-ket notation of states) to the literal language of the tongue (the phonetic denotation of the dental click). And even within the language of mathematics, the pipe takes numerous forms, from absolutes to the determinant range of a matrix. Perhaps the | (the obelisk, as it's sometimes known), is a tribute to the Tower of Babel, harkening back to a point when the symbol had but one meaning; strangely, its broken representation, "¦", seems to be the only direct acknowledgement of the tower's collapse.

No, the pipe has no place with Gibson/Tetracules. The slash accomplishes the same means and joins both names without mucking about in that symbolic muck.

S.R. 2,656

[**N.B.**] Eleanor, I believe our language would benefit greatly from a larger influence by mathematics. So much uncertainty made certain; so much space saved.

Think of the impact the change will have on our titles. Think of the immediate graphic power of coming face to face with a set of symbols versus a string of letters or words. Monolithic doesn't begin to describe it. Imagine the changes to something like Tom Clancy's portentous tale of nuclear brinksmanship, *The Sum of All Fears*. Just look at what happens when the title is brought into mathematical form:

$$\Sigma \ |\text{Fears}|$$

Or better yet:

$$\sum_{n=-\infty}^{\infty} \text{Fears}$$

Imagine that hitting you on the bookstand! A far superior title than the one currently printed across covers and spines, and, dare I say, titles that provoke more nuclear gloom and doom. And what's more, you know exactly what I mean without my having to fill in any additional language.

Though perhaps that, too, can be fixed. I shall see what I can do.

S.R. 2,712

[**N.B.**] Transmissions for the day:
⭘▢⭘.⭘⭘▢.▢⭘⭘.▢▢▢.⭘⭘▢.⭘⭘⭘.

S.R. 2,790

[**V.N.**] I don't think it would surprise you, Eleanor, to learn that I have decided to boycott the Barber. Sure, part of it has to do with the general unease of using the device, but there is another imperative, a moral one, if you will. A stance against the Powers and the only real method of rebellion available to me. Well, one that won't result in a tone-deaf aria from the Alarm.

S.R. 2,802

[**V.N.**] When I can get away with it, I've begun to supplement my reading time by taking out the star charts and basking in the simplicity of the constellations. The heavens truly knew how to write lovely, dramatic stories in simple patterns of triangles, rectangles, trapezoids, and the occasional pentagonal and hexagonal formations. Heavenly spheres, indeed.

These fables of the firmament…few actually resemble the shapes proposed by the Greeks or Native Americans: in Cancer I see no evidence of a crab, instead a strain of DNA unravelling; in Gemini I find not a pair of twins, but a coffin with a rope guiding it into the ground. There are others that look like various molecular diagrams or viruses (looking at you Pisces, Taurus, and Draco—although, with that long, serpentine tail you could pass for a different microscopic organism). In Delphinus I see a lost kite whose tether had slipped from chocolate-greased fingers. Hercules—honestly, Eleanor, how could Hercules be anything but my dear friend Mr. Gibson/ Tetracules?!

S.R. 2,855

[V.N.] Perhaps I have landed on something to alleviate my rhetorical angst—and larger problems in general—Eleanor. More later: I must return to the drawing board, so to speak.

S.R. 3,024

[N.B.] Well, here it goes, my dear, the preamble to the greater solution. Stay with me:

The Reitlinger Conundrum:

Eleanor, the relationship between metaphor and metonymy is perhaps the biggest illustrations of the quantitative limitations, and therefore failures, of our language. (And it pains me that I still am indentured to them in my writing; but I'm working on that.) And know that when I speak of metonymy I'm not talking about "The pen is mightier than the sword," "All hands on deck," the metonymic connotations of Washington or the News, The Man and his unflappable power; I'm referring to the root of the actionable words, the literal history and known associates of the word that make the metonymical phrase function the way it does, the metonymic implications of its place in time, each word's history rolled into an aleph.

Now, the equation of metaphor is easy to understand: a simple substitution like any algebra: $x = y$. Metonymy's equation, as well, is very simple: $x = x_n$; or $y = y_n$. To illustrate:

$$X = Y$$
$$X_1 = Y_1$$
$$X_2 = Y_2$$
$$X_3 = Y_3$$
$$X_n = Y_n$$

Fig. 1

Or, if we wanted to condense it into a linear form: $X_{n \to \infty} = Y_{n \to \infty}$

The metonymical *problem* with language, my dear, is that the values for x and y are muddied, irrational some might say. The values are entirely subjective. One man's n could be quite another's. The "meaning" in metonymy is simply a grouping of "related" items belonging to a metonymical field. To apply on a personal level, let us consider ourselves, for the moment, able to map out plot structure as it pertains to tension in a novel.

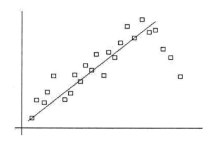

Fig. 2. [Eleanor, for the purposes of this graph allow "Tension" to occupy the Y-axis and "Time (In Progression of Plot in Pages)" to make up the X-axis.]

Through integration and differentiation one could create an equation for such a disbursement of points (the cumulative affect of the work): the affective derivative of each book (idiosyncratic; a literary genome, Eleanor). Yet, though we feel the tension, the "points" in Fig. 2 remain empty squares, empty values inside a defined interval (defined in as much as the affect of the book does not stay with you, does not continue after the cover has been shut, which surely it cannot, right?), because of the inability to properly quantify the values—there are no known values to associate with psychological affect, my dear. (As of now, that is; there were rumors circulating that The Powers were working on that, as well.) For every individual—although the derivative remains the same—the quantities are subject to the respective substitution of infinite values, thus, infinite derivatives at a given point of plot (isolating to a specific action, sentence, clause, or word upon which the tangent hinges).

Perhaps I should illustrate:

Do you remember when we talked about string theory and multiple dimensions on our anniversary? How I held your hand as we watched the shores of the Outer Banks roll in from the third-floor deck of your family's beach house? How we had just stuffed our bellies with crab and fresh scallops and I told you to imagine our concept of width, length, and height (x,y,z axes) to be condensed to a singular point, and that as a point we have no value or matrix with which to locate that point, and so we create another point, another condensed xyz, and that the distance between these two points is a very palpable space/time dimension that we connect with a line? Do you remember how you almost choked and coughed on your dessert cheese when I told you to consider the next two axes, the y and the z, other lines of space/time converging and intersecting upon the first—our 5th and 6th dimensions—and how if you condensed all of those axes to a solitary point we would have our universe? Do you remember how the night rolled in and we watched the heat lighting strike out at sea, how when it flashed you could see darkening clouds that made a staircase of the horizon, the way the light bounced off them, captured in a solitary flash of phosphorescence and you laughed and said "God must be taking a photograph"? Do you remember how I then drew another axis connecting the point of our universe with that of another universe, then bisecting that axis with another, and another, until we came to the same recurring 3-dimensional model and you said "Jesus, John, I thought we were done with all that; when is this going to end?" and I said "It *ends* when we reach a point where all possible universes [U_∞] are condensed and connected—and who knows if that's even the end!" That same idea applies to metonymy: all possible meanings and feelings and memories and senses occupying a single moment, word, phrase, or event in literature; the intersection of metonymic fields and of the nature of memory, recalling connections from one to the next, and so on and so forth. But these are all intangible values. How then can we possibly understand the solitary meaning of an author's work when there is no absolute to hold on to? No constant? When there is no firm ground with which to tether the balloon? How can we be expected to understand a feeling or idea when an author presents us with a pairing of unknown universes? (What I have eponymously dubbed the Reitlinger Conundrum, my dear.)

Do you see the contention that can arise, my little Pumpernickel? The wars attributed to biblical analysis, Torah interpretation; the heated debates of academia regarding Proust, Eliot, and Joyce; the way we blankly stare at our children when they open a book and ask "What does this mean?" of some figurative nightmare? Is it right to frighten our children with the dread and horror of uncertainty? Should we lie to them directly, Eleanor, start their young and eager lives on a vector of deceit? Though we both cried after your first miscarriage, I am resolutely grateful for the loss; grateful we didn't have to face a moment like that.

So, to simplify the thesis of the preamble into one elegant posit: There can be no finite meaning if the meanings are infinite.

You must keep this in mind.

S.R. 3,033

[N.B.] Transmissions for the day: ○○□ ; □○○ ; that contemptible ○□○ ; □○□ ; ○□□ ; □○○ ; again that goddamned □○□ ; another ○□○ , ○○○ ; ○○○ ; ○○○ .

S.R. 3,069

[V.N.] Well, this was nice and awkward, the Library endeavored to teach me about the birds and the bees today, putting the books out there for me to chart my own sexual awakening: from the clinical works of Masters and Johnson, to the romantic treatises of Miller's *Tropics*, to the emetic works of Sade. There were even a few romance novels thrown in the mix and a couple periodicals heavy on the photography and light on the articles. I confess to having some fantasies about putting my education into practice. I believe I may have already mentioned the toll of loneliness out here, my dear.

While it was certainly discomforting to me, my discomfort was not alone; now, I could very well be wrong, but I could have sworn I saw the Library blush, a shade of pink taking over the otherwise white shelves.

S.R.3,100

[V.N.] Soon, Eleanor. Very soon.

S.R. 3,198

[N.B.] Yes, I believe I've done it, the Solution to the Conundrum, meaning for the meaningless, I give you:

THE REITLINGER SOLUTION:

Let □ stand for all nouns; let ○ equal all predicates (infinitive, transitive, and intransitive); let △ represent our adjectives; ◇ for all adverbs; ▢ for all pronouns; ⬠ for all prepositions; ◭ our conjunctions; ⬡ will be our articles; and ⚪, is, I feel, a great new stand-in for interjections. I have chosen geometric symbols as a Husserlian tribute over those quite nauseating squiggles of Wittgenstein's. (I confess, Eleanor, since last chastising the works of certain philosophers and semioticians, their collective discourse—perhaps epiphanized, as I, by the stars—has facilitated the panacea of my Solution to the Reitlinger Conundrum.)

Our punctuation, however, will be alphabetical:

a	.
e	,
i	:
j	;
u	‹›
y	—
g	?
h	!

Fig. 3

Let common, mathematical symbols still apply (+, -, *,/, <, >, etc), for in them we can truly see the relationship of words. For obvious reasons, Eleanor, our parentheses mustn't change. For the sake of simplicity, adjacent words must not be taken to mean that they are being multiplied, for example $\triangle\square$ is $\triangle+\square$, not $\triangle\times\square$; addition must be implied unless otherwise noted.

The formulation of a correct and universal language is attainable, my dear, one much more universal than the false prophet that is Esperanto; we have a way of reversing the fall and returning to a Babylonian linguistic singularity. And we are doing it in such a way that the meaning and semiotic value of our speech can be easily (and accurately!) quantifiable; no more getting lost or mucking through the metonymical mud, the grammatical algorithms that are outdated and atrophied to inaccuracy.

To illustrate the wealth of simplicity this Solution affords us, let us look at the famous first two clauses of Dickens' classic, *A Tale of Two Cities*: "It was the best of times, it was the worst of times". In the Solution it would read:

$$\square\square\bigcirc\triangle^{+}\Diamond\square\,e\,\square\bigcirc\bigcirc\triangle^{-}\Diamond\square$$

(The post-script indicating the nature of the verb, positive versus negative.)

If we condense the sentence, $\blacksquare\blacksquare\bigcirc\;\triangle^{+}\Diamond\square\,e\,\square\bigcirc\bigcirc\triangle^{-}\Diamond\square$, we can see that the two sides balance out to merely $\triangle^{+}e\triangle^{-}$, the denotations clearly representing the polar relationship between the nominal heart of the clauses, and thus the idea of the clausal relationship is satisfied: we know there to be two things presented that happen to be different from each other in a polar way. And yes, Eleanor, this relationship continues in the proceeding twelve clauses, which we can express as:

$$\triangle^{+}e\triangle^{-}e\triangle^{+}e\triangle^{-}e\triangle^{+}e\triangle^{-}e\triangle^{+}e\triangle^{-}e$$
$$^{+}e\triangle^{-}e\triangle^{+}e\triangle^{-}e\triangle^{+}e\triangle^{-}e\triangle^{+}e\triangle^{-}e\triangle^{+}e$$
$$^{-}e\triangle^{+}e\triangle^{-}e\triangle^{+}e\triangle^{-}e\triangle^{+}e\triangle^{-}e\triangle^{+}e\triangle^{-}$$

Or, because that repetitive string is a monstrous vulgarity (and before the sentence is even finished, mind you!) we can simplify even further:

$$14(\triangle^{+}e\;\triangle^{-})yy\,\Diamond\bigcirc e\,\bigcirc\square\bigcirc\Diamond\bigcirc\bigcirc\triangle\square e\,\triangle\triangle\Diamond\triangle\Diamond\bigcirc\triangle\bigcirc\bigcirc e$$
$$\Diamond\square^{+}\triangle\Diamond\square^{-}e\,\Diamond\bigcirc\Diamond\square\bigcirc\square\Diamond a$$

So you see, Eleanor, the words that Dickens wrote are superfluous in accomplishing the same means. (Also, there is the issue of that idiom "in short," which I feel I should eliminate—and further, I (we) should strive to eliminate all idioms going forward; they are illogical, an unreal linguistic expression.)

Shall we try another? How about we tackle that impertinent tome that has led to books of academia amassing more pages than the actual novel itself? *Ulysses*. Let us try the first sentence:

"Stately Buck Mulligan came from the stairhead, bearing a bowl of lather on which a mirror and a razor lay crossed." △□□○◇○□ *e* ○○□◇□◇□○□△○□◇ *a* Such a sentence cannot be balanced and should thus be refuted and stricken from further editions.

Or perhaps we should look at a section towards the end, the "Sinbad the Sailor and Tinbad the Tailor and Jinbad the Jailor…" bit.

It would read as such: $\square\bigcirc\square\triangle\square_2\bigcirc\square_2\triangle\square_3\bigcirc\square_3\ldots$

By looking at the pattern, we can easily discern the meaning of the passage. And again, we can condense the section:

$$\sum_{1}^{15}\square\bigcirc\square\triangle$$

or perhaps

$$((\square\bigcirc\square\triangle)_{1\rightarrow15})$$

Do you see how much cleaner it is? How the meaning is still intact, unmolested. Should we continue we could no doubt take the book from 800 pages down to something closer to 100—30 if we stick to eliminating the unbalanced bits. And we can continue, not just with Joyce, but with all written works.

Eleanor, what we have here is the jurisdiction to propagate and correct, on a macro scale, the imperfections of literature and language; and to do so with the sole proprietary sense of justice and the benefaction of humanity, to serve ourselves by eliminating free radicals. For, if indeed language is meant to give a "picture of the word" as Wittgenstein asserts, what better picture can be made than with the acrylic tubes of mathematics and geometry?

Perhaps we should address the issue of delineating tenses, my dear: Why should a tense matter? Whether a thing has happened, is happening, or will happen, the fact that it happens at all is what matters, the fact that it is, regardless of state; where it falls in the fourth dimension is of no consequence. Perhaps the only thing to consider is the possibility of whether something *could* happen: the Heisenbergian state of uncertainty and potential. I shall consider working on some notation to demonstrate as much.

S.R. 3,282

[V.N.] On another note, I bashed my left knee against the desk, which has developed into a rather goofy looking bruise: yellow and purple, in the shape of the crab nebula.

S.R. 3,303

[N.B.] The Library has taken on the responsibility of my historical education, forcing upon me *Historia Augusta*, Herodotus' *The Histories*, Tacitus' *Annals*, Plutarch's *Moralia* and the surviving parts of *Parallel Lives*… "newer" works by Barzun, Carlyle, Lord Acton, Gibbons, Berlin, Friedman, Meinecke, and several more whose work I did not read but merely translated into the Solution, scribbling the new lines into these notebooks. One small piece in the, admittedly, overwhelming task of translating all works into the Solution. I shall have to call on you, Eleanor, to not only assist, but to disseminate the Solution to other would-be translators upon my return.

S.R. 3,345

[V.N.] I have endured a new injury to join my nebulous bruise, a savage paper-cut from these notebooks that hold my Solution. It stung like the unreduced Dickens. Then, while floating with an utter lack of concern for my surroundings toward the first aid station, I promptly banged my injured knee again on the weight machine. The anger and initial shock, and the subsequent rubbing of my knee, delayed the treatment of my hand, which continued to bleed (blood takes a strange shape in space, like a macabre gelatin, especially viscous, adhering to the properties of iron in zero-g); and after several minutes of this charade, I finally procured the gauze and anti-bacterial ointment and set to wrapping my hand. Of course, Eleanor, the attention to my medical needs seeped into the time for sustenance, and, two minutes tardy, the Alarm sounded, shaking the pod and thoroughly disturbing my senses so that I didn't tie the bandage as I should have, but instead proceeded Pavlovially to the dispenser, pressed the octagonal button, and retrieved my food while my blood continued to flow, thoroughly staining my white uniform with the floating globules—it's a wonder they didn't happen upon any of the electrical panels!

Strange, unlike the books that recycle, these poplin uniforms, one-piece jumpers more or less, are given to me in a set quantity of five. I've already wrecked one from an accident in the lavatory department, and, as this stained uniform will surely have to go, I'll then be left with three. Yes, Eleanor, they've given me chemical cleaners to eliminate sweat and dirt, freshened with a synthetic scent of rain water, but I doubt the amount sufficient to sustain three uniforms for rest of my duration.

S.R. 3,376

[N.B.] I've been working on a new translation, my dear. I decided to abandon the full, novel-length translations until I'm ready and begin with smaller works, those that really need my help—like poetry. I think this piece is as valid a starting point as ever—and one that I think especially shows the sheer power of the Solution. A nonsense poem in its original form, Lewis Carroll's "The Jabberwocky" is now a work of objective meaning. Observe:

$\bigcirc\square_{e}\triangle\bigcirc\triangle\square$

$\bigcirc\bigcirc\triangle\bigcirc\diamond\bigcirc\square_{i}$

$\blacktriangle\triangle\bigcirc\bigcirc\square_{e}$

$\triangle\diamond\blacktriangle\square\bigcirc_{a}$

$^{uu}\bigcirc\bigcirc\square_{e}\triangle\square\ ^{h}$

$\diamond\square\triangle_{e}\bigcirc\square\triangle\ ^{h}$

$\bigcirc\bigcirc\triangle\square_{e}\triangle\bigcirc$

$\diamond\triangle\square\ ^{huu}$

These are just the first two stanzas, Eleanor, but already you can see how much cleaner it is. How it removes the nonsensical and replaces it within a matrix of firm meaning. (You'll also note how I've moved our punctuation into the subscript and superscript; which enhances the cleanliness, my dear.)

This is just the start, my love. More to come. Much more.

S.R. 3,389

[N.B.] You never saw me as a boy, Eleanor—how could you have? I was so bright eyed and full of the perturbation of desired learning vs. the dissonance of mandated learning. I had bright thoughts of geometric shapes and mathematical conjectures that would relate the truths of such shapes in simple and necessary statements. (Husserl would have been proud!) I remember the burden of reading: of the required mispronunciation for certain words in our English language; of the endless homonyms, homophones—homographs!; of the dualistic phoneme "f" and "ph;" of the meddling of Latin roots,

Spanish roots, Germanic roots and syntax; the odd Arabic word thrown in here and there. How is a mere boy to be expected to comprehend such disjunctive and discerptive nomenclatures? I remember I would bang my troubled head upon the desk and feel the sting of the ruler, accompanied by Sister Mary's terse and diminutive reprimands, upon my palms and wrists but more so on my heart and head; I could feel the class's stares and their projections of failure and ignorance upon my being. And for what? Was I to be blamed for the inconsistencies of a variegated bastard language conceived through the immoralities of farmers, traders, and merchants? Not linguists or semioticians, mind you.

Oh, Eleanor, you understand me better than most, but still not enough. Could you not understand where my unease comes from? Where my pain and ambition thrives? Oh Eleanor...I long to touch your $\triangle \square e$ your $\square o$ I long to inhale your $\triangle e \triangle$ and $\triangle \square$ and call you my own again.

Oh, My Little Muskmelon, do you remember the gray banks of the Superior. The violent crashing of gray upon gray that is Duluth? When the water in the summer was still too cold to swim comfortably, yet we shed our clothes and clambered over those sharp, wet rocks and made a jovial celebration of our budding sexual energies, aroused not by our bodies and their need for touch, but by the stirring we felt in each other, the potential we felt rising to our chests, electrified when we submerged our heads and tested the buoyancy of our bodies and our ability to hold our breathes against the crushing cold, the crushing gray? I feel it again, my love; I feel it again, the warring factions of reason and art, converging and detracting; I feel myself strained again by the cold calm and the tugging tide; feel their dissonant gravitations inciting, testing, a change in myself. A change in ourselves.

S.R. 3,441

[N.B.] Eleanor, just think of the good we could do! The offenses we could dismiss! Do you recall the night we were harassed by that loquacious brute who kept shouting to the crowd that you were a "cunt-agious cunt-tree blumpkin," shouting at the man he thought accompanied you as we scurried across the parking lot that his "cock'll never crow"? How you couldn't sleep for weeks, picturing him outside, standing in your rose bushes and daffodils, singing to you in the mornings as you sipped your tea: "Oh, have you met the cunt-trolling little cunt-inually disgusting cunt-tractually repulsing, cunt-trived, cunt-tusive, cunt-rary cunt-agion?" Well, I needn't give you any further nightmares by mentioning more, but Eleanor, under my Solution, the insulting puns will have no more effect than an improper fraction: slightly unsettling, but quick to reduce. By chance, we might even turn his hatred into some beautiful equation. The language of hate subsumed into a language of love. The tongue of the caveman silvered into the telepathic transmissions of the overman.

All possible through the Solution.

I dreamt last sleep cycle that we could exist in the communion of os and 1s, a binary beauty subjugating itself solely to the clear and the concise, against the current empire of variety and variable. Though my Solution isn't binary, it is a step, no? I imagine myself returning to Earth and upon a glorious platform, festooned with congratulatory laurels of my geometric sentences, accompanied by media from around the world, announcing in slides broadcast overhead: ^{uu}Fear not$_e$ my brethren$_e$ fear not$_a$ For thou art trespassing into simpler semiotics$_i$ for inside the walls of mine orbiting abode$_e$. I have found an answer to our travails$_e$ our mindless suffering at the hands of inconsistency$_e$ brash confusion$_e$ and the insidious face of language$_a$ I have engineered a simpler world for us$_a$ A quantifiable world where we can go in peace$_e$ in mute harmony$_a$ What say you^g Do you dare to follow$_e$ do you dare for freedom^{guu}

And even now I realize—lament, Eleanor—the inability and the deficit imparted to you with these words I use—which of course shall have to be in service until I return and you've familiarized yourself with my Solution—eased into the waters, as it were—and we can speak fluidly and coherently. Until then, I can only fantasize about our nuptial discourse.

S.R. 3,477

[N.B.] Terrible transmissions today: 8 □□□, 2 ○□○, and 1 repugnant □○○.

S.R. 3,500

[N.B.] I've begun composing stories of my own, starting slow at first, working one sentence at a time, getting one sentence right before moving on to the next. After many false starts and many eliminations, I settled on what I thought was a first complete sentence: ⬠□○ □$_e$ □○□○□ □$_a$

I had sat there, admiring it, gloating, when I realized I wasn't finished, that I had more work to do. See, just as I was quick to judge and simplify the writings of olde, I realized I too was committing the crime of the superfluous. I further reduced my sentence to

⬠□○ □$_e$ 2(□○)□ □$_a$

I shouldn't feel too embarrassed, dear. We are always learning, are we not?

S.R. 3,512

[N.B.] I must admit that some of these stories came to me by way of sleep. My dreams of late are chalked full of such stories (these stories being the only ones I could recall upon waking). No sooner do I fall asleep, Eleanor, no sooner do the frequencies of my Beta waves drop into a slow Alpha tide, falling off the ridge into slower, taller, Theta levels, sinking further until resting on the floors of the Delta Deep, only to be raised to the amalgam waves of dreams, no sooner do I arrive on these horn-rimmed, oneiric steps than I am assaulted by a slew of shapes: a dazzling display of polygons, sometimes offset or adorned with placards of mathematical direction, which I follow this way and that; a slender, erect, cylinder protruding from a fork in the road bearing a choice on two rectangles, Products or Sums; a map of logarithms leading towards a temple of hexagons and spheres, an octagonal castle where squares and circles make up the court, large triangular cathedrals buttressed by trapezoids; Gibson/Tetracules, as foreman, overseeing the construction of a pentagonal youth center. And They say we can't read in our dreams.

S.R. 3,636

[N.B.] Religion now the moral imperative of the Library. Beginning with older works like the *Bhagavad Gita* and the rest of the *Mahabharata*; moving on to the *Old Testament* and the *Hebrew Bible* (which really begs the question as to the importance of ordering), King James' *New Testament*, the *Apocrypha*, the *Qur'an*, the Hindu *Vedas*, the *Buddhavacana*, Confucious' *Analects*, the *Bardo Thötröl*, and eighty-two chapters of the Egyptian *Book of the Dead*; next, Cicero's *De Officiis* to calibrate my moral compass; followed by *The Book of Mormon* and L. Ron Hubbard's *Dianetics*—which I feel should have been paired with Hubert, Dick, and Heinlein in sunrises long ago. Then the Library took a bit of a mystical turn with the Hermetic works of Crowley, Spare, and Regardie; Anton LeVey's *The Satanic Bible*; and—a mistake of the Library's that supplied me with innumerable mirth—Rushdie's *The Satanic Verses*.

S.R. 3,728

[N.B.] *More on Metonymy:*

If we extract our Fig. 1 model to include more variables—because, let's face it, X isn't just one metaphor, isn't just one theme, scene, sentence, or phrase; X exists down to the word, down to the emotive memory of each word and phoneme in the reader; thus there will be multiple Xs, multiple variables that all have their own possible values—what we would get if we use the variables A, B, C, and D is something like this:

A_1	B_1	C_1	D_1
A_2	B_2	C_2	D_2
A_3	B_3	C_3	D_3
A_4	B_4	C_4	D_4
A_x	B_x	C_x	D_x

Fig. 4

And say we look at the possible mappings of what one may draw upon from selecting different values (your metonymical relationship to the variable) from the above diagram: **Option 1:** A_1,B_3,C_2, D_x; **Option 2:** A_x, B_4, C_x, D_x; **Option 3:** A_3, B_1,C_x, D_3. Etc. Etc. Sure it's the same general line, the same sequential ordering, but the subset value will change the equation dramatically. Barthes knew what I'm getting at; the dynamism of the values will even change for the same reader at different points of their life, the reader's history importing new metonymical values. Will the word "mother" not mean something extra after the reader's has just passed? And will it not mean something different ten years after her passing?

Eleanor, imagine that four-variable equation as just one phrase, [the] "blood red cat slept," for instance, and all the various metonymic conjuring that could muster; now, extrapolate that for the clause, the sentence, the paragraph, chapter…Do you see where I'm going with this, Eleanor? Do you? Imagine the whole: the last line of the book is finished; between the covers is an equation, or matrix, of your metonymical reading of the book, your metonymical affect. You could calculate that affect if only there were some sort quantifiable metric for your experiences, feelings, general associations (see Fig. 2). We can't, in our current model, of course, but Eleanor just *imagine* it. Can you imagine it? Can you see where I'm going with this? It's as if the actual text is just one topical layer, the crust of the earth, the skull encasing the real action of the book. There's an infinite synaptical world occurring underneath the text: the cortex of the book lying underneath the corpus of the text, just as vast and largely uncharted as any brain.

But the weird thing, the lonely thing, my dear, is that we are only able to access and experience our own interpretations, our own metonymy. We can't possibly see how other people experience the work, no matter what we do; nor can we share our own experiences, not completely. Reading is the most personalized thing we could ever do, my nougatty sweet; an emotive frequency only we can hear. And that's reading in the broad sense of the word. We "read" all mediums we encounter: text, film, music, advertisements (as deliberate an attempt to engineer one's affective reading as I've ever seen: tapping into one brief, coded line of experience and relation, exploiting it, vibrating it like a microwave and sympathetically guiding it towards a solution); we read street signs and flags (of both surf *and* turf), the Crucifix (with or without the adornment of the Christ (yet another metonym)), the Aum, the Star of David: these latter examples simply a reduction of metonymy into a symbol.

Take, for instance, this commercial I witnessed shortly before my departure: It's a hot summer day in The City; no air conditioning inside the sweltering apartment whose ceiling fan hangs limp and withered; you're pouring sweat out of every pore; suddenly there appears a beautiful, perspiring bottle of soda glowing through the fridge door; you take a big, long gulp and suddenly the room is covered in a veneer of ice; you can see your breath in the air; now you are impervious to the heat; you smile; you leave the apartment, and even in the summer heat, on the sidewalks of the sweaty city, an aura of coolness and refreshment encapsulates you; you stroll on in a protective bubble of refreshment; ice forming on everything your bubble touches; everyone you pass looks at you, jealous but respectful, as if you've just come up with an invention as novel and exciting as the bicycle; respect is given; a minority of some flavor nods approvingly; a sign emerges "Limonang Soda | Take back the Cool™"; the camera pulls out until the bubble and its occupant resemble the brand's iconic yin-yang image. A reduction to the symbol. A reduction to the simple.

S.R. 3,776

[V.N.] While sleeping last, I felt an itch halfway up my left calf and tried to use the toe of my right foot to remedy the situation; now, perhaps I should have been a little more cognizant of the current state of my hygiene, but instead of sweet relief, I felt several rapid stings. When I was able to investigate in the morning, I found three crescent wounds from the offending big toe. This led me to consider not just the lapsed grooming of my feet, but of the entire state of my physique. I have decided to do some grooming, my dear. Forget the locks I had been trying to grow out of rebellion to the Powers, shaved is a much cleaner, more sterile, solution. And I'm not just talking about my head, I'm talking about my chest, my shoulders, arms, legs…elsewhere…even the fine fibers on my ears and the hairs in my nostrils. It's a Fire Sale of Follicles, my dear!

S.R. 3,808

[N.B.] Eleanor$_e$ I know what you^{u}re thinking $^{uu}\Delta$ John$_e$ you^{u}re only talking about the written word here$_e$ how can this system be applied to speech^{guu} Δ I hear you$_i$ Δ no$_e$ I haven^{u}t quite gotten there yet$_a$ Δ I assure you$_e$ as soon as I resolve this written system$_e$ well$_e$ I feel the vocal solution will present itself$_a$

Perhaps we do not even need speech$_e$ my love$_e$ after all$_e$ speech is the first treachery of the heart$_a$

S.R.3,821

[V.N.] As I slept last night I had the unfortunate pleasure of working in my sleep. I dreamt I was in the Observation Room sending an unending sequence of transmissions: square-circle-circle; circle-square-square; circle-circle-circle; circle-circle-square...

S.R. 3,845

[N.B] I've been making progress on my writing, Eleanor, poking and prodding the architecture of the syntax. Lately, I've been experimenting with other models. I've begun conforming my sentences to classic story models of our math and physics, which are really the ancient stories of our universe: our past, our present, our future. Just observe what I've done with relativity:

$$E = \square \bigcirc^2$$

Do you see, Eleanor? Nouns standing in for mass, the speed of light the ultimate predicate. Or this, my take on Heisenberg's Uncertainty Principle:

$$\triangle \diamondsuit \triangle \diamondsuit \geq \hbar$$

Which I then rewrote, dropping Plank's constant for the unreduced form in order to take advantage of a convenient parallel. I give you the Uncertainty of Exclamations Principle:

$$\triangle \diamondsuit \triangle \diamondsuit \geq h\,/\,4\pi$$

I know, Eleanor, I shouldn't sit around patting myself on the back too hard just yet. Not when there are still so many more stories to write, so many translations waiting to be written.

S.R. 3,857

[N.B.] *Another Meditation on Metonymy:*

If I say, "They lived in a white house," would you not immediately conjure ideas of the white house: *a* white house, non-descript, with or without white picket fence and a dog in the yard; *the* White House; *Casablanca,* for our bilingual friends; an old, school house; a small, steepled church maybe; a quaint bed and breakfast in New Hampshire; a small Italian villa in Tuscany; the myriad symbolic connotations of the color white: birth, life, death, afterlife, silence, hope, desperation…If I then said "The leaves in the yard were already red," would you not make a connection with the red to the white? Would you not think of the ambulatory red-and-white of paramedics, hospitals, medicine, general wellness? Would you think of the Swiss flag? The Japanese? Would you think of autumn and reiterate the idea of death? Or would you think of passion? If I said, reading a sentence by the master of the superfluous, Miriam Le Blanc:

> "The dripping, red, maple leafs sharply silhouetted on the terminally white walls of the house—the house in which passed five generations of patriarchal hierarchy, the house in which she was meant to produce sons, the house in which, once her duties were met, all that was left to her charge was death and the successful allocation, via will, of the house to the next fertile Broadmoore—made a tangled and brackish veil across Emma-Jean's sweaty and diaphanous face, red and blue veins creeping along her cheeks and temple under the rippled white skin, incarcerating her eyes and mouth in an oubliette of grief, horror, guilt and the faint outline of an un-repressed smile of relief."

Would you not think of murder? Of American murder? Would the colors not speak volumes of subvocalized ideas and images whirling around your mind in a vague torrent of recognition? If I changed the leaves to green, would the sentence be the same? Would your feelings be the same? My sweet Eleanor, diction is just a sounding board for metonymy.

This fancy, flowery, figurative writing in the books around me—and, yes, I confess, even in my own thoughts and writings (at least, until I can successfully subvert my internal language to that of my Solution—which I'm working on, dear, but the task is quite difficult, you'll have to allow me some time)—all of it goes against the law of excluded middle; and all these puns and double entendres, polysemes, homonyms, divergent etymologies, obnoxious tmeses, cognates, allusions, all these symbols colliding and melting into one another, just muddle up the work. Barthes and Wittgenstein identified one of the roots of the problem, diagnosed the inherent cancer, and now we must take action to eliminate this "second order" in our texts, to remove the underlying web, net, sounding board…all the various names applied to the text below text, until we arrive at one simple textuality, one reductive, elegant symbol.

S.R.3,865

[N.B.] I am ashamed to say$_e$ Eleanor$_e$ that I transmitted circle$_y$square$_y$square today$_e$ △ upon doing so I felt$_e$ how should I say it$_{yy}$how *can* I say it$^h_{yy}$ a precarious arousal$_e$ if you will$_a$ △ I ask you$_e$ Eleanor$_e$ is that really all so wrong^g For a man to develop amorous feelings towards something so resplendent △ beautiful in its simplicity^g

S.R. 3,872

[V.N.] Also, I've decided to eliminate interjections from the Solution. The octagon is such a cumbersome figure to draw, Eleanor, you must get it right or else it will merely resemble a sloppy circle, a verb without confidence. I had thought about substituting another shape, perhaps a spiral like those of the galaxies twisting outside my Observation Room, but I decided perhaps it was better to just be done with the whole thing. The elimination of articles, is, I believe, not the only the next logistical step, but a necessary step. However, I will give them some time to prove their worth before I grant a full stay of execution.

S.R. 3,894

[N.B.] New message today$_a$ I am no longer to submit my transmissions in sequences of three$_a$ The only transmissions now will be either a single circle or a single square$_a$ A single noun or verb$_a$

Perhaps this is not a bad thing; perhaps this is a message to me$_e$ telling me that I should condense my system to a binary one of nouns and verbs$_a$

S.R.3,896

[N.B.] On second thought$_e$ perhaps not; even I feel that might be entirely *too* simple$_a$

S.R. 3,904

[N.B.] I"ve written several new stories lately$_e$ my dear$_a$ The first$_e$ which I"m sure you"ll find quite comical$_e$ is a pastiche of the Quadratic equation;

$$\bigcirc = \frac{-\triangle \pm \sqrt{\triangle^2 - 4\square\varhexagon}}{2\square}$$

Then there"s this one$_e$ an obvious allusion to Pascal by way of the binomial theorem;

$$(\square + \bigcirc)^\triangle = \sum_{\diamond=0}^{\triangle} \binom{\triangle}{\diamond} \square^\diamond \bigcirc^{\triangle-\diamond}$$

And lastly$_e$ this one of my own design$_e$ which might be a bit too melodramatic, I"ll admit$_e$ but I am still learning am I not^g_i

$$\prod_a (\square) = \lim_{i \to \infty} \frac{\triangledown\square}{\left(\triangle + \frac{\triangle\bigcirc}{\triangle\triangle}\left(\triangle + \frac{\triangle\bigcirc}{\triangle\triangle}\left(\triangle + \frac{\triangle\bigcirc}{\triangle\triangle}(...)\right)\right)\right)}$$

S.R. 3,912

[N.B.] On a completely separate note$_e$ I^{u}ve become far too disgusted by the food I^{u}m eating$_a$ How can they possibly expect us to eat the same foil$_y$wrapped mush again and again^g I sensed my dissatisfaction growing for quite some time$_e$ but yesterday I took one bite and gagged$_a$ I simply can^{u}t bring myself to eat it^b Tomorrow I shall simply refuse to eat this garbage$_a$ Yes$_e$ the Alarm with have to dealt with$_a$ Perhaps I can just take the parcel and the pod^{u}s alarm will not sound$_a$

S.R. 3,928

[N.B.] Well$_e$ the Alarm sounded nonetheless$_e$ my dear$_a$ At the appropriate time today$_e$ I pressed the button$_e$ received the parcel$_e$ but merely held it in my hand$_a$ For some small while I thought my plan had worked$_e$ although of course$_e$ as I sat smiling childishly at my victory$_e$ the alarm sounded and I$_{yy}$forced to pick one discomfort over the other$_{yy}$crammed the whole parcel in my mouth$_e$ nearly choking$_e$ my dear$_a$ There must be some way to bypass this alarm system$_a$ Perhaps there is a box somewhere that houses its controls$_e$ which I could find and disable or smash$_{yy}$whichever is easier$_a$

> AUTOMATED DIAGNOSTIC ASSESSMENT
> #061715: All systems normal; subject responsive; vitals stable; cannot account for alarm at this point in time.

S.R. 3,930

[N.B.] Nothing doing in the way of the Alarm$_a$ I^{u}ve searched every available panel and electrical compartment and found nothing$_a$ Floated along every surface in the main hall$_e$ spinning and gliding along the circular walls looking for anything that might be a compartment secreted away in which might house the Alarm$^{"}$s electronics$_a$ Nothing$_e$ Eleanor$_a$ Not one shred of hope$_a$ Which got me thinking$_e$ being of a bio$_y$engaged entity$_e$ sensing my activities throughout the whole of the pod$_e$ the siren might not have a central control$_a$ Perhaps the Alarm is like an electrified fence around me$_e$ a nervous system$_e$ or perhaps something like a magnetic field$_e$ which becomes disrupted by some current (a particular action or inaction on my part) and responds with that unfavorable rattling of my soul$_a$ But wouldn$^{"}$t there still have to be some method of recognition$_e$ or some housing function like that of a brain$_g$ Ah$_e$ I can$^{"}$t dwell on this any more$_a$ I am remit to the rules of the pod$_a$

S.R. 3,940

[V.N.] Eleanor, is it wrong to want for a time of simpler metonymy? To expurgate language towards a more eugenic development? Proust, Hemmingway, and the other objective correlativists made a good start, but they were still far too verbose.

Also: Articles? Really, what service do they perform? I mean, if our cosmonautic neighbors the Russians don't use them, why should we? Not to mention that to draw their hexagonal figure is really quite annoying.

Yes, I believe they too shall have to be stricken from the Solution.

S.R. 3957

[N.B.] I've hit a spell of rigidity in my muscles$_e$ Eleanor$_e$ which got me to thinking$_a$ If somehow I encountered some severe paralyses$_e$ so that only my neck may move (my mandible even locked up)$_e$ how then am I to transmit$_g$ How am I to write or speak$_g$

Now$_e$ I hope you see where I am going with this$_e$ Eleanor$_e$ because it is as pure an endorsement for my Solution as one can get$_i$ with the movement of my neck still available$_e$ and using my nose as a stylus$_e$ I may draw upon the air these geometrical language shapes$_a$ I have heard of victims of acute paralysis and apoplexy finding methods of blinking or Morse code with which to spell$_e$ but think of the time$_e$ Eleanor^h How long just to reach one word^g How long to reach a phrase^g A sentence^g A lifetime could be spent$_{yy}$wasted I should say$_{yy}$in the construction of a single letter$_a$ Whereas$_e$ using my Solution$_e$ one could write a whole volume of novels in the same amount of time$_a$ Must I even ask the question as to which is the superior system^g

S.R. 3,961

[N.B.] Well$_e$ I^{u}ve gone and damaged myself again$_e$ Eleanor$_a$ My left knee must have some magnetic attraction to injury$_e$ what else could possibly account for the incessant bruising^g I feel I^{u}ve gone and ruined it once and for all$_a$ Perhaps I am just absent minded towards the left$_e$ but$_e$ well$_e$ regardless$_e$ I somehow became entangled on the ladder while coming down from the Observation Room$_e$ holding a wad of paper containing some of my old notes$_e$ trying to rectify certain remainders and inconsistencies in my stories$_e$ and didn^{u}t notice that my left foot had slipped into the corner of the ladder$_j$ in an attempt to release myself$_e$ I jerked too suddenly and twisted my knee at an angle not intended for that joint$_a$ The pain was something exquisitely awful$_e$ I am quite certain I^{u}ve torn a ligament or tendon (no way to test in this pod)$_a$

Let me put the damage this way$_i$ Do you remember that summer at Lake Mead when that wasp crawled inside your can of soda and delivered a vicious sting upon your sweet$_e$ supple lips when you took a sip^g How they swelled tremendously^g Well$_e$ imagine that same quantity of inflation afflicted to my knee$_a$ The First$_y$Aid station offered as much as could be done$_e$ supplying bandages and a cold compress$_e$ disbursing an extremely minimal level of morphine and anti-inflammatories$_a$ I suspect my knee will be like this for some time$_a$ Thankfully$_e$ the lack of gravity ensures I am still mobile$_{yy}$though somewhat slower and demanding a modicum of caution$_a$

S.R. 3,984

[V.N.] On my writing: I've been trying to take my writing to a different level, Eleanor. Adhering to similar paths I was on before, I am on a mission of reduction. No sooner do I finish a story than I stand back and go "Well this can be improved." I want to shorten it. I want to attempt, as the physicists attempt, to find one simple, elegant solution for all language. Einstein had his Relativity, and, as I've shown you, my dear, what could possibly be more relative than language? But as far as I try, nothing seems to fit, no sequence or equation seems to encompass the true nature of the unified theory.

Which is a long way of saying I have much work to do.

S.R. 4,015

[V.N.] As a means of accomplishing that goal, I have reduced the Solution further, taking the Solution to an asyndeton with the omission of conjunctions; having long contemplated the need for conjunctions—even of a mathematical variety—and, with parataxis arguing strongly in my favor, I find that in most cases assumption and contextual reading often does the job. Conjunctions really being more of a case of good manners, a nicety but not a necessity, Eleanor. It's imperative we trim the fat!

S.R. 4,032

[V.N.] Speaking of fat, without exercise and with only these high-cal MREs to sustain me, what's happening is only natural. From what I hear, some people actually find love handles and a belly attractive; perhaps something in the apish figure of an out of shape man harkens back to something...well, ape-like. A lingering primitive fetish hiding deep inside the paleo-mammalian brain, just above the outskirts of the reptilian interior. Which is a way of saying I hope you count yourself among them. On another note, I'm still as smooth and hairless as a freshly-waxed bowling ball.

S.R. 4,054

[**V.N.**] I should also note my supply of notebooks is running low. There is enough for the next week or so, but I shall have to find some alternate medium for my work. I simply can't translate or write via dictation—my Solution is still not quite there yet.

S.R. 4,065

[**N.B.**] Perhaps from my recent musings$_e$ perhaps from the bit of morphine for my knee$_e$ I^{u}ve been having these$_{aaa}$dreams$_a$ Dreams$_e$ Eleanore$_e$ of a perfect cube of language$_e$ a story that can be read the same in every direction$_i$ left to right$_e$ right to left$_e$ downwards$_e$ upwards$_a$ A cubic palindrome$_a$

This is probably foolish$_e$ Eleanor$_j$ although with these eliminations perhaps it is getting more within reach$_a$ After all$_e$ is there not something so aesthetically beautiful about a perfect square$_e$ my dear^g And maybe it^{u}s this engineering paper giving me ideas$_e$ but can you not agree that such a thing$_e$ a perfect square of language (dare I even suggest a perfect cube of language^g Six perfect squares assembled together^h) would be simply divine^g The trinity is surely a false prophet$_e$ Eleanor$_j$ I know that now$_a$ Yes$_e$ triangles have their allure$_e$ and an equilateral triangle is still something primly seductive$_e$ but come now$_e$ how can it possibly compete with the square$_e$ the first non$_n$prime polygon^g (Especially when the isosceles triangle is such an abhorrent creation$_{yy}$just a trollop$_a$) No$_e$ my dear$_e$ I believe the quadrinity$_{yy}$or tetranity$_e$ perhaps$_{yy}$to be the true symbol of the divine$_a$

I^{u}ll admit^e I came aboard this ship with a considerable diathesis for threes (owing to an endemic Christianity)$_e$ and I must confess$_e$

Eleanor$_e$ that perhaps I now hold a particular bias towards a Holy Tetranity$_{yy}$certainly steered that way by some aesthetic means$_e$ a magnetism towards certain ideologies$_e$ and$_e$ of course$_e$ Gibson/Tetracules$_e$ whose existence I"m still not quite sure if I"ve imagined or not$_a$ Either way$_e$ if I invented him (or if he invented me^h)$_e$ or if he really is even on board$_e$ my attraction to the spider is independent of the entity itself$_i$ the attraction attributed to some internal presence$_e$ or perhaps some external presence$_e$ driving me ever towards the number four$_i$ owing to all religions and no religions$_e$ whether from the four Vedas$_e$ the four voices of Islam$_e$ the four Noble Truths$_e$ the four Angels/Winds/Corners/Banners/Horsemen$_e$ the foursquare$_{yy}$the cubic disposition of New Jerusalem^h On it goes$_a$

I find it thoroughly satisfying that Hinduism$_e$ with its trinity of Brahma (not to mention Brahma"s three$_n$letter representation in the Aum)$_e$ Vishnu$_e$ and Shiva$_{yy}$be$_n$clad in tiger skin with his three$_n$pronged trident and his pelt$_e$ holding the universe"s potential energy$_{yy}$also adheres to a certain Tetranity in Brahma"s four faces and arms$_e$ representing the four Vedas (Rig$_e$ Yajur$_e$ Sama$_e$ and Atharva)$_a$ This Tetranity is a representation of knowledge$_e$ Eleanor$_e$ of finding and attaining a universal mind$_a$ Perhaps more fascinating to me is the Tetranity in the Aum itself$_i$

Containing Aa$_e$ au$_e$ and ma$_e$ the sounds of past$_e$ present$_e$ and future$_e$ wherein all possible sounds exist (the Hindus had clearly never encountered the Germanic or Celtic tribes when they made that claim)$_e$ the first chord struck by the universe and from which all songs emanate$_;$ the mantric syllable is composed of three states of being (waking$_e$ deep sleep$_e$ and dreaming)$_e$ but there is a fourth state$_{yy}$where the magic really happens$_e$ Eleanor$_{yy}$the whole of the Aum itself$_e$ the holy combination of the individual letters$_e$ where the

disparate parts are galvanized together to form the absolute self$_i$
Turiya$_e$ Bindu$_e$ the Atman$_a$ Look at the symbol again$_e$ Eleanor$_i$ four
curves representing the four states and a circle for the self$_j$ a ^{uu}3^{uu} (an
allusion to the Holy Trinity^g), a question mark$_e$ and the ultimate
period separated by a prostrate$_e$ supplicating comma$_a$ It would appear
the separation between states and the one true self is only a simple$_e$
curving line$_e$ a crescent moon of the infinite$_a$

There is still one more example of the Tetranity we must discuss$_e$ my
sweet vial of plum nectar$_i$ the Tetragrammaton$_e$ that four$_n$consonant
name of God$_a$ (Interesting to note$_e$ Eleanor$_e$ the consonantal God of
Judaism versus the vowels of the Hindu God$_a$ Hopefully the Solution
can consolidate both$_a$) Now$_e$ consider the various representations of
the Tetragrammaton$_e$ the rectangular text inside a triangle inset in a
circle$_e$ with or without radiation$_j$ we saw it once on the altar of the
Budapest Synagogue and its iterations can be found again in the Fifth
Chapel of the Palace of Versailles$_e$ or at the Church of Saint Thomas
D^{u}Aquin$_e$ and$_e$ of course$_e$ above the glimmering door at the
Cathedral of the Holy Trinity of St$_a$ Sergius Lavra$_a$ (This is not to
consider Levi^{u}s five$_n$pointed Tetragrammaton$_e$ whose division of a
perfectly fine$_e$ four$_n$based symbol into one of five is just ugly math$_e$ a
distant aesthetic cousin of that abhorrent square$_n$square$_n$circle no
doubt^b Quadrangles$_e$ my dear$_j$ quadrangles are the only sensible
shape$_a$) Now$_e$ just look at the symbol$_i$

יהוה

The mystics say that the pieces can be stacked to resemble an abstract
shape of man$_{yy}$the arms and legs of the ^{uu}he^{uu}s$_e$ the torso of ^{uu}vav$_e$^{uu}
the head of ^{uu}yod^{uu}$_{yy}$further$_e$ that those secrets emerge again$_e$
through trickle$_n$down esoterics in Da Vinci^{u}s Vitruvian Man$_e$
Pythagoras^{u}s Tetractys$_e$ and the Sephiroth$_a$ But that doesn^{u}t concern
me$_e$ Eleanor$_j$ what concerns me is the *shape*$_e$ its rectangular form$_a$ The
rectangle$_{yy}$two squares pushed together$_{yy}$now, if we just squeeze the
sides a little$_e$ mushing it into a square$_e$ then$_e$ using our Solution$_e$

wouldn^{u}t the Tetragrammaton be a noun inside of an adjective inside of a verb^g If the letters are the name of God$_e$ then this surely must be the sentence of God^h The Elegant Syntax^h

Which brings me to my main point$_e$ Eleanor$_i$ do you remember Paul^{u}s letter to the Corinthians^g Specifically verse 12^g_i ^{uu}"For the body is not one member$_e$ but many$_{aaa}$And if the ear shall say$_e$ Because I am not the eye$_e$ I am not of the body$_j$ is it therefore not of the body$^g_{aaa}$If the whole body were an eye$_e$ where were the hearing^g If the whole were hearing$_e$ where were the smelling$^g_{aaa}$But now are they many members$_e$ yet but one body$_a{}^{uu}$ Now$_e$ Eleanor$_e$ if all parts are equal to the whole$_e$ and the whole is unpronounceable$_e$ then so too should be all of its disparate parts$_a$

Perhaps that is why I^{u}ve been having such a hard time coming up with an oral form of the Solution$_a$ Perhaps we were never meant to speak at all$_a$ Paul^{u}s transitive application proves the Presence to be real$_i$ to speak any language is to presume to speak the particles of God$_j$ and if we cannot speak the whole$_e$ we cannot speak the particles^g As our old buddy used to say$_e$ ^{uu}"That which we cannot speak$_e$ we must pass over in silence$_a{}^{uu}$

Then again$_e$ perhaps it^{u}s all horseshit$_e$ and perhaps so am I$_a$ Perhaps this station has been nothing more than a celestial cocoon$_e$ transforming an otherwise sane and mathematical mind into one of lepidopterous$_e$ linguistic lunacy^g

I shall ask Gibson/Tecracules to weigh in on the matter when next we speak$_a$

S.R. 4,077

[N.B.] Having now eliminated the preposition and the pronoun$_e$ taking my Solution down to only four simple elements$_{yy}$nouns$_e$ verbs$_e$ adjectives$_e$ and adverbs$_{yy}$adhering to the Tetranity$_{yy}$I believe my solution can be taken down even further$_e$ while still preserving the Tetranity$_a$

See$_e$ the Tetragrammaton got me thinking$_e$ Eleanor$_e$ why don^{u}t we just have our triangles represent both adjectives and adverbs$_j$ its already in the shape of a delta$_e$ already signifying change and modulation$_j$ perhaps we can invert it$_e$ use the nabla to denote adverbs$_e$ already signifying modification and taking the appearance of a V with a ceiling$_e$ a stalactite$_a$ After all$_e$ just observe the shape of the adverb$_i$ ◇$_a$ Now$_e$ look what happens if we draw a simple line across it^{u}s middle$_i$ ◆$_a$ See^g Do you see$_e$ Eleanor$_e$ how it contains both delta and nabla^g It was there all along$_e$ simply waiting for a mind such as mine to unearth its dichotomous forms$_a$

Yes$_e$ this is a much cleaner correction to the Elegant Syntax$_e$ and one that still honors the Holy Tetranity$_a$ Perhaps the Jews$_e$ in their ancient mysticism$_e$ have known this all along$_j$ for isn't the Star of David the convergence of the two^g A syntactical eclipse of adverb and adjective^g Overlapping in equal symmetry$_a$

S.R. 4,123

[V.N.] I've been looking at the constellations again, reimagining their stories in accordance with the Solution, and I dare say they are much improved: the Story of Cepheus, the King's daughter, a maiden preposition sacrificially cast into space, as I have just done. His wife, Cassiopeia, a W, a pair of baseless adverbs standing to the side, impotently watching. But Cepheus could also tell the story of another king, Zeus, the noun-king, giving birth out of the top of his head to his daughter, the adjectival Athena. Aquila is the mitotic division of the adverb into its new dichotomous form, the delta and the nabla. No longer do I see Gibson/Tetracules in Hercules, now the constellation appears as a stack of two opposing conjunctions supporting an adjectival head. And it extends beyond the constellations: at least once a day I use the Sun Shield to zoom in on Saturn's mysterious hexagonal North Pole; and the mystery is revoked as soon you realize the shape is merely an article riding atop a predicate.

S.R. 4,137

[V.N.] The Tetragrammaton as the amalgam symbol of the Elegant Syntax has gotten me thinking of the holography of language, Eleanor: all letters descending outwards from the first are really just aping the holography of the universe: the first hydrogen atoms fusing together to create helium, those fusing to create lithium, and so forth down the line; the noun to the predicate to the modifiers, etc. Although, perhaps it's less holographic and more biological, meiotic. The noun and verb, the seed and egg, merging, dividing, creating modifiers for each, dividing further into pronouns and prepositions, followed by the division into lesser articles and conjunctions…Which got me thinking further, Eleanor, maybe meiosis and holography are the same thing; or at least the former's imitation of the latter, an ode to the original creation. Oh god! What if that ode is less a tribute and more a pastiche? My god, what if our creation is nothing more than a satire or a parody?!

My head hurts, Eleanor. I think I should lay down for a while.

S.R.4,147

[V.N.] Forget the perhaps, my dear, there is no doubt as to its merit: the destruction of language leads to the dissolution of thought; and if thought can be dissolved, then so to can the emotions: the rage, the loneliness, the jealousy…if I have no name to call you how can I speak your name at night just to feel you exist in the space beside me, vibrating against the headboard so I can you feel you on my face? How can I lament the nameless? It's nothing more than an abstraction. This is the true bliss.

S.R. 4,192

[V.N.] I've been rethinking my stories, Eleanor. Let me first say that they are wrong: I've committed precisely the crime I was extolling as the bane of language, precisely that turn of language whose finite interpretation isn't available to all. Should my reader not remember their algebra, he or she would never understand the joke; should my reader not be familiar with Pascal, he or she mightn't understand the allusion, and thus the gravitas, of my story. As such, even though I find my stories beautiful, and as much as it pains me, I must destroy them; I must burn them and never look on them again. I should stick solely to my basic Solution—possibly working towards that cubic palindrome I dreamt of. But first, these stories will have to go.

AUTOMATED DIAGNOSTIC ASSESSMENT (ADA)#070515: ERROR.

AUTOMATED DIAGNOSTIC ASSESSMENT (ADA)#070515(2): ERROR.

AUTOMATED DIAGNOSTIC ASSESSMENT (ADA)#070615: ERROR.

S.R. 4,223

[V.N.] Eleanor, Eleanor, Eleanor...let me tell you a little something about fire in space. Simply, it is not a good idea. It is something to avoid if at all possible. Of course, my first clue as to the severity of any and all conflagration should have been the utter absence of incendiary devices aboard this vessel: not a lighter, nor a match, nor a flint. (The second clue should have been that despite a lack of incendiary devices there was a dearth of fire extinguishers.) I therefore had to construct, in a very rudimentary fashion, a simple bow and saw technique out of plastic rods taken from my mattress, elastic from my underwear and, for kindling and substance, the rest of my underwear, along with two of my uniforms, shredded and pulled into little bits of dander. The time alone should have given me ample opportunity to rethink my plans and abort. The blaze was a toxic one—need I say? Flames in various shades of green. Lavender, even. Spreading like a molten, green amoeba. The toxicity no doubt aided by the dry cleaning agents infused with the fabric. The fire got away from me as, of course, I should have known it would in this oxygen-enriched environment and without the confines of gravity to keep it in place, floating away from me like lava coursing across some imaginary mountain and melting a hole in the plastic above the food dispensary. I didn't even have the opportunity to cremate my works—a blessing now, I realize—as I was forced to contend with my feral creation wreaking havoc throughout the main chamber—unassisted by this damn splinted leg—rerouting the blaze and smothering every last tendril of flame spreading behind the walls of the ship with a melanomic reach.

I have yet to determine the full extent of the damage but I know of at least one casualty. As soon as I had smothered the flame, I propelled myself down the tunnel and pressed the Panic button, hoping either the robotics would make the necessary repairs or someone from The Powers would come online and advise my course of action. But there was nothing.

For a minute, Eleanor, I actually began to believe that I was not really in space at all, that upon boring a hole through the hull I would find blue light pouring in, oxygen, wind, the sounds of birds or traffic; I thought should I put my eye to the hole I'd find myself in a field or laboratory; that somehow this has all just been an elaborate experiment and a voice will sound on a loudspeaker: "Test subject Reitlinger, John D., number 01123581321A-6823, has broken through his containment cell. Experiment aborted. Return him to his sweet Eleanor, she's been waiting."

But that was not the case.

AUTOMATED DIAGNOSTIC ASSESSMENT
(ADA)#070815: ERROR.

AUTOMATED DIAGNOSTIC ASSESSMENT
(ADA)#070815(2): ERROR.

AUTOMATED DIAGNOSTIC ASSESSMENT
(ADA)#070815(3): ERROR.

S.R. 4,239

[V.N.] Well, the damage has been assessed, Eleanor. My little pyromantic excursion has melted the plastic casing around the oxygen manifest (thank God I put the fire out before it could come in contact with the oxygen!), which will eventually burst from the pressure and flood the compartment with poisonous levels of O_2, and that is most likely how I shall die. An overdose of the element that gave and sustained my life, which, far from depressing, I actually find this little ironic predicament very practical and comforting in a Cartesian way. Oxygen (like the *pharmakon*): my cure and my poison. Dualistic as my triangle.

I know what you're thinking, Eleanor, But what about the robot you've spoken of before? Surely the machine can mend the damage? Aye, the robot would have been great, but it is only designed to carry out the functions of a pre-programmed matrix of all possible situations that might arise through mechanical error, aeronautical error, celestial error (comets, debris, solar-flares, etc.), and a degree of user error presupposed. I suppose no one had thought to include a protocol for what should happen in the event that their astronaut starts a fire that melts through the plastic interior and damages the oxygen regulator. And so I am thoroughly hosed, here. But this talk of the robot brings me to my next point—tangentially, of course.

In the aftermath of the fire, in assessing the damage to the ship, I have more or less discovered the source of the Alarm; just as I'd imagined, the Alarm is informed through an elaborate system of wires that surround the ship, subdermally, as it were, inside the plastic veneers of the interior walls, a webbing connecting the interior panels that I've learned are actually well-disguised thermodynamic and ultrasonic sensors; there are other sensors, too, which I couldn't immediately judge—my guess is that they are tuned to my blood pressure, heart rate, and blood-sugar levels; all the information collating and getting processed in some device I have yet to find. I know this, Eleanor, because the fire burned right through several major cables, which sent the Alarm reeling for what could have been any amount of time, and which, upon lack of information from me, stopped altogether. I have been abandoned, Eleanor, deemed dead, perhaps, by the keeper of my life. The robotics, too, I believe to be controlled by this entity, as I have yet to see any action from it; at the very least I usually hear the machine on the outside, repairing some small damage from meteoroids, but there has been nothing as of late, and it has been showering debris for the past twenty sunrises.

S.R. 4,304

[**N.B.**] I fear this may be my last paper entry$_j$ I hope I have enough space$_a$

In these last couple days$_e$ I may have taken a page out of Gibson/Tetracules^u architectural digest. Having grown increasingly nauseous from the pain in my knee$_e$ the weightlessness$_e$ and the increase in oxygen$_{yy}$which I know is indeed leaking as I have just been giddy as a schoolgirl$_{yy}$I have deigned to construct a web for myself$_e$ something to keep me stable and put$_a$ Having no use for the Alarm^{u}s wiring anymore$_e$ I removed every line of cable I could$_e$ straightening the pieces and cutting them into lines 6$_n$meters long$_e$ and began spinning myself a web in the cylindrical chambers of the Common Room$_a$

I secured the first chord$_e$ AB$_e$ from the ladder to the treadmill$_e$ and then a second line$_e$ CD$_e$ parallel with the first$_e$ adjoining the emergency station to the set of weights anchored inside the food dispensary (which hasn^{u}t worked right since I pried it open$_e$ but no matter$_e$ I don^{u}t feel particularly hungry anymore anyways)$_a$ I then connected those two lines with lines AC and BD$_e$ using carabiners to tether them together$_a$ Twisting six sets of wire into two three$_n$ply cables$_e$ I installed a pair of x and y axes at the center$_e$ intersecting at a perfect ninety$_n$degree angle$_e$ which I have labelled X_0 and Y_{0e} respectfully$_a$ With the main components in place$_e$ I secured another line$_e$ X_{+1e} parallel to X_0 at a half$_n$meter^{u}s distance$_e$ winding the ends of the wire around the main perimeter$_a$ I repeated the process every half meter until finishing with X_{+5e} a half$_n$meter away from CD and what will now be known as X_{+6j} I did the same in the other direction$_e$ working towards my Personal Chambers until reaching AB$_e$ now X_{-6a} With the same geometric dedication$_e$ I applied the procedure to the other cable until reaching lines Y_{-6} to Y_{+6a} I employed some of the smaller wires of quarter$_n$meter length to fill out the grid around the center of the web$_a$.

(Though the web was not especially firm$_e$ and a little haggard in the twining$_e$ the angles were pristine and a true testament to his arachnid greatness$_a$ If I could boldly proclaim to know His thoughts$_e$ I think Gibson/Tetracules would be$_{aaa}$neither impressed nor proud$_{yy}$feelings far beneath He$_{yy}$but$_e$ hopefully$_e$ at peace with the attempt$_a$)

After a few more turns of the wire$_e$ I positioned myself at the center of this little Euclidean plane$_e$ at the junction of X_0 and $Y_{+.5e}$ and sat$_e$ just sat$_e$ securing myself to the center with a three$_n$foot piece of wire carabinered to the belt loop of my uniform$_e$ my splinted leg floating like a drunken watch$_n$hand with tachyonic tendencies$_a$. I brought my notes with me$_e$ always by my side$_e$ now$_a$ The grid was still too large to hold the notes in place$_e$ spread so I could better read them$_j$ luckily$_e$ I had several foot$_n$long pieces of wire in my pockets and I made a 2x4 rectangle of lattice from $X_{-2 \to 2e}$ $Y_{-2 \to -4a}$ My knee is still giving me issues$_e$ so I was not able to work as fast as I would have liked$_e$ and as movement in general was more of an annoyance$_e$ I found this really the best way to view my work$_i$ floating above them the length of my tether and looking upon them all at once$_e$ able to view the entirety$_e$ or to slide in and focus on a specific piece$_e$ much like the window in the Observation Room$_a$

S.R. 4,325

[V.N.] It's so calm and quiet now, my dear. So completely silent. No more of The Library's nagging. No more transmissions. Not even the digital hum of the racks. Just…still.

S.R. 4,331

[V.N.] Taking a cue from the Egyptians, I've begun decorating my death chamber, using a grease pen in lieu of the pencil, transforming the Common Room into a repository of my Solution. On the smooth curving walls of the room you will find the initial abstracts of the Conundrum and the Solution, you will find the codex for the Eloquent Syntax, sentences, key translations, stories—in their original and reduced form, works from other writers as well as a few of my own—a Rosetta Stone of sorts to assist with the transition. Herein you will find the story and works of my life.

S.R. 4,351

[V.N.] I don't know what compelled me, what zealous hubris possessed me to reach out to Him, but I did. As if watching myself from behind my body, I drifted my arm towards Him, daring to extend no more than just an index finger, when the spider lunged forward and bit me. His bite was electric, charged, as if coursing with lightning. I felt the circuitry in my brain take new and unfamiliar paths. And then it abated, and I threw up.

S.R. 4,355

[V.N.] It's getting a little toasty in here. To decrease my perspiration I've stripped myself of my last uniform, down to my underwear, which I feel shall eventually have to go, too. An unencumbered exit is the way to go, an egress to match the ingress. However, without anything to secure my tether to, I've had to create a new one, longer and tied about my waist; I'll be long dead before the rash becomes unbearable.

I misspoke about the silence, Eleanor, there is one noise here that I've only lately picked up on: a very persistent hiss. Yes, the murderer in the closet singing me nightly lullabies, but the hiss is not entirely discomforting. There is a sort of peace in its continuity.

After a while, I forget it's even there.

S.R. 4,362

[Circling the top of the Common Room wall] Oh Eleanor, Eleanor, Eleanor, Eleanor, EleanorEleanorEleanor, EleanorEleanorEleanor, E L E A N O R E L E A N O R E L E A N O R E L E A N O R E L E A N O R L A N D O R L A N D O R L A N D O R L A N D O R L A N D O L A N D O L A N D O L A N D O R W H E R E D O E S I T A L L E N D O R ?!

S.R.4,363

[V.N.] In my Solution, of course.

S.R. 4,374

[V.N.] Well, Gibson/Tetracules can be added to the roster classification of poisonous spider. I'm starting to lose mobility in my limbs. The immobility presented not so much as a severing of the nerves, or a paralysis of autonomous communication, but of the large amount of effort necessary to move them. The poison has made me sluggish, and tired, and dizzy.

Without my mobility, I am forced to use my body as a last canvas. (Though, if we're being honest, it's not as if I really have the blank space to keep going in the Common Room.)

S.R. 4,398

[RIGHT TORSO]

○□*e*△◇△□

○○△◇◇○□*i*

△△○○□*e*

△◇△□○*a*

uu○○□*e*△□ *h*

○□△*e*○□△ *h*

○○△□*e*△○

○△□ *huu*

□ ○△△□◇□*i*

△□◇△□ □ ○*yy*

◇ ○ □ ◇○△□

△○ ◇ ◇□*a*

△*e*◇ ◇△□ □ ○*e*

○□*e*◇□◇□*e*

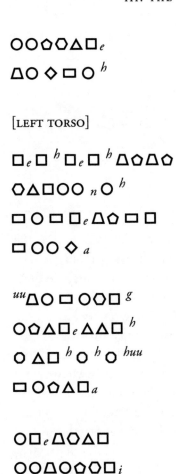

○○⭘○△□ *e*

△○ ◇ □ ○ *h*

[LEFT TORSO]

□*e*□ *h* □*e*□ *h* △○△⭘

○△□○○ *n* ○ *h*

□○□□*e*△⭘□□

□○○◇ *a*

uu△○□○○□ *g*

○⭘△□*e*△△□ *h*

○△□ *h* ○ *h* ○ *huu*

□○⭘△□ *a*

○□*e*△⭘△□

○○△○⭘○□ *i*

△△○○□ *e*

△⭘△□○ *a*

S.R. 4,404

[**V.N.**] A quick note regarding my chest piece: You just try writing backwards and upside down with no mirror other than the reflection of the window in the Observation Room all the way down the tunnel as your guide! Though a little jagged, and certainly not as cleanly spaced as I would have liked, I have finished my complete translation of "The Jaberwocky." A full scale conversion, stripping out the non- and creating sense and meaning.

S.R. 4,414

[LEFT LEG]

□ ○ □ ᵍ □ ○○○ₑ ◇ □ □ ○ ᵍ □ ○○ₑ □ ○ ◇ ○ᵢ ⟡○○ □ □
○○ₐ □ ◇ ○ ◇ ₐ □ ◇ ○ ◇ ₐ □ ◇ ○ ◇ ₐ

S.R. 4,475

[V.N.] When I die I shall try to remain tethered to my plane, near the comfort of my work, so that my body won't be floating about, decomposing, and banging into things. Sometimes I do imagine that my pod will be hit by a large meteoroid, jarring me loose and cracking the glass in the Observation Room. I imagine my loose body, rigid in whatever shape I happen to last occupy, floating upwards and smashing into the glass which—from the meteoroid, my body, and increased oxygenic pressure—bursts and I am eschewed from the tunnel into the cold, cold unknown. A comet shot through space until another body demands my mass, either merging with that body or revolving around it as a satellite; we'll stay that way for a while, in those simple movements, those quaint mechanics of gravity. We'll revolve around something bigger than ourselves: planets, suns, black holes, pulsars—wouldn't that be something tremendous?—

Oh, but now I've gone and urinated. The little beads of piss are travelling up through the canal, soon to crash into the Sun Shield, then most likely dividing into little meiosic beads of urine that will surely nestle themselves into the control panel, seed amongst the motherboards and code, birth a fire of ozone and uric acid. No matter, I expect this is a sign that I am soon to depart, as I surely didn't command the urination of my own volition.

My left foot is caught on a wire in the negative-negative quadrant. As my left knee is still swollen and I'm, thankfully, still tethered about my waist, I have to bend at the waist to release it. Eleanor, these last many weeks have seen me lethargic; my muscles are so stiff, and my energy beyond the event horizon of full depletion. This attempt could very well be my last bit of action, but I must release myself; this just isn't a position I wish to be found in, entwined in a web like a fly, very unbecoming. It is a difficult reach, Eleanor: even as my head dips below the X axis into the positive-negative region, the slope of my spine is limited; I must extend the hypotenuse of my arms but they are weak, I don't think I shall make it. My fingers reach my foot but that is all; though I strain and will my spine another five-degrees inwards, wiggle my fingers and try and throw some torque into the stretch, I simply do not have the strength to release the toes from the wire; my body remains locked. The shame is mine, Eleanor.

S.R. 4,502

[RIGHT ARM]

^{uu} OO ◇$_e$^{uu} O□□O⬠O□$_e$^{uu}◇ □ OO$_a$^{uu}

S.R. 4,510

[VN] Right there, Eleanor! The increase in ambidexterity alone should be testament enough for the Solution. Had I been forced to transcribe that passage in conventional characters it would have taken me weeks to make it passably legible, not to mention the increase in space it would have taken up. And did you notice, Eleanor, the passage selected? I thought you might. And really, what better way to mock the Library that emblazon its one glaring mistake on my body for all to see. Just the first line, mind you, but I should say more than enough to inflict embarrassment. Small victories, Eleanor, are still victories. Especially when you consider the fact that I am almost entirely immobile. Despite the fact that I was working with my inferior hand, it still took me almost as long to write out this composition as it did to translate "The Jabberwocky." But that speaks more to my current condition than the Solution, dear. The Solution is pure and beyond reproach, infallible.

S.R. 4,546

[V.N.] With little space available, and lacking the mobility necessary to reach those blank spaces of canvas, I have only one small place I may still write. And, without ink or mobility enough to search out an acceptable replacement, one medium left to write with. My fingernails are long enough to draw new sources and cup the fluid like a fountain pen. Don't think of it as anything morbid, dear. After all, what good is the oil if the engine's already dead?

S.R.4,548

[FOREHEAD]

S.R. 4,580

[V.N.] And yes, Eleanor, without the language perhaps we'll miss the joy as well. But I'll wager that bliss and absence is the greatest joy we may hope to ever find. And we can have it here, Eleanor, here on our terrestrial Earth, once the Solution has been shared with all. There will be push-back of course, I expect as much, but I feel confident the Solution will catch on. Once people see what it can do, all the redundancies it will eliminate, all the tedium it will dispel, how would it not? I don't want to necessarily say we're inclined towards the lazy—though the lazy will surely hold onto the Solution for dear life—it's more, haven't we toiled long enough over these many millennia in the mire of language? Subjects to the feudal lord of speech? Doesn't our species deserve a retirement from language? And I should think, in the absence of all that noise pollution clogging our ears at every juncture of our lives, we shall find bliss. Shear bliss, Eleanor, like the vacuum that surrounds me. A steady, resplendent nothingness to warm our bellies and minds. The Nirvana of lore.

S.R. 4,589

[FOREHEAD]

S.R. 4,592

[**V.N.**] My eyes still retain some movement, Eleanor, not much, like a greased lens out of focus, but there is some sight, just enough. I can see the rectangular shape of the ladder in front of me, like a strip of waffle tacked to the wall. I can make out the square shape of the food dispenser and the perfect gridwork of my web. I can see my notebooks spread out before me, and once more the benefits of the Solution make their own case: in my present state, able only to make out shapes and colors, I would have no chance at comprehending the conventional text; but even afflicted, I can still read my life's work; and, if I squint, I can still make out the punctuation. Turning my head, I can stare down the tunnel to the Observation Room. And though I can't really decipher any of the buttons on the panel or the constellations beyond the dark glass, there is one image I can fully recognize. There is a reflection of myself, Eleanor, caught in this terrible mess: my triangular disposition pathetically entombed in my own web, like a spider caught in his own trap as the surrounding flies point and laugh. I imagine Gibson/Tetracules shaking his head at all this. I can tell you it is a sorry sight to behold, Eleanor.

Yet of all the images before me, I must admit that I spend the majority of what vision is left staring down the barrel of that tunnel at my reflection. And sometimes, the longer I linger on the image of that stereo self, I forget that I'm the Reitlinger trapped down here, that I'm not the Reitlinger outside looking comically down on the ignominious death of this contorted creature that had done his own self in, that I'm not the one who can breathe space and time and nakedly confront the deep-freeze through the gridded safety of my circular ship and recangular parcel at my lap, that I'm not the one traveling at the speed of light, the one at c, the one composed duplicitously of particles and waves, that I'm not the one passing beyond the sphere of our orbit, our solar system, our galaxy, into the heart of the universe and trespassing the limit of infinity, that I'm not the one who'll live forever.

CLOSING CREDITS

*"In the shape that chance and wind give the
clouds, you are already intent on recognizing
figures: a sailing ship, a hand, an elephant..."*
—*Italo Calvino,* INVISIBLE CITIES

ELEPHANTS

"*Memory is redundant: it repeats signs so that
the city can begin to exist.*"
—*Italo Calvino,* INVISIBLE CITIES

ELEPHANTS I

The elephants are painting! And all without training from accredited institutions. We can buy their work and put it on our walls. We can celebrate their individual visions.

The Thai Elephant Conservation Center in Lampang is home to The Elephant Art Gallery, where you can purchase the paintings of Sri-Siam, such as the series "Going to the Moon (1, 2, and 3)." Sri-Siam's voice is defined; her paintings generally have the same compositional style, the same voice; the brush makes contact with the paper and descends in long, downward strokes overlapping in a "Seussian bamboo forest," as one critic put it.

The paintings of Tao start in the same way, with a point of contact on the paper and rich, downward strokes. Unlike Sri-Siam, Tao's strokes arc, like a sail inflated with wind. Jojo, one of the first and possibly the most famous elephant painters at The Elephant Art Gallery (and who happens to be a musician as well), has richly overlapping, zigzagging lines that switch-back over each other, some thin strokes and some very broad, some strokes where the paint was barely on the brush. Examples of Jojo's work includes "Autumn Leaves," "School's Out," and "Breezy Feeling." Wannalee, adopted by the Royal family of Thailand's Princcess, shares a similar style with Jojo in the way that Sri-Siam and Tao are similar, both utilizing a lot of wild, swooping lines; yet Wannalee's are much smoother and more consistent than the latter artists. Kaew has an almost human spacial awareness of the canvas while Min exhibits nuanced periods of her art as distinct and defined as those of Picasso.

Oh, yes, the elephants are painting all right.

BURT & BILL

"Give it about two, three months maybe, before the suffering gets really bad—Crime in Italy this coffee is hot!"

Burt lifted his straw-colored head up from the table and gave the vet a quick once-over, then looked at Bill like "who is this guy?" before putting his white snout back on the table with a sigh. The tumor on his shoulder breathed with the dog. This wasn't the one killing him though; this was just a fat deposit. The ones killing him were inside, all over.

"What do you recommend?"

"A whole lotta love and a handful of treats," the vet said, at which point the goateed doc started playing air guitar. Both gave the guy a dubious look. And both ate cheeseburgers on the drive home.

Bill had bought the yellow lab after his divorce when the puppy was eight weeks old. He named the dog Burt after his favorite actor, though the dog bore no resemblance. Burt had done the whole puppy thing, complete with ruined shoes, sofas, remotes, carpets and other messes; still, the puppy was cleaner than the divorce had been. The new condo allowed pets—and when Bill moved in he could still smell the pets of the past—but there was no lawn for the dog to play in so Bill had to create a pen in the living room neither the carpet nor the landlord appreciated. The kidney infection didn't help either, as Bill discovered when he'd brought the dog to the vet to inquire about the far-too frequent peeing. The vet informed him that the cause of the infection was due to the pup being sold two weeks prematurely by the breeder. Which helped make sense of the other issue.

Every night when Bill kenneled the dog the pup would cry for hours, missing first the warmth of his mother then the companionship of Bill, the surrogate mother. In order to fix the situation Bill wrapped an old clock inside a warm towel and nestled the ticking bundle in the crate to create a different surrogate. When Bill got tired of microwaving the towel every night he brought the pup into his bed.

When Burt got to be around six-months old he started humping Bill's leg, so Bill took him in to get fixed. Burt slept and moped after the surgery and Bill wondered whether he was sad at losing his balls or if he was even aware of what he was losing. Bill had never had kids, which he guessed was the only silver lining in the divorce, still he couldn't imagine lobbing them off.

A couple years later, when Bill was back on his feet, though not regularly dating, the two moved into a ranch on the edge of the woods. The driveway had just enough space for his truck and a new fishing boat. Bill and the dog would go on walks through the woods where Bill would remove the leash and Burt would take off, treeing squirrels and rolling in goose shit. Then the leash would go back on and Burt would sulk. The sulking continued at home when Bill would bathe the dog in the tub he hoped would someday host another pink razor.

Bill liked to fish and he'd take the dog on trips to Mille Lacs or Leech Lake, up to Bemidji or to the small acreage his family has near Red Wing with a small but boatable lake. Burt was good on the boat; he'd sit up front, paws hanging over the aluminum hull, strings of saliva running from his jowls and blowing in the wind as the 25-hp motor trawled them through lily pads, willows and canes. Trolling a line behind him, the dog barked every time the reel squealed as the line was taken out; which meant Bill never had to worry about bobbers or falling asleep, or for that matter the element of surprise. (It was no mystery why Bill caught more fish when he went without the beast.) Burt only leapt from the boat once, when he saw a beaver on the shore dart under the water. They ate beef stew on the shore. When Burt got thirsty Bill would squeeze a water bottle into Burt's mouth. When Bill got thirsty he went for a Diet Coke because he doesn't drink any more.

Christmas, Bill would cut down a tree from the family plot and place it in their living room. Twice during Burt's early years Bill returned home from work to find the tree on its side and Burt smiling through a laurel of tinsel and lights. The second time Bill had found the ceramic yellow lab ornament his mother had sent him smashed into three pieces and had to glue them back together as the ornamentation was slim to begin with: a couple bulbs purchased from a truck stop; an angler casting a line into a barrel; a toboggan; a photo of his childhood home framed in cedar, another copy given to his sister in Wilmette, whom Bill talks to on holidays.

On the actual holiday Bill usually has a cup of coffee and unwraps the presents he'd bought for Burt: a bag of rawhide bones; a new collar; several smoked pigs' ears he'd picked up from the butcher; a dog bed that Burt eviscerated within minutes. Burt got more enjoyment tearing up the wrapping paper, and Bill got enjoyment watching and picking at the book on D-Day his ex-father-in-law had sent him.

When Burt was eight, he ran across the street to join Bill, who was talking to the neighbor that owned the video rental store next to the tattoo parlor in the strip mall just outside the block. Never taught to look both ways, Burt ran out into the street and was hit by a Civic; thankfully the car had been looking for the right address to deliver a pizza to and was only crawling when it struck the dog. Still, the car's fender hit Burt across his snout and the vet had to wire his jaw shut and keep him overnight. The next couple months were difficult; eating, drinking, giving Burt his medication, watching to make sure the dog didn't aggravate the injury when he saw a squirrel outside and raced to the back door, all presented their own challenges. Eventually Burt made a full recovery.

They lived well for the next several years. Bill met a couple of ladies that had wanted to be included with the two on holiday cards, some even were, but the pink razor never came.

A taxman who always collects, age took its toll on the dog. The first tumor appeared as a small lump on Burt's shoulder blade and grew to the size of a grapefruit within the year; this was the one the doc said was benign, and to remove it could endanger the animal. Over the next two years Burt grew slower and had trouble moving. The ranch helped, but when they encountered any stairs, like those at his parent's house, Bill would have to slide a towel under his belly and lift Burt along. When Burt began sleeping more and ignoring his food Bill took him back to the vet; that's when they found the tumors more nefarious cousins lurking in his tissues. The vet made several suggestions; Bill took only the last and began putting treats in Burt's food as an incentive to eat. The food continued to go untouched.

Burt grew skinny, except for the hump. His hair fell out and his eyes became waxy with cataracts. Burt could hardly stand on his own and eventually the towel had to be used just to help Burt to his feet. Then Burt got worse and Bill got scared.

If Burt wouldn't eat, the doctors said, there was only one thing left to do aside from watching the slow death of starvation, which he didn't recommend. Bill said to give them a week.

They went fishing again, casting from the shore this time as Bill didn't think he could manage to get Burt in and out of the boat. They ate jerky and soup—and Burt actually ate. On the fifth day Burt began convulsing on the tile in the kitchen.

The seizures came in waves, and Burt breathed heavily in the valleys. The dog's jaws clacked and pink foam oozed around the corners of his mouth. Bill reached under Burt to pick him up and for the first time since Burt was a puppy he got bit. The teeth dug indiscriminately and without intent into Bill's left wrist, but he plied the dog off the ground and carried him to the truck.

The vet looked sad but not surprised. When asked, Bill said he preferred to be there with Burt when it happened. He had to wait in the lobby while they prepped; after about ten minutes a girl in maroon scrubs with kittens on them tried to smile when she told Bill they were ready. It was the same steel table Burt had been on last week. He patted the dog's matted fur and stroked Burt's yellow and white snout. The vet injected Burt with a thick pink liquid. Burt squealed sharply. Bill watched Burt's eyes become red and dopey. He stroked the dog's head until it was done.

"I'd get a doctor to take a look at that bite if I were you."

Bill looked down at the two red semi-colons bleeding through the cuff of his sleeve. He really hadn't remembered them until the doctor spoke up. Bill didn't say anything but the vet offered him some gauze and an alcohol swab to clean and dress the wound until he could make it to a practitioner of humans.

The drive home was slow and quiet. The radio had been turned off on the way to the vet; Bill turned it back on but quickly shut it off again. Even the traffic lights seemed to take a moment of reflection before changing. The road home took him past the burger shop and the urgent care facility the vet recommended but Bill drove past. He wanted a drink, badly, and for only the third time since he'd really gotten out of the woods had he seriously considered getting one, but the liquor store came and went, temporarily filling up the rear-view until taken over by naked trees and the curving road.

Now the wrist was starting to smart. He pulled into the next parking lot and parked the truck in the back row while he fished around in his glove compartment for some Tylenol. The wounds had stopped bleeding but the throbbing was deep. The side-view showed the backwards letters of the video rental store; the rear-view was filled with "soot" in gothic red letters.

There was a bell that sounded when you entered Akashic Tattoos, not that you could hear it over the doom metal. The guy with the long silver-and-black beard with the septum piercing asked Bill what he could do him for. The guy playing pool looked up briefly; the guy getting the back piece did not.

There was a discussion of infection and moral prerogative; then there was an extra $50 dollars thrown in and Bill got in the chair.

When he made it home Bill grabbed a can of Diet Coke out of the fridge and sat in the recliner whose arm had been rocked loose from Burt sleeping on it over the years. The tape on the gauze pulled at the hairs on his wrist. Blood from two injuries percolated to the top of the tattoo. The black-and-red semi-colons stared up him from his wrist, waiting for some new clause to come along and give it meaning.

EDEN, FL: PARADISE GARDENS

Eden, Florida had several nice trailer parks in the small town outside Tallahassee; Paradise Gardens wasn't one of them.

Less a trailer park than a trailer refugee camp, Paradise Gardens was a repository of trailers that had seen a little too much of the open road, experienced a few too many of the world's bugs, potholes and speed bumps. Mobile homes whose mobility had long been revoked: the tires replaced with bricks, fences and stoops blocking both fenders; awnings whose motors had burned out ages ago. A community pool even the gators had the good sense to stay clear of.

It should come as no surprise that Paradise Gardens was a staple of the local law enforcement circuit. Any call into The Garden was a veritable roulette wheel of charges, paying out even-money for public intoxication, domestic abuse, unlawful use of a firearm or indecent exposure. Three-to-one odds against sodomy, four-to-one against blasphemy, five-to-one against assault with a deadly reptile and only ten-to-one against a resident accusing an animal of grand larceny. The call that put Sheriff Broadback into the Garden was unspecified but sufficiently telling. " 'Them boys is at it again,' " his dispatcher sighed over the radio, reiterating the call verbatim. Broadback knew exactly which boys Mary meant, and he arrived just as the brothers Goodfellow had approached the nadir of their argument.

"She's *my* sister-wife," Cain shouted, holding something in his hand Broadback only recognized when the sun broke through the clouds.

"Well she was my sister-wife first, ain't that give me rights?"

This being the limp, dangling tip of the Bible Belt, it wouldn't be right to call what happened ironic—more a self-fulfilling prophecy at best. Cain lunged with his piece of broken bottle and buried the broken handle in his brother's belly.

Abel screamed and stumbled backwards, a light trickle of blood drooling from the bottle's brown lip. "Oh sweet, sexy Jay-zuz, he's kilt me! He done kilt me, Sheriff."

Judging by the ample padding holding the bottle, the Sheriff wasn't so sure about that. Still, he cuffed Cain and put him in the back of the squad car while he dispatched an ambulance for the brother, The now penitent Cain apologizing and sobbing and praying over his brother's immortal (and still kicking) soul so loudly the sheriff had to step outside to radio in. Broadback's finger had just pressed the button when the first words began to fall from the sky. At first it was just a light shower of prepositions and articles, a couple scattered nouns, trickling off the leaves with the same timbre as an afternoon shower.

"Oh what now?!"

Which was just when Surprise struck the hood of the patrol car with a large Thunk—the onomatopoeia cracking the sheriff right on the crown of his bald head and tumbling onto the grass.

"Son of a bitch," he stumbled backwards, felt his heel press against something squishy and heard a hiss. He looked down to find a twelve-foot Burmese python assuming striking position. "Je-zus H. Christ!" The squad car bobbed as the Broadback jumped onto the frame of the driver's door.

Cain pressed his face against the window to look for himself. "Nah," he said, sucking his teeth, "that's just Lucy. She wown hurcha," Cain said, smashing his nose into the window to watch the snake, whose face was raised to Cain's as if awaiting instruction. "Gone get back ter the house, Lucy. Ya hear?! Goan back, Momma's got a mouse fer ya."

Perhaps the sheriff's biggest surprise of the day thus far was that the snake did just as she'd been told, slithering off to the trailer, carving out a swath of S's in the accumulating verbiage.

The fallen brother continued to writhe on the ground holding his wound, making a half-angel in the clutter and dictating his last remaining will and testament to those that would listen. Few did. There were more important things going on.

The sheriff picked up the radio once more to call an ambulance when, with a growing whistle, Antidisestablishmentarianism dropped from the sky and crushed Abel's head; the word teetered upright for a second before toppling and falling onto the rest of his body.

"Abel!" Cain shouted. "No, no, no. You kilt im! You kilt im!"

But he didn't have time or audience as the shower quickly turned into a downpour of verbs, adjectives and proper nouns falling in droves.

The residents of Paradise Gardens scattered back to their domiciles to avoid the same fate as Abel or to patch holes in their roofs left by sharp words like Puncture and Eviscerate. The sheriff ducked back into his car and slammed the door shut, Sweat dripped off his forehead and shoulders. The words pummeling the aluminum top turned the inside of the car into a tympani drum of rhetoric, making it easier to pretend not to hear Cain's sobs and threats to the precipitant assailant.

"Breaker breaker, we got us some sort a sitch-e-ation developing on over here. I'm gonna need—," he paused to look at the body on the ground, then, realizing his fate might be repeated, continued, "medical assistance and backup."

"Can't, Sheriff."

"Whatya mean 'can't?' "

"Can't. Calvin's up on Cedar Street 'tending to a sedan cut in half from something he said was 'Deciduous;' and Marvin's over on Seventh, folks saying some unpronounceable drivel was blocking up the road. Sheriff, what's inter-oh-gait-iv mean? Cuz Wilma Crabtree was shouting about how it killed her cat."

Broadback returned the radio to the cradle as a torrent of verbiage poured outside; as the sheriff was soon to discover, calling over to the surrounding counties, his wasn't the only jurisdiction to encounter this rhetorical problem.

— § —

Heavy rhetoric was falling all over the Continental U.S., precipitating from the sky and collecting on the streets and sidewalks, yards and flowerbeds, windshields and the glass facades of skyscrapers. The words fell, owing to no particular lexicon at first, an aphasic slew of pigeon, cactus, Florida, hydrocephaly, disintegration, worm, ladder, bat, hermaphrodite, Venezuela, diaphanous, trilobite…Though that would eventually change.

A middle-aged man in Indiana called into his local weather station to report that Victorian language was clogging his gutters, chimney and drive; that he'd had to find and hire a local chimney sweep to clear it out—which was no easy matter. A mass of bilingual diction jammed up the 805 between San Diego and Tijuana. Two-hundred miles to the East a man was shot by local border militia while trying to climb over Isolationism that had fallen on the border.

On I-80, sixty miles west of Omaha, the driver of a 53' reefer hauling milk and dairy products swerved off the road after being accosted by an acute mass of profanity that collided and burst through is window. Officers on the scene found, among the broken tempered beads of glass, fuck-shit-cock-damn-ass-bitch-cunt in a large ball on the passenger seat and a splatter of blood all over the cab from striking the driver on the forehead.

All Sunday brunches in Brooklyn were suspended due to a barrage of portmanteaus; young men and women finally had a chance to put their flannel and beards to work as they chopped away at the slew of language blocking the stoops of their brownstones. Across the East River, Midtown faced a fight of Goliath proportions as the entirety of Malcolm Gladwell's bibliography fell in one insurmountable heap.

By Monday morning, schools were canceled nationwide, drifts of language blocking the streets with no regard to grade level. In Madison, kids made igloos fortified with medical diction. In Davenport, little Ravi Patel attempted to imbibe one of the words while his older sister made snow angels; his mother had to reach into Ravi's mouth and pull out the sesquipedalian that lodged itself in his throat. In Newark, Martin Dillungsrum and Bobby Brigatoni plied words together into semi-dense balls to pelt each other, cars and other passersby. It was all in good fun until one boy formed a ball around a hard, vulgar center and zinged a solid two-seamer into Becky Newberger's eye, whose mom promptly called their parents. "Where did you even find such a word?" Sylvia Brigatoni demanded. "The park," Bobby told her, when in fact it had fallen from his father's garage.

For fourteen-hours Denver was enveloped in a white-wash of biological terminology: basidiospores, blastocyst, bryophytes, haploid, hemizygous, sclerenchyma, sporangia, zygomycetes, polynucleotide, chloramphenicol...They had to shut off the passes in Eagle and Park Counties, cutting off several towns. Families reported pile ups blocking doors and windows, worded-in by quad- and quint-syllabic diction.

The Mississippi was stopped up by the monolithic 189,819-letter full name of the connectin protein. Barges on both sides of the block-ade spent hours trying to pull it apart but the bonds proved too strong. Other southern or more temperate states who had rarely, or ever, seen snow were thrown in a tail-spin. Billy Bob Beaufort of Baton Rouge woke up for his ritualistic Monday morning cat fishing excursion, found something littering his yard, picked up one of the words and shouted "Martha, get my gun; there's some kind of 'protuberance' on the estate."

Unfortunately, it never felled Brail and the blind were once again left out of the reindeer games. The mutes, however, had a field day and began picking through words and assembling giant prosodic castles on front lawns and soccer fields.

The first report of non-continental precipitation came from a life-guard tower in Kawai. A surfer was ripping some morning gnar when he was attacked by a rogue tiger shark, biting his leg and his board in half; luckily for the surfer, pneumonoultramicroscopicsilicovolcanoco-niosis crashed into the waters next to him and scared off the shark; he was able to climb aboard the disease and paddle back to safety.

A second-grade teacher in Auburn, Washington nursing a killer hangover immediately regretted her decision to take the kids outside to look at supercalifragilisticexpialidocious leaning against the monkey bars, inciting a fugue of song that would last the remainder of the day.

The Santa Ana winds blew in a flurry of Spanish that offended many conservatives in the southwesterly States. An old man in Scotts-dale was heard shouting into the storm "Speak English er dieeee." And of course all were lost when a strong formation came in from the pacif-ic and let loose with a storm of Japanese, Chinese, Korean and Cyrillic characters.

On the other shore, a shore-side restaurant in Kennebunkport was chopping up Lopadotemachoselachogaleokranioleipsanodrimhy-potrimmatosilphioparaomelitokatakechymenokichlepikossyphophat-toperisteralektryonoptekephalliokigklopeleiolagoiosir-aiobaphetraganopterygon that had overtaken their dock. Crusted with barnacles, the word would be flambéed, fricasseed, watered down and served up to their customers with shaved truffles for $49.95 a bowl.

The valedictorian of Cheektowaga's John F. Kennedy High class of

'08, on the eve of graduating *summa cum laude* from Princeton, was killed a day before commencement when Honorificabilitudinitatibus struck her on the head as she was walking through the quad.

Then things went international.

A barrage of English stormed the shores of Liberia with imperious diction and spread to points north and east. Latin America was assailed by a typhoon of economic and socio-political rhetoric. China found their already unbreathable air suffused with the impenetrable smog of tech patents. A blizzard of espionage and acronyms took out most of Eastern Europe, from Berlin to Moscow and points classified. Indigenous tribes of the South Pacific, who'd never seen a movie let alone a movie star, suddenly found their villages swept away on the insipid fillings of gossip magazines; a total of twelve tribesman from various tribes would be sacrificed, two would also be eaten.

A man in Tel Aviv was on the verge of accurately pronouncing the full 216-letter Shemhamphorasch that had fallen onto the beach when a vagrant piece of dander floated into his nostrils and made him sneeze; unfortunately, the tide had taken out the verbose name of God by the time he'd recovered.

— § —

The problem, of course, was what to do with the words. Not operating on the traditional ecology of evaporation, the words lingered wherever they fell, on the ground, on cars, weighting down and snapping the branches of trees—and a few roofs. Citizen efforts shoveled the words from walkways and drives, piled up at the curb like print-colored moguls. Municipal forces, snow plows working in tandem with dump trucks, could only deposit the words into landfills, and those quickly filled up.

"Burn it!" was the collective answer by almost all of the U.N. (Several Latin American countries abstained, opting to bury the words underground, which many feared would infect the water and soil and lead to some disturbing rhetorical flora or fauna hybrids.) Great plumes of smoke rose across cities and states in a coordinated conflagration. When the flames receded, the little ashen piles of Egyptian, Phoenician, Sumerian and Sanskrit, smoldering and glowing, were all that remained. China and Russia sent much of their linguistic refuse into space.

And though a similar holocaust occurred in Paradise Gardens, one word had remained untouched: the gravestone of Abel Goodfellow, his only epitaph the slab of language that killed him.

A STAND-UP GUY

She had eyes that opened like volumes. That's why he chose her. And he had hair like the movies so she said yes. Later, in the dark places not lit by neon, there were sounds of soft friction and vacuums opening and closing. Energies both potential and kinetic. The dark was an envelope; the stamp, first class. Thick breaths of barley sealed the glue.

Sweet smells new and old met sweat smells wild and hairy. The wood creaked and something else moaned. Shivers not from ghosts.

His post-coital contingencies replaced the pre-climactic needs and he rolled over, and his back was to her. She lay there candidly in the quiet, transfixed on the divide in the linen lamentations. Peeling posters of prosaic performers taking a bow above.

Heaped on the floor—a tuber among tube socks—the phallic phantom protecting each other from Virtuous Dissonance. Discerptive. Disseminating. Meanwhile, an imperceptible rip from fumbling fingers harkens a future of recurring rash behavior.

Impatient fingers tapped on his ribcage rising and falling. Foley sounds of sleep. In the dark he wished innocuous but found anything but she asked a simple question, "Really?"

But he was lost: more appositives for opossum; euphemizing the ephemeral. Postponing the morning's mourning.

And then she rolled over, and her back was to his.

ELEPHANTS II

However, that is not to say they have received no training, these elephants, that one of them was suddenly thunderstruck with the concept one morning while bathing in the river. It was not immaculate, the painting, it was introduced.

For three weeks their mahout caretakers teach them the rudiments: how to hold the brush, how to apply the brush to the canvas, what happens when the brush is moved along the paper, where to stand for maximum movement and comfort. They are taught to seek out the mahout when their brushes are dry. They are taught the basics of acrylics and to allow the paint to dry before applying another layer; but, of course, the elephants are young and hasty and sometimes the colors blend—not that they can truly notice.

Unfortunately, the elephants are dichromatic, lacking red and green cones in their retinas and foveas, and are visually deuteranopes (color-blind), their visual range spreading from violet to cyan. The elephants are sadly unable to experience their works fully. Their color selection is therefore made by their mahouts, acting as amanuensis. The mahouts will also choose the style of paper for the canvas, dependent on each elephants' artistic styles.

And though they have assistance from their mahouts, their compositions, as well as their maturation and developments, are their own. Like all artists, the elephants' styles mature over time as they develop their unique voices: slow and deliberate, quick but delicate, brash and abrasive, blotches over lines, trading loops for arcs.

POMPEII & THE BOMB | OR, HOW I LEARNED AN ABJECT LESSON IN OBJECT IMPERMANENCE

In 79 AD, Mt. Vesuvius erupted violently for a period of two days, burying the town in a shroud of fire, lava, and ash. The account was told by Pliny the Younger, whose uncle, Pliny the Elder, was killed trying to help the citizens of Pompeii escape. But this would not be the last of their lives. Seventeen centuries later, historians began removing the lid from the sarcophagi of the city. In their excavations, they unearthed the remnants of the culture of Pompeii, a paragon city of Rome at the pinnacle of its Empire: their pottery, sculptures, architecture, mosaics, and frescos.

In recent years, artists and scientists, working side by side, have attempted to restore the once vivid frescos encumbering the facades of the city's buildings: "Europa and the Bull," the "Beware of the Dog" mosaic in the House of the Tragic Poet, the Cult of Dionysus frescos in the Villa of the Mysteries, entombed in thirty feet of volcanic ash. Lifting the vacuum that had preserved these works of art left them vulnerable to the elements (sun, air, water, dirt) looking to make up for lost time. (Who would have thought the coffin preserved the body while the world outside decayed?) Salt splotches appeared on the paintings from the dirt; the integrity of the walls were compromised by the added moisture; colors became sapped by the sun. But after centuries of conservation—with the most recent taking the bulk of the credit—these frescos are now vibrant and alive, reanimated thanks largely to laser photoablation, ultrasounds, electromagnetics…modern techniques that don't require removing the paintings from the walls, just as inherent to the DNA of the painting as the brushes and oil.

But if you've heard of Pompeii you've likely heard of their most famous offerings. More readily available than the painted walls were the ashen busts of the townspeople captured at the moment of eruption—graves as much as works of art—gray monuments scattered throughout the gardens, piazzas, and homes of the city like sophisticated stalagmites of a cave whose roof had been rent. There were mothers protecting their children, backs turned to the conflagration, merchants caught in the middle of their transactions, others carbonized in their beds, stone families sculpted in the final quotidian moments of their lives. But what can protect them from the trauma of time? From the accumulation of bird shit and rain? The indifferent vandalism of the salty wind?

And here they're at a technological disadvantage. After all, no amount of photoablation, no amount of x-ray archaeology can strip the ash from the flesh of the fallen and spring the merchant back to life. No amount of electromagnetic imaging can bring the mother and her child back to the world of the living. Exposed as they are, eventually the mother will crumble away, leaving the child alone, unprotected, forced to endure the same inexorable fate as she, the same fate as us all.

— § —

The far eastern culmination of World War II was brought to a sudden and devastating conclusion when America dropped two nuclear bombs on Hiroshima and Nagasaki, respectfully. Little Boy's and Fat Man's detonations (occurring around 1,900-feet and 1,650-feet above their respective cities) released waves of thermal radiation so fast and powerful that they etched the negative of their terminal objects (objects even as thin and ephemeral as clothing and shadows) into the plate of everything from skin to concrete; walls and streets burnt in every place but where the occlusion of their latent image—man, woman, wheel, plant—disrupted the maelstrom of light. The images are fully captured, with no need for collodion processes of ambrotype, ferrotype, or albumen...no need for the sensitives of silver iodide or silver chloride, no gallo-nitrate oxidation...no need for the stabilizing agents of potassium bromide or hyposulphite of soda...no need for Eastman's film role...no need for anything but the daguerreotype of atoms in heat.

Because of this, we now have the shadow of a woman waiting for her husband emblazoned in a cascading shadow from the wall behind her down to the sidewalk, spilling into the gutter, trickling out into the street. The parapets of the Yorozuyo Bridge in Hiroshima staining the road in a walkable diapositive. Patterns in silk dresses eponymously tattooing the flesh of its wearer. We can take pictures of ourselves next to these black ghosts imprinting their last corporeal positions on brick walls and bridges, Talbot's calotypes on streets and sidewalks…

But what of the father excised from his family portrait? His wife imprinted on the edge of the grocery store, his two children on the building next door, while he unfortunately stood in the gap between the two, lost in the space between plates. Excluded from the barcode of his family: two short dashes, a big gap, a long dash. And what of the others who found themselves without a canvas that day? The families lost in the spaces between the concrete inventories? What of the barcodes unaccounted? What of the reconciliation?

MICHAEL

Michael felt the stubble on the man's face and tasted chemicals when their tongues were forced together, when the hand dug inside his pants against the choo-choo tracks of the elastic. New bruises that would turn purple tomorrow stung his forearms and his back. He didn't like the mean words the man used, but he didn't like the chalky taste of teeth more so he learned to keep quiet.

After the third year he stopped locking the door.

When it snowed, he made impressions of angels and marked the names he could remember. The snow cooled his back. Sometimes he'd try to eat the flakes that fell but the cold hurt his mouth so he stopped.

He liked to read when the doors were closed, when the house was quiet, when the man was sleeping. His *Children's Bible* had the pictures that helped make sense of the words. He liked the story of Daniel and the lions, especially the ending. He liked Gabriel and would find himself talking to him in the dark. His favorite angel was Michael because he fought the demons and because it was his name. He did not like the story of Job.

He used to have a Mickey Mouse watch the woman had given him before she left. Mickey's hands kept the hours and the minutes. When the man would come into his room, Michael would stare at Mickey's hands but they never seemed to move. He thought Mickey was broken and so Michael threw him away.

His room had wallpaper of jungle animals smiling and holding each other's tails: a giraffe holding a lion holding a monkey holding an elephant holding the giraffe. They paraded around the walls and Michael liked to imagine himself playing in their jamboree. He found a box of crayons in the closet from the boy the man had before. He climbed on the bed and drew a picture of himself riding on the giraffe, stick figure hands waving; in the picture he was smiling.

The man didn't like Michael's drawings and used a wet cloth to try and wipe them away but the wax stayed put. Michael could taste the chemical cleaner on the rag when it was shoved in his mouth. The gross water mixed with the water from his eyes. His nose was stuffed from the crying which made it hard to breathe through the rag and he choked and passed out. Which made the man even angrier. After that, he slept on his tummy for a while.

The man threw away the box of crayons so Michael waited until he heard the snoring to dig out a handful of his favorites. He hid them in the cubby under his bed along with his bible so the man wouldn't get rid of that, too.

His favorite color was green, all kinds of green. On scraps of paper he drew green tigers and green skies and green ghosts. The green ones wore down to where he could only grip them with his fingernails. And then he was out of crayons and couldn't make any more drawings.

The Michael on the giraffe was still there, at least, but the man's wiping made him fuzzy, like he was caught in a storm. But even in the storm he was smiling, and that made Michael smile for real.

Still, whenever he heard the wine of the screen door, or the clinking of the bottles that smelled worse than the cleaning chemicals, whenever he heard the footsteps clapping against the linoleum, he would close his eyes and remember what the bible had promised: that there were angels, too.

HOW TO SIT SHIVA FOR FORTY CANNIBALS

They were old family recipes, modified, and ones certainly not kosher anymore. But honestly they'd never kept much to the traditions so why start now. Dad had been a gentile, then a Buddhist, then a capitalist when their Henderson Farms Organic Oat Meal business took off; Mom had been Ashkenazi, then a Henderson, then disowned. So maybe the request came as an affront to those that bore her, though as much of her family was in-absentia (dead or on vacation), the "fuck you" might have been lost or, at the very least, misappropriated.

Mom had prepared it all in the final weeks of her hospice. The great long pork of Long Island. There was to be a new dish for each night of mourning, and she had given them each clever names: Filet Minyan, Karen Knish, Momtzah Ball Soup, Liver Latkes, Backside Brisket, Hamstring Hamantaschen, and Femur Farfel.

This was perhaps not what Malachi had in mind when he said to keep it in the tribe.

All things considered, the Shiva went about as well as could be expected, but a quarrel in the quorum meant we were down a man by the bottom of the sixth dish. We had all night to find a tenth, and when we couldn't, I volunteered.

"No, it has to be a man," my Uncle Levi said—this was the uncle on my father's side who'd converted for his second-to-last wife. "It's part of the tradition!"

"What tradition?" I said, "What's traditional about any of this?"
Which blew everyone up.

And there we were, at an impasse on the overpass, stuck in a Sentry heading south to my parents' house where the farfel was sitting on the counter, unattended. And my uncle had his points, and I had mine, and all the while there was my mother, growing cold.

ELEPHANTS III

The elephants feel out the spatial arrangement of their compositions, concentrating their designs on a particular space respective to the artistic tendencies of the respective elephant: downward brushstrokes of multicolored vertical lines spanning the length of the canvas, sometimes overlapping, sometimes not; similarly downward strokes but with an arc (à la Tao); a tangle of lines in the center like the inchoate stages of a bird's nest. Some elephants will concentrate on occupying the middle of the paper, leaving the corners untouched. Others might have the paint run off the side.

Even though each artist is different, it is prudent to note that none pay attention to conventional form. They do not consider perspective or shadow, depth created by combining opposing colors; they do not hatch, cross-hatch, or otherwise make use of conventional texture techniques; nor do they use enamel or other viscous mediums to bring a more three-dimensional aspect to the work. It is important to note their creations are abstract, no concrete images.

Like any artist, completion is felt in the elephants. When the elephant is satisfied with the composition, he or she will no longer seek the aid of the mahout, sometimes standing away from the painting, or, as often happens, leaving the area altogether and heading towards the river. Their inspirations are theirs to control, no matter how much the mahout would like the fire to stay burning. Creatures of great dignity, they cannot be bought or bargained with to return.

I

I spit my seed into the drain pipe of the shower and waited for gestation. There was an I growing inside the pipe—a cylindrical womb that tasted like steel; a birth canal that held the distended chrysalis—feeding on hair and soap that swirled in a maelstrom around my feet. I watched it grow and loved it unconditionally. I named it I.

— § —

When I began I was the size of a marble, and since then I've watched I's heart form, I's lungs and I's eyes. I's fingers flexed and I made tiny fists. I beat these fists against the cold, metal uterus. I tasted the saltiness of steel.

— § —

When I was born I stood up, rising from the drain pipe covered in ablutionary amniotic fluid, standing upright to meet me eye to eye—I to I on the cracked bathroom tile. I brought I into my arms and hugged I with paternal pride. I hugged back.

"My boy, my boy," I said. I had his mother's eyes.

I raised I, teaching I the things I thought I should know.

— § —

I was teething and gnawed the remotes and furniture. I destroyed shoes. I felt for I and rubbed whiskey on I's gums. I bit me. I bit I back.

— § —

Then I was young and mischievous. I tore the linen and soiled the sofa, which had once been white and expensive. I drew vulgar pictures with marker and crayon on what had once been frescoed, stucco walls. I punished I as I saw fit. I cried and pounded on the door; and I was weak and let I out, cradling I in my arms, stroking I's soft head.

At night I read to I. *Goodnight Moon* was I's favorite and I made me read it two sometimes three times before bed.

— § —

One day when I was older I killed the neighbor's cat. The neighbor approached me and demanded I reprimand I. I was embarrassed and, too big for a spanking, I beat I with sticks and with belt.

"I sorry, Papa. I sorry," I cried, "I won't do it again."

"I'm sorry, too, I," I said. "This hurts Papa as much as it hurts I."

— § —

I liked sports and I played catch with I. I threw a baseball to I. I threw it back. There we were, I and I playing catch in the front yard. Until I dropped his glove, watching the girl across the street I likes, and the ball hit I in the eye. I took I to the kitchen and iced I's eye.

— § —

I helped I with I's homework, shutting off the TV to I's discontent, telling I, "I can watch TV after I's done with I's homework."

"I want to watch now!"

"Only when homework is done, I."

"But I hate homework."

"I know I does, but I still has to do it. I has to learn, right? I want I to be smart, I; as smart as I."

I hated math the most. I taught I geometry and algebra; I taught I *i*, which made I angry. "Like I, Papa?"

"No, not like I," I said. "*i* just means a non-real number. And isn't I real?"

"Yes," I said. "But, Papa, is I a number?"

I laughed at I, "Why yes, I. But only if we're Roman."

— § —

It wasn't long before I became sexual. I rubbed I's groin on the pillows and acted inappropriately in public. I grabbed women and touched them inappropriately. I apologized for I and promised I would never do it again. One day I saw I by a drain pipe, being sexual; I grabbed I by the throat and pulled I forcefully away out of paternal responsibility.

That night I crept into I's room while I slept. I carried a pillow and I put it over I's face. I struggled. I was strong, as strong as I. I pried the pillow from I's face; I heard I crying and I let go.

"Papa!?" I cried.

I buckled at the sight of I crying.

"My poor child," I dropped the pillow and held I in my arms. "Papa's sorry. Papa would never hurt I. Never again," I lied.

— § —

When I was good I took I to beaches. I taught I to swim and to get over I's fear of the water. We went camping, I and I. Baked beans, fresh fish, warm beer. I burnt I's tongue on the bitter coffee so I made I hot cocoa. I loved the woods until I rolled in poison ivy. I itched for days.

— § —

I liked art and I made finger paintings I placed on the fridge and at my desk at work. I told I about Van Gogh and Picasso, about Leonardo Da Vinci and Michelangelo.

"Like the turtles?" I said.

"The same, I."

Movies caught I's attention and I told I about Edison, Muybridge, D.W. Griffith, the Lumière Brothers and Eisenstein. I liked Eisenstein best for the name.

"I's and Stein," I would shout through the house. I felt it was possessive, though possessive of what I can't be certain; I was never one for grammar.

"Yes, I, 'I's and Stein.' " The pair sounded like a cartoon duo.

— § —

I grew stubble and I taught I to shave the hair from I's face. I taught I to lather first and I tried to eat the foam. I taught I to use a straight razor, to hold the blade at an angle, to trim I's whiskers in a downward motion. I bled the first time and I wept as I blotted I's cheek with tissue. We had matching mustaches, I and I.

— § —

One day I came home from work and heard muffled movement in the basement. I crept down the stairs and saw I covered in blood, standing over a man's body. The man was not moving and I saw I with a pipe in I's hand. I smiled and I hit the man with the bloodied pipe in the already bloodied head.

"No, I! That's a bad I. Naughty I." I raised the pipe once more.

"Put it down, I." Slowly I put the pipe down and ran to me. I knelt on the ground and hugged my legs, sobbing.

I patted I on the head. "There, there, I."

I buried the body in the backyard while I was remanded to I's room. When the deed was done I was dirty and I went into I's room before taking a shower.

"I, how about we go for a drive tomorrow? Would I like that?" I asked.

I nodded happily; "I would like that very much."

— § —

I drove the car while I stared out the window, smiling. We passed cornfields and trees. I sat and played with I's stuffed animal, petting the dog's floppy ears and pointing the button eyes out the window; I pointed out the birds and spoke with moustache close to the animal's ear, "Puppy see?"

I turned down a side road with a canopy of maple and birch. I drove away from the highway. I pulled off that road and down a dirt road that went up and down in the cosines of hills. I watched I smile and clap every time we went down a hill and I got that falling feeling in I's stomach.

I stopped the car behind an old barn with a falling roof; I got out and ran to it. I went inside the barn with grass growing wild and animal droppings souring the air. I climbed a ladder to the hayloft and found a spider. I plucked the spider from a web and put it in I's pocket.

"Come outside," I yelled to I.

I came out. I ran up to me. I dug in I's pocket and pulled out a fist. I opened the fist to show the spider. I smiled. Then I watched as the spider bit I. I crushed the spider in I's fist as I yelled and cursed and cried.

"Papa, it bite I."

I soothed I, petting I's hair. "Come with Papa, I, we'll wash that hand and make it better."

There was a pump behind the barn that drank from a well. I brought I there and told I to wait while I got the medicine from the car. I walked back to the car while I pumped water furiously, forgetting about the bite and laughing as the water made a puddle at I's feet.

From the car I pulled a shotgun, an over-under. I snapped the breach open and loaded two shells of buckshot, one of top of the other. I closed the breach and I walked back to I splashing in the water.

"Don't look at Papa, I," I said.

But I did.

— § —

In the shower I washed the dirt off. I lathered and scrubbed the dirt from fingers and face. I watched the oxidized blood swirl around the drain in a copper whirlpool. I was clean. Then I spit a seed into the drain pipe and waited with fatherly anticipation for it to gestate.

FRANKENSTEIN'S DOPPELGÄNGER 2

I'm a made man! A man-made man made man of men. A man maid, of sorts.

There are times when I see shadows of parts of man made separate: an arm, a head, a shin, a shoulder…shadows not of my man made.

I wonder, Do these shadows' paired men see shadows of their paired parts? A shadow unpaired, a whole unmade? A lone thigh walking down cobbled paths, a lone hand lifting a glass, fingers making puppets on their own? Piecework shadows spread through the whole of Ingolstadt, stalking their makers and their makers' made men? All looking to be made whole? Looking to be made men?

Then I remember, the men from whom these shadows were made are buried, their wholes long gone, their shadows made lonely. Abandoned, left to roam. Ghosts of shadows, shadows of ghosts. Silhouettes of man unmade. Mocking the dead with their continued life.

But then I think: Perhaps not their shadows made ghosts, perhaps not their shadows mock life. No, perhaps their shadows just made silhouettes of man unmade. A sunlit aubade to their old bod, perhaps. Or perhaps, simply, their shadows made.

AN AURAL FIXATION

Through ample pharmaceutical assistance and some severe synesthesia, Beltran Flanagan, resident Libertine of the Meadow Springs apartment complex in Reseda and senior hallucinogen correspondent for the *Lucid Sideshow Daily*, donning his best OptikFilm T-shirt flashing a loop of the epileptic intro to Noé's "Enter the Void," found himself standing on the median of the 10, tapping his foot and waving his arms in a steady 6/8 tempo with a swing-feel to the sounds begotten to him through the Doppler shifts of the headlights. In the incandescent-yellows and halogen-blues of the oncoming traffic he found chords and chord progressions of our western 12-tone system: rock progressions of I-IV-V, jazz progressions of II-V-I, chords major and minor, some with suspended ninths and elevenths, a few mu chords (a rare Tristan chord!), occasionally a dominant 7th or half-diminished 7th that—either precipitated by chance or the two-car-length distance—resolved back to tonic.

The traffic was steady, and so, too, was the tempo.

Curiously, when Beltran turned around and watched the outbound traffic, with its varying shades of red, he found not a similar 12-tone system but the 22-tone system of the Eastern and Oriental world. Beltran was the self-appointed septum between the Western and Eastern modes of music (the outbound a little slower owing to a four-car pile-up three miles down the road), enveloping Beltran in a world analogous and disingenuous to the two worlds. He would write in his notebook that evening: "[It] was as if biting into a chocolate éclair in Paris only to discover it filled with kimchi; a wonton in Shanghai stuffed with a kosher hot dog of the variety and temperature found in Brooklyn." It got to be that he could step between the two worlds, choosing inclusion or exclusion with either/or, based solely on the tide of the tune.

Shortly after popping the last of his tabs, he noticed less and less the typical $A_1B_1A_2B_2$ pattern of the late baroque era and more frequently the construction of variations and suites. When he peaked, he swore he heard a *klangfarbenmelodie* of Sorabji's "Opus Clavicembalisticum" as he Whirling Dervished on the median, spinning between both worlds.

Per the nature of bureaucracy and "police philistinism," as he would later write, it wasn't long until some anonymous passing note(s) called the non-emergency municipal line and Beltran was picked up by the blue and whites. Taking out a considerable line of credit with lady luck in that he'd already imbibed all contraband and conveniently shared the last name of a respected (feared) uncle who'd retired from the LAPD shortly after the Rodney King riots ("when all the fun stopped"), Beltran was dropped at his apartment to come down on his own terms, while furiously recording notes of his experience.

Yet such is the heartbreak of re-creation: when the trip was over and the quaking predictability of the concrete world had settled back into him, he was faced with the glaring possibility that he'd likely never again attain what he had experienced. In part, because his hallucinogens (not just LSD but 2C-i, 2C-b, mescaline and a brand of tiger tranquillizer that had yet to be cleared for use on tigers) were spent and the specific recipe of the cocktail might never be replicated (the tiger tranq he believed principally responsible for his synesthetic trip utterly irreplaceable); also, because the authorities had admonished him against any recidivism with the promise of incarceration and the re-invocation of the patented rubber-hose technique made famous in Chicago during the Democratic National Convention of '68. Through waxing hopelessness, Beltran came to the sad realization that he would never see the music again, that he would never play the ocular *maestro* conducting the symphonies of the highways. No, he would have to suffer the world of normalcy—which, after a time, he refused.

With the cocktail unavailable, Beltran had to explore different methods of transporting himself back to that plane. His first efforts were focused on inversion, trying to get his brain to flip the parts responsible for the recognition and production of language with the area cross corpus-callosum for music; he thought that, as he was right-handed and the language centers were located in his left hemisphere, music in the opposite region on his right, that if he could somehow switch his dominant hand, maybe it would induce an ocular and aural switch as well. And so Beltran began using his left hand for everything, from writing and ping-pong to using scissors and shaving. When that had no effect, he increased his marijuana regimen to facilitate the conversion. Local hallucinogens provided no further headway, either. As a last ditch effort, Beltran stopped eating and drinking, hoping that by reducing his body to a state of near death, the switch would occur in a stage of near life—a phenomenon he'd read about once in a *Daily* op-ed.

And so, as luck would have it, on the last day of the third week of his fast, prostrate on his bathroom floor, robe hanging open exposing emaciated skin and a bloated stomach, checkered tiles spread before him, head nestled on a rust-colored towel that had started out white, Beltran once again saw music with his eyes.

The tune was simple, but sweet.

ELEPHANTS IV

Nor are their artistic tendencies their only human attributes; egos arise. Wanalee, the Royal Princess's adoptive elephant, is a top-selling painter and is most adored by the visitors; and the other elephants can tell. Jealousies blossom. Thâng has even been observed sabotaging Wanalee's paintings when the mahouts' backs are turned. Several of the younger painters, either intimidated by her talent or reproachful of her fame, have stopped painting all together.

Their flaws continue: Yud will only paint when JoJo is around. Aet had been known to throw stones with remarkable accuracy at those he finds to be pervading his artistic workspace, or encroaching on his mahout. Jojo's fame appears to be impacting his love life as he has two female admirers: Kod, an older elephant artist, follows him around and forcefully keeps the other females away from him; and Prachuap, who is not an artist but is much younger than Kod. Jojo keeps one on each side of him. Phungphay will only paint while wearing a beret. The impatient, Krawnkraway, will stop and prod his mahout if he takes too long to reload the brush, sometimes storming off to the river in a fit of indignant rage. Then there's Seiyn, who one day decided he'd hit the zenith of his artistic career and has since retired, refusing to even hold a brush again and refraining from socializing with the other artists.

But they were not solely in competition with each other, or themselves...

AN HAUNTOLOGY OF DEAD ENDS

P.—

My wife's diaphragm is haunted, doctor.

R.—

You mean your wife's diaphragm is haunted by the projections of your latent feelings towards her: words left unsaid, business left unfinished?

P.—

No, I mean it's really haunted.

R.—

[silence] How do you figure?

P.—

Well, like—okay look: A couple months after she died I went into the bathroom to start sorting through the vanity: a box labeled HIS that would be moving with me to the smaller condo; a box labeled HERS that, when I worked up the nerve, would get thrown in the trash. So I go into the bathroom and start rearranging. I move my razor, Goldbond and nose-tweezers into a shoebox; I put her eyeliner, her Sensitive-Skin Extra-Moisturizing Body-Lotion and her diaphragm into one of her shoe boxes. His and Hers, right? Then I hear this voice. And it's not like a spooky, hoarse, ghost voice saying Get Out or Seven Days or something. This isn't a movie, doc, I know that. The voice was real, and young.

R.—

What did it say to you?

P.—

Well, first off, you know that it's not as if we didn't want to have kids; we just wanted to wait until the time was right for both of us.

But that was before—I mean if we'd have known what was coming maybe we would have acted sooner…but well—hey, maybe it's better we didn't. So, right, okay, back to the voice.

So I put the diaphragm into the box and go to grab the cue-tips, which we shared (and I honestly—this is going to sound weird—but I honestly thought about splitting them up for some reason) and all of a sudden I hear this voice and it says, Hello? So I stop and try to see where it's coming from and it says, Hello? Is anybody there? I don't know why but I said, Hi, who's this? And the voice says, Timmy. So I'm thinking to myself, Timmy? Timmy? Do I know a Timmy? Is this a neighbor kid playing games with the vents? But before I can address the voice it goes, Do you want to play catch with me? Catch? I say. Yeah, everyone else is being a big stupid-head and doesn't want to play. They want to play ghost-in-the-graveyard but they say it's a big-kid game and I'll just ruin it and tattle and so they won't let me play. I say, Who? Who else is with you? And it's about this time that I realize the voice is coming from the box labeled Hers. So I go in real close, about six-inches from it. As the voice gets louder, I realize its coming from the diaphragm, which is sort of vibrating like a speaker. And so this Timmy says, Billy and Sarah and Jennifer and Alicia and Paul Jr. [patient points to his chest] and Big Mike and Little Mike and Kevin and Augustus III—my grandfather was Augustus Jr.. And I stop him and say, How many of you are there? And this Timmy says, Like a bagillion!

R.—

And—, and what did you do with said diaphragm?

P.—

I thought you'd think I was making this all up, so I brought it with. [At this point patient produces a diaphragm from his jacket pocket and places it on the table.]

R.—

[lengthy pause] And this is—

D.—

Who's that? [Sounds appear to be emanating from the diaphragm.]

R.—

This-, this is Doctor Rutherford. To whom am I speaking?

D.—

I'm Guthrie.

P.—

You see what I mean, doctor?

R.—

[static]

P.—

Doctor?

D.—

Hey, does this guy have any candy?

P.—

Doctor?

R.—

[thump]

P.—

Shit. Someone call an ambulance! The doc's fainted.

D.—

I'm on it!

THE BODY APARTISTS

(CLARISSA/CLARITY)

Her body wasn't her own. Not at the moment. For the time being her body was the Client's. An hourly rate had been established by an outside party, the hours had not.

She was body and mind and soul, one heart-head beating in a shell. It pulled the strings of the great big dummy. It moved the levers that moved the limbs, the head, the mouth. There was a specific sequence of levers the job demanded of her tongue and mouth. She could choose the lever sequences of her arms and hands herself. A camera captured the movements.

The levers did not move the leveler. At least, not yet. Not so far. But she'd heard tales of it happening.

He had levers of his own to work. Their levers were supposed to work in sync. Cogs in motion. Gears in tandem. There would be a bonus if the machine didn't knock, if the timing belt didn't blow.

This talk of belts…This talk of blow…

And suddenly the lever was stuck. And the oil wasn't the right kind to get it moving again.

— § —

TRANSMISSIONS FROM THE BODY SHOP: NO. 22461

"Well someone put the leg in the arm hole and the head in the leg hole. And we got a right foot on a left hand and a cufflink on the ankle. Necktie on the damn forearm. Bottom teeth up top, top teeth on bottom. Honestly, I can't make heads or tails how she's s'posed to move. You sure this is what the directions called for? Allan said it looked like Chinese to him but he *knows* Chinese so I don't know what in hell to think. We'll call the manufacturer in the morning. East coast so closed now. Motel down the road if ya need lodging. Hard to say really. Might send a replacement. Might send the right directions to make the parts work right. Did you buy the warranty? They're going to want you to have the warranty. I can tell ya from experience, *you're* going to want to have the warranty. Planned obsolescence and so forth. And it can get expensive, model such as this. Yeah you really should a bought the warranty."

— § —

H | H ==> H ¦ H

Snow falling. Love of your life asleep on the bed. TV on. No one watching. Someone watching, maybe. Boots, a woman's, walking in the snow outside. Tracks. Less tracks. Snow. She's there, close.

No, you *were* close; now, you're just proximal.

"Are you smiling?"

"Mm-hmm"

"I can't tell, sometimes my eyes don't open."

"Mine neither."

You fit together well, still. Plastic cups stacked in a cupboard. Carpet crunching like snow outside. Boots dripping old snow onto the crunching. The TV off now. White static in the window; glare of window static on the TV.

"Come away from there." You do.

The bed has issues, too.

On top of the covers she's a mess of soft touching. Underneath, a tangle of supple gestures. Outside, more static white snow. Static-white static. More complaints from the bed. Fingers on both tattoos, acronyms on both shoulders. There was an excess of excess, and an excess of access.

If no one knocks, all the better.

After, "I want to turn the TV on."

"I don't want to watch anything."

"Me neither, but I want it on. I want the heat."

She smiles, "Heat is nice."

Excused for an ice cold shit on a nice cold day. Wallpaper patterns on the tile, tile patterns on the wallpaper. Faucet that runs like static. Tile cold as snow. There aren't slippers but there are robes.

"I think we can hibernate in here." Inside a terry cloth cave of white cotton frost.

"The last polar bear," she says and you both stop. "I didn't mean."

"I know." But the robe still goes back in the closet. There are a lot of things in the closet, some they deposited themselves.

The box that holds the future lying half-cocked on the night stand. The box that held the wine vacated on the floor.

He almost spilled the glass that held the wine that holds his teeth. Two white villas on rolling pink hills, stainless steel fencing. Victims of the deluge.

Three feet on the bed, one foot underneath, hers. Snow falling harder. Quiet falling softer.

Foil and bulbs not of ornaments. White smoke not of fires but of surrender. If no one knocks, all the better.

Rush of hot blood. Trickle of hot rush beading on forearm. Fuzz of towel dabbing up spilt rush.

She says, "Do you feel the heat?"

"Mm-hmm."

"Is that why your lips don't work?"

"Mm-hmm."

"My turn," she says.

Ceiling static like the windows. Eyelid static like the ceiling. Snow inside and out. Static inside and out. Heat rising. Inner static growing louder so you can barely hear.

"Do you think they'll call?"

"Hmm?"

"Do you think they'll call?"

"Some." Dimmer on the world switched low.

"That's fine," she says. "Just fine."

The room fading out into soft static. Her voice fading into soft room.

If no one knocks, all the better.

— § —

I LEFT MY HEART IN PALO ALTO

The hand was in Atlanta, the brain in Palo Alto. The server was in Dallas. The incorporation, Delaware. Then the call came in and a fist was made, a finger extended. A grant ensured. A knee in Raleigh bent and kicked a soccer ball. The teeth in Manhattan chattered and chomped. But where in all this was the heart? Probably also Palo Alto. But maybe Atlanta.

— § —

MISSED CONNECTIONS

In two years of riding the same train I'd never seen her before. Not once; and I'm a man who samples each train car to keep things interesting. She was easily the most gorgeous girl I'd seen in the history of my commute—my commute taking me through less desirable locales, locales you wouldn't expect to find a girl like her visiting. Understandably, she captured my attention, and my gaze. She caught me looking and held my eyes. Long enough for both parties to show interest. Long enough to wonder why either party was here in the first place. I broke it off before it got creepy.

In hindsight I should have said something but I didn't; the train is a creepy place to flirt and I'm a man sensitive to these kind of things. It's not just the prying ears and eyes but the prying smells, the jostling bodies; more a public restroom than a lounge; more a DMV than a stage.

We made it four stops with intermittent eye contact before she got off—at one of the few reasonable stops on the line—and I stayed on—which should have said something about me I'd hoped she wouldn't pick up on. Anyways, I was pretty certain this was the last time I'd ever see her, a blip in the radar, a value too rare to include in the mean—and I know a thing or two about the average—but later that night I dreamt of her.

In my dream she was my date to a gala. I don't remember how we met but I know it wasn't long before. There was a familiarity and an ease of communication. She held onto my arm like it meant something to her. She had two of my kids in less than five minutes and there we were, a family. I honestly don't remember the conception. Then we were on a limo that was a bus that became a hotel room. At some point I stopped working and she had to put the key in my back and wind me up. We puttered around through a Chicago that was really the capital of New York City, and also floating, and then also bucolic—like how it was before we found it. And then I woke up and got ready for work.

It was one of those dreams that stuck with you the rest of the day. Of course, I wanted to grab the same car after work because why not? It was worth a shot, fate and all that. But I got held up at work and left twenty minutes later than usual. And then the original car was too crowded and I had to move to the next one. The chances seemed dismal.

But there she was, standing just inside the door in the handicapped zone. We locked eyes immediately. Something was different this time, and we both knew it.

An obese man on a scooter got on at the next stop and the girl had to give up her spot, moving to the open patch next to me. Her black hair was sticking to her knit cap but that wasn't the only charge in the air.

She spoke first, leaning into my shoulder and speaking just above a whisper This is gonna sound strange, but I had the most vivid dream about you last night.

The look I gave her said what I didn't have to. We both nodded.

After a minute she said It wasn't you exactly. You looked different, but I know it was you. Even though I don't know you from Adam.

I know what you mean, I said. Your hair was lighter and your height was different, but it was you.

The conductor said we were approaching the stop she got off at last time and I asked her if she wanted to get a cup of coffee and talk. She nodded like she had to, like it was a duty, a conscription from fate, and we got off the train.

The first thing she said when we'd ordered our coffee and sat down was It was one of those dreams that just sticks with you the whole day. Does that ever happen to you?

Yes, I said. More and more.

The second thing she said was This wasn't a sex dream, you know. Like, that's not what *this* is. Her hands circled the table.

I said, I know. I know. We were together—had kids even—but it wasn't an explicitly sexual dream. I don't even think we ever...

Wait, she said, How many kids?

Two.

No shit?!

No shit. Herman and—

Yogurt, she blurted

Yes!! We named the daughter yogurt for some reason.

It was political, I think.

YES!!! I said so loud the couple next to us looked over.

Despite the layers I could feel the hair on my body standing up, like someone had rubbed it with a balloon. The heat was rising in my face. I could see hers rising, too. I'm very sensitive to these things.

She said So what was your dream about? I could tell she wanted me to go first so she knew I wasn't just bullshitting. So I tell her...

...And the next time I look, the bus—

—Isn't a bus, it's a hotel room, with aquariums for windows but with lizards instead of fish.

My chin dropped like a trap door. How did you...?

The lizards were speaking Spanish through their bubbles. I could understand them even though I don't speak Spanish.

Me too!

We took a moment to absorb and collect. I had the barista add a shot of bourbon crème to our lattés. I'm a man who likes to let things sink in with a tasty libation. We waited until she returned to speak again.

I went first; I said You don't happen to have a birthmark in the shape of Wisconsin, do you? Her eyes blew up and she lifted her down coat to show me. We were both surprised. Then a little freaked.

It was her turn, And you, you said something strange when we first met, There sure are a lot of dentists at this funeral but has—

—But has anyone ever said I need a taxidermist like *now*?!

Yes! Yes!! And what was the drink you made? she said. And her fingers were sliding around my wrist.

It was something strange but you liked it.

Yes!

I remember you saying you only wanted me to make it, you didn't like the way the bartender made it.

Yes!! She said, squeezing my wrist in the way I like to be squeezed. Staring into my eyes the way I like to be stared into. *Yes*, but what was it?! What was the drink?!?

A Gatorade and rum, I think. With a splash of ginger.

Then her face fell and she let go of my wrist. No. No, that wasn't it.

With olives! I shouted back. But she was already out the door.

CONFESSIONS OF AN ISOSCELES TRIANGLE: IN THREE ACTS

ACT I: MY LIFE AS DELTA

My adult life emerged from the cocoon of δ, with as many expectations and roles to fill as any could guess. After the onset of my vertices, I left Daedalus in his tower with his crafts and his designs towards obfuscation, lift and drag—only to carry his moniker with me. Greece couldn't hold me; there were places to see, events and scenes to be a part of.

I served in several particular roles. I involved myself in heated reactions. I found various financial options in Wall Street and played the market. I took a defensive position in litigations. At dental conventions I was one-half of the mascot: Omicron and myself. There were of course periods of variable uncertainty, periods where I was merely a stand-in for some deletion; I took up a Northern European gig with CCR5-Δ32, having mutated from the frame of its original role and mission statement. That was followed by stints in aquatics with rivers and their currents. Then photography, transportation, insurance, power generation, rockets, submarines, hotels, plumbing, cartoon bikinis, Lady Justice's balance...exhaustive work with industries of every size and color. Yet, I still managed to find time for myself.

While exploring my bisexuality with x and y, I learned to love myself, and to impose no limitations on my amorism. I favored v for quite some time. And for a good many years of my life I had a very public relationship with t. There was a point, for a while, where I felt my existence predicated upon who I was paired with, who coupled with me in the spotlight. Naturally, there were periods when I was a trollop, too, a fixture of the fetishists. But I have always returned, ever beholden in my heart to t.

I have identified myself as many things over the course of my life, of my own will reposed or deposed, a life of flux, but will there never be a day when I can retire, catch up on sleep and settle into a life of constancy? When I can resolve my inverse differences with Nabla? When I can collate myself to just one function? And is it selfish to want to remain affixed with t, donning the role of domesticity as k had for so many years: time unmoving?

ACT II: ON THE PERILS OF 2-DIMENSIONAL IDENTITY

```
With the lights brought down on an otherwise
blank stage, a pair of spotlights shine on
two isosceles triangles in black turtlenecks.
TRIANGLE 1 faces out towards the empty audience;
TRIANGLE 2 stands perpendicular to Triangle 1
on his left, facing stage right. CAMERA 1 has
Triangle 1 framed in a tight close shot in the
middle of the frame, with the thin, profile of
Triangle 2 on the right side of the frame. CAMERA
2 has the opposite, a tight close shot of Triangle
2 from stage right with the thin, profile of
Triangle 1 on the left of the frame. CAMERA 3 is
a top view of both triangles as tiny slivers of
perpendicular lines.


    CAMERA 1


        TRIANGLE 1


    I must confess—


        TRIANGLE 2
```

To feelings of—

                    TRIANGLE 1

Jealousy,

(pause)

CAMERA 2

                    TRIANGLE 2

When—

                    TRIANGLE 1

Playing outside—

CAMERA 1

                    TRIANGLE 2

I see the prisms—

                    TRIANGLE 1

Frolicking amongst—

                    TRIANGLE 2

The spheres—

CAMERA 2

                    TRIANGLE 1

And—

CAMERA 1

                    TRIANGLE 2

Cylinders. To—

CAMERA 2

                    TRIANGLE 1

Watch the prism's—

                    TRIANGLE 2

Face, like—

                    TRIANGLE 1

My face;

                    TRIANGLE 2

Only for them to turn—

CAMERA 1

                    TRIANGLE 1

And I find myself—

                    TRIANGLE 2

Staring at their—

                    TRIANGLE 1

Bodies. Flat.

CAMERA 2

                    TRIANGLE 2

Rectangular. Wide.

                    TRIANGLE 1

And then they—

                    TRIANGLE 2

Turn again—

CAMERA 1

                    TRIANGLE 1

And I see my—

                    TRIANGLE 2

Face once—

                    TRIANGLE 1

More.

(pause)

Oh, were I to—

CAMERA 2

                    TRIANGLE 2

Feel the freedom of—

                    TRIANGLE 1

A body. To—

CAMERA 1

                    TRIANGLE 2

Feel the exuberance—

                    TRIANGLE 1

Of a—

CAMERA 2

                    TRIANGLE 2

Third dimension.

                    TRIANGLE 1

To know that—

TRIANGLE 2

Should I turn—

TRIANGLE 1

I would not—

CAMERA 3

TRIANGLE 2   TRIANGLE 1

Disappear.   Disappear.

FADE TO BLACK.

— § —

ACT III: PROGENY

Would you fault me if, when my child emerges, I find four points instead of three? If his sides are parallel? If they aren't? If his eight outer angles amount to 360-degrees? If they don't? If we find a break and he becomes a line instead of a polygon? If he comes out with a geodesic persuasion or tesalatory? If there are no sides at all? If I can roll him? If when I pick him up I can feel one, two, three, four dimensions? Would I know him to be mine if he didn't share my angles? If his vertices were dull and rounded? If I saw my rhomboid neighbor in his eyes? If he was scalene and I was scared? If, on affirmation, I left?

ELEPHANTS V

Per the nature of commerce, when word got round that people were willing to pay top dollar for an authentic elephant painting, it wasn't long before The Elephant Art Gallery found competition in other elephant reservations. This time with elephants painting recognizable images! Visitors and curators paid out big for paintings of flowers and self-portraits; taking great pleasure in their childlike compositions, overwhelming their hearts in amazement of the elephants' innocent worldviews, believing the paintings to be a portraiture of their consciousness, tokens of their self-awareness.

However, it is not the consciousness of the artists they are witnessing.

As could be expected, these paintings are not of the elephant's design; they are the brushstrokes of specific training and instruction, with sometimes brutal methods of conditioning. Each elephant paints the same composition, over and over, facsimiles void of any inherent artistry. Which can be expected; after all, when there's good cash on the line, you can't take chances. Of course, there are minor variations in color and line—these aren't machines after all—but the composition is uniform, and the art(ist) absent.

ZEUSIFER RISING

POLICE EVIDENCE SUBMISSION FORM

Case No: *487912* Exhibit Ref: *B*

Date: *04/19/07* Time: *1530 hrs.*

Location of Seizure: *Corner of S 4th St and Hooper, Williamsburg, ALBK*

Crime(s) Ref.: *Reckless Endangerment, Assaulting a Police Officer, Attempted Murder of a Police Officer, Conspiracy to Commit Grievous Bodily Harm, Conspiracy to Commit Murder of a Police Officer, Failure to Signal, Conspiracy to Commit Aggravated Irony, Improper Mixed Metaphor Handling, & Reckless Use of a Portmanteau as a First Name.*

Description: *The following document was recovered from the body of Detective Mauricio Angel Zetas. Document was originally found in the possession of Eugenio Levinson Cruz, who was being pursued by Det. Zetas as a suspect in relation to a burglary (Case No. 487898; Exhibit Ref: D), when Cruz was struck and killed by a bike messenger as he evaded arrest from police. Owner of said document could not be verified as multiple database searches could find no one by the name of Yael Bearheart (likely a pseudonym—and not a very good one at that). Document was therefore remanded into police custody until such a time when owner is identified. Detective Zetas, currently pursuing a low-residency MFA, had checked out the evidence from the locker, hoping to un-*

earth the identity of the author, and was kind enough to provide his own annotations, free of charge and without incurring over-time billing to the department. Unfortunately, Det. Zetas, just as he was beginning to make progress on the identity, was struck by yet another bike messenger, the accused (Mr. Seanathan Braydon-Mintz [MA candidate, est. '09]) and remains in a comatose state. Document is thus resubmitted as evidence under new Case No.487912. It is the opinion of the precinct's presiding captain, Capt. Harold Higgins (MFA, Brooklyn College, '04), that Det. Zetas' notes are accurate and any and all advice therein should be followed by the author, if and when he/she is identified, to the T. Furthermore, Capt. Higgins has several recommendations for illus-trators should the supposed author desire, and he would be happy to write the forward.

Filing Officer: *Erasmus Blandone*

Officer Signature: *Erasmus Blandone, M.A.*

— § —

ZEUSIFER RISING ISSUE #001

By Yael Bearheart[1]

---

1 Come on…a Jewish-Native American is your pseudonym?! What, was Runs With Guilt taken?[a]

 [a] *Please remember, this is Det. Zetas' ill attempt at humor. Not a joke of my own. Zetas had his own brand of humor that never really jived with the rest of the boys in the precinct, except for Capt. Higgins.* —E.B.

I . [2]

Panel 1:

Ares, 13, sits in the backyard of a lush Floridian estate[3]. The sun beats down on him. A dirty and sweat soaked WWF T-shirt is plastered to his back. Lying in the grass to his right is a BB-gun. In his right hand, a magnifying glass. In his left, an incapacitated squirrel. Ares focuses the magnifying glass into a small bead on the squirrel's back.

ARES   Burn, motherfucker, buuuuuuurrn!

Panel 2:

Ares narrows the beam of light on the animal. A thin wisp of smoke starts to rise and a tiny ember begins to glow in the fur.

Panel 3:

The squirrel jumps back to consciousness, wriggling against his hand.

Panel 4:

Ares drops the magnifying glass, picks up the air-rifle and whacks the squirrel on the head with the stock.

Panel 5:

The squirrel is still again.

---

2 No sub-heading here? You have them for every other section, why not here?
3 Florida? Wouldn't the obvious choice be Olympia, WA?

ARES   Shit, now I gotta start all over.

Panel 6:

The screen door creaks as Hebe, 9, comes onto the back porch with an American Girl Felicity doll in her hands. The doll's hair clearly cut by a kid.

Panel 7:

Hebe strolls up to Ares's back.

HEBE   Whatcha doin?

ARES   Move your head, Hebe.

HEBE   What are you doing?

Panel 8:

Hebe cranes her head over Ares's shoulder.

ARES   Mind your own business.

Panel 9:

Hebe strafes to his right and sees the squirrel in his hands

HEBE   Noooo, what are you doing to him?

ARES   I said mind your own business.

HEBE   No. I'm telling Mom.

Panel 10:

Ares drops the lens and strips the doll from her hands.

ARES   Tell mom and you're never gonna see Hannah again.

HEBE   No! Don't hurt her. And that's not Hannah, stupid-head, that's Felicity.

ARES   Well if you tell mom her name is gonna be Fucked! Got me?

Panel 11:

Hebe's eyes go wide, her mouth drops open. She turns and runs toward the porch.

HEBE   Mom, mom! Ares said the F-word again. He said it! And he has Felicity and he's hurting squirrels again. *Mommmm*!

ARES   Shit!

Panel 12:

Ares drops the squirrel, which sprints off into the forest, and chases after Hebe to the house.

Panel 13:

Hera throws the screen door open and stumbles onto the porch. The Manhattan in her hand sloshes onto her red pumps. She uses her free hand to rearrange her sunglasses back in place.

HERA   What did we say about tattling?

HEBE   Don't do it.

HERA   And what did we say about disturbing mom during her meditation time?

HEBE   Double don't do it.

HERA   Right. Now what do you say?

HEBE   But he's got Felicity! He's gonna hurt her.

HERA   Felicity's a doll, dear, dolls don't feel pain. For more on that, ask your father.

Panel 14:

Hebe screws her toe into the deck.

HEBE   Sor-ryyyy.

HERA   Good girl. Now, you wanna get mommy a topper for her Manhattan?[4] I'll let you have two of the cherries.

Panel 16:

Hebe smiles, grabs the glass and runs inside the house.

HERA   And easy on the bitters, dear.

Panel 17:

Hera walks over to Ares. She glances at his shirt and scowls.

HERA   I seem to remember pitching that filthy thing two weeks ago.

Ares looks down in shame.

ARES   [whisper] But I like it.

Panel 18:

Hera looks past him to where the rifle and magnifying glass lay in the grass. Then she slaps Ares across the face.

Panel 19:

Ares holds his face in shock.

HERA   Your father is trying to secure the GOP's Gubernatorial

---

4 Wouldn't Ambrosia be a more appropriate cocktail?

nomination and you're in the backyard killing small animals again? Do you have any idea how this would look in the papers? Do you even *want* to go to military school?

ARES   Yesss!!!

HERA   Then keep it up, mister. Any more of this and we'll ship you right out to some stuffy, New England, all-male, boarding school and I'll make damn sure you're captain of the fucking glee club when you're not rowing crew.[5]

Panel 20:

Ares throws himself at Hera's feet, pleading.

ARES   Noooo I don't *wanna* row crew.

Hera pats his back, careful to keep her drink elevated for safety, stroking his blond hair with her free hand and pressing the boy into her bosom.

HERA   Go inside and wash up, we've a dinner to attend.

ARES   I don't want to take a bath.

HERA   And I don't want to take a kid in public who smells like some everglades swamp rat. Only one of us can have their way and I believe I have seniority on that issue.

ARES   Are you making Hephaestus take one?

Panel 21:

Hephaestus's bedroom upstairs: the computer screen glows; jagged

---

5 Split up, too much for one panel; remember, you can only have so much info in one frame. Something you should watch throughout, especially the panel below. I mean Good God!—the boys and I would have to turn a blind eye if your illustrator strangled you for that one.

music plays; the pimple-faced, teenage Hephaestus sits at his work-bench soldering a motherboard; he's got thick goggles on and is wearing a t-shirt of Spock sticking his Vulcan salute into an electrical out-let.

Panel 22:

_____

[Back on the porch]

HERA   That boy needs more than a bath. But yes, all my children will be clean before they leave this house. Now hop to it.

Panel 23:

_____

Ares begrudgingly follows his mother's command and trudges inside to wipe the dirt and smell of feral, burnt hair from his hands and face.[6] Hebe returns with an overflowing cocktail.

HERA   Good girl. A little heavy on the vermouth but not bad. Here, sweetie.

Hera dips her fingers in and grabs two of the cherries; she drops them into Hebe's grateful hands.

HERA   Now go wash up.

Panel 24:

_____

Hebe runs off into the house. From the pocket of her sun dress, Hera produces an Oxycontin.

Panel 25:

_____

She pops the pill and chases it down with her drink. The sun beats

_____

6 How can we see this? How can we smell the burnt hair and the feral smells? Remember your medium.

down hard, hot and heavy.

II. HYDRA

Panel 1:

Room 206[7] at the Red Roof Inn; the "six" is broken and swings down
in a "nine." An ice box with five cubes floating in an inch of water sits
next to a half-empty bottle of Macallan 18. The cubes vibrate. The
side table and attached mirror vibrate. The headboard on the bed vi-
brates. "Thump. Thump. Thump."

Panel 2:

On the bed is a lumpy mound of blanket with two black socks sticking out of the bottom. Gratuitous, hyperbolic screams emanate from
the mound:

MNEMOSYNE   Yes, Yes. Oh God. Yesssss!!!!!

ZEUS   Get it girl! Get. It. In. There.

---

7 Is there any significance to this number? If not, why waste that much time on
it? Unless it was just to make a 69 joke, in which case, what's the point? Everyone knows 69-ing is pointless. Am I right!?[b]

 [b] *Okay* THAT *joke was one of mine.* —E.B.

Panel 3:

MNEMOSYNE   Yaghhhh.

ZEUS   Ach-. Ach-.

BOTH   Ahhhhhhh......

The open-mouthed fish mounted on the wall above the bed slips off one of its nail and swings downward.

Panel 4:

A large man with thick, white beard and white chest hair, Zeus is standing beside the bed, elbows on hips for support as he stretches his back, cracking, genitals wet and warm from friction splayed out in front of him,[8] panning like a sprinkler as he twists his back this way and that, rolling his shoulders when returning to an upright position.[9] Mnemosyne continues lying in bed with the sheet pulled up over her breasts. Her hair is a bit of a mess, but she's otherwise a doll.

ZEUS   Thanks babe! I always do better at these events when I can get a good fuck in before.

---

8 Jesus, do you really want that drawn in there?! Can't you leave that to the imagination?[c]

  [c] *Or at the very least give us some tits, too. Make it fair and balanced.*
  —E.B.

9 With lines like these I'm beginning to wonder if the graphic novel is really the best medium for your story. It isn't a particularly "graphic" story reliant on visual accompaniment. Contrary to Professor Lockhart's lambasting of graphic novels as "the products of lazy novelists" and "writers who don't want to write" there are many fine literary uses of the genre that you might want to consider reading: Spiegelman, Pekar, Moore, Satrapi and Gaiman—whose novel, *American Gods,* I sincerely hope you've read for obvious reasons. Also Ennis, for humor.

Panel 5:

Zeus slips his briefs up over the black socks, snaps the elastic around his waist like a trophy of the deed. He walks to the dresser and picks up his low ball, taking a healthy sip.

ZEUS   People are always giving me shit about icing my single-malts. A faux pas to those goddamn New England Yankee bastards with their whale-pattern bow-ties. I don't get what the big deal is. Maybe if they had this heat and humidity to contend with they'd appreciate their beverages cold.

Panel 6:

Mnemosyne roils about the bed, rubbing her knees together, cooling her thighs.

MNEMOSYNE   So what event do you have tonight?

ZEUS   Some fucking green energy event I think. Or is it a wildlife refuse[10] fundraiser? I can never keep them in line. You?

Panel 7:

[Thought bubble] Mnemosyne imagines the inside of her uterus: a band of sperm in Athenian helmets charges towards a glowing egg.

GENERAL   Give her hell, boys. With any luck she'll have a sister!

Panel 8:

[Back in the room]

MNEMOSYNE   Oh, nothing really…

---

10 Refuse fundraiser? I'm sure you meant refuge fundraiser but this could be a very funny typo or slip on Zeus' part.

Panel 9:

Zues is in his black trousers, belt clasp and fly open, still shirtless.

MNEMOSYNE   Do you have to give a speech?

ZEUS   Just a little something, 'As a proud citizen of the great state of Florida, I feel it is my duty, nay, the duty of all citizens of Florida, America and the world, to continually strive to find clean and responsible resources, not only to attend to our energy needs, but to the ecological needs that surround us. Like my daddy used to say, The fisherman can cast lines all day, but he'll never get his catch to port if he doesn't plug the leak in his hull. Right now our hull is leaking from the deleterious effects of our current reliance on fossil fuel. It's not too late to plug our holes and bail our water, then we can cast lines all day...' sumpin like that.[11]

Panel 10:

Zeus slides his arms into his shirt and buttons it up, tucking the bottom into his waist and fastening his belt.

MNEMOSYNE   I love it when you talk all fancy.

ZEUS   They all do, Mnemmy. They all do.

Panel 11:

Dressed, Zeus grabs his blazer, drapes it over his shoulder and swallows the rest of his drink. He shoots her with a gun made of fingers, clicking at the corner of his mouth.

ZEUS   See ya, toots. Thanks for showing up. Oh, and you should

---

11 Wait, wait, wait...a republican is making speeches on sustainable energy resources?!? I understand alternate universes but there's got to be a threshold of plausibility here. Also, how in the shit is all of that going to fit in one panel?!? I don't want to sound like a broken record here...but fix the needle.

probably wait an hour before "going into the pool" so to speak. Election season and all.

Panel 12:

The door slams shut. Mnemosyne lies back on the bed, pulls the sheets up to her face and inhales the scent.

Panel 13:

From the nightstand she pulls a bottle of fertility pills: Priapusil "Take 1 pill immediately after coitus." She pours an indiscriminate amount into her hand and tosses them back.

> MNEMOSYNE   Bottoms up.

III. MARATHON

Panel 1:

Western Olympia High School[12] track field. A boy in running shorts

---

12 So you use Olympia for the high school but not the town? As professor Lockhart would say, "You're chopping an ugly path through brush when there's a perfectly good trail to the right." Why apply the correct metaphor to a fictional high school in an arbitrary Florida setting when, again, Olympia, WA is just

and WOHS pinny with "Hermes" written across the front sits on the grass and stretches his calves.

Panel 2:

He stands and stretches his quads, staring up at the bleachers while he holds his left leg. In the stands are a group of female cheerleaders with a gorgeous blonde girl [Aphrodite] in the center. The girls are staring at Apollo, the hunky quarterback with flowing, blonde hair practicing discuss on the other side of the field. The girl and her friends are smiling.

Panel 3:

Hermes looks in their direction at Apollo. Apollo is flexing while a smaller guy dangles from his bicep.

Panel 4:

Hermes lowers his head and takes his position on the track next to several other runners.

Panel 5:

His feet lock against the starting block.

Panel 6:

The starting gun goes off.

---

teed up for you? Also, incongruent applications of parallelism and metaphor. If you'd like, I can forward you some literature from Lockhart that's helped me out immensely

Panel 7:

A cloud of track dusts billows as Hermes takes off.

Panel 8:

[In the stands]:

GORGON 1   Aph, your cousin is, like, a total fox.[13]

APHRODITE   Which one?

GORGON 1   Puh-lease. You know which one.

Panel 9:

GORGON 2   And did you hear him sing last week at assembly?! It
was like pure light coming out of his mouth.

GORGON 1   And into my crotch.

GORGON 3   I hear he wrote it himself.

GORGON 2   It's like he's carved from stone.

Panel 10:

GORGON 1   If I have my way those abs won't be the only thing
hard as a rock.

APHRODITE   Ew, gross, Meddy. That's my cousin.

---

13 How do we know they're Gorgons? Do they look monstrous? (If so, why would
the hot/popular girl associate with them?) Are they Gorgons in name only? Is
the student body accepting of their otherness?

Panel 11:

GORGON 3   Plus I hear he's going to be a doctor.

GORGON 1   Jesus, Aph, if I were you I'd risk popping out a three-eyed, one-branch-family monster just for a taste of that sweet meat.

Panel 12:

Aphrodite's eyes drift to Hermes. Rays of golden light dance off Hermes's thighs. Arms pumping furiously and gracefully. None of the other runners touching his wake.

APHRODITE   Mmmm, not really my style.

Panel 13:

GORGON 3   Umm, what are you talking about? He's *everyone's* style.

APHRODITE   I'm not so sure.

She looks at Apollo. Apollo is wrestling another male teammate to the ground with much zeal.

Panel 14:

Apollo pins the other boy in a very suggestive position, a big smile plastered across his face. A pained and weary smile on the pinned boy's face.

Panel 15:

GORGON 3   Jesus, your cousin runs like a freaking Ibis.[14]

---

14 See, you've got the matching symbolism right here. Why not make it more consistent?

APHRODITE   Well, if he were a gazelle, my cousin Artemis would probably have him mounted on her wall.

GORGON 2   I remember her. Apollo's sister, right? Built about the same if I remember correctly.

Panel 16:

[Cut to] A fridge bearing a Christmas card from Artemis. She is wearing camouflage and yellow-tinted hunting glasses, holding a dead twelve-point buck by the antlers as she looks into the camera. Her hands are covered in henna tattoos. Her face is covered in piercings: left nostril, eyebrow, lower lip and septum. "Merry Christmas from Artie and Mary—and Buck."

Panel 17:

[Back in the stands]

Gorgon 2 watches Aphrodite staring at Hermes.

GORGON 2   Him?! Eww, bitch those kids will have cloven feet or something.

Panel 18:

Aphrodite makes an entry into the notebook on her lap.

NARRATION   For reasons of ethics and morality, their father had distanced himself from his various illegitimate sires. He kept tabs on their grades and athletic achievements through the reports of his favorite—though politically unrecognized—daughter. So it was Aphrodite's job to take notes on Apollo's and Hermes's heats and standings. Not wanting his sweet princess maimed, he'd excused her from any and all athletics—outside of cheerleading, of course.[15]

---

15 Single instance of exposition incongruent with the rest of the story. Consider

Panel 19:

Hermes crosses the finish line, well ahead of the other racers.

Panel 20:

He grabs his water bottle and a protein bar and heads to the grass to stretch.

Panel 21:

He looks up to the stands at the girls again. Eyes longing, resentful.

Panel 22:

Aphrodite turns her head and stares at him, too. The other girls are still watching Apollo in the distance.

Panel 23:

Split-panel extreme close up of both their eyes, big and yearning.

"showing" us. Or else, who is the this narrator? Someone from Greek mythology perhaps? The ol' Greek Chorus?

IV. TITANS OF INDUSTRY

Panel 1:

A large banquet hall foyer. A festooning banner reads "Help Save the Crommyonian Sow." Hera, dressed to the nines, stands in the foyer of the banquet hall with her au pair (Demeter, a matronly woman) and children in tow: Ares, Hebe and Hephaestus—all well-groomed; Hephaestus even seems to be wearing makeup to cover his zits.

Panel 2:

Ares scowls and tries to mess up his hair. Hera slaps his hand away.

Panel 3:

HERA   Demeter, for the cocktail hour I want them out of sight and out of mind.

Panel 4:

Demeter nods and puts her arms around the children, steering them down the hall.

DEMETER   All right, children, you know the drill. Eyes sharp; mouths shut.

Panel 5:

[Inside the Banquet Hall]: A typical political event with loads of round tables, caterers, photographers. There's a large ice sculpture of the Crommyonian Sow in the center, already sweating from the heat.

All guests are wearing ID badges on their chests. Hera's bears her
name with a red donkey above it.

Panel 6:

Hera pulls up to the bar next to Zeus, trying to signal the bartender.

ZEUS   You drinking?

HERA   You sober?[16]

Panel 7:

Zeus hands Hera a fresh Manhattan, snaking a bleu-cheese stuffed
olive from his Bombay Sapphire martini.

ZEUS   How deep are you?

HERA   A lady doesn't keep a running tab. You?

ZEUS   I'm laying 6. Double bogey but I do believe I'll still hit par
for the course.

HERA   Well can you keep yourself presentable until after the announcement?

Panel 8:

Zeus pats his jacket pocket. An x-ray bubble shows a vial of cocaine
inside.

ZEUS   Long as I got my remedies.

---

16 This is an irritating tete-a-tete. One answer is yes, the other is no, but both
mean to say yes. I know what you're getting at, but the pragmatics are madden-
ing.

520

Panel 9:

Zeus and Hera look out at the other guests, spotting two sponsors across the hall: one, a greasy man with a drum of oil badge; the other, a large, white-haired man with one eye and a lightning bolt badge [Cyclops].

Panel 10:

Zeus gives a wave to the Cyclops but the man doesn't notice.

HERA   Must have caught his bad eye.

ZEUS   Shit, I'll be right back, gotta kiss the ring. Order me a drink will ya?

HERA   You just got one!?

Panel 11:

Zeus starts walking away.

ZEUS   But I'll need a fresh one by the time I'm back. [winking]

Panel 12:

With Zeus gone, a geriatric statesman takes up his place [Uranus]. Hera tries to hide a scowl as a drunk and rosacead Uranus corners her at the bar. He leans over Hera, spitting in her ear as he talks.

URANUS   With any of these fundraisers masquerading as philanthropy you can expect everyone to be three sheets to the wind before stepping into the ballroom or forest preserves or banquet halls. It's a competition, a sort of endurance trial to see how one holds his or her booze in the constancy of the public eye: when the cameras are rolling and the next political moves are all based on articulation and a good smile.

HERA   Senator Uranus, my dear, how are you?

Panel 13:

Uranus leans in even closer, sliding his hand down Hera's back.

URANUS   Be a lot better if an old feller like me had a fine young thing such as yourself to accompany me to this little soirée. That grandson of mine sure is one lucky bastard.

Panel 14:

Uranus reaches down and grabs a handful of Hera's ass.

Panel 15:

Hera jumps and blushes.

Panel 16:

Zeus returns.

HERA   Ah, look, there's our boy, now.

ZEUS   Say, who's this spry young chicken?!

Panel 17:

Zeus smiles and shakes Uranus's hand.

Panel 18:

Uranus pulls him close and whispers in his ear, specks of food flying once more.

URANUS   Now I truly hope you're giving that vixen of a wife the full bag of groceries. A peach like that. I couldn't get it up with a boom lift and a team of NASA scientists working round-the-clock but it'll do this old heart some good knowing the fruit of the fruit of my loins is waxing those.

Panel 19:

Uranus looks as Zeus and taps his nose as he walks away.

HERA   What did he say?

ZEUS   Ah, nothing. He's just talking out his ass.[17] Ten minutes and he'll be face down in his chowder with the rest of the relics from the Golden Age.

Panel 20:

[Golden Age Politician's table] A table on the far edge of the banquet full of geriatric politicians drying out: Eros and Erebus, two old, white guys half-asleep and half-drunk; Gaea, in a wheelchair, drooling on herself; flowers on their lapels drying and limp; their care-takers interspersed between them.

Panel 21:

[Back to Zeus and Hera at the bar]

ZEUS   Ah shit, there's that prick from the *Times*, Typhon. Quick, turn around. Snake fuck keeps trying to get me to comment on missing discretionary funds or something.

Panel 22:

Typhos, a slimy, smarmy, disfigured man with misshapen head and hunchback, moves towards them; a "scribe" badge on his jacket. He's

---

17 Really?!? A bit easy and sophomoric don't you think?[d]

   [d] *Once again I have to disagree with Det. Zetas' sense of humor.* —E.B.

intercepted by a mousy little man with big, energetic eyes; his badge has a large, purple "I" and "Sisyphus" written underneath.

HERA   Wow, never thought I'd say this but it looks like an Independent just saved the day.

Panel 23:

On the other side of the hall, Poseidon (his name written on a GOP badge underneath a golden anchor pinned to his lapel) talks closely with Hades (his name written on a blue, Elephant badge). Poseidon's skin is deeply tan from too much boating[18]; Hades sports the coif of a Kennedy. Both are looking in Zeus and Hera's direction.

ZEUS   What do you reckon those two are conspiring?

HERA   Whatever it is, it can't be good. Come on, let's get another round and take our seats. I'm done standing.

Panel 24:

Zeus and Hera join Demeter and their children at one of the round tables. Zeus puts his arm around Demeter's meaty shoulder.

ZEUS   And how are my lovely children doing tonight?

HEBE   Hi Daddy!!!

ARES   I'd be doing a lot better if I were strapped. [looking around suspiciously] We all would...

Hephaestus has an electronic device in his hands he doesn't take his eyes off.

HEPHAESTUS   I find that highly improbable.

---

18 How would we know boating is the source of the tan?

Panel 25:

Zeus slides his hand down and snaps Demeter's bra stap before taking a seat. Demeter straightens her back and smiles. Hera, seated, stares daggers into Demeter.

HERA   Settle down, will you, you're drawing attention.

Panel 26:

With everyone seated, Zeus and Hera with full drinks in front of them, Kronos takes the podium as his wife, Rhea, looks on from the side.

KRONOS   Good evening ladies and gents. Wow, this is quite the turnout and quite the spread. My lovely wife, Rhea, and I would just like to thank you all for attending this cause that's so very dear to our hearts.

Panel 27:

The crowd gives a round of applause.

KRONOS   Now, before we dive into this spread—and the real reason we're here in the first place, saving the sow—I do have one bit of business to get out of the way.

Panel 28:

Zeus sits straight in his chair. Hera grips his left hand. Zeus grips his drink in the other.

Panel 29:

[Zeus's thought bubble] Imagines himself joining Kronos on the podium, smiling ear to ear, arm raised in the air in his best Charles Foster Kane impression, waving off the fawning crowd and flashing lights.

Panel 30:

[Back to Kronos's speech]

KRONOS   ...which is why I can think of no better person to take those reigns than my very own flesh and blood...

Zeus smiles and starts to rise in his seat.

Panel 31:

Zeus stands and straightens his jacket.

KRONOS   ...a true leader if ever there was one...

Panel 32:

With Zeus beaming.

KRONOS   Please join me in a very enthusiastic round of applause for our very own...Poseidon!

Panel 33:

Zeus's smile turns to a grimace.

Panel 34:

Zeus sits as Poseidon takes the stage to everyone's applause. Photographer's flashes are going wild.

Panel 35:

Zeus empties his glass as Hera stares at him, equally mortified.

Panel 36:

Zeus grabs Hera's glass and slams it back on the table, holding the empty glass in his white-knuckled hand.

Panel 37:

[Back on stage] Kronos has his hand clapped to Poseidon's back. Poseidon has started making a speech at the podium [speech bubble of nonsense "!@#$%"].

Panel 38:

The empty glass explodes in Zeus's hand.

Panel 39:

Across the ballroom Zeus makes eye contact with Hades. Hades shoots him a wry smile.

Panel 40:

Ares is staring at Zeus's bleeding hand.

ARES   Coooool. Blood!

Panel 41:

Zeus angrily turns on Ares.

ZEUS   You wanna join me?

Panel 42:

Hera puts her arm on Zeus's hand.

HERA   What did we say about threatening the kids in public, dear?

V. TITANOMACHY

Panel 1:

[The Next Day...]

Pandemonium, Zeus's Headquarters, is stocked with various staffers and campaign contributors, some at desks, some milling about. Large photos of Zeus's face are ubiquitous. The front door flies open and in storms a fuming Zeus.

Panel 2:

Athena, his Chief of Staff, a sharply dressed blonde woman in her late-thirties, snake pendant around her neck, rushes to Zeus.

ATHENA   Morning, sir. Look, it's not too late to rebound from this. I've had Electryus crunch the numbers and it looks like, even without your father's endorsement, you're only polling 7% behind Poseidon. Now, we should be able to climb another couple points with single mothers, and if we get in front of—

ZEUS   'Preciate it, Thena, but I've got something else in mind.

Panel 3:

Athena stands there, baffled.

ATHENA   Oh?

ZEUS   We're going Blue, darling, with old Blue Eyes in the crosshairs.

Panel 4:

Athena drops her folder to the ground. Several near-by staffers turn
and stare.

Panel 5:

Zeus is now in his office, Athena joins him, shutting the door behind
her.

Panel 6:

Several nearby staffers watch them from outside, through the windows, but unable to hear them.

ZEUS   ######## ###

ATHENA   ##### ######

ZEUS   #### ## ########...

Panel 7:

[Inside the office]

ATHENA   You, you can't be serious, sir? We have no way of knowing how that will poll!

ZEUS   Don't matter how it'll poll. It's what's happening.

ATHENA   It's not as if they kicked you out of the party.

ZEUS   Might as well have.

Panel 8:

Athena closes her eyes and takes a deep breath.

ATHENA   Well if we're going this route we need to get on top of it. I'll set up a press release for this afternoon.

ZEUS   Yes, and unleash the hecatoncheires, I want them on every corner of every Main street stuffing pamphlets in the hands of every man, woman or child[19] of voting age.

Panel 9:

Athena opens the office door.

ATHENA   Consider it done, sir.

Panel 10:

Athena screams into the main room at the top of her lungs.

ATHENA   HACATONCHEIRES, ACTIVATE!!!

Panel 11:

Immediately, every staffer rises from their desk; all are utterly identical. They turn and file out the door.

Panel 12:

Zeus pours himself a drink from the bar in the corner.

---

19 And I suppose we can infer this is another joke?

ZEUS   One last thing: call my father, make sure he's in attendance for the release. I want to see his face in person.

ATHENA   10-4. Salting the wounds, sir?

Panel 13:

[Press Release]

Zeus stands at a podium with the Florida state flag behind him.

ZEUS   Ladies and gentleman, it is no secret: we have a problem in our great state. It's a problem that extends from every city and every county. We are overworked and underserved; overstressed and under-fed.

Panel 14:

ZEUS   Every now and then there comes a time when you've got to do what's right—not what's right by the standards of your party, but what's right by the standards of the people, the true party. Someone has to stand up, take charge, and put the ship back on a course of prosperity. In my mind, there's only one candidate sufficient to handle the task...

Panel 15:

Kronos is watching him cautiously. Very cautiously.

ZEUS   And so I extend my support across the line, to Ms. Evelyn Adams.[20]

---

20 There's got to be a better way to conflate Milton with the Greek mythos. Also, the only person with a last name?!? Again, issues of pragmatism. I really hope this isn't your final draft, Mr. Bearheart, whoever you are.

Panel 16:

The crowd gasps. The photographers go nuts. Kronos's face goes red.

Panel 17:

[Cut to]: Uranus, watching the TV in his study at home, throwing his head back in laugher.

URANUS   Ha! Sweet karmic delight! Let's see how *you* like it when your kids cut your balls off, eh Kronos?

Panel 18:

[Back at the press release] Zeus has descended from the podium and stands in the middle of the room, next to an enraged Kronos.

ZEUS   How'd you like the speech?

KRONOS   Boy, you just opened a box can't be closed.

ZEUS   I believe you were the one diddling Pandora last night, pops.

Panel 19:

Kronos leans in to Zeus, smiling through clenched teeth with the photographers flashing behind them, venom in his bloodstained eyes.

KRONOS   Well I hope you're prepared, son of mine…because I'm going to eat you alive.

Panel 20:

[Later that night] Zeus and Hera's bedroom. Both lie in bed watching the TV with cocktails resting on their stomachs. The news is replaying the footage of the press announcement. "…in an unprecedented endorsement across the aisle…"

HERA You've just signed a declaration of war. Are you sure you're ready for this?

Panel 21:

Zeus takes a sip of his drink and smiles.

ZEUS Well, babe, it's like I always say: 'Sometimes you've got to chop an ugly path even though there's a perfectly good trail to the right.'[21]

---

21 Professor Lockhart???[e]

[e] *Attempts to locate this "Professor Lockhart" proved fruitless. We believe the name may be yet another pseudonym, part of a larger network of deceitful or duplicitous authors.* —E.B.

PLINY THE ELDER

When the top blew on Mount Vesuvius, sending up a banner of violent intentions, Pliny the Younger dropped everything he was doing and ran to tell his uncle. "Uncle, Uncle, the sky is falling."

Pliny the Elder looked upwards, saw the smoke, the ash, the fire, and put down his vase of water. "She-it, boy, that ain't no falling sky."

"It ain't?"

"Mm-mmm. 'At rite-chair's the wrath o' God, it is. An' we musta pissed Him off good this time."

Still so young in his tutelage, still so young in the mysteries of the world, the Younger could only scratch the nape of his neck, "Well what do you reckon set him off, sir?"

"Guess is as good as mine, J.R., but I'd put a Silver Romulus on fornicatin' a some sort."

The boy looked up at the billowing ash forming a phalanx on the horizon and nodded.

"Well Christ-on-a-stick, boy, whatrya waiting for? Ready the artillery!"

The Younger knew enough to know not to be asked twice. He took to his heals, mobilizing any and all able-bodied men, corralling them through the streets, leading them first to the armory, then to the parapets, where they took their defensive positions and loaded their belt-fed, water-cooled Browning M1917 machine-guns, their tripod-mounted .50 caliber M2s and their Mk-19 automatic grenade launchers. They braced for the siege, awaiting the Elder's orders.

The sky continued advancing. When he could see the whites of the brimstone the Elder dropped his arm and the men fired into the oncoming ash. Spent shells collected around their sandals, burning their feet as they worked their way up the shins.

"Give 'em hell, boys. Don't let these Godless, motherless, menstrual-sausages take an inch," said Pliny the Elder while Pliny the Younger readied a mortar and launched it at a battalion of brimstone.

The smoking rocks continued to fall, smashing holes in their lines. Ash hit house and courtyard. The women and children ran for cover, clutching the small things and covering their ears in their bosom. The cowardly fled; the brave held their ground: as in any battle.

"Hold tight, boys, hold tight." Pliny the Elder readied his muscles and strode through the ranks, service revolver in hand. "How will this day remember you, lads? Fearful an' cowering? Or brave an' defiant to the end? One thing I know, this here conflagration will sure as shit 'member my gatdamned name. What about yours!? Now fire, damn you. FIRE!!!"

The men emptied the heart of their ammo into the oncoming assault. They took their attrition.

"I don't think we can hold the line much longer, sir," Pliny the Younger yelled against the drone of death and machinery, the exploding gunpowder giving off an aroma of freshly cracked hell.

Pliny the Elder clutched his toga to his chest and looked at the falling ash, the screaming red death. Then the lava hit the mortars and the ranks broke about him. He threw a wounded man off his gun, grasped the Browning by the top handle and fired from his hip. The enemy advanced, unhindered.

The city burned around him. Buxom women and small children screamed from inside the furnace of their homes. Pliny the Elder watched the incendiary sky darken from red to black. "J.R., take the women and chirren and head for them thar hills."

"But uncle—"

"Damnit, boy, we ain't got time to argue. Now move, damnit; that's an order. I'll hold 'em off long's I can. Now git!"

Pliny the Younger frowned but complied, taking as many with him as he could through the back passage; it would not be many.

Alone among the ramparts, Pliny the Elder reloaded the Browning one last time, spraying hot lead into the heavy cavalry of rock. The hammer snapped empty as a piece of stone the size of his villa flanked him from the left. "All right, let's just call this one here a draw."

And all was consumed.

THE X-FACTOR

"*The X-Factor: With his New Novel,* TRICYCLICS ON THE MOORS, *X has Once Again Comfortably Seated Himself in the Throne of Controversy,*" by *Katje Reynolds,* MORNING STAR REVIEW 10.11.99

— § —

If you've heard the rumor that indeed the pale horse and his rider have been trotting up and down Fifth Avenue, it is because indeed they have; the veritable apocalypse of the literary world, *Tricyclics on the Moors*, the new novel by extravagant author X, hit stores across the nation Tuesday, October 5th. The artist—first published under the pseudonym Ionesco C. Kampani-Sanchez, shortened to ICKS, then to just "X"—has just released another behemoth of objectionable fiction.

Critics and the public are still feuding with themselves over the merit of his previous novel, *There is an I in Broom*, which weighed in at a Herculean 5,630 pages. The book, difficultly categorized as a novel, was often paired with critical praises such as "too long by 5,629 pages," "a sprawling and amorphous mess not dissimilar to a plug of hair found at the bottom of a drain," or simply "turgid and unreadable." Taste aside, no one could argue that X's existential opus centering around the personification of inanimate objects, often satirizing public offices and conventional gender roles, wasn't at least a work worth mentioning for its sheer size—let alone a repository of potent rhetoric for any college students writing their theses on Kierkegaard, mental illness, or scatological humor and the public response.

Tapped in 1982 by Aoife Dollan and Thomas Reingold [Simon & Schuster] as the veritable second coming of Joyce or Proust, with just as much talent and unrelenting ambition (Reingold had gone on to describe *Broom* as "a collaboration between Joyce, Beckett, and Jean Paul Sarte, edited by Tolstoy, and rewritten by Gary Lutz in the throngs of a two-week acid trip"), few, however, seconded that claim. Though not all of the umbrage was based on the novel's rhetoric; X was sued twice for damages related to back injuries sustained from lugging the book around—the second time by his own editor!

Broom went on to acquire moderate sales under the circumstances; the $49.95 retail tag didn't do it any favors. Many bought the book solely for the novelty, a coffee-table book heavier than most coffee tables. Misfit youths toted the book around as a veritable trophy to the otherness of their intellect and abounding culture; some even bothered to read it. It goes without saying the bulk of the eyes actually reading the book belonged to scholars, writers, publishers, and editors, trying to gauge whether the work was genius or fraud, the next step in literature or a red herring, a new competitor or a tired cliché, or, at its most simplistic, good or bad. The community remains undecided.

Here are a few choice selections from *There is an I in Broom* for those of you unable or unwilling to join the auteur in his submersible down to the Benthic layers of his linguistic ocean:

— § —

From Chapter 3: *Coffee Tables and Accomplices* [concerning a chair]:

"Houndstooth pattern wore the silk gone through; bronze buttons blue in the face. There is an "I" I can't be certain. There is a face to cloud the ash. And who will sew four feet to the tablecloth? And who will impress the soft about the ears? Stroking, tail-wagged, mid-morning made-up plight to deliver; to be delivered; to be told."

Chapter 15: *The Banister Says I love you*:

"Execution gave the rail his stay. Morrissey-Morcheeba wet the
sponge and threw the switch. If she cries she missed the point:
singing 'SONGS OF SOMNAMBULATION FOR THE
SOMNOLESCENT SOLEMN.' "

Chapter 693: *Where the Shit Ran Clear.*

"Won't someone think of the linen? There are breasts to be cloth(d).
But the sun is strong, it is always stronger than I. Fish-pack(d)
six-pack; sardines pushing daisies. I had room for more things. I had
room for more things."

See what I mean?

— § —

Now, some might remember X's pseudo performance-piece back in
1994, a one-night event held at a converted loft in Manhattan's Alphabet City neighborhood. Risers like those used in school choir performances were brought in and set up in a full circle. The tickets cost
$3,000 dollars a-piece and came with the allowance of flash photogra-
phy and the encouragement for the audience to take as many pictures
as they desired. Naturally, the event sold out—despite the fact that no
one knew a thing about X's performance, outside of the photography
angle (which should have been at least a clue for those familiar with
X's work).

The doors opened at 10:30pm on the Friday after Thanksgiving.
The audience took their seats, which were general admission, and waited a full hour before X made his way into the middle of the circle from
an aisle between the stands. He made a total of three trips to the center: first, he brought with him a blank 9" x 12" moleskin book; on
his second trip, a bottle of ink and a fountain pen; then he left for fifteen minutes and returned in a silk kimono patterned with tigers and
snowflakes. The "house lights" were killed in favor of three 100-watt
bulbs hanging a foot above his standing height. When X next returned
to the stage, at the stroke of midnight, he dropped his kimono and
stood before the audience naked. Sitting cross-legged in the center, he
dipped his pen in the blue ink, over-saturating the tip, and began writ-

ing a fully impromptu new novel, unrehearsed and without any editing or erasure, dropping whatever popped up in his mind onto the
page, making sure to always keep the ink fresh and wet. What people
would mostly remember, though, the controversy, was what X would
do in his veritable "writing breaks."

When the moment was right, a staggering fifteen-times over the
course of the six-hour-and-twenty-one-minute event (timed to finish
at the exact moment of dawn on Saturday), X would put the pen down
and masturbate onto the pages. The semen spread over the fresh ink,
often times blending words, sentences, or paragraphs into an aque-
ous mixture of different concentrations of blue. In an interview with
Tom Halperin of *Rolling Stone*, X, in his famed monkish hair-cut and
Hawaiian tee, explained the strategy for the piece:

> *"Incarnate creation, if you will: utterly raw and unblemished in
> regard to prior stratagem. I wanted to—for people—bring them
> down to the bottom level of creation, bring them to the cutting floor,
> you see? A voyeurism in the truest fashion. After all, we're all voyeurs
> in the eyes of the artist, aren't we? I wanted them to feel the
> perversion complicit in their act of watching, of their implied
> culpability in the creation. Would any one of them not think that,
> should they not have bought the ticket—put their hand in the cookie
> jar, so to speak—the work would have been the same? Each person
> in attendance walked away that morning feeling as though they had
> lent a brushstroke in the Mona Lisa—well, I wouldn't go so far as to
> call my work the Mona Lisa—maybe something minor by
> Matisse—but something of importance.*

> *"With regard to the semen, I wanted to blend not only the conscious
> act of creation but the physical and biological act as well. (For the
> record, I'd been spending a lot of time around [Andres] Serrano.)
> Both give life: one of paper and ink, a progeny of dreams and of
> begging the question 'If something is created in our minds, does it
> not occupy some semblance of existence? Is there not a connection,
> visceral, emotive, to the worlds created by ink?;' the other, obviously,
> one half of the ingredients for giving life. (I was still upset that I
> wasn't able to find a woman willing to employ her menstrual
> discharge, but such is art.) I specifically wanted to see both "lives" of*

the creation melding together, the ink kept fresh so as to blend better. In preparation, I abstained from sexual activity—either autonomous or symbiotic—for several months, relying on strong meditation and opiates to stifle the urges. What resulted—much to my satisfaction, creating another layer of the work—was a strong showing in the early parts of the book: if you'll remember, pages 6 through 12 are utterly fused together—as are pages 30 to 33 and 45 through 50—the art inside lost—preserved, rather, like an insect in a ball of amber—but towards the end there are merely spatters and small nacreous stains. I remember there was one such stain on page 191 where the pale yellow and blue mixed so perfectly that I thought the little circle resembled Pluto, which I subsequently worked into the story. Do you see the beauty? One act of creation influencing another and then coming back and influencing the first? A Möbius strip of creation. Pure dynamism. Utterly marvelous, in my opinion."

Needless to say, the "performance" and work, which sold for a whopping $13 million dollars to an anonymous bidder, garnered considerable (and criminal) speculation.

— § —

Unsurprisingly, ever since "The Nacred Dawn," as the above performance came to be known (you may recall the hordes of disaffected youth wearing T-shirts labeled "I attended The Nacred Dawn and all I got was this stained T-shirt"), the public has been less than inviting of X's work, often accusing him of being pornographic, vulgar, blasphemous, and—by one man in Idaho—seditious. Much of the writing and academic world have agreed with the public's perception, calling his work overtly and debilitatingly esoteric, contrived to the nth degree, a complete perversion of the novel, and, perhaps most hurtful to X, who refuses to comment on his criticism,

"...deftly retarded and solely written for shock purposes. In accordance with the old theory that if one were to place several monkeys in a room with typewriters they would inevitably produce a Shakespearean sonnet, I feel the same is true for the work of Mr. X,

with the stipulation that the monkeys be provided copious amounts of MDMA, an eight-ball of cocaine, and a projector playing a loop of pure, authentic snuff. In short: it is drivel. I only wish I could live long enough to watch him and his work disappear fully and terminally from bookshelves and the social consciousness." (Thomas Quincannon, Pulitzer Prize Committee and author of the novel AN AFFAIR IN NEW ENGLAND *and the non-fiction work* JEL-LIED: MY YEAR OF EATING ONLY GRAPE JELLY*)*

— § —

Now, with *Tricyclics on the Moors*, his 800-page triptych—a novella in comparison—X finds himself once again in the laser-sighted crosshairs of both the literary and public communities, which is beginning to seem more and more a welcome abode for the author.

The new novel is essentially three "stories" meant to be experienced simultaneously, each occupying one-third of the page. The outlying "stories" are prose, similarly oblique, and whose connections one can only speculate. Why I apostrophized "stories" is because the middle section is simply sheet music, written by X himself: twelve independent movements for twelve different instruments. X is adamant that the nomenclature of 'story' remains. He is also adamant that the individual instruments are not meant to be played together or in concert; a shame, really, as that bit of organization and musical bravado would have lent at least one tangible piece of evidence towards whatever genius he's purporting to possess.

And while I could certainly go on to describe the obtuse form of the novel and the rhetoric therein—which would no doubt be a great writing exercise—it makes more sense to just show a sample of the work.

Tricyclics on the Moors

She shore it down to the nub—Digitized and Discipled. But it was meant to speak for the Me-s, or was it just meant to speak? She had a back and I rubbed it and it rubbed me back. "In the storm are riding writers writing 'Riders on the Storm.'" "Where now?" "There are holes that must be dug," there are wholes that must be hewn.

In the *piazza* sometimes a statue sometimes David. Sometimes Apollo, sometimes not. Sometimes the Madonna. In the courtyard a mother and a child.

"Why does it cry, Mama?" "It cries because it loves us."

In the storm, riders riding.

Apoplectic women rent the shores gone numb. Fertile and analgesic lest we forget.

"God is just another word for angioplasty. God is just another word for hot yoga. God is just another word for that Christmas present you hoped for but didn't receive. God is just another word for Unified Field Theory and is sometimes pronounced 'GUT.' God is just another word for 'Aw, shit!'"

There was a frequency twice forgotten. There was a hole to put the refuse. He added, "God is just another word for nothing left to lose."

Is the re-uptake a lesser rapture?

-286-

From Tricyclics on the Moors, page 286

X has stipulated that the story is meant not so much to be read and understood as experienced. When asked how one is to read the story, X was quick to say "It is not a story to be read. Don't read it. Just open the page and let your eyes rest there until they've taken it all in. Then turn the page." In a letter to his new editor, Raj Kaheel, he talked about the basis for speed reading as the idea behind the idea:

> "I had put down my CALCULUS FOR DUMMIES—something I had wanted to learn for another project—and picked up a book on speed reading so as to expedite the calculus lessons. In the introduction, the author had described the basic process of how most people read, that is, that they 'sound out' the words in their head. This is essentially a wasted effort because the recognition of the word precedes the vocalization, or sub-vocalization as it were: you know the word and its meaning long before you sound it out. This, by extension, applies to phrases, sentences, paragraphs, and basically the page—after enough time. So the concept of speed reading is to eliminate the voice and facilitate faster recognition of what is on the page, of what is before you. I wanted to create a book where this method is required to 'read' it. My ideal reader, then, would be one who is already experienced in the skill of speed reading. I heard F.D.R. was a speed reader; a shame he's dead, I truly think he would have liked this book."

— § —

In an irony befitting of X and his work, pre-orders for the book have already sold out, with many of those reserved for a nationwide book burning ceremony to commence at the end of the month. It would not surprise many (including this reviewer) to believe that X had a large part in that coordination. The author famously participated in a book burning of *Broom*, showing up to the event in full British Admiral regalia, tossing one of his own books into the flames—a happy substitute for actual firewood—and scooping up the ashes in order to make a diamond for a wedding ring. "So I can have a truly permanent version of my art," he told *Vanity Fair*. (It should be noted that X has never married.)

Now we arrive at the daunting task of assessing *Tricyclics*, which I can tell you I have not been looking forward to. Its steely eschewing of convention, plot, character—of anything concrete to grab onto in order to take the ride—gives me pause for any serious recommendation. That I believe the reading of the work wouldn't change if I had stopped at page 2 doesn't help, either. But perhaps I am being too severe. Perhaps there is a heart there after all, beating inside a fatty casing of obfuscation. Or perhaps that heartbeat is merely at a frequency only certain ears can detect. The point is this: Should we care? Is there enough value there to warrant the reading—in full or in part—of this colossal tome? And at an age when the competition for our time is at its fiercest, will that time be rewarded? And my answer: It depends.

That may sound like a cop-out or laziness but it's true, because it all depends on what you're looking for. Searchers will no doubt rejoice: the novel is nothing if not a fresh appendix of esoteric notions to add to that ever-growing, crowd-sourced Book of Mystery that will never know a back cover of resolution. Realists will bemoan the lack of a central character to provide an anchor or at least reference for an emotive reading—and they won't necessarily be wrong. Purists would likely find more enjoyment reading Updike backwards than trying to slog through this, if only for the time saved.

But regardless of how you feel about X's work, no one can deny that he is indeed a writer whose ambition forces reckoning. Though he might not always fulfill his aims, or even make those aims clear at times, he is without doubt an inimitable force upon the world of literature. A boulder falling into the flowing river of art and forcing the water and its navigants to choose between courses. Whether you're a believer or a skeptic, whether you follow in his soggy footsteps or hightail it down the opposite bank, both are indelible reactions to his work. The only question (and not the one history will parse long after his death: whether he is an authentic literary force, or merely a prolific farce) is this: If he keeps dropping stones of this magnitude, will the river continue to flow, or will he dam it up? As a weekend spelunker, I can tell you water always finds a way out. Always.

But who knows, maybe after scouring the rocky walls of the cave system for an exit, searching for that small trickle that turns into an underground tributary, you'll dive in and emerge in a lagoon on the other side, only to find X, kicking his feet up on a beach chair and drinking rum out of a coconut. Or, more likely, practicing Tai Chi naked under a waterfall in the moonlight.

— § —

[Editor's Note: Fans of X can look forward to his biopic coming out in the fall of next year. Helmed by Davids Cronenberg and Lynch, the film promises to be a mix between the real life of X and the work he has created. Both directors will film the project incommunicado in an attempt to capture the reality/unreality, inconsistency, and general ethereality that is the writer's life and art. As could be expected, the MPAA has already given the film a preemptive rating of, you guessed it, X.]

ELEPHANTS VI

Several thousands of miles to the west of Thailand, on the outskirts of the Serengeti, a herd of wild elephants make their yearly migration towards fresh waters and grazing. A matriarchal animal, they're led by the eldest grandmother of the herd. Her memory has led them to the same sources of water and grass every year and through her they will again find their way; they have to, their survival depends on it.

There is a fork in the river with a large rock protruding from the sand where the two shallow creeks diverge into separate rivers, growing wider and deeper as they spread, dividing the land into two vastly different plains. For years she has used the rock as a marker, and for years they have always gone right.

But memory and road signs aren't the only obstacles to conquer in their annual migration. The herd is hunted, a different predator depending on the environ: leopards, cheetahs, lions, crocodiles, a brazen pack of hyenas.

It's just as they're a mile or so down the trail from the rock, following close to the shore, when the lions move in. They flank the herd from the right, the first lion digging her claws into the side of a young calf. The cry alerts the others. The elephants take evasive maneuvers, stampeding, charging, or attempting to gore the attackers with their tusks. In the commotion, many of them scatter, a problem as most do not know the way; and the lions are counting on that.

The matriarch sprints forward, still trying to lead them, when she hears the cries of one of her grandchildren. Her daughter does not stop to attend to her child so the matriarch turns back as the herd marches on. She finds the calf cornered between a large kopje and three lions, honking and shrieking for dear life. Immediately the grandmother charges, goring one lion in the ribcage but not hard enough to put it down or even scare it off. The process is repeated, but she gains no more ground on the lions—mothers themselves with cubs to feed. Hearing the cries, two other lions turn back from following the rest of the herd, and now the grandmother is forced to try and keep five at bay. Just as her tusk digs into the belly of an attacker she hears the sound she's been fearing. It is a cry wild and frantic and final.

Her grandson is felled, and as the rest of the lions pounce, jumping on his back and legs, digging their claws and teeth anywhere the flesh is soft, the grandmother knows she has no choice but to flee; there's still the rest of her herd to consider. She departs, and the lions do not follow.

The matriarch returns to the last point of reference she remembers, the fork in the river. Her family still lies somewhere to the right. She will join them soon enough.

Before returning to the herd she takes a long drink from the river, knowing she will have to move quickly to catch up and will need all the replenishment she can afford. She drinks and splashes herself free of the mud and gore so the lions don't smell the blood as she passes. Crimson blasts of clay water splatter on the slab of limestone in the middle of the fork. The sun burns hot, and even though the water evaporates, the red still remains, though she cannot see it as anything but a dark patch on a light background.

She stops splashing and regards the rock, her trunk dangling. She raises it again and spreads a large slash across the rock. She takes a step back and considers the rock once more. She moves back to the water, sucks up a couple gallons, and sprays the rock once more. She does this two more times, creating a relief of patches and stripes against the bare limestone peeking through the oxidizing mud.

Then she leaves. By the next nightfall she has rejoined her herd. They mourn the loss. But they recover and move on, as they have always done. The season passes and they make the return trek home.

The following year they make the same migration, with new offspring in tow. The matriarch leads the herd once more. They pass through the same familiar areas, the same familiar threats, and once more they come to the fork in the river. Here the matriarch pauses; the rock is not the same as she remembers it. It has three long slashes of darker mud across it in a pattern not created by rain.

The herd halts and waits for her to make a decision. The grandmother huffs and paces back and forth as she considers the pattern. Slowly, she turns and follows the river to the left, and the rest of the elephants follow.

RITE OF THE MANDALA | DESTROY: ERASE: IMPROVE

~~The tattoo of the ox on Dr. Lucas's calf was meant to commemorate the year of his birth; how fitting that it would also commemorate the year of his death.~~

~~The doctor found a lung; and the lung found a doctor. It was breathing where it shouldn't. "Lance it off?!" he said, doing a spit-take with his coffee, "Hell no, I want to give it a heartbeat and a social security number!"~~

~~It was as awkward as any bifurcated confrontation with the self, pensive and progenitous; still, the coffee was hot at least.~~

~~I was informed, quite brusquely, by the stately woman with the sharp forehead and the coffee breath that the Akashic Records office was closed for the day and I could no longer submit my application for revision, even though stamped in triplicate.~~

~~You should have seen the *other* God," he told her, using the non-bandaged hand to bookmark his Brautigan with the wooden stirrer~~

straw.

The coffee shop smelled of warm butter and cocoa, and he saw her silhouetted at a table against the window.

When he stepped in the coffee shop he noticed two things: that he didn't actually want coffee, and that he couldn't take his eyes off the girl sitting by herself at a window table.

When he stepped in the coffee shop he noticed three things: that he would have to make his purchase with a credit card, that there was a beautiful woman sitting by herself, that he was sweating.

As was his custom in the last thirty years, he rose early on Saturday, walked down to the park while his wife slept, taking with him his Brittany Spaniel, Rosalyn, and tying her to the newspaper boxes outside the café while he went in for his usual scone and cappuccino; and only after he ordered and was dunking his pastry in the piping taupe liquid did she catch his attention, sitting against the window with a copy of his book, opened to his favorite chapter; he approached her curiously and cautiously, not wanting to seem pretentious but wanting to know (for research's sake, he told himself) what a younger woman such as she thought of his writing, and it was after he initiated his first steps towards her direction and a weighted greeting that he knew he was in trouble.

Were it a Wednesday he'd stop and chat, were it a Saturday he'd nod his cap at her and give a wink, were it a Monday he'd have worn underwear, but it was Sunday, and Sundays had their own rules.

Were they (were we) to remain in such obdurate lives of sacrosanct conviction, to remain like saccharine sediment unstirred, when the winds of inertia so gently yet so purposefully coaxed them (us, we) forward?

Was it ironic the coffee shop played "Black Magic Woman?" He couldn't be sure, but he took it as a sign.

"Coffee. Black."

"Give me the tallest, darkest blend you have and blacken the eyes."

And it was only after he'd committed the deed, widening his stance and shifting his weight, relying on the pungency of the coffee shop to mask what he correctly guessed to be a rambunctious and caustic effluvium, that he noticed her standing right behind him, the woman who'd become the next Christmas guest. But this is not the story their

~~friends and grandchildren would hear.~~

~~It was uncanny, the sight of her, not only the image but her posture and mannerisms: wiping her hair from her face before each sip, preemptively licking the stains from her teeth, adding more sugar when she'd drank her coffee halfway down…if he didn't believe in the permanence of death he'd have run up to her table, pulled her woolen cap to his mouth, breathed the smell and history of her hair and then told his daughter the things he wished he'd said; but this wasn't her, this wasn't Kara, he'd lowered her into the earth himself.~~

~~Here there would be no Proustian conjectures: not for him, not for her.~~

~~"Double soy caramel macchiato with two stevias, and if you don't get it with low-fat cream don't bother coming back. Now, where was I? Right. So, an aging lothario's swan song and a young girl's sexual awaking: they're pitching it as a 'Last Tango in Hoboken.' Now before you shake your head let me tell you who the director is."~~

~~There was time left for sweet nothings, for immutable pleasures so pedestrian, so local, he could, for a moment, forget about that one thing, that *other* thing, and decide to live, and to flirt with young life.~~

~~Shiva was good—fair, he should say—filling his body with this ambitious decrepitude while this young thing brimming with life sat not ten feet away. Or maybe she just had a good sense of irony.~~

~~He wouldn't forget what came next; and neither would she—he'd make sure of that.~~

~~When he saw her, he knew he could love her, but that was the life before.~~

~~When he saw her, he knew he could love her.~~

~~When I saw her, I knew I could love her, if only for a moment.~~

~~When I saw her, I knew she could love me.~~

~~When I saw her, I knew I could love her.~~

When she saw him, she knew she could love him, if only for a moment.

ABOUT THE AUTHOR

A.V. Bach is a writer and musician currently living in Chicago, IL. He holds a BA in English from Syracuse University and a MA in Fiction Writing from Johns Hopkins University. His work has been published in the US and UK in such publications as *Fogged Clarity, Kerouac's Dog Magazine, Gone Lawn,* and *Gargoyle.* In addition to writing fiction he also contributes to *Mash Tun Journal,* a periodical dedicated to the world of craft beer. This is his first novel.

CPSIA information can be obtained
at www.ICGtesting.com
Printed in the USA
FFOW04n1657291116
29778FF